THE REIGN COMETH

Dr. Trent W. Smallwood

The Reading Glass Books
1-888-420-3050
www.readingglassbooks.com
fulfillment@readingglassbooks.com

DEDICATION

I wish to express my deepest gratitude to the fantastic readers who embraced my debut novel, *Lethal Decree,* and its sequel, *Lethal Storm.* Your steadfast support and encouragement have driven me to explore my creative writing further and spawn the next era in the Sebastian Storm Series.

Lastly, I wish to thank my tremendous and faithful supporters and advisors in this work. Their advice and encouragement have been immeasurable to me.

The Sebastian Storm Series has become an extension of me in so many ways. I have been inspired to open up further the creative and imaginative pathways I didn't know I possessed until I truly tapped and explored them.

Sebastian Storm and his band of characters allow me to delve into fantasy that few will ever experience. As always, there will be love, betrayal, deception, excitement, and intrigue throughout the myriad of scenes in which Sebastian Storm is involved.

It's in his DNA and makes him who he has become and exciting to see what he will do next.

The Sebastian Storm Series will continue to live on.

Description

The Reign Cometh

With domestic anarchy weighing heavy on the balance and the current and antiquated political system failing, its ultimate implosion is imminent. Yet, a new luminary emerges from the midst of chaos. Born from a long line of staunch conservative Senators, Damian West has become the chosen hero to lead the new political faction. . . . *the Unified Party*.

As the established order and political system teeters on the brink of collapse, the people's champion, a neoteric face of optimism, emerges. Damian West arises as a beacon of hope amidst the crumbling political landscape. His charismatic leadership and strategic vision resonate with disillusioned leaders and American citizens seeking redemption. With a fresh perspective and a commitment to unity, he aims to bridge the divide that has plagued the nation for decades. His rallying cry echoes through the hearts of many, promising a new era of collaboration, effective governance, and equitable policies.

As the world watches with bated breath, Damian West emerges as a transformative energy, challenging the old guard and offering an alternative progressive path. The Unified Party becomes a formidable contender, drawing support from diverse circles and promising a government that prioritizes the needs and aspirations of the people as a whole. . . *as a nation*. Only time will tell if Damian West's leadership can reshape the political landscape and steer the country toward a brighter future.

The Unified Party, led by a determined and passionate group of key synergistic individuals, emerges as a viable alternative to the antiquated bipartisan system. With a focus on innovation and a fresh perspective, they aim to bring about positive change and efficiency in governance.

Handpicked by Damian West and his father, Senator Sam West, a team of dedicated and loyal supporters embark on a mission to redefine the values and aspirations of the United States, aiming to restore its position as a global superpower. Their unwavering dedication seeks to revive the nation's former glory and bring a new era of prosperity and influence.

Facing resistance from the Republican and Democratic parties alike, the Unified Party stands strong with its streamlined efficiency and unwavering commitment to principles of unity, racial autonomy, and a rejection of entrenched ambiguity in American democracy. Unfortunately, in modern times, the traditional parties find themselves ill-equipped to match the Unified Party's resolute stance and cohesive vision for the future.

Despite Damian West's illumination and progressive vision, hidden saboteurs lurk in the shadows, threatening his leadership and aspirations. Sebastian Storm, a dedicated ally of West, finds himself at the forefront of the battle, determined to protect and uphold the new ideals and believing in the man behind them. However, the opposing factions run deep and pose a formidable challenge to the Unified Party's agenda and evolution. The struggle for power and the nation's future intensifies as these opposing forces clash.

Damian West's dream is honed and focused; nothing will stop him or his political perspicuity, and he is determined to become the youngest candidate to hold the office of President of the United States. His optimistic and influential core group garnered unyielding potential, and Damian West will not allow anyone or anything to stand in his way. Above all, he wishes to restore the integrity and uniformity of this great nation, but it won't come without significant cost to him, his beliefs, and the sacrifices it took to get him there.

Sebastian Storm weathers the political tempest standing at West's side, but not even Storm can imagine the depth of betrayal West must endure. Sebastian Storm, a figure shrouded in darkness, emerges as a silent guardian, vigilantly observing and safeguarding the United States' future through one man's vision. Within his unwavering presence, he is resolute in fulfilling Damian West's ambitions, meticulously paving the way for West's impending reign.

Sebastian navigates the intricate web of challenges with steadfast dedication, securing a clear path to realize West's aspirations. His unfaltering loyalty and commitment are the foundation for their shared vision, poised to shape the destiny ahead.

However, within the shadows lurk new and old enemies who threaten the sanctity of the administration. Sebastian's watchful gaze pierces through the veils of uncertainty, ever vigilant and prepared to navigate the trials that lie in wait. With quiet strength and determination, he stands as a pillar of support, tirelessly working towards realizing their common purpose.

Together, they forge ahead, united in pursuing a future crafted by West's hand and the *Alternative Consortium supporting him.* Sebastian's resolute presence remains an unyielding force, ensuring that the path remains clear, allowing the inevitable arrival of West's ascendancy.

CONTENTS

Prologue

Tension Mounting

"You can conquer nearly any fear if you will only make up your mind to do so. For remember, fear doesn't exist anywhere except in the mind."
~ Dale Carnegie

Over the Atlantic Ocean
2019 Winter (Holidays)
TransAmerican Flight 368

A sudden jolt roused him from his sleep. The aircraft lurched violently, snapping him awake as adrenaline surged through his body. Despite his seasoned experience as a helicopter pilot, turbulence remained a wild, untamed force, unrelenting, always keeping him on edge. Each bone-rattling jolt was a stark reminder of the sky's unforgiving nature, challenging his resolve with every shuddering moment.

In the grand theater of life, the furor of air travel acted as a humbling overture, a poignant reminder that even the most accomplished and determined must bow to the capricious whims of nature and her whimsical moods. He couldn't help but feel a sense of vulnerability in the face of nature's unpredictable and unrelenting forces at work. For him, a man accustomed to orchestrating the symphony of his own existence, these moments above the clouds were a stark departure from the familiar.

In a world where he has meticulously engineered his own path and navigated challenges with instinctive precision, the delicate air of the stratosphere had an uncanny ability to strip away any illusion of control. It was a realm where his fate lay mainly in the hands of aerodynamics, meteorology, and the unseen forces that governed the skies.

The very essence of being suspended miles above the earth was a lesson in relinquishing the reins of control. In the cockpit, the seasoned aviators held their expertise, yet even they knew that nature's fury could be unpredictable and unforgiving. The tumult served as a vivid testament to the majesty and mystery of the world above the clouds.

This surrender to circumstance was a unique test of character for a man wired to command his destiny. It was an exercise in resilience, a chance to embrace vulnerability, and an opportunity to find grace in the face of forces beyond his dominion. In these moments, he found a newfound appreciation for the delicate balance between human ambition and nature's vast, untamed forces.

A tall, striking blond flight attendant happened to be walking by and placed her hand on his shoulder, "It's only turbulence; it should get better soon. I'm Daffni, should you need anything," she winked at him, "Anything at all," she offered a thoughtful smile after sharing her simple yet calming message as she made her way to the forward cabin.

With most of the overnight flight still ahead, he soared over the vast Atlantic Ocean, a considerable distance from their departure location in Europe. The pilot's earlier announcement lingered in his thoughts, emphasizing the imminent development of storms and the relentless turbulence caused by the ever-changing barometric pressures over the Atlantic. The pilot warned them to brace themselves for a bumpy ride for the next few hours.

Having been granted exclusive access to the ATS Division jet numerous times, he felt it a luxury he did not deserve. This particular journey held a personal significance that dissuaded him from accepting the taxpayer-funded mode of transport. Hillary Bastini, his esteemed superior, has insisted on extending the generosity in utilizing the jet, emphasizing his invaluable contributions to his country time and time again. Grateful for the offer, he graciously declined, citing a desire to maintain integrity and fiscal responsibility to the United States taxpayers. Determinedly, he embarked on a commercial flight but opted for business class. He was seated in 12B.

Amidst the hum of the aircraft's engines, he reflected on the journey that lay ahead. While the red-eye flight carried him back from his Italian residence in Lake Como, he anticipated a surge of mixed emotions and introspection. This was not just a mere return to the United States; it was a symbolic homecoming, a chance to reconnect with his roots and recalibrate his purpose.

Leaning back in his seat, he welcomed the solitude and the opportunity for relaxation and contemplation. The turbulence outside echoed the tumultuous yet exhilarating nature of his journey. With each bump and jolt, he was reminded of the unpredictable nature of life itself and the need to relinquish control and embrace the unknown. It was a lesson he had yet to master completely.

As the aircraft soared above the vast expanse of the Atlantic Ocean, he couldn't help but feel a surge of anticipation of being back in the States. There was no way he could be aware that the storms that loomed on the horizon mirrored the challenges he would face in the coming hour. Yet, always armed with determination and a continual sense of purpose, he was prepared to weather any disturbance that lay in his path. He always found strength and resilience in the face of adversity, reaffirming his unwavering commitment to serve his country and tip the scales when duty summoned his unique set of talents.

With several hours left in the flight, he delved into his more profound thoughts, contemplating the journey his life embarked upon, literally and figuratively. The clouds outside the window seemed to emulate the intricacies of his mind, shifting and evolving with every passing moment. As the airplane cut through the darkness, he didn't know the journey ahead would be a defining chapter in his life, shaping his destiny and leaving an indelible mark on his soul.

He didn't mind flying commercially. His various business ventures have been historically lucrative, and he has no shortage of resources at his disposal. With a diverse portfolio of talents and enterprises, his wealth has soared well into the high eight digits. Life has been exceedingly generous, and he maintained a deep reverence for his humble beginnings in the picturesque hills of Roanoke, Virginia.

The image of those days was just a distant memory now. He respected that time and all that came from his youth as they were his roots and also what made him the man he is today. Because of those circumstances, he had found James Woodford and his son, Sean, and they had changed his life forever with the mentoring and guidance he so desperately craved at that time.

It was 1 AM, with several hours until they landed in New York. He was eager to get to his estate in Wyoming. The thought made him smile, knowing he would spend time with his closest friend, Sean Woodford, for the holidays.

The man's nerves frayed with each violent shake. His discontentment was directed towards the flight's tempestuous nature, and the hours seemed to pass at an agonizingly slow pace, shrouded in the veil of darkness that enveloped the cabin. It was the middle of the night, and most passengers had succumbed to slumber, seeking solace in dreams that provided respite from the turbulence. Sleep had eluded him thus far.

A scattered few awake, their silhouettes illuminated by the soft glow of individual displays, or the warm radiance of reading lights scattered about. Some diligently attended to work, their concentration undeterred by the aircraft's erratic movements, sought refuge in visual entertainment, engrossed in movies that offered a temporary escape from the monotony of the lengthy flight.

As he surveyed the scene, a peculiar realization struck him. Despite its capacity, the flight appeared conspicuously empty, with only a fraction of the seats occupied. The absence of fellow passengers added to the eerie atmosphere, casting an air of mystery over the otherwise mundane flight. The sparse occupancy puzzled him slightly, lending an enigmatic quality to the night's voyage, but he cast it off as coincidence.

In the peaceful cabin, the silence held a certain tension, as if the very essence of the flight was intertwined with unspoken anticipation. While most passengers slumbered in blissful ignorance, those awake embraced their isolated seclusion, their thoughts drifting towards the enigma that veiled the flight's emptiness.

In the solitude of his seat, he found comfort in the collective silence, a shared understanding that each passenger was bound by the common thread of proximity simply by chance. In the aloneness of the cabin, he resolved to embrace the cathartic unknown, for it was in the darkest of skies that the brightest stars shone, illuminating the path toward resilience and intrigue.

In a scene that momentarily disrupted the tranquility of the business class cabin, a young Korean man in his mid-20s, his demeanor oscillating between heightened alertness and palpable anxiety, gracefully abandoned his seat. His journey unfolded like a well-rehearsed act, directing him toward the exclusive realm of the bulkhead lavatory at the forefront of the aircraft.

As he ventured forth, he seemed to be pursuing a quest known only to him, with every step marked by a sense of urgency and purpose. Within this confined space of the aircraft, his actions caught the eye of the passenger in 12B, eliciting silent curiosity and forming an enigmatic narrative amidst the hum of the engines and whispered conversations.

The lavatory door closed behind him, and the aircraft continued its flight, leaving a lingering air of intrigue as passengers contemplated the untold stories that crisscrossed the skies, often hidden within the ordinary moments of air travel.

Trained to observe every minutia of his surroundings including everyone around him, the passenger in 12B interest was marginally piqued. However, nearly at the same moment, from several rows opposite the side of the aircraft, a half-Korean/Caucasian woman emerged with her Korean romantic partner in tow.

What unfolded before him was a captivating tableau of intrigue, an enigma wrapped in the dynamic between a half-Korean woman and her companion. Their interaction, devoid of any overt romantic gestures, was a puzzle that begged to be deciphered. With a shared purpose that defied conventional norms, the pair headed toward the front of the aircraft, a journey marked by an unusual level of alertness and an almost uncanny preoccupation with any attentive passengers and flight attendants.

The half-Korean woman, a portrait of poise and vigilance, constantly swept her gaze from the center row to the right, her eyes darting like a hawk searching for prey. Immediately behind her, the male companion remained steadfastly focused to the left, as if an unwavering lookout guarding a hidden treasure. Their synchronized advancement emulated a covert precision to its rhythm, an organized and determined demeanor that was both perplexing and mildly fascinating but altogether unsettling.

As they brazenly navigated the narrow aisle, the small fraction of lucid passengers couldn't help but cast furtive glances, sensing an undercurrent of egotism. The duo appeared out of place, failing to blend in with the current environment or quietude that a typical evening flight usually provides.

Such curiosity took root in the passenger's mind in 12B, like a seed of suspicion, prompting him to remain vigilant in his observations. The enigmatic pair had ignited a sense of reservation within him, and he found himself drawn into the unfolding drama, eager to uncover the secrets that danced beneath the surface of this airborne narrative. He was never one to remain complacent.

Sitting quietly in his seat, he switched his reading light to the *off position*, making his seat appear dormant. He noticed the couple fade from view beyond the curtain on the opposite side of the bulkhead. He studied the area until a third Korean man briskly walked past him in the narrow aisle toward the approximate location where the other three had previously assembled. Now, the situation was drawing his full attention.

At this point, a trifling ripple of unease coursed through him, causing his muscles to tense. He trusted his intuition; it had rarely failed him in the past. The twilight hour cast an eerie shadow over the dimly lit cabin, heightening the suspense. The three men and woman made a peculiar group, having mysteriously converged at a desolate location within the forward cabin, moments of one another.

Their distinct behavior and appearance stood out amidst the backdrop of everyday passengers, grouped as they were, raising a flag of suspicion in his mind. Paired with the uncanny awareness of their surroundings, they were attentive to every minute detail as if they were orchestrating some intricate plan.

The seconds ticked by, but no one emerged from the shadows ahead, nor did any new figures join their enigmatic gathering. The silence was erringly quiet, broken only by the distant hum of the airplane engines. The man's intuition was piqued, urging him to dig deeper and unravel the enigma unfolding in the plane's forward compartment.

Trouble had a way of following him wherever he went, and through experience, he realized early intervention would often enhance a desired outcome. With resolve fueled by curiosity, he embarked on a stealthy reconnaissance exercise to set his mind at ease. He unbuckled his seatbelt and slowly stood up, stepping into the aisle. Like a shadow, he cautiously maneuvered his way closer, his senses heightened, ensuring his presence remained unnoticed. Each step brought him closer to the mysterious group in the forward cabin, shrouded in an aura of the unknown and mystery.

The curtains were drawn leading to the galley, lavatory, and the front-most premium cabin. He knew the layout of the Boeing 787 Dreamliner well from an altercation that he circumvented in 2017 on United Flight 211. Though a different airline, this aircraft possessed the identical seating configuration as the United flight several years ago. He thought the parallelisms of both then and now peculiar. The business class has two sections: a middle, where his seat resided, and a front, which contained the first eight rows.

Gingerly parting the curtain, he inched forward and peered into the front compartment, mirroring the familiarity of his business class section. Yet, it lay eerily silent and devoid of any airline attendants or the puzzling quartet he had observed only moments before. Their absence only deepened the air of speculation, fueling his growing apprehension and shaping his trepidation of what he feared and what was to follow. The forwardmost galley was the only portion remaining before coming to the cockpit door.

Undeterred, he pressed on with a mix of curiosity and trepidation. As he slowly made his way down the aisle, glancing down each row, his eyes scanned for any sign of the foreign passengers he had earlier identified. However, they were nowhere to be found. His fears escalated, gnawing at the edges of his mind, as he confronted the unsettling reality that things were far from ordinary.

Halting just before the drawn curtains of the forwardmost galley, he strained his ears to catch the muffled voices seeping through. The knowledge that only the galley, lavatory, and cockpit lay beyond those curtains focused his resolve for what he must do. In a calculated move, aware of his imposing height of 6'3", he purposefully slouched, subtly diminishing his stature to appear less threatening and assuming the role he wished to portray.

The anticipation hung in the air as he readied himself, to breach the barrier that concealed the answers he sought. With a steadying breath, he prepared to venture into the unknown, expecting that the revelations waiting on the other side had the potential to change not only his life but all the unknowing passengers aboard.

Gently parting the curtain, he allowed a sliver of light to infiltrate the clandestine realm beyond. In that moment, he harnessed the element of surprise, shrouded within the facade of a weary-eyed traveler searching for respite in the lavatory. Little did anyone aboard that flight realize that this seemingly ordinary passenger concealed a formidable secret beneath his unassuming demeanor. No one on the international flight knew this unassuming individual was the United States' most lethal covert asset.

He entered the galley with calculated steps, maintaining a veil of anonymity. Eyes darting discreetly, he assessed the scene before him, absorbing every detail. He immediately saw to his right the three flight attendants, the attractive blond attendant from earlier in front of the other two, and the male and female Korean passengers speaking to them. Their eyes betrayed a mix of surprise, uncertainty, and a primal instinct that something was amiss. However, the truth of his hidden capabilities remained veiled behind his unassuming facade. The enormity of his lethal potential went unnoticed, their minds unable to comprehend the preserved chaos that walked among them. They all looked at him with a minimal sense of alarm but now he had become a liability.

With an impassive expression, he awkwardly returned their gaze, acknowledging their apprehension while skillfully maintaining the guise of an ordinary traveler. Their fear, though palpable, was merely based on an additional passenger they were now forced to contend with. Disappointed, the flight attendants hoped someone *would save them,* but their new guest seemed less than confident.

He was about to say something when he sensed a sudden shift in the atmosphere. As he opened his mouth to speak, a chilling sensation crept across his temple—the touch of icy steel. "Easy, mister," came the deeply accented voice behind him.

His breath caught in his chest, as his heart skipped a beat as fear surged through his veins like an electric current. Time seemed to stand still, his mind racing as his life flashed before his eyes. He smiled inwardly; secretly, these moments made him feel alive. These were the variabilities of life that he enjoyed most.

In a symphony of tension and revelation, he hesitantly elevated his quivering palms, an act of submission to the ominous shadow that now towered menacingly before him. The gravity of the circumstance bore down on him with an oppressive force, magnifying the moment's fervor to an almost unbearable degree. Every iota of his existence vibrated with electric anticipation, and his senses sharpened to an almost supernatural keenness, hyper-alert to the delicate equilibrium teetering between existence and oblivion. It was in this crucible of extremity, this razor's edge of peril, that his true skill and abilities were unleashed, where he transcended the ordinary and touched on the extraordinary.

His eyes squinted in a mix of anticipation and adrenaline, desperately evaluating and assessing any sign or opportunity. Although appearing unassuming, all senses were sizing up the environment around him. Perception swelled within him, a tidal wave of emotions engulfing his thoughts. In that precarious instant, his existence hung in the balance, tethered to the whims of his assailants and their ability to deal with what cometh. They remained oblivious to the immense power disguised within their midst, which was all the edge he required.

As his mind raced, he couldn't help but wonder how he had come to this precipice, entangled in a web of danger and trepidation. The events that led him to this fateful encounter seemed distant as if belonging to another lifetime. Yet, in that perilous moment, the fragility of life and the stark reality of mortality were laid bare before him and where he truly thrived.

Time stood still as he braced himself, uncertain of what lay ahead. The cold touch of the gun barrel against his temple served as a stark reminder of the dangerous path he now traversed, with no choice but to navigate the treacherous depths that fate had thrust upon him.

A soft, bold, and deep voice in broken English with a strong Korean accent broke the silence, "Keep quiet and listen carefully to me." The tall passenger nods in compliance with the basic instructions, though still not seeing the man physically as yet. "Don't be afraid, but don't be a hero either. Do as we ask, and you will not be harmed. Is that understood?" Nodding anxiously, he keeps his hands raised in compliance, assuring the gunman of his submission. The attractive blond wearing a slight smile, tries her best to comfort the new addition to their group, now held captive with them.

"Go stand with the others," says the Korean man as the newest captive walks over to the other prisoners, significantly taller but seemingly far more frightened than the rest of them. He kept his hands up as the second Korean man emerged with another male passenger. "Here he is, he wasn't very difficult to spot," said the second Korean man to the leader, Ju-woo. "Did you confirm it? Get his I.D.," said the leader, still holding the gun and moving his aim to each captive's head from ten feet away.

The second soldier goes through his newest prisoner's pockets before coming to a large wallet and handing it to Ju-woo. He fumbles through the wallet while holding his gun to find the U.S. Marshal badge. He smiles, locating what he is looking for and confirming the prisoner's credentials. The second Korean man pushes the Marshal next to the other prisoners as all four hijackers move to the side, guns aimed at their captives. They were positioned off to the side so the view hole of the cockpit would look like no one was in front of the door, and the area appeared clear.

The leader trains his gun on the U.S. Marshal and says, "Are you the only Marshal on this flight?" The Marshal hesitates, still unsure how he was identified, lured to the front, and captured so easily. He was angry with himself for being such an easy target.

Reluctantly, he nods in validation of the question asked of him, his hands still raised in a gesture of compliance. The air is punctuated by the chilling sound of a silenced gunshot, its *psssffftt* muffled sound silently reverberating through the forward galley. Time stands still as the round finds its mark, piercing the forehead of the marshal, who crumples to the ground.

Shock and horror seize the two flight attendants, their muted screams betraying their unpreparedness for such unexpected violence in front of their eyes. Reacting quickly, the Korean man and woman drag the lifeless body to a secluded corner and swiftly conceal the body beneath a blanket.

Meanwhile, the group leader portrays a sinister smile, his gun now trained on the remaining four captives. "He was our only threat on this flight," he declares, his voice laced with cold determination.

"Now, the rest should be easy." With a menacing gesture, he motions for the captives to move to the opposite side of the galley, where the corpse of the marshal serves as a haunting reminder that their own lives hang in the balance and can be extinguished at any moment.

The female hijacker turns back to the open laptop on the counter and presses several buttons before looking up at the leader and saying in perfect English, "Got it! We are now controlling the aircraft as the third Korean hijacker looks beyond the curtain and turns back, "Everyone's asleep or preoccupied." The leader nods, then looks at the woman, "Heading 088, make it a soft turn as we discussed so the passengers won't be alerted to the plane changing course," "Copy," replied the woman as she punches in commands within the keyboard initiating the order. The gradual turn commences as the aircraft begins to change course. He can feel the turn, but it is subtle, and he ventures to guess that none of the passengers would be aware after a few moments pass.

A chilling revelation unfolded before him as he contemplated the potential thoughts of the pilot and co-pilot. The pilots will soon realize they have lost control of the aircraft if they haven't already.

The Korean couple, their expressions hardened, swiftly redirected their guns toward the four remaining prisoners. Simultaneously, the two other Korean men re-positioned, their weapons now trained on the sealed door leading to the cockpit. The leader's low and commanding voice cut through the tension in a cryptic, icy fashion.

"Kill whoever emerges from that door first, and then breach the cockpit. We'll have only a brief moment to take control, and we cannot afford to let that door close. And remember, accuracy is paramount. A stray bullet could spell catastrophe for all of us."

As the weight of their mission bore down, the group shared a collective understanding and unknown agenda, but their reward outweighed their risk. In that charged atmosphere, every passing second brought them closer to a pivotal moment where lives hung in the balance. The outcome could tip the scales between success and disaster, with no margin for error.

Amidst the tense anticipation, he realized the harsh reality that casualties were likely inevitable. However, his steadfast intention remained to minimize the loss of life and to navigate a path that struck a delicate balance between achieving their objective and preserving the well-being of those involved but innocent.

With a somber determination, he mentally prepares himself for the grim possibilities that lay ahead. His focus honed on navigating the situation's complexities, seeking to mitigate harm and make choices that would yield the most favorable outcome.

In that moment of uncertainty, he found consolation in his commitment to preserving life where possible, even amidst the dark circumstances that enveloped them. It was a solemn duty he shouldered, a responsibility to honor the value of every individual caught in the throes of this harrowing ordeal.

The hijackers braced themselves in the face of danger and uncertainty, poised to execute their chilling instructions to the letter. Their collective resolve forged a bond, an unspoken understanding that failure was not an option for them. With hearts pounding and adrenaline coursing through their veins, they steeled themselves for the critical moments that lay ahead.

As predicted, the cockpit door begins to open as the captain emerges and asks, "Ryan, Daffni, are you . . ." As two silenced bullets rip into his chest. He staggers backward as both men file in after him and subdue the co-pilot immediately. The passenger in 12B was hoping for an unexpected opportunity to save a single life, but he needed to think of the needs of the many. However, his ambitions were dashed as both the woman and man had their guns honed on the three attendants and himself, unfazed by the commotion within the cockpit, not even drawing a glance from the rigid fanatics. They were professionals. Their job was defined and simple: detain or kill the prisoners if necessary, anything necessary to maintain their objective.

He realized he was dealing with highly trained operatives but was still determining whether they were soldiers for hire or radical extremists. He kept his cool but asked with a cracked voice,

"May I put my hands down?" the woman nodded, and he obliged. She cocked her head and looked at him peculiarly, studying him closely for the first time. It was then that he was afraid; she may have recognized him. He knew they wouldn't hesitate to end his life if they had killed a passenger already. After a moment, she shook it off and turned back towards her computer, tracking the aircraft's turn.

The hijackers gained access to the cockpit and killed the U.S. Marshal and the captain. The entire ordeal was achieved without disruption and unbeknownst to the remaining 200 passengers.

With a glimmer of hope, the attractive blond flight attendant stepped forward, her voice laced with a desperate plea for negotiation and a desire to remedy the situation. Unbeknown to her, the hijackers' motivations rarely left room for compromise, whether driven by monetary gain or a fervent cause. Their resolve remained resolute, resistant to any attempts at a peaceful resolution. She began to speak but misread the environment completely.

In a swift and brutal motion, the female hijacker's hand met with the flight attendant's cheek with a resounding slap, a stark reminder of the power dynamics at play. The tension in the air intensified, threatening to ignite a volatile spark. Despite the surge of adrenaline coursing through him, he managed to maintain his composure, a mask of calm determination, veiled behind his true emotions.

His mind calculated the delicate balance between compliance and defiance, recognizing the need to bide his time to seize an opportunity when it presented itself. The hijackers' aggression underscored the seriousness of the situation, reminding him of the danger that loomed over all of them. He remained patient. He would have his moment . . . *he always did.*

As he held his ground, he vowed to remain vigilant, his senses attuned to the shifting dynamics within the confined space. Every fiber of his being coiled with readiness, prepared to act decisively when the moment for action inevitably arrived.

He focused on all four terrorists as the female remained looking at him, studying him, strangely yet intently once again. Knowing what she was thinking, he had failed in his attempt to downplay his display of fear and worry over the given situation. "Ju-woo, I need to speak with you privately," the woman said to the leader who was in the cockpit with the other terrorist, named Jae.

The leader, Ju-woo, was clearly annoyed but came out into the galley and, in Korean, asked, "Gi, what is it?" Her eyes darted back and forth from Ju-woo to the tall captive, and in Korean, she slowly said, "This tall man, ki keun namja. I have seen him somewhere before. He has been in the news, but I don't remember where or why." The Korean boyfriend, Sang, responded in Korean, "I'm sure you are mistaken, Gi, and even if true, it doesn't matter; we have a mission. Stay focused. He has guns focused on him; there is nothing he can do."

Not reacting to their dialogue, he understood Korean well enough that she was referring to the hijacking he had derailed two years before on United Flight 211, and it was just a matter of time before she remembered where she placed him, and his life would be forfeited. Then, the leader said in Korean, "Gi and Sang, watch the prisoners; Jae, get the passenger manifest and bring it to me." Jae exited the cockpit as Ju-woo took a few steps toward the co-pilot, watching him closely, "Fly the plane. Do not look behind you or you will be shot." The co-pilot remained looking forward.

Aware that time was slipping through his fingers, he felt a surge of urgency. Engrossed in reading the manifest, Jae gave the man a moment to focus on his strategic calculations. Closing his eyes for a fleeting moment, he visualized the positions of those around him precisely.

To his left, the woman and man sat roughly six feet away, their proximity presenting a potential opportunity for action. On his right, at a distance of eight feet, stood the formidable figure of Ju-woo, the leader commanding the group. And directly in his line of sight, Jae would soon traverse the galley, his path intersecting with the leader's, manifest in hand. His fate rested on that sheet of paper, not yet realized by his captors.

———

Every detail burned into his mind; he recognized that this upcoming encounter carried with it, immense significance. The manifest held the potential to unlock crucial information, and seizing control of that document could tilt the balance of power in their favor. The unfolding moments would require audacity and precision, a seamless execution of his plan.

A surge of determination coursed through his veins as he prepared himself mentally. Time pressed upon him, urging him to seize the opportunity that lay just ahead. With heightened senses and a resolve that afforded little compromise, he readied himself for the decisive moments that awaited, poised to disrupt the meticulously laid plans of his captors.

It was then the blond flight attendant put her hand gently on his shoulder, comforting him, "It will be okay, Sir," as he opened his eyes and smiled and softly replied, "Yes, it will, in a moment." She looked at him oddly based on his enigmatic words and the expression accompanying them as Jae walked in front of the captives, holding his silenced gun while reading the manifest.

Jae's mistake would be his opportunity. In a blur, the tall man lunged forward, grabbing the Jae's gun and smashing his face with the barrel and fist, then whipped around with the assailant stunned but in the line of sight of both Gi and Sang. They hesitated to fire with their team member in the line of fire paired with the surprise of a hostage uprising. Still, that mistake and hesitation ended up being their downfall as he moved backward with Jae's gun in hand and fired a well-placed bullet into Sang's forehead, killing him instantly as Gi turned to her fallen comrade. He used that moment of hesitation to put a round into Ju-woo's shoulder, and his hand holding the gun, firing as Ju-woo's gun fell to the ground and Ju-woo dropped to one knee.

Gi turned her gun toward him as he shifted his weight, and her fired round hit Jae in the neck, blood spattering across the wall. A second round from her silenced gun hit Jae in the shoulder as the tall passenger returned fire, hitting her in the sternum with his second shot through her right hand, losing her weapon as she slumped to the floor.

Dropping his human shield, Jae slumped to the ground as the tall passenger felt a weak punch to the back of his kidneys and immediately turned and crushed Ju-woo's nose with his elbow, knocking him to the floor.

The flight attendants watched in awe as he handled all four terrorists with relative ease. They were all surprised by the prior display of fear and anxiety the passenger in 12B seemed to emulate. "Give me something to tie this one up; the authorities will have some questions for him and cover the others with blankets and leave them where they lay." Gathering up all the guns save for one, he entered the cockpit and dumped them in the empty captain's seat.

He looked at the co-pilot and winked, "Looks like you are our new captain and weapons keeper. You okay with getting us on the ground?" The co-pilot looked at the guns, then at his guest, "Yes, I can handle it; I'll notify air traffic and the authorities in New York about the circumstances," looking at him closely, "and thank you." "You are welcome. Don't let anyone in here unless it's me, and lock the door when I leave," came the reply as he closed the door.

When he emerged into the galley, the blond flight attendant twirled handcuffs around her index finger and looked at their hero, "I had these in my purse. Will they do?" He smiled as he grabbed them from her and cuffed Ju-woo's wrists tightly. Ju-woo grunted at the pain, but his captor had little sympathy. He looked up at Daffni with a strange look, questioning why she had handcuffs in her purse, and then stood up. He handed the remaining gun to the blond attendant, then looked at Ju-woo and said to the blond attendant, "Daffni, if he moves, just shoot him." "Gladly," she replies, hoping he would do just that.

The tall man walks over to the woman lying on the floor, Gi, who is weak from bleeding out, a puddle of blood pooling next to her, and crouches down, "I remember you, now," said the woman in a faint voice, looking into the man's eyes. He felt her pulse as it was becoming weaker, yet she continued, "You were the one that saved all of those people on that flight to Miami. Sebastian . . . something. I remember how handsome you were on T.V. That was what made me remember you . . . *finally*," as her eyes fluttered. "Sebastian . . . Storm is my name," he replied.

She looked at him and softly asked, "We never had a chance, did we? Bad luck for us this time." Sebastian Storm looked into her eyes and slowly nodded his head.

"No, you didn't, Gi . . . . *Sleep well*," She nodded, somehow content in finally knowing, giving her some sense of comfort as her eyes closed for the final time.

After a moment, Daffni came up as Sebastian stood, "I agree with her, Mr. Storm. You are quite a hero and very handsome, I might add."

Sebastian smiled, "I couldn't just sit idle, plus I needed a coffee." She smiled as she kneeled to grab the manifest lying on the floor, blood smeared all over the page, "I'll get you a coffee any time you like . . . *Mr. Storm*. And anything else you might require. You need just ask," She winked as he retook his seat.

After a few minutes, he finally got some sleep until the wheels hit the runway four hours later.

He never did get his coffee.

Chapter 1

Armageddon

"Change will not come if we wait for some other person or some other time. We are the ones we've been waiting for. We are the change that we seek."
~Barack Obama

Seattle, Washington
2018 Summer

She looked at him, immediately attracted to his ruggedly handsome face, chiseled jawline, and toned physique. She had made her choice. She could see the muscles bulging in his arms, which was always an attractive quality she found in a man. She imagined he was younger, in his late twenties, with pre-mature graying of his hair and beard already setting in. He wore a tailored black suit with a white shirt. Right out of a GQ magazine, she thought. He would be perfect. She needed to pull him away from the other two men with which he was consorting. He would notice her; they always did. . . . *eventually.*

She gave him a casual smile before taking a sip of her glass of Chardonnay. She had set the bait; now, the question was whether he would bite, but she already knew the answer.

It had been some time since she had traveled to Seattle. However, duty called, and her company relied on her expertise to guarantee the flawless execution as the world's largest semiconductor firm selected this site to launch its groundbreaking next-generation technology the following year. A lot was riding on this union, and every detail had to be checked and rechecked.

It was Friday, and the last of the work had been completed. Everything was in order, and the state of Washington was more than happy to be selected as the test site for the implementation of Dymitron's newest innovation. It was a technology disruptor and would change the face of how everyone communicated.

Fueled by a week's worth of exciting and stress-inducing transaction details, Mila craved an electrifying escape. The notion of returning to Texas that evening felt mundane and lackluster, so she made a bold decision to immerse herself in the thrilling underbelly of Seattle's entertainment scene. Determined and eager, she set out on a quest for an experience that would make her heart race and her senses come alive, if only for the evening. Her work in Seattle had certainly earned her that small luxury.

Mila Dmitri had a darker side and explored it on occasion, or when the mood was tempting her, she couldn't shake the urge. She was dressed in a short skirt, revealing her toned legs, and a tight top with just a hint of her midriff revealed. At 29 years old, she had been blessed with height and curves, the envy of any other woman in the room and the object of every man. Long, trim legs from hours in the gym each week were apparent as she was often mistaken for a runway model. She loved the attention but wasn't interested in a commitment. Her vocation was far too straining and demanding of her time; she didn't entertain a long-term relationship but was more than willing to satisfy her carnal needs occasionally when the mood struck her.

Residing at the Four Seasons Hotel in Seattle for the week, she was always satisfied with the caliber of men she had observed during her stay. She dressed every bit the part commanding attention. As she strolled into their lounge, Mila drew the attention of every man and woman within the establishment. She felt their eyes upon her as she walked through the lounge.

She had chosen a seat at the end of the bar; the dinner crowd had already dispersed for the evening. Often avoiding crowds, her timing was specific and deliberate, knowing the lounge was less than busy. None of the men present impressed her until the distinguished gentleman in the black suit caught her eye moments before.

Making eye contact with him several times in the minutes following only ensured him of her interest. At that time, two men approached minutes between one another to attempt to strike up a conversation, but she politely declined the offers of their company or their proposition to buy her a drink. She was confident he would make his move. She knew what she wanted and would be patient, hoping he would not dissatisfy her. Her fear was always primarily in being disappointed.

The bartender brought her another cocktail. Knowing she had not ordered the drink herself; she hoped it wasn't another arbitrary suitor hoping for a chance at a conversation. She wasn't in the mood for that type of dance that evening. She had her own agenda.

Fortune smiled upon Mila as the bartender referenced the intriguing man she had been discreetly eyeing all evening. It turned out he was the one who had sent her the drink, a gesture accompanied by a flirtatious wink and a playful "cheers" with his own cocktail. Though the interaction was cliché and predictable, it was a gesture Mila knew well—a means to an end in her pursuit of distraction and amusement. All that mattered to her was winning the affection of the one she had chosen. All the rest were mere noise to her, an annoying distraction.

She enjoyed her glass of wine, and after nearly finishing it, from behind, she heard the question, "Seems rather unfortunate, a woman as beautiful as you are here all alone." She turned and smiled, slightly repulsed by the platitude, but seductively replied, "Who says I am . . . . *alone*," as she took another sip of her wine. "Oh, touché," his response.

She quickly realized the conversation wouldn't be the strong suit in this union, so she modified her angle and seductively said, "Sit down and keep me company," which the attractive gentleman promptly did. "My name is Steven," as he introduced himself, and she replied in kind. They talked for a time, light and surface in content over another two drinks.

Mila found him entertaining, with a touch of amusement lingering in her thoughts. While his physique and handsome face attracted her initially, his intelligence was not her primary focus. It was physicality that would serve the purpose she had in mind. After an hour of banter, she put her hand on his and softly said, "It's getting late; you should walk me to my room." Steven eagerly paid her bill, and they walked arm in arm to the elevator. The door opened, they stepped inside, and as the doors closed, Mila pressed her floor button and activated with her passkey, then turned to him and kissed him passionately. Her aggressive, forward behavior both shocked and excited him.

"You are just what I need right now; don't disappoint me," she said as she pushed him back against the wall. They surrendered to the hunger that consumed them, their bodies pressed together in a passionate embrace. He met her intensity with equal fervency, spinning her around and melding her body against his own. The forceful contact ignited a surge of exhilaration inside of her, and she reveled in the exquisite intensity that enveloped them. Would this one be different from the rest, she considered? A question she often asked herself.

Her skillful kisses left him breathless, an artful display of desire eclipsing any deficiencies in verbal expression. For a brief moment, they broke the connection, their eyes locked in a mutual anticipation of the pleasure that lay ahead. Without hesitation, she leaned in again, driven by an insatiable eagerness to prolong their fiery connection or at least pursue the possibility.

———

The pulsating energy between them was palpable, and she delighted in the unmistakable sign of his arousal as his leg pressed against her thigh. It only heightened her excitement, intensifying the primal magnetism that drew them closer together.

As they stepped out of the elevator, their eyes darted around, relieved to find the corridor deserted. A shared excitement pulsed between them, intensifying the anticipation of what awaited them. Steven's urgency became evident as he pulled her into the ice machine room, swiftly shutting the door behind them. A decision that ultimately may be his undoing.

In the confined space, the air thick with anticipation, he pressed her forcefully against the wall. Their bodies pressed together, creating a delicious friction that electrified the atmosphere. Mila's hand embarked on a sensual journey, tracing a tantalizing path down his chest, her fingers dancing along his taut chest and stomach. With each passing moment, desire surged within her, compelling her hand to venture further, tracing the contours of his thigh, yearning to feel the undeniable evidence of his arousal below his belt.

Mila's eyes sparkled with a mischievous glimmer as she unbuttoned his pants, the anticipation swirling between them. Her alluring and seductive smile locked with his gaze, silently conveying her intentions. In a deliberate motion, she unzipped him, revealing the desire that awaited her touch.

With a firm yet gentle grip, she held him within the confines of his boxer briefs, exerting a pressure that startled him. Meeting his eyes, she uttered her wanton desire, her words punctuating the charged atmosphere, "I want to taste him." A smile crept across his face, a mirrored reflection of the fantasy taking shape in his mind. Little did he know, Mila held the power in the moment, her strategy cunningly executed. *Men*, she thought, were such simple creatures, easily swayed by their primal desires.

Kneeling, Mila indulged in the pleasure she had longed for since first laying eyes on him at the bar. Her touch was tender, yet purposeful, as she caressed him, fully aware of the pleasure she bestowed upon him. Well-versed in the art of pleasuring a man, she savored every moment, her cravings driving her actions and intentions.

As she gazed up, her lips tantalizingly close to him, she reveled in her power and the control she wielded over his pleasure. His taste, shape, and curve ignited a primal need within her, compelling her to delve deeper into her desires. With each sensation, she reveled in the fulfillment of her craving, embracing the sweet intoxication engulfing her senses, exciting her further.

She had chosen her partner carefully; her selection was calculated to fulfill her deepest desires and orchestrate an evening of escalating pleasures. As she took him into her mouth, her strokes deliberate and unhurried, a sense of delight surged deep within her. Pleasing him excited her in ways she couldn't deny, but a secret truth resided beneath the surface.

In pursuing her own gratification, she reveled in her control over him. Every movement and caress were a testament to her dominance, a manifestation of her insatiable cravings. It was a pirouette where she set the rhythm, her yearnings took precedence. He was merely a tool, a means to fulfill her coveted desires.

But amid her conquest, a subtle shift occurred. A momentary pause revealed her need for fulfillment, her desires demanding attention. In the moment, the focus shifted, and she slowed her movements, savoring the anticipation of her satisfaction.

This encounter was not solely about him but rather her; however, her hidden desires were unleashed in a passionate act of self-indulgence. With each passing second, the realization grew stronger, fueling her determination to embrace her cravings and ensure her yearnings were met.

Behind her enigmatic facade, she reveled in the knowledge that she held the power, the ability to mold the experience according to her whims. And as their desires intertwined, the boundaries blurred, meshing pleasure and control in a symphony of primal urges as they erupted . . . . *as they always had in the past.*

With a deliberate grace, she gradually rose to her feet, her gaze fixed upon him, her fingernails lightly scratching as she ascended.

As her eyes met his, she could discern a flicker of disappointment lingering within his gaze, a silent plea for her to continue the pleasure she had momentarily initiated. Yet, she had grander designs in mind, a more elaborate tapestry of experiences awaiting them both if he met her expectations.

Unfazed by his longing, she held his gaze, a subtle smile tugging at the corners of her lips. She bit her lip, only enticing him more. In that moment, she conveyed a promise of something greater, an unspoken assurance that their journey together would transcend the immediate gratification of the moment.

Her pause was deliberate, a calculated decree to heighten the expectation, to build the anticipation that would make the forthcoming pleasures all the more exquisite. She had crafted a vision, a master plan that would envelop them both in a symphony of desires, orchestrating their passions with a meticulous touch, but she had yet to see his talents. He appeared confident in himself, but it was his turn to show her. She licked her lips, inviting him, beckoning him to show her his abilities.

As she stood before him, her eyes locked with his, the air pulsated with an electrifying tension. Unbeknownst to him, she held the key to a realm where their desires would intertwine, where ecstasy would find its culmination in the dance of their souls. And with that realization, a glimmer of anticipation sparked within his eyes, mirroring her own hunger for the adventure awaiting them.

Mila kissed him and whispered, "I want you to pleasure me, Steven." He seemed oddly confused by her request as he pulled up her skirt, revealing nothing underneath, arousing him further. She anticipated feeling his tongue, but he appeared consumed more with his immediate gratification, entirely missing the bigger picture that would unlock her carnal eruption.

He grabbed her by the thighs, lifted her as she straddled his waist, and slowly guided himself deep inside her. She let out a small moan as he entered her fully. Pushing her hard against the wall, she looked into his striking, chiseled face as he thrusts in and out of her methodically and firmly. He missed the opportunity to show her his talents and poorly misread what she truly desired. However, his aggressiveness was impressive in the moment, but she desired to know more about his endurance and determination behind his lovemaking. Much of the sexual experience was in the energy as it built up between them. That was yet to be defined, especially in light of the moment's spontaneity.

Smiling, Mila enjoyed the moment as she considered the notion of letting him stay with her for the evening, but then, in an instant, he began to groan and tremble as he orgasmed quickly. Mila opened her mouth in surprise, wanting to say something, but then thought better of it. He looked at her face, knowing he probably had disappointed her but was hopeful he could make it up once they got to her room. He smiled and gave her a soft kiss.

He let her down gently as she eased her skirt back down; simultaneously, he pulled his pants up and buttoned them. She smiled at him as she placed her hand by the side of his cheek and gave him a peck on the opposite cheek. "Thank you, Steven," was all that she said, confusing him further.

She then walked to the door. With a gentle pull, Mila slowly opened the door to the ice room, her eyes scanning the hallway with caution, listening and looking for anyone in their proximity. The surroundings exuded an air of serenity, undisturbed by the bustling of the outside world twenty floors below. Meanwhile, Steven's excitement simmered, the evening's promising start fueling his anticipation for what lay ahead.

Little did he know.

Taking hold of his hand, Mila guided him into the hallway, her intentions veiled in secrecy and elusiveness. Steven's bewilderment was palpable, his curiosity yearning to unravel the enigma she presented. He wanted more of her, and she could feel her ambiguity and mystery intoxicated him. They walked silently, holding his hand as she proceeded a step ahead of him, almost dragging him behind her, each step carrying them closer to their destination and toward her suite, or so he thought. He assumed her eagerness to get him to her bed, and the thought excited him.

As they reached the elevators they had emerged from earlier, Mila unexpectedly stopped and hurriedly pressed the *down button* on the wall. The subtle humming echoed in the quiet corridor, and the awkward silence between them was obvious.

Steven cocked his head as to why she summoned the elevator but thought it might be another impulsive gesture, curious about what was to follow. The weight of his expectation hung in the air, both of them awaiting the arrival of the familiar chime . . . *for far different reasons.* The anticipated chime signaled the arrival of the much-anticipated elevator. The seconds ticked by slowly.

Thankfully, only moments later, the familiar melodic tone resonated softly, harmonizing with the hushed atmosphere, and the doors gracefully slid open, unveiling a portal to their next chapter. He took a step in, but she hesitated, not following him into the awaiting elevator. Silent anticipation enveloped them as they embarked on a journey filled with possibilities yet to be discovered.

Puzzled, Steven turned to look at her, "Aren't we going together . . . ." His words hung in the air, but Mila maintained her composure, collecting her thoughts before answering. She held the elevator door open, but instead of reciprocating his anticipation, she leaned forward and placed a finger to his lips, silencing him before he could utter another word.

With an air of finality, Mila spoke, her voice filled with a blend of gratitude and detachment. "Well, Steven, it appears our paths diverge here. I appreciate the temporary diversion you provided, though it was regrettably shorter than I had envisioned . . . *and hoped for.* No regrets, but our brief moment has come to its natural end."

Her intent was clear. Mila moved her fingernail from his lips to his chest, deliberately, gently urging him backward into the middle of the elevator while she stepped back and remained just outside its doors. Steven's hands rose in a gesture of confusion, his face a picture of bewilderment as he tried to make sense of the unexpected turn of events. He shook his head as he looked at her, not understanding what he had missed in the last ninety seconds.

———

Meanwhile, a subtle smile played upon Mila's lips, her eyes sparkling with a hint of cryptic obscurity. "C'est la vie, Steven," she murmured, her voice laced with a mix of benevolence and appreciation. With those parting words, she watched and smiled as the double doors slowly closed just inches before her face, separating them once and for all.

Steven's bewildered expression lingered in her mind as the doors sealed shut, a testament to the enigmatic nature of their passing encounter. She wondered what he would think during the long ride, descending the twenty floors to the street level. Mila embraced the transient nature of their connection, content in the knowledge that she had taken control of her own narrative. She left behind a moment that would only momentarily remain etched in her memory but lasting far longer in his, she was sure.

Mila reached into her purse, retrieved a tissue, and gently wiped away her lipstick as if erasing any lingering trace of their encounter as she made her way to her room. A profound yearning for a warm bath consumed her, an urgent desire to cleanse herself of the filth and regret she felt, still haunted by the remnants of his undesired scent clinging to her skin and clothing. She longed to wash away not only his physical presence but also the memory of their rendezvous, as if immersing herself in warm water could absolve her of the lingering traces of their connection on all levels.

Compartmentalization of any positive or negative memory had always been a skill she possessed, a mechanism to store away memories she deemed unworthy of her consciousness and long-term subconsciousness. Living in the present, she embraced the spontaneity each passing moment offered, and this instant wasn't different from any in the past.

However, this particular experience was one she yearned to erase from her mind as swiftly as possible. The desire to forget was a relentless flame that burned within her, propelling her to seek comfort in the fleeting nature of time, hoping it would carry away the unwanted remnants of their transitory moment, leaving her refreshed, renewed, and free to embrace the future unburdened by the weight of the past.

She was unsure why she wished to forget this particular occurrence with more insistence other than she was disappointed in his tenacity and stamina. She surmised it simply as male weakness, his selfishness of being unable to endure and succumbing to his egotistical pleasure while disregarding hers.

She made her way back to her room.

With the room key in hand, she deftly waved it over the lock of room 2003, digital and mechanical parts reacting, promptly unlocking the door. Stepping inside, she closed the door behind her, enveloping herself in the privacy and sanctuary of her suite. A sense of relief washed over her, knowing the man she desired to keep at a distance would unlikely gain any access to her inner sanctuary. She thought it peculiar her interest in the evening only repulsed her now and in such a short time.

Confident in her decision, she recognized the layers of security that shielded her from his presence. He remained unaware of her last name, rendering it impossible for him to locate her suite within the hotel. Furthermore, she assumed he was not a hotel guest, eliminating the possibility of possessing a passkey to the elevator or bypassing her defenses. And lastly, she didn't recall mentioning her suite number, though he knew which floor. It would be quite a feat and endeavor to locate her.

In the solitude of her suite, she breathed a sigh of relief, reassured by the layers of security fortifying her refuge. Here, she would find solace, untethered from any unwanted intrusions.

A sense of relief washed over her, knowing she had successfully eluded the evening with a stranger and the awkwardness that would have undoubtedly followed. Everything had unfolded according to her meticulously crafted plan. She placed her purse on the entry table and embarked on the short journey down the hallway to her spacious two-bedroom suite.

Stepping into the living room, she was greeted by a breathtaking panorama of the Seattle skyline spread before her. The expansive windows framed the city's splendor, inviting her to immerse herself in its beauty. As she made her way to the kitchen counter, a pang of realization struck her when she saw the bottle of wine sitting solitary atop the smooth surface of the countertop. She had forgotten the bottle of Caymus, a thoughtful gift presented to her earlier in the week by her boss, Anthony Voss, on her successful campaign in Seattle.

Pausing for a moment, she contemplated her options. The allure of the wine beckoned, promising a moment of indulgence and relaxation. With a decisive nod, she resolved to retrieve the forgotten bottle, refusing to let the opportunity slip away to enjoy the robust flavor she knew the bottle would provide her. In addition, she desired a method to drown out her impending guilt from the evening which loomed over her.

However, she had her priorities. With purposeful steps, she made her way to the large bathroom, the anticipation of a luxurious bath enveloping her senses and maintaining her focus. Turning on the faucet within the tub, she unleashed a stream of hot water, watching as the bathtub slowly filled and steam began to saturate the room, soothing her in the process.

Her fingers gracefully gripped the soap bottle, pouring a generous amount into the rising water, releasing a captivating fragrance as the bubbles ascended. As she eased off her clothing, her outfit slowly cascaded to the floor; she shed the layers concealing her bare essence, embracing the vulnerability of her exquisite nakedness.

Mila saw the candle on the counter and lit it with the matchbox lying adjacent to the fixture as she turned off the lights, the glow from the candle creating an amatory mood. Adding soft and tranquil music only added to the allure of her moment. The rich bouquet of plumeria immediately began to fill the room, bringing a smile to her face and reminding her of the islands of Hawaii.

Leaving the bathroom momentarily, she ventured back into the kitchen, the promise of indulgence beckoning her. Uncorking the bottle of 2011 Caymus Cabernet, she poured a generous measure, savoring the opulent aroma and the promise of its velvety taste.

Glass in hand, she retraced her steps, the sensual elegance of her stride embodying confidence and allure.

Returning to the bathroom, the warm glow of candlelight danced upon her exposed form in the dim light, casting shadows that only enhanced her allure. Gazing into the mirror, she studied the flawless figure standing before her. She knew with unwavering certainty that any man fortunate enough to cross her path would be forever altered, unable to compare to the depths of her appeal. Yet, despite her power to captivate, no man had ever truly claimed her heart in a way that would make her exclusively his to possess. She had never allowed anyone to get close enough to her to claim her heart. That notion was an enigma to her.

It was a bittersweet realization, for while she embraced her independence and the freedom it brought, a part of her longed for a connection transcending a mere moment of passion. Pride and melancholy intertwined within her, creating a complex tapestry of emotions as she navigated the delicate balance between self-assuredness and the unfulfilled yearning for a love that would envelop her completely.

As she turned, the delicate rim of the Cabernet glass danced along the contours of her lips, an enticing accent to her already mesmerizing magnetism. In that fleeting moment, she indulged in self-admiration, marveling at the sculpted masterpiece her body had become. As she approached 30 years of age, bestowed upon her was a genetic advantage, but she refused to rest solely on that fortune. She worked diligently to maintain her exotic elegance and appreciated every moment.

With unyielding dedication, she had sculpted her captivating physique through a rigorous routine of disciplined choices. The strict adherence to a meticulous diet and the relentless pursuit of challenging workouts, blending the finesse of boxing and the transformative power of Lagree, had forged her lithe and toned form. It was a magnetic attribute that constantly drew desire from the opposite sex, a testament to her ravenous appeal. Yet, it held a more profound significance—a symbol of external validation interwoven with her unwavering pride, a tribute to the unyielding spirit that had fueled her remarkable journey of self-preservation and personal triumph.

Mila slipped a toe into the steaming bath, followed by the rest of her leg, the heat tingling her skin and senses as she slowly descended. She luxuriated in the scorching embrace of the water, relishing its intense heat, which enveloped her every curve. She reveled in the sensations as she eased deeper, surrendering herself to the comforting depths, the bubbles swirling around her in a playful cavort.

Setting her glass of wine on the adjacent table, she reclined further into the steaming liquid, feeling it gradually enshroud her body, caressing her skin and enticing her senses. With each passing second, the water became an effervescent elixir, washing away his lingering scent, liberating her from his hold, and leaving her cleansed, renewed, and ready to embark on her journey of sensual self-indulgence.

Relaxing in the moment, her body was fully enveloped, and the sting of pain, like needles upon her skin, diminished as she adjusted to her new environment. Mila stared at the ceiling, her ears barely below the water level, amplifying the distorted sound to her ears from even slight movements she made within the tub.

In these moments, she indulged in vivid fantasies, longing for her encounter to unfold precisely as she craved. Deep within, she held onto a desperate hope that this serendipitous meeting would finally fulfill her most intense desires, for she had never experienced the elusive pleasure of an orgasm with a man. Disappointed by past experiences, she had resigned herself to the belief that such satisfaction might forever elude her. Recognizing her unique ability to stimulate herself in a way that ignited her sensuous desires, she understood she alone possessed the key to unlocking the depths of her own pleasure.

She closed her eyes and concentrated on the few moments with him within the ice room as she tasted him, drawn simply from her memory. Her hand moved between her legs as she felt what she already suspected: the smoothness of her skin and the slickness present of her fluids, as well as his. Even underwater, her fingers lubricated as they stimulated her feminine button as she thought of him inside of her, stimulating her further. Her opposite hand was now squeezing her breasts and slightly pinching her nipples, and her ecstasy began to rise. She needed the vision of him to satisfy her basic need.

Visualizing her arms around his neck as her back slid up and down the wall, rhythmic to his thrusts and penetration. She chose a far different ending than the reality of her night. In her version, she enjoyed him as she slid up and down him, delighting in his aggressiveness as he pushed her from wall to wall only to finish against the ice maker itself as the squeezing and thumping were surely heard from outside the room.

Her fantasy then continued with them running to her room, kissing passionately along the way, barely able to get to their intended goal of reaching her suite. Once inside, the physical manifestation would continue into the second chapter of obsession and excitement.

The music was distant in her mind but added to the excitement. She continued to touch the warm water around her, thinking of the delight in the moment as images filled her mind of seduction and sexual arousal. She would think of christening every piece of furniture within the suite but noticed her fantasy no longer was of Steven but of someone else. An image of a different man began to fill her thoughts.

This new man's face had an increased passion and verve she had not felt before. As her dream escalated to its climax, she now envisioned the man above her, inside of her, looking into his deep green eyes and feeling all of him and his essence. Still, his eyes concentrated on her and only her. Their rhythm aligned and in sync; as he penetrated, she held his gaze as the image became more precise and more relevant.

She couldn't hold on any longer and burst out as her orgasm exploded, and she moaned in her ecstasy and her excitement. She trembled, and her entire body spasmed; every nerve firing within her body, and she wanted to feel it all before it stopped. She embraced her contractions as the bath water spilled about the sides, but she didn't care.

All she could think of was the sensation she had never before felt. She knew it wasn't only because of the physical element of her experience but equally because of the mysterious man who ultimately materialized within her vision, filling her thoughts. How did he creep into her fantasy, she wondered? She didn't mind; she welcomed it, even embraced it. Her senses formed a coalition that created the perfect storm, locking in her pleasure on every level.

As the tremors diminished and her surroundings became tranquil, his image filled her thoughts again. A man she had never met but had heard so much about. What did it mean, and why did he appear within her fantasy? It didn't matter; she knew what she must do. She had to meet the man who was filling her dreams.

The reoccurring image was of Governor Damian West.

Los Angeles, California
2021 Summer

A sense of tranquility filled the room as Ryker Davion lay back against the pillow, comfortably in bed beside his wife at their luxurious Bel Air estate. The elderly couple, both in their early 70s, savored the rare moment of respite. Ryker engrossed himself in the pages of an advanced copy of the Wall Street Journal, relishing the opportunity to stay ahead of the financial world. On the other hand, his wife found comfort in the guilty pleasure of watching the latest episode of the Real Housewives of Orange County.

With their dedicated staff having departed for the night, the Davion's enjoyed the serenity and intimacy of their private oasis, enduring the quiet conversation and bickering that often preceded their restful slumber. Although, after as many years spent together, they annoyed one another more than cherished their union, despite it lasting nearly 50 years.

Ryker Davion, a boisterous and prolific figure in Democratic circles, and his strong support for the party was no secret. One of the country's wealthiest hotel chain moguls and entrepreneurs, he commanded a measure of respect in all cliques. Whether his opinions were sought after or not, Ryker never hesitated to express them to anyone regardless of interest, leveraging his power, prestige, and considerable influence to make his positions known on local and federal matters. His outspoken nature enjoyed no bounds, and he took pleasure in flaunting his vast fortune, biases, and political judgments to anyone who would listen, or not listen with equal indifference.

He had long grown tired of President Trump's arrogance and bravado and was elated the Democratic Party regained the White House in the 2020 election the year before. He had felt hopeful that Joe Biden, having announced his intention to run in April 2019 and promising to continue Barrack Obama's legacy, would make him a considerable favorite, and it paid off with his victory over Donald Trump in 2020.

He would miss the endless arguments and debates with his longtime friend, Republican Senator Samuel T. West. They always concentrated on the good fight and continuously maintained their friendship first and foremost, but he was glad the Democrats prevailed, and he let Senator West know it whenever possible.

With the exception of Senator West, however, with his colorful opinions, Ryker had amassed a long list of adversaries throughout his life, while his supposed friends only lingered around to further their own personal agendas. This kind of scenario was all too familiar in the Los Angeles area. Ryker thrived in the company of like-minded individuals who only fueled his sense of entitlement and power.

Meanwhile, further down the block, three figures, attired in black, systematically and methodically made their way along the rear of the expansive backyard of the Davion estate, the security cameras disabled easily. They continued along the side of the house before coming to a side entrance, glass door.

The leader, a tall and muscular man, towered over the other two, ensuring they maintained and respected their tight schedule. *Nerek König,* codenamed *Inferno,* was no stranger to combative warfare and kept a tight ship with all missions executed under his command. He has Fury to answer to and didn't want to disappoint his superior. "Sapphire, get us through that door," whispered Inferno. "Yessir," came the soft response. The third, Onyx, observed from behind them for any activity or movement.

The only woman of the trio went to one knee, pulling from her backpack a specialized circular glass cutting device, and attached it with a suction grip to the section of glass just below and to the right of the handle. Given enough time, Sapphire could break into anything. The other two figures maintained their vigilance, scanning the surroundings for any signs of alarm.

The two men stood, studying her as she meticulously performed her objective on the glass door. Methodically working the apparatus, she measured the circle's radius at roughly 3", giving a diameter of 6" for the cutting mechanism to perform a completely unobstructed circular tract. Rotating the diamond cutting tip, she swiveled counterclockwise four times, cutting the glass seamlessly before detaching the device and the 6" piece of glass itself, giving her access with her hand to the locking mechanism within, just below the handle without activating any sensors in the older home. She softly opened the door as the three of them silently slipped inside. A slight and quiet beeping sound was emitting, allowing time to disarm the security panel.

With a sense of urgency, the trio swiftly made their way toward the location of the security panel. Their steps were calculated and deliberate, minimizing any noise that may draw attention.

As they reached the designated area, the woman skillfully produced a small device from her pocket designed to override the security system. With precision, she connected the device to the panel, bypassing the alarm code requirement within a few seconds, and the beeping ceased. The three exchanged glances, a silent acknowledgment of their accomplishment. They had cleared one obstacle, but their mission was far from over.

The group hesitated momentarily, listening for any disruption that broke the solitude enjoyed by the quiet evening. Now, with unhindered access to the house, they proceeded deeper into the residence, their true intentions yet to be revealed.

"Did you hear that, honey? It sounded like a door opened downstairs, and something is beeping, but now it has stopped, did you hear it," asked Gwendolyn, Ryker's wife. "I'm sure it's nothing, Gwen," responded Ryker, displaying a boldness solely for her benefit, as if to say, "Who would have the audacity to invade *our* home?" Gwendolyn shook her head at her husband's outward display of arrogance, "Oh shhh, Ryker, go check it out, please." In an effort to satisfy his wife and avoid any additional complaining, he grabbed his .380 snub-nosed revolver from the nightstand in a vague attempt to flex his masculinity. Still, the effort was lost on Gwendolyn as she quietly said, "Oh, Ryker, what are you going to do with that? Is it even loaded? Probably just shoot yourself in the foot, you old fool."

He sheepishly glared at his wife, secretly loathing her very existence, as he turned in a huff and made his way outside their room, down the vast hall, to the stairway. The three figures detected the old man descending the stairs as they silently waited for him to come within range.

Out of sight of Gwendolyn now, Ryker was visibly frightened as the gun grew heavy in his outstretched hand, causing it to shake uncontrollably. Upon coming to the last stair, Ryker turned to his right, only to see the incoming fist of the larger man hit him squarely in the face, knocking him unconscious; Ryker's image faded to black as he collapsed to the floor. His unloaded gun fell to the ground, sliding across the marbled floor.

"Wake up, Ryker, wake up, you idiot!!!" His subconscious focused on Gwendolyn's voice, desperately calling out to him, seemingly so far away, but as he regained awareness, he realized it was far from a bad dream he had been experiencing. Ryker found himself atop his bed, sitting upright, their backs against the headboard. His wife beside him, both of their hands bound in front of them by nylon ties, the salty taste of blood in his mouth. His upper lip was swollen from the blow he had suffered earlier.

The three figures stood at the foot of the bed, masked all, holding silenced handguns in their right hands; the woman had hers in her left. Ryker and Gwendolyn looked at one another, uncertain what was happening before Ryker finally said, "Take what you want . . . take it and leave. Please don't hurt us."

Inferno looked at his two prisoners and replied, "We aren't interested in anything you have, old man; we are here to make a statement. You are the first of many . . . examples until the government begins to listen, and the people rise in retaliation. It is the fate we have chosen and will follow as destiny has determined. Things must change in this country, and your sacrifice, and others like you, will serve its purpose and get their attention. Some may call you martyrs, but most won't care. In a month, you will be all but forgotten. You are a means to an end, a small piece in an otherwise larger puzzle. Your boisterous words will be your downfall, Mr. Davion, and for your big mouth and lofty opinions, your wife will suffer as well. *Your opinions* have forfeited . . . *both* of you."

The man's words were cold and cryptic in his monotone voice, and Gwendolyn and Ryker just looked at one another, unsure what to say, but as the masked figure's words began to sink in, they both realized their captors had only one intent.

Ryker always prided himself on being quite the negotiator. He could reason with these people; he was certain of it, "Please, let's talk this through, I'm sure . . ." As Inferno raised his silenced gun and put a single round through Gwendolyn's forehead, a perfect trickle of blood dripped from the 9mm hole as her eyes slowly closed, a final reflex as her last breath of air expended.

Ryker stared in disbelief at what was happening; everything progressed far too quickly to process. He looked at the gunman, knowing he was going to die at that moment; there was no way out of this, but true to his nature, he had to, at least, try. He began to open his mouth to speak, and as he did, the second round from the ominous man's gun ripped through the air into Ryker's right eye, extinguishing his life without him uttering another word.

The shorter of the two men pulled out an old medium-sized paint brush from his backpack and removed it from the sealed Ziplock bag it had been stored within. The ample space above the couple's large bed provided the ideal spot for their message.

The taller man pulled out his phone and typed a message, "The Davion's have been dealt with." The text received 2,750 miles away, signifying their targets were eliminated.

"Paint the message," we need to get out of here barked Inferno to Sapphire and Onyx.

New York, New York
2021 Summer

A sense of contentment washed over him as he admired the breathtaking cityscape from the 64th-floor penthouse. The hefty price tag of his luxurious loft seemed insignificant compared to the joy it brought him. The spaciousness, the stunning view, and the comforts it offered were all worth the 19.7-million-dollar investment.

Still fixated on the view, hearing the clinking of the ice cubes colliding with his glass of Clase Azul tequila, familiarly calming him, he softly said, "The Davion's have been handled. It's all coming together." Fury was proud of his young protégé, Inferno, having executed the objective in Los Angeles, as he muttered to himself,

"Tobias would be proud of the young man," as Fury looked out over the bright light illuminating the concrete jungle below. Inferno would arrive back at their base in a few hours.

Later that evening, Inferno's arrival being discreet, the private jet touching down under cover of night, adding to the mystery surrounding his arrival along with Onyx and Sapphire. They emerged from the aircraft, his ominous stature silhouetted against the dimly lit tarmac with the two in tow as he was met by Fury. Despite the late hour, their movements had a sense of urgency, a determination that belied their fatigue.

All three bore the unmistakable signs of exhaustion, their faces lined with fatigue and their bodies tense with the memory of a successful mission. They looked as though they had faced trials that would break lesser men, their physical presence alone enough to command respect and instill fear in any that came before them.

As they made their way through the city streets to the penthouse, a palpable aura of danger always surrounded them, a reminder of the darkness they had confronted and the demons they had battled in their life past. Theirs was a world of shadows and secrets, where every step could be their last and every ally could be a foe in disguise. They knew Sebastian Storm, HB, and the Anti-Terrorist Special Division (ATS) were always on the lookout for them, and Fury and Inferno desperately remained only a step ahead of them and ATS's radar.

Despite their weariness, Inferno remained vigilant, knowing Fury would want a full report of the Davion mission. Their senses sharp and their minds alert, they knew that their journey was far from over, that new challenges lay ahead, waiting to test their resolve and mettle. Their success was built on one mission at a time, but they also knew they were ready to see their objective through to the end.

Arriving at their building, Sapphire and Onyx went their separate ways. Fury and Inferno entered the penthouse foyer, their figures fading past the front door.

Fury and Inferno were not just soldiers; they were forces of nature, unstoppable and unyielding in their determination. Wherever they went, the flames of their passion and fortitude would burn

---

brightly, lighting the way for those who dared to follow. And now, with their new objective, they would be forever modifying the American landscape in the months and years to follow.

Inferno softly said, "I think Tobias would be pleased with our progress." Fury sighed, "I think he would as well, more so because of our resourcefulness. No disrespect, but we will do it better than he did; we won't make his mistakes. Of that, I can assure you, Inferno."

Fury changed the subject, "How's the pain in the jaw?" "Still pretty numb and occasional aching that comes and goes, but it is what it is; pain doesn't bother me," replied Inferno. Fury nodded, "Mine is almost gone, but glad that is over." Inferno nodded and snickered, "Yeah, no more of that shit."

When Inferno and Fury escaped Dublin, Ireland, and slipped through the fingers of Sebastian Storm and Hillary Bastini, their immediate destination was Colombia. Fury knew that HB's Anti-Terrorist Special Division (ATS) would be on a manhunt for the two of them after Tobias was eliminated, thereby cutting off the figurative head of the successful Fenris Organization that Tobias Teague had spent over a decade building. They had spent a small fortune getting to South America undetected through private air transit, ground, and sea to reach their destination. Their attention to detail had gotten them there unscathed and well off the grid.

In Bogotá, Colombia, a specialized doctor, unknown to most, had a unique gift for altering the identity of anyone who passed the vetting process and produced the one million dollars in cash, due and payable upon the consultation.

Fury and Inferno met with the doctor in his private facility, which was state of the art and contained all the modern advances medicine has to offer. They walked in, with only the doctor sitting in wait within the anteroom anticipating their arrival. Fury dropped the satchel containing two million dollars upon the desk. The Doctor's demeanor seemed cautious and serious.

Dr. Leonardo Rendón smiled and unzipped the bag, seeing the $10,000 stacks of $100 bills. He estimated that the entire 200 stacks seemed to be contained within. Upon his visual verification, his outlook changed. "Welcome, my friends," he declared in his strong Colombian accent. An educated man, his English appeared to be exceptional.

"Oh my, you both big men, grande, that may be extra. Just kidding, same price. That was a bad joke, " as Leonardo looked at the men, they did not find the comment humorous at all. Dr. Rendon thought it best to get to business. He took a few photos of each and loaded them into his computer.

"Please, please, gentlemen, sit down," he gestured to the two seats in front of him. He looked at both of them, studied their facial features, and, after a few moments, explained his proposal. "Gentlemen, you are both. . . . fierce men, strong I can see. For you," as he referenced Fury and his monitor with Fury's face, he showed the manipulation of extending his chin, giving him a cleft in the process, widening his jaw and reshaping the nose, lastly removing multiple scars and offering him a prosthetic eye for the one he lost on the mission in Australia. For Inferno, accentuating the zygomatic arch above the cheek, thinning the nose, and taping the ears back tighter against his head.

He also suggested tattoo-type melanin darkening of the skin that would make them look more European and less Caucasian, fading into their chest to appear normal or suntanned. They would receive a different set of teeth using veneers so that dental records could not be verified, and their eye color would also change.

As a last measure, their fingerprints were to be removed, and specialized implants were placed upon each finger, altering their unique ridge patterns, varying loops, whirls, and arch form. All of these physical effects would essentially erase their given identities. The final component included within the price was the documentation to support the alterations made. Dr. Leonardo Rendón concluded his discussion after 30 minutes of talking, very proud of himself for this thoroughness and expertise.

Fury stood up along with Inferno, towering over the man before them, "When can we start, Doctor?" Looking up, Rendón softly said, "Tomorrow, if you wish? The process will take five weeks total."

———

Fury put both hands on the table as he leaned forward, "Dr. Rendón, we will each have the various procedures done on alternative days as one of us will watch over the other . . . . and we will be watching you. In addition, your records, conversations, images . . . all of it, will be destroyed in our presence upon completion. Any deviation from this will initiate your prompt termination of life. Do you understand me completely, Doctor?" Dr. Leonardo Rendón shook as he slowly replied, "Yes, Sir. I assure you." "Good," responded Fury, "We will be back in the morning," then turned and left. Dr. Leonardo Rendón sat down in his chair, looked at the bag of money, and wondered if this case was worth the risk. *"What had he gotten himself into,"* was his parting thought as the door closed behind them.

Fury and Inferno were still recovering from the host of surgeries and procedures, but neither were strangers to pain. They both knew it well, embraced it even. But now, in light of Dr. Leonardo Rendón's work, they could walk more freely, more confident that their true identities were protected.

At least, for the time being.

Despite the artificial eye that Fury now had, he preferred the ominous black patch. He wore it with pride, the badge of honor that reminded him daily of that man that did it to him and at some point, he would ultimately satisfy his vengeance. He knew, someday, his path would cross with Sebastian Storm.

Fury and Inferno clinked glasses and took a pull, looking out over the New York skyline, enjoying the beginning of what they both hoped would be their legacy.

The following morning, the Davion's Lead Chef, David Jeromy, prepared their breakfast as he had done for the past 15 years. He made his way promptly at 7:30 AM toward the large hallway leading to the immense stairway heading to the master bedroom. As he walked with the breakfast tray, his foot kicked the small chrome snub-nosed .380 revolver across the floor. He abruptly stopped, placed the tray down, retrieved the gun, looked at it for a moment, then placed it on the tray and proceeded upstairs.

Mr. Jeromy historically never had to knock as the Davion's were always up to greet him, usually both irritable and bickering with one another when he entered. However, as he opened the door that day, all was uncharacteristically quiet and peaceful. He couldn't remember the last time he had entered their vast bedroom without Mrs. Davion complaining about something concerning her husband.

He walked down the short hall that opened into their lavish bedroom but stopped suddenly and dropped the tray upon the floor. Before him lay Ryker and Gwendolyn Davion, sitting upright, both shot in the head, blood platter on the headboard behind them.

The scene before him was disturbing and filled with a bizarre and twisted set of details about the dual murders. The grotesque, distorted faces of Ryker and Gwendolyn staring, lifeless, along with the eerie words written on the wall with what appears to be their own blood, creating an unsettling and chilling atmosphere. Their eyes had been taped open, making the scene appear eerie and unnatural.

Hours later, the lead homicide detective spoke with the coroner while forensics was still piecing together the crime scene. "What's your take on these two, as far as the cause of death, anything out of the ordinary?" The Detective asked. "I don't expect much other than the obvious bullet to the head lends to an open and shut. What about you, Detective, any motive or suspects," asked the coroner. "I wish. Nothing appears to be stolen or out of the ordinary from what the employees are saying. No, this one worries me the most; this crime was personal and came from pure hate or some fanatic. We have no leads and no witnesses. We have nothing." Replied the Detective, shaking his head as he knew he had something far bigger going on here. They both stared at the words written in blood above where the victims had been lying for most of the night.

The coroner looked at the words on the wall as if they would speak to her in some way or explain their meaning, but nothing came. She cocked her head and read aloud, *"It's time for change. The Reign Cometh. He will reveal himself soon. This is merely the beginning . . ."*

"What do you suppose that means, Detective?" asked the coroner.

"I really have no idea, but there can be nothing good about it . . . . *Nothing good at all*," replied the Detective.

New York City, New York
2021 Early Summer

Joseph R. Biden was elected the 46th American President of the United States and had taken possession of the Oval Office only months before in January, winning the Presidential election in November 2020. With the Democrats now controlling the White House, Senate, and House of Representatives, everyone thought the American people would be settled and satisfied, but nothing could be further from the truth. Possibly because of the unilateral control, followed by further political gridlock, the American people had become even more disenchanted and angry. Nothing was changing, and the confidence of the American people was eroding with each passing day.

All came to a head as of May 2020. The George Floyd's incident fueled an onslaught that would affect cities nationwide for the following year. Floyd's senseless death further catapulted chaos to every corner of the nation. The cities were burning and the politicians simply watched the slow decay of a dying nation.

The larger cities seemed to be the hardest hit. Molotov cocktails erupted in a synchronized display of chaos, shattering storefront windows along downtown New York's 5th Avenue. The shopping districts and SoHo bore the brunt of the devastation, with extensive damage inflicted massively throughout the city and similarly in other states. The surreal scene was a rallying cry for the thousands of rioters and looters, fueling the mayhem and disorder that swept through the city like wildfire.

Amidst the vandals in downtown New York, the police force found themselves severely constrained in their efforts to control the dissidents and protestors. They faced immense regulatory setbacks and limitations, hindering their ability to maintain proper order and safety for their inhabitants. The scrutiny and media attention surrounding allegations of police brutality and related deaths only exacerbated the situation. As a result, the country was descending into pandemonium, with cities such as New York on the verge of self-destruction, unraveling with each passing day, cannibalizing themselves one city at a time.

The crowds exuded an overwhelming sense of confidence and arrogance, almost taunting the police enforcement, testing their resolve. Criminal incidents were captured on countless videos and phones, quickly spreading across social media platforms, exposing the upheaval on a global scale. The widespread documentation showcased the extent of the vandalism and protests as they engulfed the streets and businesses in the area. The viral nature of these recordings further fueled the defiance and brazenness of the crowds, amplifying the challenges faced by law enforcement. Their wings clipped, and the public took advantage of that notion.

The government was losing its grasp on martial law as vandalism, protests, and rioting were on the rise, increasing in frequency, and many anti-governmental factions were growing in popularity and evolving as these organized groups were acting out far more than had been witnessed in the past. Much of the tension seemed to converge around the growing separation between the wealthy and the poor, its escalation in segregation, tax hikes, inflationary increases, racial inequalities, diminishing economy, governmental inefficiencies, inadequate home and student loan programs, and the ever-increasing unemployment rate.

People had grown disillusioned with their government, witnessing politicians amassing wealth and prioritizing their interests over the well-being of the people they swore to serve. The population yearned for improvement in their lives, yet all they witnessed was empty political rhetoric and a widening gap between the politicians and the people they governed. The demand for change was palpable as the public grew weary of the broken promises and self-serving actions of those in power. Chaos was quickly becoming the norm in American's everyday life.

He zips up his jacket, covers his head with his hood, and ventures into the evolving Armageddon developing around the city. Happening upon an ideal spot, Malcolm removes the red, white, and blue paint canisters from his grimy backpack, and amongst the disorder and ruin before him, he finds, quite by chance, a portion of brick wall unscathed and unmarked despite the fires, broken glass and destroyed property strewn about. A perfect canvas for his latest masterpiece.

It must be an omen, thought Malcolm as he smiled inwardly. Amongst the wreckage and devastation, he was fortunate to discover a pristine backdrop amidst the chaos. To him, it's a sign, an opportunity to convey his message and expression through art. In its simplicity, his creation will speak volumes. Well, at least, for those that will appreciate it.

His intention wasn't to loot, steal, burn, or destroy per se. His mark was more of the creative variety. He simply wanted to exercise his 1st Amendment right of *freedom of speech; he* had been born into that right as an American citizen. He spent the better part of thirty minutes designing his masterpiece in an artistic form that suited his mood at the time and reflected his views of the crumbling world around him.

He knew law enforcement was too preoccupied with more pressing issues along 5th Avenue and those high-dollar storefronts to give him any attention or hassle. His work complete, he stood back, critiquing his creation, content in his manifestation, displayed for all to see and hopefully value but more so, poignant in its simplicity and the message it illustrates for those that happened upon this particular spot in New York City.

A disheveled vagrant approaches Malcolm from behind, unaware of Malcolm's newly crafted artwork. He's holding a makeshift Molotov cocktail, looks at Malcolm's picturesque wall, and reads it aloud, "Cease All Tyranny, Stand Up Americans. Stand and Be, Unified All . . . . . . Hell yeah, man!!" and yells out loudly as he lights the strip of fabric dangling from the bottle and throws it at the wall saying, "Let em' burn, all of them. Burn! Burn it all down," as the wall ignites from the accelerant splattered from the impact of the bottle as Malcolm's words burn with the irony reflected in the message written. Malcolm tried to stop him, but it was too late. The damage was done as he was mesmerized by the burning wall before him.

Symbolic in some form, as the man runs off to cause havoc somewhere else. Malcolm studies the drifter as he runs down the street, fascinated by the man, seemingly liberated on some level. After a moment, he turns back to his partially distorted artwork, the still-wet paint burning and dripping now. Altered and charred, the image looks more relevant and heartbreaking, symbolic of the anarchy surrounding them.

His country was falling apart, a far cry from the time in his youth when he had served in the Marine Corp. Saddened by all humankind, Malcolm has little hope as he stares sadly at his work. He peers down the street in both directions, fires everywhere, their lights dancing along the walls of the night. Above, soot and ash fell like snow from the sky, and it was then that he realized they were all at fault, and all he had ever stood for, now teetering in the balance. This great country was dissolving into nothingness right before him. With all this disarray and mess, he wondered how people could live this way and accept such a worthy nation's gradual devolution and deterioration. He looked down, something caught his eye. A New York Times newspaper lay nearly perfect, a second sign he witnessed that evening. He knelt down grabbing the paper and upon its cover a picture of the handsome and charismatic new Senator from Wyoming . . . Senator Damian West with the headline . . . *The Newest Shining Star – Will He Save Us All?* Malcolm smiles and says under his breath, "I hope so . . . . but hope more that, there will be something worth saving."

As Malcolm ambled away, a heavy burden weighed upon his shoulders, causing his typically confident stride to falter. His head hung low, not just in submission but also in contemplation, as he grappled with the profound weight of reality. For a man who had always worn his American identity as a badge of honor, this moment marked an unprecedented shift in his perspective.

It was a watershed moment, a crossroads of disillusionment that had etched itself deeply into his psyche. The soil he had proudly stood upon and defended, the land that had nurtured his dreams and ambitions, had now become a desolate source of shame. It was a sensation that pierced his soul, a stark departure from the unwavering patriotism that had defined his existence for so very long.

The realization was like an acrid pill to swallow, leaving an acrimonious bitterness in his mouth. He had witnessed a side of his country that challenged his convictions, an America that diverged from the ideals he had held dear. The dissonance between his principles and the harsh truths before him was an internal struggle that gnawed at his conscience.

Yet, despite the pain and disillusionment, Malcolm knew that his feelings were not born out of apathy but of a profound love for his homeland. This love compelled him to confront the flaws and contradictions, demand better, and contribute to the hope of making America a truer embodiment of its ideals.

As he walked away, head hung low. Malcolm carried with him the weight of his newfound awareness. He was not just an American; he was a steward of its future, a torchbearer of its potential, and a voice that refused to be silenced in pursuing a more just and equitable nation. His nation desperately needed someone to lead them.

From his commanding vantage point atop the towering edifice, Fury gazed out from the 64th floor of his penthouse, reveling in a perspective that granted him an unparalleled view of the swirling disorder below. The city stretched out before him, a tapestry of tumult and madness. The rancorous aroma of smoke and the fiery tendrils of destruction wafted upward, filling his lungs with a familiar scent that transported him back to another time, years before, in a myriad of countries and wartime conflicts that circled the globe. He enjoyed the smell of death and destruction.

As he inhaled the intoxicating mixture of burning embers and the city's smoky exhalations, his mind wandered to a distant past, a time when his own life had been irrevocably altered, and death was everywhere around him. Memories of another land, far removed from the towering skyscrapers and frenzied streets of New York City, danced at the periphery of his consciousness and made him miss those days. He thrived in that environment and missed it greatly.

As he surveyed the panorama of destruction, Fury's thoughts meandered back to the distant landscapes of Afghanistan, a place where he had once witnessed burning buildings and smoldering vehicles. The parallel between those memories and the scene before him was eerie as if fate had drawn an intricate web connecting past and present.

For Fury, the turmoil unfolding below was not a scene to be feared or despised; rather, it was a spectacle to be embraced. That arena provided to him the platform to remove the scum of the earth. Wartime morality possessed a far different face. He was a killer, and those were his killing fields so long ago.

The fiery spectacle before him reflected a nation that had turned its back on him, rejected his talents, and cast him aside with callous indifference despite his sacrifices and suffered for it. The fractured society, the bedlam in the streets, was a testament to his resilience, a vindication of his abilities that had been discarded and undervalued.

He stood at the precipice of his balcony, a silent observer of the firestorm that swept across the city like a vengeful force of nature. The cacophony of sirens and the kaleidoscope of flashing lights below served as a symphony to his ears, a serenade to his vindication. He welcomed all of it and spread his arms wide, welcoming it all within, basking in the suffering before him.

He was content in the anarchy.

He reveled in the realization that he had played a pivotal role in the design of this orchestrated chaos. His hand had set the wheels in motion with the simple removal of a Governor out of Wyoming, his vision that had guided the unraveling tapestry of turmoil. With a sardonic smile curling upon his lips, Fury embraced the sounds and fragrances of bedlam saturating the New York City streets below, relishing his role as the architect behind this grand spectacle of societal upheaval.

His plan was all coming together. It was but one piece of an elaborate and intricate puzzle. The one-piece fundamental in lighting the spark that would ignite the beautiful picture he was to create when it was all completed.

Dallas, Texas
2021 Late Summer

Dymitron Solutions had achieved an extraordinary feat, solidifying its position as the premier manufacturer of semiconductors and computing solutions on a global scale. With their exceptional performance in the semiconductor industry, they outshone industry giants such as Intel, Taiwan Semiconductor Manufacturing, and Qualcomm, establishing themselves as the unrivaled leader in that competitive sector. Their dominance extended to the computing solutions market, surpassing renowned companies such as Microsoft and IBM.

Acquiring large media companies was next on its list, and it was rumored that a deal to acquire Google was an aspiring possibility. The company's profitability soared, surpassing Microsoft by a staggering 5:1 ratio in mid 2020. Dymitron Solutions emerged as the most robust and influential American-based company, setting new benchmarks for success and innovation in the technology industry. With a new product established and successfully implemented and tested in Washington state, they would widen their gap further in the next 36 months.

Their products were superior in quality, they maintained the capacity to mass produce and satisfy demand, and their leadership was undeniably efficient and well-oiled in every form. Large profitable companies like Dymitron were often targeted and were rarely beyond significant perils and obstacles along their evolutionary path. As a result of their growing fiscal vigor, they had become the focus of multiple class action and antitrust lawsuits. Still, the company was solid in its position defensively and held its ground time and time again. However, they knew it wouldn't last forever.

They cornered the market, and the American Government didn't appreciate Dymitron's executive prowess and growing capital strength. These types of companies weakened governmental stability and control. With the presidential election having just come to a close, matters seemed to look even less favorable in the interest of big Corporate America. With the Democratic party prevailing and Joe Biden securing the presidency over Donald Trump, Dymitron would only attract more scrutiny and regulation.

Anthony Voss, the CEO of Dymitron, stood proudly in front of his executive board late one Friday evening at their headquarters in Dallas, TX. "Anthony, this is bullshit; we can't sit still on this. We need to act. What should we do?" asked Andy Feyd, Dymitron's CFO, concerning the lawsuits and injunctions received that very day. The better part of two hours was spent as Voss explained his idea and logistical rollout of a possible headquarters and manufacturer relocation for Dymitron to Singapore. This meeting was held with the strictest security, as leaking this information could devastate the company's viability. Anthony Voss still had to secure the votes from his Board of Directors to initiate the plan and potentially the move. It would be an enormous undertaking. With the presidential election past, time was of the essence.

"We have simply become too large and powerful for the U.S. Government, and this is with the Republicans in power. Imagine how the Democrats will be once the election dust settles. They honestly just don't know what to do with us and are more than afraid that our insurmountable global strength will challenge their position if they are not properly aligned with Dymitron. Hence, the lawsuits are simply attempting to bog us down and halt our momentum. They are afraid of Dymitron's influence on the global system and domestic and foreign markets. And you know what? They should be afraid, terrified even. Look what Elon Musk and Tesla achieved in manipulating their own stock when he leveraged a strong position with Bitcoin. That was brilliantly maneuvered and orchestrated by Musk. Tesla is an infant compared to us; the government knows what we are capable of and isn't sure what to do. We are an enigma to them. When you don't understand . . . *you regulate and tax*."

The fight is what Anthony adored most as he smiled, enjoying where his company was positioned. "Our movement of this corporation to Singapore will be a blow to the United States economy and a slap in the face of the current Administration. They know we can manipulate the market as Elon Musk did earlier this year, and they can't afford to have that liability. With Singapore's fair taxing practices, ample labor force, and our 100% retention of stock, we will save billions upon billions in the years to come with a move like this. The U.S. can't compete with those figures and benefits. They only burden us with lawsuits, increased taxes, and frustration at every turn. They are working against us instead of *with us*. And the American people will not allow any embargo on our product line. This country will unravel if the government tries that angle. The transition will take some time, but we need to make the move. This is why I called you all here tonight," he recapped. "This announcement will hurt us in the short term as the NASDAQ, and naysayers will invariably beat up on DYNI Stock for a time, but our profits are strong, we are sitting on nearly a trillion in equity, our range is long, and we are only picking up more momentum. Our infrastructure is sound, our future is hopeful, and we are well on our way to a 37% projected increase in profit this year. We all know what is in the pipeline. It could triple our profits in the next seven years."

Anthony Voss made his pitch, and it was impressively presented. He had always had the support of his executive board as he had never failed them in the past, and he didn't plan to with this decision either. The board then voted to relocate the corporation to Singapore over the following five-year period.

The votes would take a few moments, and this was the only time Anthony could ever remember being nervous about anything in his life. He needed this vote to go his way. This decision would shake the United States on a global scale when announced. The key would fall upon Anthony Voss as to *when* that announcement would occur. The United States of America would suffer a tremendous financial blow when this news eventually went public.

It was then that the vote was taken as minutes ticked by, and the silent vote was calculated. Anthony waited anxiously until all the votes were tallied. A unanimous decision was made *to relocate* Dymitron. He had the Executive Board's complete support.

He sighed in relief.

He closed his eyes, thankful and relieved about the decision, and smiled, put his hands together, and bowed to the group with a simple, "Thank you."

His excitement wasn't entirely realized because of the work this endeavor would take, but he knew he had the undying support of every man and woman sitting in front of him, and they would follow him into the fiery depths if he called on them, too. They trusted and respected him either out of adoration or fear, or both, but he didn't care which, but at that moment, he also knew he, alone, controlled this company and paved the way for its prominent future.

That vote and single confirmation was the only thing he needed. . . . . and he got the outcome he desired.

The move would undoubtedly shock and hinder the United States and the global economy. Its impact would surpass the infamous Stock Market crash of 1929, which plunged the nation into a prolonged economic downturn. While the crash affected the financial realm, this scenario strikes at the very core of the human psyche, instilling fear and trepidation on a personal level concerning the ability to keep its most prolific company from moving to another country.

Its repercussions would reverberate across society, sparking a wave of public uproar, demanding the essential need to support and bolster American companies, not cripple their progression. The ripple effect captured by the media's collective attention would prompt the relentless quest for answers and scrutiny from the government. Its long-term ramifications would hinge upon the answers given as to why the United States lost its greatest company to foreign soil.

———

However, that would be saved for another day when they went public with the news.

The American people would not forgive the U.S. Government for losing Dymitron and forcing them to relocate.

Chapter 2

A Dynasty Created

"We must adjust to changing times and still hold to unchanging principles."
~ Jimmy Carter

Jackson Hole, Wyoming
2018 Fall (Three Years Before)
Senator Sam West Private Estate

As Senator Sam West admired the picturesque scenery, his mind wandered to the pressing matters awaiting his attention in the political arena in Washington, D.C. The United States was in a state of constant unrest, violence, and turmoil. It pained him to watch his own country suffering, and he knew it would only get worse unless something drastic occurred.

Like his father before him, he was revered as a devoted Republican, driven by conservative values and a dedication and declaration of loyalty to his countrymen. Having represented Wyoming for several terms, he earned a reputation as an unwavering and influential figure within the party, both in his home state and at the Capital.

Despite the idyllic setting and the serenity it brought him, Senator West knew the world outside his estate was filled with challenges and complexities that would compound in the years following. He pondered the intricate issues demanding his attention—economic policies, national security, healthcare reform, and the ever-present tug-of-war between party politics and compromises for the greater good.

On a more social level, the people were unhappy with the current government policies and agendas of the Republican Administration and were beginning to retaliate with riots and violence in clusters throughout the country. There was no question President Trump was rebuilding the economy, but his methods were constantly scrutinized by American voters and leaders worldwide. His country was unraveling before his eyes, and it broke his heart to watch; he wished he could do more. . *but, then again, maybe he could.*

Taking a deep breath, Senator West silently vowed to continue his unwavering commitment to his constituents and the conservative principles he held dear. He knew his role in shaping legislation and making decisions impacting the lives of millions required persistent determination and a clear vision for the future.

He never tired of his view before him. With the stunning landscape of Jackson Hole as his backdrop, Senator West gathered his thoughts, preparing to face the political battleground once again, armed with his convictions, experience, and desire to make a lasting difference. The Republicans currently controlled Congress, with only two years remaining in Donald Trump's administration, who knew what would happen next. However, Senator West was less than confident Trump would remain in office despite the fact the Senator was primarily the reason the man had even been elected President of the United States in 2016. He owed the Senator a tremendous favor, and Senator West *never* forgot those who owed him.

Never.

Peering through the window, Senator West always experienced a certain sense of tranquility in these moments, caught in a trance as the trees swayed back and forth in the afternoon breeze. The vacillating waves of branches and leaves were emulated almost methodically in their movement as if choreographed to the beautiful overture of Chopin or Mozart. The leaves had begun to change, with hints of yellow, orange, and brown peeking through the green that had dominated for months.

The Fall was in full swing, and the 2018 elections had just ended. He had taken a tremendous gamble, but it had paid off, and the ripple effect would be felt for years to come. It was the first step of many in his quest for the winds of change the country desperately needed. A change in the political tapestry had arrived, and he was both excited . . . and terrified in the same beat.

The view, sprawling nearly 1000 acres, located just outside the town of Jackson Hole, Wyoming, had provided his family with countless memories for three generations and had scarcely changed in nearly seventy years. He appreciated the historical fact, although he assumed many may argue the point if given the opportunity with all the tourism flooding the area in the last twenty years.

His land had remained largely undeveloped, except for the two large estates on his property, which was all that mattered to him. Sam entertained numerous offers to sell his valuable land over the years but always inevitably declined any offers. He often enjoyed considering their propositions to watch and observe the style and enthusiasm the prospective paramours would put forth with luxurious pitches about why they deserved to obtain the land and their lavish intentions once Sam agreed to sell it to them. But he never did, never even came close.

The West dynasty stood as a testament to the unwavering commitment and dedication of the West family to public service. Senator Sam West followed in his father's footsteps, continuing the family legacy and upholding the values they held dear. Together, they had tirelessly championed conservative principles and fought for the interests of Wyoming and the nation equally.

The West family's enduring presence within the political landscape showcased their resilience and deep-rooted connection to their constituents. Their unwavering determination and sacrifices earned them the respect and support of the people they served. The reign they had built spanned generations, demonstrating a profound understanding of the intricacies of governance and a commitment to leaving a lasting impact.

Through their collective efforts, the West family navigated the turbulent political tides surrounding their family, overcoming challenges and shaping policies aligning with their conservative ideals. They had weathered the storms of controversy, earned the trust of the people of Wyoming, and left an indelible mark on the nation's political history. They were also positioned to become a significant component of its future as well; Senator West was laying the groundwork that would shake the nation in the years to follow.

As Senator Sam West peered out over the rolling hills of Jackson Hole, he knew his family's legacy was secure. The baton had been passed to a new generation, ensuring the West Dynasty would continue to shape the political landscape in the coming years. With each passing day, they would strive to honor their predecessors' heritage and serve the people of Wyoming and their great nation with integrity and unwavering dedication.

Sam had supported his state of Wyoming attentively over the years, but his true talents lay within the covert undertakings deep within the underbelly of Washington D.C.'s political culture. As a powerful and influential sub-committee member, he thrived on making the difficult decisions necessary for the betterment and protection of his country. Disciples he possessed in people like Hillary Bastini and Sebastian Storm saw his goals were being met, and any foreign and domestic adversaries were dealt with using those effective instruments.

Senator Sam West understood the hidden clout and weight within the political underground. He was well versed on Washington's major and minor players and, more importantly, how to win them over if the need arose. While the public perceived political deals and decisions as occurring primarily within the formal setting of Congress, Senator West knew the actual negotiations and agreements took place in the less formal and more personal settings of social events, late dinners, wedding, funerals and cocktail receptions.

Whether it was on a campaign trail, a political rally, a sporting event, or even a sweet sixteen party, these gatherings provided an opportunity and platform for politicians from different parties and backgrounds to interact in a more relaxed and candid manner. Here, they could set aside their partisan differences and engage in genuine conversations about their shared interests, emerging agendas, and the nation's future.

Amid the unassuming and often overlooked realm of social gatherings, a remarkable phenomenon unfolded—a space where Democrats and Republicans, despite their entrenched differences, discovered a common ground. Here, far removed from the hallowed halls of Congress, they shed the weight of partisan pressures and the adversarial atmosphere that so often defined their interactions and often stunted progress.

Within these seemingly ordinary moments, a vastly different type of dissertation thrived. It was a discourse steeped in meaning, where the divisive rhetoric of the political arena yielded more constructive dialogues and genuine exchanges. Here, individuals representing opposing ideologies could sit at the same table, breaking bread together while engaging in substantive discussions transcending party lines.

These gatherings were not merely social affairs but the crucible of cooperation. In this melting pot of ideas and perspectives, alliances were born as political foes discovered the common ground on which they could stand. It was in these private, off-the-record conversations the seeds of compromise were sown, often leading to groundbreaking agreements that would shape the nation's course.

In the shadows of the grand political theater, these unassuming events became the incubators of progress. It was here the essence of democracy was palpable, as individuals from diverse backgrounds and beliefs demonstrated that, despite their differences, they could find unity in the pursuit of a shared goal—advancing the greater good of the nation.

In these hidden chambers of discourse, politics transcended partisanship, and the art of statesmanship blossomed. It was a testament to the enduring spirit of democracy—a reminder that even in the most divisive times, the human capacity for collaboration and consensus could light the way forward, forging a path toward progress, one meaningful conversation at a time.

Senator West recognized the value of these interactions and understood they held the potential to shape the political landscape far more than the public spectacle of congressional proceedings. In the political underground, where personal relationships and trust were cultivated, the true art of negotiation and deal-making thrived and prospered at every level.

In these informal locales, he could navigate the complexities of bipartisan politics, forge alliances, define and identify enemies, and work towards advancing his own agenda while finding common ground with others.

The political underground became Senator West's arena for crafting meaningful and impactful agreements, away from the public eye but with the potential to shape the nation's progression. The method, tried and true for years, was beginning to take a new shape. This new perspective was not necessarily evolving but rather devolving, feared Senator West.

Sam West always thought of Congress as a governmental circus, the political dressing fabricated and essential to make the American people sleep better at night. The true grit occurred outside of Congress. It was always curious to Sam that the self-interests of Congressmen from both sides of the aisle could be leveraged, manipulated, and traded like common baseball cards.

Feeling a sense of nostalgia and melancholy, Senator Sam West reflected on the changing political climate surrounding him. He acknowledged he was becoming a relic, a dinosaur of an earlier era, in an environment constantly evolving and transforming.

Gone were the days he longed for, when politics seemed more predictable and stable, and adversaries looked you in the eye, but those days were long past. The landscape had shifted, and new voices and ideas were emerging, challenging the established order behind the scenes. Fresh approaches replaced the once-familiar strategies and tactics, and the electorate's demands were manipulated more covertly and often secretly.

However, amid this changing model, Senator West found solace and hope in his son, Damian. He saw in him a reflection of the passion and drive that once fueled his own political journey. Damian represented the new, emerging generation with their own perspectives, ideas, and aspirations.

Through Damian's eyes, Senator West witnessed the energy and enthusiasm that characterized the progressing political environment. He saw the potential for new solutions, innovative approaches, and a different leadership style. Damian became a source of inspiration and a symbol of the ongoing legacy of the West family in the new and emerging political arena.

While Senator West acknowledged his place in the past, he also recognized the importance of embracing change and supporting the next generation. He realized his role now was not to resist the transformation but to provide guidance, wisdom, and support to his son as he navigated the tumultuous and unyielding political terrain.

In Damian, Senator West saw the continuation of their family's commitment to public service and their shared values. He found comfort in knowing the West's line would carry on, albeit in a different form, adapting to the needs and demands of the present. He recognized the necessity for change, as it was essential for progress. He made it his goal and obligation to pave the way for his son to emerge unscathed from the perils of modern-day political rigors.

As Senator West embraced this realization, he became determined to contribute to the political conundrum in innovative, neoteric ways. He recognized the importance of staying informed, listening to diverse perspectives, and remaining open to fresh ideas. In doing so, he aimed to bridge the gap between the past and the future, ensuring the West family's impact would endure in a constantly evolving world.

The changing political environment may have made Senator West feel like a relic, but through his son, he found renewed purpose and a sense of optimism. Together, they would navigate the ever-changing environment, adapting to the times while staying true to their shared values and commitment to public service. It was time to move the West family into the next level of American history. To secure further the birthright, Sam West envisioned for his son and the betterment of his country.

Damian West was to be his legacy and the architect of his beloved country's . . . . . *Future*. That was all that mattered to him now and remained his only focus. The United States was long overdue in adopting a new influential domestic political bloodline to emerge as the nation's unrivaled royalty, a reign he felt the people needed, the country selected, and even the world desired.

The nation desired a hero they could stand behind with unified support. The Kennedys were the most prolific family of American nobility to broach the possibility but were plagued with tragedy and conspiracy; their lineage suffered an unraveling from which they never fully recovered. It was time for a new protagonist pedigree to arise, and Sam felt there was no better option than . . . . *The West Family.* It was their time to lead this suffering and sickened country back to health and cement his family's place in history.

Senator Sam West couldn't help but feel a sense of longing for the intricate world of politics that had defined his career for so many years. He recognized that it was within the nuances and exploitations of the political game that he had thrived and wielded his power, contributing to the strength and influence of the United States on the global stage.

The intricate labyrinth of manipulations, deals, and strategies had been the cornerstone of his political journey. Sam had never shied away from stepping on toes or leveraging his position to achieve his goals and advance his political agenda, never for personal gain but rather for the good of his country. He understood within the world of politics, it was often necessary to make calculated moves and navigate the complex web of power dynamics to bring about change and progress.

Throughout his career, Sam mastered the art of negotiation, skillfully maneuvering alliances and calculating political risks. He adeptly influenced policy and steered the nation's direction, utilizing his experience and connections. Unapologetic about the ruthless nature of politics, Sam recognized it as a competitive arena demanding hardball tactics and tough decisions. His calculated moves and strategic alliances left a significant mark on the political landscape, firmly embedding him within the American political mainstream.

While others may have been intimidated by the myriad of challenges and potential backlash, Sam had always embraced the game. He saw it as a means to an end, a vehicle through which he could bring about meaningful change and leave a lasting legacy.

However, as Sam reflected on his career and the evolving political climate, he also acknowledged the rules were changing. The dynamics of power were shifting, and the old strategies were no longer as effective as they once were. The world's interconnectedness, the rise of social media, and the demand for transparency are reshaping the political landscape daily.

Sam realized he needed to adapt and evolve with the changing times. He needed to find new ways to leverage his influence, engage with the public, and navigate the complexities of the modern political arena. This challenge both excited and discouraged him. Sam was determined to find his place in this evolving reform, utilizing his experience and skills to continue making a difference and leaving his mark on the political stage long after he was gone.

At seventy-three years old, Sam West was still a towering figure in American politics and thrived in the intricate game of power and manipulation. He walked a fine line between the two but always remained grounded and true to his cause. With ten successful elections under his belt, he stood as the United States' most gallant patriot, relishing the combative spirit and the strategic dance of the Senate arena.

———

Despite the tumultuous political backdrop, Sam remained a formidable force, adept at building alliances and securing support. He navigated the challenges with finesse, leaving a lasting impact on the nation's history.

Sam's unwavering commitment to his principles and the American people earned him respect from colleagues and constituents alike. With charisma and strategic prowess, he played the political game with excitement and zeal, never fearing the toes he stepped on or the battles fought.

Senator Sam West, an exemplar of patriotism and valor, etched an enduring legacy in American politics. He served as a vivid reminder of the electrifying essence of the political arena and the transformative power of unwavering leadership. Every ounce of his wisdom, connections, profound understanding of American history, and the intricate playbook of politics was meticulously bequeathed to his sole heir, Damian West, and years of mentorship, intense debates, and comprehensive education had prepared Damian for this very moment—a culmination of his journey.

As Senator West looked back on his role as his son's guide, he realized with a sense of profound humility that the tides had shifted and the time had come for him to assume the role of a student, to glean valuable lessons from the very child he had nurtured and raised. The realization washed over him, a humbling recognition that parenthood's dynamic had evolved, transforming him into a humble pupil ready to absorb the knowledge and insights his son had acquired.

Senator West embraced the profound significance of generational exchange at this poignant juncture. With his son's education now complete, he acknowledged his cherished offspring held a treasure trove of wisdom, fresh perspectives, and innovative ideas that could reshape the political landscape in the years to come. The torch had been passed, and the torchbearer had become the beacon of enlightenment, guiding his father and those he touched toward a new frontier of understanding and growth.

———

Senator Sam West recognized the indomitable spirit and leadership witnessed in the actions of his son. As he embarked on this new phase of his journey, the senator embraced the opportunity to learn, evolve, and forge an even stronger bond with Damian and his future—a testament to the enduring power of love, mentorship, and the ever-unfolding tapestry of American politics.

A sense of sadness overcame him as he looked out over his land. He knew his time was growing short, and the final phase of his plan had just begun. It was the end of an era but the forging of a new one he had crafted for the new breed of politics he was to unveil in the years that followed.

As thoughts and feelings swirled within Sam's mind, it was at that moment he sensed a presence approaching him from behind and knew immediately it was his greatest accomplishment —*his son, Damian West.*

"That view never gets old, does it, Dad?" Said Damian quietly, knowing his father was immersed in thought and didn't want to disrupt him. "No, Damian, it sure doesn't," replied Sam as he turned halfway towards his son, expressing such adoration for the young man.

He smiled and continued, "How does it feel? To be the youngest Senator in U.S. history? Handedly trouncing Democratic candidate Gary Trauner. That's quite a feat in and of itself, especially securing the seat as an *Independent*. Your Grandad would have been proud. All this at only thirty-one, Damian, a truly amazing accomplishment." Pausing momentarily, Damian replied, "Surreal, maybe; I honestly don't know. Switching from Republican to Independent was a bold move and risky, but you called it. It went exactly as you said it would. I'm kind of numb to it all, I suppose, but I certainly couldn't have done it without you, Dad."

Sam pondered his son's response, "I disagree. I only provided some guidance and maybe a little familial reputation, Damian, but you have achieved your success and the win all on your own, and I'm very proud of you. Your mom would have been as well." Damian smiled at the thought of his mother. They had lost her fifteen years prior, just as he was finishing high school. A rare and inoperable brain stem cancer claimed her far too early. Sam West had never remarried and was never the same since her passing.

As the public speculated on Sam West's retirement and the potential successor to his Senate seat, Damian West emerged as the favored candidate. With Sam's strategic endorsement and the momentum it generated, Damian gained significant exposure and support in the year leading up to the election. It was clear Damian had his father's backing and was poised to carry on the West legacy in Wyoming's political evolution.

Six months before the election, the switch to the independent ticket was announced, causing a stir and a slight drop in the polls. However, Damian quickly regained the loss. A few strategic speeches grabbed the hearts of his statesmen, and the national exposure became a windfall, earning precious momentum.

Damian's father certainly paved the way, as his grandfather had before him. Still, Damian was an eloquent and colorful orator himself, well-versed and eerily comfortable within the political showground. Inspired by the political legacy of his father and grandfather, Damian West carved his own path in the world of politics.

While he greatly valued his father's guidance, Damian's own qualities and achievements set him apart. As an eloquent and charismatic speaker, he commanded the attention and respect of those who supported and listened to him. Despite his relatively young age, Damian had already earned a remarkable level of professional esteem. With inherited wisdom and unique talents, Damian was poised to impact the political stage significantly. He was the one to watch, and their expectations of him were very high, being Senator Sam West's only son.

His political resume was impressive in and of itself. Finishing high school early, Damian quickly navigated his way through his undergraduate studies after being accepted early to Stanford, then on to Cambridge, where he graduated at the top of his class at Harvard Law School at age twenty-three. Sam insisted Damian spend a few years as a state prosecutor to acquaint himself better with state and national law and understand the political system more intimately, thus impressing his superiors as he moved up the legal ladder within Wyoming's District Attorney office.

Progressing rapidly, after just a few years, the driven Damian West had already gained significant clout as the youngest district attorney in Wyoming's history at the mere age of 25. He served the office aggressively before adding to his dossier.

In early January 2016, he became the youngest Governor of Wyoming, appointed at the age of 27 after the Governor-elect, Steven Hathaway, had been tragically killed in a car accident with his wife while driving home on New Year's Eve, leaving the important position open for several months until the upcoming election. Damian was an up-and-comer and knew the position well while aiding Governor Hathaway. A few strategically placed phone calls from Sam West all but guaranteed his son would assume the Governor's post until the term ended months later and went on to win the re-election handily. He then held the office for another two and half years before his aspirations took another upturn.

Holding the prior record for youngest governor for some 35 years, past President Bill Clinton was elected governor of Arkansas in 1978 at age 32. Damian had trampled the record by nearly four years. The turn of events sealed his fate and catapulted his career quickly, where he satisfied the position for nearly three years after winning the Wyoming Governor election, and would have won the re-election ably, had it not been for the opportunity that arose to take over his father's soon-to-be vacated senate seat.

Under Governor Damian West leadership, the unemployment rate decreased by high single digits, revamped the state budget, and decreased state taxes, making him popular with the people of Wyoming and the rest of the country was watching this young politician closely, amazed at his ability to woo politicians on both sides of the aisle with his candidness and sincerity during his 2-year term serving in the governor's post.

With his innovative, creative, and robust ideas, newly appointed Governor Damian West displayed unparalleled direction, guiding Wyoming's governmental system with eloquence and brilliance. While much of the country remained stagnant in its progress, Governor West's visionary approach propelled the state forward, setting an example for others to follow.

In the face of complacency and inertia, Governor West defied the norm, introducing his groundbreaking ideas that breathed new life into Wyoming's governance. His innovative strategies addressed pressing issues and paved the way for future advancements. Through his unwavering determination and forward-thinking mindset, he transformed Wyoming into a bastion of progress, where the seeds of change blossomed into tangible results.

Governor West approached challenges with unconventional angles, devising inventive and pragmatic solutions. His ability to think outside the box and outthink his colleagues enabled him to tackle complex problems with ingenuity and overcome obstacles others deemed insurmountable. Most fiscal reform came from governmental inefficiencies that hadn't evolved in decades and reorganizing budgets.

The strength and effectiveness of Governor Damian West's leadership were evident in the perceptible outcomes he achieved. His initiatives sparked tangible improvements in Wyoming's infrastructure, economy, and quality of life. The state thrived under his guidance, becoming a shining example of what visionary leadership could accomplish if properly honed and focused.

Amidst a national landscape of slowed inertia and limited progression, Governor West's dynamic leadership brought about a renaissance in Wyoming's governance. His transformative ideas, characterized by their ingenuity and effectiveness, propelled the state forward, creating a beacon of hope and progress at a time when many regions struggled to keep pace.

As the undercurrents of social unrest surged, the call for astute and steadfast leadership echoed across all tiers of government. At the helm of his state, Damian had exemplified brilliance in governance, tirelessly steering the ship for his entire governorship. His tenure had been marked by a resolute commitment to the welfare of his constituents, a dedication that had earned him both respect and admiration.

However, as the storm clouds gathered on the political horizon, a new chapter beckoned. Damian's decision to enter the race for the Senate seat was far from impulsive; it was the culmination of a strategic chess game that had been unfolding behind the scenes for decades and part of Sam West's long-term plan. The pivotal moment was set in motion by his father's wholehearted endorsement and the impending retirement of a political patriarch who had clung to his seat for over 50 years.

For his father, the decision to relinquish a position he had held dear for so long had not come easily. It was a seat steeped in history, a seat that held the weight of legacy and tradition. Yet, he recognized the need for a transition, a calculated move in a larger political gambit.

The torchbearer of their shared vision, Damian, was the logical choice to step into the Senate race to replace his father. His father's endorsement was more than a passing of the baton; it was an act of trust, a testament to Damian's readiness to take on a mantle that had been carefully prepared for him.

It wasn't just a tactical maneuver; it was a strategic masterstroke transcending the realm of individual aspirations, resonating with the grand symphony of a far more elaborate plan. Damian's pivotal decision to vacate the Governor's office was no trifling matter. It was a meticulously calculated step, an integral move in the intricate choreography of a vision reaching far beyond the boundaries of personal ambition. The irony within it all was Damian's lack of true understanding of his father's end game. His true masterpiece was yet to be revealed even to Damian.

As Damian set his sights on the Senate race, he became a linchpin in a grander tapestry where leadership at the highest echelons of government would become the architects of a brighter tomorrow. While the nation grappled with the tempestuous tides of both social and political transformation, Damian embarked on a journey that held the promise of reshaping the very contours of governance.

Yet, beneath the surface of this political odyssey lay a labyrinth of hidden layers and undisclosed trials for Damian's father. Damian, the poised statesman, remained unaware of the full extent of his father's sacrifices and the high-stakes stratagems that had paved the way for this moment. The intricate dance of politics had woven a complex array of risks and detriments, all orchestrated by the veiled maestro, Senator Sam West.

As Damian ventured into this uncharted terrain, he could only glimpse the tip of the iceberg, for the depths of his father's endeavors were shrouded in secrecy. The sacrifices made, and the calculated risks taken were the foundation upon which Damian's ascent was built. The stage had been set, concealed, and hidden from Damian's astute eye. And while he might never fully fathom the depths of his father's endeavors, he carried with him the torch of a profound birthright, a beacon of hope in a world where leadership was both an art and a science, and where the future held the promise of transformation.

In addition, the American people were becoming increasingly disenchanted with recurring city riots and the brutal deaths of media icon, Ryker Davion, to simply make a statement, in the early part of the year struck close to home. Opposition to the current bipartisan system was becoming more openly and publicly challenged. They needed champions within Congress as much as it needed reformation.

In the carefully orchestrated choreography of their political strategy, both Damian and his father understood seizing the Senate seat was the key that would unlock a coveted place at the illustrious table of Washington's powerbrokers. It was the passport to a realm of influence stretching far beyond the confines of state politics, where decisions carried the weight of a nation.

The Senate, Damian recognized, would be his launchpad into a sphere of unparalleled leverage on the national stage. It was here his ambitions would take flight, unhindered by the limitations of state-level governance. The very thought of it fueled his determination and steeled his resolve, for he knew within the hallowed chambers of the Senate, he could shape policies that extended well beyond mere state boundaries, leaving an indelible mark on the nation's course.

Damian had proven himself to be a rising star with each stride along the path to political prominence. His unswerving commitment to the principles he held dear had resonated with supporters and constituents alike. As the election loomed on the horizon, his campaign gathered momentum like a locomotive hurtling down the tracks, fueled by the hopes and aspirations of those who saw in him a guiding light.

In the ever-shifting landscape of American politics, Damian West was not merely a participant; he was a force to be reckoned with, an emerging embodiment whose trajectory knew no bounds. The seat in the Senate was not just an opportunity; it was the culmination of years of dedication, a chance to etch his name into the annals of history, and a testament to the enduring spirit of ambition in the heart of a desperate nation.

Once victorious, his leadership skills, charisma, and progressive thinking captured national coverage, and everyone wanted to know more about this young, newly elected Senator from Wyoming. Senator Damian West quickly began attaining celebrity status, but he always maintained his humility; he felt he was serving his country the best way he saw fit. There was a genuine sincerity about him few politicians possessed. Damian West radiated the authenticity making a select few presidents legendary, such as John F. Kennedy and Teddy Roosevelt.

While Damian's decisions, philosophies, and affiliations remained formidable, one enigmatic aspect lingered, making him vulnerable to public scrutiny. The question loomed: Why, in all the years leading up to this pivotal juncture, had he not found a suitable partner with whom to share his life? It was a query that resonated in hushed conversations, whispered behind closed doors, and even posed discreetly by the curious.

In the face of this delicate inquiry, Damian was known for his artful responses, laced with a subtlety suggesting this territory was off-limits to prying eyes. With a creative and articulate flourish, he would deflect the question, delicately reminding his audience that the boundaries of his personal life were his to define.

"I appreciate your desire to peer into the intimate corners of my existence," he would begin, his words delivered with a measured and calculated grace, "but it's essential to acknowledge my quest for a semblance of privacy is a value I hold dear. While those who hold public office must accept a degree of openness in their personal lives, my dedication to my position remains my utmost priority."

He continued, emphasizing his commitment to the responsibilities that came with public service. "Whomever I choose to share my life with, at some point, God willing, will need to embrace not only me but also my unwavering devotion to my calling."

Damian's principled stance on this matter was articulated time and again, woven into various interviews and conversations. His responses were rarely met with challenge, for they emanated from a place of undeniable sincerity and authenticity. It was difficult not to admire Damian West, a figure whose soft-spoken demeanor and authentic presence had a calming effect on those he encountered.

In a world where public figures often walk a tightrope between transparency and privacy, Damian's ability to navigate this delicate balance with grace and poise only added to his appeal. He remained a figure of admiration, and his enigmatic personal life, a puzzle, only added to the intrigue of a man whose dedication to his position was unwavering, even in the face of probing curiosity.

On that particular sultry evening, bathed in the dimly lit ambiance of her surroundings, Mila Dmitri found herself positioned at the rear of the room, her vantage point offering an unobstructed view of Damian West for the first time. Her gaze was an ardent caress, tracing the contours of his mannerisms and expressions with a hunger simmering beneath the surface. With every subtle gesture, every artful word, Damian captivated her, a magnetic force drawing her deeper into his orbit.

Mila had been an ardent follower of Damian's illustrious career; her fascination ignited during his meteoric rise to the Governorship at an age when most were still navigating the complexities of early adulthood. She had been an avid observer for three years, trailing his trajectory through the chronicles of power and influence. But it wasn't just his political prowess that ensnared her; it was the enigmatic allure he exuded, a charisma that had invaded her most intimate fantasies for over a year.

The wait had been an exercise in patience. An excruciating journey had finally led her to this moment: close enough to see the contours of his features, savor his voice's cadence, and witness the effortless grace with which he navigated the interview. Mila's heart quickened with each passing second, her senses attuned to the seductive dance of power and attraction swirling in the air.

As Damian's presence enveloped her, Mila felt drawn into a whirlpool of desire, which intertwined reality and fantasy. The room may have been filled with dignitaries and onlookers, but it was a clandestine world of longing and anticipation in that stolen moment. The allure of Damian West had become an intoxicating elixir, and Mila was poised on the precipice of an encounter promising to transcend the boundaries of mere admiration.

As she watched Damian West, a tidal wave of awe surged through Mila. He stood before her, a commanding presence, a natural in every sense. It was as though he had been born for the stage, a performer in the grand theater of politics, and she could now comprehend why the entire nation was captivated by this charismatic young Senator.

Taking advantage of the attended charity event and catching Damian West in a tuxedo, the journalist seized the opportunity to put Senator Damian West on the center stage for those attending to enjoy that evening and to get some insight into his innovative rise in popularity.

The interview was Damian's domain, a realm where he reigned supreme, and he knew it. The harsh glare of the camera lights bathed him in a molten glow and did nothing to dim his composure; if anything, they seemed to amplify his allure. He possessed an uncanny ability to exist in the limelight, to thrive in the furnace of public scrutiny, where others might wither.

Damian West was more than just a gifted orator; he was a maestro of language, a virtuoso of rhetoric. His words were not merely spoken but imbued with a resonating power that commanded respect. With every assertion and explanation, he wove a tapestry of conviction and knowledge that left an indelible mark.

The interviewer herself harbored no doubt regarding the integrity of Damian West's victory. It was evident he had earned his place in the spotlight, a seat he had claimed on his own merit, transcending the shadows of his father's generous bequest. The election had been a testament to his prowess, a resounding affirmation he was more than capable of carrying the torch forward.

In those moments, as Mila watched Damian's magnetic presence, she couldn't help but be drawn deeper into the gravitational pull of his charisma. It was a seductive dance, a fusion of intelligence and charm leaving her breathless, and she knew then the allure of Damian West was a force she could not easily escape.

As Damian eloquently addressed the audience, microphone in hand, his discerning gaze hesitated as he happened upon Mila, a vision at the rear of the room. She was draped in a violet splendor of a dress, its neckline plunging provocatively between her breasts, the form-fitting dress tracing the seductive curve of her voluptuous hips and accentuating the mesmerizing contours of her figure. Her stature, standing tall at 5'8", bore the exquisite blend of European and Asian heritage, bestowed with high cheekbones, only added an air of aristocratic elegance to her presence.

Always the epitome of professionalism, Mila carried herself with a grace that was nothing short of impeccable. Yet, her magnetic allure was impossible to ignore, and it was evident Damian found himself momentarily unmoored by the magnetic pull of her penetrating focus on him. For a man who had mastered the art of composure, her presence was a tantalizing distraction that played havoc with his concentration.

As the reporter's question hung in the air, Damian was compelled to ask for clarification, his words betraying a momentary lapse. "I'm sorry, Angela," he began, his voice laced with a hint of disorientation, "could you please repeat the question?"

It was a rare occurrence for Damian West to be thrown off balance, but Mila Dmitri had achieved what few could claim. In that electrifying moment, it was clear the enchantress in the violet ensemble had successfully disrupted the poise of a man who had been considered unshakeable.

It was then she knew she had captured his attention, her mission complete.

Mila was captivated by his charm and poise and knew she needed to learn more about Senator Damian West. As Damian took the question, he eloquently explained his position on terrorism, looking at those in attendance until he casually looked back in Mila's direction, but she was no longer there.

Damian expertly regained his composure addressing the questions asked. His voice was entrancing, a siren's call beckoning those who listened to surrender to its seductive cadence. Damian's words flowed with a fluency bordering on poetic, each syllable a brushstroke in the masterpiece of his eloquence. His diction was nothing short of flawless, a testament to his mastery of the art of oratory.

As he engaged in verbal parries with the local news anchor, it was evident their exchange was akin to a high-stakes game of wit and intellect. Damian's responses were a symphony of insight and magnetism, leaving those present in a state of rapt attention. The seasoned news anchor interviewer found herself eager to prolong the discourse with this rising young political luminary.

Several minutes later, Damian West concluded his interview without a hitch, his performance a testament to his polished communication skills. All in attendance applauded and were impressed with his genuine delivery. As the interview concluded, he graciously entertained additional questions in private, further solidifying his reputation as a politician who captivated on the public stage was and accessible and engaging in more intimate settings.

A gentle tap on Damian West's shoulder interrupted his thoughts, prompting him to turn and reveal a warm smile when he saw his father standing there. However, his smile transformed into mild surprise as he noticed the presence of the exquisite Mila Dmitri at his father's side.

———

"Damian," his father began, his tone laced with a hint of excitement, "I'd like you to meet someone. This is Mila Dmitri. I had the privilege of knowing her father quite well; he was the former CEO of Dymitron. Mila is currently one of the foremost lobbyists in Washington, D.C., representing Dymitron, of course. She's been lobbying on behalf of Anthony Voss, the current CEO of Dymitron, headquartered in Dallas, Texas. I believe you might be familiar with the company?"

Turning his full attention to Mila Dmitri, Damian West found himself entranced by her exquisite beauty, which appeared even more striking from mere inches away. He couldn't help but be momentarily disarmed by her presence, a rare occurrence for a not easily intimidated man. Mila had, without a doubt, managed to disrupt his customary composure, leaving a subtle ripple in his usual self-assured demeanor.

In an attempt to regain his footing, Damian smoothly redirected the conversation, acknowledging the subject at hand. "Ah, yes, Dymitron," he began, his voice carrying a measured cadence and assertion. "If memory serves me right, Dymitron was founded in 1981 by Napoleon Avante. However, in 1986, your father, Ms. Dmitri, Salvatore Dmitri, assumed the CEO role and orchestrated a remarkable ascent of the company's profitability. Under his leadership, Dymitron became the second-largest semiconductor business globally, trailing only behind Taiwan Semiconductor Manufacturing Company Limited (TSMC)."

Damian's eyes sparkled with a deep well of knowledge as he continued, "Dymitron's reputation was further solidified by its pioneering *StreamLINE*™ technology, a breakthrough setting it apart from the competition. This milestone, coupled with Anthony Voss taking the reins six years ago, propelled Dymitron to the summit, surpassing TSMC and establishing itself as the unrivaled leader in the semiconductor industry worldwide. Did I get most of it right?"

A hint of curiosity danced in Damian's gaze as he turned the spotlight back onto Mila. "I can't help but wonder, Ms. Dmitri, do you play a pivotal role in Dymitron's incredible success story?"

His inquiry carried an air of intrigue, a desire to unravel the enigma behind Dymitron's meteoric rise and Mila's role in its ascent.

Mila Dmitri smiled, impressed with the senator's knowledge of her company. "Most impressive, Senator, you do your homework. And yes. . . ." "Yes?" repeats Damian, as she continues, "Yes, my father put Dymitron on the map, and *yes,* I may have had a little something to do with its success, but Anthony Voss our CEO, has blown off the doors with what he has brought to the company and its market share. And pulling to number one with StreamLINE™ has proven that point." Damian smiled, knowing it had become his turn to throw her a precarious volley.

He liked her spunk and verve, and the way she expressed herself was confident yet poised and elegant in her demeanor. He tried to throw her off balance since she clearly had attempted to do so with his father's introduction after looming in the rear of the room during his interview.

"I'm curious, Ms. Dmitri. . ." "Please, call me Mila," she interrupted. He smiled again as Sam West watched the two interact but dismissed himself, giving them privacy. "Yes, sorry, Mila, there is a rumor Dymitron may leave the States and Anthony Voss has become disenchanted with American politics and tightening grip of Congress. Is there any truth to the rumor?" She narrowed her gaze, curious how he would have obtained the data, but replied coolly, "Mr. Voss is an American through and through, Senator . . ." Now his turn to interrupt, "Please, Mila, call me Damian." She smiled back at him in a demure way and looked up at him, "Damian . . . yes, of course. I've never been privy to those decisions, but I know Anthony is intelligent and shrewd. If there is some reason, then I suppose he would entertain the notion, but I am unaware of any such news, Damian." "Fair enough," he replied with a wink, wondering if there was far more to the story but would let it go.

Damian looked at her closely and said, "I have an easier question for you, Mila. What are your thoughts on *spontaneity*?" She turned her face in such a way, "Well, it would all depend on what spontaneity you are referring too, Damian . . . ."

It was then, Senator Ren Cosner came up with his wife, Angela, to say hello, and Mila Dmitri knew their small window of conversation had closed, at least for the moment. Damian said to the Senator, "Senator Cosner and Mrs. Cosner, so happy to see you," as Mila nodded to the Senator and his wife and began to step back and make her exit.

At that moment, her arm was grabbed, and she turned to see Damian's handsome face looking at her, "We will continue this conversation at a later date, Ms. Dmitri. There is so much more I would like to know." She smiled, "Come find me when you have time, Senator, and I will enlighten you further." And with that, she slipped into the crowd, disappearing.

He turned back toward Senator Cosner to engage in their conversation, but his mind drifted to the beautiful woman who had been the highlight of his evening.

From an early age, Sam had diligently educated young Damian, and their mentorship continued well into Damian's twenties. They would often delve into discussions about the United States' political landscape, engaging in candid and unrestricted conversations behind closed doors. In this private setting, honesty and frankness prevailed, free from judgment of any kind. The bond between Sam and Damian West transcended mere family ties over the years. Their connection ran deep on an intellectual and ideological level, fueling their late-night conversations that often took place in the Senator's study.

They examined the complexities of the United States' political platform, unafraid to confront complex topics and engage in passionate debates, both mainstream and controversial. Their discussions touched upon various subjects, from racism and economics to business and philosophical viewpoints. Despite the depth of their conversations, they shared a mutual respect that allowed them to engage in fruitful and dynamic dialogue, even when their opinions differed. Through these discussions, Sam continued to mentor and educate Damian, shaping his understanding of the political world and its complexities and preparing him for the challenges ahead.

Ensuring Damian was ready for this stage in his young life, Sam also knew Damian possessed the qualities vital to maneuver quickly through the various political contrivances he would be confronted with on a daily basis. Sam had always felt Damian was a better, more polished version of himself. He had bred Damian that way and knew he . . . . *was the best of their bloodline.* The mere thought made Sam smile.

Beyond the formidable influence of his father, Damian had another powerful force that had been intricately woven into the tapestry of his structured upbringing. As the years unfurled, the connection between Julian Chambers and Damian West also deepened, guided by a shared recognition of the profound value in their respective journeys held when viewed through the lens of the legal and political perspective.

Julian Chambers, respectable in the realm of legal scholarship and advocacy, had been a confidant to Damian since the early days of his legal studies. Their relationship surpassed the boundaries of mere friendship; it was a partnership forged within the commonality of jurisprudence, where ideas and principles intersected.

In their shared exploration of the legal landscape, Damian and Julian embarked on a journey extending well beyond the confines of statutes and precedents. They explored the intricacies of justice, dissecting the ethical dilemmas often accompanying legal decisions. Their discourse was a symphony of intellect, where arguments were honed to a razor's edge, and counterarguments were met with unwavering scrutiny.

Through countless hours of debate and contemplation, Damian came to appreciate the depth and nuance of the legal system—a structure that was not just a framework of rules but a living, breathing entity with the power to shape societies and safeguard liberties.

For Julian Chambers, he valued the West family more than a mere friendship; Damian was a guardian of the legal conscience, a sage whose wisdom illuminated the path of justice. Their shared journey was not just an exploration of laws and statutes but a voyage into the heart of fairness and equity, a quest to uphold the principles underpinning a just society.

In the frequently heated moments of their legal discussions, Julian discovered not only the intricacies of the law but also the profound impact it could have on individuals and communities. Together, they sought to navigate the labyrinth of political legalities, armed with a shared commitment to justice and integrity and the belief that the legal perspective held the power to shape a better future for all.

Julian was accepted to Michigan University and later Columbia University School of Law, which was no easy feat with his less-than-favorable upbringing, but diligent dedication and hard work earned him a spot in the top 10% of his graduating law class. Julian Chambers would never know he wouldn't have gotten into either school without the silent support and influence of Senator Sam West. Sam also had a plan for Julian Chambers, but it was vastly different than the one Damian's journey would take him.

Julian embarked on a new chapter in his life, leaving his tumultuous past behind and entering the realm of politics. He started his political journey by working as an aide to Senator Cosner from Indiana, gaining valuable experience and insights into the workings of the political system for several years. With his determination and dedication, Julian caught the attention of others in the political arena, including his close connection with Damian West, who was rising as a political superstar. He would have been foolish not to ride on Damian West's coattails.

With a formidable blend of knowledge and unwavering passion, Julian Chambers was nothing if not an opportunist. In the year 2016, he seized a golden opportunity that presented itself—a chance to vie for the open position of State Representative in Indiana's relatively unopposed 16th district. Leveraging his astute political acumen and his close ties to Damian and his father, Julian embarked on a relentless campaign under the banner of the Republican ticket.

His campaign was nothing short of a tour de force, marked by vigorous rallies, compelling speeches, and an unwavering vision for positive change. Julian wasn't as a masterful orator as Damian, but he was more than capable of engaging audiences with his eloquence and rallying support from constituents who yearned for a brighter future. He found interviews and questions focused more on his affiliation with the West family and his ties to Sam and Damian West directly than his own accolades. He weathered the questions but privately resented the avoidance of the media to what his own story entailed and his own rise up the political ladder, not that of the West association.

Yet, it was his association with the West family that truly set Julian apart, whether he liked it or not. The connection to Damian and his esteemed father lent an air of gravitas and credibility to his candidacy, which was impossible to ignore. The voters of the 16th district saw in Julian Chambers not just a promising candidate but also a bridge to a dynamic duo whose potential in Washington was boundless.

Sam West, the patriarch of the West family, played his own role in this political ballet, deftly pulling the strings necessary to ensure Julian's campaign gained the traction it required. His influence, carefully wielded behind the scenes, was an invaluable asset elevating Julian's bid for office. He did Julian an immeasurable favor, but Julian would have to return it one day.

But Sam West, with his keen political acumen, understood favors exchanged in the world of politics were akin to currency. He knew one day, the time would come for him to reciprocate his support to Julian. It was a chess game played with the future in mind, a game where alliances were forged, debts were incurred, and the dance of politics unfolded with calculated precision.

Through hard work and strategic maneuvering, Julian won the election and became a State Representative from Indiana. In the following years, he fought hard to earn his right despite rumors that he prevailed over a weak district, and the West family greased his way into the Representative seat. He resented the notion, and despite Sam West influencing various aspects of Julian's successful securing of the 16th District, Julian was confident he had done it primarily on his own.

His journey from a Senator's aide to a respected elected official was a testament to his determination, skills, and the weight of his association with the West family. Julian dreamed he and Damian would someday create a formidable team, working towards their shared goals and bringing fresh perspectives to the political environment.

All those hours of discussion brought them to this point— Damian, now a United States Senator, and his closest friend, Julian Chambers, a respected State Representative. The next chapter of understanding was but the last for Sam West to teach his son, "Now, the difficult work begins, Damian . . . reshaping the political machine as we know it and changing the perspective of the old guard who only sees it the way it's always been. Despite my influence with the conservatives, I can only get so far with my endorsement of you, and your limited, though impressive, experience will also inhibit you. You must be ready for these obstacles, as they will certainly come. A good leader knows his strengths but understands his limitations and weaknesses even better. Thankfully, several key players are watching you from afar and poised to clear the way for your progression. Your victory today as an 'Independent' was a calculated gamble but essential to our strategy, and the wager paid off brilliantly. They will all feel you are riding on my coattails, undoubtedly. At least for a time until you can rest on your own merit. We must make you a respectable presence in Washington and among all your contemporaries. We will begin to build your reputation, brick by brick, allowing it to stand alone above my influence and on your own virtues and fast and fierce in its execution. Our training and discussions will now be critical in implementing and integrating you within the system. I've thought a lot about this, and I think a masterful way of achieving this is getting you on a few critical committees and strategic groups in the Senate, and I can help with that as well. I also think it's time we bring Julian into the fold. He will bend to our wishes and share our perspective." He looked at his son, engrossed by what his father could still teach him. He nodded in agreement concerning Julian and also felt the time was right.

Senator Sam West continued, "We need you in front of groups that will grant you the attention needed and turn the heads of those in persuasive and instrumental positions." Damian smiled, placed his hand on his father's shoulder, and replied, "It will work, Dad. We have worked tirelessly on this venture, and you have mentored and formed me in the image this new party will represent. I know I will not fail you on this point. I am honored to be your son and carry the West name into the history books, and I know our timing for this change is critical. We are right where we need to be. I will make you proud, Dad." "You already have Damian; you always have," replied Sam.

There were never any disagreements between them. Sam made vitally certain Damian viewed the world the way Sam intended, which was all part of Senator Sam West's design. It had to be . . . .

. . . . *Though Damian West did not yet know it yet, his father was grooming him to become the next President of the United States.*

Chapter 3

The Political Spectrum

"Liberty and Union, now and forever, one and inseparable!"
~Daniel Webster *(U.S. Senator)*

Cleveland, Ohio
2016 July 18-20 (Four Years Before)
Republican National Convention

Damian and his father found themselves amid a whirlwind of political fervor as they made their way to the Republican National Convention in the bustling city of Cleveland, Ohio. For Damian, this journey was not a mere excursion but rather an opportunity to immerse himself in an electrifying political arena. Having assumed the role of interim Governor of Wyoming just a year prior, his aspirations had been ignited, and there was no grander stage to stoke the flames of his political objectives than the national convention.

The Republican National Convention Hall buzzed with a palpable energy, a symphony of voices and ideologies converging in a cacophony of debate and discourse. Damian and his father navigated through a sea of political heavyweights, mingling with the who's who of the Republican Party. Sam West was at the top of the heap, making Damian realize just how important his father was to the nation and the people that governed it. It was an experience unlike any other, a front-row seat to the theater of American democracy and all its grandeur.

As Damian rubbed elbows with the political elite, he absorbed the wisdom and insights from the myriad of seasoned statesmen. It was a masterclass in political maneuvering, a chance to witness the intricate dance of power and influence that defined the world of American politics.

For Damian, this convention was far more than a mere steppingstone; it was a consortium of validation, a vibrant arena where his ambitions were recognized and celebrated. It was a realm where his dreams were not merely encouraged but emboldened, infused with the vigor of possibility. Within the dynamic space, every interaction, every exchange of ideas, was a spark that ignited his passion, transforming aspirations into tangible visions.

The knowledge he gleaned from seasoned experts and the connections he forged with like-minded visionaries would serve as the foundational blocks for his future endeavors, each encounter a brushstroke in the masterpiece of his burgeoning career. This was not just an event but the genesis of a journey, a pivotal chapter in the unfolding story of Damian's pursuit of excellence.

Within the sea of delegates and pundits, Damian West stood as a rising star, a beacon of promise in a realm where aspirations reached the highest-power echelons. The convention was more than an experience; it was a platform that would shape the trajectory of his political journey, setting the stage for a future where his ambitions knew no bounds.

As Wyoming's Governor, he was more in an observatory capacity. Still, the political arena intrigued him greatly, and he always enjoyed the socializing aspect the conventions brought with the exposure. His father would often tell him, "Connect with as many of these Senators, supporters, and contributors as you can, Damian, and always establish a lasting impression within their minds when you meet them but more so. . . . *when you leave them*. Make them remember you. Stand out. It may prove useful at some point."

Damian smiled inwardly at hearing his father's voice in his head time and time again. Hosting the colossal event, only the Quicken Loans Arena (currently the Rocket Mortgage Fieldhouse) would accommodate such a large gathering and support such a caucus. The convention marked the third occasion Cleveland had hosted the Republican National Convention and the first since 1936.

During the 2016 Republican National Convention, which took place from July 18 to July 21, Donald Trump was formally nominated as the Republican Party's candidate for President of the United States. Senator Sam West proudly announced Trump's endorsement as their candidate for President for the 2016 election. In his speech, Senator West defined the state of the new political era and the need for a candidate not swayed by the antiquated political system, and Donald Trump emulated such a persona. They desperately needed a leader that was truthful, vigilant, and valiant in his efforts to improve this country. Indiana Governor Mike Pence was selected as his running mate for the position of Vice President. Standing proudly beside his father, Damian West listened to Trump's speech in which he outlined his campaign's challenges and emphasized his slogan of *Making America Great Again.*

Further back in history, the year was 2000. At only twelve years of age, Damian West also stood proudly next to his father and mother as his father took the podium at the National Convention in Philadelphia, PA, to introduce Governor George W. Bush as their selected Presidential Nominee. With glowing adoration upon the stage, Senator Sam West spoke proudly and eloquently about their Republican Nominee and ensured the American people that George W. Bush, come November, would prevail to become their 43rd President of the United States. His victory over Democratic candidate Al Gore seemed a foregone conclusion. Yet, despite the eloquent rhetoric, Sam harbored deep resentment toward Bush's nomination. Months earlier, Bush had dismantled the meticulous plans that Sam West and his consortium had crafted to ensure the nation's endurance and prosperity. Bush's failure to fulfill his obligations and uphold the Republican Party's promise to endorse their new presidential candidate left Sam's carefully laid groundwork in ruins. However, that argument would be saved for another day, they would have to press on and support their Republican Nominee.

Senator Sam West predicted the results of both outcomes correctly. Many theorized George W. Bush and Donald Trump won their respective elections on Sam West's endorsements alone, but Sam never gave the notion credence. It was widely publicized Sam West was initially the heavy favorite for the Republican Nomination in 2000 and 2016. Still, he humbly declined the formal offers, much to the party's surprise in the Fall of 1998 and 2014, respectively.

Earlier in the month, Damian and his father had been sitting in his study in Wyoming, and young Damian asked his father, "Can you help me understand something? I'm confused, Dad. The Republican Party wants you to be the next President. They have asked you on several occasions, but you declined their offer every time. It's a testament to their confidence in you; I can't wrap my head around why you would decline such a tremendous offer?" Sam eased back in his forty-year-old high-back leather chair, squeaking from years of use, smiled at his son, and appreciated his articulacy even at his young age. He was already a gifted and incisive young man, masterfully delivering his charismatic charm even with the questions he asked.

In the quiet and intimate exchange between father and son, Sam West's words carried wisdom instilled through a lifetime of political maneuvering and astute observation. As they sat together, the room took on an aura of solemnity, as if it were a sanctuary where the truths of the political world were being unveiled.

Sam's deliberate pause before speaking emphasized the importance of what he was about to convey. It was a moment of mentorship during which the elder West sought to impart the insights that guided his remarkable career.

"Son," he began, the affection and pride for Damian evident in his gaze, "I don't expect you to fully grasp the intricacies of what I'm about to explain, at least not right now. But trust me when I say there will come a time when the pieces will fall into place, and all of this will make perfect sense to you."

In his measured tone, Sam underscored his confidence in his own abilities and his genuine desire to serve the nation. "Make no mistake, Damian, I believe I would champion the everyday pressures and challenges of the Oval Office. I know I would be a competent President who would make you and your mother proud and leave a lasting mark on this country."

However, as Sam continued, his words revealed a deeper philosophy and weight that had guided his political career. "But here's the truth, Damian. My most impactful work, the work that truly shapes the course of our nation, is done in the trenches. It's behind the scenes, in the art of negotiation, deal-making, and diplomacy. All those attributes have, at least in some form, manipulated and influenced the acting President. It may have been the President-Elect making the speeches and conveying the narrative publicly, but few of them were the architects behind the scenes. They weren't the ones rolling up their sleeves and getting their hands dirty. We haven't seen the likes of that since Reagan, JFK, or Roosevelt. Those were true leaders, true Presidents. It's about finding common ground with political adversaries, leveraging it to achieve a greater good, and manipulating the President to see that end is commonplace."

With the gravitas of a seasoned statesman, Sam elaborated on the significance of his behind-the-scenes role. "Whether brokering deals on important legislation or strategically positioning individuals of merit in key roles, this is where real change occurs. It's the heart of political influence, where we work to better our country and uplift the American people."

His words carried an air of humility as he admitted his preference was to operate discreetly. "The President, Damian, is under an unyielding spotlight. Every move they make is scrutinized and judged, and they often become a symbol more than a true agent of change. That's where I differ. I prefer to move in the shadows, where I can most effectively navigate the horizon."

Sam's voice held a profound conviction as he concluded, "Presidents have their role, and they are undoubtedly important and are the face of our nation. However, it's crucial to recognize true power in politics often lies in those who operate behind the scenes, in the shadows, orchestrating the intricate ballet of governance. It's a world where loyalty, strategy, and influence shape destinies, and we haven't had a president who has been able to achieve both, or either, successfully in some time."

He turned to Damian, his eyes full of adoration and earnestness. "So, Damian, as you navigate your own political journey, remember that the presidency is just one part of the intricate puzzle. Embrace the shadows, for it is where the most meaningful changes often take place. I have yet to meet a President who has been able to equalize all aspects . . . *and execute them effectively*."

The room reverberated with the weight of Sam West's words, leaving Damian to ponder the depth of his father's insights and the profound knowledge he had inherited.

Sam observed young Damian's reaction and feared his words may confuse his son on some level. How could he expect an adolescent boy to understand the ways of the world when he had so much more to learn? "I think I do, Sir. In short, are you saying you are better a kingmaker. . . . . *than a King?*"

Sam narrowed his gaze, focused on Damian with such intensity Damian felt he was burning a hole right through him, and softly said, "Exactly, Son . . . . Bravo . . . . *that's exactly what I'm saying.*" Sam sat back in his chair, amazed at the understanding and comprehension of his son as he took a drink of his Bourbon sitting on top of his desk.

After a moment, he looked at Damian and thought, "And my hope, someday, Damian, is I will have a hand in *making you that King.* This is my dream and goal, but there is much to be done before we get to that point." There was much Sam West desperately wanted to say to Damian, but it was all too early for such weighty Conversation in theoretical underscores and political manipulation. So, instead, he stated, "The making of Kings, Damian, is no effortless task. There are so many people, agendas, and manipulations that must be organized, placed, synchronized, and tested. Honestly, it's a daunting process to think about, and I'm not sure it can even be accomplished with the political gridlock we face today. There are so many moving parts to consider. The game has changed tremendously in recent years."

"I know, Dad. Watching you announce Mr. Bush made me proud and opened my eyes to what may be achieved if properly orchestrated. I want to go into law after Stanford and get into the political arena as soon as possible, and I want you to teach me everything you know," explained Damian.

Sam rose from his chair with deliberate slowness, a man accustomed to the weight of his own authority. He crossed the expanse of his study, a sanctuary lined with shelves that groaned under the weight of countless tomes filling the wall—each volume a testament to his insatiable thirst for knowledge and a symbol of his legal prowess. Leaning against this fortress of wisdom, he fixed his gaze upon his son, a mirror of his younger self, hungry and ambitious.

"That pleases me to hear, Son," he began, his voice a blend of pride and caution. "But be forewarned. The path you've chosen is fraught with obstacles. It is a journey marked by hardship, disillusionment, and, at times, blatant injustice. The political arena is a battlefield, merciless and unforgiving. It will challenge your resolve, exploit your weaknesses, and test your mettle. Are you prepared to endure such trials?"

"Yes, Father, I am. Well, I feel I am," came the resolute yet humble reply. "But I also know that under your guidance, I will learn to navigate these treacherous waters. Teach me the intricacies, the pitfalls, and the triumphs. I want to understand the inner workings of this vast machine and master the art of bending it to my will. While others may learn through trial and error, I have the privilege of being mentored by my father. There is no greater teacher and no more admirable ally than you. I am determined to excel, and with your wisdom to light my way, I will not only succeed but become a figure of respect and appreciation. Help me to achieve greatness, Father, for I am eager to learn and ready to conquer. I will be your proudest pupil."

Damian smiled as he said those words and believed every single one of them as they fell from his lips. Sam understood his son was gifted beyond most and would provide the ideal vessel for Sam to unfold his masterful plan.

The moment was surreal to Damian as an adult, as he reflected sixteen years prior and pondered that poignant historical moment while attending middle school. It was roughly during that time that Julian Chambers came into his life.

Philadelphia, Pennsylvania
2016 July 25-28
Democratic National Convention

It had been over ten years since Philadelphia hosted a presidential convention, and the city was primed to host the 2016 Democratic National Convention. In 2000, Philadelphia hosted the Republican National Convention, of which Texas Governor George W. Bush became the party's nominee, as announced by Senator Sam West.

Being 2016, as usual, the convention was shaping up to be a star-studded event featuring big names in American politics alongside Hollywood celebrities. According to the press release from the convention's committee, the first night of the convention kicked off with First Lady Michelle Obama and Senator Bernie Sanders, Clinton's fiercest primary rival, as the headline speakers. On Tuesday night, there would be the roll call vote would officially nominate Hillary Clinton. It was expected President Obama and Vice

President Joe Biden would deliver their remarks on Wednesday. It was also traditionally the night the attendees heard from the vice-presidential nominee; Hillary Clinton was to announce Tim Kaine, Senator from Virginia, as her running mate on Friday.

It was scheduled that Chelsea Clinton would aid her mother in wrapping up the convention on Thursday, and Hillary Clinton was expected to speak about her vision for the country that night.

Throughout the multi-day convention, actors and singers who were Clinton supporters would grace the stage, including Katy Perry, Eva Longoria, Alicia Keys, Demi Lovato, Tony Goldwyn, and Lena Dunham, to name a few.

Other political influencers would also take the stage throughout the week, including Senator Elizabeth Warren, Senator Cory Booker, Senator Al Franken, Governor Andrew Cuomo, former Maryland Governor Martin O'Malley, and New York City Mayor, Bill de Blasio.

Bernie Sanders's presidential campaign may have ended earlier in the year, but the movement he started continued as Hillary Clinton would carry the torch until the Presidential Election in November. The City of Brotherly Love felt "the Bern," as supporters held a week of rallies to show their support for the Vermont senator. In the later stages of Sanders' campaign for the Democratic nomination, many of his supporters expressed anger about the party's system of using superdelegates, as use of the unbound delegates who typically hold, or have held, elective office within the walls of Congress, as a governor or the like were free to vote for the candidate of their choice during the formal nominating process. The utilization of these super delegates exercised a tremendous amount of power in selecting a nominee to represent their party. The support of these unpledged delegates, combined with bound delegates distributed due to the caucus and primary vote totals, pushed Hillary Clinton over the threshold to clinch the nomination. "It is time for the DNC and its Rules Committee to ensure the voices of voters, not party insiders, will always be the deciding factor in our nominating process," said Aaron Regunberg, a Rhode Island state representative and DNC Rules Committee member.

Despite the Democratic Party's best efforts, Donald Trump and Mike Pence went on to win the general election, defeating Hillary Clinton and Tim Kaine's Democratic ticket. Their reign, however, would only last one term.

Following the election, Sam and Damian had lengthy discussions on the growing separation of the bi-partisan system, and the disparity between the Republicans and Democrats grew exponentially.

They passionately debated over a fresh and innovative rise of a disruptive formation of a third party to stimulate the political unrest of the bi-partisan system and how it would be shaped. Several prominent political issues resonated with voters and shaped the national discourse. They spoke for hours about the reform needed in the various areas most affecting the American people.

Economy and Jobs were among the leading topics: addressing income inequality, stimulating economic growth, and providing more opportunities for the middle class. Healthcare reform also posed issues with The Affordable Care Act (ACA - Obamacare), which remained contentious. Immigration policy, particularly related to the issue of undocumented immigrants and border security, was indeed a hot-button issue needing more resolution. It was an issue that generated significant debate and shaped the political discourse, from building a wall along the U.S.-Mexico border and enforcing immigration laws to providing a better path to citizenship for undocumented immigrants.

National Security, terrorism and gun control: The proliferation of ISIS and global security concerns prompted more aggressive solutions to the growing issues surrounding terrorism. The issue of gun control received significant attention following several high-profile mass shootings in the United States. Candidates had different approaches to balancing Second Amendment rights with the need for stricter regulations to prevent gun violence.

Climate change, specifically environmental issues, gained prominence in the 2016 election. A myriad of different views exists on the extent of human impact on the climate and the role of government in addressing environmental challenges. Rounding out the critical components were that of Criminal Justice Reform. The public demanded criminal justice reform, including addressing issues such as police misconduct, racial disparities, and sentencing reform.

Charlotte, North Carolina
2020 Republican National Convention
August 24-27

While the COVID-19 pandemic significantly impacted the election process in the United States, altering the traditional format and protocol commonly used in years past. However, the 2020 Republican National Convention, which re-nominated President Donald Trump and Vice President Mike Pence as the party's candidates, was initially planned to be held in Charlotte, North Carolina. However, due to the pandemic, the format and location of the convention were modified. The main portion of the convention took place in late August 2020 at the Andrew W. Mellon Auditorium in Washington, D.C., where President Trump officially accepted the nomination. Other elements of the convention were held remotely or at various locations to comply with health and safety guidelines.

The convention was initially planned for the Spectrum Center in Charlotte, North Carolina, but it was moved after disagreements over crowd size and health measures. Some scaled-down proceedings took place in Charlotte, but the rest, including Trump's acceptance speech, were held remotely from various locations like Fort McHenry and the White House. The convention followed the Democratic National Convention, and Trump secured the Republican nomination with little opposition in the primaries.

Washington D.C.
2020 Democratic National Convention
August 17-20

The stage was set for the much-anticipated 2020 Democratic National Convention, a political extravaganza initially slated for Milwaukee, Wisconsin. However, the specter of the COVID-19 pandemic had cast a long shadow over the event, leading to a major pivot in its format. What was once envisioned as a bustling gathering with throngs of enthusiastic delegates was transformed into a largely virtual affair, with only limited in-person activities.

Despite the unprecedented circumstances, the convention remained pivotal in American politics. It served as the formal nexus for the Democratic Party to nominate its candidates for the highest offices in the land—President and Vice President of the United States. As the nation grappled with a health crisis and a deeply divided political landscape, the stakes were higher than ever.

The convention's agenda was laden with highlights that drew the attention of political enthusiasts across the country. Key among them were the speeches delivered by prominent Democrats, whose words carried the weight of their collective experience and vision. The roster included luminaries such as former President Barack Obama, whose oratory prowess was legendary; former First Lady Michelle Obama, whose eloquence resonated deeply; former Secretary of State Hillary Clinton, a trailblazer in her own right; and Senator Bernie Sanders, a figure who had ignited a passionate movement.

Yet, the pinnacle of the event was undoubtedly the nomination acceptance speeches. Joe Biden, a seasoned politician with decades of public service, took to the virtual stage as the Democratic Party's nominee for President. His speech was not merely a formal acceptance of the nomination; it was a call for harmony amongst all, a plea for healing, and a blueprint for the future.

Equally historic was Kamala Harris's nomination as vice presidential candidate, which was groundbreaking in American history. Her acceptance speech was imbued with a sense of purpose as she embarked on a journey to shatter glass ceilings and inspire a new generation.

The convention was not merely about the individuals on stage; it was a platform to rally the Democratic Party behind a common vision for the nation's future. It was an opportunity to lay out a comprehensive platform that addressed pressing issues such as healthcare, climate change, racial justice, and economic recovery.

Throughout the event, the speakers passionately emphasized the imperative need for accord between them. They highlighted the stark differences between the Democratic Party and the incumbent Republican administration, presenting an alternative path for the nation. In a time of turbulence and uncertainty, the convention sought to offer a beacon of hope, a roadmap to a brighter and more equitable future.

As the virtual lackluster applause echoed through screens across the country, the 2020 Democratic National Convention left a sense of status quo on the political landscape. It was a testament to the stagnation and age old rhetoric of American democracy, a reminder that even in the face of adversity, the democratic process would continue to remain unmoving and idle.

After one of the most prolonged and drawn-out controversies in election history, on November 3, 2020, President Donald Trump and Vice-President Mike Pence went on to lose the general election to the Democratic ticket of Joe Biden and Kamala Harris. Though riddled with arguments and accusations, the American people and candidates eventually went on to accept their new President and Vice-President.

Damian found his father in his study early that evening, the day after the announcement that President-elect Joe Biden was to be the next president of the United States. It was a bittersweet moment for Senator Sam West, who was proud that his only son had won his Senate seat as an Independent. However, he was also deeply burdened by the thought that Joe Biden would lead his great nation with no direction or vitality backing the prevailing party.

The 2018 Wyoming election of Damian West with a distinctive margin, winning the senate seat, and having his father's endorsement to succeed him. A seat he had held for over fifty years was both an honor and a testament to the West dynasty. The bitter truth, however, was that with his son's election, Sam West would eventually become a political relic. The strategic move was to have him step down and hand over the reins to his successor. It was ultimately a sacrifice he took for his son's progression.

Now, he would no longer be in the position of power and influence to which he had become accustomed. He would remain a formidable force as a leader and retired senator, but, officially, he would no longer carry the same weight and influence he was accustomed to wielding. He sacrificed that right when he put his full advocacy behind his son to replace him as Wyoming's representative senator. The prior two years of retirement was spent forming Damian, educating him, in the nuances of replacing him in his Senate seat and paving the way for the next chapter that was about to unfold.

The significance of the nation's future bore heavily on Damian's mind as he noticed his father's growing worry. His concerns were palpable, like a looming storm on the horizon. Sam West had dedicated his life to the service of his country, and his devotion ran deep. He had weathered the tides of politics, navigating the turbulent waters of Washington with a steady hand. But now, as the election passed, the transition was at hand, and it carried a significance that Damian had not fully anticipated.

For Sam, the election was more than a mere changing of the guard; it was a momentous turning point in the nation's history. It symbolized a gradual decline from the lofty ideals upon which the country had been founded. The significance of his years in public service gave him a unique perspective, allowing him to witness the shifting sands of politics and power.

As the campaign season was in their rearview mirror, Sam couldn't help but reflect on the principles guiding his career. He had always endeavored to uphold the values of integrity, honesty, and bipartisanship. But in the current climate, where polarization dominated the political norm, those principles appeared to be increasingly elusive.

Damian sensed his father's deep-rooted concern, stirring a similar unease within him. He felt that the election was not a mere contest of political ideologies; it was a referendum on the very soul of the nation. It was a moment when the ideals of unity and compromise were being put to the test, and the outcome would shape the course of the country for years to come. It was the *calm to the proverbial storm* as Sam was close to unleashing the next phase of his elaborate plan.

As the campaign rhetoric intensified and the nation's divisions became more pronounced, Damian couldn't help but wonder if the America his father had served so faithfully was slipping away. The burden of responsibility weighed on his shoulders as he contemplated the role he would play in the nation's future.

In the midst of this political maelstrom, father and son shared a bond that transcended politics. They shared a profound love for their country and a commitment to its betterment. The election was a passing event and a platform for discussing their shared values and convictions.

Together, they stood on the precipice of change, grappling with the realization that the nation they cherished was at a crossroads. The election was a defining moment, and the burden of safeguarding the nation's ideals rested on the strength of the new administration.

The room was quiet, the occasional crackling of the fire in the hearth the only sound. The quietude calmed him and provided the tranquility he needed most to weather this new change. The fire's glow illuminated the space sufficiently, tossing shadows as they pranced upon the walls and overhead beams of the vaulted ceiling.

The aging Senator sat quietly alone in front of his large fireplace, a glass of bourbon in his hand, lost in his thoughts. It was a picturesque moment, perfect for a painting depicting the weight of the world on a singular soul. The fire's warmth and flickering light emulated a melancholy state of serenity where Sam West often retired to ponder life's challenges. He enjoyed those moments since he had lost his wife nearly two decades before. Since her passing, he appreciated the finer moments most took for granted.

The sizzling and popping of the embers had a trance-like effect on Sam West. Not hearing Damian enter the room, he softly asked, "You okay, Dad?" Sam West slowly pulled his attention from the fire as it danced about the logs perfectly placed within the manicured hearth. "Of course, son. Come, sit down. Sit and talk with me for a time." Damian West respected his father's wish and eased into the plush chair next to his father as they watched the fire in silence for a moment more. So warm and cozy inside, yet just feet away, six inches of snow outside covered the landscape around the estate. An early snow for the season, which usually meant the winter would be rigorous. The snow continued to fall on the cold November day.

"It's an end of an era, Damian. A changing of the guard, in a sense, with your arrival effectively equates to my . . . . release of my official duty. However, now after two years of retirement, counseling you, it is finally time . . ." I always knew this was how it would occur. I just never thought I would have this dismal feeling about it all, I suppose." Damian looked over at his father sorrowfully; he seemed somehow older in the light as it shone through as dusk began to settle in.

Despite their hours of lengthy discussions in the years before about this very moment, Damian knew when the time finally came when his father was no longer there, it would feel like the loss of a close friend he had held dear for his entire life.

In an effort to improve his mood, he offered, "Well, it's because of you that I won the seat. We will make the West name legendary in the years to come. Now is when our work truly begins. You may not hold the actual seat, but your work will be more substantial in the coming years than it has ever been. We have discussed this, Dad."

Sam West smiled at his son, proud of him and the man he had become. "It's simply a phase and a moment of dejection is all. I'll get over it. Now, on to more important matters. Yesterday set this country back, and with the Democrats returning to power, it may be good timing for me to nudge those a little harder that owe me favors and accelerate our plan somewhat, but it will make your job a little more difficult. The race in 2024 should be interesting, depending on how Joe Biden fares during his term. 2024 will not have a lot of front-runners from the Republican side. Only former Vice-president Mike Pence, Governor Ron DeSantis, and former President Don Trump have any chance in my estimation."

Damian considered the list of candidates, "I like the list. I don't think Pence or DeSantis will gain much in the popular vote, but Trump is somewhat of a loose cannon, and his approach can come out of anywhere." Sam looked at Damian closely, deep in thought, "Agreed. The points in contention are Trump's border wall proposal and its effects on immigration and its enforcement. The DACA (Deferred Action for Childhood Arrivals) initiative is also a dicey area that will need to be built out and defined better as well." Damian added, "Immigration reform will also play a big part in the coming years."

Sam considered these long-standing topics, such as climate issues, terrorism, and the economy. They had a lot of work to create the infrastructure for their new party and make it palpable for the American people to witness its value and benefits. There was far more to the plan that Damian was not yet privy to, but he was brought up to speed in due time; he simply needed the aid of his dear friend, the Speaker of the House, Congresswoman Regina Alvarado, to help when the time was right.

"The question remains, when will we release the Unified Party, officially?" asked Damian. Sam considered the question, "I give us a year to put it all together and recruit those we hope will be loyal to the cause. There will be leaks, Damian; there always are, so we must be ready to launch far earlier if given the opportunity. The fluidity will be an ongoing fluctuating dynamic, and we need to be ready for any and all of what comes at us. Your governorship has created a well-oiled machine that has worked well as a model for this state, and we need to push the idea that it can also work well on the national front. The amount of time we spent creating reform has worked brilliantly here in Wyoming and is gaining headway nationally. People are watching you and want to see what you will do next. That increased interest will be our goal and challenge, and we will be scrutinized heavily for it. Be ready to take the gloves off, son."

Damian looked at his father, "I'm prepared to take the Unified Party to the end. I want people to see there can be an evolution beyond that of the Republican and Democratic mentality." Sam West smiled, "I like that spirit. We will need it, believe me."

Restrained, Sam West's face became solemn, "It will get worse . . . . . *before it gets better, Damian.*"

Chapter 4

A New Alliance

"Freedom is the open window through which pours the sunlight of the human spirit and human dignity."
~Herbert Hoover

Dallas, Texas
2020 December

As the clock struck 6 PM on the chilly Friday evening, she found herself enveloped in a cocoon of comfort and tranquility within her downtown brick stone residence. The world outside was bathed in winter's cold embrace, but indoors, a warm and inviting ambiance reigned supreme. She had carved out this moment, a sacred sanctuary of relaxation and indulgence. No distractions were the focus of her evening.

With a glass of Cabernet in hand, its deep red hue shimmering in the soft glow of the fireplace, she settled into her favorite armchair in the living room. The flames danced and crackled, casting a mesmerizing play of shadows on the walls. It was a tableau of cozy perfection, a retreat from the demands of the outside world.

Her choice of evening pastime was a literary indulgence. She had immersed herself in the pages of "Jian," a mesmerizing work of fiction penned by none other than Eric Van Lustbader. It was the fourth installment in the Sunset Warrior Cycle series, a literary journey that initially captivated her imagination.

In "Jian," Van Lustbader wove an elaborate blend of words and imagination that transported her to a world far removed from her own. It was a realm where the strict and intricate array of Japanese culture served as the backdrop for a tale of epic proportions. The book delved deep into the nuances of honor, tradition, and martial prowess, painting a vivid portrait of a society where every gesture held profound significance.

What had initially drawn her into Lustbader's literary universe was the seamless blend of fantasy and Asian culture, reminding her of her upbringing. It was a heady concoction that had the power to exhilarate and captivate. But it wasn't just the action that ensnared her; it was Van Lustbader's masterful storytelling that truly held her in thrall.

The author's writing style was a wonder, characterized by its high-energy narrative, intricate plotting, and meticulously researched detail. Van Lustbader left no stone unturned in his quest for authenticity, and it showed in the rich tapestry he wove in his work. His characters were not mere archetypes but complex beings with their own motivations, flaws, and virtues.

As she turned the pages, she reveled in the thrill of the story's twists and turns. It was a journey of discovery for the characters and herself as a reader. Van Lustbader's exploration of complex themes and the human condition added depth to the narrative, making it a literary experience transcending mere escapism.

In her living room, with the firelight casting a warm and inviting glow, she savored every word, every sentence, and every chapter. Eric Van Lustbader had once again transported her to a world of wonder, where the boundaries of reality blurred, and the magic of storytelling held sway. It was a moment of pure bliss, a communion between reader and author, a testament to the power of literature to transport and transform. She breezed through the first 70 pages, refilling her wine glass, engrossed in the story.

As she settled back into her cozy chair, the unexpected knock at the door startled her, momentarily pulling her away from the alluring world she had been immersed in the moments prior. She was more than a little annoyed at the disruption and well within her right to not answer the door at all in hopes the interrupting visitor may saunter away, but a second rap at the door made her realize she would need to deal with the intrusion directly.

Still light outside, she cautiously approached the door and opened it. A well-dressed man in a suit and sunglasses introduced himself. "Ms. Dmitri, I am Secret Service Agent Benjamin Lee. I didn't mean to surprise you, but Senator Damian West has requested your presence tonight."

Taken aback at the request, she hadn't seen, nor heard from Damian West since they met at the charity benefit. It had been nearly a month, and assumed he had forgotten about her or wasn't interested and she certainly would not chase him. She looked at Agent Lee and cocked her head, "Is he here in Dallas?" Agent Lee hesitated at the question, looked to either side, and said, "Well, no, ma'am, he would like you to visit him at his cabin." She looked at him strangely, "Cabin? I'm a little confused. I am unaware of any cabins or lodges in Dallas," Agent Lee elaborated, "His cabin is in . . . . well, it's in Jackson Hole, ma'am."

"Jackson Hole?" She repeated. Agent Lee softly said, "Yes, ma'am, that's the one . . . it's in Wyoming." Mila smiled, "I know where Jackson Hole is located, Agent Lee, just a little mystified and possibly slightly offended."

He continued, "Senator West said you might say that, so he wanted me to tell you that he thought it would be nice for you to meet him there and have a chance to get out of Dallas and . . . *relax for a bit.* . . were his words, I believe, Ms. Dmitri."

"Oh, he does, does he?" Mila. Agent Lee added, openly awkward but understanding her hesitation, "He suggested you pack a small bag for the trip; dinner will be ready when you arrive . . . . *also, his words*." He shrugged while looking at her. "I can't believe he would expect me to drop everything and simply leave. Please tell him thank you, but no thank you." Agent Lee replied, "Yes, ma'am, I will give him your response," as he turned to walk away.

As she gently closed the door. She put her head on the doorframe, thinking about the situation, then opened the door a moment later while Agent Lee was beginning to open the door of his SUV. He stopped when he saw her emerge from the doorway.

She sheepishly walked out a few steps and quietly said, "Agent Lee . . . Please give me a few minutes to get some things together." Agent Lee smiled and replied, "Of course, ma'am, take your time. Bring something warm to wear. He said you will return on Sunday if that helps." She looked at him and grimaced; two days alone with a man she barely knew, what was she even thinking as she closed the door and turned off the fireplace, leaving the full glass of wine and book on the coffee table.

In a whirlwind of impatience, she dashed up the staircase of her charming brick stone residence. Minutes later, she emerged, the door locked securely behind her. Her hurried descent down the stairs was matched only by the rapid thumping of her heart, a telltale sign of the excitement coursing through her veins.

Outside, Agent Lee's black SUV waited patiently for her arrival. Even the sophistication of his vehicle, with its sleek lines and polished exterior, was a testament to the luxury and style she anticipated from the Senator. With a sense of purpose, she slid into the plush leather seat, the engine humming to life, ready to whisk her away to a destination shrouded in furtive anticipation.

The journey to the private airstrip was a mere twenty-three minutes, but it offered ample time for introspection. She couldn't help but mull over the intriguing invitation she had accepted. It had come from none other than the magnetic Senator from Wyoming, Damian West. Handsome, charismatic, and enigmatic, he was a figure who captured her attention in more ways than one. Secretly, he ignited a spark of excitement in hearing from him, despite it being an indirect invitation. She would have never declined his offer, she just didn't want to give in too quickly.

As the cityscape whizzed by, her thoughts meandered through the labyrinth of her desires and curiosity. What had propelled her to embrace this opportunity, to step into the enticing unknown with Damian West? It had been tugging at the corners of her mind since she had first received his invitation.

In the end, she had decided to throw caution to the wind. Damian West's allure was undeniable, and she couldn't resist the chance to be in his company. Something about him, something charming and irresistible, had drawn her in. It wasn't just his rising as a political star that fascinated her; it was his energy, passion, and unbridled ambition.

Mila assumed the evening promised more than just an ordinary encounter. It was a rare opportunity to have Damian West all to herself, free from the distractions and clamor of those who sought his attention. In the world of politics, where every move was scrutinized and every word analyzed, their private rendezvous offered a glimpse into a different side of Damian West, a side reserved for those who dared to venture beyond the public persona.

The anticipation in the air was palpable as the SUV glided toward the private airstrip. Mila couldn't deny the rush of eagerness that coursed through her. She was embarking on an adventure, guided by her curiosity, and growing desire for the unknown, and an undeniable attraction to the perplexing Senator from Wyoming. It was a journey that promised to be unforgettable, a night where two worlds would collide, and the sparks of intrigue would set the night ablaze.

She was very curious about his brazen demand and summoning to his home but also intrigued by why he had sought her out only weeks after they had met at the charity fundraiser. She eagerly awaited the evening as the private jet made its way down the runway to arrive a few hours later in Jackson Hole, Wyoming.

The jet arrived in Jackson Hole at 9:15 PM. She freshened up well before her arrival with a shower and rested in the provided bedroom on board. Upon landing, Agent Lee knocked on her door to announce they would be ready in five minutes. She politely confirmed and opened the door a few minutes later.

Mila Dmitri emerged from the doorway, stunning and elegant. She wore a black skirt with pantyhose and a sweater to match. Her full-length white jacket with black fur along the collar and clear eyeglasses gave her a sophisticated look, which was precisely her intention. She walked through the aisle as Agent Lee turned, taken aback by her beauty.

All he could muster was, "Nice choice, Ms. Dmitri," as he escorted her down the stairs into the black SUV waiting below. He opened the door as she stepped inside and closed the door behind her. A maintenance employee brought her roller bag to Agent Lee as he loaded it into the rear door, and then they were off.

Jackson Hole, Wyoming
2004 (16 Years Before)
Senator Sam West Private Estate

"The two-party system mentality is a perpetually antiquated, a dying dinosaur, Julian," explained Damian. "I would agree, although it's been a fairly well-balanced platform for many years. However, both parties struggle with the notion they may become antediluvian in this evolving society. Sadly, neither party will accept or even consider the possibility that they are becoming obsolete. There is a lack of diverse representation: The dominance of the Democrats and Republicans often limits the range of political perspectives and hampers the representation of minority parties or independent candidates. This can lead to limited choices for voters and a lack of diverse voices in the political arena. Then, there is the consideration the two-party system can contribute to heightened polarization and partisan divisions. The focus on winning elections and maintaining party unity can often overshadow the need for constructive dialogue and compromise, leading to a gridlock in policymaking. This has especially worsened over the years. The idea of bi-partisan goals and focus appears to diminish daily. My father often speaks of a time, not long ago, when the system worked well and operated within a healthy environment. Democrats and Republicans would practice a healthy competitive nature between them. They would take their *figurative gloves* off during campaign season, for example, fight the good fight, and the winner determined outright and not disputed or argued, but rather, accepted, and life moved on. It was a respected system. The victor would be publicly announced and *accepted by all in good form.* The losing candidate would call the elected winner and offer his concession, and the new administration would execute their term for the common good of the nation. The parties would put their gloves back on and move forward ceremoniously and in unison as if it was a ritualistic dance between these two mighty factions. It was a magnificent idea and concept, Julian, and to listen to my father describe it to me is a thing of beauty." Damian shook his head.

"Now, both parties are simply exhausted by the other. Inextricably connected, chained together, antagonistic, becoming one another's ball and chain. They have inadvertently become one another's burden, unable to separate from the other. Also, with only two major parties, the range of policy options presented to voters can be limiting. Some argue this restricts innovative ideas and alternative approaches to addressing societal challenges we face now we didn't recognize or entertain, fifty years ago." Julian Chambers nodded as his best friend spelled out the difficulties facing the two-party system.

Julian added, "Don't forget, Damian, the influence of money and special interests, too. The two-party system is often associated with a significant influence of capital and special political interests. Wealthy donors and powerful interest groups can exert substantial influence over the parties and their candidates, potentially undermining the democratic principles of equal representation and fairness. This can lead to the exclusion of alternative voices as a result. Third-party candidates and independent voices face significant barriers to gaining traction and visibility in the two-party system. Access to debates, media coverage, and campaign financing can be challenging, as you know. This makes it difficult for alternative perspectives to gain widespread support."

Damian carries the point further, "All so true. Ingrained was a respect, *always the respect*, within the bi-partisan system, but not anymore. It appears to be fading as the years pass. Each subsequent administration is hell-bent on dismantling the prior one and anything they put in motion during the preceding administration. It's time for a change, Julian. The political system needs it, the country is thirsty for it, and the people are beginning to demand it. They are tired of the empty promises and rhetoric; they need to see something significant occur in the way of change and reform, or they will stand up and rebel. The government will be powerless if it occurs."

"Yeah, powerless, that's an issue too," replied Julian, "Man, I just love to listen to you speak, Damian. There is such passion and excitement in your explanations and reasoning. You are going to be President someday, I swear."

Damian laughs and holds his hand up, "Let's not get ahead of ourselves, Julian. We are only sixteen, and our views are far too simplistic and unrefined and saturated with an unobtainable *ideal in logic*, don't you think? I mean it, though, the people won't stand for it. They will demand, at some point, the balance this country needs."

Julian shook his head slightly and scowled, "Yes, but the people are weak; they are a mass of conjecture and selfishness, believing everything they hear. The media has made them all sheep. The Government should take a stronger position on martial law. I feel we are far too lenient in our control of the people, their beliefs . . . . . their *stupidity*. The United States should be more regimented in its governing. Hell, maybe the Nazis were on to something . . . ." Julian says, testing the waters, then immediately began to awkwardly snicker at the reference, and Damian joined in, thankful Julian was simply recklessly flippant over the thought the Nazi regime was anything but catastrophic and barbaric. The two young men would talk for hours in Damian's father's study.

Sam West had orchestrated this home office venue deliberately, down to even the furnishings: the old walnut bookcase and desk, coffered ceiling, and walls encased in stained walnut. One might contemplate this setting when considering an old law library. Sam's desk sat quietly, unoccupied, immense in size, situated in the back of the room and beyond it, sprawled the beautiful country landscape.

Three large cow hide-covered chairs were situated in the middle of the spacious room, facing a large mantle where a fire would often be roaring to life within the hearth below. The intimate setting was conducive to hours of discussions, arguments, teasing and even laughter, bountiful and flowing. This was a sanctuary of complete candidness and strictly devoid of judgment. You spoke your mind within these walls and were never judged for one's candor.

Years before, Sam West set up the only variable "rule" was everyone had to respect one another when entering the study. Anyone within the confines of the study could speak their peace without censorship and scrutiny. It was the truest haven of safety in individual expression. Anything said within the room was sacred, and its confidence was respected above all. Sam referred to the room as his *Sanctuary,* and everyone was aware of the rules of that room, which were few, and all respected its nature and referred to the study as such.

So, too, had Sam made this room unique in less obvious ways as well, not just on the surface by means of its function and aesthetic but also for another purpose entirely. More covert in nature, Sam had a less known, devious, and calculative side to him, certainly with a touch of paranoia. When the home was built in 1964, Sam had the acumen to protect his conversations with people above all and limit his exposure. Therefore, he initially secured his interests by placing small listening devices and later, in 1996, upgraded to full video within various hidden areas. The recording devices initiated and activated by voice and movement; these sensitive devices recorded everything transpiring within his study. It proved invaluable when discussing delicate and often classified issues with fellow Senators, campaign supporters, diplomats, or past and current state governors. This practice was strictly forbidden, but Senator Sam West didn't care in the least. When it came to protecting himself, his family, and his country, he would stop at nothing to ensure its sanctity and proliferation. Recording conversations was his insurance policy.

Although these listening devices provided immeasurable security and leveraged over the years, Sam had never anticipated a far more relevant use for the technology until 2001. Having just finished Thanksgiving dinner that year, Sam and his son Damian retired to the study when Damian, at only thirteen, had asked his father why he had declined the nomination for president of the United States the previous election. They had spent hours discussing Sam's reasoning, and by the end of the evening, exhausted from the day's festivities and the lengthy discussion, they both decided to call it a night.

"I'll be up in a few," with a nod from Sam as Damian excused himself from the study and bid his father a good night, leaving him in front of the fire with his thoughts. After a few minutes, Sam stood from his chair, walked to the large walnut French doors that led to the hall, closed and locked them, and went to sit at his large desk in front of the sizable bay window that looked out over his vast Wyoming property. He could see the waving trees beyond the green in front of him, well-lighted by the full moon that night. The hour was late, just after midnight.

After sitting at his desk, Sam felt with his right hand for the hidden fingerprint sensor beneath the desktop, located the pad, and placed two fingers necessary to verify the security mechanism. Confirming authenticity, a panel slid open on the top portion of his desk with an alphanumeric keypad on the right, fully exposed. He typed in "B-E-R-L-I-N" within the exposed keypad, and a secondary panel opened, revealing several additional buttons, two small video screens, a digital timer, and an earpiece. He placed the bud within his right ear to listen to the short meeting with the governor that had transpired two days prior and took some notes as the recording terminated.

As he sat at his desk, meticulously jotting down his thoughts and observations concerning a meeting earlier that week, Sam West was unexpectedly interrupted by a new recording that had begun to play. It was a recording of a lengthy conversation that had taken place earlier that evening with his son, Damian.

In all their years together, there had never been a conversation Sam deemed important or significant enough to warrant recording. However, as he listened to the playback, he realized discernments existed and subtle nuances in Damian's words that had escaped his notice during their face-to-face discussion in front of the fireplace.

Sam leaned in closer to his computer screen, his curiosity piqued. The audio and video recordings allowed him to delve deeper into the intricacies of their conversation, offering a perspective that had been hidden in plain sight. For the next hour, he listened intently, occasionally reversing and fast-forwarding to key moments in the dialogue.

As the recording played on, Sam's astonishment grew. He had always believed he knew his son well, but this newfound perspective was akin to peering through a different lens. Damian's words took on new meanings, and Sam began to pick up on subtle non-verbal cues and communicative attributes that had eluded him during their original conversation.

The insights gained from this playback were invaluable. Sam realized that his son was a complex individual, with thoughts and emotions that ran deeper than he had previously realized. It was as if a veil had been lifted, revealing layers of Damian's personality that had remained hidden.

Sam knew this newfound perspective would be instrumental in the years to come. Armed with a deeper understanding of his son's inner world and convictions, he was eager to engage in further relative and poignant discussions with Damian. Their conversations would no longer be mere exchanges of words; they would be opportunities for Sam to analyze and connect with Damian profoundly.

Sam's determination to strengthen their bond and nurture their relationship grew with each passing minute of the recording.

He recognized that as a father, there was always more to learn about his son, and he was committed to embracing this newfound insight to deepen their connection in the years ahead.

Jackson Hole, Wyoming
1998 (Damian West's Childhood)
Senator Sam West Private Estate

Julian Chambers had been Damian's closest friend since early elementary school, where they met after a peculiar incident on the first day of school, a late summer day in 1998. It was the first year Damian had attended school, attending private school up until that point. He quickly determined Julian led the class in popularity. Both boys had strong personalities, true to their convictions and stubborn as young boys often were at that age.

A rope in the schoolyard roughly 20 feet high, secured at the top, knotted every 12" for leverage extending to the top. The popular yard game between all the boys was to clock how quickly one ascended the entire length of the rope, arriving at the top and tagging the highest knot where the thick rope tied into the platform above.

As the first recess of the school day unfolded, a sudden commotion at the base of the rope caught Damian's attention. Children were packed in to view the spectacle. With casual curiosity, he sauntered over to witness the exhibition unfolding before him.

There, amidst a gathering crowd of classmates, was Julian Chambers, embarking on a daring ascent of the rope. Each knot presented a new challenge, a test of strength and agility. Damian's eyes were fixed on Julian as he methodically scaled the rope, one knot at a time. It was a mesmerizing display of determination and skill.

With unwavering focus, Julian strategically used his feet, pushing off each knot as he ascended higher and higher. The feat demanded both physical prowess and mental fortitude. The onlookers below hardly contained their excitement, and their cheers and hollers echoed through the schoolyard.

Julian reached the final knot with a burst of energy, a triumphant grin spreading across his face. The jubilant cries of his classmates served as a testament to his achievement. He had just shattered a record on the first day of school, a remarkable feat that spoke volumes about his dedication and the hours of practice he had committed himself to bettering his performance over the summer.

With grace and confidence, Julian began his descent down the rope, each careful movement met with applause and eventually enthusiastic pats on the back from his admiring peers. His pride was evident, and he basked in the attention and admiration washing over him.

In that moment, Julian Chambers became the undisputed hero of the schoolyard. His thirst for recognition and the admiration of his classmates had been quenched, at least for the time being. Damian couldn't help but admire the resilience and determination displayed by the confident Julian. It was a testament to Julian's unyielding spirit and relentless pursuit of excellence.

Julian had held the record at 13.5 seconds for two years and bested it that morning at 12.6 seconds. Damian looked at Julian quizzically, drawing his attention as Julian bestowed his confidence. He proudly concentrated on the new kid in the yard. . . . . *Damian West*. Julian taunted, "What are you looking at, new kid?" One of the boys standing by said, "Julian, that's the Senator's kid." "I don't care who he is. What are you staring at?" replied Julian.

Damian looked directly into Julian's eyes and said, "You should climb two knots at a time, not one, and using your legs only slows you down unless you don't have the upper arm strength. It's, well, inefficient." The crowd got quiet as Julian recognized the pressure of the confrontation and walked a step closer to Damian and said, "Maybe you think you can do better than me, huh? New kid?"

The small crowd waited silently for Damian's response to the challenge. With a wry smile, Damian replied, "I'm certain, actually." Julian smiled back and shook his head at the sheer arrogance of the kid and gestured Damian to the base of the rope, then stood back several feet to give him space, "Well then, by all means, please go right ahead, but your father won't be here to save you when you fall on your face, rich boy." Damian disregarded the taunt as the muted, nervous laughs fell over the crowd from Julian's remark. This was a telling moment that day on the small Wyoming school grounds.

Damian held the rope with both hands and looked up at the 20 feet of rope above him, wondering what he had gotten himself into. The distance appeared a lot further from this perspective, but his conviction focused as one of the school kids holding the stopwatch spoke, pulling Damian from his trance. "You ready, kid?" Said the boy, and Damian, still looking up, nodded. The boy began his countdown, "3 . . 2 . . 1 . . *GO!*" as Damian leaped high, leveraging his vertical range, grabbing the 6th knot, legs straddling the thick rope as he quickly ascended the rope in the manner in which he had described, using his upper arm strength to climb the rope.

The kids yelled and screamed, both in wanting Damian to succeed but equally anticipating his failure, thus preserving Julian's record. The seconds ticked by as Damian seemed to effortlessly climb the rope as he tapped the final knot signifying his task's completion and effectively stopping the clock. He quickly descended the rope as the boy holding the stopwatch opened his eyes wider in amazement as he scrutinized the figures before him.

Impatience radiated from Julian as he barked at one of the boys in the crowd, his eagerness to know the results palpable. The hushed murmurs of the onlookers ceased once more as another boy seized the stopwatch, his fingers deftly navigating its dials and buttons. Tension hung in the air, everyone waiting with bated breath for the crucial piece of information.

In a moment that felt like an eternity, the boy's eyes widened, and he announced the time with a mix of astonishment and excitement, "10.5 seconds, the new kid has the record!!!" The words hung in the air, electrifying the atmosphere with anticipation.

Julian demanded to see the clock himself, unable to contain his disbelief. With trembling hands, he took hold of the timepiece, his eyes scanning the digits confirming the astonishing time. A disbelieving shake of his head followed as if hoping to dispel the reality of what had just transpired.

The schoolyard erupted into chaos again, but this time, it was a symphony of awe and adoration. The children's voices blended into a chorus of amazement and celebration. The new kid, the one who had not only broken Julian's record but had obliterated it, was now the center of attention, bathed in the spotlight of admiration from his peers. It was but a glimpse of Damian West's entire life and the charisma he possessed.

It was a moment that would go down in schoolyard history, a triumph of determination and skill that had left even the formidable Julian Chambers in awe. The new kid had proven himself as a worthy contender and etched his name into the chronicles of schoolyard legends, a hero of the highest order.

A few moments passed, Julian walked over to Damian amongst the mayhem, hesitated, then smiled as he extended his hand and said, "You won fair and square; you were right. But don't think I won't try to beat your time now that I know your secret. What's your name?" Damian shook Julian's hand and replied, "My name is Damian, Damian West, and you are Julian Chambers, I'm guessing? I've heard of you." "And I, of you too. Your dad is a big Senator, right?" said Julian. "I suppose he's something of a big deal to most."

From that day on, their friendship matured into their adolescence and well beyond, and Julian would become Daman's greatest confidant, except for his father in the years to follow.

Julian Chambers's drive and ambition came easily to him from a young age. An attribute he did not inherit from his own father, Carl Chambers. His mother, Kate, a relatively simple woman, largely raised Julian and his younger brother, Kane, while working at the local grocery store in Jackson Hole.

Julian's father led a contrasting lifestyle, prioritizing his desires over parental responsibilities. He was largely absent in raising his two boys, focusing on his work in construction during the warmer months and indulging in his role as a seasonal ski instructor during the winter season in Jackson Hole. While construction provided steady income in the warmer months, the upcoming ski season offered him opportunities for personal enjoyment, particularly with vacationers seeking thrill and excitement during their winter getaways. He had his pick of the vacationing coeds and hapless cliques of impulsive housewives itching to satisfy their urges that only their 'girl's trip' would satisfy.

Carl Chambers lived for those winter months and distraught when they ended. Julian and Kane didn't see much of their father during the ski season as he would be absent most nights, succumbing to lavish parties and social events in town to which he had been invited. It was the one time of year Carl was able to feel he was something more, occupying a higher station in life, if even for a short duration every season. The socialites didn't know who he was; he played the part brilliantly, and he fabricated a persona well enough to fool all in attendance for those few short months. Carl was a fraud, a fake, but none of those partygoers had any idea. To them, he was a handsome ski instructor with talents on and off the mountain. For them, he became a part of their . . . *vacation experience.*

Vacationers were there for long weekends, sometimes a week or more, then back to their mundane lives elsewhere only to be replaced by a new batch of lonely wives that were all too eager to enjoy an attractive man's attention, and Carl was more than happy to provide them the escape they desired.

Julian's mother knew better than to ask, but the boys often heard their parents fighting and yelling after their father stumbled through the front door after a wild night of drinking and women.

The boys shared a room adjacent to their parent's room, the walls thin as their mother and father would yell and scream just feet away in the small house. It wasn't a healthy environment but their modest life, with all the comforts and stereotypical parallels of a modern dysfunctional American household. Julian often fantasized about something more out there than this; he just wasn't sure what it was at the time, he just knew he was desperate to get out.

His younger brother idolized his father, but Julian wasn't impressed and held a far different opinion of the man. Julian did not doubt that Kane would most likely stay in Jackson Hole and likely fall into his father's pattern and when Kane came of age, he was being groomed to become his father's primary drinking companion and that seemed to suit the two of them perfectly. Kane could not wait to share his father's adventures in the coming years, but Julian wanted no part of that life. He set his sights far higher.

Although most attributes were vastly different, one aspect that Julian and Carl Chambers shared, and Julian could not escape, was a darker and opportunistic outlook on life. They both suffered from control issues and narcissistic behavior, and Julian detested these personality flaws. He was determined to find a way to evade it as it was the one thing that tied him to his father and the attributes that could keep him from achieving his dreams. He would get out of Wyoming; its stifling simplicity and monotonous lifestyle were beneath him; he would find something more.

He had to leave; he could not let the limitations of his parents trap him within this recreational prison that surrounded him. There was only one person he knew could be his way out: his release. Damian West was his savior, and he needed to foster that relationship. He would find some way . . . . *To escape.*

There was no other option for him.

Chapter 5

The Unified Party Emerges

"Four score and seven years ago our fathers brought forth on this continent, a new nation, conceived in Liberty, and dedicated to the proposition that all men are created equal."
~Abraham Lincoln

Jackson Hole, Wyoming
2020 Early Winter - Weeks After Presidential Election
Senator Sam West Private Estate

"I was a little worried there, honestly. By initially launching my campaign as an *Independent* and experiencing the full brunt of the media backlash, I was uncertain. Not to mention, I've been a faithful Republican my entire life. I shocked a lot of people by the move, Dad. I wasn't certain I'd weather it. Then, when Trauner took advantage of the situation and pushed hard on that fact to weaken my resolve, I began to doubt myself. The pressure was starting to get to me," explained Damian, reflecting on the prior six months leading up to the election. Democratic candidate Gary Trauner had been a thorn in his side from day one and took advantage of his independent status because it wasn't a popular affiliation. If you weren't a Republican or Democrat, you often didn't command as much respect within the political circle.

Sam West considered his son's words, then nodded and responded, "Without question, Damian, those moments defined many things for this campaign as this political climate has made for perilous times as we waver on the precipice of self-destruction across the country, it appears. Coming from a strong and historical lineage of Republicans, breaking the line to move to an *Independent* made for a dicey gamble for us, but especially for you." Senator Sam West smiles and continues, "And yet, you sit here a Senator, son. You pulled it off beautifully."

"I know, Dad, we had tremendous momentum, and we had . . . *you,* in our corner, I think that's what got me here. You campaigned for me as much as I did myself. It's a wager we had to make. None of this, *our plan,* would have worked if I had been elected on the Republican ticket. I think your endorsement and your publicly displayed views on the traditional two-party mentality being at risk put you directly into the line of fire and consequently pulled the focus from me just enough," explained Damian.

"Ahhh no," Sam began, his tone reflective as he leaned back in his chair, his gaze fixed on Damian. "The timing was perfect for me to publicly voice my concerns about the direction of politics in this country. It was a calculated move allowing me to express my reservations while diverting some of the attention away from your transition from Republican to Independent. And, if I may say, it played out exactly as we had anticipated."

Sam's words carried a weight of strategic wisdom. He continued, "Had I been seeking higher office or even contemplating re-election, those comments would have potentially dashed those hopes. But now, as I approach retirement, I'm grateful for the freedom to speak my mind without restraint. I relish the newfound liberty I have in that regard."

He paused, his eyes locking with Damian's as he revealed their next audacious endeavor. "But, Damian, those public statements were not just about venting frustrations. They were necessary to pave the way for our next substantial challenge—launching our new Unified Party."

The words hung in the air like a forbidden secret, a revelation meant for their ears alone, away from prying eyes and judgmental ears. The notion of a Unified Party was a radical departure from the established norms of American politics, and its mere mention sent ripples of intrigue and anticipation through the room. It was a concept nurtured behind closed doors, a daring vision having the potential to reshape the political landscape.

Sam's eyes gleamed with purpose as he discussed their clandestine plan. The prospect of uniting disparate ideologies and factions under a single banner was a formidable challenge, requiring both to navigate treacherous waters. It was a gamble, a leap into the unknown, and Sam West and his son, Damian, were determined to make it a reality.

Sam continued, "That will be our biggest wager yet, and truly the one worrying me most. I do have to say you handled the press well and put your biggest competitor, Trauner, right into his place. I loved watching the debate between the two of you. It was poignant and relevant to what we are trying to achieve here. And what a stroke of luck the national networks covered the event, put your face in front of the nation, and displayed your tenacity in front of *all* Americans. It was beautiful to follow, Damian, and you could not have gotten any better national coverage than that debate. It's all falling together beautifully. You decimated Trauner on every point; it's honestly what clinched it for you. The people here in Wyoming beheld your strength and conviction in your desire and verve, and they knew they had the best man representing them in Washington despite changing your political affiliation. They didn't care; they witnessed the man and what he represented, and the rest was just a backdrop. But better yet, the exposure you received nationally where all the American people witnessed this *new star* rising. It made me the proudest, in the moment, watching *my son* effortlessly navigate the interview and debate beautifully. We are right where we want to be, Damian. Just a little more time, paired with your leading Wyoming and implementing programs, receiving national exposure for you all while improving the lives of the residents of this great state. We need more of those opportunities to begin getting the word out. We want people talking about you, your ideas, and the wisdom you bring to the table concerning this country's reform. The American people are hungry for it. The Unified Party will emerge, rising from the ashes the Republicans and Democratic parties have created in their wake."

The pride emanating from Senator Sam West as he spoke about his son was unmistakable. This very sense of pride formed the bedrock of their unified front, the cornerstone upon which the new party had been founded. The concept they championed symbolized the fusion of old and new beliefs, a powerful amalgamation of time-honored values and innovative ideas.

In many ways, their vision mirrored the evolution of society itself—an ongoing process of shedding antiquated philosophies still holding sway within the current, faltering American political framework. The landscape of American politics had become increasingly divided, marred by impasse between the prevailing parties, and plagued by a deep-seated discord seemed insurmountable.

Sam and Damian West's Unified Party theory represented a bold departure from the status quo. It was a rallying cry for change, a call to transcend the rigid boundaries of partisan politics. Their party sought to bridge the gap between conflicting ideologies, recognizing progress would only be achieved through a willingness to adapt, compromise, and embrace fresh perspectives.

As they embarked on this audacious journey, they were acutely aware of the challenges ahead. They understood reshaping the political landscape would require unwavering dedication, resilience in the face of adversity, and an unshakable belief in their mission.

The Senator's gaze bore into his son's, a silent affirmation of their shared commitment to this transformative endeavor. They were united by a common purpose—to breathe new life into American politics, to forge a path where unity and progress would flourish, and to leave a legacy transcending the boundaries of party lines and partisan divisions.

"So, this fall will be the opportune time to let the public know of our intention to move the *Unified Party* into the fold and bring its full focus to light," but Damian also thought privately, "*Fall . . . . is so far away.*"

"I would estimate another year would be best, as we still have some finer points to work out on the full reform. Also, as we have discussed, it will give us time to get you involved within these committees and develop your reputation in the Senate. These past two years you have built a reputation as a young Senator looking for change and demanding of it from your constituents and you are earning their respect. You are asking all to toe the line as you have done yourself and it is making an impact. It will take some favors being called in with the members of the steering committees and a lot of pampering and recruiting, but some key players can help, and others still need impressing in the Senate as a whole. There is an entire faction within the government, Damian, that seeks this change. They need a leader to see it through. I am confident we will gather momentum once we announce it as well. I've laid out most of the groundwork with the steering committees and committee chairs to have you take my place. Three of the five committees I was involved with have agreed to allow you to take my position, as expected, and the votes are secured to ensure the transition, as these individuals are your supporters. Per the law, I was permitted to participate in only two Class A and one Class B committees but was advised on two other Class A committees. Senators Cosner, Arnold, and Porter have all committed, all of which have been your greatest advocates, as you know, over the years as you have been climbing the ranks. The other two, Nagel and Pfeiffer, are still reluctant to accept the notion based on your lack of political experience and independent status, which you would expect. Many of these 'old boys' uphold these assignments must be earned in merit and years of service.

They insist that one 'does your time' and won't be as open to your immediate initiation. They aren't considering you have served as a prosecutor, district attorney, Governor's aid, Governor, and now Senator over the last decade—an impressive resume, to say the least, Damian. Even if Senators Nagel and Pfeiffer don't come around, the other committees will be invaluable for you. And we always have the wildcards in Senators Jacobson and Billings who may come through and a host of other Senators who need to hear our stance. Those are key appointments that will give you a direct pulse into political life and the nuances of tenure. It isn't always pretty, and you must keep your hands clean with these committees. We want to steer clear of another Iran Contra affair and what happened to Oliver North and Richard Secord in 1986. Maintaining a strong sense of separation and cleanliness is essential when maneuvering through these covert subcommittees, Damian. I have had a few close scrapes with Hillary Bastini's group, the Anti-Terrorist Special (ATS) Division."

Damian knew he had a lot to learn but had his father to weather the storm alongside him as he navigated the tumultuous terrain lining his journey. He had always been a quick study and he planned to align himself with the like-minded Senators desiring change and would be open to a new and fresh perspective Senator Damian West would provide. . . .

. . . . *if he could only convince them to see his vision.*

Jackson Hole, Wyoming
2002 (Damian West's Childhood)
Senator Sam West Private Estate

Damian's thirst for knowledge and intellectual stimulation was nurtured by his father's educational moments and tutorials during his formative years. From early adolescence to young adulthood, he relished the opportunity to delve deep into the intricacies of political culture instilled by his father. Their lengthy discussions became a treasured ritual, spanning various topics that captivated their minds and sparked intense debates and tested perspectives. Despite the subject, Damian cherished these intellectually stimulating exchanges with his father, who fostered his curiosity and shaped his understanding of the world from a young age.

With his vast knowledge of American political history, Sam West took every opportunity to impart his wisdom and shape Damian's understanding of their country's power and influence as well as its evolution. Damian vividly remembered first introducing his friend Julian to his father in 2002. Senator Sam West didn't take long to lead them into his study, eager to discuss their interests and political views. Damian sensed that his father had three motives for these conversations. First, he wanted to assess the intelligence and understanding of those around him, evaluating their political acumen. Second, he saw it as an opportunity to educate and showcase his own political insight and range of understanding, cementing his reputation as a formidable political figure and authority. And lastly, it was Damian's father's way of assessing who Damian confidants were. Sam West was a big believer in the notion of asking the relevant question: *Tell me who you walk with, and I will tell you who you are.* Sam West always instilled *in Damian to associate himself with like*-minded and meaningful people.

As the conversation unfolded in the study, Sam West had always taken a genuine interest in Julian Chambers, impressed with the young man for overcoming his own familial limitations and not allowing his socioeconomic status to adversely affect his upbringing or sway his goals and ambitions. Senator West enjoyed probing him about his family background, interests, and aspirations.

Julian, who had meticulously researched Senator Sam West from an early age, was determined to impress him with his depth of knowledge and understanding of the intricate workings of the American governmental systems. Julian's maturity, intelligence, and grasp of the foundational principles upon which the nation was built left a lasting impression on Sam West. Thriving on these enlightening discussions, Sam began to paint a vivid picture of the evolution of the political system as he saw it, delving into the rich history and intricate nuances that shaped the country in the last 250 years. The meeting became an engagement of intellectual minds, where knowledge and ideas were interwoven to form a tapestry of political wisdom for all three to share and deliberate.

Observing the two boys, merely teenagers at the time, hungry to learn, sitting up to catch every word the seasoned historian would spell out for them.

Sam began, "The United States government is a complex system, and the Founding Fathers pulled from many different global legislative philosophies at the time to create what they thought would be best for their young government and their newly formed nation. I won't bore you, gentlemen, with the intricacies of that quintessential constitutional evolution, but in those initial days of our country's inception, it was a turbulent time for America."

"In the beginning, they needed some structure to mold their new government. George Washington, Alexander Hamilton, and John Adams formed the Federalists in 1789, and the National Republican and Whig Parties eventually succeeded them. They sought to ensure a strong government and central banking system. Thomas Jefferson and James Madison instead advocated for a smaller and more decentralized government and formed the Democratic-Republicans. The Democratic and the Republican Parties were rooted in this early faction." Sam could see the intense interest building within the boys as he continued. These were the stories and opinions that didn't ever make it to academic teachings or textbooks.

"It wasn't until Andrew Jackson emerged that the two-party system began to evolve and take shape." He looked at the boys hanging on to every word he uttered and smiled, appreciating their attention. Sam continued, "The seventh president to occupy the U.S. presidency, Andrew Jackson, was instrumental in establishing the Democratic Party in 1828, becoming the oldest of the two largest U.S. political parties. Nearly thirty years later, the Republican Party was officially founded in 1854. Still, the histories of both parties are inherently connected, tracing the two parties' historical backgrounds back to the Founding Fathers. Differing political views among U.S. early adopters eventually sparked the formation of two distinct factions as controversy and conflict often occur between its constituents."

"At the beginning of the 19th century, the Democratic-Republicans were largely victorious and dominant nationally and only gaining momentum. The Federalist Party, in turn, slowly faded after 1801, eventually dissolving in 1812. Because the Democratic-Republicans were so popular, the party had no less than four political candidates pitted against each other in the presidential election of 1824. John Quincy Adams won the presidency despite Andrew Jackson winning the popular vote. This sparked a strong political division within the party, which eventually caused the party to split into The Democrats and the Whig Party. As assumed, the Democrats were led by Andrew Jackson, which went unchallenged. He was bitterly opposed to the existence of The Bank of the United States, and he largely supported state's rights and minimal government regulation. The Whig Party stood in distinct opposition to Jackson and the Democrats and supported the national bank."

Sam sat back in his chair and watched the boy's reaction, noticing their eagerness for him to continue, "As the country emerged into the mid-nineteenth century, slavery was a widely discussed political issue. The Democratic Party's internal views on this matter differed greatly from one another; Southern Democrats wished for slavery to be expanded and reach into Western parts of the country, but Northern Democrats, on the other hand, argued that this issue should be settled on a local level and through a popular referendum. Such Democratic infighting eventually led Abraham Lincoln, who belonged to the Republican Party, to deal with the disparity, winning the presidential election of 1860. This new Republican Party had recently been formed by a group of Whigs, which were essentially composed of influential Democrats and other politicians who had broken free from their respective parties to form a party based on an anti-slavery platform. At that critical time in history in the United States, tensions were high between Northern and Southern states, causing the Civil War to break out in 1861, in the immediate aftermath of Lincoln's inauguration. During the Civil War, seven Southern States formed the Confederate States of America and fought for detachment from the United States. However, the Union won the war, and the Confederacy was formally dissolved. The issue of slavery was at the center of political disagreement during the Civil War. This caused Republicans to argue for the abolition of slavery, and Lincoln signed the Emancipation Proclamation in 1863."

"At this point in history, the U.S. South was predominantly Democratic and held conservative, agrarian-oriented, anti-big-business values, which were largely popular with the Democratic Party at the time. The majority of Northern voters, on the other hand, were Republican, many of which fought for civil and voting rights for African American people. After the Civil War ended, the Republican Party became more oriented towards economic growth, industry, and big business in Northern states. At the beginning of the 20th century, it had reached a general status as a party, supporting more wealth within the various social classes. Many Republicans, therefore, gained financial success in the prosperous 1920s until the stock market crashed in 1929, initiating the era of the Great Depression. Many Americans blamed Republican President Herbert Hoover for the financial damages brought by the crisis. In 1932, the country elected Democrat Franklin D. Roosevelt president."

Looking at Damian and Julian, Sam asked, "Shall I continue?" Julian was first to respond, "Absolutely, Sir, please do." Damian laughed and said, "My father is a lot more interesting than our history teachers, isn't he, Julian?" "Without question," replied Julian enthusiastically, looking at Sam and Damian. Sam just smiled and continued with his dialogue, "In an attempt to get the country back on track, Roosevelt introduced his *New Deal* to the American people. The New Deal launched several progressive government-funded social programs, ensuring social security, improved infrastructure, and minimum wage requirements for business employees. As a result, many Southern Democrats, whose political views were more traditional and conservative, didn't support Roosevelt's liberal initiatives and joined the Republican Party instead, many of whom did out of spite. Roosevelt's progressive, liberal policies played an important role in framing the party's political agenda to evolve it into the now-modern Democratic Party. After Roosevelt died in 1945, if I recall, the Democrats remained in power with Harry S. Truman becoming president, guiding the Democratic Party into more of a progressive direction with a pro-civil rights platform and desegregation of military forces, thereby gaining support from a large number of African American voters, who had previously supported the Republican Party because of its anti-slavery platform."

"The Democratic Party largely stayed in power until 1980, when Republican Ronald Reagan was sworn into office. Reagan's socially conservative politics and emphasis on cutting taxes, preserving family values, and increasing military funding were important steps in defining the modern Republican Party platform. Following Reagan's two terms in office, his Vice President, George H. W. Bush, was elected as his successor in the White House, as you know, and I have an idea he will win handily his second term in a couple of years as no strong candidates are opposing him, save Democrat, John Kerry. Since then, Republicans and Democrats have been evenly rotated through the White House. The 2008 election should prove interesting, as Bush cannot run for a third term, and the strongest candidate is most likely Arizona Republican congressman John McCain. Democrat Barack Obama is a real up-and-comer, and it may make for an interesting pairing potentially if he was nominated by his Democratic constituents in 2008. Well, that is my prediction, anyway." Senator Sam wouldn't know it then, but his predictions would ultimately come true in the years that followed.

"That is six years away, Senator. Impressive, you have already thought that far ahead," stated Julian. "Oh, Julian, my father has thought far beyond that already." As Damian glanced at his father. Sam West smiled as he stood up to coax the fire. The embers were beginning to die out, and he always made it his mission to keep them burning. Sam hesitantly opposed his son's comment, then replied, "One can always speculate, but the political map is not difficult to follow, gentlemen. It's important to study the trends, and even more so, the players within the game as they will tend to give you the most valuable insight as to where agendas, whether apparent or hidden, actually lay." Julian and Damian enjoyed the discussion and were eager to learn from any opportunity Sam West would provide them.

"Tell Julian your other theory Dad, the one about the need for a new unified third party to emerge and how the Democratic and Republican Parties have devolved in their beliefs and ideals, becoming obsolete in their thinking." Upon hearing this, Sam shot a stern glance toward his son. That theory was private, and Damian should know better than to discuss it in mixed company despite Julian being a permanent fixture in their home over the past five years.

He looked at his son for a moment, forgetting the boy was only fourteen, and didn't think of the magnitude and weight of his words. Sam quickly recovered, "Oh Damian, that thought is just me rambling and throwing out the 'what ifs' of our constantly evolving political circus. There is really no substance to it."

Damian looked confused and slightly shaken, but then, at that moment, he realized his question came without thinking through the ramifications of the question posed. He was aware his father was not a trusting man, and it was then he realized Julian Chambers had not yet earned the right to hear their deepest and darkest opinions or perspectives.

Damian's mind raced with regret as he realized the gravity of his mistake. He understood the delicate nature of his father's perceptions and ideas, knowing that if they were misinterpreted or taken out of context, it could have devastating consequences for his father's reputation. The West family had learned to trust no one, as the political landscape was filled with pitfalls and potential adversaries. Damian chastised himself for his recklessness, realizing that he needed to appreciate the importance of preserving his father's trust and confidentiality.

His father's circle was very tight, and Damian thought himself very fortunate that he was included within that circle, but his best friend had not yet earned that right. As his father explained away their conversations as mere conjecture and rhetoric, Damian could see the disappointment in his father's eyes. The trust that had been broken would take time and action to rebuild, and Damian vowed to himself to honor his father's expectations and protect the sanctity of their private exchanges.

But Damian was proud they were considerable and potent in theory, but he needed to maintain faith in his father, who knew how it would all transpire. Julian picked up on the exchange and disconnect between father and son and was eager to learn more and instill confidence in Sam and Damian to confide in him further in the coming years. Knowing the West family was the bloodline he should have been born into, Julian wanted nothing more than to cultivate that integral connection and become a part of whatever they were involved in the future.

They were his opportunity . . . *his fate was tied to them.*

———

Chapter 6

A Theory Revealed

"Yesterday is not ours to recover, but tomorrow is ours to win or lose."
~Lyndon B. Johnson

Jackson Hole, Wyoming
2021 Late Spring/Summer
Senator Sam West Private Estate

Damian and Sam West worked closely with the current Governor of Wyoming, Megan O'Malley, who had been a Wyoming State representative for two terms before replacing Damian West when he was elected Senator. She was a well-respected politician of American Indian/Irish lineage, coming from humble roots. Some considered herself a hardline conservative but had followed and respected Senator, Sam West since she entered politics. She considered him her most worthy and trusted mentor and always highly respected Damian as well.

They invited her to visit Senator Sam West's home in Jackson Hole to discuss the matters at hand and a deep discussion of the future of Wyoming and their national agenda. They felt they could trust her but also wanted to test the waters and thought it best with someone with a strong belief system.

When Sam and Damian sat down with her to discuss his exit from the Governorship, they wanted to ensure she embraced their work in improving the quality of life for Wyoming residents.

Out of respect for both men, she openly discussed and understood the changes within the state and was impressed the platform had been working well during Damian West's short tenure as Governor. It took a few months, but after some time, she stood firm as a believer of the new system, and after hours of discussion, she became the first significant disciple of their new order. She saw the value in their goals and pledged her support privately and publicly when the time came.

Both father and saw the discussion as a favorable accomplishment. They felt Governor O'Malley represented the change she desired to see in the government and was flattered they approached her first. She was their sounding board on how they would plan to approach many other key and influential members of Congress.

With the honed model, they would begin to manage key opinion leaders, influential Congressmen, business moguls, and the like, one at a time, enrolling them into the ideals encompassing the Unified Theory for American reform in the following months.

The Speaker of the House, Regina Alvarado, and some key Senators were among their next stops, and their involvement would be critical to their cause.

In mid-summer, Damian was in Washington D.C. for an arranged interview with *PBS News*, scheduled to last for fifteen minutes. It was meant to be a minimally exposed interview, but a far different result occurred.

Robert Figora and Shay Simpson were hosting the segment and were eager to have Senator Damian West attend the program.

The show was progressive and poignant, and the people selected were purposely not given the interviewer's list of questions so that the responses would come in their truest form. They wanted the replies to come from the heart, unrehearsed, forthright, and honest.

The primary objective was pertinent yet relevant in its design. Its principal intention was to focus on the recent statewide improvements through structured reorganization and give Senator Damian West a platform and exposure on the national level. Damian West's exploits in Wyoming were a hot topic but hadn't received a lot of national coverage until the PBS interview. Being an Independent, Senator West was in a difficult position with no party backing. Independent or third parties often got pushed behind the mainstream Republican and Democratic focus, but young Senator West planned to change that historical fact that evening.

Sam West made every stride to ensure his son was getting the exposure essential for the next major step of their strategy. They were still months away from the formal reveal of their new party and outlay the specifics and mechanics behind the concept of the Unified Party, but subtle hints were orchestrated and unveiled to roll out the concept of an emerging Unified Theory and the party philosophy slowly and deliberately.

The main topic concentrated on his state's restructuring of statewide spending and how the state of Wyoming and its people benefited without compromising funding for necessary programs such as transportation, education, unemployment, and welfare. Senator West initiated the change while serving as the Governor of Wyoming but had lobbied hard to implement numerous changes through state legislation. The public and Congressmen alike were following the young Senator, not only talking about change but actually getting it done in his home state. The venue for this interview was an informal setting with three soft chairs for the two interviewers to one side, and Damian West sat on the other over a platform.

"Senator West, the programs you have implemented were originally met with some opposition. But now, your constituents have widely applauded you as you have lowered Wyoming's state taxes by 7%, cut unemployment by 4.5%, and decreased state spending by nearly 18% in less than two years, beginning with your Governorship. How do you explain the widespread success of the state-wide reform?" Asked Robert Figora with PBS News.

"The concept is basic, really, Robert. I'm simply bringing the economics of Wyoming back to the basics. My home state, and the entire country, for that matter, are riddled with antiquated inefficiencies and corruption, and some politicians are more concerned with their own agendas and getting themselves re-elected than with what their offices truly represent and what this country was founded on. I'm confronting all governmental officials and their respective offices to *toe the line* in Wyoming, and I hope all this great nation's leaders do the same in their respective states. Governor Figora and I have had lengthy discussions and strategies on these changes and reform, and she is also on board with the vacillation in policy. I have her largely to thank for moving this legislation through the process here in our great state of Wyoming and carrying the torch since I moved to Washington. Although I also have my own agenda, admittingly, Robert. I aspire to make residing in the state of Wyoming and this entire country beneficial in every way to all Americans, and I won't stop until we meet and overcome the challenge. As an *Independent*, I feel like I can move more freely, *unified if you will*, with both the Republicans and Democrats, and I think both parties can see the clear path I have set forth is for the good of all and with no personal gain. My programs create jobs and decrease ineffective state spending habits we have adopted, which can also lower our taxes. *It's an everybody-wins mentality*. I do not see the downside."

As Senator West expanded on his methodology and ultimately finished his response, he noticed the reaction of Robert Figora and Shay Simpson, purposely hesitating for any rebuttal, but Robert and Shay simply nodded in agreement and seized the opportunity to ask her question. Damian had heard she was the more aggressive of the two and would immediately come at him. Capturing Damian's attention, Shay Simpson began as predicted, "Thanks for coming on the show, Senator . . . . . Senator West, what of this Unified Theory, can you shed some light on what it is and what it means?"

Damian wasn't prepared to let the public entertain his weighted and detailed view on the subject of the *'Unified Theory'* as he and his father both made vitally certain of that fact. However, with everything seemingly in politics, keeping a tight lid on anything significant in Washington wasn't easy. Damian and his father had approached enough of the heavy hitters in Washington, D.C., and nationwide for it not to eventually find its way to the media. Damian also knew he could simply dodge the question; However, it would be far more damaging and precarious if he skirted around the topic on everyone's mind. He pondered the question momentarily, softening his demeanor and approach as if he were about to reveal something of significant importance to the people in attendance. His skills as an orator were tested that evening, but it was also an opportunity he decided to run with, and hoped his decision was the correct one. There were roughly twenty-five people standing behind the cameras as his audience, not the usual size for Damian West, but it would have to do. He had a lot riding on this answer.

Damian West softly grinned at the group, capitalizing on its effect and hesitation; the camera zoomed in and captured the handsome face of Damian West from several angles, all complimenting the presence of the man who stood before them. Damian West's smile was always a crowd favorite and, capturing the moment, he kindly replied, "I think it best not to get into that right now, Shay, as the focus of tonight's discussion is concentrating on what has transpired in my home state of Wyoming, all for the better, I might add, and I don't want to steal its thunder. I respect the time and effort of the many people who have worked tirelessly to that end; however, I also know that answer alone will not satisfy the appetite of everyone watching this program, so I'll leave you all with this . . ."

He slowly stood up, unorthodox in a television program, but the producers simply watched and behind the scenes exclaimed, "Stay on him and roll with it. . ." The interviewers briefly looked at one another, unsure how to react, but remained silently sitting in their chairs watching the Senator.

As Senator Damian West looked out over the people in attendance and the viewers watching the program, he continued, "Three generations of West Senators have now proudly served this country and me being the last in the long line of humble servants of my great state and country. That said, I will tell you we desperately need change, not change that we simply talk about or that is theorized and then forgotten, like so many before me have promised. No, we need change to bring together this celebrated nation under a common purpose and ambition with that intent alone, like our founding fathers strived and even died for only two centuries ago. Our country has changed tremendously since that time. So, too, have our politics and mission to help the people of these United States. We must evolve as a people and a nation. This is essential to our future as we are deteriorating as a country. Slowly, but certainly, and without question . . . *decaying.*" Damian looked up as if to gather his thoughts.

"Americans need their government to help them thrive and flourish for those less fortunate, but also for those strengthening and fortifying our infrastructure through commerce, innovations, and taxation. It all must be balanced. We are currently out of balance, which is toxic for our nation. Racial conflicts, financial disparity, and corrupt institutions leading to governmental frustrations must give way to the greater good and the goal for us *all* to stand together as Americans, unified and strong. *Unified* . . . is the key term here. We must cast aside these ingrained differences and remember we are a young country, but we need to gain a new level of maturity, as a whole, committed, and above all . . . . . *Unified.* This undertaking will be our legacy, our salvation, and we must make it so and follow and foster the dream we as a country can all be proud of once again. My father instilled this ideal in me, and we have worked diligently to begin the process, as witnessed in Wyoming. As all can see over the last twenty-four months, it has progressed and has its ability to sustain . . . . *through change.* Simple and basic, hence my mantra . . . *Back to the basics.*" He took a moment to flash his magnetic smile.

"My vision is honed on this endeavor, and I will remain committed and dedicated to its end, but I know the Republican Party isn't the answer any longer, nor are the Democrats and even the Independents have been far too non-committal towards one ideal. I humbly call on every American to open their eyes and truly see what we have become as we cannibalize ourselves through social media, hate, inequality, and malaise. We will require far more than this historic linear reasoning model; we need to advance ourselves and our maturity as a nation for what the future holds for us. The days of disparity, we need to leave behind, our new outlook needs to be of one voice and one goal, cohesive, and this can only be achieved through our faith in one another, and above all . . . *Our Unity.* I ask all of you to consider. . . .Would you rather we have unity within our great nation or calamity? Ask yourself which one would give you peace. Unity will create the gift of advancement and evolution. Our core government platform was built on sticks and mud, and it must evolve in the technical age we find ourselves within. Our worst enemy is simply . . . . *ourselves.*"

He looked out over the crowd, and in his final words, he said, "So, I implore you all to consider this. Truly ask yourself this simple question. Is your political model the Republican Party, which largely stands for limited government, fiscal conservatism, strong national defense, individual liberty, conservative values, states' rights, free trade, and a belief in personal responsibility? Or the Democratic Party generally standing for social justice, civil rights, economic equality, expanded government role, environmental stewardship, healthcare access, multilateralism in international relations, and protecting voting rights and democracy?"

For effect, he hesitated and then softly continued, "Or would you consider a party that encompassed all of those ideals? What would you call such a political party. . . I have an idea, maybe . . . *The Unified Party.* I like the sound of it, simply even uttering those three words. The question I pose to all of you is, would the American people allow enough change and maturity, along with forgiveness of this young country, to allow such a party to exist? Not a party to

serve one sect or group of Americans but rather a party to serve . . . .
all Americans. I ask you again. Is America ready for just such a party
. . . . *A Unified Party* that will bring us to the twenty-first century? I
have every confidence in the American people that we are ready to
evolve, flourish, and fill the shoes that every other country looks at
us to become. Thank you for hearing me dream."

Damian looked out over the group. Silence prevailed from
his words as they hung in the air, striking the hearts of every human
being within that room, within that moment. They drank it in,
mesmerized by this young man's words, clarity, and confidence in
seeing this plight through. He was already proving it in his own state
and was praised for his efforts. If he could do it in one state, why
couldn't it be done with the nation as a whole? A *Unified Approach*
to an evolving country. Damian captured the moment of silence
and demanded it, but then he realized the weight of his words. He
wished only to abscond the setting he had just created. He feared
he had said too much.

Seizing the opportunity to end the session on his heartfelt
note, he leaned forward, the cameras zooming in again to capture his
sincere expression, "Good night, all, and thank you for listening this
evening." With a wave and smile, he quickly descended the stairs to
the hallway adjacent as Secret Service Agent Benjamin Lee gestured
him to follow the escorting agent. The room fell silent; he heard his
own footsteps on the concrete as he made his exit behind the stage.

Robert Figora and Shay Simpson stood up, perplexed by what
they just witnessed, and simply began applauding. After a moment,
the rest of the staff and employees joined in as the room filled with
noise, and the deafening sound of clapping could be heard within
the entire building. The customary barrage of questions that usually
ensued from the hosts gave way to the respect given to someone
worthy of admiration.

It was a moment remembered comuch like John F. Kennedy's
speech in January of 1961 asking the people, "*And so, my fellow
Americans: ask not what your country can do for you – ask what
you can do for your country*."

Down the hall, Senator Damian West slowly stopped and turned to listen along with the Secret Service Agent Lee assigned to him. Although out of the line of sight of the myriad of people he had just left, he was used to the unfailing diminishing energy he felt as he made his departure. However, this time, he heard something completely different and unexpected. "Do you hear that?" asked Damian to no one in particular, but Agent Benjamin Lee had also stopped with him and listened. "Sir. . . . . sir, are they . . . Applauding and cheering? Yes, they are clapping for you, Sir." And they were supporting him and his claims; the young Senator and his entrancing and charismatic words affected those in attendance in a way he could not have foreseen.

Agent Lee gently nudged Senator West's elbow in an effort to move him along as he had a 6 PM flight back to Jackson Hole that evening. They exited the back door, still hearing the rhythmic cadence of people applauding in the background. He was quickly filed into an SUV, waiting for the Senator and his team.

Damian's staff took the back seat, Damian grabbed the middle for himself, and Agent Lee took the front seat across from the driver. They drove the 21 miles to the airport for their flight scheduled to depart in 54 minutes. After the SUV pulled out onto the main freeway, leaning over his left shoulder, Agent Lee asked, "Sir, in my 22 years of service, four presidents and 17 Senators, I have never witnessed, even once, *any* Senator receive applause following a televised interview. *Never.* Did you mean what you said in there, Sir?" Damian West looked at the veteran agent and, with the utmost sincerity, replied, "I do, Ben, but the only way I can truly prove it is not by any empty words but rather, measured by my actions. I would expect nothing less." Agent Lee looked at him and nodded, accepting that commitment as Damian turned his head and looked out the window at the beautiful landscape he had come to know in Washington. The monuments formed a backdrop in the distance of Washington, D.C., and always made him feel proud being within the mecca of American politics. Those monuments were symbolic to him, representing the sacrifices made by the Americans before him.

He wasn't expecting to divulge anything about his plan that evening, but he was sure that the short interview would create a stir within the political arena that he would have to address on some level. He had no idea the magnitude of that small program on PBS News would end up having as his world would now never be the same. He had awoken a sleeping giant, and that giant was hungry.

Sam West's jet sat upon the tarmac quietly as he awaited his son's arrival. They had planned to leave for Jackson Hole together. Sam hadn't been this incited in some time, but the events that transpired just an hour prior would change the scope of their vision and tighten up their timeline. He was fixated upon the television as the various channels covering the live program on PBS surrounding the young Senator from Wyoming unintentionally stirred up the political scene enough that the national networks were volleying for the coverage of the remarkable and historic speech.

The interview had been reserved simply to explain some of the recent successes the state of Wyoming was experiencing but shifted abruptly when the interviewer's questions clearly steered Senator West into a political maelstrom that he expertly navigated, seemingly unscathed and even extending his nationwide character and popularity, significantly within hours of the broadcast.

As the cameras rolled, capturing every word and nuance, CNN had successfully secured the pivotal segment of Damian's dialogue and broadcast it to the world. Sam West, a seasoned strategist and connoisseur of opportunities, leaned back in his chair with a confident smile, a glass of bourbon in hand. He couldn't help but feel a surge of pride as he watched his son effortlessly command the stage. Damian's innate talent was nothing short of extraordinary, surpassing even Sam's highest expectations.

In an ideal scenario, Sam would have preferred to bide time, waiting several additional months, perhaps even longer, to unveil their carefully crafted plan. However, he understood that, on occasion, the stars align in the most unexpected ways. This unscripted and authentic moment, masterfully orchestrated by Damian, was a gift they couldn't have hoped for, nor was its impeccable timing. It was a golden opportunity to set their intricate blueprint into motion, which had been meticulously designed to reshape the future.

What struck Sam most about his son's performance was Damian's ability to reveal just enough without giving away too much of their plan. It was a delicate dance, an art form that Damian had mastered perfectly. This tantalizing glimpse of their intentions would undoubtedly leave the world hungry for more, creating an insatiable appetite for what was to follow.

However, the interview accelerated their timeline, forcing them to expedite their strategy. The premature release of their agenda had ignited a sense of urgency. The list of influential individuals they aimed to recruit was still extensive, and every moment counted. Sam felt they had to move swiftly and decisively to secure the backing and support they needed for their rousing vision of the future. The machine had been set in motion, at least in some form, and they would need to stay ahead of it.

Following the brief speech, the press praised Senator West's address, which was a rarity, not with current thinking but with the politicians of late. Sam studied the news clip as it went to a reporter on location. Aaron Acosta, the political correspondent for CNN, initiated the news spot, giving the back story before switching to the reporter on sight, "Sherry Holden was covering a routine interview with up-and-coming Wyoming Senator Damian West in Washington, D.C. earlier this evening. Senator West's speech riled up the house there in Washington. Sherry Holden reporting. . . . Sherry?" Sherry took the lead and continued with the story, "Well, Aaron, something you don't see every day. A politician receiving applause from every cameraman, producer, and staff, regardless of party affiliation attending today's televised interview of Senator Damian West. *Dare I say Unified Party?"* The segment shot to a video which was from the segment included the questions posed by Robert and Shay and Senator West's calling out that *change* needs to occur within our nation. Sherry Holden continued after the clip, "Senator West spoke of politicians *'Toeing the line'* and reform as well as some vague insight to this mysterious Unified Party that is the buzz of the political fabric as of late but not in a way or method like we have heard in the past from aspiring politicians. Senator West spoke from his heart, with poise and passion, as you could see in the clip. He believes this, Aaron, and he has proven the model can work in his home state of Wyoming."

The segment cuts to Shay Simpson with PBS News, who did the interview for a brief clip of her thoughts on the interview. Sherry asks, "Shay Simpson with PBS News and one of the two interviewers who instigated the historic event with her question directly aimed at Senator West. Ms. Simpson, what are your thoughts on what transpired here today?" Without missing a stride, Shay Simpson seizes the opportunity to express her critique: "I'm trained to ask the difficult questions, Sherry, as you well know, and when asked about the 'Unified Theory' that has been floating around, well, the Senator seized his opportunity. Although not overly exhaustive in his explanation, he responded in such a way that it will bring on far more questions pertaining to this mysterious Party and what it represents. Is a new Party set to be unveiled? Admittingly, Senator West is the real deal, Sherry. He has a strong vision and a goal to get there, and his words today shook everyone in that room. Look at his pedigree. They believe in him; you can see it in their eyes. I think my question served him right up, and he will have the platform now to delve further into this idea of his in the future, and now that it's out there, the questions will be far fiercer than when I asked earlier." Sherry follows up, "How so, Shay? I mean, what made this interview any different than other discussions or the message spoken by any other politician?"

Shay added, "He really appears to be genuine and sincere, Sherry, and to get a group full of random, mixed political affiliations to applaud his monologue . . . . was miraculous and surprising. It sent quite a message. It makes us all want to know more, what this potentially new party will represent, and what effect it will have on the Republican and Democratic foundation. Kudos to you, Senator West, and good luck; you have your work cut out for you. In other news, more riots break out in central L.A. . . ." Aaron Acosta followed her segue, taking over for Sherry, knowing he needed to move on to other news, keeping on schedule.

Watching the news piece intently reduced the volume when Aaron turned his focus to other news in Los Angeles. Sam beamed inwardly; this type of coverage was priceless, and at that moment, the striking brunette flight attendant emerged into the cabin and announced, "Sir, Senator West will be arriving in a moment. He just cleared security." "Thank you, Sasha," affectionately responded Sam, appreciating Sasha, who had served his family for almost 18 years. "Also, Sir, the journalist, Barbara Walters, is on the phone and would like to have a word with you," as she handed him the phone and then took leave.

Sam West leaned back in his chair, put his ear to the phone, "Barbara. . . It is so wonderful to hear from you. Well, thank you, he did a marvelous job. . . . How's retirement?. . . . .you know I can't discuss those things, just yet Barbara . . . No. . . Oh my no. . . . .Well, that's an interesting idea. Let me think on that . . .Can I get back to you after I speak with Damian?. . . . Tremendous, talk soon." And the line went dead as Sam pondered the significance of Damian's speech and how it caught the eye of one of his era's most respected news interviewers.

Barbara Walters wanted to interview Damian West.

After a moment, Sam could overhear the brakes engaging from the SUV arriving outside containing Damian and his team. He couldn't remember when he was so excited to see his son and discuss the interview.

The vehicle doors opened and closed, replaced by the bustling of people ascending the jetway stairs. Sam stood up as two of Damian's staff were first to enter the cabin, followed by Damian. Sam acknowledged the staff as they nodded and continued to the back of the plane, and when Sam saw his son, all he could do was smile and embrace him like he hadn't seen him in ages.

"A big day for you, Damian," said Sam, and Damian smiled back at his father and replied, "It sure was Dad. For all of us, I did not foresee this chain of events unfold like this today; I thought it would just be another normal conventional interview, but was I far off." Sam had fixed Damian a drink and gestured him to the oversized chair opposite his own. The team was aware of letting the father and son talk this out privately and immediately closed the rear cabin door, giving them complete privacy. "Wheels up in 5 minutes," said Captain Angler over the intercom as Sam gave his son a minute to settle into his seat and pull from the provided drink. Damian gestured his crystal glass to his father out of respect and acknowledgment of a good day for the West family.

"The interview went a completely different way than I had anticipated," explained Damian. "The news coverage has been very flattering to you, Damian. The moment was perfect, son, and your words will make the history books. I haven't witnessed that since John F. Kennedy's speech sixty years ago," replied Sam. "You have seen the piece already?" asked Damian, "It's all over the news, Damian, nationally too; you positioned yourself as a major player today with the reply to Shay Simpson's question. You have captured the interest of the American people, and you are the one they are watching now."

Talking aloud, Damian continued, "I felt the timing was perfect with the question coming from Simpson, and I thought this is the opportunity for us to, at the very least, give them a glimpse of our 'Unified Theory' as they have so aptly coined. Someone had to leak it to the press, though, Dad. Do you have any idea who?"

Sam twisted his smile before answering, "Actually, *I leaked it* through a third-party source. I just didn't think it would air so quickly. I thought the reporters would vet the information further before publicly announcing it. So much for due diligence. And in that, I wanted you to be natural in your responses, so I didn't mention I had leaked it to Tom Brokaw as I was certain he would know who to contact. Barbara Walters also reached out and remarked how brilliantly you performed, as well," replied Sam. "Those two have been tremendous advocates of mine for decades and have been following your career. They are both good to have on our side, though getting up there in years," offered Sam.

They both clinked their glasses and laughed at the significance of the small piece of critical information released that would begin a chain of events changing history forever in the months and years to come.

Damian's phone began to ring, and he pulled it from his breast pocket, looked at the name on the screen in front, and smiled, pressing the 'accept' button. "Representative Chambers, happy you called." Glad to catch up with his oldest and dearest friend.

Julian couldn't hold back his enthusiasm, "That speech was something to behold. It honestly brought a tear to my eye listening to your words, Damian." Damian glanced at his father, and he nodded, knowing what his father wanted, "That means a lot, Julian, thank you. Speaking of, I'm here with my dad, and we discussed you. We would like to sit down with you and discuss . . . our future."

There was a hesitation on the line before Julian responded, "I'd like that; let's meet next week." Damian responded, "Sounds good. We will set it up. Let's have dinner. Have a good night and thanks for the call, Julian." Damian hung up and looked at the phone, excited at the thought of bringing Julian into the circle, one ring closer, for the next phase of their plan.

When Julian hung up the phone, a wave of numbness washed over him, leaving him momentarily stunned. They had finally extended an invitation, albeit indirectly, welcoming him into their inner circle. He had yearned for this moment for fifteen long years, and now it had finally arrived. The significance of being asked, particularly after the remarkable speech delivered by his lifelong friend that night, was not lost on him. He could sense that they had something substantial in store for him, something that could reshape his destiny. In the same vein, he would have hoped he earned it by now. Julian had devoted a tremendous amount to the West family and was due a return on his own investment. Senator Sam West owed him.

Yet, beneath the excitement, a subtle undercurrent of jealousy coursed through Julian's thoughts. He didn't want anyone to misconstrue his achievements as mere byproducts of his association with Sam and Damian West, but deep down, he acknowledged their undeniable influence on his journey. He grappled with the idea that he might be perceived as someone riding on their coattails, leaving him with a sense of inner conflict. He had done the bidding of Sam West; the risks he had taken were substantial. Julian Chambers had done more than his part for the West's. The West family owed him success and was happy they involved him after all he had done for Damian. He may have owed Sam West for his political advancement, but unknown to Damian, he owed Julian for much of his own political ascension.

Despite this internal struggle, Julian recognized that he had played an active role in his own accomplishments. He had worked diligently, honing his skills and forging his own path, and he was determined that people would eventually come to recognize this fact. Perhaps not immediately, but someday, he vowed, they would all see the extent of his personal achievements and the greatness he could attain.

He was aware he needed patience, for greatness did not materialize overnight. Julian was resolute in his commitment to proving himself as someone who could achieve something remarkable and substantial. He believed in the potential within him, and he was determined to rise above any shadows of doubt or lingering feelings of dependency. In time, Julian was certain he would emerge as a force to be reckoned with, a testament to his own capabilities, and a living example of true greatness.

Agent Lee emerged from the rear cabin and looked directly at Sam West, "Mr. West, a senior Agent from the Anti-Terrorist Division, is on the line for you and says it's urgent," extending the phone to the older man. "Sam West here . . . Ah yes, it's good to hear your voice. Thank you for getting back to me; now that my son has a seat on the Class A covert operation committee, I think it would benefit both of you to meet on less of a social stance this time and with more of a professional capacity. I'll be in an advisory role on those committees for the next three years, and then Senator Cosner will take the helm completely. Yes, I appreciate you remembering. Agreed, long overdue."

There was a hesitation on the other end of the line for a few moments, and then Sam continued, "Tremendous. I'll coordinate it for next week in Jackson Hole if that works for you. Great. Thanks for calling. Of course, I'll pass it along." Sam hung up the phone and looked at Damian, unsure how to explain the conversation. Damian looked at his father sardonically as he didn't think his father had any secrets from him.

"Who was that, you have me curious?" Damian looked at his father, questioning all the cloak-and-dagger ambiguity lingering between the two of them until Sam softly answered, "That was a dear friend and ally, Damian. You have met before, but only on a surface level. He is probably the greatest weapon and patriot this nation has ever known. I thought it was time for the two of you to meet in more of a professional capacity. He is an asset with no equal and someone you want in your corner. And after your interview, he is reaching out to us, which should be significantly flattering to you."

Damian raised his hand, "The man needs no introduction, Dad. His reputation precedes him. I assume you are speaking of . . . . . . *Sebastian Storm.* I've been looking forward to this moment.*"

Sam West looked at his son, "Mr. Storm said he saw your speech and was impressed. And I would imagine few people have that distinction, Damian. However, he followed with, *'Your son is going to need me.'* If Sebastian Storm deems it *important* for you to meet him, then it is damn well important."

———

Chapter 7

The Unified Theory

Jackson Hole, Wyoming
2021 Early Fall
Senator Sam West Private Estate

Retired Senator Samuel T. West, Senator Damian T. West, and Representative Julian Chambers were all sitting in front of the fire, talking politics as usual, when Susan Lee, Sam West's housekeeper of twenty-five years, announced Sebastian Storm had arrived. They all stood to greet the most infamous guest to attend the small gathering.

Sebastian Storm entered the study, and his stature commanded a level of respect in and of itself. He was easily the tallest in the room: dark, esoteric, standing just short of 6'3", and athletic, toned, after years of duteous attention to his body, mind, and honed abilities. All those attributes were respected, sharpened, and acutely developed through his dedication. His demeanor was commanding even within this auspicious group of men.

Commanding attention effortlessly, Sebastian Storm was the kind of individual who possessed a magnetic pull on those around him. His mere presence was a force to be reckoned with, a tantalizing blend of rugged charm and undeniable authority leaving a lasting imprint on everyone he encountered.

A short, well-maintained stubbled beard framed his chiseled jawline, enhancing his rugged appeal. A hint of silver gracefully threaded through his hair and facial hair, adding an air of distinguished maturity to his subtle handsomeness. His sun-kissed, tanned skin spoke of adventures under the open sky, hinting at a life filled with daring escapades.

Sebastian's striking features were a work of art. His eyes, a mesmerizing shade of hazel, held a depth hinting at a wealth of life experiences. When he looked at you, it felt as if he could peer into your soul, an uncanny ability making every interaction intensely personal.

Though he made every effort to maintain a stoic exterior, an electric energy surged from within him, impossible to conceal. It was as if the universe itself conspired to amplify his presence. When he entered a room, people couldn't help but turn their heads, drawn to the enigmatic aura surrounding him.

In conversation, Sebastian Storm possessed a magnetic charm impossible to resist. His voice, a deep and velvety baritone, possessed the power to captivate anyone within earshot. His words flowed like a carefully orchestrated symphony, each syllable laden with an irresistible charisma.

Sebastian Storm left an indelible mark no matter where he went or what he did. He was more than just a man; he was a force of nature, a living embodiment of vigor, and an allure one could only dream of encountering. In his presence, those around him felt more alive and vibrant. He and Damian West shared in those qualities, however in very different ways.

That evening, he wore black slacks and a form-fitting matching turtleneck under his Overland long Toscana gray thigh-length Sheepskin coat.

Sam West took the lead, "Thank you, Susan, and good night. Congressmen, I present to you Sebastian Storm," as they all shook hands. Susan took his coat, excused herself, closed the French doors behind her, and turned in for the evening.

Sebastian Storm was a master of restraint and calculation, a man who meticulously evaluated the individuals around him, regardless of his prior familiarity with them. It was a deep-seated paranoia he always seemed to hold close. A trusting limitation that may be a fault but had also kept him alive countless times.

As he found himself in the grand and opulent study, surrounded by a gathering of men whose faces were mostly unfamiliar, he couldn't help but engage in his customary assessment. The verbal and non-verbal exchanges would tell a tremendous amount about a person, and Sebastian Storm mastered the ability at a young age.

Among the sea of strangers was one familiar face he held in high regard—Sam West. He vividly recalled the pivotal meeting in 2017, a clandestine rendezvous centered around a sensitive matter involving the then-Saudi King, Abdul Fahad Khalid. The memory of the encounter remained etched in his mind, a testament to the gravity of their discussions and the trust formed between them several years prior.

On the other hand, Damian was a figure he had encountered only briefly during those same intense discussions with Sam concerning classified military operations. While their paths had crossed, Sebastian couldn't claim to know Damian well. His impression of Damian West was that of a shrewd, calculated, and enigmatic individual who operated in the shadows with expertise commanding respect.

Sebastian maintained a distinctive air of composure as the room buzzed with subdued conversations and the clinking of glasses. His sharp, analytical mind never ceased its evaluation, understanding the people assembled here were undoubtedly players in a complex and intricate game. Each face held secrets, each voice carried weight, and every interaction concealed a multitude of agendas.

In this world of covert diplomacy and clandestine maneuvers, Sebastian Storm was a formidable presence, always on guard, assessing, and forever ready to navigate the treacherous waters of power and intrigue.

He always made it a point of knowing everything about those people significant in the room, and he had done his research on Damian despite the two of them meeting three years before at the request and insistence of Sam West.

Sebastian had already learned a fair amount about Julian Chambers as well. He and Sam West had become immediate friends, and their relationship had deepened in the prior four years, often dealing with sensitive national security matters. There was an earned, mutual respect for one another. It was apparent Sam and Sebastian had spent a lot of time together; they had a familiarity to them witnessed by all in the room. Their close friendship had grown to the point of appreciating the respective talents each possessed. Sam considered Sebastian as if he was his own son their professional relationship had certainly spilled over to that of a deep-seated personal nature.

When they had first met, Storm and Sam West designed a delicate staging to remove the Saudi King from power. Sebastian Storm executed the mission expertly, almost losing his life in the process. His actions restored the fragile balance of power in the region and regained the equilibrium in the relationship between the United States and Saudi Arabia. Sam West was already impressed with Sebastian Storm well before their meeting years before, but the hallowed feat made him indebted to the man indefinitely. Sam West had no greater respect for anyone than Sebastian Storm.

The retired Senator offered Sebastian a drink exactly how he liked it. "McCallum, 21 year with a large cube, if I remember correctly." Sebastian smiles, "You remembered, Senator; that's correct, thank you." He took the drink, and they all sat down around the fire. They spoke for several minutes, and Sebastian used the time to determine the mettle and verve of Damian West and Julian

Chambers. He was already aware of Damian's sincerity and strength through their limited interactions, but both men possessed tremendous intelligence and understanding of their respective political arenas.

Something troubled Sebastian about Julian Chambers. It was subtle and faint, but something small disturbed him about Damian's closest friend; he just couldn't put his finger on it. He would have to consider that further or spend more time with the Congressman to determine whether there was some merit to the notion.

Following the pleasantries, Sebastian Storm took another drink of his Bourbon and cut to the chase as he had been historically known to do from time to time. Because he was the one to call the meeting, he took the initiative. Sebastian had not anticipated Representative Chambers being present, but he gathered why Chambers had been included in the meeting. It only further solidified Sebastian's belief and added substance to what he wanted to discuss with the group. The Wests had brought Chambers into their circle of confidence. That was a significant move, and Sebastian noted it as such.

Looking at Damian, keeping the meeting professional, he began, "Senator West . . . . ." Damian interjected, "Please, Sebastian, first names. I only use *Senator* to get restaurant reservations; we are all friends here, and this is an informal setting. First names, please, I insist."

Sebastian smiled, liking the young man more with every meeting, although they were only separated by roughly five years. "Fair enough, Damian; firstly, as you are aware, I've had the privilege of knowing your father for a few years now, and I have the utmost respect for him." Looking over at the retired Senator, who nodded in appreciation, Sebastian continued, "He and I have never minced words, straight-shooting, and don't get offended if we don't see eye to eye on some things, though rare, I'll admit. Would you agree, Senator, er, I mean Sam?" That's an affirmative," came the retired Senator's response and a laugh over his son's rule of using first names.

Sebastian continued, "That said," he hesitated, taking a moment to look at every individual sitting in the room, and repeated, "That said . . . I can see right through all of you and what you are planning, and if I can, then others can as well, and that is where my concern lies. That's why I called this meeting, and that's why I wanted to speak with the Senators . . . and you being present, Congressman Chambers, only solidifies my assumptions. Please listen to what I have to say. I am only laying out facts and observations, but I think what I say will be of significant interest to you."

The three men looked at one another, slightly taken aback by what Sebastian may be inferring. Sam West began to speak, but Sebastian stopped him with a subtle raising of his hand. "Respectfully, let me continue, Sir, as I think it will be clearer in a moment." Sam West gestured for him to continue, respecting that Sebastian had a plan. Sebastian Storm always had a plan. Julian Chambers squirmed slightly in his seat, unsure of what Sebastian Storm would reveal.

"Damian, you have ascended the political ladder sure and fast, most of which has been by your own merit. You are a seasoned and gifted orator with an understanding of the people you govern and a keen comprehension of the challenges bureaucracy poses and the red tape it is encumbered with. You have found a way to circumvent that and fast-track agenda items that implement significant change. I applaud your efforts in that endeavor. However, your ascension also has been because of your well-respected father here, which, if given the opportunity, has its value, and it was insightful of you to leverage that asset. You have also successfully tested your theory and resolved it in your home state. Your litmus test, if you will." Sebastian shot a glance at Julian. "Your rise, Congressman, also has been largely the result of your affiliation to both men. Make no mistake, Congressman, although your tenacity and vigor have been admirable." Sebastian paused for a moment and looked at both Senators as well.

"I say all of this not to recognize privilege, choice, or even in light of the opportunities bestowed upon each of you but rather to recognize the need for change and that all of you possess the system, determination, and mechanism to actually make that difference. You have recognized your unique abilities and appreciate your limitations in implementing your goals. For example, Damian is coming from a long line of conservatives and still securing the election win . . . *as an Independent*. That's an amazing feat in and of itself. This means the people aren't trusting only your views or your faith in your respective party, but rather they are trusting more . . . *the man behind them*. Your televised interview was a testament to that belief."

He looked at all of them as they were drawn to his words. "To take it one step further, you are indirectly casting away your conservative views, or at the very least, modifying them and furtively snubbing the Republican Party by your election as an Independent. That was a ballsy move, Senator. Very assured . . . and assertive, and it impressed me."

He continued looking at the senior Senator, "Senator West. Having been a Republican for your entire life but then endorsing your son to take your place as an Independent was both brilliant and risky, to say the least. Still, it all paid off, and with all the political unrest facing our nation, it was skillfully timed. The country is primed for something new as the two party system is failing the evolving United States of America. A third party that could possibly reshape the political landscape and tip the scales at this point could potentially rescue this crumbling nation.

When I finally saw your speech a few days ago, Sebastian, it moved me to the point where I finally felt change could occur if properly orchestrated and implemented by the right people. As your father knows, I have never been a big fan of politicians or our country's political framework, but he has made me consider a different perspective, and I have come to appreciate his education in this matter. And being your father's son, I also recognize the same qualities in you. We have even had our own discussions on the topic ourselves, Damian, though minimal. This is why I contacted your father to expand upon this further. To make these changes, you must formulate a well-executed plan and implement it with strategic and well-positioned people, which I'm certain you are well aware. A new and innovative party formed that will craft the message that makes it palpable for the people to understand the benefit to not only themselves but also our great nation and serve those in power unwilling to perceive the benefit of such change. All of this would have to come together perfectly. A virtual *perfect storm* for all of it to work."

Sebastian looked at retired Senator West again and softly said, "Do I have it about right, Sir?" Senator Sam West swallowed hard as he looked at Julian, then at Damian, and quietly replied, "Yes. Yes, you do, Sebastian." Damian was most surprised watching his father's reaction. He had never before witnessed his own father at a loss for words.

In silence, Sebastian turned back toward Damian West and asked him directly, "Are you confident, without pause, you can pull this off, Senator? Win the adoration of the American people and champion the hearts of both the Republican and Democratic parties, and go on to become a progressive leader that our country desperately needs at this moment?"

Damian West looked hard into Sebastian's eyes and responded after a moment, "Yes, Mr. Storm, I do believe I can. More than anything, I want to turn this great nation around."

Sebastian Storm smiled at the Senator's response and hesitated before slowly responding, "Good, then . . . . *I'm going to help you make that happen.*"

Damian West explained, "As you all know, the bi-partisan system refers to a political system or environment in which two major political parties dominate the political landscape and effectively control the government. For years, this system has worked, but it is no longer viable. These two parties have significant influence and power, but it's diminishing, and their competition with one another to win seats in legislative bodies and to hold executive positions is dwindling in weight. It was meant to keep both parties on their toes, which breeds a healthy element in our otherwise stagnant political platform, but that has changed." Damian looked at the group and then continued.

"Also widely practiced within a bi-partisan system, the two major parties usually represent different ideologies, policy positions, or interest groups, providing voters with a choice between two distinct options. They debate, negotiate, and compromise to pass legislation and make decisions. This system worked well in the past, but now, the two major parties are at constant odds and conflict, and the nation is suffering as a result. The system is antiquated in design. They are essentially in a spiraling gridlock of distinctive polarization."

"In some cases, a two party system can lead to a more stable political environment, and for generations, it has served well this country as both parties work together to find common ground and reach consensus. However, it can also create a rigid, stagnant, and divided political landscape, with little room for smaller parties or alternative viewpoints, and this is where our challenge will lie. Our new party is largely untested and new to the political backdrop, but it represents change and a platform to make that occur. Change that has eluded us up until now, except what I have been able to accomplish in a relatively short amount of time here in Wyoming. The model could simply be modified nationally, streamline budgets, trim needless expenses, establish a sound budget, and lastly, trim the fat of those abusing the system."

"It's important to note that a bi-partisan system doesn't necessarily mean that both parties unanimously support all decisions and actions. Disagreements and conflicts between the two major parties are common, but the system typically relies on cooperation and collaboration to govern effectively. We no longer have that respect between the respective parties, and as a result, we are in a perpetual stalemate and have been for nearly two decades."

They talked well into the night, and much like his speech, Damian and Sam West recognized their challenges and the core of where the country had strayed in the last 25 years. With the bourbon flowing, the opinions and philosophies became deeper and more entwined within the fabric of what the new party would represent.

Damian continued, "I strongly recognize so much of the cog of this country lies within the antagonist views both parties appear to have for one another. So many Congressmen on either side of the aisle will sacrifice their own beneficial legislation for the sake of an opportunity to undermine one of their countrymen simply because he is a member of the opposite party. How can that be beneficial to anyone? My ideas and methodology don't seem to be the focus of the media because of the simple truth that I don't claim either party as my own; therefore, my agendas are viewed as they should be . . . . for the betterment of the all the people, they affect."

Julian chimed in, "Case in point, The impact and effectiveness of the Affordable Care Act (aka Obamacare) is a subject of ongoing debate and depends on a myriad of factors and perspectives. The law aimed to increase access to healthcare, improve affordability, and implement reforms in the insurance market, but I don't think most are convinced that, in fact, occurred. Since its implementation, the Affordable Care Act has achieved certain outcomes, sure. It expanded health insurance coverage by providing subsidies to lower-income individuals and expanding Medicaid eligibility in some states. This led to a significant reduction in the uninsured rate in the United States. However, the government also introduced consumer protections, such as prohibiting insurance companies from denying coverage based on pre-existing conditions and allowing young adults to stay on their parent's insurance plans until age 26."

"It's the elephant in the room. Opinions on the effectiveness of Obamacare vary, as you all know. Advocates highlight the positive impact of preventive care and the ability of individuals to seek necessary treatments without fear of being denied coverage." The consensus was that the plan needed revamping and easier to navigate.

"Critics of the law contend that it led to higher premiums for some individuals and businesses, limited choices in the insurance market, and imposed burdensome regulations on healthcare providers. They argue that it did not do enough to address the underlying issues of healthcare costs and failed to provide truly affordable coverage for all. Minorities, geriatric, businesses, and undecideds will be heavily weighted in the 2024 election and will be an important and defining point in a few years." The universal agreement was that the plan needed revamping but would be a significant and important topic when the time came. Sam West shifted the discussion to more current circumstances.

Sam recognized the political shift of the presidential election a year before, "With Donald Trump not getting re-elected, it left Biden to run this country and the Democrats back in power which his administration is off to a lackluster start. As he has already initiated, Biden will spend his entire term dismantling Trump's policies and progress as a bureaucratic puppet. I would expect as much as Trump did with Obama before him. It's become a vicious cycle of inefficiency and ego-driven chaos. I fear Biden won't be respected by the American people or his party either for that matter."

The hour was getting late. It was 3 AM when the group decided to retire for the evening, but Sebastian had a lingering question he needed answered before they disbanded. Sebastian had to ask, as it had been weighing on his mind for some time all evening. "So, will this new party change it all? Bring all the factions together: race and creed, young and old, wealthy or destitute? *What will you call this new party?*"

Damian and Sam looked at one another, surprised this discussion hadn't come out in the evening and with all the discussions swarming around the room.

Damian West looked directly at Sebastian Storm and replied, "Sebastian, that is why it is humbly called . . . . *The Unified Party.* Simple and memorable, emulating exactly what it's meant to represent within an already ailing system. The Unified Party will end the bi-parison regime, or at the very least make people question its validity."

Sebastian smiled as he stood up and put on his full-length Overland jacket, anticipating the brisk air he would encounter in Wyoming Fall once outside. "I like it, Damian. It says it all within the simplicity of its name. It will be a battle, but I believe in what you are doing. I will be your biggest advocate." As they shook hands, Sebastian bid Damian and Julian good night.

Sam West winked at Sebastian, "I'll walk you out." They walked to the front door alone, a lengthy walk from the study and well out of earshot, not to mention the ailing Senator moving a little slower these days. He occasionally grabbed Sebastian's arm for stability, but he didn't mind. Sebastian noted the Senator had aged tremendously in the last several months since his retirement. The office he served so boldly and proudly for so many years kept him young and served his vitality. Without serving office, the Senator was now aging like everyone else. His mind was still sharp, but anyone could discern his body was beginning to fail him. Sebastian valued in the senator a tremendous warrior, not shrouded in bullets and brawn like Sebastian Storm but of intelligence and wit paired with an unwavering desire to serve his country.

When they reached the front door, Sebastian turned to Senator Sam West as Sam grabbed Sebastian by both arms, "We will need you in our corner when this all comes to light, Sebastian." Sam smiled at him, "Damian, more than anyone, will need you. I won't be around forever, Sebastian, and he needs people like you and Julian to follow this through and protect him, as he won't be popular with many of the old guard, especially if we manage to pull this off."

"I know, Senator, but Damian has a gift and sincerity about him. I will make it my goal to see it through and protect him as much as possible. HB is also on board; she values the benefit here," referencing his boss, the head of the Anti-Terrorist Special Division (ATS Division). She had answered to Senator West for many years, and they had come to respect one another immensely.

Sam West sighed, "The work you do at ATS is substantial, and I don't want to take away from that, but this could change the face of our great nation, Sebastian." Sebastian responded, "Senator, if she is lending me to you and this campaign, she must value its importance." Sebastian shook his friend's hand. Senator West smiled, knowing that with this man on their side, he would protect them with his life if he were ever presented with such a threat.

Sebastian tilted his head, "I also think HB is concerned there is more to the story concerning the death of your friend, Ryker Davion, a few months ago in L.A. The people's tolerance these days is mounting, and figureheads appear less engaged these days." Sam West nodded, "He was made an example, oh how they must have suffered, and the message written. What was it . . . Something like, *It's time for change. The Reign Cometh. This is merely the beginning. . .*” Sebastian simply shook his head, “I don't know Sam, but it worries me.” Sam pursed his lips, nodded, and squeezed his arm, acknowledging the statement.

Opening the front door, Sam said his goodbyes as Sebastian walked to his awaiting SUV. The driver held the door open as Sebastian hopped in the vehicle and saluted to the Senator waiting in the doorway to see him off.

Sebastian's SUV sped off as Damian approached him and stood in the doorway with his father, watching the brake lights fade off in the distance. It was then he noticed the first snow of the season had just begun to fall not minutes before. Sam West thought it a symbolic evening, their meeting that night and all that transpired.

“He is a good man, Dad. I like him more as I get to know him better. He wasn't as reserved tonight; he believes in in our vision. I can see why you value what he brings to the table,” said Damian of Sebastian Storm. Sam West puts his arm around his son, “Yes, he is, son, and someday you will probably hear about the myriad of stories of his heroism and patriotism surrounding the man. He has saved two presidents' lives, a plane full of passengers. . . *twice*, and acts of terrorism that would have imploded this country many times over. He has given the ultimate sacrifice for life and liberty. There is no more extraordinary patriot than Sebastian Storm.” Damian West was impressed and even more fascinated with Sebastian's decision to help them with what some would call a hopeless endeavor.

“Well then, I'm glad he is on board with us and seeing our dream through,” replied Damian West. His father stood silent momentarily as he looked at the snow falling, just beginning to accumulate on the surface as the darkened ground slowly turned white as the snow continued to fall.

Sam West turned to his son, “That very commitment in serving our cause may end up being the greatest accomplishment in his already colorful career. You are the future, Damian, and despite all the incredible people in your corner, Sebastian Storm may be the most valuable of us all.”

They both looked out over the driveway as the snow fell, "We have a lot of work to do, Dad," his father simply nodded in agreement.

The snow was the first of the season and symbolic of their crucial forging of relationships. Relationships that would define a country in the following years. None of them could know the twists and turns surrounding the next part of their plan.

Chapter 8

The Master Plan

"Some men see things as they are and ask why. I dream of things that never were and ask why not."
~ Robert Kennedy

Jackson Hole, Wyoming
2021 December
Senator Damian West Private Estate

The drive was relatively short, only 19 minutes to Damian West's estate. Exterior lights illuminated strategically the outside, and she wondered how the terrain looked during the day. As if reading her mind, Agent Lee softly said, "You will enjoy the view in the morning. It takes my breath away every time I see it, Ms. Dmitri. You won't be disappointed." She smiled at him from the backseat as he looked at her through the rearview mirror.

"The West family owns roughly 1000 acres here in Jackson Hole, with only two properties occupying the entire acreage. Senator

Sam West has the property to the South that his family has occupied for three generations. As his only child, Damian has the Northernmost property, which he built five years ago, and it's quite the estate. The two Senators don't ever seem to be far away from one another and are very close. Their respective homes are about a fifteen-minute drive from one another."

Mila decided to capitalize on the opportunity to gain some insight about the mysterious Senator from Wyoming, hoping she may charm any sliver of information out of the Secret Service Agent. He appeared talkative, so she hoped she was trusting enough to hear anything he may be willing to divulge about her mysterious host.

She began a simple line of questioning, "How long have you been working with the new Senator, Agent Lee?" He looked at her in the rearview. She couldn't see his smile but saw the crow's feet along his eyes, "Please, call me Ben. I have been with the West family for over 12 years. Started with the old man in 2008 and have gotten to know the family well. I've watched Damian West grow up essentially. They both thought it best that my detail transfer to the younger Senator once he was elected." "So, you know them well, I see," responded Mila.

She decided to probe a little further, "I'm curious, Ben, why hasn't the Senator taken a wife? He is certainly attractive and quite the eligible bachelor, I'm assuming?" Ben glared slightly in the mirror before looking forward, watching the road, "We thought he was close once. He dated a nice girl for 6-7 years sometime back, but she required a lot of his time, and with his District Attorney appointment and eventually the Governorship, time was a luxury he didn't have a lot of for her. As Senator, he would have far less time available to her. He knew he couldn't give her what she needed."

Mila nodded and said, "Did he love her, Ben?" He looked at her and cocked his head, knowing none of it was his business nor did he want to engage in any telltale, but he also thought all of it was common knowledge. "I think he did, in his own way. He never appeared madly in love with her, but she was an attractive woman from a good family here in town. His life has been his work, and

I'm not sure a woman has yet been able to steer his focus from that endeavor. But I'm not entirely certain; we didn't talk much about those things......Ahhh, we have arrived, Ms. Dmitri. I present to you . . . the West Estate." He was relieved their arrival had interrupted the discussion of Senator West's private life.

She sat up and looked out the window as Agent Lee turned off the main road, arriving before a massive iron gate with stone supports that displayed a simple 'W' in the center where the gate separated in two and opened magically for the SUV as it passed through. They drove a mile or so in silence up a mild incline, then began their descent when passing the top of the hill. The large home, well-lit, looked more like a compound than a home. The contemporary cabin was well over 10,000 square feet and beautifully designed in every detail. Even at night, the dwelling took one's breath away. Mila could only imagine what kind of views would be unveiled with sunlight highlighting its surroundings. With nearly a foot of snow on the ground, the winter wonderland looked like something out of a Christmas movie. The driveway was clear as Agent Lee pulled up to the front door and hopped out to open the door for Ms. Dmitri. He grabbed her small bag, escorted her down the walkway to the front door, and opened it, allowing her inside the main foyer.

Mila Dmitri immediately became overwhelmed by the height of the foyer and the grand pair of stairs on either side of the large archway leading to the kitchen. The second irresistible sensation was the aromas emanating from the kitchen, making Mila realize how truly famished she had become. Agent Lee gestured to the large guest room to the right of the stairs as she followed him past the large French doors into a beautiful large and ornate room with an oversized fireplace already lit in front of the king bed. The room was warm and cozy, and she felt like she could stay there in its peacefulness forever. She was impressed that she was not escorted to the Senator's room which would have been far too presumptuous.

Captivated by all its splendor, Agent Lee again repeated, "Ma'am. . . Ma'am. Let me take your jacket," as he did so and hung it up in the closet along with placing her luggage on the shelf within, gently closed the closet door and turned to Mila. "I think you will find the Senator in the kitchen. You have been fully vetted, so explore freely as you will. I apologize for the precautions." Sniffing into the air, Agent Lee's nose raised upward, and he smiled, "He is familiar with the kitchen. A skill he picked up from his mother, Jenny, as a kid. I wish you a good evening, Ms. Dmitri. It was a pleasure speaking with you tonight." And with that, he was gone like a puff of smoke.

She turned slowly toward the fireplace and stared for a moment, thinking that just a few hours prior, she was sitting on her sofa, a glass of wine in hand and a novel in the other, ready to ease into the evening at her home in Dallas. Yet, now she was 1300 miles away at the base of a snow-capped mountain in Jackson Hole, Wyoming, in the same home where one of the most talked about men in America resided. Life had an interesting sense of humor sometimes, she thought.

She slowly sauntered out of her room back into the foyer, appreciating its magnificence once more as she made her way underneath the large cascading stairways upstairs, and the light in front of her began to expand. Smelling the bouquet of rosemary, basil, and garlic filled her senses as if she could almost taste it already. She continued to walk until she arrived at the base of the substantial archway that defined the base of the stairways above.

There, she saw Senator Damian T. West working diligently with his back to her. An Italian aria played softly from above as he sampled his sauce in the large pot. He wore navy pants, a slim cut, a white open-collared shirt, tan shoes, and a belt. Nicely dressed but casual at the same time. It was widely recognized that Damian West always dressed impeccably, and she recalled seeing an article where the author questioned if he owned any sweatpants or tee shirts. She laughed at the thought and wondered the same.

Pondering the sample of his sauce, yet apparently not entirely content with its flavor, he added a few specific spices to his Bolognese to give it just the right zest he was searching for to complete his dish. He mixed in the spices and stirred, trying he blend once again, and let out a soft "Ahhhh," and she smiled, knowing he found his combination. She was fascinated, watching him momentarily, enjoying the view and his culinary aptitude. She watched him for a few moments relishing him navigating the kitchen and enjoying his music in the background.

"You got me all the way out here, Senator. That sauce had better be amazing," Mila softly said as Damian West slowly turned around and smiled. She first noted his handsome face and charming smile when he turned. The smile was witnessed on every tabloid, television, and social media outlet available to man in the last month, and she was experiencing it firsthand. "You made it, Mila; I was beginning to think I may have all this as leftovers for the coming week," as he gestured to the small mess and chaos surrounding him.

Damian quickly recovered and walked a few steps to the island, where a bottle of Cabernet Sauvignon and two glasses sit. Damian asked about her trip as he poured the wine into both glasses and handed her one as she reached over the island to grab the glass he offered.

"I am hoping you might like this Cabernet," he said as he toasted her and said, "To a successful meal and wonderful company." They both took a sip, savoring the deep reddish/purple liquid and enjoying the moment. "This Cabernet, Mila, comes from Napa and received excellent ratings from wine critics, and it's respected for its depth, complexity, and aging potential. . . ." Mila respectfully interrupted, "Let me have a guess." "Be my guest. . ." he replied as she sniffed the glass's bouquet once again and smiled, ". . . . . *Shafer Vineyards Hillside Select Cabernet Sauvignon. . . A 2016, I* believe?" Damian West's eyes opened wide in amazement, astonished her guess was spot on, on every point. He turned the bottle so she could see the label, verifying her correct response. "I will certainly refrain from making any bets with you, now knowing your skill in wine selection."

They tapped glasses once again and took another sip, looking at one another. She admitted, "I have a confession, for I cannot tell a lie. I did cheat a little. I know the selection intimately and have a half case of it back at home. In fact, I was about to lose myself in a much anticipated Van Lustbader novel, paired with a healthy pour of the identical selection you offered me tonight. However, I was rudely interrupted by an assiduous Secret Service Agent summoning me, incessantly over the persistence of an even more relentless Senator demanding an audience with me in the evaporating hours of the evening. I was then whisked away to a location where the inhabitants dress in full-length down jackets and snowshoes."

Damian laughed at the description of her alleged abduction, "I will fire him tomorrow for his . . . *Incessant summoning*? Relentless Senator? I had no idea the suggestion to come to Jackson Hole was so overpowering," he winked and asked, "Are you hungry?" "Very! I thought you would never let me savor what's in your pot." Was that a double entendre, he wondered? He enjoyed her light and playful humor. He had not entertained a woman in his home since he had broken it off with Natalia nearly eighteen months before.

Mila helped him as he transferred the Bolognese over the penne pasta and vegetable sides with the salad and vinaigrette to finish. They sat in the dimly lit formal dining room with the roaring fireplace off to the side, drank their wine, and savored their meals. The laughing and toying with one another during dinner were palpable and comfortable, lasting hours.

"This Bolognese is amazing, Damian. And so is your home." He smiled at her and said, "It's the least I could do due to my demand of you to come to where the *'inhabitants dress in full-length down jackets and snowshoes.'* I mean, that is a big ask . . . to tear you away from your book reading, Friday night agenda." He looked at the empty bottle and asked, "Shall I open a second?" She looked at him and cocked her head, not wanting the night to end, "Should we. . ." and nodded as he got up to retrieve another of the 2016 Shafer Vineyards.

Her appetite was fully satisfied following the wonderful dinner, but his entrée was too delicious to leave anything remaining. Wanting to stretch her legs a bit, she pushed the chair back quietly and stood up, knowing exactly where she wanted to explore.

Her eyes drifted into the opulent living room, an area she had glimpsed earlier, where the soft glow of the fireplace accentuated the grandeur of the space. Drawn by curiosity, she rose from her seat, the gentle strains of Italian music still caressing her senses and ventured into the living room alone. Her gaze was immediately captivated by a gallery of photographs adorning the walls, each a snapshot of Damian West's remarkable life.

The images told a story of a man intimately acquainted with power and influence. There were photographs of Damian alongside his renowned father, captured in moments of history and shared ambition. Past presidents, foreign dignitaries, and renowned business figures featured prominently in the visual narrative. It was evident that the West family had shared close ties with these influential figures, each playing a role, however minor, in the young Senator's ascent to success.

As she perused the photographs, her attention was suddenly arrested by a particularly intriguing image. It portrayed Damian, his father, and her own superior, the CEO of Dymitron, Anthony Voss, captured during the Republican National Convention in Cleveland, Ohio, back in 2016. Surprise coursed through her; Anthony Voss had never mentioned his association with either Senator. Such a revelation had never been brought up in all her time spent with Anthony Voss.

Tonight, however, was not about digging into the intricacies of these connections. It was an evening designed for them to acquaint themselves with each other more personally. The question about their shared history could wait for a more appropriate occasion when the conversation would naturally steer in that direction. For now, the focus was on forging new connections and unraveling the mysteries within this captivating gathering.

She gracefully moved closer to the roaring fireplace, savoring the comforting warmth it exuded as the flames waltzed across the intricate stonework of the hearth. The ambient glow cast a bewitching spell, and she found herself spellbound by its mesmerizing dance. Silent and enigmatic, Damian materialized behind her, his arrival perfectly timed with the vintage grandfather clock's twelve resounding chimes, each strike resonating with the passage of another hour.

The abrupt sound startled her, momentarily dispelling the trance the fire had woven around her, paired with the healthy amount of alcohol in her system. However, the moment Damian's presence enveloped her, a sense of tranquility washed over her like a soothing balm. He deftly refilled her wine glass, a gesture that reflected his intuitive understanding of her unspoken needs.

Mila's eyes remained fixed on the flames; their flickering allure dulled slightly by the effects of the rich Cabernet she had been savoring. The potent combination of the wine and the tantalizing ambiance gently swayed her senses.

In a voice that barely rose above a whisper, Damian's words reached her ears like an intimate secret shared in the stillness of the night. "Let's sit down."

Mila nodded in agreement, her gaze finally shifting to meet Damian's. Beyond the undeniable physical attraction, she deeply appreciated his sharp wit, profound intelligence, and sense of humor that had effortlessly drawn her in. Damian was a complex enigma, a puzzle she was eager to solve. He revealed glimpses of his inner self, but it was clear that he approached their connection with a level of caution that only heightened her curiosity.

As she chuckled inwardly, Mila couldn't help but imagine that others might view her similarly—a woman with layers, guarded yet revealing, a captivating mystery waiting to be unraveled. In this enchanting dance of secrets and allure, she was drawn ever closer to Damian, a magnetic force that promised thrilling discoveries and passionate encounters.

They talked for hours about their childhood experiences, parents, the loss of people close to them, hardships, challenges, friends, and mutual interests. Little about politics or the state of the country was mentioned, keeping the conversation flowing and without conflict or overt opinion. They laughed as she would touch him on the hand or knee. The alcohol was certainly lowering their inhibitions as she turned to him and asked him where the closest bathroom was located. They both stood up as he said, "It's in the main hall, the 2ⁿᵈ door on the right, Mila," as she looked up into his eyes, captivated by every part of him.

It was then that she knew she must have him, "Will you take me, Damian? I don't want to get lost in this big house." "Of course," came his reply as he gently took her hand and guided her through the dimly lit hallway to the door he had described a few moments before. "Wait for me," was all she said as he nodded. She handed him her glass of wine and then slipped into the bathroom, smiling at him as she closed the door behind her.

She finished, then looked at her image in the mirror as she dried her hands, knowing he was waiting for her, stimulating her slightly. He exuded an air of elegant handsomeness that left her breathless, a captivating blend of refinement and allure. As the evening unfolded before them, she couldn't shake the notion that it held the promise of something truly extraordinary. It was a sensation she hadn't experienced in a long time, the kind of magnetic attraction and genuine admiration that seemed to defy memory.

A few minutes later, she opened the door and slowly walked out. Before her, he was leaning against the wall, waiting patiently as she had requested. He smiled, unmoving, as she slowly made her way to him. His soft smile was so disarming as she took the glass from his hand and looked up to him as she inched closer, taking a sip but never losing eye contact. The Grandfather clock chimed, startling her once again, signifying three gongs; it was already 3 AM. The night had flown by, and she didn't want it to end.

Damian grabbed her hand. "Follow me," he whispered as he led her through more of the unexplored home and finally out a back door onto the terrace. Above them, the moon shone full and large in the clear night. What made it spectacular was the 14,000-foot-high Grand Tetons in the distance, with the white snow reflecting from the moonlight illuminating the backdrop of Damian's property beautifully. Not another house was in sight, viewing the spectacle the same that evening as settlers did 250 years before.

———

It was a magical setting, and Mila was mesmerized, her eyes wide in wonder as she turned to him to say something of the splendor before them, and he softly grazed his lips with hers. His left hand gently came to the side of her face as he kissed her more deeply this time. She eased into him further, craving his touch and the softness of his kiss. Their embrace intensified as he slightly pulled her neck towards him.

She sensed his cologne and recognized the instant animal magnetism to him, but then a sense of fear rushed over her. Would he disappoint her like all the others had in the past? She adored his passion, and it continued for several seconds, then their lips parted for a moment as she looked up at him, both taking a final drink of their glasses of wine.

He looked down at her, appreciating her exquisite features; her igniting brown eyes, with a hint of yellow, sparkled in the moonlight, captivating his attention. She shifted her legs slightly, knowing he was arousing her and knowing he was equally attracted to her. "What an incredible night . . ." he began as she pulled him to her again and kissed him hard, wanting and hoping for more as their bodies came together. She could feel the effects of his excitement as his body pressed against hers, and it stimulated her even further. He eases her back again, hoping to invite her for more as he takes her hand and retraces the steps they had taken just minutes before.

They arrive in her room. He takes her wine glass, places it on the dresser, and turns to her, pulling her firmly to him. They kiss passionately as she begins rubbing her body against his, his excitement palpable and growing even further and intensifying her own, enjoying every minute. He can feel her breasts pushed against him, her warmth, her passion all wrapped in his. Their connection is electric and palpable beyond words.

He has both hands on her neck and cheeks and her arms around his waist as he eases back, then softly touches her lips once again with his own, looks again into her eyes, and smiles.

"I had the most incredible evening with you, Mila Dmitri, and tomorrow. I have some incredible things to show you. All designed to take your breath away." Like tonight, she thinks and is amazed at the notion that he may be ending the evening. Parting from her lips, he whispers, "If you should need anything, I will be upstairs. . . ." as he kisses her one last time, a bewildered look on her face was the last image he saw as he backed out and closed the French doors in front of him and in an instant, he was gone, and she was all alone.

Mila smiled to herself. She could not recall when a man had rejected her advances. Although she was disappointed, she was impressed by the notion that Senator Damian West had not disappointed her, which excited her even more.

She unpacked her things and showered before slipping into bed, wearing nothing at all. The warm fireplace calmed her as she lay in bed looking at the ceiling, watching the lights dance upon the ceiling from the fireplace below. She was covered from her waist down, but her breasts were exposed, soothed by the warmth from the wine and its effects, paired with the heat of the fireplace.

She looked at the clock at 3:24 AM and knew she needed sleep but couldn't get the evening out of her mind and was mildly hoping he would come through the door at any moment. She thought of the last few minutes as their lips touched, instantly exciting her with the spark between them. She was certain he experienced the same but wondered why he pulled away at the end of the evening. She fantasized in her mind about the thought that . . . *if only he had remained.*

The evening was perfect with their chemistry and connection, the strongest she had ever connected with someone. She closed her eyes at the thought of the evening and had he only closed the doors with him inside them. . . . instead of outside.

Jackson Hole, Wyoming
2021 December - Earlier the Day Before
Damian West Private Estate

"Our timeline has been moved up, and here is the list of remaining key individuals we need to approach," Sam West handed a copy of the list to Damian, Julian, and Sebastian.

Within Damian's own study sat a massive, yet rustic round conference table with large chairs he affectionately referred to as the "Round Table" in reference to Arthurian legend and medieval folklore. The idea of the Round Table itself symbolized equality and fraternity among Arthur's knights, as there was no head or foot on the table, emphasizing that all knights are equal in status and importance. The concept of the Round Table emulated a powerful symbol of unity and the unwavering cipher of chivalry, and that code Damian West felt strongly was the backbone of their approach to the new Unified Party.

They all perused the lengthy list for a few moments. Damian spoke initially, "We currently have 18 Senators on the list, 4 confirmed on board, 66 House Representatives with 21 confirmed, and a host of contributors, donators, and influencers in business and media. The most important person on this list is the Speaker of the House, Regina Alvarado. She holds the key in the swing of a lot of people. If we can convince her to see things our way, it would be a windfall for us and our establishing this Party as a hitter. We have our work cut out for us, without question."

Sam smiled within; Regina Alvarado wouldn't be an issue. He was certain but didn't want to disclose the specifics of his confidence just yet. Sam West stood up and said, "I will work on SOH, Alvarado. She and I have had some lengthy discussions in the past about the change this country needs, and she has always been a big supporter of yours, Damian. If we hit her with a one-two punch, we could have her. I'll soften her up, and you come in and work your charm, Damian. We have an appointment in a few days with her in D.C. We have good headway on this list and have been meeting with nearly all the names on this list over the next few months, but the timing, media, and rumors will accelerate everything, I'm afraid."

"You also have the additional possibilities in the wildcards," suggested Sebastian Storm, "Once this goes public, there will be backlash, and party loyalties will come into play along with heavy scrutiny."

"Sebastian's correct," replied Damian, "as some people on this list will be unable to bear the weight or pressures of such a political move and will be guilted into staying within their respective party. Switching parties is a risky move. We are essentially forming a coup, and the risks for all on that list can either catapult them into a progressive way of thinking if we succeed or a quick and painful political death if we don't. That risk alone will diminish the list; however, others unforeseen, or predict, to come over will also materialize. That is the unknown we will have to navigate as the fluidity of this dynamic unfolds."

Julian looked at Sebastian, curious about another angle they hadn't considered or discussed, "Sebastian, what is your take on the security surrounding this endeavor?" They all looked to Sebastian as Damian said, "Good point, Julian. Thoughts on that, Sebastian?"

Sebastian Storm then stood up. An imposing man, even in black jeans, a ribbed navy sweater, and a white tee shirt barely showing through at the neckline. He paused a moment before answering, "A shit show, in all honesty, gentlemen. Any major political upheaval draws out the dregs of society. It's their moment to shine, and if they can make an example out of a high-profile target, then your head, Damian, on a platter is what they shall seek. Political unrest attracts the fanatics of one party rising against the other, but a new party emerging and one that gets traction will attract the most menacing zealots from both parties, which worries me the most. At some point, I'll need to sit down with HB and the Secret Service on how to best protect this environment and the unknowns it will present. I'll coordinate that with Agent Lee, who we will eventually need to become privy to our plans and involved directly with this team.

He can provide some valuable insight, providing he is onboard." In unison, Sam and Damian replied, "He will be." Sebastian smiled, "Good, I was hoping so." The West family certainly displayed a strong loyalty to Secret Service Agent Benjamin Lee.

Damian continued, "The next items come down to third-party assimilation into the current bi-partisan system. And this one is a big hurdle. Potentially our biggest. As historically witnessed with the Green and Libertarian Parties, they have been plagued with various obstacles. Having a third party political status, we will have limited electoral success, struggling to secure ballot access and media coverage, but I think we have found some ways to circumvent this impediment."

"Our positives in this regard lie in strong contributions and donor networks thanks to my father, so that should help in keeping the machine running . . . . and coursing hot, preferably. We must throw everything we have at the American people, the opponents, and the media. We have to somehow make it favorable to all Americans. Our electoral representation will depend on the list we discussed earlier and who we can secure."

Sam West explained, "Some voters may perceive third-party candidates, including those from the Unified Party, as less viable in elections. This perception can deter people from voting for Unified Party candidates in the future, as they may believe their vote would be more effective if cast for a major-party candidate. Also, many states have ballot access laws that make it difficult for third-party candidates to appear on the ballot. We will have to push hard with this one, and your recent popularity, Damian, may play in our favor in this aspect. If we impact from the top, it will only trickle down from there. I believe this is where the Green and Libertarian parties failed. They began at the local level with a hope to slowly build upwards, but that is too slow and narrow in focus; we need to think opposite of this tact." He looked at all in attendance as they were fascinated by his depiction of the process.

Damian then took over, "These individual state laws often require third parties to meet strict signature requirements or achieve a certain percentage of the vote in previous elections, which we will obtain if necessary. We may need a couple of strong national news conferences to seal it. This, too, will push for more public awareness, and our donors list may be heavily leveraged. I feel if we can receive more exposure in the media, all media, it will only fuel our cause. We want the people starving for more of what the Unified Party stands for and the change in insurance through my message. The various media will want to satisfy that demand. Americans will not be largely familiar with the Unified Party and its platform, and the party faces challenges in raising public awareness and educating voters about its positions and candidates. We need to saturate the media on every front."

"Above all else, we will not prevail in this endeavor, I fear, if we do not get on the national debates when the time comes, and we have a viable candidate. We must do everything possible to make the American People demand an open debate platform. My concern is the criteria for inclusion in presidential debates for any candidate we choose to represent us in the future are set by a commission that tends to favor major-party candidates, making it difficult for Third Party candidates to gain exposure on a national stage," explained Damian. "Dad, you could be influential on this one besides Senator Cosner. The private, non-profit Commission on Presidential Debates (CPD) organizes and hosts the presidential debates during the general election campaign. The CPD was established to ensure that presidential debates are conducted fairly and without the influence of any political party or candidate. Let's hold them to that responsibility. Despite the CPD never allowing a third party to debate in the Presidential Debates, this may be the time to influence a change with them and their historic policy. They must let us into the debate if we make enough noise. Allow our voice to be heard, and we have to make it worth hearing. Despite not ever being associated with the commission, you know Senator Cosner well, who has co-chaired the CPD in the past for the Democratic Party, not to mention everyone on that commission respects you, and your influence carries a lot of weight. If we don't get on those debates, we are dead in the water. We also have to create a shortlist for potential presidential candidates who could be the first to represent the party in 2024 or, if not, then in 2028."

Sam West nodded; he knew what he must do, "I'll get it done. It won't be easy, but I'll call in every favor that is owed to me. As far as Presidential Candidates, let me handle that one personally. I will share that list later." He knew things about the Commission and Senator Ren Cosner that Damian was unaware of. He also knew Damian was less aware of his father's list of potential presidential candidates. It was a bit of the puzzle Sam West held close to the vest for the time being.

Julian Chambers noted, "In their defense, the CPD has never had a third party worthy enough to consider including within the debates. I don't believe any third parties have garnered more than 5% of the popular vote, making them unworthy of a Presidential Debate bid. While the Green Party hits hard the environmental angle, social justice, ecological responsibility, and grassroots democracy, whereas the Libertarians being platform based on limited government intervention in both social and economic matters, personal freedom, individual rights, and a philosophy of self-reliance and individual liberty, we are primed to be the hybrid that satisfies the majority of both of these views common to both Libertarian and Green. If we spin it correctly, we could obtain many of their key members if they see us making headway, but they won't want to support a weak horse and waste their votes. These groups will be the first to jump ship and align themselves with us if we can make it enticing enough and worth their while. People must believe that this party, the Unified Party, can go far. Every vote the Unified Party secures is a vote lost from the Democrats or Republicans."

"Those are observable points, Julian, and true. We need the support of some of the big hitters, which my father and I will hit hard," replied Damian. "The challenge is the historical precedent of the American political system: The Democrats and Republicans have a long history in American politics and have entrenched themselves in our country's political fabric. That current political system is antiquated. But people are growing tired of them and their ineffectiveness. Violence and outrage are at an all-time high in this country. This historical precedent makes it challenging for third parties to break through and gain widespread support. American politics has become increasingly polarized, making it difficult for third parties to attract a broad spectrum of voters. However, voters, more of whom are gathering on the fence because of the increasing alienation they are experiencing from the extreme positions of the major parties, are prime to make a political affiliation move. We must target this group with social media, mainstream media, debates, interviews, articles, and news conferences. And we have to hit it out of the park. I think we need at least 20% of the popular vote to gain any traction, and that's lofty when no third party has tallied more than 5%, as Julian mentioned."

Damian shook his head at the daunting amount of work they would need to endure. Changing the entire country's perspective in an otherwise differentiated atmosphere was no simple task, but deep down, retired Senator Samuel T. West had been preparing for this moment for nearly a quarter century. He hadn't shown his hand up until this point, but he would soon reveal the true architecture of his plan . . . .

. . . . And the sheer genius of it all.

The four men spent the majority of the day hashing out the specifics of how each obstacle would be addressed, who would approach, or deal with their respective challenges, what the possible outcomes would be, and how they would navigate through them. After which, the group settled by the fireplace and burrowed into a marathon of political and historical discourse. The hours waned, and the conversation delved into the rich tapestry of political philosophy, the lessons etched in history's archives, and the speculative paths that lay ahead for the United States. Sebastian Storm, a man whose name echoed the very essence of strategic defense, lent his profound insights into the military's indelible role in shaping the past and present.

His colleagues listened as Sebastian expounded on the interplay between military might and political doctrine—the sword and the pen in an eternal dance of influence. With the acuity of a scholar and the precision of a tactician, he illuminated how force had been the silent architect behind pivotal moments that altered the course of history. His understanding went beyond the mere acts of aggression; he spoke of the necessary equilibrium between strength and diplomacy, the art of wielding power without undermining the pen's capacity for peace and progress.

His peers, seasoned in various spheres of influence, found themselves captivated by Sebastian's discourse on the occasional necessity of force—not as an instrument of oppression but as a guardian of liberty and an arbiter in times of inevitable conflict. It ultimately led him to the ATS Division (Anti-Terrorist Special Division) and his fight against the global threat that affected all humans.

It was a perspective that added depth to their strategy, reminding them that the path to a peaceful future often required the wisdom to know when to deploy the sword, as much as the pen, in the service of their nation's enduring ideals.

At 3 PM, the meeting began to break, and Secret Service Agent Benjamin Lee entered the room and stood before Senator Damian West, and quietly said, "Ms. Dmitri has been thoroughly vetted, Sir. I was about to board the jet to retrieve her." Damian nodded, and Agent Lee left.

Sebastian Storm overheard the short conversation and turned to the young Senator, "Damian, look for me at 8 AM sharp on your back patio; I have something special for you and your . . . date in the morning."

Damian smiled at Sebastian, "Well, that is, if she shows Sebastian, she seems to be quite the tenacious one, but if she does, we will be there." They laughed at hearing Damian's pessimism. Sebastian added, "She will show. But, if by some chance she doesn't, then it will just be you and me. Be there at 8 AM regardless," he said with a smile.

Chapter 9

Mila Dmitri

"Excitement is the spark that ignites our passions, the fuel that propels us towards our dreams, and the energy that electrifies our journey through life."
~Author Unknown

Jackson Hole, Wyoming
2021 December
Damian West Private Estate

As Mila stirred from her restless slumber, a distant clatter in the kitchen disrupted her tranquil morning silence. Her eyes instinctively sought out the clock, its illuminated digits revealing the ungodly hour of 6:33 AM. It was a cruel reminder she had managed to snatch only three hours of sleep the night before, a fact further underscored by the faint throbbing sensation that began to pulse at the front of her head from the wine consumption.

In that quiet moment, her thoughts drifted back to the enchanting evening that had unfolded just hours ago. It had been nothing short of perfection, an intoxicating dance of words and shared glances with the charismatic Senator from Wyoming. She had reveled in his company, basking in the warmth of his presence, all the while searching for the smallest chink in his seemingly impenetrable armor.

It was a night that had left her in a state of tantalizing sexual frustration and a hint of anxiousness. Damian, a man of undeniable allure, could have had her at any moment during their encounter, yet he had chosen not to, a gentleman possessing insurmountable control. The gesture impressed her. It was a choice that both baffled and intrigued her, leaving her with lingering questions and a burning curiosity.

In her moment of contemplation, doubt began to creep into her mind. Perhaps Damian didn't find her as attractive as she had hoped. However, a spark of determination ignited within her. She had yet to meet a man who could resist her charms, a fact serving as her unwavering truth throughout life. Amidst this uncertainty, she couldn't help but wonder if Damian would prove to be the exception to the rule, a man who would challenge her in ways she had never imagined nor experienced.

Mila granted herself a few precious moments, closing her eyes and allowing her mind to wander into the depths of her desires. Her thoughts wove an intricate tapestry of fantasies, vividly depicting how she hoped the evening would unfold. A sensuous sigh escaped her lips as her fingers gently squeezed and caressed her breasts, each delicate touch sending a shiver of pleasure coursing through her body.

Her mind, ignited by the tantalizing possibilities, danced with the intoxicating imagery of Damian and the effect he had on her the night before and in her dreams well before meeting him. She imagined his gentle touch, his fingers tracing the contours of her body, igniting a fierce passion smoldering deep within her. Her nipples responded eagerly to her sensual reverie, hardened and sensitized by the vivid mental images. He would never know she had been fantasizing about him well before they even met. If he only knew.

As her hand trailed downward, the heat and anticipation built within her, her skin moist in perspiration as she reveled in the intoxicating slickness greeting her fingertips. Her legs parted slightly, a subtle invitation to her own desires, and she found herself lost in a world of pure sensuality. Her fingers ventured deeper, seeking the elusive spot propelling her into the realms of ecstasy.

In her mind's eye, Damian's presence loomed large, his touch firm and possessive, stoking the flames of her fervent longing. The intensity of her fantasy quickened her ascent, and an orgasm, swift and intense, claimed her surprisingly quickly. She surrendered to the waves of pleasure, each contraction and spasm rendering her body ablaze with electric excitement.

As the tremors gradually subsided, Mila basked in the afterglow of her desire, her body bathed in warmth and satisfaction as the moment passed. A sense of hope and anticipation filled her, the fantasy now a beacon of possibility in her mind. She yearned for Damian as much as she craved every aspect of him, eager for their connection's potential.

With a satisfied smile lingering on her lips, she allowed herself a few more moments of reflection, lost in the glow of her own desire. With a renewed sense of purpose, she decided seeking out Damian in the immense home was the next tantalizing step toward bringing her fantasies to life. He stimulated her mind and body, and the combination excited her.

Mila luxuriously cast her sheets aside, the silky fabric sliding effortlessly over her naked imminence as she rose from the bed. A hint of her moist arousal remains saturating the sheets from where she lay. A figurative badge symbolizes her attraction to the character dominating her fantasy.

With a graceful stride, she carried herself toward the expansive, picturesque window dominating the room, where the world beyond beckoned with breathtaking allure. The view before her was nothing short of spectacular, the Grand Tetons gracing the distant horizon, their rugged peaks framed by the crisp, clear morning sky. Not a single wisp of clouds dared to mar the azure expanse.

There was a captivating magic to the morning hours, revealing an entirely new world compared to the shadows of the night. The scene unfolding before her now was nothing short of exquisite. The majestic vista held her in its thrall. Mila couldn't help but lose herself in the beauty of it all, her gaze locked onto the panorama as she stood by the window for a few precious minutes, absorbing the grandeur of nature's majestic masterpiece that lay before her eyes.

With the serenity of the morning seeping into her soul, she finally tore herself away from the view and made her way to the bathroom. The steaming cascade of the shower's waters enveloped her in a warm embrace, washing away the remnants of a restless night and leaving her refreshed and invigorated.

Emerging from her personal sanctuary, Mila was the epitome of casual yet chic, clad in beige leggings accentuating her lithe figure, fur-lined boots exuding a touch of luxury, and a cream sweater paired with a snug brown vest. Her hair was artfully gathered atop her head, revealing the elegant contours of her neck, while a pair of sunglasses held in her hand would add a dash of mystery to her ensemble.

As she ventured into the main foyer, bathed in the soft glow of daylight, it was as though she had stepped into an entirely different world. The space, so familiar from the previous night, now took on a fresh and vibrant appearance as the sunlight saturated the vast interior, revealing new details and nuances that had been hidden in the shadows. Mila was ready to embrace the day ahead, her heart brimming with anticipation for the adventures awaiting in the luminous embrace of the sun and to meet the man who made her heart flutter at the mere thought of seeing him.

As she passed the foyer, she looked into the living room where she had spent so much time with Damian the night before. The room appeared far larger with the sun coming in. She turned to see the grandfather clock and scowled once again as the chime hit at 7 AM, startling her for the 3rd time in 12 hours. She walked into the spacious kitchen as an elderly woman had prepared a myriad of breakfast items ranging from fruit to toast, eggs, and even waffles.

The woman looked up, and Mila entered the kitchen and smiled, "Hello, young lady, my name is Helen. I kind of look after the Senator. Keep him sharp," she said with a wink, "Grab whatever you would like in front of you. The Senator is on the terrace. Can I get you a coffee or hot tea?"

Mila smiled back, "Hello and good morning, Helen. I'm Mila, and yes, hot tea sounds wonderful. English Blend with mint, if you have it?" "I do," was the reply, "I'll bring it out to you. The Senator is sitting outside already, and do not worry, dear, the view is spectacular and heated out there. Go enjoy it. It's really quite pleasant." "Thank you, Helen." As she grabbed a few breakfast items and walked outside.

Damian immediately stood and walked over, "Good morning," taking the items from her and placing them on the table as he pulled her chair out and got her situated. Mila looked at him, and her butterflies fluttered as soon as he sat down. Trying to keep it together, she said, "The view here is absolutely mesmerizing, Damian. It honestly takes my breath away." She was referring more to him than the view, but he seemingly took the bait. Damian smiled at hearing her comment and replied, "That is the intention, Mila," as they both laughed at the obviousness of it. "Touché," she simply replied.

Helen brought her tea and winked, then nodded before leaving them to their privacy as they laughed and teased over the various topics they enjoyed the night before. The hour was approaching 8 AM when she said, "I have a confession, Damian. You had me in quite a tizzy when you left me last night." He sheepishly looked at her and shook his head, "Well then, I'm glad I wasn't the only one. I had to get out of there before I did something I regretted. . . ." She interrupted and said, "Would it have been so bad?" His eyes opened wide, and he was about to say something when a loud roar of a jet engine only a few hundred feet above them broke the silence and frightened them both as they heard the reverberation of the helicopter before seeing the large Eurocopter pass over the roof and continue over the back yard. They observed in awe as the sleek aircraft, outfitted in all black but with a gray underbelly, dominated their view. The aircraft came low to the ground, impressively coming to a hover in an awesome acrobatic display, quickly moved sideways, finally rotating while still accelerating, displaying the expert abilities and talents of the pilot operating the aircraft.

After 90 seconds of exciting virtuosities, the aircraft came to a hover, facing the couple as it slowly descended until the skids softly landed with a perfect touchdown. The rotors began to slow, and the noise softened to subtle swishing as Mila looked at Damian. He looked back at her, "I present the impressive piloting talents of the remarkable. . . . *Sebastian Storm.*"

Mila looked at Damian, having heard the name Sebastian Storm in circles before but never having met. The stories were vast, from official accountings of his bravery and patriotism to the lesser-known tales of the countless times the man had pulled the fate of the United States from the shackles of despair. She was unsure of which were true or which were exaggerated, but the man's reputation proceeded him more, in fact than even Damian's famous father. "You know Sebastian Storm, Damian?" She asked as he laughed, "As a matter of fact, I do. Here, I'll introduce you to him. But judging from the look on your face, Mila, please don't be awestruck; he is less than interested in starry-eyed groupies." She hit him in the arm when he mentioned the quip, and they both began to walk down the stairs toward him. Sebastian stepped out of the cockpit as the blades slowed to a steady turn.

When within twenty feet, Damian smiled at Sebastian, "An impressive entrance, Sebastian. You trumped my beautiful view with your display of impressive rotary acrobatics." Sebastian laughed as they came together, "Just wanted to make sure you two were up. You probably talked this poor woman's ear off for hours last night."

They both looked at one another, perplexed by how he would know as if he was omnipotent, thought Mila. Sebastian shook Damian's hand before turning to Mila, "And you must be the lovely Mila Dmitri. It's an honor to meet you, Ms. Dmitri," as he took her hand and slightly bowed, making her blush slightly, hoping they wouldn't notice as a result of the cold, crisp air biting their skin.

"Please call me Mila, Mr. Storm; believe me, the honor is all mine. From what I know, the country will never be able to repay the debt you have served and sacrificed over the years." He nodded in appreciation and waved it off; however, he never accepted praise well. Damian quickly took the reins and followed up with, "Sebastian, to what do we owe the pleasure?"

"I was on my way back to my place in Montana, and I thought I would stop by and take you two on a little helicopter ride to see this mountain range from a slightly different perspective?" Mila's eyes lit up as she loved new adventures, and this would make the perfect morning. She quickly nodded with enthusiasm as Damian answered for both of them, "We are in, Sebastian."

They all filed into the helicopter, Damian giving Mila the front left seat as Sebastian took the pilot's seat in the front right, and before they knew it, the rotors were in full rotation as Sebastian spoke to his passengers through the headsets provided to them. Aviator sunglasses on, Sebastian looked to his right, then to his left, slowly lifted the helicopter to a five-foot hover, and said over the mic, "This is flat ground, so I'm going to get some airspeed, and it may make your heart race a bit, but it will get better in a moment, I promise."

Exactly as he described, he began tilting the cyclic forward as he pulled up the collective, and the helicopter began creeping forward until it got to 30 MPH, accelerating up to 100 MPH in under ten seconds. The sensation was riveting as the ground was only feet below as the helicopter expertly skimmed over the surface with the sensation of the skids sliding over the snow. Once he hit 110 MPH, he pulled up on the cyclic, and the helicopter immediately began accelerating upward. The sensation was like being on a rollercoaster, and Mila and Damian embraced the experience to the fullest.

The helicopter scaled the Grand Tetons at just under 14,000 feet within a few minutes. Sebastian got on the mic, "The Grand Tetons from only a few feet away. Few people have ever been this close," as the snowcapped terrain blurred by only feet below them. He trailed over the ridge for a few minutes before tipping over the summit and descended quickly to give his passengers the ultimate experience and most unique helicopter ride they would ever encounter.

———

He brought them to where they had taken off 30 minutes before as he softly landed the helicopter and turned, "Senator, I am going to let you off here, and Mila, it was a pleasure to meet you. Mind the tail rotor when you get out. Only walk toward the front of the helicopter, in the direction of the stairs." They both hopped out of the aircraft and proceeded as instructed. Once they were at the stairs, they waved to Sebastian, and he saluted back. Then, in a whipping fashion, he took off the same way he had before, but this time going backward until he reached the desired speed, then flipped it sideways for a moment before heading forward in an awesome display of piloting and control. After 60 seconds, he was over the ridge and disappeared. Sebastian headed back to his place in Montana, a 90-minute flight by helicopter.

Mila so enjoyed the moment but also wondered why one of the United States' most famous Anti-terrorist agents was at the West estate to begin with. It all appeared a little too coincidental.

She looked at Damian West as they ascended the stairs and thought about all the mystery surrounding this man. She knew she had not even scratched the surface of who he was or the plan he had put into motion.

They spent most of the day visiting the sights in downtown Jackson Hole before ending the day at the Blue Lion, where Damian had made reservations. It was an early dinner, and both were dressed casually as they walked through the front door, greeted by the maître D', Angus Parman. Angus was delighted to see the Senator, "Good evening, Senator West and ma'am. I was so happy to see your reservation, Sir." Angus proceeded to escort the couple to a tucked away corner towards the back of the restaurant. They took a seat somewhat secluded from the rest of the patrons.

"Today was amazing, Damian. You showed me so much," she said as she smiled and instinctively grabbed his hand over the excitement. Realizing it might be a presumptuous gesture, she squeezed his hand, however, began to pull away as he held her hand, holding it firmly, liking the physical touch. She smiled as they teased one another until the waiter came by, asking them what they would like to drink. Looking at the list, Damian found a selection and turned to Mila, "The 2013 Cabernet Sauvignon by Pernod Ricard Winemakers out of Australia? What do you think, Mila?" She squeezed his hand and simply nodded as he confirmed their selection with the waiter.

They talked for a time as the wine arrived and poured before them, enjoying their first sample and impressed with the vintage and year. Her inquisitive mind always working, "So Sebastian Storm. He seems an interesting friend to have and seemingly so close to you. You both operate in vastly different governmental capacities. I'm curious how you met," testing the waters as Damian looked deep into her eyes curious her angle on the question but played along. "I've not known him for a long time, but he has been close to my father for some time and, understandably, how we met. They work together on some super-secret spy operations. My father thought it best we get more acquainted after replacing him in the Senate and I am now part of a subcommittee that uses Sebastian's . . . er, *talents* from time to time. I have to admit that Sebastian offers a unique perspective on several fronts, but I genuinely like the man and appreciate the integrity and honesty he brings to any environment. He is cunning and extremely intelligent and a master at interpreting. *. . . people and situations alike."*

Mila's keen intellect never ceased probing, and she pondered the intriguing dynamics between the two men. Their connection had an unspoken complexity, a tale lurking beneath the surface, begging to be unveiled. Yet, she was no stranger to the art of discretion and knew better than to pry too deeply into matters not freely offered. She decided to steer the conversation in a different direction, her curiosity still simmering beneath the surface.

Her voice, laced with a subtle blend of charm and intrigue, ventured into the realm of Senator West's personal life. "Fair enough. And your dating history, Senator West," she began, a knowing glint in her eyes, "could you enlighten me on why the most eligible bachelor in the room hasn't yet found the perfect woman?"

Her words hung in the air, a playful challenge daring him to share a glimpse of his inner world. It was a question that touched upon his personal desires and aspirations, a subject revealing more layers of the enigmatic man before her. As Mila observed his reaction with a knowing smile, she was prepared for whatever revelations the charismatic Senator might choose to divulge.

He looked at her intently and softly said, "Maybe I already have found her, Mila . . . ." With a wink, he took another sip of the Pernod Ricard Cabernet. She laughed at the comment, "You are quite the mystery and charmer, Damian. And yes! You just may have met her; don't let her go," as she squeezed his hand, "So, tell me, Senator, tell me about your past relationships. They can't be easy, being in the public eye and with so many people watching and scrutinizing your every move, but then again, the public loves a politician with a traditional mindset. Wife, kids, the white picket fence. You know, all the mumbo jumbo. Doesn't it hurt you, politically, not being in a relationship or even married?"

He nodded, "It does actually, and probably one of the weakest attributes I appear to be burdened with. An albatross I seem to be carrying around my neck concerning my personal life. I was in a relationship for seven years. Wonderful woman but would have never dealt well with the challenges I face with my professional responsibilities. It takes a special partner to see the value of what I do and is willing to adapt to being in a second position sometimes. I don't like it, but I did sign up for it, so I have to accept its personal limitations and sacrifices. She deserved more, primarily in time, and my efforts appeared to fall far short of her expectation." The failure of the relationship visibly saddened Damian. She suspected he hadn't experienced many setbacks in his life, but that relationship suffered because of him and his failure to save it and provide her with what she needed from him.

He smiled and steered the conversation back toward her, "Now you, Ms. Dmitri, what of your past relationships? I'm sure with your line of work, you must have little time for personal endeavors?" She smiled, "Oh, I can make time if the individual is worth the sacrifice, but none have been thus far, Damian." Her honesty was true and unfaltering, "I have had my fair share of trysts in the past, but few, if any, have ever held my interest for more than a few months. I suppose I'm rather picky."

"I see. So, have you ever been in love, Mila?" She thought for a moment. Damian's question hung in the air, a subtle inquiry into the depths of Mila's heart. She pondered it for several seconds, a suitable response eluding her as her gaze locked with his, weighing her response. She was slightly embarrassed in her response, "I'm not entirely sure," she admitted, her tone thoughtful. "*Love . . . to me, is marked by an unwavering desire to be with someone, to think of them constantly, or at the very least, for them to occupy most of your thoughts. Personally, I've never experienced that kind of consuming love. How about you?*"

Her question, delivered with a hint of playfulness, caught Damian off guard. He considered her query, his mind retracing the contours of his own experiences. "I thought I might have been in love once," he confessed, the words carrying a touch of vulnerability as he looked up slightly, reminiscing of a time long ago. "With Natalia, my longest relationship. I loved her, certainly, but I can't say I was truly *in love with her*. I don't believe I would have let her slip away if I had been. I concur with your perspective, Mila; love should encompass a ceaseless consideration of the other person. If your thoughts aren't consistently filled with them, perhaps it wasn't the love we often romanticize it to be."

Sensing a connection surpassing mere words, Mila reached out and gently took Damian's hand in her own, her touch a silent affirmation of their shared understanding and deeper connection. They continued their conversation, delving into the complexities of modern relationships, challenges and where the pressures of contemporary familial obligations intertwined with the trials testing the endurance of love in a rapidly changing world.

Their exchange was a dance of intellect and emotions, a vibrant exploration of the intricate tapestry of human connection. In each other's company, they found a depth of understanding transcending the ordinary, drawing them closer and forging a bond that promised to navigate the complexities of the modern age with grace and authenticity.

Damian turned serious for a moment, "I have to ask only one more question of you because I am so curious, Mila." She wasn't sure what road he was taking but curious what his question was, at the very least, "Ask away, Prince Charming. . . ." He smiled before continuing, "What is Anthony Voss planning to do with the Dymitron? Are the rumors true about him possibly relocating its headquarters overseas?"

She smiled at his question, inwardly pondering her response, "You know I adore you more than anything, Senator, but that request is laden with deep-seated, insider information and on a very, very private need-to-know basis. I could never discuss the specifics as much as I would love to. Of course, you must know, I am sworn to secrecy?" To push and tease a little further, "I would be willing to consider discussing a small shred of information with you if only you discussed with me why you had a visit, presumably earlier yesterday, with our helicopter pilot this morning. I imagine a man like him rarely makes house calls unless it's for important reasons."

She had him dead to rights in his equally valued secret of Sebastian Storm's true reason for visiting the estate. They were at a stalemate, and it was pointless to continue, and any tension between them was of no interest to him while they enjoyed their evening.

"Looks like we both have a few valuable secrets tucked away, my dear. Let's agree to leave it behind us. . . at least for the time being?" She grabbed his hands once again, "Agreed. Take me home . . . . *Senator*," Damian West's eyes lit up.

Damian was captivated by her intelligence, wit, and spunk. Mila was a driven woman and germane in every aspect of her life, seemingly except for her romantic history. That part appeared to elude her, but Damian couldn't fault her in that aspect as he was experiencing the same fate in his own historic romantic chronicles.

She enjoyed their chemistry and connection, was eager for the next chapter to begin with him, and wondered where it would lead. He captivated her, enthralled, and stimulated her. She felt a sense of sadness as they left the restaurant, realizing she would be leaving the following day.

Agent Lee opened the door of the black SUV and loaded them in, closing the door behind them. Sebastian looked at her, "I'm ready to slip into something more comfortable," she liked his thinking and anxiously nodded her head like a young girl. Once home, Damian opened the door of the SUV and gave Agent Lee a "Good night" as they filed into the front door, cold from the outside, knocking the snow off their shoes as he closed the front door. "It's so cold tonight," shivered Mila, sparking a thought with Damian.

Damian turned to Mila, "I have an idea," he grabbed her hand and walked out to the back deck where they had been the night before and that morning. Another clear night as the moon shone again, reflecting off the snowcapped terrain and mountainside.

Once again, she was mesmerized by the image, fixated on its beauty, almost in a trance as the imagery and magnificence pulled her in. She was startled by a soft thud in the back of her vest as she looked to her right and saw Damian throwing snowballs at her like a schoolboy. She squatted down, grabbed snow of her own, balled it up, and hurled it at Damian, missing wide as another snowball lightly hit her in the thigh. Her frustration becomes apparent as she misses time after time; coming closer to one another, she finally lands one on his arm as he laughs, gently grabbing her and pulling her to him.

As the tension between them reached its zenith, Damian couldn't resist the magnetic pull any longer. His fingers slid to the back of Mila's neck, his touch commanding and possessive. In response, she yielded willingly, her body instinctively gravitating towards him, a silent confession of her desires.

Their proximity intensified, her breaths becoming shallow and rapid, her heart pounding with an exhilarating mixture of anticipation and longing. Mila leaned into Damian, her chest pressed against his, her gaze locked onto him with an unspoken yearning.

The moment hung in the air like a charged current, the world around them fading into obscurity. Damian's lips brushed tantalizingly against hers, igniting a spark reverberating through their souls. A surge of heat and passion coursed between them, their mouths melding in a fervent kiss, deepening with each passing second.

Mila welcomed the damp warmth of his breath mingling with her own, a heady concoction sending shivers of delight down her spine. Their tongues danced in an intimate tango, a symphony of desire leaving them both intoxicated by the intensity of their connection.

In the timeless moment, neither of them wanted it to end. Their passion was a roaring fire, a conflagration of desire consuming them both. The pleasure of their union was electric, a fusion of bodies and souls that defied words. It was a sensation begging to endure, an insatiable hunger that craved the sheer bliss of their connection.

Finally, their lips parted, leaving the taste of one another lingering as Damian delicately licked his lips. Mila's gaze drifted momentarily to the right, her smile radiant with satisfaction and a hint of mischief. Then, as her eyes returned to Damian, she conveyed a promise of more to come, an unspoken agreement their passionate encounter was far from over.

"You know what I'm in the mood for, Damian?" The mysterious question potentially had a myriad of various answers as they swirled in his mind, seizing his tongue, not even being able to muster a simple answer. She turns again to her right, "Let's get in the hot tub right now," as he also turns to look at the steam rising from the large hole in the ground, beckoning them to immerse themselves. His conservativeness comes out, "Well, I would, but we don't have suits, Mila . . ."

"Fuck the suits as well as the formalities, Damian, don't disappoint me," Mila breathed in the sultry challenge, her voice a sensuous caress that hung in the air, laden with irresistible allure. A knowing smile curled on Damian's lips; the die had been cast, and there was no turning back. There was no way he would allow her to be disappointed in any form.

Mila's fingers interlaced with his as if they were carefree teenagers, guiding him with an electrifying anticipation toward the spa's edge. She stepped backward, standing just a few feet away, a portrait of seduction as her lingering gaze met his.

With deliberate slowness, Mila's fingers traced the zipper of her vest, unveiling the treasures beneath as she smiled at him, seducing him, catering to his carnal desires. Damian, equally undaunted, shed his light jacket, his eyes locked onto Mila's with an intensity that could set the night on fire.

The act of divesting themselves of their garments became a mesmerizing dance. Each layer was slowly removed, a teasing revelation. Damian stood, clad only in a tee shirt and pants, his physique a testament to desire. Mila, dressed in leggings and a bra leaving little to the imagination, exuded a magnetic allure holding Damian spellbound.

In synchronicity, they cast aside their boots and peeled off their socks, their feet grazing the cool stone surrounding the spa, a tactile reminder of their brazen adventure. A moment of hesitation hung in the air, both of them locked in a rapturous exchange, their gazes unwavering.

Then, with an erotic flourish, Mila unbuttoned her bra without hesitation, exposing herself to Damian's unrelenting gaze. Her erect nipples bore testament to her desire, and she reveled in the tantalizing thrill of being watched as she slowly eased down her leggings, revealing a daring secret – the absence of panties, a detail that did not escape Damian's hungry attention.

In response, Damian shed his remaining inhibitions, unbuttoning his cargo pants and guiding them down along with his boxers, matching her earlier initiative. They both stood naked, stripped bare in every sense, their desire palpable and intense.

In a silent pact of mutual surrender, they retrieved their discarded clothing and placed them on a nearby chair. It was a declaration of their willing adventurousness, eagerly stepping into the intoxicating unknown. They studied each other with hungry anticipation, the air charged with an unquenchable desire, welcoming the threat of setting their world ablaze.

Her figure is exquisite and toned. Years of attention in maintaining both mind and body. Her long, toned legs capture his eye along with her small waist and full hips framing her mons, bare and glistening in the moonlight.

He was far from a typical Congressman, far from sedentary, gluttonous, greedy, or lustful. Damian was quite the antithesis, being lithe and sculpted like an athlete and lean with a stomach displaying the strength of his core. He was trimmed and beautiful, and she enjoyed watching the effect she was having on him looking downward.

She walks over to him, seemingly shorter even without her boots, and enjoys his smooth, trimmed chest, absent any gray hair to speak of despite the daily stresses the man must endure. He again pulls her to him, their skin touching, almost electric as their skin contact, but his warmth is intoxicating as he connects with her still more, their combined energy matched.

Then, the kiss eclipsed all others. It was intimate and passionate but, most of all, genuine and sincere as she put her arms around him, not wanting their kiss to end. She notes the chill at her back, forgetting for a fleeting moment they are both without a stitch of clothing in the freezing cold enveloping them.

As if he's reading her mind, he lifts her as her legs open to straddle him, skin to skin, erotic in its form. His hands move to the underside of her thighs to support her as he steps down the three steps into the steamy waiting water below. She holds his gaze the entire time, trusting his and enjoying their bodies so close and intimate. She had envisioned this moment before she ever met him, but she would never tell him of her ongoing fantasies. Those secrets were for her only to know. Yet, her dreams were now becoming her reality.

He gracefully descends into the steaming water, the contrast biting with the frigid exterior temperature intensifying the vigorous experience awaiting him. Each step led him closer to the final destination within the scalding embrace of the bath below his feet. As he settles in, the hot water envelops his cold skin, creating a breathtaking sensation of both pleasure and pain.

The heat of the water searing their cold skin is an exhilarating prelude to their electrifying connection. Bodies intertwined, skin against skin, their very essence charged with an undeniable electricity. She takes control, straddling him, drawing him further into the whirlwind of passion engulfing them as they descend into the water.

His lips meet the delicate curve of her neck, planting fiery kisses as she gently rubs her pelvis against his, a slow, sensual dance of desire. Her longing is palpable, a desperate yearning for him to be inside her, yet she hungers to savor this moment, to let their natural rhythm unfold at its own pace. Her impatience, a familiar foe in the past, has no place here. This time, she yearns for something different, something unique with Damian.

Mila's heart aches to cast caution to the side, to rewrite the story defining her historical encounters with the countless, faceless men peppering her past. She craves a passionate narrative, an experience beyond the ordinary, mundane ritual haunting her for years.

His hands drift to her firm rear as she smiles at him, enjoying how he touches her and knowing he will not be disappointed once he explores every unknown part of her. She craved his loins being aroused for her, growing as it throbbed between her thighs, almost torturing her, driving her senseless with anticipation. Their lips continue to brush the skin of the other in various ways. His tongue laps over her neck as she arches her back, inviting him to lick her breasts. Her nipples are erect as his tongue laps over her areola, then the nipples themselves. Holding the back of his head, she pulls him ever so slightly toward her, wanting him to savor every part of her. Their passion grows as his hand drifts to her inner thigh, finding her outer folds as he begins to feel her wetness even within the warm water; he senses her excitement growing within.

She puts both hands on his face, kisses him, and whispers in his ear, "I want you, Damian, but not here; take me to your room. "I thought you'd never ask," was his response as she stood up, her beautiful mound directly in front of him. As she looked down and winked, offering her hand as he stood up as well. They both stepped out of the spa, grabbing two towels from the heated box adjacent to the bar, and she welcomed the warm towel as he draped it over her and then himself, tying it to his midsection. She started for the door as he grabbed their clothes and was right behind her, eager to escape the biting cold.

Damian grabbed her hand, realizing she didn't know where she was going. She followed him up the stairs and down the long hall to his bedroom behind the French doors. He laid their clothing on the side chair in front of the fire as they entered the room, dimly lit with the largest stone fireplaces she had ever seen situated in front of the bed. As if reading her mind, he attempted to explain, "I really like fireplaces, Mila," as she laughed, "I can tell there is no shortage of them in this home." She looked at him, "Come with me. . ." As she led him to the large bathroom and turned on the shower. It heated up quickly as she wanted the chlorine rinsed off her, always having an aversion to the sterile smell of chlorine.

They dropped their towels and slipped inside the expansive shower as he pushed her against the glass, immediately kissing her and drawing her in closer to him. The water fell over their bodies as she grabbed the soap, lathering him up as he did the same to her. They massage one another sensually, not missing a spot, then rinsed as she backs up, pulling him from the shower, looking at him up and down as he does with her.

He grabs a towel and begins drying her off from behind. The tips of her hair are wet as he dries her, followed by her neck, and finally down her back and legs as she turns, and he towels her as he moves upward, getting her arms and breasts. She focuses on his eyes as he slowly covers every inch of her body. Taking the towel from him, she begins to dry his chest, holding his gaze as she moves to his arms, slowly begins to squat, getting each leg and enjoying watching his manhood rise to the occasion as she stands up and kisses him while rising up on her toes as the towel falls to the floor. Her right hand gently encircles him, enjoying his erection within her hand as she gently strokes him while maintaining their sensual kiss.

Damian can't wait any longer as he grabs her hand and leads her out of the bathroom to the bedroom, stopping in front of the fireplace. She accepts the warmth from the fire and equally as much from Damian's body heat; both give her a strong sense of serenity and pleasure.

"I'm so glad you decided to come this weekend," as his hands slowly stroke her neck, and she smiles while looking up at the handsome Senator, "I'm glad the Van Lustbader book could wait. . ." He pulls her upward and kissed her, stopping her words, taking in her scent, and enjoying the softness of her kiss as well as her skin against his.

He slowly eased her backward until the back of her thighs came into contact with the bed as they continued to kiss one another. He gently lifted her onto the bed and eased her to the middle, hovering over the top of her.

He begins to caress her neck and moves to her breasts; his tongue brushes her nipples as she instinctively opens her legs for him, inviting him to enjoy her very essence. He moves lower to her stomach, appreciating her toned features. Mila closes her eyes as she enjoys his attention to every detail, using his tongue to take her to a place of immense pleasure. He hits her spot with precision, bringing out her womanly urges to the verge of exploding, but he eases off slightly, driving her to the point of ecstasy once again. She is fighting to stay in control, but she can sense he is enjoying the effect he is having on her until he, too, grips her thighs firmly this final time around. She is unable to hold back as her orgasm reaches its peak. She arches her back, accepting the muscle spasms take over and drive her to the breaking point, losing control. He lightens up with his tongue, not wanting to stop but also not wanting to overstimulate her either. The perfect combination of his touch brings her orgasm to an erotic and sensual completion as she thinks to herself no one has ever brought out her womanliness until that moment, and she already knew it would not be the last with Damian. She intended to seek far more from him in the future.

He slowly begins to ascend to her stomach once again, her breast before giving her nipples a slight nibble before coming to her lips once again and kissing her. She could taste her own arousing fluids on his lips, which excited her even more. In addition, she was reminded of his hardness upon her inner thigh. She wanted so badly to take him, all of him, but she wasn't ready to accept all of his manliness just yet.

Mila's fantasies had been brewing long before this auspicious evening. A potent cocktail of desire and anticipation had steadily consumed her thoughts well before she met Damian. The relentless yearning to taste him within her mouth had become an irresistible craving, and she was determined to quench the thirst before allowing any further indulgence. It wasn't just about her own satisfaction; it was about showcasing her abilities, revealing her prowess in fulfilling his deepest impulses. She desired to be everything to him. This was a crucial aspect of their connection, a testament to her desire to take control and leave an indelible mark on his yearnings.

With a slow, deliberate movement, Mila pushed him gently to one side, her body rolling with his until she found herself straddling him. Atop him, she gazed deeply into his eyes, her own brimming with intensity and longing. The anticipation between them crackled in the air, an unspoken promise of passion and intimacy.

Their lips met in a kiss that transcended the ordinary, a kiss delving into the depths of their desires. It was a connection that conveyed a multitude of unspoken messages: longing, lust, vulnerability, and trust. As their mouths melded together, they became lost in a world of sensation and connection, each touch igniting the flames of their shared desire.

Mila was determined to make this moment unforgettable, to imprint herself upon his memory in a way that would resonate for a lifetime. Their union was a symphony of passion, a dance of bodies and souls, and Mila was ready to lead the way with a combination of intelligence, sensuality, and a profound understanding of both of their desires.

As she eased down between his legs, she took both hands and encircled his member, slowly stroking up and down and enjoying his breadth and length as her tongue grazed his tip, stimulating him before she took him between her lips completely. She softly strokes as she savors his tip, enjoying him grow even larger, verifying his satisfaction with her skills and the effects it is having upon him. His hand rests gently on her head as she looks up at him, loving the image before her as all she can think about is him ultimately inside of her.

Faster, then slower, her cadence fluctuating so as to not allow him to commence his orgasm too quickly, disappointing both of them if he did. She begins to fantasize about him deep within her when she knows he may not be able to hold on to it any longer. She could tell he was getting closer as he let out a slight groan, and she began to slow her rhythm further. She continues to stroke him as she moves her body upward, kissing his neck, followed by his lips for a moment, continuing to stimulate him as he whispers, "I want you inside me, Damian." His eyes light up at the mere suggestion as she begins to straddle him. She holds his focus intently as she teases his tip within her hips and folds, saturates him with her natural lubricant, and takes him in just a little deeper.

His hands drift to her hips as he pulls her closer, selfishly wanting to slide deeper within her as now, she groans as her womanliness accepts all of him. Moving her hips back and forth slowly in a gyrating motion, she stimulates him in a way he hasn't experienced before. She finds the perfect spot as her skin flushes in how perfect he feels within her.

Flawless in their harmony and beat. Immediately stimulating her spot to the point of initiating a succeeding orgasm as she shudders again as she tightens around him and continues to stimulate Damian focusing on him now and murmurs, "Give it to me, Damian, give me all of it. . ." As if freeing him, he releases it all as she puts her hand upon his chest, accepting all of him inside of her as she leans over and kisses him again, sliding him as deep as he can go.

She sits back up, with him still inside of her, as she turns, facing away from him in one failed swoop, grabbing his hips as she rolls over on her side, pulling him with her as he spoons her from behind, still remaining deep within her feminine folds. Mila's intention all along. Gently grabbing his arm, she pulls it around her, reaches for the cover, and squeezes his arm as his body completely engulfs her.

———

He smiles to himself, noting her need to have everything just right. Facing away from him, she whispers, "You were amazing, Damian." "As was you, Mila . . . . " as she abruptly, though methodically, disrupts their unruffled position and turns toward him as their faces are now only inches apart. "I haven't ever met anyone like you before, I don't know what to think of it . . . . Senator." They laugh at the comment, "Is that all bad, Mila? Sometimes, the unknown can be rather exciting and electric." A wry smirk comes over her face, "Just what a mystery man would say, but I have my mysteries as well, so be forewarned, Senator. "You really need to stop calling me that," he sneers, then tickles her under the sheets as he leans in and touches her lips and kisses them. Just a simple kiss would excite him, and she knew he was enamored with her as much as she was enchanted by him.

Their lips touched, savoring one another's warm breath as her hand drifted, locating her target, happy he was again aroused for her. "I don't think he is ready to go to sleep just yet," as she eased under the covers. Damian turned on his back, looking up at the ceiling and watching the dancing lights from the fire. He enjoyed the warmth of her mouth engulfing him as he shook his head, "What was this woman doing to him," was his only thought as he quickly succumbed to her stimulation and was quite certain neither one of them would get much sleep that night.

And he was more than content with that notion.

Chapter 10

Their Work Begins

"The will of the people is the best law."
~Ulysses S. Grant

Jackson Hole, Wyoming
2021 December
Flight to Washington D.C.

"You appear a little distracted this morning, Damian," his father asked, an hour into their flight from Jackson Hole to Washington D.C.

"I suppose I am for a few reasons, but I will pull it together, I always do," smiling at his father. The senior Senator knew his son well and was aware when he was skirting his questions. Sam West was far too intelligent for such tactics, "Spill it, boy. I've been through all of it and more, Damian, you can't shock me. What's on your mind?" Damian laughed; he never got anything past his father.

He was far too crafty and perceptive to accept anything from Damian at face value. There was always more to the story.

"Honestly, two things, Dad. The first is the pressure to enroll the people as supporters of the party we have selected for our list. Despite my confidence in what we are attempting, if we fail, we will be hung out to dry, and that reality is first and foremost for me. I know we have considered every angle, but the downside is our political suicide. I would imagine my career will be forfeited."

Sam West considered his son's concern, "There is no question you are correct, Damian. Your young career would be, most likely, sacrificed, and mine . . . well, let's just say that all I have worked for, and my legacy would all be for naught. We would both suffer greatly but the reward is colossal. The difference is my clock is running out as I am not getting any younger and I'd have little time in which to endure my social sentencing. You, on the other hand, Damian, would have your entire lifetime to live with the political scrutiny of this endeavor, and that alone is an enormously heavy price to bear. Ultimately, you have the most to lose. You aren't having reservations about this, are you?"

Damian paused, the weight of his father's words settling upon him like a heavy mantle of responsibility. Each syllable carried the echo of decades of shared dreams and aspirations, of a legacy that intertwined their destinies. He felt the gravity of his father's trust, a trust not only in him as a son but as a bearer of their shared vision for a better future.

His mind danced with the intricacies of his father's conviction, parsing each layer of meaning behind the words spoken. It wasn't only about the present moment, but a culmination of years of shaping and molding, a testament to the intricate dance between mentor and protege . . . . *father and son.*

As he contemplated his response, Damian couldn't help but reflect on the journey that had brought them to this pivotal juncture. From the tender age of ten, when his father had first whispered of possibilities beyond the ordinary, to the present, where the weight of their collective ambitions rested upon his shoulders.

The notion of being the catalyst for change, the driving force behind the realization of their shared dreams, stirred something deep within Damian's soul. It was a reminder of the immense power he held, not only as an individual but as a vessel for the hopes and aspirations of generations past, present and future.

His father's words resonated with a profound truth, an acknowledgment of Damian's unique blend of resilience and insight, qualities instilled in him by his mother's gentle guidance and his father's unwavering determination.

With a sense of purpose renewed, Damian met his father's gaze, a silent promise and confidence etched in the depths of his eyes. It was a pledge to honor the legacy they had built together, to wield the tools bestowed upon him with wisdom and grace.

As Damian was about to respond, his father added, "However, that said, if anyone else were my son, I would have not the confidence to take this risk, Damian. You, alone, are the catalyst that has brought this notion to fruition. If you were any less of a man, any less of a . . . . *force*, I would never have introduced this possibility, and my dream for the future would be lost to a memory and a hope of something better. Hell, you were only a boy, ten years old at most at the time when I began discussing the idea of an emerging third party. But you, son, have breathed new life into the fragileness of what might be. It was a lot to lay on you, but even then, I was certain you would be something special. Unique in the ways of the world and the understanding of what would make this country grand, once again. Those qualities, thank God, you got from your mother. I simply molded you into the presence you have become. You always had all the tools, I simply showed you how to use them."

"Always a King maker, but never the King . . . ." replied *Damian, the phrase he mentioned so many years before,* and his father smiled remembering the moment, "Exactly, son . . . *exactly.* I'm a King maker; I was never meant to be anything more than that. Our combination is what gives us the chance to see all of this work and potentially change the scope of American politics. Anything

less from either of us, and we would have never been given the opportunity to pull it off."

Sam looked at his son and realized he needed some encouragement, ". . . . And pull it off we will, Damian. Yes, we will. There is also another component in all of this I have yet to reveal, and when I do, the picture will become far clearer to you. And that, I can promise, son. Give me a few days and the clarity will come for you and everything we are doing."

"Fair enough, Dad. I know, with certainty, we can achieve something great, and you are correct; we are a package deal." Sam West patted his son on the back, "And the second thing on your mind?"

"*A girl . . .*" replied Damian.

"Oh fuck, well that is a problem then, and I can't help you with that one, whatsoever. Good luck," they both laughed, knowing there was probably some truth in the statement.

Washington D.C
2021 December
Regina Alvarado, Speaker of The House's Office

"We need this one, Damian. Let me start with her, then you come in with the charm," as they sat within the waiting room of *third* most powerful person in the United States, the Speaker of the House, Regina Alvarado. He was certain this meeting had a far greater significance than Damian was aware but wanted his true agenda to play out naturally in the coming meeting. This day would be the day that started it all. He was more interested in Damian's reaction to the meeting than the meeting itself, for he knew why they were both there, but Damian did not.

Regina Alvarado had earned her spot at the table over the years. Beginning her career in politics lobbying hard against the NRA (National Rifle Association) after her older teenage brother and father were killed in a home invasion in Memphis, Tennessee in 1972. After a few years, she set her sights higher, winning the Republican State Representative seat in Tennessee, and retained the seat ever since, remaining loyal to the great state of Tennessee where she had lived most of her life.

She stood as a defender of justice, a beacon of hope amidst the tumultuous currents of political intrigue and power struggles that made up the American political fabric. Her commitment to the greater good transcended personal ambitions or desires, her heart beating in rhythm with the pulse of the nation she swore to serve and protect. Unfettered by the conventional trappings of domesticity, she found solace in the relentless pursuit of righteousness, her unwavering dedication earning her the title of their guardian, their champion.

For decades, she had stood as a sentinel against the encroaching shadows of corruption and injustice, her resolve unyielding, her spirit indomitable. The halls of Congress echoed with the resounding reverberations of her impassioned pleas, her voice a clarion call for change, for progress, for the realization of the collective aspirations of those she represented.

Yet, amidst the clamor of political machinations and the ceaseless demands of her duties, she remained solitary, an exemplary figure standing against the tide of compromise and betrayal. Her heart belonged not to the fleeting promises of traditional romance or familial bonds but to the noble cause she had pledged her life to uphold. No husband or heirs proved her commitment to her plight.

In the labyrinthine corridors of power, where loyalty was a commodity traded with reckless abandon, she found comfort in the steadfast friendship of Senator Sam West. He was more than a confidant; he was a pillar of strength in a world rife with treachery and deceit. Their bond, forged in the heart of adversity, surpassed the superficial alliances that crumbled at the first sign of difficulty.

Sam West was a rare breed in the cutthroat world of Washington, his integrity unblemished by the stains of duplicity and self-interest. In him, she found a kindred spirit, a soul whose steadfastness mirrored her own unwavering commitment to her principles. He appreciated her, not the color of her skin or her socioeconomic upbringing, but rather measured by her resolve and determination. Sam West loved a fighter, and Regina Alvarado was all of that and much more. Together, they formed an unbreakable alliance, a beacon of integrity amidst the murky waters of political expediency.

As the last bastions of honor in a landscape besieged by cynicism and opportunism, they stood as a testament to the enduring power of righteousness, their bond serving as a reminder that, even in the darkest of times, the light of truth would always prevail.

They were so close; in fact, it was rumored that if they found themselves on opposite sides of any pending legislation, they would bow out of the vote, stating merely a conflict of interest and simply let the Bill be voted on without their involvement. She and Sam had been close friends since her Senate debut as a State Representative in the mid-'80s, and everyone in Congress was aware of their undying loyalty to one another despite being affiliated with opposite political parties. Their relationship was constantly scrutinized for being so well aligned while maintaining conflicting political perspectives. They emulated the epitome of what the bipartisan system stood for, but the hope of that unity was long lost generations before. The Senator and Speaker's relationship was a rarity that walked the halls of Congress.

She had studied closely Damian West moving up the political chain, making a mark along his colorful journey. She helped along the way, unbeknownst to him, but her ever-watchful eye always kept close tabs on the young emerging star. She was proud of his accomplishments and his success and rightly expected it as well, for Damian West wasn't any young up-and-coming emerging luminary; he was also . . . . *Regina Alvarado's only Godson. She expected nothing less from the young man.*

Congresswoman Alvarado's personal assistant came to the reception room and requested that Senator Damian and Sam West follow her down the hall to Congresswoman Alvarado's office. They entered the large office and saw her on the phone at the far end of the lavish room. Congresswoman Alvarado put up a finger to her guests as if to apologize for the call interfering with her meeting with them, but Sam put up a hand, brushing off the inconvenience. He was more than privy to the demands of her station, it being unrelenting at times.

She ended the call, her voice commanding, "Get it done, Senator, don't half-ass on this. I need for you to get your shit together and secure the votes. Period. This should have been handled months ago." As she hung up the phone, her entire demeanor changed, seeing Sam and Damian walking toward her.

She quickly runs around her massive desk, almost in a dance, shuffling her feet as she meets them, "Here we have my oldest friend and my only Godson," as she hugs Sam West and gives an even bigger hug reserved just for Damian. He thought sure she was going to grab his cheek and shake it, but thankfully, she thought better of it.

Countless Christmas and Thanksgiving gatherings they had all shared over the years and many a late night in front of the fire with Sam and Damian at the West estate in Jackson Hole. They talked about life, the future, victories, and failures in those days, and often about American politics and its challenges and where it was heading in the future. Regina Alvarado was generally grim about the future of the United States and was always honest with the two of them. She kept a positive outlook and face for her constituents, but Sam and Damian knew her true beliefs on how she felt about where the country was heading.

She ushers them both over to her sitting area, where four chairs sit with a coffee table in the middle. Her secretary was just leaving them, having placed, juice, tea and coffee out for the group. The secretary leaves the group but props the main office door open in case the Congresswoman should need her, sitting at her desk just outside.

"Please sit down, gentleman. Sam, you and I run in the same halls for years, and barely have a chance to ever talk to you these days. I miss our weekly *Bourbon talks*." Sam West looks at her and smiles, "After you listen to what we have to say today, I'm hopeful we can start that tradition up again, Regina."

She slaps his knee, "You know I would love that. Damian, your dad here taught me about everything I know about politics and all the games associated with it." She winks at Sam, the obvious appreciation and adoration she has for the man is unquestionable. She turns to Damian, "And you should also be made aware, Damian, as you are aware, I also have two Goddaughters, but they are entitled little bitches . . . Senator's daughters. You are definitely my favorite, without question, Damian, but keep that to yourself," as she slaps his knee as well.

Damian had always cherished Regina Alvarado and idolized her influence with people around her. She had taken a more active role with Damian after his mother had passed away and he always appreciated her for that gesture. Regina was the most dominating female figure Damian had the pleasure of knowing, and he was proud to have her as one of his biggest advocates and the privilege, if not bragging rights, for calling her his Godmother.

Damian hadn't had a chance to speak as yet, "You know, Regina, I have always been proud to call you my Godmother; it's bought me a tremendous amount of clout over the years." She smiled, "Whatever I can do to help my Godson get in those little co-ed's panties, I am more than happy to be of service."

"Regina!" shouts Sam West but they all are aware Regina Alvarado was as direct as they come. Some say she coined the phrase, *straight shooter* and she didn't much care what people thought of her crass remarks. Damian's wit always sharpened, "Well of course it did, Aunt Regina," he lied, as they all laughed, and Sam West shook his head.

"Have some tea, or coffee," as Regina Alvarado stood up and walked to her office door, peered outside as they heard her say behind the door, "Hold all my calls and no interruptions. Oh, and move my meeting with Senator Howard to tomorrow. No interruptions." She ran a tight ship, and they were more than certain there wouldn't be any disruptions unless the city was under siege.

As she walked back to her seat, the air within the room appeared to change. The dynamic of the mood adorned more of an uncomfortable silence now between them, confusing Damian.

Regina Alvarado took her seat and looked at Sam West as her demeanor grew more serious. She hesitated, then acknowledged, "It's finally time, isn't it, Sam? The day has arrived. That's why you are here today. It just hit me. It has finally come?" Sam swallowed hard and nodded to his old friend, "It has, Regina. Our moment has arrived." She sat back in her chair as if she had received the gravest of news. Damian's glance bounced back and forth between them, searching for some explanation for the silence.

Regina hesitated, then slowly turned to Damian, collected herself, then cocked her head, and nodded back at Sam, considering the weight of his words as she contemplated, then paired it with a faint smile before looking back at Damian. She sat up in her chair, rigid, unwavering, as she focused on him directly, though the question was directed at his father, "You think he's ready, Sam?" Without hesitation, Sam replies, "Yes, he is Regina, he is ready . . . *and we are ready*." Damian seemed perplexed but held his composure. Then Sam turned to Damian, "It's the final part of the puzzle, Damian. The final piece I've kept from you for your entire life. . . . *until now*."

Damian looked at them both, confused to some degree at what was transpiring, before saying, "Can someone please enlighten me as to what's going on?"

The Speaker of the House, Regina Alvarado put her hand on her Godson's knee, "Are you ready, Damian . . . . . ready *to become our 47th President?* "

Washington D.C
2021 December
Métier Restaurant
Senator Ren Cosner's Office

After leaving Speaker of the House Regina Alvarado's office, Damian's mind was reeling, "I need something to eat . . . . and probably something to drink." Sam West says to the driver from the back seat of the SUV, "David, take us to the Métier Restaurant." He then turns to Damian, "We are a little early, but I know the owner there; I've arranged a private booth in the back for our meeting with Ren Cosner in an hour." A few minutes later, they arrive at the Métier.

The restaurant owner, Sagé Atherin, quietly greeted the Senators, shook hands, and ushered them into one of their private back rooms. *The Métier:* An upscale, Michelin-starred establishment offered a tasting menu in an intimate setting and secluded. Sam West had conducted a tremendous amount of business in years past at the Métier. Sam looked out over the people sitting there for lunch and wondered if many of them knew the number of laws and legislation that had been created or quashed between the walls of that establishment.

"Such a pleasure to see you, Senator West. It's been far too long," and glancing over at Damian West, "And it is a tremendous pleasure to meet you as well, the young Senator from Wyoming. I recognize you from television, Sir. I saw your speech a few weeks ago. I was most impressed with your words and sincerity and more excited to see what you will do in the coming years." Damian shook his hand again, thanked him for the kind words, and gave him the smile that was becoming a common fixture and brand of who he was becoming and for what he embraced within the tumultuous world of politics.

Looking back at Sam, "When the Senator arrives, I will announce him, Sir." "Thank you, Sagé, and for your discretion as well. It would be most appreciated if you would be so kind as to bring us a bottle of the Caymus Vineyard Special Edition from my wine locker. We will wait to order some lunch until the Senator arrives. Maybe some bread to tide us over." Sagé nodded, "My pleasure, Sir," as he dismissed himself, giving the Senators the privacy they desired. It was a large room reserved for the larger dinner crowd that would fill the restaurant several hours later. They had the time they needed to discuss the matters at hand.

"I'm still a little perplexed over the consideration of it all . . . . the thought of running for President of the United States. I would be lying if I didn't say I have thought about it; of course, I've also fantasized about it, but it's an older man's game, or so I always thought. Possibly in 2040 or 2036, but I never even considered 2024. It just seems so early to me," as Damian sat back in his seat, his mind reeling at the possibility of it all.

Sam West could read the concern on his son's face, "It is early, no question, Damian, but it's also a good time to strike and strike hard. The 2024 election will have Biden desperately defending his seat, of course, and it's hard to say who will oppose it, but DeSantis and Trump may try again depending on how Biden's administration performs in the coming years. I think 2024 will be the year to make the move, and honestly, 2028 is too far away to know who the major players will be, and I don't know if I'll be around by then, son. Lastly, I don't want to miss this for the fucking world. I've worked my entire political tenure for what will happen next."

They both laughed as Sagé returned with the bottle of Caymus, offering the nod from Damian on the pour and cork over his father as a sign of respect to the new guard. Both Damian and Sam appreciated the gesture.

After Sagé left the table, Sam explained many nuances of where the thought began. "I realize your age is a factor. I believe John F. Kennedy was the youngest elected president at 43 years of age; you would beat that by a sizable margin. To give you some scope and history, there has been a major machine at work well before you were even born, Damian. There has been a deep-seated consortium, an underground syndicate that has been vying for change, evolvement, and progression of our political framework in the last half-century. We tried to launch with a portion of our faction covertly with the Libertarian movement in the early 1970s, but it was laden with too much ideologic diversity within the party and still does today. Then, we attempted it again in the mid-1980s with the Green Party, but their focus was too specific, and the infighting and divisions within the party also inhibited their growth and potential. Political greed infected both of those emerging parties, and neither party got much steam as a result. They are ultimately just a diluted version of the democratic party and really not substantial enough to gain the momentum needed to overthrow the bipartisan mentality." He looked at Damian as his son held on to every word fascinated by his father's dialogue and explanation. Sam went on to paint the colorful history of the political undertone their focused group symbolized in the early years. It was a part of the political fabric very few people knew about and very hush hush.

Damian shook his head, "So you are saying that your group, *this consortium*, created those groups to attempt to divert focus and eventually overthrow the current bipartisan system?"

"Yes, Damian, I will no longer keep any more secrets from you. We are a very private and secretive group known as the *Alternative Consortium*. Historically, it was our solution for creating a lasting dynasty we hoped would bring us into the 21st century, but sadly, we failed that endeavor. At the time, there were 32 of us initially, all Congressmen, big business, and our biggest advocate, President Ronald Reagan. We controlled the White House and most of the influence within the walls of Congress. President Reagan was our last, great hope. The failure of the Libertarian and Green Parties to gain market share was their lack of unity. Far too much ego and drama within the parties gave way to any momentum they could muster. Humans are greedy by nature, not only in a monetary way. Greed can also come with power and influence," added Sam. Looking at his son, Damian was captivated by the story.

Sam continued, "Our plan was simple. George H. W. Bush was to get the presidential nod in 1988, following Reagan's two terms. Bush was also a member of the Alternative Consortium and held the distinction of Vice President to Reagan; he was a clear choice for us, and like 2024, it was the time to strike as Michael Dukakis was his democratic opposition and a weak candidate at best."

Sam sat back in his chair, reliving the moment like it was only the day before and shaking his head, "That spineless bastard had the presidency in his sights and locked in, and when it was time to pull the trigger, announce his running for president and unveil the heart and passion of the new Alternative Party, he folded and couldn't go through with it. He would have had the backing of the current president, who was adored by all Americans, and all of us in hiding would have gone public to support him. But sadly, he failed all of us and our system. He ended up keeping the Republican Party affiliation and won handily over Dukakis 4-1 in the electoral college vote. We had two years to promote it and George H.W. Bush killed it all by fear and selfishness. We failed in 1971 with the Libertarian Party, then again in 1984 with the Green Party, and lastly in 1988 with Reagan's successor not having the balls to move forward . . . . it was utter ruin for our plan. Needless to say, the consortium lost hope, dwindled in number, and constituents died off, retired, or just lost interest. Well, lost interest . . . . . *until recently.*"

Sam took a long draw from his Cabernet and reflected on the tumultuous two decades long since passed. "The time was reminiscent of today, with the economy in a state of flux, high unemployment, and recessions in the early and late 1970s. The energy crisis was on the rise, and oil prices were angering the American people. The Environmental Protection Agency (EPA) was created to address environmental issues. Women's rights, desegregation, and LGBTQ+ rights were all active and volatile topics. Sadly, the start of it all was Watergate, which prompted concern for government office, its transparency, and accountability. Add the drug epidemics, with crack cocaine affecting the larger cities, immigration policy primarily surrounding Central America, and the Cold War ever present with the Soviet Union. The world was in chaos, and the United States was at the core of it all, unraveling. Those years created a tailspin for the American government, and they needed a savior, someone to give the American people hope, but George H.W. Bush let all of us down, and all remained status quo after he took office." Damian looked as if he had seen a ghost, but he was both mortified and intrigued simultaneously. He wanted to hear it all until he understood the entire story.

Sam smiled, knowing he had fascinated his son like he had for years. This was a new story for him to hear, and he was enthralled. They both appreciated the history of the United States and all the trials and challenges the great nation had faced and overcome through the decades. "For nearly twenty years, a small group of us have kept the *Alternative Consortium* sentient yet dormant and quiet. However, when Barrack Obama was elected in 2008, it stirred our group after the questions of his citizenship, religion, voter ID Laws, and his stance on the Afghanistan and Iraq wars rekindled a spark within our circle. Our heated discussions caused us to consider a new and fresh perspective of our country's direction and instilled a fresh an innovative and creative stimulation within our small group. We began to build on to the developing notion of a new group, or party, that would inspire the ideals of the majority of Americans. A feeling of conformity, yet under the ideal of unity of all. For twelve years, we have cultivated the philosophy, Damian. We have fostered the platform that led to you having such a successful governorship in our home state. It has led to the philosophies you have put forth already under the unified understanding and have ultimately led . . . *to you*. Though a terrible tragedy, Governor Hathaway's death paved the way for our re-emergence, to put it bluntly. His death served a greater purpose." Sam wanted to make sure his son fully understood what he was explaining. Damian's expression saddened at the thought that someone's death benefitted his own career.

"You are the future, Damian. Many of us under the *Alternative Consortium* have slowly molded you over the years to take the helm when the moment was ripe. It wasn't coercion or manipulation as much as our attempt to aid you in processing this idea. We appreciate the value of how it came to be and how it could ultimately benefit everyone." Damian West looked at his father, "What are you trying to say, Dad?" Sam looked at him and, with a straight face, said, "For over a decade, Damian, we have groomed you, educated you, and paved the way for you to become our president under a stronger Unified Party. Our Consortium may argue and debate that point, but we ultimately accept what the majority seeks. You are the chosen one to lead this country to the greatest era of its young history. Regina Alvarado is but one cog in this system. There are so many who have watched you, aided you, and guided you since the beginning to see this one purpose go the distance in the 21st century and achieve what we could not in the 20th century. This is your moment; this is your beacon that we will all follow. And you, son, will be at the pinnacle of the entire movement."

Damien looked at his father and simply said, "Then, Dad, we need to take this all the way. Once and for all, for the people, for all Americans."

Sam winked at his son, "I believe you. . . ." Sam nodded over Damian's right shoulder, then looked at Damian and whispered, "And now, our first being Regina. Here is our second champion of the day." Sam slowly stood up as he said, "Senator Cosner, so glad you could join us today. . . ." Senator Ren Cosner walked to the table to join them. Damian also stood to greet his long-time mentor and pay his respects.

Senator and majority whip Ren Franklin Cosner was born in the projects of Chicago, Illinois. Growing up in a destitute black family, he was the youngest of six siblings. He barely knew his mother, keeping down three jobs to keep her children fed, and never met his father, unsure of what fate bestowed the man after abandoning his siblings and mother. He was determined to break out of his given stereotype and did whatever he could to stay out of trouble, maintain good grades, and get into a small college playing football with a partial scholarship and student loans to subsidize the rest.

He was a champion of the people and well respected by all Congressmen for the journey he had endured. He was pragmatic, calculated, and smart, and he had cemented his legacy within the government but was also secretly disenfranchised by contemporary politics. He ran for president in 1992 and 2000 and was close to attaining the nod, but Bill Clinton edged him out in 1992, gaining the nomination from the Democratic Party, and in 2000, Al Gore was given the distinction over Ren. America was simply not yet ready to see a black president run the most powerful nation on the planet. Ren Cosner was simply born too early.

Senator Cosner had long followed the budding career of Damian West and helped where he could aid the young man along the way, like many others, to open up his potential to become a part of the larger influential circle that was growing around the young Senator. They all sat down, ordered their lunch, and spoke of the new Senator's acclimation into the congressional mainstream.

After a few minutes of pleasantries and catching up, Senator Cosner was eager to get a glass of the Caymus but knew they had a full docket to discuss, "Damian, your father has worked tirelessly to pave this expertly veiled road we have well trekked for a few decades now, atoned with gold I may even add, but it won't come without its perils especially after we let the cat out of the bag, so to speak. By now, you probably understand the significant reach and influence of the Alternative Consortium, what it represents, and your quintessential role within the mechanism of its potential of what it could become?"

Damian nodded his acknowledgment and took a deep breath, "I'll admit, Ren, I was a little in the dark, but Dad has illuminated its origin along with the Speaker of the House and her perspective of its significance and my role within our intention for the next few years."

"Ahhh, yes Regina Alvarado. She is a significant player in our faction and well respected, as is your father here, but we have all played a part in helping you along the way, but soon," as Ren looked at Sam, ". . . soon, I fear our loyalties will be questioned, chastised and tested and we will need to maintain a unified front. After this all goes public, the whole lot of us could be lynched overnight." Damian then asked, "Ren, I've always thought of you as an uncle, a mentor, and my friend. Why keep me in the dark about all of this for so long?" Ren turned more solemn, much like Speaker of the House Alvarado did when her words held a particular weight and his role to implement their dream.

Ren Cosner chose his words carefully, "Son, your father, the Speaker, and I felt it best that you found your way . . . on your own, and without the pressure of bestowing our objective upon you." Sam added, "We obviously exposed you, Damian, to this perspective, but we had to see if you embraced it upon your own accord, in your own way, and without us coercing you in any direct way. Indirectly, of course, but we needed to watch you evolve on your own. If you did not align with our thinking, we wouldn't have this conversation today. Life would have commenced as it had already, died in the wind or possibly continued with another candidate. We had a few considered, but you have been the front runner for some time, and your speech in Washington D.C. a few weeks ago made us all realize . . . . you were the one."

An awkward silence came over the table for a moment as the significance of their discussion sank into the thoughts of all three men, especially Senator Damian West.

Damian was the first to break the silence, "I will do what needs to be done, gentlemen, to see this mission through. You have seen the potential in me to carry the torch and weight of this campaign from here forth, and I don't want to disappoint you and, least of all, myself. I agree, Ren; you, my father, and Regina will also have a lot to lose, so we will all have a tremendous amount of skin in the game. We have a lot riding on this move."

Senators Cosner and West nodded, and Ren continued, "But here is the key to all of this. Unlike our attempt in the early 70s with the Libertarian Party, again in the early 80s with the Greens, and late 80s with H.W. Bush, we had far too much incongruency built within the various factions." Ren smiles and looks at Sam, "But now, young Damian West, we have the esteemed Four Horsemen, all focused, attaining a completely seamless concentration and determination for the future."

"As in the fabled Four Horsemen of the Apocalypse, Ren, what do you mean?" asked Damian. He felt there was so much for him to learn, and every moment shed a new chapter of the past and the future slowly revealing itself.

Ren laughed, "Ahhh yes, the Four Horsemen of the Apocalypse . . . . . *of the old ways*. And new, I suppose." Taken from the New

Testament of the Bible, specifically from the Book of Revelation. The Four Horsemen appear in Revelation 6:1-8 and are symbolic representations of four calamities that will occur before the world's end. Each horseman rides a horse of a different color, and they have various interpretations.

"I think we prefer to think of us as the American re-awakening," explained Sam West, "From the Bible, the Four Horsemen each representing war, conquest, famine, and death, which is ever present in today's society, our reawakening concentrates on commonality, acceptance, peace, and unity. The Four Horsemen of our reawakening constitutes Ren, me, Regina Alvarado, and lastly and most importantly . . . . *you*." Ren Cosner put up his hand, "No, Sam, I don't have that part of the fight in me any longer, you need an enforcer, a protector."

Damian smiled, "Sebastian Storm," Sam spoke up, "Yes, Sebastian, he will be our knight and guardian."

Ren continued, "Excellent choice. You now are the infamous Four Horsemen, and with it comes enormous influence. Many will commit to our unveiling, waiting patiently in the shadows for such a move. Others will see the value as it gains momentum and popularity, as we feel it will with the wisdom this Party will bring. Your father served as Republican Majority Whip for nearly two decades and 12 years for me on the Democratic side. We have amassed substantial continuity in thinking in that time."

Sam West took the reins, "As we discussed in Jackson Hole, Damian, we have committed roughly 18 Senators on the list; 4 have confirmed they will change affiliation. An estimated 66 House Representatives possible with 21 confirmed and tremendous depth in contributors, donators and influencers in business and all media."

"Funding this campaign has been a daunting task, to say the least, and we will need to double traditional campaign budgets as we need to be in front of every American at every moment leading up to the election. Historically, in the 2020 election cycle, Joe Biden's campaign raised around $938 million during the 2020 election cycle. This figure includes campaign funds and affiliated committees. On the Republican end, Donald Trump's campaign raised approximately

$811 million during the same cycle. In the 2016 Presidential Campaign, Hillary Clinton raised about $1.2 billion, making it one of the most expensive presidential campaigns in history, whereas Donald Trump's campaign raised around $647 million. Going back even further, in 2012, Barack Obama was over $1 billion compared to Mitt Romney's $992 million." Damian West simply shook his head at the staggering figures.

The question lingered in his mind, "And of the Unified Party, have we received firm contribution commitments that even approach those numbers?" Both Ren and Sam sat back in their respective seats and smiled after glancing at one another. "Tell me, gentlemen," asked Damian.

Sam leaned forward, "We have commitments of 1.1 billion, but we need more." At the utterance of that number, Damian also sat back and simply said, "Amazing." Ren looked at Damian, "Your speeches and inspiration will draw twice that I anticipate."

Sam explained, "We will hit hard on multiple facets and a wide range of activities, such as advertising, campaign staff salaries, travel, and event costs. The costs associated with presidential campaigns can vary significantly depending on the race's competitiveness and the amount of money raised, but we will blow away traditional spending. Additionally, independent expenditures from political action committees (PACs) and other groups can further influence the total spending in presidential elections. Though the Republicans and Democrats benefit greatly from this, we must rely more on the private sector. The presidential campaign typically involves significant expenses for advertising (television, digital, and radio), campaign staff and infrastructure, travel, and other operational costs. We will allocate resources strategically, focusing more on competitive states and regions and hit media the hardest. We need to get on that presidential debate. Damian will crucify Biden or DeSantis, but Trump may pose more of a challenge if he enters the race. Robert F. Kennedy Jr. may try to run as an independent but doesn't have the backing. I think it will come down to Biden and Trump."

Cosner added, "This will be where I can potentially sway and manipulate that key element. The Commission on Presidential Debates (CPD) has been a private, not-for-profit organization since the 1980s and has remained independent of governmental control. If we make enough of a splash, they will have no choice but to let the Unified Party within the debate in either a separate pairing of two candidates or a free-for-all with all three. But we have to fully engage the American people to do so. We need for them to demand that the Unified Party has a voice and a voice worth hearing. There is no other option. We need a substantial level of support in national polls to have the Unified Party even be considered. Janet H. Brown is their current CEO, and I have a very solid relationship with her as you do, Sam, and that may be our "in" with enough pressure to have you represent the Unified Party within the Commission. The Democrats and Republicans have solid representation upon the commission, and with the Commission's nonpartisan approach, the CPD has always emphasized its nonpartisan nature and is committed to ensuring that debates are fair, impartial, and not influenced by any political party or candidate. It operates independently and does not receive government funding. That will be our key. In addition, the CPD has faced enormous criticism from some quarters for its debate criteria and for not including third-party candidates or independent candidates in the debates historically. Critics argue that the CPD's criteria can limit the diversity of voices heard during the debates, but no parties in the past have maintained any stature, so the CPD was warranted in their third-party omission. However, I don't think they will be able to ignore it this time."

Damian noted, "The Commission on Presidential Debates plays a significant role in the U.S. presidential election process by providing a platform for candidates to discuss important issues with a national audience. However, the CPD's criteria and practices have been a subject of heated debate and discussion, with calls for changes to be more inclusive of third-party candidates and to further ensure the impartiality of the debates. We are primed as a strong third party for them to use the excuse to allow the Unified Party if the American people insist upon it."

Sam mentioned, "When we finally announce we will have lost a lot of support and the shift in power and influence that has served us for years will be challenged. Friendships and alliances will be examined and may be shattered in some cases. We must also consider a suitable running mate for VP, which is well down the road, but we should consider some options."

Ren turned to Sam, "Our Majority Whip days, Sam, are upon us again. It's time to bring them all together and finish what we began all those years ago. It's finally time to take the gloves off one last time. For the good of the American people, we must fight for the unity of this nation."

Both Ren and Sam turned to young Damian West. He was their future; he was their destiny.

With the confidence and humility this country needed, Damian replied, "The fate of this country rests not only in us, gentlemen, but in the unity of all Americans. For us to, once and for all, rise to a level beyond the color of their skin or their religious beliefs but in the sanctity of humankind to rely on our intelligence and evolution to adore the American standing proud beside you and embrace them for what they contribute to our society. Rise above the hate, the jealousy, the privilege, and the history of what has crippled this great nation. I will lead in spirit, where my trust will be without state borders and beyond the colors of one's skin. We need to look onward and upwards not behind us and the picture of what our history created. It is time we fall under one flag, a united people, unified and just all with one goal under the banner of the Unified Party, once and for all."

Chapter 11

The Launch

New York, New York
2022 Mid-January
Fury's Manhattan Penthouse

Fury pressed 'end' on his encrypted cellular phone and turned his attention to the figure seated across the large room before the fireplace. Inferno, a formidable presence, was ensconced in contemplation before the crackling fireplace, his mind seemingly lost amidst the flickering dance of flames.

As Fury approached, he noted the restlessness simmering beneath Inferno's stoic facade. A warrior by nature, forged in the crucible of conflict by the tutelage of Tobias Teague and Fury himself, Inferno epitomized action, a force of nature unleashed upon the world to bestow his own brand of destruction and chaos. But deeper still, he wondered what his role was without Tobias to guide him. He was lost in some form and didn't like how it made him feel. He was lacking a vision . . . . *a purpose.*

Yet, their roles had shifted for over a year and a half since Tobias's death. Instead of the thunderous footsteps of chaos, they had become phantoms, orchestrating their clandestine machinations under the shroud of secrecy woven by their enigmatic employer. The loss of Tobias Teague in Dublin had cast a shadow over their endeavors, a stark reminder of the dangers lurking in the shadows. Tobias Teague had been their leader, and without him, the nature and effectiveness of their talents lay dormant and largely useless save for the single client that was utilizing them for the long game, which meant moments of action but then followed by months of stagnation. Inferno struggled during those prolonged periods, lacking inertia, laden with insignificant minutia.

Sebastian Storm's vendetta in Dublin had left scars upon their souls, driving them deeper into the shadows and forcing them to adopt an invisible existence. It was a life of meticulous planning and cautious maneuvering, a far cry from the visceral thrill of combat Inferno craved and Tobias supplied in abundance before the Dublin attack. However, he reminded himself of the importance of this current, sole mission objective.

Fury understood the fire burning within his companion, the yearning for action gnawing at his core. However, he was aware patience was the key to their success. Their contact had been met, a crucial step in the intricate web of deception they had spun over the years. But to reveal such a connection to Inferno prematurely would be to cause disaster and compromise their client's purpose and secrecy.

And so, Fury watched the flames dance within the hearth, a silent witness to the turmoil raging within his pupil's soul and spirit. The time for action would come, he was certain. But for now, they remained bound by the threads of their elaborate scheme, biding their time until the moment was ripe for their reemergence into the world.

The genesis of their current mission could be traced back to a clandestine conversation held years ago, shrouded in the cloak-and-dagger world orchestrated by Fury's mentor and superior, Tobias Teague. In the twilight of 2015, their organization received a covert summons, an enigmatic proposition surrounding the governor of Wyoming and his strategic and manipulated demise, thereby lighting the match that would ignite the United States political maelstrom that was to follow. The intricacies of the plan had been woven with meticulous care by Tobias, a mastermind whose strategic acumen was legendary within their secret circles.

Fury's initiation into the clandestine world of their organization marked a pivotal moment in his life's narrative. The threshold he crossed, guided by Tobias Teague's sage hand, was not merely a transition from one phase to another but an immersion into the depths of intrigue and subterfuge defining their covert operations, with this operation emulating the pinnacle of all they had ever achieved. It was an operation to be remembered for a millennium, although most would never know their names. Fury and Tobias had singlehandedly arranged it all.

With each step into the inner sanctum of their organization, Fury experienced the weight of responsibility settle upon his shoulders like an ancient mantle. It was a burden borne by those who dared to tread the murky waters of surreptitious affairs, where every word spoken carried the weight of a thousand unspoken truths, and every action held the potential to shape destinies.

In those early days, as he absorbed the wisdom imparted by Tobias, Fury grappled with the realization the path he had chosen was fraught with peril. Yet, amidst the uncertainty, there was a sense of purpose, a clarity of vision illuminating the darkness shrouding their objectives.

As he cast his gaze upon Inferno, he saw a reflection of his journey mirrored in the younger man's eyes. The torch of knowledge passed from mentor to protégé, forging a bond transcending mere allegiance, binding them together in a shared quest for mastery over the clandestine arts.

The weight of responsibility now rested upon Inferno's shoulders was not merely a burden to bear but a testament to his resilience and fortitude in the face of adversity. Like a phoenix rising from the ashes, he had emerged from the crucible of training and trial, honed into a weapon tempered by the fires of experience.

And as Fury stood beside him, he was acutely aware their journey was far from over. As they began the final chapter together, they would navigate the treacherous currents of deception and betrayal, their resolve unyielding, their purpose unwavering. For in the world of shadows where truth was a rare commodity, they were the arbiters of destiny, sculptors of their own fate in a realm where power and influence held sway overall.

And yet, amidst the uncertainty, there had been a glimmer of hope, a spark of potential revealing the path ahead. Fury remembered the fire burning within him, the drive to prove himself worthy of Tobias's trust, to stand shoulder to shoulder with the titans of their organization. Fury underwent a surge of camaraderie with his companion's apprehension, vividly recalling the adrenaline-fueled rush he experienced when initiated into their covert operations. As the plan unfolded in secrecy, he too, had been swept up in a whirlwind of uncertainty, the thrill of navigating uncharted territory electrifying his senses like a bolt of lightning.

As he glanced at Inferno, he saw echoes of his own journey reflected in the younger man's eyes. Once just a boy, barely into his teens, Inferno had been thrust into this world of shadows and intrigue, forced to navigate its treacherous waters with only his wits and determination as his guide. Tobias had created a killing machine in Inferno. The young man was fueled by pain and the suffering of others. Tobias had seen to that.

But despite the trials and tribulations that lay ahead, Fury was certain they would emerge stronger, forged in the blending of adversity. They were not merely soldiers in a grand game of chess but architects of their own destiny, masters of their fate in a world where the lines between friend and foe blurred with each passing day.

Years before when Tobias ran point on the specific operation, he was often in the dark, just as Inferno was as well. The principle was so secretive, it was insisted Tobias meet with the client privately.

It was the first and only time Fury had not been allowed to attend the meeting to discuss the specifics of their objective, and he was unsure who the identity of the high-ranking individual could possibly be and what role was undetermined.

Fury harbored suspicions a notable figure within the intricate web of the U.S. Government wielded influence over their specific and secretive operations. However, he understood the delicacy of probing his employer for specifics, acutely aware of Tobias's formidable disposition. The last thing Fury desired was to incur Tobias's wrath; thus, he exercised discretion, refraining from prying into matters beyond his purview.

Respecting Tobias's authority was paramount in Fury's code of conduct. If Tobias deemed it necessary to keep Fury in the dark regarding the mission's finer details, Fury would dutifully comply. He recognized Tobias possessed insights and foresight beyond his own and, as such, deferred to his judgment with unwavering loyalty and commitment.

However, there lingered a tantalizing curiosity within Fury's mind, a relentless urge to unravel the enigma shrouding this particular mission. He couldn't shake the feeling there existed a compelling rationale behind the veil of secrecy, a puzzle waiting to be deciphered. Until Tobias deemed it opportune or the client-sanctioned disclosure, Fury resolved to navigate the murky depths of uncertainty with patience and vigilance.

In the intricate dance of covert operations, every shadow concealed a secret. Every silence whispered a truth yet untold. And as Fury awaited the revelation of the mission's clandestine underpinnings, he remained poised, ready to heed the call to action when the moment of revelation finally arrived.

All those years ago, sitting in Tobias's office, Fury waited patiently until, hours later, Tobias entered the chamber at their compound in Dublin, Ireland. Fury stood up upon hearing the large blast door open and shut, "Take a seat, Fury," as Tobias came to the chair behind his desk, and they both sat down at the same time.

Tobias took a long look at Fury, "This is the mission ensuring our place at the global table and defining the aptitude of our abilities. It's a long reaching political agenda, and the dream and opportunity we cannot allow to fail. Its impact could have substantial effects on the United States, as a whole, for decades to come. Its ripple effect will be appreciated by the entire world." Tobias shook his head at the magnitude of the operation, pondering the significance of the operation and its long reaching effects. He continued, "In addition, it will cement our place and our end, or at least, mine. This last mission will thrust us into the final stage, and my life's work will be completed. I will have fulfilled all I wish in my lifetime, and I will then pass the baton to you and Inferno. My days will then come to an end in this arena." Fury began to speak, and Tobias held up his hand, "It's my decision, Fury, and it is final. I will tell Inferno when the time is right."

Back on point, Tobias continued with his objective, "This final mission has to be executed in stages, specific to a particular and unique agenda and spanning over the next several years. I can only tell you small portions of the objective for the time being, but it will all begin with the elimination of an insignificant Governor from Wyoming. The client wants it to occur on New Year's Eve, flawlessly executed, and made to look like an accident. No ties, no margin for error, Fury. Immaculate in every detail."

Fury looked at Tobias, "Yes, Sir. That's just a few weeks away." "That it is, Fury," as Tobias handed Fury the dossier on the Governor. "That is all, Fury, make us proud," as Fury got up to leave and made his way to the door before Tobias said finally, "No mistakes on this one, Fury. This contract will allow us to write our ticket." "Yessir, Boss," came the reply from Fury as he headed out the door.

Tobias Teague wouldn't see his accomplishments manifest as he was killed by Adriana Mercer when Sebastian Storm came to rescue her in Dublin, Ireland. The legacy of the mission came down to Fury and Inferno completing it in Tobias's honor and their vision was to make him proud.

$\mathbf{F}$ury thought of that moment seven years before, and despite Tobias's death, the machine was already set into motion. Tobias had left all instructions and relevant information surrounding the objective and directives to covertly communicate with the elusive client to continue the objective where Tobias had left off. The day after Tobias's death, as Inferno and Fury quickly exited Dublin, Ireland, they retrieved the encrypted laptop Tobias had secured in a hidden safe house location. Only Fury had known about the laptop in the event of Tobias Teague's untimely death. Contained within the computer was the information surrounding open contracts as well as the most significant political contract had originated five years before. Lastly, slightly over 500 million dollars had been left for Fury and Inferno allowing them complete autonomy to continue his dream if they chose to continue his legacy.

Mesmerized by the prancing flames of the fire before him, Fury looked at Inferno, "I want to shed some light on what was to be Tobias's greatest dream and objective, Inferno. It started seven years ago with the simple elimination of the Governor of Wyoming. Tobias and I initiated a sequence of events bringing us to where we are today." Inferno turned his gaze toward Fury, curious about the story and eager to hear more.

Fury detailed for Inferno the elaborate series of events from the fateful New Year's evening in Wyoming. Governor Steven Hathaway and his wife left the New Year's party at 11:34 PM, hopeful to miss the intoxicated mass exodus that was sure to commence following the New Year's festivities.

$\mathbf{T}$he Governor's driver, Antonio, waited quietly in the SUV, listening to a classic Blues channel on his radio. Only several minutes remained in the year 2015 as the dawn of a new year was quickly approaching. on his radio. It had been snowing all week in Cheyenne, and the Christmas that year enjoyed twelve inches of newly fallen snow blanketing the countryside and roads. The lower temperatures maintained the drifts for the following week as New Year's approached. In the span of a few hours, freshly fallen snow had accumulated a few additional inches along with the temperature drop, making for somewhat of a hazardous landscape for any driving that evening.

Antonio spilled his coffee as he saw the Governor and his wife quietly emerge from the front door without warning, swearing under his breath. He was somewhat angered the Governor nor his wife warned him they were planning on leaving the party early. Nonetheless, he put his coffee in the holder, wiped his hand on his pants, scrambled to open the door, and hurriedly ran around the rear of the SUV, nearly slipping on the icy ground to open the rear door for his passengers.

Nodding as they stepped into the vehicle, "Ma'am . . . Governor," said Antonio as the Governor responded in a low breath, "On a whim, we decided to get out of there early, Antonio; sorry if we surprised you," the Governor noticing Antonio's haste.

"Not a problem, Sir," replied Antonio as he eased the door shut and then ran around the rear of the SUV, but not learning his lesson the first time as he slipped and hit his rear hard, swearing again and quickly got up, brushed himself off suppressing his pain knowing it would feel worse later in the evening once he got home. He had a fifth of Jack Daniels Black Label waiting for him on his table beside his Laz-e-boy recliner in front of the television.

"You okay, Antonio," asked the Governor as Antonio winced, "Never better, Sir. We will get you right home in a jiffy."

Fury had his sight fixated on the small bridge covering Crow Creek on the outskirts of the city, providing the optimum location to complete the mission objective. The bridge was a common route leading to the Governor's mansion and the most likely and fastest trek the Governor's driver would have taken to the Governor's home. Unassuming people were predictable, thought Fury. A fair amount of detail was implemented by Fury and his team of three to create a weather-ridden pothole in the pavement, hidden by the newly fallen snow, masking their intent masterfully and adding to the effect nicely.

Fury had been lying in the cold, flattened terrain for well over an hour waiting for the call that the Governor was leaving the party. "Black Sheep, the gate is open, in on four," came the message over his earpiece. The message translated to the. . . . *Governor's ETA was roughly four minutes away.* "It's about time; it's getting downright unbearable out here," said Fury under his breath but then replied, "Copy White Sheep."

He eased up the M2010 Enhanced Sniper Rifle (ESR), adjusting the scope, focusing on the pothole in the middle of the lane of the bridge as his team set up the pylons and warning sign denoting a hazard on the road, then hopped over the side of the bridge remaining undetected. He knew he had some time but the clock had started.

Activating the fingerprint reader on the top of the container sitting beside him, he triggered the small pressure-sealed case. A faint *whooshing* sound could be heard as it opened, revealing four unique underlit rifle bullets called *NitroB rounds.* The .300 Winchester Magnum round was a specialized bullet made of compacted nitrogen-frozen material and arranged in a linear row within the case. Fury carefully pinched one round with his Kevlar-coated gloves, loaded a single round into the M2010 Sniper Rifle, and slid the bolt forward, locking the round within the chamber.

The specialized nitrogen-frozen bullet was meant to withstand a high-velocity discharge and was designed to fragment upon impact or vaporize within seconds of striking a warm target. The small metal base of the bullet contained a volatile charge used only once per round. The propellant aluminum base remained in the chamber after the round was expended, unlike a standard shell case. The system was clean and simple. It was essentially an invisible bullet, capable of leaving no trace of its impact and its immediate evaporation upon contact. The sound of the discharge was a subtle *whisp,* virtually silent and was accurate up to 1500 yards, nearly a mile.

In the cold, arid climate, Fury was aware he had roughly three minutes before the frozen round would denature within the chamber, and he would be forced to replace it with a new round. The ETA of the Governor was less than 90 seconds.

It was the headlights Fury spotted first, rounding the corner before approaching the bridge. He steadied his sights upon the pothole as the SUV containing the Governor and his wife approached.

Antonio stared at the road ahead of him, fixated on the falling snow that seemed to reflect back at him from the beam of his headlights. The snowflakes descended and danced as whisks of wind would constantly deviate from their paths as they fell, creating an erratic pattern upon their descent.

As Antonio neared the familiar bridge, a path he had traversed countless times, an unexpected sight disrupted his routine journey. A cluster of warning pylons, accompanied by a vivid hazard sign, stood defiantly in the center of his lane. The peculiar arrangement, never before encountered on this well-trodden route, hinted at an unseen danger lurking ahead. He was compelled to swerve sharply to the left, narrowly avoiding the sudden obstacle.

A silent crack of the bolt propelled the liquid-frozen bullet, less than 150 yards away, toward the driver's side front tire, striking the rubber tread, popping the tire while it simultaneously hit the pothole beneath. Antonio then lost control of the wheel and tried to overcompensate as the SUV whipped and hit the curb adjacent to the guardrail in the opposite lane, flipping it up from its momentum and completely over the side of the railing, spiraling the thirty feet to Crow Creek below.

As the SUV slammed upon the rocky creek below, the force of the impact pushed the engine into the driver's compartment, crushing anyone in the front two seats and killing Antonio instantly. The SUV came to rest upside down in the icy cold water. Despite the creek being only a few feet deep, the cab began quickly filling with water.

Neither the Governor nor his wife had been wearing their seatbelts, forcefully smashing them into the back of the front seats. The Governor couldn't move; he attempted to reach for his wife, but both of his arms were broken. Her cryptic face staring at him, eyes open, her head contorted, breaking her neck from the impact. He called out to her as the frigid water began to rise from the broken windows on both sides of the vehicle. He was unable to help either of them.

Governor Steven Hathaway felt utterly helpless, unable to move other than lifting his head, buying himself a few precious seconds before his head submerged below the icy water. The water level stabilized just a few inches above his head, but he was unable to lift himself any higher as his air quickly began leaving his body.

His final image was of his wife's face staring at him, tranquil somehow as her life was extinguished. Governor Hathaway's final thought was he was content his wife did not suffer. He thought it strangely poetic that he should pass alongside his high school sweetheart. It was their 30th wedding anniversary that evening, and the sadness overcame him. He would never share another anniversary with her or walk his two daughters down the aisle. All those moments dashed in that fleeting moment.

He wished he could touch her one last time as his last breath left him.

The pylons had already been removed, and any trace of their existence was eradicated with minimal disruption to the environment. "Get down there and verify status, then meet back at point Alpha for extraction," barked Fury to his team. Fury packed up his gear, did a final check of his surroundings, and made his way to the rendezvous point. Sixty seconds later, "Black Sheep, all occupants deceased, verified," came the report. "Copy," replied Fury as double timed to extraction point Alpha, their objective completed.

The first part of the puzzle had been fulfilled. However, little did Fury know that the events of that evening would disrupt the course of the future for the United States and change it trajectory beyond any other moment in history.

Returning to the present, Fury looked at Inferno who had sat up hanging on Fury's every word. "When do I get to meet this elusive client of ours, Fury," asked Inferno. "In due time, young man. Don't be too excited, for when you do eventually meet him, your life may be irrevocably changed as a result not to mention expendable, I might add. Knowing his identity makes you a liability. I have been pulled into the web because I was Tobias's number one. I don't wish the same for you, if I can avoid it in any way," explained Fury.

Inferno rarely spoke but when he did his words had passion and meaning, "If Tobias wanted this, Fury, then we should honor his wishes and stand behind what he started. We owe him that much."

Fury nodded knowing the young man was correct, "We both would not be standing here today had it not been for Tobias Teague. We will both see his vision through, no matter what the cost. I promise you that, Inferno."

"Our client has called a meeting for midnight tonight to discuss the next steps. You will accompany me to this encounter. I will let him know you will need to be a part of the team from here on, the question is when, or if, he will allow you to know his identity," explained Fury.

Washington D.C.
2022 February
Damian West Downtown Residence

Damian lifts Mila onto the marble slab of the kitchen island, "Fuck, that's cold, Damian," he laughs, knowing the frigid stone would startle her. "I think you need a little cooling off after the last hour," he replied with a wink.

It was 3 AM on a Saturday, and they both became thirsty after their late return from dinner and rigorous sexual tryst lasting several hours.

The evening weighed on her mind, and she thought it the perfect time to ask about it. Despite knowing Damian's father, she had not spent much time with him while in Damian's company but that evening, they had shared an elegant dinner, the three of them at the Fiola Mare, located on the majestic Georgetown waterfront. Popular for its elegant seafood dishes and stunning views of the

Potomac River, Fiola Mare provided a sophisticated locale for her to get to know the famous retired Senator from Wyoming and provide some more insight into the illustrious son she had come to adore.

Within the kitchen sans any clothing, they rummaged around the kitchen like high school kids looking for snacks and something to cool them off. Damian grabbed a couple of bottled waters from the refrigerator and handed one to Mila, "You were insatiable tonight, Senator." Damian stood between her legs, cutting apples to the side as she sat upon the counter, smiling, knowing 'insatiable' was a common denominator in their relationship over the last ten weeks. He smiled to himself as she always referred to him as *Senator,* as if it held some kind of sordid sexual innuendo. He grabbed an apple slice and eased it between her lips, which she happily accepted.

He looked into her eyes in the dimly lit room as her hand came up to his face, "What am I going to do with you, Damian?" His smile softened, "These last couple of months have been the most amazing time I have ever shared with anyone, Mila, and I wanted to thank you for that." She looked at him intently, knowing she felt the same, and it both excited her and frightened her as well.

No man had ever possessed any control over Mila Dmitri. There were moments in her adult life when she thought there might be a chance of something more, but those possibilities were quickly dashed within a few months of the budding relationship. However, there was something different about Damian West. She had always easily found the flaws in men from her past in some form, whether it was intelligence, charisma, sexual awareness, or humor, but Damian held her interest on every point and made her lust for more from him. She found herself fantasizing about their next encounter as he stimulated her intellectually and sexually, and she had never found a man that satisfied both as he did. She was cautious yet more intrigued by every moment she shared with him.

Never longer than a week had passed between visits as she longed to be close to him, captivated by his charm and wit on a level she had never experienced in any other relationship. In the last few weeks, she found herself becoming increasingly saddened when their time together would draw to an end. As she looked into his eyes, she realized she knew so much about him yet still so much still left unknown about the man peering back at her.

Mila reflected on their dinner a few hours before. It was then that she recognized Damian's charisma was a trait carried down from his father. The two men bantered in such a way that she could tell their appreciation for one another ran deep and was unfaltering in their adoration. They were both fascinating to listen to, and the elder man was a wealth of knowledge surrounding American history and the political spectrum. Damian would chime in, equally conversant about the array of partisan topics and well-versed in the deep understanding of the doctrinal undercurrents of modern politics. She enjoyed watching them debate but they were largely congruent in all significant electoral philosophies.

Because she enjoyed stirring the pot, she saw her opening and took it, "So gentleman, what's all this talk and rumor about an emerging concept of this Unity Party, United Party or whatever its name?" Both Sam and Damian West turned toward her, then one another, before taking a bite from their dinner. Awkward and odd in form, never had she witnessed silence coming from either of these two men . . . . *She had hit a nerve,* throwing them off balance, and she smiled, enjoying the moment of silence as they pondered her question.

Sam West was the first to break the silence, "Ohh, young lady, whatever can you be referring to. We have a bipartisan system, living free and strong within this country. Any reference to unity simply is an urging of our camp to embrace such a concept between Americans all."

"Well, it's been quite the buzz on the Hill for several months now, as well as about every media outlet out there trying to piece its meaning from your handsome son here." Mila grabbed Damian's hand and winked, trying to keep the conversation light.

Damian squeezed her hand in response and looked at her, "Would it be so terrible to give the antiquated bipartisan system something of significance to think about? It's important to consider that while the United States has a current two party system, the level of political polarization and the dynamics between the two major parties have devolved slowly over time. In recent years, political polarization has increased, leading to greater partisan division in the country's politics. This has also led to the emergence of independent and third-party thinking and perspectives."

Damian had her attention, "Several points affect the system today. One of the most significant weaknesses of the bipartisan system is that it limits voters' choices to just two major parties. This can lead to a lack of diversity in political representation and can make it challenging for voters to find candidates who align with their specific views and values. Additionally, the Democrats and Republicans have contributed to increasing political polarization. Candidates often cater to their party's base only, which can lead to extreme positions and a lack of willingness to compromise. This position is folly; polarization can hinder effective governance and lead to gridlock in Congress, which is more than apparent currently. Consequently, third-party candidates and independent voices often struggle to gain a foothold in the political system. The winner-takes-all electoral system and the challenges of ballot access can make it difficult for alternative parties to compete on a level playing field, which is far from fair for the American people and their respective choices. This bipartisan dominance can stifle competition and limit opportunities for new parties to emerge and this inhibits national growth and evolution. This can lead to a sense of voter disillusionment and a feeling that the political system is controlled by a small group of elites. In a two-party system, there may be less incentive for the major parties to innovate or adapt to changing demographics and issues facing all of us. They may become entrenched in their positions and resistant to change. As a result, many voters may become frustrated with the choices offered by the major parties and may choose not to vote at all. Voter apathy and low voter turnout can be consequences of the limited options presented in a bipartisan system. Complex problems often require clever solutions, but in a two-party system, the emphasis is often on presenting clear, contrasting positions. This can make it challenging to develop comprehensive, bipartisan solutions to issues such as healthcare, immigration, and climate change."

Sam West then took over, and their two-pronged response to the issues mentioned made them such a formable pair when debating any issue. "You see the conundrum, young lady? The winner-takes-all electoral system can lead to a lack of proportional representation, where parties that receive a significant share of the vote may not win any seats or representation. This can discourage smaller parties from participating in the political process." Damian seamlessly took the reins.

"The two major parties have a vested interest in maintaining the status quo, Mila," continued Damian, "Which can make it difficult for new ideas and voices to gain traction in the current political landscape. It's an antiquated system and honestly quite oppressive."

Mila considered their words and then added, "However, it's essential to recognize that while the bipartisan system has its weaknesses, it also has its strengths, such as providing stability and predictability in the political process, but ours is currently gridlocked and only getting worse, year after year. Many countries around the world have multiparty systems that come with their own set of advantages and challenges. Public discourse often revolves around debates on how to address the shortcomings of the bipartisan system and whether electoral reforms are needed to foster greater diversity and representation in American politics."

Sam West smiled and sat back, "Well, Damian, we apparently have a political intellectual among us," as they all laughed at the comment. Another bottle followed, and their discussions continued for another hour before Mila squeezed Damian's thigh under the table, letting him know she wished to have their own version of dessert to follow. She was ready to call it a night.

Mila excused herself to freshen up, as she went to stand, both men also stood, and Damian pulled her chair to allow her to exit as they both waited patiently for her make her way to the restroom. Both men silently appreciated her as she left, their eyes lingering a little too long, awkwardly so, basking in the elegance her figure displayed in simply walking away. Her long black dress, outlining her contoured backside as she walked away, was mesmerizing to watch and admire. Her long hair falling well below her waist only added to the allure and sensuality of the woman.

Damian looked at his father and smiled inwardly, knowing his father used to look at his mother in the same way when Damian was younger. Captivated and enthralled by the woman who captured the older Senator's heart for the better part of 40 years. Damian felt for his father, knowing he still loved the woman who enchanted his life before she succumbed to the cancer that consumed her and left his life shattered and empty. After he lost her, he had only his career and his son left to occupy his time. Damian allowed the old man a moment of enjoyment as his gaze followed her for a few seconds, fulfilling his contentment.

After a moment Sam turned to his son as they sat down, "She is an extraordinary woman, Damian. She comes from an exceptional family and her father was a shrewd businessman when he was at the helm at Dymitron."

"Thank you, Dad," replied Damian, "She has held my interest for nearly three months now and never ceases to inspire and mesmerize me."

Sam treaded lightly asking but not imposing, "You haven't said a word to her, have you about our plan?" Sam was curious about the loyalty of his son in holding to the strict silence they had placed upon their directives and was simply testing the waters of where his allegiances lay.

Damian sat back in his chair as he took a drink of his wineglass, "I'm insulted you would even ask, Dad. Have my loyalties ever been in question, or have my directives and focus ever been laden with any doubt? In this endeavor, I have trained, deliberated, studied, and focused, and it has consumed my entire existence. Why would I ever jeopardize that with pillow talk of an outsider I've only known a short while." Damian shook his head, clearly upset with his father for mentioning the possibility of such a notion.

"I apologize, Damian. I didn't mean to insinuate that you have mentioned it. We have so much at stake, and we are just weeks away from delivering the largest political bomb this country's political platform has ever witnessed. It was wrong for me to assume any less devotion and dedication from you. I won't question you again, but I would be remiss if I didn't mention that Mila Dmitri is extremely intelligent and far from a fool. If she hasn't pieced a lot of this together already, based on her questions and discussion tonight, then I would be more than surprised if she didn't wonder if something is developing. It will come in a subtle way, in pillow talk, as you say. Don't be naïve to the wiles of an intelligent and beautiful woman. I know, believe me. Your mother had me so wrapped she ran circles around me when it came to astuteness and manipulation. I'm not saying it's bad, but women like Mila can be steps ahead of where you think she is."

Damian laughed, "I'll keep that in mind," then hesitated as Mila walked back toward the table. Both men again stood up as Damian quipped, "Mom ran circles around you, huh, Dad?" They both laughed as Mila approached the table with a smirk, "Ahhh, talking about women and their superpowers, I gather, gentlemen? We are the superior sex, there is no question, don't forget that," as Damian and Sam looked at one another astounded Mila Dmitri put the truth together so quickly.

"Mila . . ." She heard Damian's voice, then blinked several times. Pulling herself from her trance, recalling the discussion of the evening. She looked into Damian's eyes and kissed him hard upon his open lips.

She slightly pulled away, both hands upon his face, appreciating the handsome man before her. The conversation from dinner with Damian's father continued to seep into her consciousness, gnawing at her inquisitive nature. Her thirst for understanding the depths of this man apparently possessed no limits, and after spending time with his father, she realized they were both vital extensions of one another.

They fed off of the same energy, it was apparent. She wanted to test him, push his buttons more, and delve deeper into his soul. She desired to understand all of him, all his strengths and all his weaknesses.

She pushed a sliced apple into his mouth this time, cocked her head slightly, appearing inquisitive. "You and your father, Damian. You are both so interesting, so thorough in the understanding of our history . . . *and our future*, it appears." And so it goes, thought Damian. She is phishing about what lies beyond our discussion from tonight, what Sebastian Storm was to him, and the significance of his counsel while at his home several months before. A soft smile formed on the side of his mouth, "Let me ask you, Mila. Do you feel the current state of our country is moving in a positive direction?"

Mila pondered the question as she stuck another slice into his mouth. "Not even close, Damian," as she thought of her CEO, Anthony Voss, announcing the news of Dymitron's departure from U.S. soil in a few weeks' time. The announcement would have a major disruption on the U.S. economy, and the ripple effect would be substantial when the news broke. "This country is crumbling and falling apart at the seams. We need a great white hope, something to save us from the catastrophic events that are encircling this great nation. We need a savior," as she looked into his eyes, knowing he agreed with what she said.

Senator Damian West was well aware of what she meant, the deeper undertone of it all, and he agreed with every word and was more than impressed with her aptitude in understanding what their country was facing. Their philosophies aligned along with most other attributes they shared.

In a few weeks that followed, the announcement both were secretly privy too would come and would shake the very ground they walked upon. However, little did either of them know that their worlds would become more entangled and . . . dependent on one another as the United States was about to be tested . . . . and changed more than it had ever before, and both Mila and Senator West would be within the eye of the storm when it arrived.

Russia – Invasion of Ukraine
2022 February

On February 24, 2022, the world witnessed a seismic shift in the geopolitical landscape as Russia embarked on a fateful journey, crossing the border into Ukraine. This marked a harrowing escalation of the long-standing Russo-Ukrainian War that had been smoldering since 2014. What unfolded was nothing short of historic; it was the most extensive military assault on a European nation since the tumultuous days of World War II.

The consequences were dire and heart-wrenching. Tens of thousands of Ukrainian civilians perished, and hundreds of thousands of brave soldiers paid a heavy toll in the conflict's early days. By the time June 2022 approached, Russian forces had laid claim to roughly 20% of Ukrainian territory, redrawing the map of Eastern Europe.

The true cost extended far beyond borders. Ukraine's population endured unprecedented upheaval. Approximately 8 million Ukrainians were forcibly displaced within their own homeland, while over 8.2 million sought refuge beyond Ukraine's borders. This massive displacement gave rise to Europe's most significant refugee crisis since the dark days of World War II, with implications that rippled across the continent.

The ecological fallout from this conflict was equally alarming. Many described it as nothing short of an "ecocide," as extensive environmental damage compounded existing global food crises.

Leading up to the invasion, Russia had amassed troops along Ukraine's borders while officially denying any intent to launch an attack. However, Russian President Vladimir Putin's announcement of a "special military operation" turning rhetoric into reality. The operation purportedly aimed to support Russian-backed separatist enclaves in Donetsk and Luhansk, regions embroiled in the Donbas conflict since 2014.

Putin's inflammatory pomposity questioned Ukraine's right to exist, alleging governance by neo-Nazis who oppressed the Russian minority. He justified the operation as a move to "demilitarize" Ukraine. Russian forces launched air strikes and ground offensives with a multi-pronged approach involving northern, southern, and eastern fronts.

The conflict's twists and turns were as unpredictable as they were devastating. By April 2022, Russian forces faced logistical challenges and fierce Ukrainian resistance on the northern front, ultimately retreating. However, the southern and southeastern fronts witnessed Russia capturing strategic cities like Kherson and Mariupol following grueling sieges. Throughout the winter, Russian forces continued to unleash air strikes far from the frontlines, targeting both military and civilian infrastructure, including Ukraine's energy grid.

In a stunning reversal, Ukraine managed to regain parts of Kherson Oblast, including the city of Kherson, in November. The conflict's ever-shifting dynamics continued to leave the world on edge.

Internationally, condemnation rained down upon Russia. The United Nations General Assembly passed a resolution in March 2022, unequivocally denouncing the invasion and demanding a complete Russian withdrawal. The International Court of Justice ordered Russia to halt military operations, and the Council of Europe expelled Russia from its ranks.

A global response emerged, with nations imposing sanctions on Russia and its ally Belarus while extending humanitarian and military aid to Ukraine. Anti-war protests erupted worldwide, but Russia countered with mass arrests of demonstrators and media censorship measures. Over 1,000 companies ceased their operations in Russia and Belarus, inflicting economic repercussions.

The International Criminal Court (ICC) stepped in, launching investigations into potential crimes against humanity, war crimes, child abductions, and even genocide.

In a stunning move, an arrest warrant for Putin was issued by the ICC in March 2023, adding another layer of complexity to this multifaceted global crisis and in June of 2024 Putin declared the United States and "Enemy" of the state. Foreign relations was at an all-time low.

Chapter 12

The Speech That Fostered A New Era

"Ask not what your country can do for you—ask what you can do for your country."
~John F. Kennedy

Jackson Hole, Wyoming
2022 March
8 PM MST
Damian West Private Estate

The much-anticipated interview with Barbara Walters was promoted for the better part of three months. Senator Damian West stood with his father, Regina Alvarado, and Sebastian Storm in his room as he put on his jacket and made last-minute preparations. No cards, no prompts, no rehearsing; Damian West shot from the hip and with honesty when he spoke. He fully lived the mantra; always *telling the truth kept you from having to remember what you said.*

A saying he would often recall his mother mentioning from time to time. The American people deserved that much from him.

Looking at his son, Sam was proud of the man and what he had become in such a short time. He matured tremendously in the last 24 months. "Everything we have worked for has culminated to within this moment, Damian. Even Barbara Walters, coming out of retirement to interview you, is something of a marvel, but after watching you last summer, she thinks you are our great hope." The IT tech threaded the mic, hid it under the lapel, and walked away, giving them privacy.

Sebastian gave Damian an approving nod in his characteristic way. He knew this was Damian and Sam's moment, but Damian had asked Sebastian personally to attend of which Sebastian Storm was deeply honored and accepted the invitation.

Damian West had come to enjoy having Sebastian Storm around during critical moments. Regina added, "This is your moment, your time, Damian, and we all support the man you have become and the movement you will create," as Damian hugged his Godmother, always appreciating her sound and controlled words. She always gave him peace when he needed it most.

"What's your take on all of this, Sebastian?" Singling him out, Sebastian hesitated, choosing his words carefully, "Well, you are becoming more and more of a celebrity, Damian. Just don't ever think you can ask me to put your slippers on for you or bring you M&Ms in the middle of the night because, frankly, that's where I draw the line," they all laughed. Sebastian was always one to provide comedic relief during stressful moments. Sebastian's smile faded, knowing his friend needed something more, "I think the timing is perfect, Damian, make an impact. Be profound tonight. Impress Barbara, and you will impress the people watching." "Well said," replied Sam, patting Sebastian on the back.

Damian shook his head, "I can't believe you persuaded her to do this, Dad." "Oh, but I didn't, Damian. She reached out to me the night of your enlightening speech, planting the seed with me on making this happen tonight. Come to think of it, both Barbara and

Sebastian contacted me immediately after the speech which started it all. You impressed her, and I know she wants you to excel. This is your moment, son," As Sam stood in front of him, hands on both arms, "This is where our future begins. We take another step for the Unified Party tonight."

Damian West looked at his father, appreciating his advancing years and wisdom yet saddened, wondering at that moment how much longer he had with him. He was exceptionally fortunate to have such a worthy mentor protecting him, advocating, and inspiring him from an early age. He smiled at his father, "You have been the single greatest thing in my life, Dad, and I will always strive to make you proud of me and our mission. Tonight, we find out who truly are our friends in all this and who forsakes us. This night is the pinnacle of our movement, and I will not fail you or us. Of this, I promise and commit to you."

"I know you do . . . . *Make me proud, son.*" Damian turned to see the three looking at him. This auspicious group was made up of the Four Horsemen: the pioneer, the voice of reason, the enforcer, and he himself was their shining beacon.

Damian smiled one last time as he walked out of the bedroom, down the stairs, and sat in the living room where Barbara Walters sat patiently, waiting for him to arrive. She stood up and shook his hand as she waved off her assistant, giving Ms. Walters and Senator West a moment alone.

She smiled at him, "You nervous, Senator?" "No, ma'am, rather excited, actually." Barbara Walters laughed at the confidence, or arrogance she wasn't sure which. Out of earshot, she whispered, "Be yourself, Senator. There are a lot of people watching, and those that don't will at some time soon. We are making history here tonight."

She grabs his hand and leans in, "The Unified Party needs their leader now, Damian. Show them what you're made of. The Alternative Consortium is supporting you fully. Make us proud." As she turned and took her seat and gestured with her hand for him to do the same. Damian, rarely shaken, was shocked at her words at the moment; how would she know anything about those secretive groups unless . . . . .

Upon hearing those words and glancing to his right, he saw his father and Sebastian standing proudly. He was suddenly aware the interview was set up only for him, for his benefit, and to emerge as the people's champion, and, lastly, for those who needed their liberator to rise in the moment. The level and depth of influence of the Consortium amazed him, more so every given day. Everything had been laid before him to pave his success in his journey. They had all thought of everything, not a detail missed or omitted.

He took his chair opposite Barbara Walters as the cameras began to roll. Signifying the magnitude of the iconic Barbara Walters to seduce out of retirement to do what could be the last great interview of her life. "3. . .2. . . ." and with fingers gesturing to signify they were *live* with television feed.

Barbara Walters began with an introduction, then personalized it in the classic intimate demeanor only Barbara Walters could deliver, "Well, Senator West, thank you for allowing a moment to speak with an ailing journalist. I will admit this interview I've looked forward to more than most in my long career. After seeing you speak in the Capitol late last summer, I believe it's been on the minds of all Americans, certainly mine, and little has been shed on your Unified outlook. It was enough to bring me out of retirement just to have this interview with you. Welcome, and thank you for being here tonight."

Damian smiled in his charismatic yet humbled demeanor as he looked at her as well as the camera, playing his charm masterfully as he answered, "Well, Barbara, I am more than honored to be asked to speak with you this evening. Your list of esteemed subjects is quite impressive, far more extraordinary than me. I am a mere Senator and steward of the people. Far from the past presidents, celebrities, dignitaries, and Nobel Peace winners, you have interviewed historically. I respectfully appreciate your gracious invitation to be here tonight."

"Well, that may be true, Senator West, but you have made some strides few Senators, or past presidents for that matter, have been able to achieve. Your system has worked wonders for Wyoming. And now, I have heard a few other states, such as Montana, Nevada, and Arizona, have found similar results using your method of revamping the governmental system. Please tell us what your secret has been," inquired Barbara.

"The country, Barbara, needs an honest change and reform. My system, when implemented, removes the toxic part of what the government has become. Back to the basics as it were . . ." Damian spends the next few minutes describing how and what those changes were and its method of integration and putting pressure on current state governments and key political positions as it being their fiduciary responsibility to improve the issues facing Americans today. He spoke from the heart and why his plan was working and the people of several of these western states were seeing the change almost immediately.

Barbara then switched gears, "Senator West, it's been widely publicized you don't appear to have a special person in your life, can you shed some light on that area for our listeners?"

Damian was certain the question would come up, and he chose to meet it head-on, "I'd much rather talk about your Havanese dog . . . *Cha-Cha*, isn't it?" Barbara laughed, impressed he researched her dog's name, "Hahaha, yes, Cha-Cha is my little baby Havanese, you charmer."

Pressing forward, Damian didn't want to skirt the important question, "Actually, Barbara, there is someone. She is someone special to me, and I've been seeing her for several months now. Out of respect for her and her privacy, I won't delve any further into such subjects, but rest assured, I'm every bit normal in that arena, and when I'm ready to share more of it with the rest of the world," he then turned to the camera and continued, "Then I will, but I would hope the American people will respect my privacy and hope the best for me in my time as my relationship develops."

Barbara Walters smiled, moving the focus, "I think that's fair, but as you know, Senator, your private life, or that of any celebrity, is often an open book. I certainly know from experience." "Fair enough, Barbara, give me time. It's still early," Damian replied. She smiled, knowing the next few questions would define the evening.

As the clock struck the anticipated thirty-minute mark, the excitement in the air was palpable, with viewers from every corner of the globe hanging on to each word uttered. Barbara Walters, renowned for her ability to capture the essence of the moment, held the audience in the palm of her hand, steering the conversation with the finesse of a seasoned journalist.

In the midst of the fervor, the hottest story of the moment loomed large, casting a shadow of intrigue over the proceedings. Yet, despite the mounting anticipation, the most critical question remained conspicuously unaddressed: the rumors swirling around the enigmatic Unified Party.

Speculation ran rampant, fueled by whispers in the corridors of power and clandestine conversations held in the dead of night. But amidst the chaos of conjecture, one thing remained certain: Barbara Walters held the key to unlocking the truth, her penetrating gaze poised to pierce through the veil of secrecy shrouding the elusive faction.

As the world held its breath, eagerly awaiting the revelation promising to redefine the political landscape, Barbara's poised demeanor betrayed none of the urgency coursing through her veins. With a subtle nod, she signaled the impending moment of truth, a tantalizing glimpse into the heart of the story captivating the world's attention.

And as the cameras rolled and the spotlight focused, all eyes turned to Barbara Walters, the consummate storyteller primed to unravel the mysteries lying hidden beneath the surface. For in that fleeting moment, the fate of nations hung in the balance, and the power of journalism stood as a beacon of truth in a world fraught with deception and intrigue.

"Senator West, there have been increasing rumors, much of which was from your own speech last summer and this concept of a unified front and focus for all Americans. The American people want to know. Is this a party wishing to rival the deep and entrenched bi-partisan system, and if so, what is your goal?" Barbara sat back in her chair, knowing this topic was the pinnacle of the evening. Her crescendo was well composed and served up to young Senator West.

Damian West, in the moment, felt as heavy as history itself, interlaced his fingers and leaned forward. There was a brief interlude as he collected his thoughts, and then, with the air of a man stepping onto the world stage, he addressed the millions of people watching with a conviction that seemed to reverberate against the walls.

"Barbara," he began, his voice steady and imbued with a sense of urgency, "we stand at a critical juncture, a precipice of despair for many Americans. The bi-partisan system, once the bedrock of American governance, is no longer fulfilling its promise and obligations to the American people. We find ourselves outpaced by other nations in the very arenas that define a society's progress: education, technology, innovation, and policy."

He paused, allowing the weight of his words to sink in before continuing. "The Republican and Democratic parties, ensnared in perpetual gridlock, have become vanquished in their efforts, each administration fixated on dismantling the legacy of its predecessor rather than building upon it. This cycle is not only unproductive; it is a harbinger of decline, a toxic ritual poisoning the well of political discourse."

West's gaze swept from Barbara to the camera, capturing the attention of all with the gravity of his assessment. "The polarization has become so entrenched that mutual respect and the pursuit of a common good have become casualties of a partisan war. The malignancy of this division runs deep, threatening the vitality of our political system—a system, I fear, is beyond resuscitation in its current form. It is an antiquated machinery, crumbling beneath the weight of its own obsolescence."

In this stark portrayal, Damian West didn't just diagnose the ailments of the American political system, he surgically dissected its failures to the people; he articulated the sentiments of a population yearning for rejuvenation in their governance—a call to action for a new chapter in the annals of American democracy. Spoken with all the truth and sincerity, defining the political climate facing all Americans.

Barbara asked what those were thinking, "So, do you feel, Senator, there is a better way? A healthier way for our country to flourish once again?"

Damian West leaned in, his expression a blend of resolve and anticipation, as he addressed the crux of Barbara's inquiry. "In a word . . . . *yes*. I share your concern, Barbara, and yes, I do envision a transformative blueprint for our nation. Together with some of the sharpest minds of our time, we've been architecting a comprehensive strategy—one transcending race, creed, and economic status, promising a future where every American has the opportunity to prosper."

His eyes, alight with the fire of innovation, continued, "We are crafting a system where the government and its people march in lockstep towards shared aspirations. Imagine a healthcare system that genuinely works for all, a tax framework that equitably distributes the burden and benefits, irrespective of social class to name a few."

Damian spoke of responsibilities, as well as rights, of a social contract renewed, "We envisage a society where the citizenry and state exist in a symbiotic relationship—each playing their part in forging a collective success. Picture initiatives bold enough to lift every homeless individual from the streets, integrating them into society through employment programs and enacting measures balancing the right to bear arms with stricter regulations to ensure the imperatives of public safety are met. And yes, we will tackle the sensitive debates surrounding reproductive rights with the compassion and nuance they deserve."

West's tone took on a professorial edge as he unveiled his vision, "The Unified Theory isn't a panacea. It's a pragmatic step forward from the partisan stagnation we're mired in. It's a leap towards something substantially more significant than the sum of its parts, more consequential than the hollow rhetoric that's become the hallmark of our current parties. It's time for actions that speak louder than words, for policies that do more than just promise—it's time for solutions that deliver."

Barbara interjected, "So are you saying, Senator West, you have a new and emerging third party that could resolve many of these issues Americans face today?"

Damian's pause was a dramatic prelude to a profound connection with the audience beyond the lens. As he gazed intently into the camera, his gaze seemed to pierce through to the very heart of the nation. "To the people of our great nation," he began, with the gravity of a statesman aware of the historical weight of his words, "I stand before you with a resolve to dismantle the bi-partisan gridlock stifling our collective progress. Barbara, you question whether I have a plan. It is far more than a plan—it is a widespread movement. It's the inception of a new party poised to excise the entrenched toxicity of our current political landscape."

His voice, firm and impassioned, continued, "We will forge a path where every citizen is seen, heard, and valued equally—without the specter of segregation. We'll cultivate harmony between the people and the government, a true representation of the will of the electorate, not the charade we witness today, where governance is a commodity traded among the elite. No more shall our system be one trampling over its citizens in the rush to fill its coffers. This is the dawn of a new epoch, an era of unity and integrity."

Damian West's declaration reverberated with the promise of a new political dawn. "This movement," he proclaimed, "will not merely rise—it will soar, infused with hope and bound by the unshakeable principle of unity. We will extract the wisdom of our forebearers and the strengths of existing parties, discarding the decay undermining our nation's ideals. Barbara, I stand before you and the American people ready to champion a party embodying this vision—I impress upon the people of these United States, I present to you . . . *The Unified Party.*"

His voice swelled with conviction and passion as he continued, "Today, I cast off the mantle of an Independent, as I did with the

Republican Party before it, and I pledge my allegiance to a party representing not just the few but of . . . . *every American.*"

Barbara Walters, momentarily taken aback by the audacity of the announcement, regained her composure, her journalistic instincts piqued. "Senator, on live television, you're forsaking your Independent status to embrace the Unified Party?" The astonishment was clear in her voice, but it was swiftly followed by intrigue. "This is a formidable leap, Senator. How do you intend to rally the public behind such an ambitious endeavor?"

Damian leaned in, his eyes alight with strategic fervor. "Barbara, momentum is built on boldness and belief. We will galvanize support through unwavering commitment to the people's true needs and by demonstrating our policies are crafted not for power but for progress. We will engage in dialogue directly with the citizens, listening and learning and showing politics can be a noble call to service. Through transparency, integrity, and action, we will inspire a coalition across the entire spectrum of society, united under the banner of the Unified Party, ready to restore the republic to its people."

In an unpretentious manner, Senator Damian West expertly explained, "Barbara, the American people have been demanding it and have been lied to for many years regarding our inability to move forward in this current political platform. With the riots, murders, and mass exodus of key companies from U.S. soil, we are losing the battle to create an environment worth living in and a country worth defending. The Unified Party was founded upon the ideals of the founding supporters for change to occur. Those who are tired of the rhetoric are rising up within this party, and the world will see the emergence of an imposing force challenging the Republican and Democratic parties poignantly and exposing them for their contemporary mediocrity. We will stand tall and openly face the opposition." Damian West looked at Barbara, who appeared amazed at the honest and determined focus of her young guest as he so eloquently explained. She simply wanted to hear him speak and was eager to learn more.

In Barbara Walters's hesitation, Damian continued, "We have all been diligent students in knowing the Republican and Democrats repeated display of their weaknesses, as they have worn them like badges for decades on end. The Unified Party holds true the idea of what it is to be an American and won't cower behind the mask of obscurity. We will meet our challenges head on, and we feel we will prevail under the guise of understanding the people making up this great nation."

Finally, Barbara Walters had regained her composure, "Senator West, you keep mentioning *'we.'* Who is encompassing the supporting cast for you in which to build and propel your new platform?"

Damian smiled, hoping to be asked the question, "We, as a group include people sympathetic to the cause and dream and have been for decades. This includes Senators, large corporations, and public figures. The list, of which will be impressive once disclosed. There has been a support structure for many years, ready when the time was right and when the American people had finally had enough."

"Today is that day, Barbara. The emergence of the Unified Party has ventured forth. *With the people, and for the people, it will become one with the people and has always been our goal.* The betterment of all Americans who wish to help themselves and fortify their country through a unified front with one another and aligned with government."

Damian West turned away from Barbara Walters and looked directly into the camera, and with seriousness and conviction, he proclaimed, "To the American people, I make this pledge. Though daunting in the process, I promise to make the Unified Party follow through on the change and progression and not just oratory from other emerging third parties. Our focus is centered on you. The elected government officials we choose must always remain stewards of their commitment to serve in a capacity striving to make this country great . . . its people and business enterprises. The Unified Party strives to make the government, the businesses, and its people a synergistic platform to flourish and work together . . . *unified.*"

The energy within the room was overfilled with inspiration and curiosity. Senator Damian West had a charisma not witnessed in generations and captured the hearts of Americans and foreigners alike. His humility and genuineness were apparent, and the viewers could sense it. Over 126 million people tuned into the Barbara Walters Show to watch and witness what they had been hearing about for months concerning the charismatic Senator, exceeding her interview with Monica Lewinsky in 1999, which attracted an impressive 49 million. The expectations were high, and Damian performed exceptionally in every way possible and exceeded the expectations of all who watched the historic event.

Barbara smiled, "If I didn't know better, Senator West, I'd say you are almost insinuating a presidential run. Is that a possibility in 2024?" Damian smiled back at her, hesitated for a moment, "I will serve this country in the best way I can, Barbara. This is my mission and my focus. I have no idea what the future holds, but the American people need only know the interests I share as well. My job is that of a congressman, and I will do everything in my power to uphold the office in the way that benefits this country the most."

"Ambiguous as expected," replied Barbara Walters, "And with that, I thank you, Senator West, for spending this evening with us and enlightening everyone watching about this exciting emerging party that seems most impressive. I wish the best of luck to you and your endeavor. You can get more information on the Unified Party on the website below. Thank you, Senator West, for being on the show." "My pleasure, Barbara," replied Damian West as the feed faded too commercial.

"Wow," was all Barbara Walters could muster as the production crew all began clapping for Damian West. He stood up and put his hand to his heart in an effort to thank them all for the kind gesture.

Barbara also stood out of earshot of the others, "You played all of the interview brilliantly, Damian. You have the next year to reel them in before you announce your presidency." Damian looked at her curiously, wondering how she knew of their plan as she added, "The Alternative Consortium will be the force you will need to see this through. God bless, young man, and good luck," as she began walking away, grabbing the hand of Sam West as he walked towards them. She squeezed his hand in passing and looked up at him, "He has a gift, Sam. Guard him well," and that was it, as one of her assistants escorted the ailing woman out of the room.

Barbara Walters wouldn't live long enough to see her prediction come to fruition as she would pass away on December 30, 2022, just a few months later. However, her last interview with Senator Damian West was deemed the most significant of her career, surpassing interviews with Monica Lewinsky, Ronald Reagan, Michael Jackson, and Barack Obama. The significance of the moment is forever captured in history as one of the most inspiring discussions ever recorded.

Dallas, Texas
2022 March
9 PM MST
Dymitron Headquarters

Mila Dmitri intently viewed the television, along with the other 150 million viewers watching the Barbara Walters Special Edition Interview, entranced with the words of the eloquent Senator from Wyoming bestowed to all who cared to listen. The viewership had reached over 177 million by the end of the interview, no doubt from the buzz over the social media frenzy to view the young Senator's interview. When the segment finished, she smiled inwardly, amazed the 60 minutes had passed so quickly.

Mila experienced a rush of flattery upon realizing she was the subject of his discussion and romantic reference, a wave of validation coursing through her veins as she recognized the significance of his narrative with millions of viewers. The knowledge that her presence had sparked intrigue and interest in him ignited a glimmer of excitement within her, fueling her with a sense of anticipation for what was to come.

Yet, beneath the surface of her elation, a shadow of surprise and hurt lingered, casting a cloud over the moment of recognition. The revelation he had chosen not to share the important news regarding the unveiling of the Unified Party with her beforehand struck a chord of disappointment, leaving her feeling excluded and overlooked in a matter of significance.

As she grappled with the conflicting emotions swirling within her, Mila couldn't help but question the foundation of their relationship, a subtle undercurrent of doubt creeping into her thoughts. Had their connection been as strong as she had believed, or had she misjudged the depth of their bond? But then again, they had not known one another long, and she had her own secrets. Secrets that would soon be revealed to the public in the moments that followed.

In the midst of her internal turmoil, Mila resolved to confront him, to seek clarity and understanding in the face of uncertainty. For she refused to allow her feelings to be disregarded, her presence relegated to the periphery of his world. As she prepared to address the issue head-on, she steeled herself with determination, ready to demand the transparency and honesty she deserved.

She was both adulated and angered by the fact she had no idea all of this was brewing since they had met. She felt betrayed he didn't confide this vital information to her despite her mentioning several aspects not aligning, such as Sebastian Storm's presence on the property or a deeper understanding of his extempore speech in which he divulged the initial concept of unity to the public in the famous Washington D.C. interview the summer before.

As she thought about it further, she realized she couldn't blame him fully; she had her own enigmas, she supposed, the most significant of which was moments away from being announced, and Senator Damian West would be equally upset with her once the news reached him. They both had skeletons in the closet, and hers may even be more significant. She would know in a few minutes.

There was a knock at the door, and then it opened slightly, "Pardon me, Mila, he's going on soon; he wants you close to him," said the producer as Mila followed her from the media room. She followed the young lady through a labyrinth of hallways and rooms to the main stage, where the frenzied mass of news reporters sat in multiple rows of seats, waiting for the news conference to begin. Mila walked to the back room, nodded to the guard who opened the door, and she walked in closing it behind her.

There, Anthony Voss stood alone, confident, and styled with a custom blue tailored suit and white open shirt. He portrayed and emulated the consummate CEO, poised, focused, and serious in the moment. "I was beginning to think you may not show, Mila," teased Anthony. "Sir, you know I wouldn't miss this for the world," replied Mila, smiling at her boss.

"Would you believe I am a little nervous? Who would have *thunk*," jokingly teasing himself. "'Thunk,' haha, well, at least you haven't lost your sense of humor, Anthony. You have that, no question. We have had this in the works for a long time. We knew this day would come," added Mila.

"True, but what I say tonight will shake the world and most likely cripple the market," said Anthony. "Well, it would be the second time tonight then . . . . the world will be shaken, I mean," replied Mila.

"Second time," asked Anthony, a little confused, cocking his head as he looked at her. He had been so wrapped up in his own news conference he had blocked out the rest of the world.

Mila hesitated, then replied, "Senator Damian West announced in an interview with Barbara Walters he has formed a new faction called the Unified Party. It appears he has substantial backing, enough to make the move against the Republican's and Democrats' stagnation. Nearly 200 million viewers watched him with anticipation."

Anthony Voss was dumbstruck at the news as he sat in his chair, "Holy fuck, his news may actually trump my announcement. The American people are being hit with two thumps tonight. Although his news has more of a positive slant than mine. Jesus Christ, Damian West, you are a maverick." He shot a glance at Mila, forgetting her relationship with him, "And you didn't know? Honestly?" No, no, I didn't, Anthony, it's all news to me. Then again, he doesn't know ours either," she said, shaking her head, knowing he was hinting at the possibility.

"Well, that, along with this news, should make for some interesting pillow talk next time you see one another. I sure as fuck don't envy you, Mila," as he laughed. She flips him off as the young female producer from earlier knocks and pokes her head in, "We are ready, Sir." "Bravo, game time, Mila, wish me luck," said Anthony as he stood up. "Break a leg, boss," she said without looking at him, turning her gaze to the large monitor in the corner of the room. Her best spot to view the news conference: secluded and private.

Several seconds later, the CEO of Dymitron enters the side entrance, hops eagerly up the stairs, walks to the podium in the center, and waves to the news reporters as they rise to their feet.

Anthony gestures to them to quiet themselves and to take a seat with his hands in a downward motion. He takes a deep breath and slowly says, "Thank you all for being here tonight. I am going to make a brief statement, and upon its completion, I will not be taking any questions. It has been decided after substantial consideration and unanimously voted upon by our Executive Board of Directors that Dymitron Solution will be moving our Corporate Headquarters and substantial manufacturing division to Singapore to explore more competitive options in labor costs, supply costs, ongoing U.S. regulatory restrictions, and various reduction of operational expenditures. As CEO, I have realized the significance and impact this decision will have on the U.S. economy, but the longevity and legacy of this company are my fiduciary responsibility. I am ultimately responsible for, and I owe it to, our clients, employees, and most of all, our shareholders. The move will occur over the next three years. Thank you and have a good night."

Anthony Voss walked off the stage as the barrage of questions and flashing lights hounded him until he was safely behind the security doors, safe from their anger for not answering their questions. He was glad it was finally over. The burden he had been carrying for months was finally lifted. The word was finally out, and the corollaries following was the next step of the announcement.

Mila Dmitri turned from her screen to greet him as he entered the room. She smiled, "I think they loved it," Mila suggested sarcastically. Anthony Voss smirked and cocked his head, "Yeah, I'm sure. Longest 60 seconds I have ever had to endure. Now the stock price will plummet." Mila replied, "Futures are already down $7 a share."

Anthony shook his head, "The carnage begins. Well, we knew this would come, and we all need to weather the storm. Only hope we don't dip below $37 a share.

The Special Report news switched to the announcement of Voss only minutes later, as Mila and Anthony listened to Lester Holt from NBC Nightly News. The image of Laster Holt appears, "This just in from Dallas, Texas. Dymitron Solution's CEO, Anthony Voss, has just announced the company will be moving off U.S. soil over the next three years to Singapore based on labor costs, U.S. regulatory issues, and supply costs. Voss refused all questions following the announcement. Let's take it over to news correspondent Tori Caspian in Dallas . . . ." "Thank you, Lester. Yes, there has been a buzz about this rumor Voss is considering taking Dymitron Solutions, the largest and most substantial of American businesses, away from American soil itself, which is a crushing blow to the Biden Administration as they were unable to meet the needs of Anthony Voss and company specifics surrounding the growing tax implications, regulatory restraints and labor/product costs facing the semiconductor company. Most will recognize the name Dymitron Solutions, having launched the StreamLINE^{TM} technology a few years ago, revolutionizing the world in the Semiconductor business. Voss's relocation of the Headquarters and Manufacturing plant could cripple the U.S. economy if he follows through with his announcement to move the company overseas. The Biden Administration isn't commenting at the moment, but it doesn't bode well in not taking care of the United States' most prolific and lucrative companies, and President Biden won't be happy a company like Dymitron is leaving on his watch, I'm sure."

"Thank you, Tori," replied Lester Holt, "And never before occurring in my career, a simultaneous secondary Special Report concerning the Barbara Walters special featuring the up-and-coming Senator from Wyoming, Damian West, son of prominent Senator Samuel West. The interview brought iconic interviewer, Barbara Walters out of retirement with the most widely attended interview of her illustrious career. The Senator shook the viewers, announcing his new Unified Party's immanent release and dodging the question of entering the presidential race in 2024. His interview created quite a stir, and rumor has it he has depth in his ranks supporting the new party. Should be interesting to see what develops in this story in the months to come."

Damian and his father retired to his study the night following the Barbara Walters interview. Already waiting within sat Senator Ren Cosner, Speaker of the House Regina Alvarado, State Representative Julian Chambers, Senator Gideon Arnold, and Media Mogul Harrison Stensrud. Lastly, though not a member of the auspicious group, their protector, Sebastian Storm, was their overwatch. They all waited, seated each within the large round table, discussing the interview as Sam and Damian entered, the first meeting since Damian learned of their endorsement of him for the 2024 Presidential Campaign.

Gideon Arnold was added to the group, an influential and respected Democratic Senator from Washington state. A Republican by affiliation but more moderate in style. Senator Arnold held the wide respect of Congressmen on both sides of the aisle for his even temperament and sound advice on sensitive matters. Involved with multiple committee chairs, Gideon possesses a quick wit and charismatic banter with his continuants and a powerful alley within the Alternative Consortium and a key player in the orchestration of George H.W. Bush to announce the emergence of the Unified Party in the presidential election in 1988, but Bush failed the consortium over the Republican influence and keeping congruent with his Republican affiliation and loyalty, essentially dismantling the movement to push the emergence and evolution of the Unified Party. As a result, Gideon Arnold lost significant confidence in the Republican party after George H.W. Bush was unable to follow through with the Alternative Consortium's plans to bring the Unified Party to light.

In addition, also present was Harrison Stensrud, a shrewd media mogul and considered one of the most influential businessmen of the 21st century. He had been a long-standing member of the Alternative Consortium and worked diligently to get the Libertarian Party much-needed coverage as they emerged. There was not enough strength internally, and inner party dramatics inhibited the party from going further as a substantiated third-party worthy of recognition.

Everyone took their seats, the image surreal as the seven legendary members sat around the circular table. An imposing group represented the idealistic nature of what the Unified Party emulated and stood for as a significant force demanding a new and refined United States of America.

Damian West, the youngest of the group, stood at his chair and addressed the group for the first time as their leader. No longer the young disciple as he had been to many who sat within the illustrious group but now crowned as their champion. Crafted and created at the hands of the leaders who sat around the table and had formed much of the political framework supporting the new regime.

Senator Damian West emerged as a prolific figure, a beacon of truth and justice amid a sea of uncertainty, heralding the dawn of a new era the Alternative Consortium had long envisioned. For years, they had awaited a leader who passionately galvanized their movement, a victor to carry their ideals forward into the turbulent waters of the next decade. In Damian West, they found not only a politician but a symbol of hope and progress, destined to become the linchpin of their aspirations.

As Damian commanded the attention of the supporters gathered around the table, their gazes brimming with admiration and reverence, it was evident he embodied the very essence of what their party stood for. His presence exuded charisma and authority, a potent combination that resonated deeply with those who had placed their faith in him.

———

Among the onlookers, Senator Sam West felt an enormity of pride swell within him, his heart ballooning with paternal pride as he beheld the remarkable journey his son had undertaken. Damian's achievements surpassed those of most individuals twice his age, a testament to his unwavering dedication and unyielding resolve.

Surveying the impressive gathering of luminaries and leaders, Sam couldn't help but reflect on the pivotal role they had played in shaping Damian into the formidable leader he had become. As mentors and guides, they had nurtured his talents and honed his skills, laying the groundwork for the momentous occasion unfolding before them.

But now, as Damian prepared to take the reins of leadership, the dynamics had shifted. No longer the pupil, he stood poised to lead the charge, to guide his allies and comrades-in-arms into the next chapter of the American narrative. As Sam appreciated the scene before him, he couldn't help but feel a sense of awe at the magnitude of the journey that lay ahead, knowing Damian was destined to leave an indelible mark in the records of history.

With great strength and confidence, Damian petitioned, "Thank you all for being here tonight. We made a significant stride last night with the Walters interview, and now we all have passed the point of no return. Before all of us . . . . . *the seven of us* will be the next great challenge we must address. As all of you know, Dymitron Solutions announced their relocation to Singapore over the next few years. This may offer a golden opportunity for us if we could woo Anthony Voss and Dymitron to possibly stay in the country. If we end up brokering one of the largest deals to keep our largest, most significant American company from leaving U.S. soil, it could be another shot in the arm of what we are trying to create here."

Sebastian Storm spoke up, "Damian, that's a masterful plan. Anthony Voss is a practical man, and if you make it worth his while and cater to his sense of pride in being an American, you may secure his commitment to stay. It has to make sense to him and for the betterment of Dymitron."

Sam spoke up, "Voss would need to see the fiscal upside and reduce the restrictions Biden's administration has put upon Dymitron . . . . . *all of this may all fall into place.*"

Damian gestured to the empty eighth seat, the only remaining spot they had yet to fill, "Possibly the opportunity he is looking for if he can recognize the benefit of potentially becoming a part of this distinguished group.

"He would make a substantial addition, especially if his interests aligned with the Unified Party lines," offered Julian Chambers. Damian continued, "That it would. However, we will wait until he approaches us, for at that time, we will know his true intention. To align with us, follow our creed, and reveal he would rather stay within the U.S. border if at all possible. We must remain vigilant and patient."

"Once we have the eighth position filled, we will have our Executive Board in place," explained Damian West, "Our group will ensure the integrity of Unified Party is held true, certify the American people receive fair and dedicated stewards representing their needs and we regain the sovereignty of what our great nation holds as our focus. The eight at this table will be the watchmen and guardians of what the Unified Party holds dear.

I have decided to call this auspicious group. . . ."

"*. . . . The Watchful Eight.*"

Chapter 13

The Unified Party

"One man with courage makes a majority."
~Andrew Jackson

Washington, D.C.
2022 May
Senate Floor

For the next month, the media remained in a state of frenzy. Senator Damian West's inspirational interview with Barbara Walter's sent shockwaves across the country.

As promised, upon his delivery of the new party, an immediate shift within Congress commenced, disrupting normal flow and loyalties across the already tumultuous aisles separating the two political heavyweights.

Americans were confused and unsure what this disruption meant in the grand scheme of the political fabric they had been accustomed to.

Many remained reluctant, unsure of where this new party would fall as many third parties had tried yet failed in their attempt to gain any footing within the established two party system. Slowly, additional Senators and State Representatives switched their alliance and were immediately taken under the protective wing of the Unified Party, offering political asylum for those brave enough to weather the sacrifice they made in publicly denouncing their respective political affiliations.

It was no surprise Damian West was scrutinized the heaviest along with the Speaker of the House, Regina Alvarado, but they were both ready for the onslaught that followed along with Senators Cosner and Arnold. All masterfully led any interviews and press conferences down a road of party certainty and confidence, instilling curiosity in the American people. Americans and foreigners alike were intrigued by how a superpower could be so exposed to the emotional upheaval such a new party seemed to be bringing to the media circuits across the globe.

Within days of the Barbara Walters interview the initial polls were astounding as Americans were shifting their thinking after Damian announced the formation of the Unified Party. Republicans and Democrats felt confident the inspirational delivery of Senator West would fall on deaf ears, lost in the noise of historical political upheaval, much like the Green and Libertarian parties in the past. As a result, the bipartisan system gave little credence to the Unified Party and knew full well the uphill battle the small and new party would face in gaining traction against the political heavyweights.

A subtle shift and fear occurred and piqued the interest of the Republicans and Democrats once the initial polls were released. The early polls showed that 82% of Americans agreed significant change needed to occur in the current political platform and reform was needed. The poll results offered an interesting perspective:

9% of Americans believed the Unified Party emulated the changes needed to initiate reform effectively.

38% of Americans were unsure of the Unified Party and its claims accomplished.

———

32% felt no third party could penetrate the historical and substantive age-old Republican and Democratic parties.

And 21% were undecided yet, curious, and needed to hear more.

In a swift and calculated countermove, both the Democrats and Republicans mobilized their vast networks and resources in a coordinated effort to tarnish the reputation of the Unified Party. With a nationwide campaign that echoed with the reverberations of political warfare, they sought to discredit not only the party itself but also its figureheads, chief among them being the Speaker of the House and the recently elected Senator, Damian West. Targeted also was Sam West, questioning his loyalties despite all his years of service.

The air crackled with tension as smear tactics and propaganda machines whirred into action, their sights set squarely on undermining the legitimacy and credibility of the Unified Party's leadership. In the months following the Walters's interview, no stone was left unturned as the opposing parties delved deeply into Damian West's background, seeking to exploit any hint of inexperience or youthful indiscretion to cast doubt on his ability to lead.

But as the onslaught intensified, Damian West stood undaunted, a bastion of resilience in the face of adversity. His youthful exuberance tempered by a steely resolve, he refused to be derailed by the barrage of attacks aimed at his character and reputation. For Damian, this was not just a battle for political survival but a testament in which his mettle would be tested, and his convictions forged anew.

Meanwhile, the Speaker of the House found herself thrust into the spotlight; her leadership was called into question by opponents eager to exploit any perceived weakness for her indecisiveness in changing her party affiliation. Yet, like a seasoned general on the battlefield, she marshaled her forces and rallied her allies, determined to weather the storm and emerge unscathed from the onslaught of political intrigue.

As the titans of the political arena clashed in a high-stakes game of brinkmanship, the fate of the nation hung in the balance. With the eyes of the world upon them, they grappled for supremacy, each maneuver and countermove a testament to the cutthroat nature of modern politics.

In the swirling maelstrom of accusations and recriminations, alliances shifted, and loyalties were tested as the battle for the soul of the nation raged on. And amidst the chaos and tumult, one thing remained certain: in the demonstration of adversity, true leaders would rise, their resolve unshaken and their vision undimmed by the tempest of political strife.

Unbeknownst to both the Democrats and Republicans, lurking beneath the surface of the political landscape, the Unified Party had amassed a formidable arsenal of resources, dwarfing any other third-party contender in the past. With a war chest overflowing with funding—exceeding tenfold the assets of its third party predecessors—the Unified Party stood poised to defy convention and challenge the entrenched pillars of bipartisan dominance that had endured for generations.

But it wasn't just the sheer magnitude of their financial backing that caught their adversaries off guard. It was the meticulous orchestration of their master plan, carefully crafted to unleash a calculated assault of revelations shaking the very foundations of the political establishment. Each detail was meticulously calibrated, and each move was strategically timed to maximize impact and sow seeds of doubt within the established order.

As accusations flew and partisan barbs were exchanged with fervor, the Unified Party bided its time, waiting for the opportune moment to unleash the full extent of its power. Like a coiled spring, it remained poised to strike with precision and force, delivering the intrigue and momentum that would reverberate throughout the corridors of power.

As the Democrats and Republicans grappled with the unexpected resurgence of their upstart challenger, they found themselves outmaneuvered at every turn, blindsided by the depth and breadth of the Unified Party's influence and organization. What they failed to realize was they were not just facing a political opponent, but a formidable adversary armed with a strategic vision and the resources to see it through to fruition.

In the unfolding drama of American politics, the stage was set for a showdown unlike any other. With the Unified Party poised to rewrite the rules of engagement, the battle lines had been drawn, and the fate of the nation hung in the balance.

Nearly every day following the Barbara Walters interview, one of the Watchful Eight would follow suit with a public message as Regina Alvarado was the second to announce her loyalty, followed by Senators Arnold and Cosner. All putting their careers on the line, yet strong in their conviction of supporting the new incipient philosophy and guidance from the young Senator from Wyoming. Their stature and changing of affiliations spoke volumes about the seriousness of their personal political shift.

The genesis of the seismic shift in American politics commenced with a seemingly innocuous press conference, where the venerable retired Senator Samuel T. West stepped into the spotlight, casting aside the traditional trappings of the age-old Republican Party in favor of a bold new allegiance to the Unified Party. His decision reverberated through the hallowed halls of power, sending shockwaves across the political landscape and igniting a firestorm of speculation and intrigue.

With the gravitas of a seasoned statesman, Senator West articulated his reasons for this historic defection, each word resonating with the weight of decades of political experience in every interview or discussion. Citing the guidance and inspiration of his own flesh and blood—his son, Damian West. In addition, Sam West went on to paint his compelling narrative of generational change and ideological evolution. In the validation of familial bonds and shared convictions, he found the courage to chart a new course, shaping the destiny of a nation, and he knew his son represented the future of the nation.

But Senator West's decision to have Damian replace him was far more than a mere act of political expediency; it was a symbolic gesture, a rallying cry for a new era of unity and progress. With his unwavering support, the Unified Party found itself catapulted onto the national stage, its ranks bolstered by the endorsement of a revered elder statesman.

As the cameras flashed and reporters clamored for insight, Senator Sam West stood resolute, a beacon of hope amid the tumult of partisan discord. His inspiration reverberated throughout the Capitol, challenging the entrenched status quo and heralding a bold new era of possibility.

In the chronicles of American history, this moment would be remembered as a turning point, a watershed moment where the old guard yielded to the inexorable march of progress. And as Senator West stepped down from the podium, his legacy secured and his convictions reaffirmed, he knew the journey ahead would be fraught with challenges and obstacles. But with the unwavering support of the Watchful Eight and the burgeoning momentum of the Unified Party at his back, he was ready to face whatever trials lay ahead, confident in the righteousness of their cause and the promise of a brighter future for all Americans.

Julian Chambers was the last of the Watchful Eight to announce his change in political affiliation, citing the loyalty he possessed to the West Family leadership displayed over the years and his trust in their beliefs and dedication. The less prolific of the rest, he tended to keep matters close to his vest. Their strength was in their continuity between all the Watchful Eight.

Interparty issues and commotion within the other parties tended to be their worst enemy and often stunted the growth they had hoped to achieve. The Watchful Eight entertained none of those issues, but if they were ever to arise, they all agreed to address them swiftly or make any necessary adjustments to circumvent the altercation. They could not afford any discontinuity within their auspicious group. Their strength was in their diversity. Past Republicans and Democrats, black or white, male or female - they were all unified in thought and were not encumbered with limited perspectives like the Republican and Democratic parties.

What the polls revealed after six weeks would send Washington into a tailspin, and the timing was poised for the second half of the plan to drop. The new poll results offered a varying perspective following key figures making their switch to the emerging party. The statistics were astonishing and evolving:

22% (previously 9%) of Americans believed the Unified Party emulates the changes necessary to uphold effective reform for the country.

24% (previously 38%) of Americans were unsure of the new Party and its claims.

21% (previously 32%) felt no party could penetrate the history and substance of the Republican and Democratic parties.

And 33% (previously 21%) remained undecided.

The new polls shocked members of the bipartisan system's way of thinking, and it was apparent the new party was gaining momentum despite a range of efforts to suppress them. It could not be explained how the numbers in support of the Unified Party could be increasing, but Senator Damian West was diligently promoting the new party and gaining interest from minorities, millennials, the elderly, and undecided voters. These demographics needed a political home, and the Unified Party provided the infrastructure and innovative programs supporting these diverse groups and their varying interests.

At the very least, the Unified Party was piquing the awareness and curiosity of the American people, and they were impressed with the substantial Congressional leadership's favor and applauded the infrastructure of the Unified Party. Leaders spoke of the confidence and innovative perspectives surrounding the changes promised by the unsullied and well-organized group.

However, despite the American people being curious about the emerging party, Congress, internally was undergoing a violent undercurrent within its core. Arguments and confrontations, even in the most mundane of monthly political affairs, were heating up, and it was apparent the two largest political powers in the United States were threatened by this small and seemingly insignificant pest of the Unified Party. This was the battle of David and Goliath, and the tension was mounting.

And then it all came to a head as a special session was called to order by Senator Theo Camloc.

Sitting patiently, Damian respectfully listened to their rhetoric on the Senate floor until he had had enough and stood up, invited by Senator Theo Camloc to state his position on the value of the Unified Party.

His vernacular was passionate and fierce in delivery. Senator Damian West defended his position to all of his constituents, "Your opinions are incorrect, Senator Camloc, the two party system has been crippled and largely ineffective for decades. These days, all we see is political gridlock, and polarization is running rampant within both the Democratic and Republican parties. Your parties are complacent and ineffective in dealing with key focus groups," as Damian looked out over his continuants, the faces sprinkled with equal numbers of Democrats and Republicans.

Damian West had found his voice, and it was more of a roar as his statements were heard and his conviction strong. It was hard to argue with the young Senator because he possessed a unique way of exposing the underbelly of policy ineffectiveness but was respectful in the method by which he delivered his points and arguments. Further supporting his convictions was the work he had accomplished as Governor of Wyoming and neighboring states following suit.

In the hallowed halls of Capitol Hill, where tradition and hierarchy reign supreme, it was nearly unheard of for a young Senator to make audacious claims without facing relentless scrutiny and opposition from senior constituents and rival factions. However, Damian West was no ordinary force. What set him apart was not just his youthful vigor or ambitious aspirations but the formidable backing and unwavering encouragement of prodigious champions who stood steadfastly in his corner. The Watchful Eight carried enormous weight, and that alone demanded substantial respect from the Senators before him, regardless of which side of the aisle they sat.

These influential figures, poised at the pinnacle of power and influence, lent their formidable support to Damian and their unified cause, their endorsement serving as a powerful testament to his credibility and potential. With their support, Damian found himself partly shielded from the relentless barrage of criticism that often befell newcomers to the political arena, his position bolstered by the weight of their collective prestige and influence.

But it wasn't just the endorsement alone of these prodigious champions that set Damian apart; it was the symbiotic relationship they shared—a dynamic interplay of mentorship and protege, wisdom and ambition. Under their guidance, Damian honed his skills and sharpened his political acumen, navigating the treacherous currents of Capitol Hill with the poise and finesse of a seasoned veteran.

As the whispers of skepticism and doubt reverberated through the halls of Congress, Damian remained undaunted, secure in the knowledge that he had the backing of some of the most influential figures in American politics. With their guidance and support, he charted a bold course forward, his eyes fixed firmly on the horizon as he strove to make his mark on the archives of history.

In the cutthroat world of politics, where alliances shifted like sand and loyalty was a rare commodity, Damian's unique position as the protege of prodigious champions afforded him a rare advantage—a potent blend of legitimacy and clout set him apart from his peers. As he prepared to embark on his journey of transformation and change, he did so with the unwavering assurance he was not alone but rather part of a formidable coalition of visionaries and leaders united in their quest for a brighter future.

His father, for one, stood proud and was respected by all, as was Regina Alvarado, the Speaker of the House. Senators Arnold and Cosner rounded out Damian's corner and it was difficult to gain any ground against the young Senator with the four pillars of political power standing behind him. He was well protected in voicing his opinion, and the senior guard was forced to listen, and he was only gaining momentum with each passing week.

In addition to the weighty constituents supporting the Unified Party, the group was also gaining strength from the fact the Republican and Democratic parties had been at odds with one another for so many years and split on many topics they could never effectively join forces to effectively abolish the Unified Party and the Watchful Eight relied on this factor to hone their momentum.

This fragmentation and segregation of the bipartisan system and antagonistic platform in which they had both been built only gave the Unified Party a stronger position to handle both parties in varying ways instead of one ominous and formidable opponent. They could come together to argue the points directed at the members of the Unified Party, but at the end of the day, there still remained a bitter age-old rivalry between the Democratic and Republican Parties.

Surfaced and identified arguments with the leaders of the Unified Party often gave way to bickering between Democrats and Republicans that would steer the focus away from the argument initially launched against their new adversary. The Watchful Eight would often observe in amusement as the arguments would predictably ensue between members who were known to routinely argue amongst themselves, only further solidifying the ineffectiveness of the bipartisan platform and historical ineptitude.

The Watchful Eight were very strategic and shrewd with regard to their timing in dropping substantial political weights in the form of news and party developments at critical times and to poignant media outlets to maximize their effectiveness. When the time came, those key party promotions would push the needle of the American public's awareness, letting them have a glimpse of the growing political unrest and a certain dread of the Democratic and Republican parties and the positive emergence of the Unified Party.

The complacency of the large parties was finally being tested and called out for their lack of progress and condemned for their ambiguity and outmoded thinking. The American people had finally had enough and were no longer simply accepting what rhetoric the Republican and Democratic parties were dolling out and expected all to accept. Their verbose and trifling excuses were no longer acceptable. It was now challenged and debated at every turn.

The Republican and Democratic parties had fought against one another for so long that their battle tactics had become dull and ineffective, bordering on mundane and predictable. The Unified party carried with it the edginess and determination to change the ways of the old, and the staunch and stale bipartisan system was ill-equipped to handle this new and fearsome antagonist, and they were beginning to realize they were facing a far more crafty and agile foe.

The political platform was evolving far too quickly, and the Democratic and Republican parties were unsure how to deal with such a fast-spreading political wildfire that was consuming the political arena as they knew it. An arena that had been forged over generations and seemingly now exposed to an entity that could bring it all crashing down with their fresh perspective and argumentative spirit. The status quo was no longer an acceptable excuse for the normality, explaining the lack of political progress plaguing the system for generations.

Democratic Senator Theo Camloc had called a special closed session to debate the validity of this so-called Unified Party, and every Senator and every state was represented and in attendance. The month before, within the Senate, 48 seats were held by the Republicans, 47 were held by the Democrats, and 5 being the Unified Party, one being Senator Damian West, but just prior to the special session, the numbers had changed considerably, and the fluid dynamic of party officials changing the affiliations needed to be addressed and Senator Camloc felt this special session was essential to cease and subdue the Unified Party's increasing momentum.

Nearly two months after the revered interview with Barbara Walters, the climate had changed significantly in the Senate. As of May 2022, within the Senate floor, there stood 42 Republican seats and 40 Democratic seats, and the 2 Independents moved over to the Unified Party. 16 Democrats and Republicans switched their respective affiliations to the Unified Party, making it now 18 strong. This switch in balance was threatening the very existence of the bipartisan system, and the momentum only seemed to be growing.

In a stunning turn of events, the entrenched bastions of the Democrats and Republicans, long embroiled in their perpetual political tug-of-war, suddenly found themselves united by an unexpected and unifying challenge. The emergence of the Unified Party, spearheaded by the charismatic and strategically astute Damian West, had rapidly escalated from a mere political curiosity to a formidable threat looming large over the traditional two-party system.

This newfound adversary was unlike any they had faced before—a movement exceeding the typical partisan divides and appealing to a broad cross-section of the American populace, disillusioned by the status quo. The Democrats and Republicans, sensing the seismic shift in the political landscape, were compelled to recalibrate their strategies. No longer could they afford the luxury of their destructive squabbles; they had to address the tidal wave of emergence and momentum the Unified Party was drawing.

In hushed conference rooms and over urgent phone calls, strategies were drafted, and alliances reconsidered. The two parties, historically adversaries, found themselves in an unprecedented détente, their focus redirected toward mitigating the influence of this new, dynamic force in American politics. Discussions once centered around outmaneuvering each other now revolved around a common strategy to counter the surging popularity of the Unified Party.

An unexpected alliance between the Democrats and Republicans highlighted the transformative impact of the Unified Party. It had not only challenged the existing political paradigm but had also inadvertently sown the seeds for a potential collaboration between the two parties that had long forgotten the art of bipartisan cooperation. The American political landscape was on the cusp of a significant evolution, with the Unified Party acting as the catalyst for change, compelling the traditional powers to adapt or risk obsolescence in this new, dynamic era of American politics.

Senator Camloc shook his head, "We have been doing this a long time, son, since before you were even in diapers. Ask your father, he is well aware. A third party simply cannot co-exist within our political system. A system, mind you, originating with our founding fathers. The emergence of a third party has been tried before . . . . *and failed*. The Green and Libertarians are probably the most noteworthy and look what has happened to them. They haven't even secured a 1% penetration between them."

Damian's reply to the Senator was a masterclass in restrained intensity, his voice steady yet underpinned by a palpable determination. "Senator, the reason I stand here today is a testament to a systemic stagnation. The bipartisan system, though well-intentioned, has become a relic, paralyzed not by a dearth of effort but by an absence of progress. And that, Sir, has been occurring since before I was in diapers. The once-lubricated gears of your parties have succumbed to the rust of inefficiency and the corrosion of corruption. You're so entangled in the cobwebs of your own, making you fail to see the crumbling foundation below your pedicured toes, Senator. You have failed to perceive the grinding halt of the political machine lining the underbelly of this nation—a stagnation persisting since the Reagan era. We have become cumbersome and gluttonous in our convictions."

He leaned forward slightly behind the podium, his eyes reflecting the fervor of his belief as he looked out over the other Congressmen. "This isn't just about political disagreements or ideological differences. It's about a fundamental breakdown in the way we govern, a failure to adapt and evolve. The landscape of the world has shifted dramatically, yet our political system remains stubbornly rooted in the past, unable to move, unable to address the needs of a rapidly changing society progressing around it."

Damian's critique was more than an indictment of the current political order; it was a clarion call for a new era of governance. An era that acknowledged the failures of the past and embraced the possibilities of the future, driven not by partisan gridlock but by a united vision for progress and innovation.

He turned, casting a respectful glance toward his father, Sam West. "My father," he continued, invoking the elder West's wisdom, "would often recount tales of a bygone era when Democrats and Republicans waged the noblest of battles. They would fiercely debate, yes, but then extend a hand across the aisle to pass legislation propelling our nation forward. Deals were struck and compromises made, all in service of the American people. Where have those days gone, Senator?" Damian turned his head to look at Senator Camloc, yet uninterested in an answer, and looked away.

Damian's voice grew more impassioned as he painted a picture of the political camaraderie that once was. "Elections were a time for vigorous contention between the respective parties, but once the dust settled, regardless of the victor, all would unite, ready to contribute to the great American enterprise. But those days have receded into the chronicles of history. Now, we witness a perpetual cycle of dismantling rather than building, a relentless deconstruction of predecessors' administration and any progress secured, rather than a collaborative effort to uplift the nation."

He paused, allowing the gravity of his words to resonate. "This is why the Unified Party must emerge—not to reminisce about what was, but to revive the spirit of progress and carry it into a new age. An age where the political machine is not fed with the fuel of discord, but with the energy of unity and the relentless pursuit of the common good." Damian's statement was more than a critique; it was an inspiring call to action, an invitation to restore the tenets of democracy and forge a path to a brighter American future.

Damian stood at the podium with Senator Camloc to his right. His passionate delivery held conviction and logic and they all knew his words were coming from his heart and fueled with honesty and merit.

Damian continued, "So, *no*, Senator Camloc, I will not dismiss what this party represents and what it stands for and hopes to accomplish. You referenced the Green and Libertarian parties and how we should observe and take note of their failure when, in reality, you should be forced to look at your own. You state that our fate will likely mirror their eventual fall from grace. But know this: their numbers don't hold a candle, if even combined, to the interest this party has commanded in a very short time." Waving his hand across to all the senators before him, "Our views and focus, in just 7 weeks' time, constitute 18% of the Senate seats as of this moment, and our numbers are only growing as this belief and the wisdom of the Unifides gain more traction."

Uncharacteristic of the floor of Congress, several whistles and hoorays came from the background. Inspired Unified Party members vocalized their excitement as Damian's enthusiasm only increased his dynamic, "Therefore our answer is a resounding . . . . *no*, Senator Camloc. We will not vacate this dream or for which it stands. We have achieved more, a hundred times over, than what the Green and Libertarian parties *ever* accomplished. We will not go quietly into the night, Senators. You only have yourselves to blame, for we would not be here tonight if the Democrats and Republicans had been doing the job they were elected to do. We are here, Sir, because of a failed system, and many people within this room contributed to that collapse. The system is broken, a system ineffective and largely because of your stewardship of this fractured platform. We are here because the machine no longer works for the betterment of this country and the benefit of the people who feed it. We are here, Senator, because of the collapse of your ideals and your laurels. We exist because someone has to now step in and retire this system or revamp it entirely." Damian looked out over the faces of the men and women who largely were hungry for change to occur, and he knew then he was the man to fulfill that dream.

Damian's posture was unwavering as he addressed his constituents and Senator Camloc specifically, his tone a deliberate balance of poise and intensity. "We remain steadfast, Senator, unyielding in our dedication to the mission summoning us to serve. We stand here today not out of choice but necessity, propelled by the inertia of this system's shortcomings in serving the citizenry and this distinguished nation. The time has come to confront the hard truths, to shoulder the responsibilities we have long evaded."

He paused, allowing his gaze to sweep across the room, every eye fixed upon him. "It's our time to embody the accountability that has been long absent, to enact the reform and change this country cries out for. This, Senator Camloc, is the mandate of the Unified

Party—a commitment to action, to reformation, to the resurrection of a governance worthy of its people."

Damian's voice rose, not just in volume but in fervor. "The old guard, the Republicans and Democrats, have squandered the reverence they once held. Their actions—or rather, inactions—have eroded the trust and respect once granted to them by default and have spawned our evolving party as a result. They no longer perform to the standards this nation requires, nor do they serve the interests of its people as they have taken a vow to pledge."

His declaration was more than a statement; it was a rallying cry, a call to the hearts and minds of the American people, urging them to recognize the dawn of a new political epoch. The Unified Party, he assured, would not only fill the void left by the old parties' failings—it would carve a new path, one of integrity, efficacy, and unwavering commitment to the true spirit of democracy.

As a final word, "This, Senator, is my response to your demand for us to vacate. I give to you an unequivocal . . . . *No, to your request.* Rejected with prejudice. Good day, Sir." Damian West had made his peace and was not about to accept defeat . . . *nor the respect of a response.*

The chamber erupted as Senator Damian West concluded his impassioned speech, the assembly rising in unison to deliver a standing ovation by many, thundering through the august hall. West had not merely spoken; he had kindled a fire in the hearts of those present. His vision, crystalline in its clarity, had outshone the luminescence of any other in the room, and his resolve was unassailable—a beacon of determination that would not be dimmed by opposition or obstruction. Senator Camloc's attempts to stifle Damian West had exactly the opposite effect he desired.

Senator Camloc pounded his gavel to demand order to the point of the wood block falling to the ground. Senator West had been called out in front of Congress and made his point, there was nothing more to say.

The thunderous applause cascaded like a tidal wave, spilling into the corridors beyond the chamber's doors, a testament to the transformative energy West had unleashed. Adjusting his tie with a cool, collected movement, he looked out over the crowd and acknowledged the assembly with a nod, a silent affirmation of the path he was set upon, straight and true to his vision. Damian West peered over at Senator Camloc still pounding his gavel garnering no effect from the audience attempting to quell the fervor were swallowed by the roar of approval, the voices of change drowning out the last whispers of the old guard.

Damian West had made his peace.

Descending from the stage, Damian was flanked by figures of equal conviction: his father, the indefatigable Regina Alvarado, the astute Julian Chambers, and Senators Ren Cosner and Gideon Arnold. Their procession behind him was not just an exit; it was a powerful statement, a physical manifestation of the momentum the Unified Party was gathering. They were a phalanx, with Damian West at the vanguard, blazing a trail through the morass of a beleaguered political landscape.

As they moved up the aisle, the doors of the chamber swung open—not just wooden panels on hinges, but portals to a new epoch. The moment was imbued with the kind of surreal majesty often reserved for coronations, a king not of lands and titles but of ideas and progress enveloped with purpose as he departed his court. The applause that followed him was not mere clapping of hands; it was the sound of barriers breaking, of old structures crumbling, of a new era being heralded. It was the sound of a society poised on the brink of a renaissance, with Damian West, unflinching in his stride, leading the charge. His reign within this emerging party was defined.

From the upper observatory level, Sebastian looked on and smiled, appreciating Damian West for his purity and dedication. He didn't let anyone push him around, and Sebastian respected him highly for this characteristic. Sebastian had never been a fan of politics, along with most politicians either, but this one, he thought, was a rare breed and worthy of the distinction. Damian West was a natural-born leader, and his genuine demeanor and candor compelled people to listen.

Sebastian Storm knew the road would be treacherous as Damian gained ground and political momentum. He was easing into the role nicely and it came effortlessly for him.

Watching from a seat by himself, he observed Senator West's entire monologue following the Democrat's and Republicans' arguments on how to handle the emergence of the Unified Party.

All of the Unified Party members had followed Damian West out of the room, leaving the senators in chaos in their wake. Sebastian found it interesting the disparity between the two groups and how they couldn't agree on any measure, defining and validating their own gridlock. Nothing could be accomplished between the two parties, and it was apparent.

As Sebastian watched the circus before him, he thought of Damian West and the loyalty he decreed with those closest to him. Damian West possessed a charisma that drew people to him, and he humbly leveraged his ability.

The party still had to increase its validity to the American people, but Sebastian assumed after today's display that Senator Camloc's attempts to stifle the party only fueled Damian West's dedication further and most likely inspired some additional sway of affiliation loyalties on the Senate floor.

The stage was set, knowing Damian West would be announcing his candidacy for President of the United States in the months following. There was much work to be done and spreading the word of the party's intent was a daunting process.

Despite the challenges they would face, Sebastian Storm was confident Damian West would deliver on the promises made, and he knew patience in the process was the key. When the dust finally settled, all would watch in awe as they would finally witness the reform the country desperately needed.

Damian West and his powerful Watchful Eight would lay claim to the throne, and a new dynasty would emerge, long-awaited as Damian West's . . . . . *Reign Cometh.*

As Damian West began to exit the Congressional floor, Sebastian popped up to meet him at the chamber doors below and safeguard the man he had vowed to protect.

Outside of the Capitol Building, the air was alight with the energy of a special session adjourning minutes before. It was a session that would be etched into the accounts of history as Damian West, Julian Chambers, Regina Alvarado, Ren Cosner, and Gideon Arnold, along with various staff, descended the grandiose steps of the Capitol Building. A throng of VIP news media and aids buzzed around them, each playing their part in the unfolding drama, hoping for a soundbite that would make the headlines. The group moved with a purpose, their steps a rhythmic echo on the stone, as the golden hour cast a cinematic brilliance over the scene.

Sebastian Storm, a figure of composed vigilance, led the entourage, his earpiece a lifeline to Secret Agent Ben Lee and the other agents on the detail, all custodians between the descending mass of people to the awaiting fleet of SUVs stationed at the foot of the stairs.

The setting sun painted the sky in hues of burning oranges and pinks, a backdrop that seemed to celebrate the dawn of the new era Damian West had heralded. The fading light draped the group in an almost celestial spotlight, shadows stretching long and dramatic across the marble steps.

And then, in a moment, the serenity of the evening was pierced; a sound shattered the calm—a sniper's round, slicing through the air with deadly intent. Sebastian's instincts kicked in before his mind fully processed the sound. He watched in horror the effects of the bullet fired and its impact as it met with flesh and bone of its intended target. It was the unmistakable echo of a threat made manifest. The bullet met its mark with harrowing precision, turning the tranquility into chaos.

Panic ensued, but Sebastian's training took over. With a swift motion, he was on the move, even as the accompanying Congressmen, governmental aides, and journalists scattered. A step behind, Secret Agent Ben Lee sprang into action, their protocols a well-rehearsed dance in the face of danger. The group converged protectively, their movements a blur of urgency to protect themselves from the unknown of what lurked beyond their midst.

As the sun continued to sink behind the cityscape, its light fading like the final act of a play, the Capitol steps became a blood-spattered stage for a starkly different type of spectacle—one resonating with the shock of betrayal and the grim reality of the risks borne by those who dare to lead change. The gravitas of the moment was palpable, charged with adrenaline and the fierce instinct to protect. It was a stark reminder the path to change is often perilous, lined with the shadows of opposition strikes from the most unexpected of places.

As the last reverberations of the sniper shot dissipated into the dusk, Fury slowly withdrew his eye from the reticle, a faint satisfaction settling in his chest. Time was now the currency of his escape, and he spent it sparingly. With the grace of a shadow, he rose, swiftly collecting the spent casings, their metallic bodies still warm with the echo of their recent flight. His hands were a blur, breaking down the faithful Dragunov SVD rifle with mechanical precision, each component sliding into the embrace of his custom-fitted backpack as he moved toward the stairwell.

He took to the stairs, his boots a mere whisper against the stone as he descended the spine of the Smithsonian Museum's grand structure. Each step was calculated, the descent an orchestrated symphony of his evasion. He slipped on his helmet, now his guise, the leather jacket his cloak in this urban theater of espionage.

A trifle few seconds had passed—a lifetime in his line of work— as he checked his watch, his heart still betraying no haste. He slipped through the exit door to the alleyway, his senses heightened, scanning for any untimely witness to his passage, but there were none. The side alley offered some sanctuary, where his sleek Suzuki 750GSXR motorcycle lay in wait, its carbon-fiber body a sliver of night itself, which was quickly approaching and only aided in his evasion.

The turn of the key was a symphony of anticipation, the engine's roar a declaration of his fleeting presence. With a twist of the throttle, Fury was off to the edge of the alley, then swiftly melded into the flowing traffic, his exit as enigmatic as his arrival. The city, oblivious for the moment, would soon awaken to the chaos he had sown, but by then, he would be a mere ghost, his presence fading into the growing traffic along with the setting sun, leaving behind only the whispers of a specter in the twilight.

No trace of him would be left behind, only the mystery of his intention.

Quantico, Virginia
2022 June

"We haven't caught a single lead, Sebastian," lamented Hillary Bastini, the seasoned Director of the Anti-Terrorist Special Division, her voice heavy with frustration. "Our shooter is like a phantom. There is no camera footage, no tangible evidence. Basically, no footprint on this guy at all. It's as if he vanished into thin air. We're grasping at straws, suspecting the shots might have originated from somewhere near the Smithsonian Museum. There's a theory that the shooter made a swift escape on a motorcycle, but even that's a shot in the dark. We've had HALO scouring every inch, but they've come up empty-handed. This shooter is a wisp in the wind."

HB had a long-standing bond with Sebastian Storm, dating back to his youth. She had played a pivotal role in shaping his early career, stepping in as a mentor after James and Sean Woodford had imparted their wisdom. Under her guidance, Sebastian had ascended to unparalleled heights in his field, becoming the crème de la crème of agents in her eyes. Their relationship had deepened over the years, with Hillary consistently championing Sebastian as her top operative.

Together, they shared an unwavering belief in Senator Damian West, dedicating significant resources to ensure his safety. In the face of this elusive threat, their resolve was put to the test as they navigated the murky waters of uncertainty, determined to shield the senator from harm.

"Damn, I was afraid of that. For some reason, Fury and Inferno and their escape in Ireland last year still resonate in my mind, and I feel we haven't seen the last of them, and this attempt makes me wonder about those two. It's totally their MO," explained Sebastian.

"Good morning, Mr. Storm," came the monotone voice and now with a refined and realistic human image, a hologram of a man's face upon the screen beside them. "You appear to be constantly evolving by the minute, HALO," replied Sebastian, "and good morning to you as well." Sebastian cocked his head, questioning why he was wishing a computer A.I. a *good morning.* HALO was an ever-evolving enigma to Sebastian, and he hadn't gotten entirely used to him over the last 20 years. But there was no question the A.I. was evolving exponentially in the last few years.

HB, turning the conversation back to the present, "Let's stay on point, gentlemen. I would agree, Sebastian, but those two have vanished completely. Nothing has come up on either of them on any level, and it would only put them at risk to surface now. Nonetheless, this assassination attempt doesn't add up. There was a relatively clear shot on West with the second round fired, but your intervention caused Chambers to take the bullet to his leg, but only after the victim, Jenifer Honnoly, was fatally hit. HALO, what's your take on this?"

As the situation unfolded with clinical precision, HALO delivered its analysis with a sterile detachment, heightening the gravity of the event. "The parameters of the round fired align with the capabilities of a sniper with intermediate capabilities, considering the half-mile distance and the myriad of factors involved," HALO began, its voice devoid of emotion yet rich with calculated certainty. "Taking into account the target's slow movement, ambient temperature, time of day, wind conditions, bullet drop over distance, the complexity of the shot reduces significantly for a skilled marksman."

HALO⊙ paused, processing terabytes of data in a digital blink. "Furthermore, Ms. Honnoly was situated approximately 12 feet from Senator West when she was struck by the first round, indicating that she was the intended target of the initial strike. The subsequent shot, which was notably delayed, deviated from its trajectory and impacted Mr. Chambers in the left femur. The shot was not aligned to hit Senator West even if all the parameters had been ideal."

HALO⊙'s analysis continued, its algorithms dissecting the chaotic variables of human conflict with dispassionate logic. "The ballistic profile and my A.I.-powered re-enactment of the scenario suggest that the second round was not meant to be lethal. The angle and impact analysis indicate a non-fatal wound was the likely outcome, suggesting that the intent was to incapacitate Mr. Chambers rather than to terminate him."

In the cold light of HALO⊙'s digital dissection, the incident was transformed from a violent assault into a series of calculated variables. Yet, the tension hung heavy in the air—a chilling reminder that behind the data and trajectories were real lives, teetering on the edge of a knife's blade or the fatal tip of a bullet.

The data stream from HALO⊙'s meticulous analysis cascaded into the secure room, casting a new shadow of doubt over the incident's narrative. Sebastian, with his experience in covert operations, and HB, a master in tactical assessment, exchanged a glance that conveyed volumes. The cold, hard facts delivered by HALO⊙'s Artificial Intelligence opened up a labyrinth of new and sinister variables. The incident had become more of an enigma, a myriad of pieces that didn't quite fit the expected pattern of an assassination attempt.

"HALO⊙'s input suggests a level of complexity we haven't considered," Sebastian offered, his mind racing through various scenarios. "The precision of the shot on Ms. Honnoly was deliberate and lethal. It's almost surgical in nature, a message, possibly rather than a murder attempt on Damian?"

HB nodded, her analytical mind processing the implications. "And the second shot," she added, "it was off by a measure that doesn't align with a sniper of any decent caliber. It's as if the shooter was choreographing the chaos, not aiming to take the obvious target but to orchestrate an intended outcome. However, baffling, what was the intention behind this attack?"

"Could it be a diversion?" Sebastian pondered aloud, "A calculated act designed to trigger a political ripple rather than a casualty? But to what end and why?"

HB's eyes were back on the screens, her fingers dancing across the keyboard as she cross-referenced data. "Or perhaps a power play," she speculated, "sending a stark warning to certain players in this political game. The shots fired were not just bullets but signals, each with a specific recipient in mind and to follow a specific pattern, possibly."

The more they delved into HALO's deconstruction of the event, the more they realized that the incident was not just a matter of public safety but a convoluted web of political strategy and manipulation. The implications were disturbing, suggesting that the sniper's agenda was far more concerning than a simple desire to harm—it was a nuanced move in a game where human lives were pawns on a chessboard, and the endgame was still shrouded in mystery.

Washington D.C.
2022 June
Damian West Downtown Residence

"I know, I know, we have already discussed this," reminded Damian as he sat back in his chair sitting with Mila at the dining room table. "And don't forget, you not mentioning to me that Voss was leaving the country, his significant business in tow," continued

Damian. Mila cocked her head, "That's different, Damian. That's a business move and doesn't have anything to do with you. On the other hand, your move to the Unified Party is, ah, kind of a big deal, don't you think?" "Not really," hinted Damian, and Mila grabbed him by the tummy and tickled him until he relented, "Ok, ok, maybe mine was a little worse." She tickles him again out of spite.

They had discussed the details surrounding his party's unveiling and hers being the significant move of Dymitron to Singapore, but both agreed the sensitivity of both events warranted complete discretion, but they also agreed transparency between them was also important and vital to their respect for one another beginning from that moment forward. It was a game of trust and they agreed they would adhere to complete clarity between them from that moment on.

She looked at him with a look of genuine concern, "Then, the attempt on your life last month. Damian. So many fanatics will struggle to accept your vision. Maybe this is all too dangerous. I worry for you." He grabbed her hand, "I realize the incident last month frightened you. That day scared me, too, and Julian caught the second bullet, which was meant for me. I have Sebastian to thank for that. I still can't believe poor Jenifer wasn't so fortunate. She had been my dad's aide for years. Sebastian has our security all buttoned up, please don't worry, okay?" He said it to comfort her but also was aware Sebastian would never be able to always protect him.

With a wry smirk, the gesture silently communicated a complex message to him, a mixture of resignation and quiet concern. It was her way of acknowledging, despite her outward composure, that a part of her would always be tinged with worry. She had come to terms with the fact his chosen path was fraught with danger. The occupational hazard was an inescapable part of his life. Her smirk was a testament to her acceptance of his perilous profession, a silent pledge of her unwavering support despite the ever-present shadow of concern lingering in her heart.

Damian faced her, his expression earnest, an unspoken acknowledgment of the danger shadowing his every step. "I'm constantly reminded of the risks, but the chance to make a real difference, to change things for the better, for all Americans . . . it's a reward that calls to me, beckons me, Mila. I have to see this through, and Sebastian Storm has been my steadfast guardian from nearly the beginning. My faith in him is unwavering. I trust he will do whatever it takes to keep me safe, or, at the very least, he will do everything he can to protect me."

She couldn't mask the fact her smile was tinged with worry, a silent testament to her internal battle between support and fear. "Damian, it's merely that politics have a way of exposing you to the extreme elements, and sometimes all it takes is one misguided bullet or one simple mistake or a dedicated extremist with a death wish. A single bullet snuffed Jenifer's life in an instant. The thought of losing you in the same way . . . . *it's unbearable for me.*"

In her eyes was a depth of concern only deepened the gravity of his pursuit. "Please, you have to promise me to be cautious. Your dreams are precious, but so are you, to me, and to many people. The tragedy that befell Jenifer and Julian is a constant reminder the path you've chosen is fraught with risks. Promise me you'll stay vigilant." Her words were not only a plea for reassurance but a reminder of the delicate balance between chasing a dream and remaining alive to see it come to fulfillment.

Mila could feel the discussion bothered him, so she chose to shelve it for another time. Her hand slid down his leg as she winked as she changed gears, "I loved our dinner tonight."

Lately, she found herself reveling in their intimate moments at home with a newfound appreciation. Their routine had often included dining out, but as Damian's popularity surged, these outings became a challenge to their privacy. The ever-watchful eyes of the public made it increasingly difficult for her to enjoy the undivided attention she craved from him. The thought of sharing him with the rest of the world was becoming an unwelcome reality, a stark contrast to the cherished solitude they found in each other's company at home. She treasured every second of their time together, and she was certain he felt the same, holding onto those precious moments as a sanctuary from the relentless demands of his growing fame.

Damian poured two glasses of Cabernet and handed one to her, lightly grabbing her hand, "I don't want any more secrets from you, and I don't want you to worry, Mila. That said, I have something very important to tell you. Something I think you should hear from me, in light of all that has transpired and especially as a result of our conversation." She looked at him intently, "Is there someone else? Are you secretly a spy or running for president?" He cocked his head and looked at her strangely, "How did you know . . . . . *I was a spy*," he joked, but then his eyes took on a more serious demeanor.

"My father and some of the most influential people in the nation have groomed me for something bigger, for something that will potentially change the trajectory of the United States. They seek a symbol for all American people to instill hope for a better world and significance they can believe in and work toward achieving."

Mila squeezed his hand, "For such a gifted communicator, you are beating around the bush, Damian." He smiled, knowing she was right, "I'm running for President of the United States in 2024, Mila."

The words hung in the air for a moment as her mind swirled from the news. It wasn't as if she hadn't thought the possibility could manifest for him at some point. She had considered the probability in the years that followed, depending on how his career progressed . . . but in 2024, it was almost unthinkable. With the assassination attempt the month before, this news would only bring out more vulnerability for Damian, but she wanted to concentrate on the bigger picture for him. She realized he valued her support.

"I realize it's a lot and overwhelming next year, in so many ways, but I am announcing in November, symbolic of when I was elected to the Senate." She was still numb to the idea and wondered where her place was in all of his plans but chose to shelve the topic for another time.

Mila leaned over to kiss Damian, "I'm proud of you, Damian. The Presidency would be an amazing accomplishment, and I will support you in every way." She turned her head as if something sparked within her mind as Damian saw it, "What is it, Mila?" She looked back at him, "I have an idea I could arrange to show you, my support. It's a long shot, and I can't guarantee it will work, but if you could manage to pull it off, Damian, it would be an incredible boost to your campaign."

"Oh, Mila, do tell," asked Damian. Mila wanted to articulate her idea, hesitating, then explained, "I sense, deep down, Anthony Voss doesn't want to move Dymitron off American soil, but because the current administration has launched the Anti-trust suit and placed so many regulatory restraints on Dymitron, paired with tax incentives all but yanked away from so much of big business, he was compelled to make a statement with his decision to move out of the U.S." Damian followed her logic, eager to learn more of her idea. The Watchful Eight had theorized this possibility but didn't have a significant enough influence within Voss's camp. Yet, Mila was just beneath their nose the entire time and a direct conduit to Anthony Voss.

"If your candidacy gains momentum to where you begin to craft some kind of offer where everyone prevails, you would win the heart of Voss and his Board of Directors and potentially retain his business here in the States. I mean, I have no idea the specifics or if he would even entertain it, not to mention the tumultuous task of sifting through all the opposition for such a deal, but if you could manage it . . . I don't know, it could be amazing. Imagine the implications of you brokering a deal of that magnitude. You have some of the most incredible minds and influencers in your corner, Damian. The effects of such an outcome benefit so many people. You would be the hero that kept Dymitron from leaving."

Damian looked at her, thinking about the possibility, "That's a brilliant strategy, a daunting task, no question, but if it would work, the magnitude is unimaginable." He squeezed her hand and kissed her, "You have such an incredible mind, Mila." He further explained to her the notion of the Watchful Eight and how it comprised a significant consortium of political and business heavyweights, but there was still one seat left unoccupied. "We actually have considered Anthony Voss for the remaining spot but were unsure how it would play with his recent decision to relocate his company, which, if he did, would be a dealbreaker, of course."

"You could leverage the position to sweeten the deal if it comes to fruition. Knowing Anthony as well as I do, I think he would be honored to be a part of such an auspicious group. Let me lay the groundwork to set up a meeting. What do you think?" Damian nodded, the potential swirling around in his head, "Possibly broach the subject in a month or two. I need to think about how we would approach him this early," replied Damian.

"Good . . . . but now, Senator West, I want you . . . inside me," as Mila slowly stood up. Her casual black dress expertly fits her elegant contours as she looks at him intently. She reaches for the zipper on the back of the dress and slowly unzips it as she captures his gaze while doing so. He grabs his glass of Cabernet, eases back in his chair, and is fascinated by the sultry exhibition Mila displays for him.

Once fully unzipped, she tugs the fabric at her waist, easing the dress down as the straps release over her shoulders, exposing her breasts. He smiles at her, approving her seduction as she slowly eases the dress below her flat stomach, hesitating and noticing his disappointment as she stops. She is aware of what he wants, and she enjoys making his dreams come true in any way she is able.

Not wanting to disappoint, she pushes the dress below her waist, exposing the space between her thighs, sending him over the edge, almost unable to contain himself. Her beautiful plump mons, a few feet before him as it beckons, as images of what she has done to him in the past swirl in his mind, arousing him further, knowing she is able to bring him to the highest point of ecstasy he has ever experienced.

Without warning, she turns, revealing her firm, contoured rear, almost pushing it out at him as she begins to push her dress the rest of the way to the floor, giving him a perfect view of what lies between her legs. Coming to her heels, she lifts a leg, followed by the other, stepping out of the dress as she throws it over the chair, not ruining the glimpse she has graciously and seductively provided to him in the process.

She looks behind her as she is bent over, smiling at him, knowing he is enjoying it all as she slowly undoes the clasp of her right heel. Her leg is slightly bent as she removes the heel, then the other, pushing them off to the side, completely naked now.

He looks up at her long legs extending to her perfectly round, yet firm, rear as she slowly begins to straighten up, looks over her shoulder one last time, lifts her finger, and gestures for him to follow her as she erotically begins to walk away, ensuring he is lured in completely with her sensual and voluptuous walk towards the bedroom.

Chapter 14

The Circle Complete

"Peace and justice are two sides of the same coin."
~Dwight D. Eisenhower

Washington, D.C.
2022 September
Damian West Downtown Residence

The political landscape was undergoing a seismic shift as the Unified Party gained unstoppable momentum. By late September, a remarkable transformation had taken place within the Senate. A dozen Republicans and eight Democrats had defected from their traditional affiliations, embracing the Unified Party's vision, accounting for a staggering 22% of the senate seats, along with the two Independents who had already pledged their allegiance.

The wave of change was even more pronounced in the House of Representatives, where the Unified Party's presence had swelled to 24%. This surge was spearheaded by the enthusiastic

Indiana Representative Julian Chambers and the tenacious Regina Alvarado. With Julian Chamber's instant hero status in full bloom after the assassination attempt, he leveraged his crippling body to the masses garnering sympathy along the way. Together, they formed a formidable pair, their voices resonating with a growing number of their peers and constituents.

However, their journey was far from over. The old guard of the bipartisan system still held sway over a significant portion of the political landscape. To truly revolutionize American politics, Chambers, Alvarado, and their allies needed to wield their influence even more effectively. They had to persuade those still clinging to the antiquated two-party paradigm to embrace a more unified, collaborative approach to governance. The stakes were high, but the potential rewards for their nation were even higher.

Constant petitioning of the Watchful Eight was paramount within the press and all social media outlets, but the Republicans and Democrats cease-fire amongst themselves to concentrate on this new threat before them, resulting in positive effects as well. The excitement of the Unified Party's initial release had subsided, and now the heavy work had to be implemented to continue the momentum and continually educate the American people about its value and its place within American politics.

The Republicans and Democrats eventually resorted to televised and social media smear campaigns, and the sinister messages portrayed were surprising to the Unified Party and its supporters. They soon realized the fight would not remain fair and respectable. The Unified Party was gearing up for the biggest announcement to date and wanted everything in order.

The smear campaigns concentrated on the newness of the party, the inexperience of their leader, Damian West, and their inability to be able to saturate the bipartisan platform and protocols to gain weight in the 2022 Congressional Primaries. The debates were largely occupied by the Democrats and Republicans, and few gave the Unified Party candidates the platform to be heard, which hurt them considerably. The Unified Party had anticipated the limitation in Primary platform exposure time, so it was always considered that general promotional propaganda would be released to the masses in an effort to sway and educate the voters through social media and mass media.

The Unified message was honest and forthright to the American people. The Watchful Eight insisted on not smearing the bipartisan system; they simply laid out the facts surrounding the inefficiency to get the job done and focused on the fact it was a dying platform, archaic in design and antiquated, and required much-needed reform.

Damian West declared, "Smear campaigns are the low road in politics." Sam countered with a raised hand, "But it's the American political tradition. The nastier the presidential campaigns get, the worse they fare in the polls. Let our opponents sling mud; it's only fueling our cause and propelling us forward."

Regina Alvarado added, "To change gears, gentlemen, our newest obstacle is that I'm on the chopping block in a few months with an uphill battle in maintaining the Speaker of the House position under the Unified affiliation. I've held it handily for 10 years, but with my move over to the Unified Party, it won't take much to oust me unless we can pull a miracle."

Damian stated, "We knew we'd hit this barrier. With the major parties divided, our focus should be on winning over the undecided Congressmen. Regina has steered the House with unmatched stability for over a decade. Displacing her now would be more than just a strategic misstep; it would play right into the hands of partisan politics. Despite her recent party switch, her leadership remains as respected as ever, and a Vote of NO Confidence seems unlikely. Remarkably, her popularity within the Republican ranks remains largely intact."

Julian added, "The Democrats will most likely offer up Steny Hoyer out of Maryland, I would imagine, and Elise Stefanik for the Republicans." "I agree," offered Regina Alvarado, as did Sam and Damian West.

"We have to appeal to the undecided group and the votes wavering. Senator Nagel has come to the Unified's; however, Senator Pfeiffer is still holding out. This is where we will need to hit our entire sphere of influence of the Watchful Eight. We just need 218 votes; we must focus on this victory to help Regina maintain her position as Speaker," stated Damian. "Here is a list of all the Representatives in the House. Let's all take a list and determine where we stand on numbers," as each member filled out a list of approve or deny Regina Alvarado's maintaining the Speaker of the House position.

Once the votes were tallied based on each member determining how the 435 votes would sway one way or another, it was determined that 140 votes would affirm, 200 votes against, and 95 undecideds.

As they surveyed the daunting task laying before them, Damian and his team were keenly aware of the Herculean effort required to sway the 95 undecided Congressmen to their cause. With the stakes at an all-time high and the outcome of their campaign hanging in the balance, they understood every vote counted, and every ally gained could tip the scales in their favor.

But it wasn't just the undecided they needed to win over; they also recognized the imperative of securing support from those firmly entrenched on the opposition's side—the "against" list. To achieve their goals, they would need to employ a multi-faceted strategy combining persuasion, negotiation, and political maneuvering to turn the tide of allegiance in their favor.

With a clear-eyed focus and unwavering determination, Damian and his team set out to court potential allies, leveraging every resource at their disposal to make their case and win hearts and minds. Whether through impassioned speeches, behind-the-scenes negotiations, or strategic alliances forged in the crucible of political intrigue, they left no stone unturned in their quest for support.

And so, with steely resolve and unwavering determination, they pressed forward, confident in their ability to overcome the odds and emerge victorious in their quest to reshape the political landscape of the nation.

———

Party loyalties were not as adversely affected as they had anticipated, with members switching to the Unified Party. Big and small businesses, minorities, the elderly, undecided voters, and the newly acquired millennials were key groups the Unified Party was primarily appealing to. Those groups never appeared to have a strong stance, change, or significant policy reform within the Republican or Democratic framework. They were tired of the oratory but always disappointed in the unkept promises made by politicians and administrations alike.

While the intricacies of Congress were certainly a pivotal battleground, Damian and his cohorts recognized the true fulcrum of power lay within the hearts and minds of the American people. As disillusionment with the stagnant status quo reached a fever pitch, an unprecedented wave of interest and curiosity began to swell around the Unified Party—a beacon of hope in a sea of political disillusionment.

What set the Unified Party apart was not just its lofty promises but its unwavering commitment to tangible change and meaningful reform. Unlike the tired rhetoric and empty platitudes of the Republican and Democratic parties, the Unified Party offered a fresh approach—a pragmatic blueprint for progress resonating deeply with a populace weary of broken promises and political theater.

The Unified Party ignited public trust with its unwavering commitment to impactful action and innovative problem-solving that transcended traditional party lines. Focusing on inclusive and cooperative approaches, it aimed to craft policies that served diverse interests without unintended consequences—a fresh take in the polarized realm of politics.

Gaining traction, the Unified Party became a symbol of hope, rallying Americans around a new vision of politics marked by practical solutions, integrity, and a deep commitment to the public interest.

Committed to reform, the party tackled the misuse of internal resources and the corruption involving third-party contractors that burdened taxpayers. They aimed to realign with ethical companies and ensure government contracts served the nation's true needs.

Senator West, first as Governor and then as Senator of Wyoming, waged a relentless battle against the mismanagement of tax funds. His rigorous audit reclaimed hundreds of millions through cutting state budget fat, addressing fund misappropriations, renegotiating third-party contracts, and tackling inflated billings. His efforts inspired other states to follow, rigorously evaluating every cost, and ensuring every dollar was justified.

The Unified Party delivered where Democrats and Republicans had stagnated, bringing tangible reform and benefits to the people. They shone a light on the failings of the established parties, pushing for the changes that the old guard knew were needed but had long neglected. Now, the Unified Party was here to hold the line or clear the stage for a new era of promised improvements and genuine reform.

Regina Alvarado and the Unified Party braced for the headwinds of the mid-term elections, knowing the stakes were high. Her bold leap from the Republican to the Unified Party was a calculated risk they all deemed necessary. With the shift, the loss of Republican backing loomed large, threatening to strip away campaign funds, party networks, and leadership endorsements. The Watchful Eight knew running a lean campaign would test their mettle.

Regina Alvarado's leap to the Unified Party risked alienating allies and raised eyebrows among her new colleagues. Despite the potential fallout, she remained resolute, her fair committee assignments lending her credibility amidst the switch.

As Speaker, she navigated the tightrope of partisan politics, aware that her decision might complicate her re-election. She faced the task of justifying her switch to voters and colleagues alike, knowing that her ability to lead and legislate hinged on maintaining the House's support.

A party switch can have personal consequences, although because of Regina Alvarado's unique ability to maintain bipartisan loyalty, the number of strained relationships with former colleagues and the potential for political isolation appears to be at a minimum.

Damian West highlighted the seismic impact of Regina Alvarado's party switch, acknowledging the mixed reactions from their constituents and its potential to reshape the House's political dynamics. "This shift could be a game-changer for us," he admitted, recognizing that the true test would come in the upcoming elections.

Sam West interjected with a strategic diversion, "Damian, an early announcement to run for President could shift the focus and amplify the Unified Party's presence. It's a bold step that could balance the scales among the three parties as elections near." The suggestion captured the room's focus, presenting a dynamic new front in their political strategy.

"I know I speak for everyone in this room when I say we all share a palpable concern about the passionate desire of the American electorate to provide an open platform encouraging more spirited and substantive debates. What's worrisome is the criteria governing participation in future presidential debates, which currently appear to favor major-party candidates, thus erecting a substantial hurdle for third-party contenders, like the Unified Party, which seeks nationwide recognition," Damian conveyed with evident concern.

"Ren, I'd like to know where we stand in terms of securing a potential podium in the Presidential debate when we enter the race, as its significance cannot be overstated in our case. The Commission on Presidential Debates (CPD) shoulders the vital responsibility of orchestrating and hosting presidential debates, guided by its founding mission to ensure impartial, equitable discussions free from external influences. It is incumbent upon us to demand accountability in upholding this fundamental mandate," Damian continued, his tone resolute and unwavering.

"What's truly remarkable is despite the CPD's historical reluctance to include third-party candidates in the Presidential Debates, the current political climate offers a unique window for transformation. Through vocal advocacy, we have the potential to compel the CPD to expand the debate stage to accommodate the Unified Party. While we may lack direct affiliations with the commission, our close association with you, Senator Cosner, who holds the esteemed position of co-chair on the CPD, commands profound respect and wields considerable influence," Damian asserted, directing his gaze toward Ren Cosner. "Should we fall short in securing our place on that stage, our prospects may be rendered inert, and this may all be over before it started."

Ren Cosner rose and said with conviction, "I have a good connection with key members of the Commission like Frank Fahrenkopf and Janet H. Brown. They, along with others like Kenneth Wollack and Dorothy Ridings, value a fair contest and are receptive to third-party inclusion, given we demonstrate strong support in Congress and sustain it through upcoming elections. They're open to the idea if we can show significant public interest and maintain our seats. It's still uncertain what numbers they're looking for, as we haven't officially announced our 2024 Presidential run. But the crucial point is, they're considering it. My position on the commission could be at risk, but if we secure the numbers, I could be at that debate representing the Unified Party. We need to hit those numbers—they're key."

Sebastian Storm had remained quiet until that point, "Gentlemen, speaking of unchartered territory, I have another component or technology that could aid us here. Strictly speaking, it's A.I. tech we utilize at the Anti-Terrorist Division and certainly gives the Unified's an edge over the Democratic and Republican parties, but the bipartisan advantage of years in existence and the political framework certainly gives them the advantage. I feel what I have will somewhat level the playing field. I will explain it, and we can vote on it, and know what I'm proposing is a one-time offer. I need to make myself perfectly clear: is everyone in agreement to discuss the A.I. tech, then following, there will be a vote." All agreed with the Watchful Eight, and all were eager to hear more. Only Sam West and Sebastian were aware of its capabilities. Sebastian nodded, then moved to the center of the room.

He positioned his phone on the table, put his face close for facial recognition and verified by retina scan, then placed two fingers on the screen and said, "Request: Sebastian Storm TS2509596. Summon, HALO." The software performed its verbal audio verification. Sebastian Storm stood up and walked backward a few steps, then said, "Image rendition." At that moment, a dapper individual of Spanish descent appeared in a holographic image, vivid and lifelike in appearance, materializing before them, appearing as another individual at the table, "Mr. Storm, looking rather fit today, I see," responded HALO.

"I could say the same of you, HALO, nice identity selection today," replied Sebastian. "Thank you, Sir, I certainly try. How can I help you this evening," was HALO's response.

Sebastian didn't answer but instead looked at the group, smiling within from the reactions the group was displaying around the room. Sebastian Storm continued, "Gentleman, I present to you the ultimate Artificial Intelligence interactive platform, otherwise referred to as . . . . HALO . . . . . It stands for *Heuristic Artificial Logistical Optimizer.* He is essentially a supercomputer on a dynamic Artificial Intelligence platform."

Then, as if listening and not fully accepting the description, HALO added in a refined, methodical, monotone masculine voice, "You make me sound so cold, calloused, and rigid, Mr. Storm," interrupted HALO. Sebastian smiled, "And equipped with a heavy dose of sarcasm, you can see. Nevertheless . . . HALO processes at an exponential rate. He creates complex algorithms, models, and systems enabling HALO to understand, interpret, reason, learn, and make decisions autonomously."

"You make me blush," replied HALO as Sebastian shook his head, always good-natured about HALO's responses, although often strange and awkward. The group laughs at the realistic exchanges between HALO and Sebastian.

Sebastian continued, "In addition, HALO encompasses a wide range of techniques and methodologies, including complex human and processed learning and cognitive understanding, natural language processing, computer vision, facial recognition, terrorist methodologies, and more. These techniques enable HALO to analyze vast amounts of data, patterns, anomalies, probabilities, human language, non-verbal, perceive and interpret images, and even interact with the physical and digital world. In short, he's exemplary in every way. We just recently initiated a hologram physical form, as you can see. He appears to be testing his options these days."

HAL⊙ added, "I'm quite impressed with my physical manifestation, Mr. Storm. Of course, I deliberately refrained from making my physical portrayal as physically attractive as you, Sir. I didn't wish for you to develop any insecurities on my behalf." Sebastian shook his head, slightly taken aback at the sheer brazen comments that HAL⊙ uttered, often surprised at what HAL⊙ would say, "And quite the aspiring comedian, as well," said Sebastian as the entire group laughed at the comment.

Sebastian cocked his head, "HAL⊙, based on polls and the current political climate, what is the chance the Unified Party will be able to participate in the 2024 Presidential debates if we announce our intention for Damian West to enter the race? I also wish for a thorough explanation of any details validating your answer?"

The hologram of HAL⊙ tilted his head as if to think, then stated while looking about the room, "Well, Sir, you know this isn't my area of expertise, but I'll give it a go. I estimate roughly a 31% probability based on current polls, Senate and House saturation, undecided votes, popularity and interest amongst Americans over the age of 18, and the current Congressional climate at the moment, to name a few of my parameters reconsidered in my analysis." One could hear the stammering and murmurs of the people in the living room of Damian West's large condominium.

Sebastian was fluent and very familiar with the A.I., and versed in what questions to ask, "Fair enough, HAL⊙. your analysis, please, and what probabilities may occur in the next several months to increase the percentage?" HAL⊙ once again tilted his head, as would a human, pondering the question, then softly and methodically answered, "If Senators Ren Cosner, Sam West, and Gideon Arnold increase their promotion and support of the Unified Party, the Speaker of the House instills more of the ideals she has implemented in the House of Representatives thus far, the increase would be approximate, 11%. Securing Dymitron's CEO, Anthony Voss, to ally with the Unified Party would increase the percentage by an additional 6%, and brokering a deal to retain Dymitron to remain within the United States would garner an additional increase of 5%. Lastly, Sir, the probability can be most increased with Senator Damian West announcing his candidacy for the office of the President of the United States in 2024 before December 7, 2022. That specific announcement, followed by a thorough and well-canvased campaign strategy, will increase the chance of the Unified Party forcing the hand of the Commission on Presidential Debates (CPD) to accept Senator West to partake by a measure of 27%. Those parameters combined will increase the overall probability to 80% Senator West will be included in the 2024 debate, Mr. Storm. Of course, these are only estimates, but I'm usually fairly accurate."

Damian uttered, "That's impressive." "Thank you, Senator," came the reply from HALꙨ, slightly startling Damian. Sebastian decided they had had enough of HALꙨ for the moment, "HALꙨ, rest," "Have a good evening, Sir, good night, everyone," and with that, the image disappeared.

Sebastian could see from the expressions before him the group was generally awestruck, "We use HALꙨ for complex mission scenarios such as missile strikes and ground attacks in a way minimizing our human casualties as well as mechanical assets. HALꙨ runs military tactics for us at ATS and best and worst-case scenarios. He's invaluable in our mission planning, and then I thought, what is the difference between those military combative scenarios and situations surrounding political agendas and probabilities? The pen, or the progression of this party, is mightier than the sword, it's been said, has it not? Therefore, if HALꙨ can operate on both battlegrounds, so I theorized, why not utilize him to benefit this mission? He can be the probability member of the Watchful Eight until you fill the last seat with a suitable replacement."

Julian Chambers noted, "Sebastian, did you supply any specific Intel to HALꙨ concerning bringing Antony Voss into the fold?" "No, no, Congressman Chambers, I did not," replied Sebastian

Storm. They all appeared impressed by the consideration of Voss, as Gideon Arnold expressed what all in the room were already thinking, "So, HALO extrapolated all the data and determined based on who was present, and Anthony Voss would be the single best selection to fulfill our Order to the full eight? And, not only that, but the percentage points also gained would come with his addition as well as the possibility of him retaining the business location within the states. . . . *remarkable.*"

Sebastian added, "And gentlemen, I've never known him to be wrong, maybe off a point or two, but never wrong.

Damian finally concluded, "Well, I think we know what to do. Listen to the man, er, I mean, the machine. His points make sense. We need to hit those lingering Congressmen and I need to . . . . . *Announce to the nation I'm running for the President of the United States under the Unified Party in 2024.*"

Chapter 15

Unified Or Die

"What I've learned is that real change is very, very hard. But I've also learned that change is possible - if you fight for it."
~Elizabeth Warren (U.S. Senator)

Washington, D.C.
2022 November
Press Conference

Over the following month, tension was running high as the elections were quickly approaching, and Regina Alvarado, Senators Cosner, Arnold, and West were pushing for her to retain the Speaker of the House position. The Unified Party was gaining steam and secured a few more seats, but more were promised after the election to secure the Congressmen's re-election, which was a conservative and safe move.

The Unified Party needed numbers, and they were witnessing a gradual increase in interest, but not as fast as they would have liked.

Senator Damian West briskly sauntered up the stairs to the podium for the much-anticipated press conference, enthusiastic over the short speech he was to give that day. Sebastian Storm and Sam West looked on as pride washed over Sam's face. "You should be proud of him, Sir," whispered Sebastian to the senior Senator. Sam leans over to Sebastian, "You know I am, Sebastian. He has all the attributes I don't possess . . . . *He is a better version of me*." They stood in silence as Damian West expertly explained the programs and the outline improving the economy and how the Unified Party system was working to improve the lives of the Americans it served.

Seven states had implemented his systems for improving governmental efficiencies, programs to aid the impoverished, small businesses, and healthcare. The Unified Party addressed the issues neglected by the bipartisan system for years. The popularity of the *Unified Party's Principles*, affectionately referred to by Senator West as his UPP's, addressed, head-on, the issues facing the country itself and each American today.

When Damian West discussed the transformative reforms and revitalized policies his Unified Party proposed, his words carried both substance and conviction. His enthusiasm and passion were palpable as he painted a vision of what these principles could achieve for the American people. Yet, he also issued a stark warning about the entrenched opposition ready to fight against the change and progress he championed.

"Change and reform challenge the very core of the entrenched status quo that Democrats and Republicans have skillfully crafted and preserved for decades," Damian West declared with commanding authority. His voice, a dynamic mix of intelligence and charisma, captured the undivided attention of the gathered reporters. "This isn't merely a flaw; it's a fundamental defect embedded in the DNA of our antiquated bipartisan system—a system that once served us well but now operates on broken logic. Today, it caters only to the interests of politicians, neglecting the very people it's supposed to represent—the true power driving our nation."

As he articulated his vision, their recording devices and cameras were aimed at him, capturing every moment, each nuance, as if they were witnessing a historical event. They hang on his every word, enraptured by the man before them, who exudes an almost divine presence akin to a modern-day prophet sent from the heavens. At this moment, Damian West is not just a man; he is a phenomenon, a beacon of hope and change, leaving an indelible mark on all who listen.

Sebastian's admiration for Damian overflowed as he shook his head in awe, his voice tinged with reverence as he spoke to the elder Senator. "He possesses a rare gift—an innate ability to inspire and captivate with his words. Watching him speak is like witnessing a force of nature, raw and unbridled, pouring forth from the depths of his soul. His passion is palpable, his conviction unwavering. Every word he utters is infused with a profound sense of honesty and authenticity, a testament to the depth of his belief in the causes he champions."

Sebastian's eyes sparkled with fervor as he continued; his admiration for Damian was evident in every gesture and expression, "He's a beacon of integrity and sincerity. You can't help but be drawn to him, to believe in him and the transformative potential he holds for our country." Sam nodded in agreement.

As Damian spoke, his voice intensifying with passion and verve, it was clear Sebastian's admiration for Damian ran deep. For him, Damian was more than just a politician; he was a visionary—a leader who possessed the rare ability to inspire hope and ignite change. As Sam looked at Sebastian, his eyes burning with fervor, knowing Damian's words had struck a chord not just with him but with countless others who yearned for a leader they could truly believe in.

Sam West added, "He is a product of our purest notions, Sebastian, not a puppet, mind you, but educated and taught within a vacuum on the precipice of an ideal we have all contributed to, ensuring the purest view was carefully deep seeded and formulated on how we can improve as a people and a country."

As Sebastian listened, he couldn't help but marvel at the dynamic interplay between father and son—the seamless synergy of experience and innovation defining their partnership. In Senator Sam West, he saw the embodiment of a bygone era—a nostalgic figure whose legacy loomed large, casting a long shadow over the political landscape. And in his son, Senator Damian West, he witnessed the promise of a new generation—a voice of fresh perspective and boundless potential, poised to chart a bold new course forward.

Together, father and son formed an unbeatable team—a formidable combination of wisdom and vision that resonated deeply with the American people. For Sebastian, they represented the very essence of what leadership should be—a harmonious blend of tradition and innovation grounded in the values of integrity, compassion, and progress.

As he contemplated the significance of their partnership, Sebastian couldn't help but feel a surge of optimism coursing through his veins. Here, before him, was the model for a new era of American politics—a blueprint for leadership transcending party lines and ideological divides. With their united front and unwavering commitment to the common good, father and son embodied the hope and promise of a nation yearning for change.

In their hands, Sebastian saw the power to inspire and unite—a force for good breaking through the barriers of cynicism and apathy and igniting a spark of hope in the hearts of all who dared to dream of a better tomorrow. And as he looked to the future, Sebastian knew that with leaders like Sam and Damian West at the helm, the American people had every reason to believe in and embrace the promise of a brighter, more inclusive future for all.

Immersed in the inner sanctum of political discourse, Sebastian found himself enveloped in a whirlwind of intellectual exchange and ideological exploration over the prior year. With Damian and Sam West as his guides, he embarked on a journey of discovery—a trek well beyond the confines of mere mentorship to become a profound odyssey of enlightenment and growth.

In the hushed confines of private discussions, Sebastian delved deep into the recesses of political theory and strategy, absorbing the wisdom and insights of his esteemed companions like a sponge. Their conversations spanned a vast array of topics, from the intricacies of policy formulation to the nuances of coalition-building and beyond. Each exchange was a masterclass in its own right, a symphony of intellect and passion leaving an indelible mark on Sebastian's psyche.

Sebastian was not just awestruck by the vast knowledge imparted by the West family; it was their profound wisdom and genuine convictions that truly resonated with him. From Damian, he mastered the art of passionate advocacy and the critical importance of adhering to one's principles amidst adversity. Sam West taught him the value of pragmatism, the essential nature of compromise for progress, and the power of diplomacy and persuasion in politics.

As days melded into weeks, and weeks into months, Sebastian's grasp of the political arena deepened, molded by the wisdom of his mentors. More crucially, he found his purpose and a clear vision for leadership and service to the American people.

In a dominion of discourse and debate, Sebastian discovered not just knowledge but inspiration—a fire within, propelling him toward a brighter future. With Damian West at his side, he felt unstoppable, ready to transcend limits and transform visions into reality.

As Sam West watched his son captivate the room, his eyes were focused on the words his son was about to utter, shocking the world with the information he was aware was about to follow. In a low voice, almost to himself, within earshot of Sebastian, "He emulates the ideal of me, the best version of what we stand for." It was then a single tear fell from his eye as he raised his hand to wipe it away, hoping no one took notice, but Sebastian Storm witnessed the sentiment; he was acutely aware of the effect Damian West's words were having on his ailing father.

Sebastian remained steadfast, focusing on the speech, not wanting to acknowledge the pride the older man displayed and respecting his dignity. Sebastian revered the retired statesman's adoration and sacrifice he made for his country as well as his son and felt it was his moment, his time. They both listened, knowing Damian was coming to the end of his speech.

He was approaching the conclusion of his monologue, and a few questions were asked about specific programs or elaborations on key points from various reporters. Then Keith Morrison from *NBC's Dateline* put up his hand as Damian pointed to him," "Senator, your programs have been widely applauded, though some naysayers claim the methods aren't realistic despite your well-documented results, but with the Unified Party's growing popularity and the theory widely curious by many Americans out there, the question begs to be answered . . . . *Is Senator West going to enter the Presidential Race in 2024?*"

Sam West stood a little taller and looked at Sebastian, "This is it, Sebastian, this is the moment I've been waiting for. . . . it's taken us decades, but this is what it has all come to." Sam West's hands rose to his lips, palms together as if in prayer, closing his eyes for a moment as he listened to his son navigate the question.

Senator Damian West grinned and eased back from the podium, quiet and calculated, slowly scanning the room, searching for the words. This moment was completely his, and he embraced it, cultivating the moment and building its impetus.

The room, was once loud and bustling with reporters clambering away to ask follow-up questions or recognized by the now-famous Senator from Wyoming. All was erringly quiet and still as if the room was vacant. Everyone waited for the Senator to answer the question everyone wanted to know.

Hesitating longer than normal, peering out into the crowd but locking eyes with no one in particular until he glances at his father in the back of the room and smiles, yet holds his focus as Sam West nods slightly back at him as if to say, *"Tell them, Damian, tell them all."*

A flash of thoughts rushed through his mind from his childhood to the saddened walk down the hospital hallway the evening he lost his mother. His memory of climbing the rope in the schoolyard yard, where he gained the respect of those around him, as well as Julian Chambers, his friendship forged, came into view and, as quickly, diminished.

He looked into the lights above, recalling his graduation from high school with Julian by his side to the flash of lights, graduating at the top of his class at Harvard Law. The slab where Governor Steven Hathaway stood motionless, Damian being the first to be called to identify the body that chilly New Year's Eve. And lastly, being sworn in as the youngest Senator in history from Wyoming, carrying on the West family legacy, to this moment in time as his eyes came to rest upon his father's eyes once again, watching him now. The vibrant emerald green shared between both men was a distinguishing physical attribute they both possessed. His father was a mirrored image, just 40 years Damian's senior, handsome and distinguished, both. Senator Damian West was simply a younger version of his famous father. It all came to light in that moment.

The pride his father held was palpable as Damian slowly pulled himself toward the microphone, "For a long time now, I've studied this country: its history, its independence, its proliferation, its egotism, its frailty, and lastly . . . . *its inevitable extinction*. They all represent different visions within my mind. The nation has been cashing checks from those possessing no merit, no integrity . . . . and no honor, and this nation is fiscally and emotionally bankrupt as a result. This great country's value has diminished. It's been diluted to a point of no remaining potency. It's become a farce . . . . *a fraud*, even," Damian West looked out over the crowd as the room remained tranquil and calm, hanging on to his every word.

"However, there is a plan in all this. A promise to the American people to pull back the reigns inhibiting us as a thriving nation. There are people, leaders, and citizens alike who recognize our fate and still hold true to the value of what we once were and could be again. Dare I say it is not the Republicans or the Democrats that will save us but rather the unity of those who don't recognize any longer a difference in the color of one's skin, socioeconomic differentiations, age, or creed but rather stand together in a unified form, as one voice, above all others demanding the winds of change and not accepting anything less from those leading them and those standing beside them. It's time to purge the ailments that plague our various cultures and beliefs and embrace the totality of unity of this amazing country." Damian West pauses again, no one wanting to interrupt him as he speaks his inspiring words.

"Our country hungers for strong leadership that will not rest until its objectives are met and will not rest until the cancers within our government are cut away. We will not rest until the people, as a whole, are heard, yet are willing to accept compromise as well. We must all do our part. All of this defines what it is to be unified. It won't be perfect; I won't make such a claim. We are flawed yet committed and resolute in our endeavor. This country needs something to hope for . . . . it needs trust, unity, and appreciation for what the man or woman standing next to you can provide beyond himself. But, above all it needs . . . . *hope*. The Unified Party was destined to carry the burden as all others have failed in doing so. Now, the torch has been accepted with dignity and responsibility, enflamed with accountability to its people and to this nation."

"This obligation, I have accepted, and it has become my mantra, my battle cry to wake all Americans, seize our day, and place our country back to a wholesome place. The Unified Party is the new light in a seemingly dimming society, wrought with our historic mistakes and misgivings."

"With this, I pledge . . . honesty and integrity as I enter the race for President of the United States of America . . . If my country will have me in 2024." He flashed his signature smile, not accepting any more questions, and finished with a simple, "Good night," as Damian West held up his hand, then skipped down the stairs, Sebastian Storm in tow, after him.

Sam West stood alone, watching the podium where his son stood only moments before, proud beyond belief of what his legacy had accomplished. It certainly wasn't over yet, but the Alternative Consortium had achieved more in those two years than all their efforts combined historically over the last four decades, and their bold move tonight would commit to the world of their seriousness to this endeavor.

They would not fade into the fray. They were here to show the world the strength of unity, and the solidarity ran deep within their veins, and the American people, once again, witnessed the true inspiration and awe of Damian West.

Damian West had become the symbol, instilling hope in the American people. His journey would become far more tumultuous and rigorous, but his announcement to enter the 2024 Presidential race would send a significant ripple through the political landscape, and Damian West's name would be revered when simply uttered.

It was time for Damian West to take his rightful place.

Jackson Hole, Wyoming
2023 January
Damian West Private Estate

They lay staring at one another in bed, the first weekend together in three weeks and the time apart had been especially difficult on her. He had already begun a soft campaigning schedule, promoting his vision and perspectives, despite the height of the election being more than 23 months away.

She put her hand upon his face and smiled. She was proud of him and what he had accomplished in such a short period. The press conference 5 weeks before had sent him and the Unified Party into a frenzy of media coverage, and Paparazzi had become relentlessly camped outside his Washington condominium 24 hours a day.

The press conference had catapulted him to the spotlight well beyond what the interview with Barbara Walters had achieved. He was on the cover of *Time Magazine* with a broad and lofty headline that read, "Senator Damian West . . . *Is He America's Savior?*"

The *press conference* and *Time Magazine article* had meticulously exposed the inner framework of the Unified Party, and it appealed to many Americans, including eight additional Congressmen switching their political affiliations to the Unified Party.

Despite all the efforts the Party attempted, the increased interest and popularity weren't enough to preserve Regina Alvarado's retention as the Speaker of the House in the mid-term election. The position fell to Republican Steny Hoyer of Maryland, barely edging out Regina Alvarado by a vote of 224 to 211. This set the Unified Party back, but they had anticipated the chance she would lose the speaker position.

The Watchful Eight realized it was a possibility, but upon hearing the news, Damian was determined to get her back into the position she adored by the next election in 2024.

As they looked at one another, he held her hand and sometimes just enjoyed looking at her. "You must suspect . . . . *I love you*, Mila," he softly smiled as he said it. Taken aback, her hand resting upon the side of his face, "I know . . ." was all she could think of to respond. She had heard those words dozens of times before from as many men, but never had she with the same words in response. Mila Dmitri had never felt deeply enough for someone to tell them she loved them in return, and yet this man was the only one she had ever wished to share her true feelings with. She was simply ill equipped to reciprocate the gesture.

He smiled at her, knowing the struggle she was experiencing, and he didn't want to make her uncomfortable any longer. Changing the subject, "I'm going to make you the best breakfast you have ever had. Waffles or pancakes, my dear," he asked.

"Definitely . . . . *waffles*. You are amazing, Damian," as he excitedly hopped out of bed, threw on his robe, came to her side of the bed, and gave her a soft kiss as she leaned up; then he was out of the door to embark on his culinary mission and to mesmerize her with his crafty waffle making abilities. She could hear him clambering down the stairs to the kitchen.

As she slowly reclined against the plush pillow, her thoughts swirling with a tumultuous mix of emotions, she couldn't help but replay the tender moment in her mind. With a sigh, she buried her face in her hands, her words a soft whisper lingering in the empty space he had left behind.

"*I love you too, Damian,*" she confessed to the silence, her voice tinged with a hint of regret and longing. In the solitary moment, she struggled with the weight of her own emotions, grappling with the realization she had never experienced love quite like this before, but she didn't possess the strength to him she felt the same of him.

Her heart ached with the memory of his departure; her mind was plagued by the knowledge she had let the perfect moment slip through her fingers. It had taken courage for him to bare his soul, to lay his feelings bare before her, and she couldn't shake the notion of disappointment in herself for not seizing the opportunity to reciprocate. There was no question about how she cared for him.

But, as regret gnawed at her, there was a glimmer of hope flickering deep within her heart. She theorized love was not a race to be won or a game to be played, but a journey—a slow and steady unfolding of the heart. And though she had missed her chance to speak those three precious words in the heat of the moment, she was determined to find the courage to say them when the time appeared right as she had never uttered those words to anyone before.

For in Damian, she had found a love that transcended words—a love that spoke volumes in the tender moments they shared, in the warmth of his embrace and the sparkle in his eyes. As she lay in bed, lost in her thoughts, she smiled, knowing their love story was just beginning—a tale of passion, perseverance, and the unwavering belief love would always find a way.

With a daring heart, Damian mustered the courage to bear his soul, professing his love for her with raw honesty, leaving him vulnerable. His words, filled with passion and sincerity, were a testament to the depth of his feelings. On the other hand, she found herself in a tumult of emotions, always equally smitten yet unable to voice her affections. Her heart raced with the same fervent love, but fear held her back, rendering her fainthearted in the face of his open declaration. The intensity of their unspoken bond was palpable, a silent dance of love and hesitation leaving them both yearning for more.

Mila got out of bed several minutes later, put her robe on as she put herself together and walked down the stairs toward the kitchen to help the man she can come to love and adore. She entered the kitchen, the aromas emanating the air activating all of her senses and making her realize how hungry she had become.

Looking around, Damian was nowhere to be found until she came across the note with a heart shape on the top of the kitchen bar with an arrow leading outside. The house was empty, save for the two of them, and she figured Damian had given his staff the day off. Mila walked to the door and looked outside but couldn't see anything as she peered through the window door. The cool winter breeze stung her face as she cracked the door ever so slightly, peering outside, then located Damian by the outside firepit.

His position looked odd from her perspective until she realized he was kneeling on one knee as she stepped into the frigid cold. The sun was out, not a cloud in the sky as she could see the steam from her breath billowing upward as she stepped on to the heated deck with only her robe and a thong and looked at him strangely. He smiled at her as she approached, still confused by what he was doing, until he extended from behind his back a small black box.

"Mila Dmitri, I have been so blessed with so many wonderful things happening to me over the past 12 months, but you, by far, are the best thing that I have experienced. I can think of no woman that would make a better wife, a better mother, and a better . . . First Lady, than you. Make me the proudest man in all of the free world by accepting me as your devoted and loving husband forever. Will you marry me, Mila?"

Mila's hands immediately went to her mouth to subdue her excitement, shocked and almost weak at the thought someone loved her enough to make her his forever. He reached for her left hand, sliding the elegant 3-carat solitaire diamond over her finger despite not yet giving him a response.

The sunlight reflected perfectly, making the stone brighten her face further as she looked at it for a moment, mesmerized as she walked a step closer to Damian, took his hands in hers, and urged him upward as he began to stand, unsure of what her response would be.

She looks up at him as she places both of her hands on each side of his face. She smiles at him and softly says, "Damian West, I think I have loved you from the first moment I met you. I should have said it this morning, but despite my silence. . . . please know I love you too."

He took her hands in his and replied, "I can sense you do; I can feel it all the way through me. It was in that instant this morning that I realized you have never loved anyone before. Not like me. Your hesitation in responding in the same way was strangely my confirmation that you love me the same way I do of you. You just needed a moment to realize it, but I was certain you would. But Mila, the question still stands. Will you marry me?"

She looked up into his eyes and smiled once again, "There is nothing that would make me prouder than to become. . . . Mrs. Mila West. Yes, yes, of course, I will marry you, Damian."

Mila Dmitri had never been more certain of anything in her life. It was the first time she had ever experienced a sense of complete enlightenment and happiness in a person that fulfilled her in every way.

Then it hit her, she could end up being the youngest First Lady to ever live in the White House and the thought both excited her . . . . . . *and frightened her.*

New York, New York
2023 April
Fury's Manhattan Penthouse

Inferno and Fury quietly enter the vacant elevator. Fury presses the penthouse button, along with providing the retina scan to activate access to the penthouse floor. The elevator door begins to close as a frail, elderly man inserts his cane between the closing doors to open them, his hand shaking in the process.

Fury steps forward, blocking the old man's path, "Take the next one . . . ." as the bewildered man nervously looks up at the two towering men standing before him and instinctively backs away. Their glares are ominous as Fury and Inferno stare back down at the meager old man in disgust and annoyance. The doors close, and the elevator ascends to the topmost floor. After 45 seconds, the doors open into the private hall with the front doors automatically open to their lavish Penthouse within.

After a few minutes, Fury fixes a drink for both of them and hands Inferno his glass as they sit on the couch, enjoying the warm fire, their palliating sanctuary. The warmth of spring was slowly approaching, but far too frigid to sit on the balcony. Inferno reflected upon the meeting that had occurred just an hour before.

The meeting, orchestrated by their enigmatic client, was set in a secluded alley off Canal Street, downtown New York City, maintaining the usual veil of secrecy. The location was a moving target, changed frequently and sometimes at the last moment to dodge any pattern or undue attention. With their high-profile client, a certain level of paranoia was expected. Despite having met the individual multiple times, Fury was accustomed to a stringent code of silence. The client had not yet allowed the presence of Inferno.

While Fury engaged in the clandestine negotiations, Inferno stood guard, a silent guardian ensuring their privacy from a modest distance. His encounters with the mysterious figure were brief and from a safe distance, ensuring secrecy. He had noticed the man's stature in shadows, along with a distinctive limp that caught his eye. Yet, there was an unsettling familiarity about the man that lingered in Inferno's mind, a puzzle he eventually set aside, respecting the veil of anonymity. He kept his observations to himself.

Their focus was singular: the mission at hand. After each covert meeting, Fury would debrief Inferno, sharing the essential details as they navigated the murky waters of their covert operations.

Fury looked at Inferno, "The next phase begins next month to bring the focus more on the politically prolific. The client wishes to make them an example using certain key targets. It's finally time for you to get your hands dirty again, Inferno."

Inferno smiled; he enjoyed when Fury would let him out of the cage from time to time. It had been 18 months since he had been given a significant objective which was eliminating hotel mogul, Ryker Davion in Los Angeles two summers before. Other than a reconnaissance, the year and a half were strategizing, though contracts had come up occasionally. Their primary objective was the timing of tactical objectives to further the cause of their primary client. There was some exclusivity with the client until their objective came to fruition. Fury made sure they were cautious to not accept any contracts that could jeopardize or conflict with their primary mission.

Fury handed over the dossier as Inferno perused the relevant information. "A prolific rapper, huh," asked Inferno. "Yes, this one's a loudmouth Republican. However, as you know, Inferno, we are equal opportunity killers, so we need to maintain a strict sense of balance." "Of course," replied Inferno, giving him a cheers gesture with his glass.

Neither Inferno nor Fury was particularly political or possessed any interest in the arena. They both felt American bureaucrats held the position of a relative nebula, insignificant, interwoven with corruption and indolence spread throughout. Their current client emulates that very profile. Any political dominance within a party was inconsequential to either of them and insignificant to the overall trajectory of the American journey and evolution but if either party could benefit from Fury and Inferno's particular set of skills, the highest bidder would prevail. Ultimately, the contract price mattered most to the two of them; the political agenda was of little use or concern.

Miami, Florida
2023 June
Apocalypse Private Residence
11:34 PM

At the pinnacle of his musical ascent stood *Apocalypse*—a prodigious talent who had risen from the gritty streets of Indianapolis, Indiana, to become a formidable force in the world of rap music and its wide influence. At only 31 years old, he had captured the zeitgeist, captivating audiences with his raw talent and unapologetic authenticity. He was respected for his unfiltered outlook, often depicted through his lyrical undertones and media interviews.

As a black artist navigating the turbulent landscape of America's heartland, Apocalypse brought a unique perspective to his music—a sincere expression of the trials and triumphs of life in the urban jungle. His lyrics resonated with a generation hungry for truth and authenticity, striking a chord with both Generation Y and Z, who found solace and inspiration in his words. People were moved and influenced by his work, and this only fueled his drive to produce more and to be heard by his listeners.

But it wasn't only his musical prowess that set *Apocalypse* apart—it was his unyielding commitment to using his platform for social and political change. In an era marked by division and discord, he emerged as a flicker of optimism—a voice of dissent and defiance against the status quo. He fought against the government and was often at the pinnacle of demonstrations, using the platform to challenge laws, governing agencies, and strong political issues facing all Americans.

He felt his musical and lyrical prowess was a gift, and that gift should be used to illicit change and people's perspective.

Drawing political inspiration from trailblazers like Public Enemy, Eminem, Tupac, Sinead O'Connor, Talib Kweli, and U2's Bono, Apocalypse fearlessly tackled taboo subjects, challenging the prevailing norms and shining a light on the injustices that plagued society. From racial inequality to police brutality, he fearlessly tackled the controversial issues, fearless in speaking his truth about those in power accountable. His view and lyrics were relative and poignant and stimulated his listeners to demand their rights and expect more from those governing them.

To his legions of fans, Apocalypse wasn't just a musician; he was a symbol of rebellion and renewal, a revolutionary wielding melodies like torches in the darkness of a world crying out for change. He became the chosen voice for a generation yearning to be heard, embodying their hopes and frustrations. Each lyric he crafted wasn't merely sung, but wholly felt—a momentous voice that stirred the souls of his listeners. With every powerful verse and stirring chorus, he lit a fierce blaze in their hearts, urging them to stand up, to raise their declarations together in a resounding chorus demanding justice and equality. His music became a rallying cry, a pharos guiding them toward a brighter, more inclusive future for every American, exceeding the boundaries of race and uniting them in their shared quest for a better tomorrow.

As he stood on the precipice of greatness, Apocalypse knew that his journey was only beginning. With his music as his weapon and his passion as his shield, he vowed to continue fighting for justice, equality, and freedom for all—a true force to be reckoned with in the ever-evolving landscape of music and activism.

His music hit hard the views of both right and left political ranges, and much like Eminem, he gathered speed and momentum from his music's popularity. Multiple Grammys, Golden Globes, BET, MTV, and two Academy Awards for Best Original Song in 2019 and 2021 pushed him to the top of his celebrity status and made him as popular with his political perspectives, lyrics, and confrontations as his music. He dominated all media. People wanted to hear his words on every medium. People believed in him and his cause.

Early in his career, Apocalypse didn't advocate any solid position politically; however, in 2016, his position and outspokenness escalated when complications with the Affordable Care Act (ACA) or Obamacare affected his mother's treatment and her ability to get access to an adequate provider leading to a late cancer diagnosis. Sadly, the delay eventually led to her passing from breast cancer and sent Apocalypse into a tailspin of despair and pushed his political polarization to the hard right position because of the inability of the ACA and the Democratic machine to help his mother when she needed it most. The ACA failed her and he blamed the Democrats general malaise for her untimely death.

Apocalypse deviated from traditional political affiliations, being liberal in his views, but later evolved to the more extreme political variance to the right of center. His perspective was becoming more active and relevant within the controversial lyrics of his music. He was becoming bolder and more brazen as he attacked the American Government and its lackluster support for Americans.

As of late, Apocalypse was becoming increasingly vocal about his endorsement of Senator Damian West and the Unified Party's beliefs. They had not met, but the young musician expressed his interest in the Presidential candidate as the only visionary within the political spectrum who could see the future in its clearest form. He was impressed with his Barbara Walters segment and well-publicized speech in Congress calling out the inadequacies of the Democratic and Republican parties.

Prior to Senator West entering the race, Apocalypse's support subtly validated Donald Trump's position, yet only marginally. Senator West's announcement to enter the 2024 Presidential race swayed Apocalypse's position to put his full weight behind the young Presidential hopeful.

"Nah, man, it's a new time. . . . a new era. Things are changing, and this dude, West, man, he gets it, bruh," Apocalypse explained to his childhood friends, Garrett and Nicky. They had been a close group since childhood, running the streets of Indianapolis, getting into trouble with the law before taking a turn, and making promises to one another to make something of themselves. Apocalypse, born James Fogler, respected Garrett and Nicky as they were best friends before Apocalypse had acquired his acclaim and had never once asked anything of their infamous celebrity friend. However,

Apocalypse saw the value of keeping them close; he trusted them beyond all others.

Garrett was the most levelheaded of the three, and he and Apocalypse would delve into deep philosophical debates depending on how *"high"* they were on a given evening. Their beliefs usually aligned on most topics, but Garrett enjoyed pushing his friend's hot buttons on political and social debates. Nicky was the quiet one, always watching and not as interested in the deep discussions his two closest friends often engaged in, but he was present, nonetheless. Tall in stature and an early disciple of Muay Thai fighting, Nicky was a tall man at 6'5" and 240 lbs. He took his childhood anger out at the gym and had recently begun competing in (Mixes Martial Arts) MMA fights and was currently with an impressive 23-1-1 amateur record and a 5-0 record in professional fights over the prior two years.

As a result, Garret had become Apocalypse's most trusted advisor and Nicky became his bodyguard. The three were inseparable.

Garrett always enjoyed getting under Apocalypse's skin, "But this West character doesn't have the track record, man, too much of a newbie and a privileged white man to boot." Apocalypse took another pull of his Indica Marijuana pen, "Nah, you don't get it, man, he's legit, got it all covered. West is the real deal, and he is grabbing the hearts of the American people . . . black, white, yellow. . . they all be unified. That's how it should be. Color means nothing to him, and I respect that. Half his advisors are minorities and equal in Democratic and Republican past affiliations. The Speaker of the House is a woman and hell man his fiancé is half Asian. This dude don't care what color, gender or creed you are, he just wants the folks that see his vision for the future."

"You two sound like an old married couple," declared Nicky as they all laughed. Apocalypse blurted, "Tricky Nicky always got all the random hilarity coming out. But Garret here, be the ole' lady. I'm dashing and debonair. Let's dish that off." They all laughed as they took another draw from the CBD pen.

Apocalypse begins a lyrical improvisation paired with an impromptu melody.

The tides are turnin'.
People are burnin'.
The sun be risen'.
But people is dyin'.
West be speakin'.
And people believin'.
He know the way.
His words be slay.
West will show the way.
His vision is here to stay.

"Haha, that is sweet, man," says Nicky, "Don't know how you bust that shit out on a whim, man." All three laughed before becoming quiet, enjoying the cloud created above them and savoring the moment.

All three sat in their individual recliners in Apocalypse's 30-seat cinema room, watching Gladiator for the 50th time. Apocalypse's mansion was sprawled over 10 acres and 21,000 square feet on Star Island overlooking Biscayne Bay in Miami. Since childhood, Apocalypse always wanted a mansion in Miami, and a few years before, he decided to buy himself one.

At Apocalypse's lavish parties, he often boasted that he hadn't actually visited every room in his estate nor driven every vehicle in his 30-car garage and was extremely proud of that fact. The kitchen and master bedroom were the only rooms utilized with any frequency. However, the cinema room is where Apocalypse spent most of his time along with Garrett and Nicky when he wasn't touring or recording new material.

The small boat coasted covertly, without any lights, to the front of the expansive property. Inferno's team, including Onyx and Sapphire, all systematically exited the boat with silenced handguns at the ready as they all took a knee. Clad in black, they were firm in their objective and waited for their leader to initiate the mission.

Indicating to switch to mics, he pinched his throat, "Let's roll out, Sapphire, 3-click us when you have disabled the system, clear the house one room at a time, let me handle who you find," as they all acknowledged the affirmative of the order. Inferno pointed to each side of the home with his two fingers as Sapphire and Onyx made their way to the north and south sides of the home. Inferno waited and 60 seconds later received the 3 clicks on his mic as instructed and made his way to the center of the back of the home. Each waited, watched, and listened for occupants and, after finding no sign of activity, picked an exterior door and stepped inside. The home seemed quiet and dark from the outside.

Inferno looked at his thermal wrist piece and could track Sapphire and Onyx in their designated locations, but no other thermals were appearing within the home, but he knew Apocalypse was on the premises. Inferno explored the main level and Sapphire and Onyx the upper bedrooms in addition to the master bedroom/bath. "All clear, upper level," came the soft female voice of Sapphire. "Clear. Main," came Inferno's response, "Meet at the stairs. They must be in the basement."

Their silenced weapons drawn, the three eased down the stairs hearing the laughing and sound effects from the theatre room, down the hall.

As the trio entered the room from the rear, Garret, Nicky, and Apocalypse were in the front row, engrossed in the movie and teasing one another, completely unaware of the intrusion. They fully relied on the security system and cameras, which were easily skirted by Sapphire.

"What the fu. . . ." exclaimed Apocalypse when Inferno put a bullet into the screen, cracking it and causing it to short out. Sapphire and Onyx came to the front of the room; Inferno was the last to approach them. Sapphire and Onyx had their guns trained on both Garrett and Nicky.

Apocalypse was the first to speak, "Not sure how you got in here, but I won't say a word if y'all just turn right around and walk outa here. I've got no cash in the house and no quarrel with any of you," offered Apocalypse. Inferno pulled his gun up and put two rounds into Garrett's chest as Nicky popped up, "Ahhh nah, you didn't," as he took a swing at Inferno and missed.

Inferno holsters his gun on his hip and looks at Onyx and Sapphire, "Let me have this one." Nicky squares up on Inferno, "You one big boy, Mista, but you ain't seen what Tricky Nicky can do; I got moves," as he attempts to sweep Inferno's legs with a variation of Muay Thai, but his attempts prove ineffective.

Inferno's talents were many, but his most useful was that of learning his opponent's tactics and using it against his adversary. Nicky swings again, missing wide, and Inferno puts a solid combination right then left into Nicky's face, causing him to fall to the ground. He shakes his head and looks up, his face mangled with two front teeth missing. His face already a bloody mess.

He attempts to get up, wavers, then rushes Inferno, but at the last moment, Inferno sidesteps the large man's trajectory and grabs Nicky by the scruff of hair on the back of his head and belt, and shoves his head into the wall and through the drywall into a plumbing pipe, knocking him out cold as the water begins to puddle around the wall where the unconscious Nicky lay. Inferno pulls out his gun and, in a cold and calloused execution, empties two rounds into the back of the big man's head.

Apocalypse looks at his two murdered friends, stunned and mortified over what has happened in mere seconds. Inferno walks up to the famous vocal recording artist, and looks him in the eye. Apocalypse shakes his head, "Why, man, why would you do this to me? Garrett and Nicky were my best friends, wasted, and for what? What possible good can come from this?"

Inferno cocked his head, "No good came from killing them, none at all," referring to his two friends, "They are nobody's and died because they were with you. You died to make a statement," as Inferno raised his silenced 9mm and fires a round right into Apocalypse's face, killing him instantly.

Onyx pulled out his paint brush, "What are your words of wisdom today, Boss?" Inferno thought about the question, but he and Fury had already decided, *"Our day of enlightenment is upon us, The Reign Cometh."*

"Position them as I described," barked Inferno as Sapphire and Onyx executed his orders.

Chapter 16

The Sentinels Align

"If men were angels, no government would be necessary."
~James Madison

Miami, Florida
2023 June
Apocalypse Private Residence
12:28 PM (The Following Day)

Jamie Bellamy had not heard from her one and only, exclusive client all morning. Apocalypse was scheduled to be in the recording studio for the entire day, detailing the final touches on his latest album, *Reckless*.

She had represented him for nearly five years, and he had never failed to return her texts when she needed him and certainly never missed a minute spent in the recording studio. However, today was the exception. It wasn't like him.

Babysitting him was her job, and Apocalypse was her meal ticket, and she wasn't about to let some drunken binger with his less-than-favorable friends, or a drug-induced coma keep him from finishing his album. She needed to keep him in tip top shape, and it was no easy achievement. He was an artist through and through and more of an activist as of late. People listened to him like he was the second coming of the Messiah. She didn't understand why, but if it sold albums, that was all that really mattered.

Jamie Bellamy kept the *Apocalyptic Machine* in motion, and he was well aware she was the reason it all ran smoothly. Jamie appreciated, more than anyone, the value of her investment in the Apocalypse franchise and also why he paid her 5 million dollars a year to handle all of his problems and keep him on the straight and narrow which was no easy task with his celebrity status. Thankfully, he kept pretty much as a recluse. Minimal parties, but when they did, they went all out. Her biggest obstacle were his two friends, who glommed on to him more than anyone. The girls, opportunists and the partygoers would come and go, but Nicky and Garrett never left his side.

He affectionally called Jamie his *GlitchSmith* as she fixed all the issues Apocalypse, or his posse, often created, and she felt like she deserved every penny she received. This year she would ask for a portion of the revenue he would receive from the new album. She was certain he would agree because they both appreciated her value to him. Jamie was as much a contributor to the new album as the artist himself, as her job was to keep Apocalypse healthy, sober, and recording, and she performed her job diligently.

He had boasted that the soon-to-be-released Reckless album was going to be his best compilation to date, and there was no question it would go multiple Platinum when it was released in the Fall. Jamie was banking on it.

She stepped through the front door when no one answered the doorbell. He gave her a key years before as he and his friends were often in a stupor of sorts, usually imprisoned within the basement. With loud music often blaring or various movies running 24/7, they were often oblivious to the outside world. The world could be ending outside, and the three of them would never know.

Jamie called his name several times with no response, and the house appeared erringly quiet, surprisingly for Apocalypse and his freeloading friends.

"James . . . . Garrett . . . . Nicky," sometimes Jamie loathed babysitting these three, but her payday would soon come. She just had to remain patient. *Eye on the prize . . .* She often told herself.

She figured they were passed out in the basement, a common occurrence but unusual for a recording day. Apocalypse enjoyed those moments more than he enjoyed his friends and their shenanigans.

Hitting the bottom of the stairs of the basement, she slowly walked towards the cinema room. Everything was still and quiet, "James . . . . Apocalypse, Garrett?" There was no response as she knocked on the opened door, walked into the cinema, and immediately noticed the broken big screen with what appeared to be a bullet hole in the center of the glass.

Jamie Bellamy looked to her left as her hands came to her mouth in horror, instinctively seeing the grisly sight before her.

Upon the back wall, she witnessed the body of Apocalypse strung up in only his boxers, like Jesus upon the cross, hands and feet nailed to the wall, crossed over the other. Garrett and Nicky were positioned below him, backs to one another, looking forward as if humble servants serving their master. A true interpretation of the three of them in life . . . . *and in death.*

Horrified but curious, she walked closer to them and read the words spraypainted above Apocalypse's head . . . .

*Behold my ultimate sacrifice, laid bare for all to see—
an offering to you, the world. Change is not merely
on the horizon; it is inevitable. A new era is about to
unfold, one that promises to reshape the very fabric
of our existence. This is not just a transformation;
it is a revolution, an evolution, a powerful tide that
will sweep away the old and herald the dawn of*

something extraordinary. Prepare yourselves, for the winds of change are gathering strength, ready to usher in a reign of innovation and rebirth. The Reign Cometh. . . .

Jamie Bellamy didn't understand the message but then thought it peculiar, lying upon the floor between Garrett and Nicky a bloodied newspaper with Senator Damian West's picture filling the entire page, his renowned smile unmistakable, an odd fixture in an otherwise grotesque display.

She stepped backward, retracing her steps, not wanting to touch anything and disrupt the environment; as she left the room, pulled out her phone and dialed 911. After ten minutes, she hung up. Still standing just outside the room she then called her attorney, he picked up on the second ring. "Franklin, what do I stand to gain from Apocalypse's estate if he were to die?"

Washington, D.C.
2023 July
Senator Damian West Private Residence

"Social and political unrest is beginning to run rampant, and with this Apocalypse issue last month, the people are wanting justice and looking to you, Damian, to guide them through this tumultuous time. There is tension even, on a global scale as conflicts in Ukraine and with hostility on the precipice of collapse in the Middle East, it just appears the world is unraveling," explained Sam West.

Damian shook his head, addressing both Julian Chambers and his father, "I can't wrap my head around the murder of Apocalypse in any way and don't understand how they have tied his martyrium to me and my campaign." Julian sat down, his leg still sore from the assassination attempt on the Capitol's stairs over a year before. He had just ceased using his cane but retained a slight limp from the ordeal and surgery that followed to repair his shattered femur. He looked at Damian and Sam West, often wondering why the Wests hadn't been more empathetic of the bullet that Julian had taken, most likely meant for Damian West. He often had to remind himself that they had gotten him to this point, but his verve and dedication were what helped him keep the seat. Julian Chambers still had a job to do.

Julian made the point, "Strangely though, his death has brought with it an entire movement capturing the Millennials (Generation Y) and Generation Zers. His agent, Ms. Bellamy, is relentlessly pushing publicity with this impending new album release in a month or two. The hype on it has been incredible since his death, which is directly affecting your popularity, Damian. Bellamy and their publicist have pushed his death into a media circus surrounding his new album, which supposedly has a strong political slant toward needed change and reform. It's playing right into our campaign. We need to leverage Apocalypse's momentum to work in our favor and our campaign."

Damian looked at his long-time friend, seeing a different side to the man and curious over his lack of empathy for a person so brutally murdered, let alone manipulating his death for Damian's benefit. Damian was about to say something, hesitated, then realized he must.

Damian West looked at them and shook his head, "I can't profit from the brutal murder of this artist." "You must, Damian. You didn't cause or create the hype," said Julian Chambers, "But you must capitalize on the opportunity you have been given. We need any edge that comes our way. Any publicity can only help our cause."

Julian added, "You don't need to cite him or acknowledge it happening; simply embrace those groups, Damian, and welcome into the idea your endorsement for what Apocalypse believed in and the dream that he envisioned. That message, his message, is true and honest and very powerful. I think if it is spun in the right way, you will have championed this voting group. Remember also, Damian, we both fall within this demographic ourselves. We are in between both groups, so we can sympathize with them and empathize with his vision."

"Julian is right, Damian. We need to seize the moment," added Sam. Damian West nodded, "I see your point and agree as long as we don't come off opportunistic and spin this in a way simply acknowledging the young artist's sentiments." Damian looked at Julian and smiled, "You are a pretty smart guy, Julian. Maybe a little conniving and sinister at times, but sharp. You know, I've been thinking about who would make a good running mate when we hit the campaign trail in a few months and I have talked about it with several of the Watchful Eight and think you would make a fine Vice President, Julian. You were on the shortlist, a very short list, mind you, but I wanted your thoughts first. What do you think about that?" Sam also smiled, "You two would make an incredible team, no question." Julian wasn't sure this discussion would ever come, but finally, it did.

Julian Chambers was shocked at the idea of even being considered, and with so much time having passed, he assumed they were looking closer at other options for the Vice-President slot. He was humbly honored and a little astonished at the thought, but it was the opportunity he had always desired and felt he had earned it. He would finally be given a chance to make something of his name and show the world the potential of his own legacy recognized.

Damian and Sam West let him think about the possibility for a moment, and when he finally looked up at both of them, he too smiled, "Well, of course, I will accept if given the opportunity. I have to assume you have other strong options, but if you do nominate me, I'll accept, and I'll make you both proud . . . and never regret this decision." He looked at the senior retired Senator, walked over, and shook his hand, "Thank you, Sir. Thank you from the bottom of my heart for your consideration. Thank you for everything you have ever done for me." Then he turned to Damian, "My lifelong friend, thank you always for believing in me. You have always been the better man, and I've always strived to live up to your expectations. Damian, I promise you I will not fail you on this one." Julian looked at Sam, and he nodded his approval, their understanding carrying a far deeper meaning to both of them.

———

Damian looked at him, "I'm certain you would make us proud, Julian, and also why we are extending to you the nod to be my Vice-President. We will formally announce our selection next week and formalize the decision in the coming weeks."

It was a Wednesday night, and it was getting late; they both had a session on the floor the following day, so Julian excused himself and bid them both a good night.

They said their Goodbyes and Julian Chambers exited Damian's home and as he waited for the elevator to arrive, he thought . . . *He had come a long way, indeed.*

As he rode the elevator down to the street level he walked outside as the brisk cold air of the fall struck his face like razor blades. The winter cold was coming early as he stepped into the awaiting black SUV.

He decided to call his mother and tell her the good news, "Mom, hi, yes, sorry, it's late. I wanted to tell you that Damian has asked me to be his running mate for the 2024 Presidential election. With a little bit of luck, I may be the next Vice President of the United States." He had to pull the phone away from his ear from her excitement as he could hear his father in the background asking who it was and her proudly telling Julian's father how their son was going to be the next Vice President. Julian heard growling and arguing as his father, Carl, grabbed the phone from his wife, and with an alcohol-laden response, he shouted, "Vice President, second best as always, Julian. If you aren't first, it doesn't much mean anything to anyone. Second to that bastard West, aren't you? No one remembers who a Vice-President was, they are just puppets. Is that what you are, Julian . . . . *a puppet*?"

Carl Chambers dropped the phone, obviously inebriated, before recovering it once again and continuing his dialogue, "Yep, no one remembers who came in second, Julian. Call us back when you become President," as Kate grabbed the phone back from her husband, pushing Carl away.

It only took a moment for Julian's father to begin to fall back into his alcohol-induced stupor as Kate turned away and pulled the phone close to her ear as she walked out of the room into the kitchen, "I'm so sorry for your father, Julian. I am so proud of you and always will be. You took a terrible childhood and a selfish father, and still, you made something of yourself, and for that, I am so honored for what you have become."

"Thank you, Mom, that means more than anything to me. You don't need to defend him. In his eyes, I will never measure up," answered Julian. "Don't pay him no, never mind, he is old and a fool, and more than anything, he is jealous of you, above all. Keep that light shining bright, honey, and I am always so proud of you." "Thank you, Mom, you have always been too good for him," as he hung up the phone.

Julian Chambers sat back in his seat and thought about everything that had transpired and his ultimate goal had finally been achieved, to run with Damian West as his Vice President, only one position away from the most revered world leader in the free world. So much had transpired for him to get to this place, he thought, and it was all becoming worth the significant risk he had taken, but it was all coming together.

For years, they had all coddled the golden boy to emerge as the country's favorite, but his moment would come; he just had to remain fortitudinous. It was all about patience and Julian Chambers had learned that all good things came in good time.

Everything was falling into place.

Dallas, Texas
2023 Late September
Anthony Voss, Dymitron CEO, Private Residence

Damian West, Sam West, and Sebastian Storm all sat within Anthony Voss's expansive two-story library, waiting for their host to arrive. He was finishing a call in another part of the estate. The lavish property was located in one of the most prestigious residential areas in Dallas, Texas . . . . *Highland Park*, located just north of downtown.

While the others sat waiting patiently, Sebastian Storm stood and peered at the thousands of books filling the walls around him when Anthony Voss walked in and answered the question Sebastian Storm had already been thinking, "*Yes*. In case you were wondering, Mr. Storm, *the answer is yes*, I have read every book you see within this room," then referencing a different style wall, "And those over there along the entire wall, I read before I was 12."

They all stood to greet their host.

"Impressive, Mr. Voss," replied Sebastian. "Please, call me Anthony," as Anthony made his way over to Sebastian Storm first, "Your reputation more than precedes you, Mr. Storm. An honor." Sebastian smiles, "Sebastian . . Anthony, just Sebastian. And thank you, however, unnecessary."

Anthony Voss then turned to Sam and Damian West, "Sam, always a pleasure, and Damian West, it's been far too long, my friend. I have enjoyed watching you seduce the American people of late. I have been so curious about this meeting, please sit down," as he gestured for all of them to take a seat.

They took their seats and spoke for a time, catching up and discussing various social and political perspectives, the campaign, and Sam West's retirement. After some time, Anthony pushed his limits somewhat, "So, Damian, you are stealing my right hand, Mila, who, as you are aware, is a key part of Dymitron. She holds this entire machine together around here. You up and marrying her will take her away from all this," as he gestures to his surroundings.

"Oh no, Anthony, don't be mistaken, she is all yours unless, of course, I win the Presidency, then she will have a completely different role," they all laughed. "Fair enough, but honestly, I am ecstatic for you two. You are of respectable pedigree," as he glanced at Sam West. "She is special to me, and I know Mila Dmitri very well, and if you have captured her heart, then you must be something extraordinary. She is a free spirit, and none have tamed her . . . until now. Bravo, Damian West, you are the only one I'm aware of who has ever captured the woman's heart."

Hearing the story, Sebastian Storm was reminded of his own similar narrative in meeting Adriana Mercer and the captivating adventure they shared spanning from Vienna, Austria to Dublin, Ireland, while enslaved by Tobias Teague, ultimately bringing him and Adriana together. He greatly valued the bond he shared with her and was enlightened to hear of Mila and Damian's unique relationship as well. Although he had only met her once, he was more than impressed with Mila Dmitri.

As Anthony delved into the depths of Damian's political philosophy, his questions served as a gateway to a spirited and impassioned dialogue—a discourse well beyond mere conversation to become a symphony of ideas and ideals, a collision of intellect and inspiration between them.

With each probing query, Damian seized the opportunity to articulate his vision for the future—a future defined by unity, progress, and, above all, hope for the American people. He spoke of the challenges facing the nation, from the pervasive gridlock of bipartisan politics to the ever-shifting landscape of domestic and geopolitical affairs. And with a fervor bordering on evangelism, he outlined his vision for the Unified Party—a vision rooted in the belief that true change could only come through unity and collaboration.

Damian's words crackled with electric fervor as he spoke, each infused with purpose and conviction. He envisioned exceeding the bitter divides of partisan politics to carve a new path marked by inclusivity, empathy, and a shared commitment to the greater good. As he delved into his vision for a progressive future, his passion was unmistakable, his voice amplifying with every call for change. To Damian, the rise of the Unified Party was more than a political shift—it was a detailed dream of a brighter tomorrow. His compelling vision sparked a fire in his listeners, igniting inspiration and a steadfast belief in the transformative power of united action.

Anthony Voss studied the younger man as he spoke and was impressed with his beliefs, his perspectives, and his rousing words.

Damian West didn't speak as a politician but more as a visionary. He looked about the room at the others in attendance, and it was evident the young Senator's words had influenced all of them in the same way. They were all dedicated to the end in serving Damian West and the Unified Party.

Looking at Damian, Anthony then turned to Sebastian, "This will shake this country to its foundation if you can pull it off, Damian. However, Sebastian, I can imagine you are more than aware of the enemies this will surely summon from the darkness?" Sebastian's expression grew grim, "The worst kind of fanatics, I'm afraid, Sir." Anthony agreed, "Damn right, gentlemen. I love the vision and the inspiration behind it, but as this campaign ramps up, the true crazies will start to unhinge. Of that, I am certain."

Damian nodded in agreement, "That's why we have the infamous Sebastian Storm on our side, Anthony. He is taking every precaution." Anthony nodded as if accepting the response as a viable solution to an evolving and seemingly dangerous issue surrounding Damian's candidacy.

There was a pause before Anthony decided to cut to the chase, "I'm respectful of your time as all of us are busy men, but what do I truly owe the honor of having you all in my home and so far from Washington? What is the real agenda here if I can be so bold?"

Sam decided to field the question and, for several minutes, launched into the history of their group, the failed historical attempts at the emergence of a prolific third party, and the fact they had orchestrated a substantial congressional coup of key leaders to the Unified Party on both sides of the aisle along with the prior Speaker of the House. Sam West went on to explain the Watchful Eight and the one position still left unoccupied. He concluded with the single spot left open intentionally, hoping Anthony Voss would consider himself worthy of potentially winning the final seat within the illustrious group.

Damian West continued the dialogue and went on to ask Anthony the question they had all come to ask, "So tell me, Anthony, what would it take to keep Dymitron here on U.S. soil? What would you require, within reason, to keep the move of the largest company in the world from happening?"

Anthony Voss looked at Damian intently, then at Sam before slowly standing up, pondering the question. He assumed the reason for their asking for this meeting may very well surround the decision to move Dymitron to Singapore. He walked over to the window, peering out over his large backyard. "That's a hard question, Damian, and with a myriad of moving parts precipitating the decision to move the company. As I am certain you are all well aware, the current administration is imposing tremendous regulation and taxes on U.S. businesses and overtly manipulating their control. Covid-19 and the initiatives directed will ultimately be covered by businesses such as mine because the government sure as hell can't pay for it. The cost to move Dymitron will have a price tag of roughly one billion, but the taxes saved and regulation ease will pay for the move in three years. You ask me what it would take to keep my business here Senator? It would take an easing of regulation, to put it bluntly. I realize regulation is necessary, but not in the sense of what the government wants to do. I mean, we aren't the FDA; we aren't curing cancer here. We are simply making the quality of life for all humans, in general . . . *better*. Second, tax incentives for businesses would be nice. For example, using money contributed by American businesses to help those in need in our country, homeless, low-security prison work programs, etc. I don't know, letting our tax dollars actually be utilized to do something to help people, not filling the government coffers or funding exorbitant civilian contractors where it will be invariably mismanaged or misappropriated. I wish to refine the system so that taxing high-worth individuals and corporations can incentivize them to want to see their tax dollars moving toward something of significance. You ask what it would take to keep the business here; it would take making it worth my while and for that of Dymitron, to keep the company on U.S. soil. The Republicans and Democrats perpetual and chronic conflict only breeds hostility, and it trickles down to the American people feeling as if their leaders are doing nothing . . . *which they are. . . doing nothing.* Amidst a political storm, we face a scenario where President Biden's mental capacity is under scrutiny, and Democrats are in a frenzy to find a strong contender for 2024—or decide whether to stick with an incumbent shadowed by two tumultuous years. As a moderate, I've consistently challenged both parties, much like Elon Musk, and we've both become focal points under the intense scrutiny of public and political lenses—yet our perspectives remain our own, a private matter not open for public dissection. Aligning with any one group could be disruptive to my business, and I don't take that lightly."

Damian viewed the reactions of the group in front of him, afraid of what he may see, but was surprised to observe nodding heads and validation for Voss's concerns and observations. Above all, Anthony Voss was aware if he moved Dymitron, many other companies would follow suit. He was to be the first to blaze the trail, and the trickle effect would cripple the United States, but the current administration had backed him into a corner and he was forced to make momentous decisions.

As Damian rose to his feet to make his point, a sense of purpose radiated from him, his every movement deliberate and calculated. He fixed his gaze on Anthony Voss, his eyes ablaze with a fervor demanding attention—a passion born of conviction and a burning desire to effect change. Sam's smiled with avid anticipation and satisfaction of what was to follow. He knew that Anthony Voss was about to witness the full spectrum of his son's emerging prowess—a display that was rapidly becoming legendary. The stage for this encounter was set in an intimate, exclusive venue, with the audience comprising none other than the most famous businessman in the world. The significance of the moment was not lost on Sam or the others present; this was a rare opportunity for his son to showcase his talents in front of a titan of industry, and Sam relished the thought of the impression it would undoubtedly leave.

"It's often been said the backbone of our great nation lies in the strength of its businesses—both large and small," Damian began, his voice commanding the room with its resonance. "For centuries, American entrepreneurs and innovators have been the driving force behind our prosperity, fueling modernization, creation of jobs, and bolstering our economy. But in recent years, we've witnessed a disturbing trend—a trend of neglect, of disregard, and of outright hostility towards our nation's businesses and their leaders."

He paused, allowing his words to sink in, the weight of his message hanging heavy in the air. "The benefits once afforded to American businesses have been systematically eroded, stripped away by a government who has lost sight of its duty to support and celebrate the entrepreneurial spirit. Instead of fostering an environment conducive to growth and innovation, our government has chosen to burden businesses with excessive taxes and suffocating regulations, stifling their potential and hindering their ability to thrive or worse . . . *the desire to thrive.*"

Damian's voice rose with each passing moment, his passion igniting a fire in the hearts of all those present. "And you, Anthony, and Dymitron, are a prime example of the injustices that have been perpetrated against our nation's businesses. Despite your contributions to our country—your revenue, your reputation, and the jobs you've created—you've been met with nothing but disdain and indifference from those in power."

He paused, his gaze piercing as he locked eyes with Anthony. "But it doesn't have to be this way. Our government should be looking to businesses like yours—innovative, forward-thinking, and successful—for guidance and inspiration. Instead of burdening you with onerous regulations and punishing taxes, they should be learning from you, emulating your successes, and working alongside you to build a brighter future for all."

Damian's words hung in the air, a call to action reverberating throughout the room. He sensed he had captured their interest, especially that of Anthony, who appeared poised to absorb every word of the young Senator's impassioned plea for change. As he continued to speak, Damian realized he was not just speaking for himself but for every entrepreneur, every business owner, and every American who dared to dream of a better tomorrow.

"I have shown a better way within my own state. Other states have now followed suit and still more will over the next year. This is the model I wish to take with me to the White House. A method to and for the people of this great nation. A nation taking pride in its businesses and helps them to foster more, knowing the government, the people, and the nation will stand taller as a result, and the global eyes will see benefit also in the unity and products and services we can also offer them. Everyone wins. Those who have pilfered and stolen, or those who have learned to manipulate this government for their own personal gain, will find folly in that thinking with me at the helm. I will not stand for it and will not allow it anywhere my path leads me. So yes, Anthony, I want you to keep your business here; I want it to prosper, and I want to share in your success as it will carry over to the advancement of this great nation as well. I want to lean on you to help us as a nation and government thrive and flourish for all. Government can help the people, but so can business if we create environments and incentives releasing the tax burden on businesses and individuals in an attempt to help those less fortunate than we all win, and that is my ultimate goal."

"As we contemplate the possibility of Dymitron's departure from the United States, Anthony, we must confront the stark reality such a move would have far-reaching corollaries—consequences extending far beyond the confines of the business world," Damian declared, his voice resolute and unwavering. "For too long, our government's policies have served to undermine the very foundation of our economy, weakening the delicate financial infrastructure upon which our nation's prosperity depends."

He paused, allowing his words to resonate in the room, the gravity of the situation hanging heavy in the air. "The overregulation and over-taxation of American businesses have eroded the integrity of our economy, threatening to plunge us into a state of chaos and disarray. If Dymitron were to leave, the vacuum it would create would send shockwaves through the financial markets, destabilizing the complex fabric of our society. This country is already economically bankrupt. Your departure would be the final nail within our fiscal coffin. Your move will initiate a domino effect we may never recover from."

Anthony nodded, "I am acutely aware of the far-reaching effect this move will have, and although I am not happy about it, my hand has been forced, Damian. I must make a stand and hold my ground. This is not a bluff."

Damian's eyes burned with intensity as he continued, his fervency for the cause evident in every word he uttered. "I know it has, and it pains me to think we have driven you to this end. But the true tragedy lies in the realization our government's shortsighted policies have not only jeopardized the stability of our economy but also undermined the fundamental principles upon which our nation was founded. By neglecting to provide businesses with the support and incentives they need to thrive, they have effectively abandoned the people who drive our economy forward—the entrepreneurs, the innovators, and the risk-takers who dare to dream of a better future."

He paused, his gaze sweeping across the room, his words resonating with all who listened. "It is time for a change, Anthony. It is time for our government to recognize the invaluable contributions of businesses like Dymitron and to implement policies fostering innovation, rewarding hard work, and creating opportunities for all. Graduated incentives must be put in place to encourage businesses to invest in our nation's future, to create jobs, and to lift up those who have been left behind."

As Damian spoke, his words carried the weight of conviction and purpose, a rallying cry for change in a world desperately in need of it. As he concluded his impassioned plea, he was aware he had ignited a spark in the hearts of all those who listened—a glimmer of hope, determination, and unwavering belief in the power of collective action to shape the destiny of a nation.

Anthony Voss looked at Damian, "If you could make that happen, ensure it would happen, then yes, I would keep the company here, and the Executive Board and shareholders, I'm certain, would accept it. However, we all know one cannot simply wait for that to happen, Damian. For one, a promise is an empty vessel to me; the action is what proves the promise, and second, it cannot happen quickly with this bureaucratic nonsense happening on the Hill. Nothing gets done quickly within congressional congestion permeating Congress like a disease."

"That will change, Anthony, I can assure you, if I get into office. No longer will this be a puppet position. I will not stand for it. I won't mince words, Anthony. We want you and Dymitron on our side. We aren't looking for donations or financial support, we want you as a player for our team, plain and simple. We wish for you to be a part of our future, unified and true to what we stand for and what we hope the country can once again become: a place of prosperity and hope. We would be honored to have you as a part of our Unified Party if you felt so inclined."

As Anthony Voss nodded in response, a complex tapestry of personal history and political ideology unfolded behind his eyes. Born into a family with strong Republican roots, he had been raised on the stories of his father—a German immigrant who had found refuge and opportunity in the land of the free. It was a narrative of resilience, hard work, and unwavering belief in the promise of the American Dream.

Over the years, Anthony had navigated the shifting currents of political discourse, evolving from a staunch Republican to a more moderate position within the party's ranks. Yet, as time passed, he found himself increasingly disillusioned with the state of American politics—profound cynicism that ultimately led him to break away from party lines and embrace more of an independent status.

For Anthony, politics had become a source of frustration and disappointment—a somber reflection of the dysfunction and divisiveness pervading every corner of the political landscape. The characters who once commanded his admiration now appear a little more than actors on a stagnant stage, their words and actions falling short of the ideals they professed to uphold.

But despite his disenchantment with the American political stage, Anthony remained steadfast in his commitment to his principles. While he may not have been overtly vocal about his beliefs, his disillusionment fueled a quiet resolve—a resolve to seek out truth and integrity in a world plagued by deception and hypocrisy.

And as he listened to Damian's impassioned plea for change, Anthony felt a flicker of hope ignite within him—a hope that perhaps, amidst the chaos and uncertainty, there was still room for redemption. For in Damian's words, he saw the glimmer of a brighter future—a future defined not by partisan politics but by unity, compassion, and a shared commitment to the common good.

As the conversation unfolded, Anthony was cognizant as he stood at a crossroads—a moment of reckoning, shaping the course of his political journey for years to come. And as he contemplated the path ahead, he resolved to lend his voice to the chorus of change—to stand up for what he believed in and to fight for a better tomorrow, not just for himself, but for all those who called America home.

"Damian, in the next year, gain some more support, and if you get elected, you implement your reform and see through the various points we have made today, then you will have my support. I plan on completing the move to Singapore in the next three years, so you have some time to show me the changes that are occurring and make me a true believer in the Unified system."

"Fair enough," replied Damian West. They all stood up, and Anthony asked softly as he patted Damian's back, "What would it take to secure the last seat on the Watchful Eight, Damian?"

"Oh, that's simple, Anthony, join our party, and the seat is yours. That's what we came here to do, but it appears we have failed. We hoped for a declaration of your support to the Unified Party today and to join our innovative group."

"Don't count us out, Anthony," replied Damian. "Oh, is hardly my intention. In fact, I'm rooting for your collective success," replied Anthony.

Anthony Voss saw them all to the door. As he shook hands with all of them and bid them farewell, he grabbed Damian's hand once again and held it a moment longer, saying, "You haven't . . . . failed yet, Senator," as a smile washed over Senator West's face. Damian West smiled back and nodded, then turned and left.

Israel
2023 October
Israel-Palestine Conflict

The Palestinian-Israeli conflict emerged as a powder keg of tension, following in the wake of the Russia-Ukraine conflict just 18 months before. In the volatile global landscape, friction was on the rise, and a palpable sense of apprehension began to cast a shadow over the world stage.

On the dawn of October 7, 2023, a covert rocket assault orchestrated by Hamas struck Israel with stealthy and well-orchestrated precision. Hamas, a formidable Islamist Palestinian political and militant entity, predominantly operates within the intricate territories of the Gaza Strip and the West Bank. Within the enduring Israeli-Palestinian conflict, Hamas stands as a pivotal and enigmatic player within the region.

Born during the First Intifada in 1987, Hamas is rooted in Islamist ideology with ties to the Muslim Brotherhood, aiming to establish an autonomous Palestinian state under Islamic governance across the West Bank, Gaza Strip, and East Jerusalem.

Hamas operates with a dual approach: it engages politically within Palestinian territories and governs Gaza since 2007, but it also has a military faction, the Izz ad-Din al-Qassam Brigades. These brigades have been involved in continuous armed conflicts with Israel, resulting in their designation as a terrorist organization by Israel, the United States, the European Union, and other countries.

The group's refusal to recognize the state of Israel fuels ongoing tensions and violent confrontations, marked by rocket attacks and clashes that have had severe consequences for both Gaza and Israel. This ongoing conflict underscores the complex and volatile nature of Hamas's role in regional politics.

Internationally, Hamas is embroiled in controversy, widely designated as a terrorist organization, which heavily impacts its global standing. Despite this, diplomatic efforts by some countries contrast sharply with the staunch non-engagement stance of others.

Efforts to stabilize the region through ceasefire agreements have seen limited success, with peace remaining elusive due to frequent violations and escalating violence. Hamas's central role in the Israeli-Palestinian conflict continues to fuel intense debate and significantly influences Middle Eastern security dynamics and the broader peace process.

The region's volatility was heightened by the second Intifada in 2002, leading to Israel's reoccupation of West Bank cities and was further destabilized by Yasser Arafat's death in 2004. Subsequent years saw repeated conflicts, including Israel's war with Hezbollah in 2006 and several major operations in Gaza. The violence reached a peak with significant international repercussions following clashes on Nakba Day in 2017 and 2018, the latter prompting a UN investigation into potential war crimes.

The situation took another turn with the election of Donald Trump as the U.S. president in 2016. His alliance with Israeli Prime Minister Benjamin Netanyahu at that time resulted in the relocation of the U.S. embassy from Tel Aviv to Jerusalem, signifying recognition of the city as Israel's capital. Trump also controversially designated the Golan Heights as Israeli territory, disregarding the broader international consensus that viewed the region as illegally annexed.

Further complicating matters, Trump curtailed American funding to the UNRWA and entrusted his son-in-law, Jared Kushner, with the ambitious task of formulating a Middle East peace plan. Kushner's unorthodox approach only added yet another layer of complexity to an already intricate geopolitical landscape.

The international community had mixed reactions to Trump and Kushner. Some countries supported the U.S. moves, while others condemned them. The decisions contributed to debates about international law and the status of Jerusalem.

The effects of these decisions were and continue to be a subject of debate and discussion. The Israeli-Palestinian conflict remained unresolved, and the region's geopolitical dynamics continue to evolve. The impact of these choices extends beyond the immediate actions themselves, influencing the broader context of the conflict and regional diplomacy.

Washington D.C.
2023 November
Sebastian Storm's Private Residence

Sebastian Storm sped down Highway 1 before merging onto George Washington Memorial Parkway. Driving more than twice the posted speed limit, his nerves calm and collected as he shifted the gears methodically. Sebastian didn't hesitate as he weaved in and out of traffic, heading toward his newly purchased penthouse located in Kalorama, downtown Washington, D.C.

Being an avid performance car enthusiast, his *McLaren Speedtail* was a limited-production supercar with a price tag of just over $2 million. Recognized for its exceptional agility, innovative design, responsiveness, and cutting-edge technology, the Speedtail is the epitome of technical prowess. Powered by a hybrid powertrain consisting of a 1,055 horsepower, 4.0-liter twin-turbocharged V8 engine combined with an electric motor. This hybrid system made the Speedtail one of the most powerful production cars in the world. Delivered from Dubai that morning, Sebastian had just taken possession of the new car. He was eager to break her in, curious and saddened he wouldn't reach its top speed of 250 mph within the cement jungle surrounding him.

The car's design was characterized by its streamlined, innovative appearance. The model featured dihedral doors, opening upward, a long tail section, and a centrally located driver's seat, similar to the McLaren F1 from the 1990s. The look and performance suited Sebastian perfectly, and to that point, he was more than satisfied. On a whim several months before, he had chosen yellow for the exterior color, an unusual selection for him.

Turning onto Key Bridge, then onto Whitehurst Freeway before exiting off on Connecticut Avenue, Sebastian pushed the accelerator further to the floor, letting out the clutch, provoking his Speedtail to over 120 mph, savoring the longer stretch of road with minimal traffic, beckoning him to tame the unhindered freedom of the pavement stretching before him. Adrenaline surging, the city landscape and stop lights sped by in his peripheral vision as Sebastian expertly traversed around traffic as if they were stopped.

Sebastian reveled in the thrill of navigating high-performance vehicles of varying types through the bustling urban landscape, an experience that rivaled his adoration for soaring through the skies in rotorcraft. For nearly two decades, he had been intimately acquainted with the art of helicopter piloting, but the allure of speeding through city and country roads or taking to the skies never waned. Whether it was the symphony of engines or the exhilarating sensation of flight, Sebastian's insatiable appetite for speed and adventure found its fulfillment both on the ground and in the air.

In Sebastian's discerning eyes, all other vehicles on the road were mere spectators, insignificant obstacles begging for a display of the McLaren's unparalleled gallantry and precision handling. With the finesse of a virtuoso, he effortlessly navigated his high-performance machine around them, leaving a trail of bewildered motorists dumbfounded as he passed them, all in a blur, a whisp of yellow racing by the unsuspecting motorists.

As the world outside became a haze of yellow, the intoxicating surge of acceleration coursed through his veins, the RPMs dancing into the fiery red zone. The distinct whine of the Speedtail, teetering on the edge of its limits, was music to his ears, a concerto of power and control.

Unperturbed and fearless, he executed a lightning-quick downshift, engaging from sixth to third gear in an instant with a deft flick of the clutch to avoid a turning car that wasn't anticipating his excessive speed. The RPMs soared, and with unwavering precision, he swerved around the vehicle, his heart rate never waning.

A mile later, he approached the Kalorama limits far more quickly than he would have liked. A gentle left, an immediate right, and then the final straightaway, unleashing a surge of power catapulting him from fourth to fifth gear, followed by the sixth and final gear in the blink of an eye. The opus of speed, control, and exhilaration echoed in the engine's responsiveness, and Sebastian remained the unchallenged conductor of this thrilling automotive performance. He slowed as he saw his building approaching on the south side of the street.

Kalorama, an affluent residential neighborhood respected for its grand historic homes and estates. A popular and much sought after choice among diplomats and high-profile individuals or for those providing the hefty price tag of the real estate within.

He flipped his visor downward as he pulled up to the large steel garage barricade, then pressed the door control. Sebastian slowly eased Speedtail in and found his spot among the two additional stalls reserved only for him. His other vehicle, a 750 GSXR motorcycle, and the Rezvani SUV, parked perfectly beside one another.

The *Sentinel Towers* were aptly named and made Sebastian smile, enjoying the creative moniker of his new residence. He felt comfortable within his new home environment as he should; with a nearly 8-digit value, the property demanded the amenities be top-notch. He purchased the Penthouse after looking at several, knowing he would be spending a fair amount of time in Washington D.C. during Senator Damian West's Presidential candidacy, extending over the following 12 months and potentially beyond, depending on the outcome.

The property afforded him a sound and secure defensive position, and security was paramount despite adding his own brand and complexity to the four-bedroom design. From any position upon the balcony, the views of Washington D.C. downtown were mesmerizing, with a terrace encircling the entire unit and a private elevator from the 22nd floor to the street and garage level.

Sebastian Storm enjoyed the comforts of his properties. They all provided a sanctuary to him in one way or another. Among them was his waterfront estate on Lake Como, 1500 acre Montana lodge, and now his expansive Washington, D. C. Penthouse. None of the assets could be supported on a mere Governmental Agency's paltry annual income but Sebastian had always been fiscally resourceful, even as a boy growing up in Roanoke, Virginia.

At a young age, Sebastian designed and later patented several creative and humane animal traps and ultimately created a lucrative business venture along with his mentor, James Woodford. They later sold the business for tens of millions of dollars, securing his financial security for a lifetime. Sebastian then parlayed the sale of his company, Bearhugger^{TM}, with imaginative and various profitable ventures, including real estate projects and brokering rare gems to amass a sizable estate valuing several hundred million.

Sebastian Storm thrived in his governmental role, driven by a relentless pursuit of justice and crippling those aggressors that abused, persecuted, and tormented those less fortunate. With time, he had not only earned but fully embraced the unparalleled autonomy granted to him and his surrogate brother, Sean Woodford. For more than two decades, their unwavering dedication had become the backbone of the nation's security. Terrorists came to fear the ATS Division (Anti-Terrorist Special Division) and Sebastian Storm and his elite team, specifically.

In the world of covert operations, Hillary Bastini, possessed a reputation resonating far and wide for many past presidents and Congress's interests alike. Her recruitment of Sean Woodford, a formidable talent hailing from the exclusive ranks of the Navy S.E.A.L's Sniper Division, marked a pivotal moment in the annals of counterterrorism. Together with Sebastian Storm, they formed an indomitable partnership akin to a modern-day wrecking ball, poised to shatter the very foundations of terrorist organizations worldwide.

Their union wasn't only about combining skills; it was a fusion of unwavering dedication, razor-sharp intellect, and an unyielding commitment to justice. With HB's strategic brilliance, Sebastian's planning and execution, and finally, Sean's unparalleled marksmanship, they operated as a synchronized force, striking trepidation into the hearts of those who threatened global security.

Their track record spoke volumes as they relentlessly pursued and neutralized global threats with surgical precision. To terrorist organizations, the mere mention of their names sent shivers down spines and left a trail of shattered networks, terrorist cells and dismantled plots in their wake. Their partnership had become synonymous with resilience, cunning, and an unrelenting pursuit of global harmony.

In a world where shadows concealed the heroes who safeguarded the realm of the everyday world, Sebastian Storm and Sean Woodford stood as sentinels, a beacon of hope in the fight against darkness. Together, they forged a legacy that would be recounted in hushed tones and revered as a testament to the power of human resolve in the face of adversity.

The country owed a significant debt of gratitude to these extraordinary heroes. The United States of America stood taller, their contributions immeasurable, standing as an indelible testament to the nation's security and prosperity. Yet, as time unfurled its relentless tapestry, a new chapter beckoned—an epoch where their unwavering commitment would find a profound purpose, one resonating deeply with the sanctity and welfare of the American people.

The transition was a pivotal moment, a shifting of gears from safeguarding the nation's physical borders to fortifying the very essence of its strength and unity. Their resolve, once directed outward in defense of the homeland, was now turned inward, focusing on nurturing a force transcending the tangible—a force founded on principles, ideals, and the enduring spirit of the American people and their future.

Sebastian Storm had taken it upon himself to become the steward of this new regime and assume the role of custodian of this transcendent force. He understood the well-being of the nation was not solely dependent on external threats but also hinged on the resilience of its core values. His new mission was to safeguard against not only global threats but also focus more on the heart and soul of America itself—a force so strong and meaningful that it would ensure the nation's enduring legacy, echoing through the chronicles of history.

Damian West was that legacy.

In this new chapter, he would not be battling tangible foes but standing as a protector against the erosion of principles and the corrosion of American unity. His commitment, once measured in covert operations and tactical victories, now found expression in preserving the very foundation upon which the United States of America was built. The debt of gratitude, ever-present, was now woven into the fabric of his profound purpose—to protect, empower, and fortify the nation for generations to come. This was his charge and his conviction.

Sebastian Storm, respected for his unyielding nature and formidable presence, was not easily influenced or swayed by others. His personality and approach to life were such that he stood apart, a figure whom others frequently found intimidating and often difficult to connect with on a deeper level. However, a select few managed to break through his resilient exterior and reach the depths of his inner core, revealing the depth in which Sebastian Storm held his veritable spirit.

Among them were James Woodford, Sam West, Hillary Bastini, Adriana Mercer, and Sean Woodford. Each of them, in their own unique way, had a profound effect on Sebastian over the years, influencing him in ways that were rare and deeply significant. James Woodford, with his insightful wisdom and calm demeanor, offered Sebastian a perspective on life that was both insightful and enlightening. Sam West, admired for his wide range, scope, and trust, challenged Sebastian's intellect and expanded his political horizons. Hillary Bastini, with her strategic and visceral approach and relentless pursuit of excellence, provided a sense of confidence in Sebastian's early development. Sean Woodford, a dynamic and charismatic figure, ignited a sense of ambition and drive in Sebastian he admired and respected. Lastly, Adriana Mercer provided the greatest quality of all in her emotional support and keen intellect.

She helped him to see further within himself. Their tutelage kept him balanced and honed and made him the best in covert operations.

Recently, Damian West emerged as a new and influential figure in Sebastian's illustrious life. Damian's impact was immediate and profound, fostering a connection extending well beyond mere acquaintance or friendship. Their discussions were deep and meaningful, spanning a wide range of topics from intellectual debates to technical discussions, and these interactions solidified Damian's position as a pivotal figure in Sebastian's existence despite being the youngest of this revered list.

What set Damian apart was not only his intelligence or his ability to engage in dynamic conversation but also the way he understood and appreciated Sebastian's complex nature. He recognized the layers beneath Sebastian's tough exterior and connected with him on a level few others could. This understanding and mutual respect fostered a deep-seated devotion in Sebastian, a loyalty so strong he vowed to protect Damian at any cost and with his own life if necessary.

Their relationship was a testament to the power of genuine connection and the impact a few select individuals can have on someone who is otherwise seen as unapproachable and impenetrable. Sebastian's interactions with Damian and the others who had circled within his life were more than mere meetings of minds; they were the kind of deep, meaningful connections that shape and define a person's actuality and essence.

Damian West embodied the potential to chart a new course, one that could either revive the nation or his failure could hasten the gradual demise of the United States of America. To Sebastian Storm, this was more than a mere candidacy; it was a pivotal moment in the nation's history, a crossroads where principles hung in the balance, poised on the knife's edge of transformation and teetering on the precipice of evolution or, rather . . . *devolution.*

Sebastian's commitment to this cause remained profound, fueled by an unwavering dedication to safeguarding the principles underpinning the nation's very identity. It was a mission he embraced with unyielding determination, a duty to protect the core values upon which the United States had been built.

The journey that lay ahead was fraught with a myriad of challenges, akin to vigorous and unrelenting trials and tribulations melded into a formidable test of mettle and resilience. However, Sebastian's unwavering determination remained steadfast, unshaken by the daunting obstacles looming before him and Damian West's candidacy. He possessed an insightful comprehension extending far beyond the confines of a mere political campaign; he grasped the reflective reverberations the outcome would likely produce, transcending the realm of any singular candidacy. Sebastian Storm felt Damian West was the man to bring the dream to fruition.

The challenges lying in wait were formidable adversaries capable of sowing doubt and despair. Yet, Sebastian saw them not as insurmountable obstacles but as opportunities to test the strength of character and the depth of conviction. With every trial that arose, he stood prepared to confront it head-on, for he knew the destiny of a nation rested in the balance, and he was committed to ensuring that the outcome would be one honoring the ideals shaping the United States throughout its storied history.

In the face of adversity, Sebastian would stand as a consummate guardian, an unwavering defender of Damian's principles, ready to navigate the treacherous waters of politics and power to ensure Damian West's candidacy reached its culmination. This was a commitment overshadowing the mere politics it was a pledge to protect the very essence of the United States of America, no matter the cost.

And Sebastian Storm was committed to see it through.

Chapter 17

Pressures Persist

"I have sworn upon the altar of God, eternal hostility against every form of tyranny over the mind of man."
~Thomas Jefferson

Washington D.C.
2023 December
Damian West Private Residence

Sebastian Storm, Damian West, Sam West, Gideon Arnold, Regina Alvarado, Julian Chambers, and Ren Cosner sat in attendance, along with HALO, advising on statistical support. They all took their respective seats around the formal dining room table, their focus on determining the best method to expose the Unified Party to a greater concentration of American people. HALO's virtual hologram image sat within the empty seat provided to him, a usual fixture in their meetings and discussions as of late, offering alternative perspectives and theoretical analysis.

Donald Trump had been actively campaigning for his attempt at re-election since November 15, 2022, more than a year before. He was gaining momentum but more at the cost of incumbent Joe Biden's steady decline in popularity and diminishing capacity to lead the country.

Back in the 2020 United States presidential election, the then-serving President Trump sought re-election but was defeated by Democratic nominee Joe Biden, by nearly 80 Electoral votes. Trump contested the results, alleging election fraud and refusing to concede.

Additionally, in January 2021, during the final week of his presidency, Trump faced impeachment by the House of Representatives for incitement of insurrection in connection with the January 6, 2021, Capitol Hill attack. He was ultimately acquitted in the Senate with a bipartisan vote of 57-43, falling short of the required two-thirds majority.

Towards the end of his term, there were discussions about Trump potentially forming a third party referred to as the "Patriot Party" to compete against both Democrats and Republicans, although Trump's spokespersons later denied such a strategy. Nevertheless, Donald Trump began his candidacy early and was on a hard push to expose the inadequacies of the current President. He never considered Damian West, representing the Unified Party, to carry much weight within the bipartisan system. Emergence of a third party was a far reach and Donald Trump and Joe Biden gave the Unified Party movement very little credence.

In August 2023, former President Trump faced indictments at both the federal and state levels, including charges related to his alleged involvement in attempts to overturn the 2020 presidential election. These indictments accused him of engaging in a criminal conspiracy to manipulate election results and pressuring officials to alter vote tallies.

Before these election-related charges, on March 30, 2023, Trump was indicted on 34 felony counts of fraud related to falsifying business records tied to hush money payments to Stormy Daniels during his 2016 presidential campaign. Trump denounced these indictments as political persecution.

Subsequently, on June 8, a federal grand jury indicted Trump for mishandling classified documents and destroying evidence related to a government investigation at his Mar-a-Lago residence. Additionally, Trump was found liable in a civil lawsuit for sexual abuse and defamation against journalist E. Jean Carroll on May 9. Trump vowed to appeal this decision, characterizing it as an unconstitutional silencing and political persecution.

In contrast, President Biden faces a daunting task with less than a year to persuade voters that their well-being has improved during his tenure, and the early signs aren't in his favor.

Interest rates had decreased during Trump's presidency by 32% to Biden's increase of over 200% in just three years. Rates were a hot topic as they approached 2024, and Americans were fed up with the increased rates and fluctuating fuel prices.

Recent polls showed concerning trends for the president. He constantly scrutinized the accuracy of surveys indicating he's trailing Donald Trump in crucial states for the 2024 election. His job approval rating has dipped to 40%, down from 46% in January, according to an NBC News poll. Even within his own party, some Democrats are showing disapproval of his performance, while a surprising 20% of black voters express openness to voting for Donald Trump or Damian West, compared to the 12% Trump secured in 2020.

While the economy has experienced some positive indicators, including GDP growth and wage increases, many voters remain skeptical. Inflation and rising prices for essentials have eroded the perceived gains. The administration's handling of crime and immigration issues further complicates the narrative, with concerns about safety and border security not reflected in official statistics.

Ultimately, voters are assessing their own experiences, and President Biden was attempting to bridge the gap between the data his administration highlights and the incensed realities of everyday Americans if he hopes to improve his approval ratings.

Damian West posed an interesting question to HALO☉ to gain its perspective, "HALO☉, how does my candidacy compare with Trump and Biden currently, and how does the Unified Party rival with the current bipartisan platform?"

HALO☉ hesitated, seemingly calculating his answer before delivering his message, "Interesting question, Senator. Drawing from current news programs, the internet, analysts, and lobbyists, I have compiled my assessment, Senator West," announced HALO☉. After a moment, HALO☉ continued, "The current political landscape has changed tremendously over the last few months. Former President Donald Trump has gained significant ground in the last year, chipping away at President Biden's diminishing popularity and added widespread concern for his rational and cerebral capacity to lead the nation. However, the Unified party has now gained considerable traction diluting interests in the Democratic and Republican parties respectfully."

HALO☉ acted as if he needed a breath, which appeared awkward, as everyone was well aware this was less than a necessity for an artificially intelligent personality. HALO☉ endeavored to appear as human as possible when given the opportunity.

HALO☉ then continued, "In the 2020 United States presidential election, the percentage of the national popular vote received by Joe Biden (Democratic Party) was roughly 51.3% and Donald Trump (Republican Party) approximately 46.8%. As of today, those percentages have shifted considerably to Donald Trump securing an estimated 41.3% of the popular vote, 32.7% for President Biden, and an impressive 21.8% for you, Senator West, with 4.2% remaining undecided. Interestingly, the overall popular vote for Republicans has reached 35% and nearly the same for Democrats, while the Unifides have increased to 25%, impressively. The murder of the famed artist, Apocalypse, also brought about an intensified focus for the Unified Party that was not anticipated. The Unified Party, with you as its leader, Senator West, is steadily gaining ground."

Damian turned to the group in front of him, "Thank you, HALO☉. I think that is better than we had expected by this point, but we need to turn up the heat. Damian West turned to Senator Ren Cosner, "How are we looking on the Presidential debates, Senator?"

"They are being cautiously elusive. Hopefully, with this mounting focus on our view and objectives, our momentum will only increase. I remember talking a few years ago about this, and we predicted that we would have to garner at least 20% of the popular vote, which we have now achieved.

Julian Chambers suggested, "With over 20% of the popular vote solidly supporting the Unified Party and Damian specifically, it's evident that we've become a potent political force to be reckoned with, and the CPD can't deny or avoid any longer. As we prepare for the upcoming presidential campaign, it's essential that we address the role of the Commission on Presidential Debates (CPD) and let us debate our views. The people want to hear our message and our perspectives in the televised debates."

"The CPD was established with a crucial mandate: to organize and host presidential debates during the general election campaign. This responsibility carries immense weight, as these debates serve as a cornerstone of our democratic process, providing voters with insights into the candidates and their policies should be paramount to them."

"One of the core principles underpinning the CPD's mission is to ensure that these debates are conducted fairly and without the undue influence of any political party or individual candidate. This principle is fundamental to maintaining the integrity of our electoral system and preserving the people's trust in it."

"As we move forward, it is our collective duty to hold the CPD accountable for upholding these principles, and Senators Cosner and West should be able to instill this integral obligation. Our pressure on them needs to be constant and relentless. By doing so, we can ensure that the upcoming presidential debates serve their intended purpose, providing voters with a clear and unfiltered view of the candidates and their visions for our nation. We need to stay on this and will require constant updates on the development."

Damian West looked at his father and Senator Ren Cosner, "Gentlemen, please make it so. We need this to have any chance of

influencing the swing states and those Americans who still remain on the fence. There are so many moving parts. We need to hit hard with our impetus and push back this political line the bipartisan system has created. Put me in front of the people, and I will make them see."
The entire group had no hesitation in believing that truth.

Maui, Hawaii
2023 December
Grand Wailea Hotel

Nestled amidst the awe-inspiring ocean landscapes of Maui, Hawaii. The Grand Wailea Hotel stands as a veritable sanctuary of opulence, tranquility, and serenity. The boutique gem transcends the ordinary, redefining the very essence of privacy and elegance in the realm of hospitality. Its vibrant tropical gardens, basking in the Hawaiian sun, form an enchanting backdrop, setting the stage for an idyllic romantic escape.

Every location of the Hotel Wailea exudes an aura of quietude and refinement. Ocean vistas, framed by swaying palm trees and lush flora, weave a mesmerizing tapestry of natural beauty from all vantage points. Here, the gentle symphony of the waves serves as a soothing accompaniment to one's stay, an irresistible invitation to relax and savor every precious moment offered to its guests.

In this realm, where tranquility and sophistication seamlessly converge, the property beckons, extending an invitation to delve into the true essence of Hawaiian luxury and local culture. The resort's unwavering commitment to privacy ensures that all who grace its halls can revel in each other's company, forging cherished memories in the seclusion of this esteemed paradise. Within these hallowed grounds, time appears to slow, affording guests the opportunity to rekindle connections and rediscover their inner sense of vitality.

For those in search of an oasis of calm, the Grand Wailea Hotel epitomizes the spirit of a romantic hideaway. Damian couldn't help but remain certain that his selected locale provided the perfect setting for the union of two souls, as he envisioned making Mila Dmitri his wife.

Their wedding was simple, overlooking the ocean as the sun began to set. Brilliant and beautiful, the vibrant colors dancing across the blue-lit sky behind them, a perfect setting to forge their commitment to one another. The picturesque backdrop paled in comparison to the beautiful bride that Mila Dmitri emulated. Her sequined white dress with full sleeves but a mid-thigh cut and sweeping peekaboo skirt. The look was edgy but mildly suggestive and definitely caught the eye of all those who beheld the exquisite ensemble. Damian wore a classic tuxedo with a stylish white vest, and Sam West served as his best man during the proceedings.

Three years to the day, he had unexpectantly flown her one evening from Dallas to his home in Jackson Hole, Wyoming, a seemingly arrogant and pretentious move that ended up winning her heart and making her fall in love with what could be, the next President of the United States.

It was December 29th, and they became married at 6:43 PM with only close family and friends in a secluded part of the hotel. It was difficult to keep the ceremony a complete secret, but they were able to enjoy, not only their wedding ceremony but a reception for the small group for a few hours before the paparazzi eventually got wind of the affair.

It was then that Damian grabbed Mila and pulled her close, "Let's get out of here." She looked at him quizzically, ". . . . But our guests?" He didn't care as he grabbed her hand, and they ducked out the back exit into a service alleyway.

Sam West notices their departure out of the corner of his eye and starts after his son, but Sebastian stops him, "Sir, it's their wedding night; let them have their moment." Sam stopped abruptly and smiled as he looked up at Sebastian, who was significantly taller, "You are right, Sebastian. Just keep an eye on them for me."

———

Sebastian winked, "I won't quite do that, but I'll make sure they are safe, Sir," as Sebastian began walking in the direction of Damian and Mila. Sebastian had a gifted ability to move within the shadows, he would ensure that the Senator and his bride remained protected as well as uninterrupted.

Damian looked around as she pulled him to her and kissed him passionately as they both eased backward against the wall. She looked at him intently, "I want you, Senator." Smiling to himself as he always did when she called him that, he kisses her neck as she grabs his hand, removes each of her heels, and runs barefoot toward their spacious oceanside villa.

As he unlocks the door with the keycard, she begins to enter. As he softly pulls her back, he places his hand behind her back, the other under her knees as he lifts her abruptly. "Tradition," Damian whispers as he carries his bride across the threshold.

He gently lets her down as her feet softly touch the floor, as she pushes him upon the bed, then slowly back up a few steps as he leans on his elbows, watching his new bride slowly remove her sheer dress skirt off first, revealing her firm legs underneath. She eases the upper portion of the wedding dress above her arms and head as it drops to the floor.

At that point, she is down to only her skirt and bra as she walks over to the side table where a bottle of champagne sits chilled along with a note, lying beside, from the hotel wishing them heartfelt congratulations for including them in their wedding plans. She hits a button on her phone resting on the nightstand, and sensual soft music begins to fill the room.

Mila pops the cork on the bottle and pours its contents into the two glasses accompanying the bottle as Damian looks admiringly at his new bride, drinking in her beauty as she pours the bubbly liquid, carefree and without a worry. She hands one of the flutes, filled full, to Damian where he winks at her as he takes the glass from her hand.

She nonchalantly walks back over to where her dress lay on the ground and clumsily eases her white skirt down her thighs off along with her bra with only one hand, the other holding her own glass. Only a dainty pair of white sheer panties remain, arousing Damian, making her smile, knowing the effect her image is having upon her new husband.

She laughs slightly at the mere utterance of the word 'husband', as she is less than accustomed to the term but adores the sound of it, nonetheless. She looks at Damian and begins to move her hips to the music watching as his eyes light up, never having witnessed this side of Mila in the past. Her hands move over her body as she sensually moves her hips in an erotic and suggestive way, often stealing a glimpse of Damian as he consumes her elegance and sensuality.

Her hand moves to her neck as one finger enters her mouth, and she licks it before she brings up the glass of champagne, swallows it all, and throws it on the bed next to Damian. Both hands now move slowly to her breasts, all while her hips slightly gyrate to the constant beat of *Enya* emitting from the nightstand.

She turns as her hands ease down her thighs, and her perfectly round rear taunts him and beckons him as she moves, torturing his spirit and his sense to remain still and relaxed, displaying her ability to dance for her man and seduce him in the process. He fights the urge to sit up and reach out to her but thinks better of it, unsure why he would want to ruin such a beautiful spectacle she is providing for him.

She bends over now, exposing herself further for his enjoyment as she touches her feet, looking back while in front of her knees, knowing she is luring him in further into her web of seduction and mystery. Easing up slowly, Mila's hands move from her outer thighs to cup each of her rear cheeks, squeezing them softly as her fingers intertwine with the white lace as she carefully and seductively eases her panties down as well. They slide down her legs to her knees, dropping the rest of the way to the floor. She carefully steps out of them and looks back again, ensuring she still has his attention, but she already knows the answer to that question.

Mila smiles again as she turns toward him, somewhat shy as he takes a large drink from his glass of champagne and looks at Mila, bare and exposed . . . beautiful in her elegance yet inhibited now as his wife, she felt for a moment that her role had changed.

<hr>

Sensing her unease, Damian rose up to sit along the edge of the bed and pulled her close to him as she leaned over and put her hand to his face, "I've never loved anyone before, Damian. It excites me and scares me all at the same time."

"I know," came his response as he kissed her hard and deep in the moment, knowing he, too, had never loved a woman as deeply as he did Mila, and there was a part of him that was equally as excited and frightened by it all as well.

As she remained kissing him, her hand drifted to his shirt. As she began to unbutton it, he undid his pants and removed them, and she found the final button on his shirt. Their lips separated as he looked into her eyes, easing his white shirt off, exposing the toned physique he meticulously maintained, and she more than appreciated his efforts. Beyond his sharp mind and wit was a physical specimen she enjoyed admiring, especially while they shared imaginative, intimate moments together.

With one hand, she gently eased her fingers inside his waistband and slid off his boxers, satisfied that he was as bare as she. Mila was more than satiated that he was also as aroused as she was, making him a little embarrassed as well now, as the tables now turned.

Mila looked down, licking her lips, excited for what was to follow. Her hand drifted from his face to his chest, encircling his member, and gently began stroking him. Watching his eyes and biting her lower lip, he was entranced with her as she lightly licked her lips and kissed him once again as her head moved down, still stroking him, then her moist lips as they met his tip, and he slowly began laying back on the bed. He looked down at her as she kissed him, smiling at him as she stroked him, making him more and more erect. Easing her knees on the bed, she straddles his legs as she begins taking more of him within her mouth. Her cadence increases as his hands rest upon his stomach, barely able to contain himself.

She is reminded the effect she is having on him is directly affecting her own arousal, and she is aware he will not be able to last much longer, but her intensity makes her realize she won't as well.

Stroking faster as she enjoys every inch of him, he grows harder with each passing moment.

Mila continues to stroke him as she lifts her head, her saliva drenching him as she sits up and moves forward. She positions her hips in just the right position and slowly inserts him into her. He enjoys the warmth of her inner cavern as he slides deep into her. She begins to sit up fully, rotating her hips in a circle and back to front in such a way he knew he would be unable to hold back any longer.

Looking at him, Mila whispers, "Give me all of it, Damian. Release it into me," her words trigger the reaction she was hoping for within him, and she craves what is to follow as he releases all of his seed deep within her eliciting an orgasm from both of them at the same time as their muscles mutually contract. He grabs her thighs firmly as she takes all of him deep within her as the seconds tick by, both settling into their tranquility as she slides to the side of him, draping one leg over his thighs as the music comes more in focus, listening for the first time, in silence to the lyrics of the song as it played.

After a moment, Damian breaks the silence, "Mrs. Mila West, I like the sound of that." Mila looks up at him and smiles, "I do as well, Damian. It was meant to be, I think."

"Yes, it is, Mrs. West . . ."

"However," responded Mila, "There is no way I am doing your laundry, Senator," as they both laughed at the comment.

Miami, Florida
2024 March
Faena Hotel

Sebastian Storm scanned the crowd, ever weary of public events, and Miami was a virtual nightmare with regard to any worthwhile security. The Faena Hotel Miami Beach was hailed for its theatrical design and opulent interiors. The venue offers unique and artistic accommodations, a stunning pool area, and a world-class theater, but maintaining the safety of his assets more than concerned him and his team.

Sebastian pressed his neck mic, "Navy, blue hoodie, a man in his 30's, brown hair and beard, south of stage, thirty feet from the southeast edge. He has his hands in his hoodie pockets." "I'm on it," came a voice from the Lead Secret Service Agent on the other end.

Sebastian observed when a few seconds later, two Secret Service Agents approached the man in question from either side and behind the subject. Watching intently the man's reaction as the agents came and spoke with him and asked for him to take his hands out of his pockets, only to see the mace canister in each of his hands. One agent grabbed one of the man's arms and swept his feet as the other agent grabbed the other arm and quickly laid him upon his stomach, wrists behind him as they cuffed him and lifted him up and escorted him away swiftly and precisely in such a manner to alert few people around him.

Not remotely aware of the altercation, Senator Damian West addressed the sea of faces before him. A palpable sense of anticipation hung in the air, felt by over 4,000 individuals gathered in the vast auditorium. Each word he uttered resonated with the weight of conviction and the promise of transformation, captivating and commanding the rapt attention of every attendee. His eloquence was not merely a matter of rhetoric but a profound demonstration of his ability to connect with the collective consciousness of his audience.

With a voice that carried the gravitas of history and the urgency of the present moment, Damian spoke of a future not as a distant dream but as an imminent reality—a future shaped by the hands of reform and rejuvenated by the spirit of collective endeavor.

He invoked the legacy of the slain musical icon, Apocalypse, whose lyrics once stirred the hearts of a generation, "Reform is the necessary sacrament of change." This powerful line, immortalized in song, was repurposed by Senator West to encapsulate the shared aspiration for a new era characterized by equity, justice, and progress.

Senator West's speech was a tapestry woven from the threads of past wisdom and contemporary insight, illustrating his deep understanding that true change is sacramental—it requires faith, commitment, and the willingness to renew one's beliefs and actions. He delineated a vision that was at once a homage to the struggles that preceded this moment and a clarion call for a day of reckoning—a day where the status quo would be challenged, and reform would be embraced not only as a policy initiative but as a moral imperative.

His narrative was not one of empty promises; it was a well-orchestrated blueprint for dynamic change, reflecting his comprehensive understanding of the complex sociopolitical landscape that surrounded their nation. Senator West's dialogue with the crowd surpassed the conventional boundaries of political discourse, entering a realm where each phrase, each anecdote, was a catalyst sparking the intellect and emotions of his listeners.

In the moment, Senator West was more than a politician; he was a visionary leader, echoing the transformative desire of a society yearning for restructuring and embodying the very essence of leadership that both honors the past and forges a new path forward. His message was clear: the time for restructuring was now, and it was an endeavor that demanded the collective will and action of all.

As Sebastian watched, he was content with the result of the apprehended individual and turned from Senator West and his speech to look for any other people of interest within the crowd.

Sebastian Storm was a master at seamlessly blending into the background, like a chameleon in its natural habitat. He possessed a deep fascination with the bustling pace of human life, and the campaign trail supplied an abundance of stimuli. He always made it a habit to position himself strategically, granting him an unparalleled vantage point from which to scan the ebb and flow of the world around him.

From his carefully chosen vantage point on the rear of the stage and off to the side, he meticulously analyzed the people in the proximity and the layout of the venue, contemplating the most likely exit routes in the event the unexpected occurred.

This was the essence of his profession, an art of being intimately attuned to his surroundings and hyper-aware of every detail, every individual, at any given moment. To Sebastian, the world was his stage, and the dynamic was fluid and indiscriminate in nature.

He carried a perpetual concern for the possibility of unknown figures lurking behind him, a concern that made him deeply appreciate the support of a sturdy wall or solid surface at his back. It was a constant, reliable source of protection upon which he often leaned. Sebastian sat in quiet solitude, his presence intentionally unobtrusive, all in pursuit of his ultimate goal: to remain unnoticed by those who might be watching.

He operated in a perpetual state of assessment and calculation, meticulously analyzing each individual through a complex web of parameters. From physical attributes, size, gender, and even stature to the less tangible qualities, such as intensity, energy, fluidity, and interactiveness, he contemplated it all. Even the subtleties of their engagement, poise, posture, and demeanor were all taken into account.

To Sebastian, every detail was relevant, for in an unforeseen crisis, anyone within the vicinity could potentially pose a threat. Human temperaments could shift in the blink of an eye, which is why he remained vigilant, observing everyone wherever he looked, both obvious and obscure. These factors, carefully assessed and compartmentalized, allowed him to categorize each person and gauge their level of potential danger or threat to Senator West.

Understanding and deciphering the chaos of people was not only a skill but a deep-seated core value for Sebastian Storm. It was this intricate process of scanning and evaluating each individual that kept him sharp and honed in his craft. Though it demanded his strictest attention, it was a labor he cherished and regarded as one of his most vital intuitive abilities. These talents had, on numerous occasions, been the difference between life and death, leaving no room for complacency.

Senator West was wrapping up his speech, ". . . . And that is why I will serve you, the people of this great state of Florida, and the rest of the nation as your next President. . . . Thank you."

The roar of the crowd and applause rang through the large auditorium. The amphitheater was standing room only as Senator West turned to leave the rear of the platform, and Secret Service Agent Benjamin Lee ushered the Senator to follow him to the stairs at the back of the stage.

Sebastian did a final scan of the environment before following behind Agent Lee and Senator West. They quickly exited from the rear exit and filed into the awaiting SUVs. Once inside, Senator West asked, "Sebastian, what was the issue with the guy in the blue hoodie?" Sebastian turned from the front seat, "Looks like mace canisters, but I'm not sure of his intent. He wasn't that difficult to identify. Agent Lee?" Agent Lee was sitting next to Senator West, "No, he is still being debriefed, but it appears to be a small, insignificant event. I think he was simply trying to make a statement or get his 15 minutes of fame, but Sebastian caught on to him too quickly. Not sure how you do it, Sebastian, you have a sixth sense about these things."

One of Sebastian Storm's remarkable talents lay in his ability to seamlessly adapt to diverse situations, akin to a skilled performer effortlessly shifting roles on a grand stage. Seeking neither praise nor admiration, such accolades were not in line with his demeanor. Instead, he found deep satisfaction in his innate capacity to subtly manipulate the dynamics of various scenarios, gently nudging them along the course dictated by human nature. The recent incident with recognizing the individual in the audience had clearly showcased his expertise, as he had skillfully averted a potential threat, though seemingly minimal in scope, averting a complex series of events the questionable subject had intended.

Washington D.C.
2024 March
Commission on Presidential Debates Executive Meeting

In the realm of American politics, the enigmatic and non-profit entity known as the Commission on Presidential Debates (CPD) held the power to make or break a potential presidential candidate. This shadowy organization holds a vital and captivating role within the presidential infrastructure, orchestrating the high-stakes spectacles showcasing the presidential debates during the heated frenzy of the general election campaign.

With a responsibility of such monumental significance, the CPD navigates the tumultuous waters of democracy, ensuring the nation's most influential leaders face off in a battle of words and ideas, a manifestation viewed by millions, shaping the course of the nation's future and ultimately determining who the nation's next president may, in due course, win the rights to the Oval Office.

The CPD was established to ensure presidential debates are conducted fairly and without the influence of any political party or candidate. This election, above all else, would test their resolve and integrity to the purity of the institution.

Janet H. Brown, the astute and forward-thinking CEO of the Commission on Presidential Debates (CPD), had just concluded a strategically significant conference call with an influential cohort of Senators: Ren Cosner, Sam West, Gideon Arnold, and the emerging political luminary from the nascent Unified Party, Damian West. The discourse had been a deep dive into the political undercurrents shaping the landscape for the upcoming 2024 Presidential Campaign.

With the insights from the call still fresh in her mind, Janet convened the CPD's Executive Meeting, a gathering of minds poised to dissect the political prowess and public appeal of the potential Democratic and Republican candidates. Her role was to facilitate a discussion that would not only anticipate the direction of the national dialogue but also shape the platform from which the American people would hear from those vying to be their next leader.

Janet's leadership was characterized by an incisive intellect and a dynamic approach to the ever-evolving political arena. In this meeting, she aimed to spearhead a comprehensive analysis, leveraging the collective expertise of her team to scrutinize the policy positions, campaign strategies, and public personas of each prospective candidate. The goal was to ensure the debates the CPD would host were not only informative and fair but also reflective of the crucial issues that mattered most to the electorate.

She understood the gravity of the CPD's role in this pivotal electoral process — the debates were a cornerstone of democratic engagement, a platform where rhetoric would be tested against the reality of national and global challenges. In this light, Janet's leadership took on the responsibility of crafting an environment where substantive discourse could flourish and where the contrasts in leadership styles, visions for the country's future, and the practicalities of governance could be clearly articulated and understood.

She was experiencing tremendous pressure from all three parties, fully aware of and navigating the various agendas they expressed. Each conflicting with the other, she was navigating the arguments expressed by all three perspectives. The stress of it all was getting to her, finding it difficult to balance a trio of parties when two were difficult enough and with varying motivations and perspectives.

As the meeting unfolded, Janet steered the conversation toward not just the candidates' competencies but also the broader socio-political dynamics at play, including the public's sentiment, the media's influence, and the historical context within which the 2024 campaign was set. The meeting was not merely a procedural affair but a strategic session crucial to the integrity of the election process, setting the stage for a presidential race that would be keenly observed and scrutinized by the nation and the world at large.

The Democrats and Republicans possessed solid representation upon the commission, and with the Commission's non-partisan approach, the CPD had customarily emphasized its neutral nature and its commitment to ensuring the debates remain fair, impartial, and resistant to influences by any political party or candidate. Operating independently, it did not receive any governmental funding, ensuring its objectivity above all else, but one would be remiss to assume the Republicans and Democrats didn't place heavy pressure on the CPD to exclude the Unified Party.

In the vibrant and diverse landscape of American politics, the push for greater inclusivity and urgent reform was intensifying. Janet and her board recognized that the legitimacy of the Commission on Presidential Debates (CPD) depended on its ability to adapt to these demands. Presidential debates, crucial for democratic engagement, were at the heart of public discourse and pivotal in shaping the nation's direction.

As political discourse broadened, the case for including voices beyond the traditional two-party system strengthened. Advocates argued that a true democracy flourishes with a variety of perspectives, and excluding these from the national debate stage shortchanged the electorate.

Janet was keenly aware of these criticisms and was strategically planning how the CPD could introduce transparent policy changes to align with public expectations while preserving the debates' integrity and educational goal. The challenge lay in harmonizing the CPD's core standards with the growing calls for wider representation.

Facing this complex issue, Janet was poised to lead with diplomacy and vision. Reforming the CPD's policies represented a significant, transformative step requiring thoughtful deliberation and an inclusive approach. Janet was ready to spearhead this crucial conversation, aware that the CPD's adaptability would not only demonstrate its commitment to democratic principles but also enhance the richness of political discourse, ensuring its relevance for the 2024 Presidential Campaign and beyond.

The emergence of the Unified Party had dramatically shifted the political landscape, compelling the Commission on Presidential Debates (CPD) to take notice. No longer could they overlook the growing influence and presence of this new political force. The Unified

Party was rapidly carving out a significant niche for itself, capturing the attention of a nation eager for change. As they gained momentum, their innovative ideas and fresh perspectives resonated deeply with a wide swath of the electorate, making it clear that they were not just participants in the political arena but formidable contenders shaping the future of American politics. The nation watched with bated breath, keenly observing every move of the Unified Party as they challenged the status quo and redefined what was possible in the dynamic theatre of American democracy.

In November of 2023, the CPD announced the debates would be held in Texas, Virginia, and Utah, respectively, between September 16th and October 9th, 2024.

As the Board Meeting convened the discussion unfolded, she wasted no time in delving into the heart of the matter—the rise of the Unified Party and its growing significance in the political landscape. With precision and insight, she painted a vivid picture of the shifting dynamics, highlighting the formidable challenges posed by the entrenched establishments of both the Democrats and Republicans.

In a closed session, Janet continued her discussion with the executive board sitting before her, "It's abundantly clear the Democrats are poised to stick with their incumbent, President Biden, while the Republicans are once again rallying behind Donald Trump," she began, her voice tinged with a sense of urgency. "But amidst the chaos and polarization of our current political climate, it's the Unified Party that has surprisingly emerged as a potent force advocating change—a force that cannot be ignored any longer."

As she spoke, her words carried the weight of undeniable truth, each syllable resonating with the gravity of the situation. "In just two short years, the Unified Party has captured the hearts and minds of a significant portion of the electorate, amassing roughly 27% of the popular vote and gaining momentum with each passing month."

She paused, allowing her words to sink in, the significance of the Unified Party's rise becoming increasingly apparent. "Much of this success can be attributed to Senator West's unwavering inspiration and motivation, coupled with the impressive backing of his supportive team, all of which are heavyweights in the political spectrum," she continued, her voice rising with conviction. "With Senator West at the helm, the Unified Party has struck a chord with a diverse array of demographics, connecting with the people on a level well beyond traditional party lines. They are a force, there is no question."

As she spoke, the energy in the room palpably shifted, the Executive Board leaning in with rapt attention. "While the Democrats and Republicans remain entrenched in their respective camps, the Unified Party is surging forward, propelled by the momentum of change and the promise of a brighter future," she concluded, her voice ringing with passion and determination. "And as we navigate the turbulent waters of the upcoming election, it's clear that the Unified Party—and Senator West specifically, wish to play a pivotal role in shaping the course of our nation's destiny and certainly appear to have a plan to do so."

Amidst the labyrinthine corridors of political strategy and public sentiment, Janet Brown found herself at the confluence of a pivotal discourse within the CPD. The hours were marked by rigorous and multi-layered debates centered on the emergent Unified Party's claim to a place in the national political theater. The crux of the discussion: had the Unified Party, bolstered by the charismatic appeal of Damian West and his supporters, achieved a significant enough presence in the national consciousness to merit inclusion in the traditionally bipartisan Trump-Biden Presidential Debates?

With the clock ticking towards the debates — the first slated for September, followed by a second in October, and a third yet to be scheduled — the CPD was pressed to make decisions with about half a year's lead time. These forums were not mere events but were landmarks in the democratic process, critical in shaping the electorate's choice for the nation's leader. The inclusion of a third voice representing the Unified Party could potentially recalibrate the dynamics of the political landscape.

The agenda was further complicated by the logistics and format of the debates, with three Presidential and one Vice Presidential debate to coordinate. The decision-making process was not only about whether the Unified Party had garnered enough of a "market share" of public interest but also about the implications of such a decision for the conduct and format of the debates themselves. There had never been a debate with three podiums in the history of the United States Presidential Election. It was unprecedented.

Adding another dimension to the deliberations was the nomination of Julian Chambers as the Vice-Presidential candidate for the Unified Party. His potential participation in the Vice-Presidential debate added another layer of complexity to the negotiations. The CPD had to consider various factors — from the potential impact on voter education to the logistics of debate staging — in order to ensure a fair and equitable platform for all candidates.

The CPD's role required Janet Brown to synthesize a vast array of data points — polling numbers, legal precedents, historical data, and the evolving public discourse — to guide the CPD's decision. The intelligence and dynamism she brought to the table were pivotal as she steered the organization through these uncharted waters. Her leadership would not only reflect the CPD's response to immediate concerns but would also set precedents for the inclusion of emerging political entities in the foundational democratic practice of televised debates. The pressure was mounting for her and seemingly coming from every angle.

In this era of rapid political evolution, the decisions made in those hours would reverberate through the current election cycle and beyond, potentially reshaping the CPD's role in facilitating a more inclusive and representative democratic dialogue.

After careful and detailed deliberation, it was decided by the Executive Board representing the CPD that they would limit the debate for the time being to only the Republican and Democratic Presidential candidates to maintain a sense of normalization, not allowing access to the Unified Party in the 2024 election.

They felt at this juncture, the Unified Party had not yet withstood the resilience and tenure to warrant a position on the primary platform, and despite the nearly 30% saturation of the voters, it wasn't enough yet to satisfy the committee's requirements to allow a third party within the debating venue for September 2024 Presidential Debate matchup six months henceforth.

As Janet H. Brown reluctantly stepped up to the podium, the weight of the CPD's decision heavy on her shoulders, she knew the announcement she was about to make would ignite a firestorm of controversy. With a deep breath, she addressed the gathered press and the world at large, her voice steady but tinged with apprehension.

She would announce the CPD's decision in a press conference following the executive discussion. "Ladies and gentlemen, after three days of deliberation and debate, I must announce the CPD's difficult decision regarding the participation of the Unified Party in the Presidential Debates occurring in the fall," she began, her words echoing in the hushed silence of the room. "Despite the overwhelming support and clamor for their inclusion, the CPD has unanimously chosen to deny the Unified Party their application to participate at the debate table in 2024."

As the words left her lips, a wave of outrage rippled through the crowd, the palpable sense of injustice hanging thick in the air. Social media erupted with condemnations and accusations, condemning the CPD's decision as an affront to democracy and a blatant disregard for the principles of fairness and equality.

With over 500 people in attendance, the tension in the air was palpable, each individual bracing themselves for the inevitable backlash that would follow. As Janet concluded her announcement, a lone unopened soda can flew through the air, striking her squarely in the face and knocking her to the ground.

A deep cut upon her forehead, blood dripping down her face was the picture on every newspaper and social media feed that afternoon.

Chaos erupted as police rushed to her aid, swiftly ending the briefing and escorting her to safety. But the damage had been done, the violence and unrest spreading like wildfire as outraged citizens took to the streets in protest. From coast to coast, small riots broke out, fueled by a sense of righteous indignation and a demand for justice and fairness to all parties represented in the fall Presidential Election.

In the aftermath of the press conference, the nation stood on edge, teetering on the brink of upheaval. As the sun set on a day marked by turmoil and dissent, one thing was clear: the fight for equality and fairness was far from over, and the Unified Party's struggle for recognition had only just begun.

The following day, social media was buzzing with millions of posts denouncing the value of the CPD and its unbiased position that largely was construed as heavily biased towards the current bipartisan platform. If a new and emerging political party had been able to secure 30% of the public support, then that should be telling the world there was a new formidable player in the political arena.

The CPD began receiving hate mail and emails and was chastised on Twitter, Instagram, Facebook, and all other media outlets.

The times were changing, and the CPD and Janet H. Brown underestimated the backlash that would occur from the decision they had made.

The following day, Janet H. Brown resigned as acting CEO at the CPD.

Washington D.C.
2024 March
Senator Damian West Private Residence

When the disheartening news of the Commission on Presidential Debates' restrictive decision regarding the Unified Party's eligibility for the upcoming presidential debates reached Sam and Damian West through Ren Cosner, their dismay ran deep. It was a bitter pill to swallow, and it stirred Damian to immediate action.

Summoning the Watchful Eight to an executive meeting the same evening, Damian West gathered the formidable group comprising Ren Cosner, Regina Alvarez, Sam West, Gideon Arnold, Harrison Stensrud, Julian Chambers, and himself. As they congregated in Damian's chamber, an air of somber contemplation hung heavy. The CPD's perplexing choice to diminish the significance of the Unified Party's political and national standing, despite the progressive and popular ascension, left everyone mystified. The energy in the room was unmistakable—they had unequivocally earned their rightful place on the debate stage despite the CPD invalidating their respective recognition.

"We shall not be ensnared by the shadows of this event and the CPD's reckless decision; our focus must remain steadfast upon the horizon of possibilities." With those words, Damian stirred the room with his resolute optimism.

In a moment of unexpected entrance, Anthony Voss was announced to the party by Agent Lee. The visionary CEO of Dymitron made his grand appearance, causing astonishment to ripple through the gathered assembly. Damian, acknowledging their distinguished guest, extended a welcoming nod and declared, "Anthony, your presence here is a true pleasure."

Voss, whose presence in the room carried with it a sense of quiet authority, chose a moment of rhetorical calm to make his presence appreciated. With a discreet but deliberate hand gesture, he commanded the floor, addressing Senator Damian West directly with a tone of measured consideration. "Senator," he began, his voice steady and assured, "I stand not yet committed to the cause, but I cannot overlook the perceived injustice the CPD has executed upon your party and what you, as a group, have accomplished. It's a mockery of what your group has achieved."

His interjection was more than a mere comment; it was a critical inflection point in the dialogue, introducing a nuanced stance that acknowledged the complexities at play. Anthony's appearance produced a bold statement and was a masterful articulation of a position, while non-committal, recognized the legitimacy of the grievances held by the Unified Party against the CPD's established protocols. Anthony was a firm believer in fair play and a strong stand that the Unified Party wasn't receiving their just rights and entitlement. Anthony was there showing his support to a group of individuals he admired and worthy of respect.

The gravity of his words did not merely hint at but openly heralded the significant discussions that lay on the horizon. Anthony's choice of language — particularly the term *"perceived injustice"* — did not outright accuse the CPD of wrongdoing but rather pointed to a widely held sentiment that warranted consideration and debate. Anthony's strategic intervention transformed the meeting's focus, skillfully navigating the discussion from mere policy details to the broader implications of fairness and perception. His intelligent and dynamic approach reframed the issue, suggesting a deep dive into how the CPD's actions impact democratic representation and its role in ensuring a fair electoral process. This shift promised a more nuanced exploration of the issues at hand, highlighting the importance of perspective in shaping policy outcomes.

The subtext of Anthony's statement was clear: the conversation was no longer about whether the CPD's actions were just but about how those actions were perceived and the effects of that observation on the political landscape. This shift set the stage for a more profound examination of the CPD's practices, the Unified Party's emergence as a political force, and the evolving expectations of an electorate increasingly attuned to issues of inclusivity and equity in their democratic institutions.

Harrison Stensrud greeted their guest with a dignified nod, his words carrying the weight of collective gratitude. "Mr. Voss, your presence among us is deeply appreciated, and we can only hope to convey the profound significance of the Unified Party's aspirations and goals."

A knowing smile graced Damian West's lips as he added, "I believe, Anthony, that your curiosity about our mission alone is what demanded your presence here today." Anthony Voss offered a simple yet eloquent response, "Touché," as Anthony Voss looked out over the group, "I'm here, at least for the moment . . . . *Inspire me, gentlemen.*"

"The assembly of the Watchful Eight is now complete. Well, I hope that it is if Mr. Voss will accept." Damian noted, casting a meaningful glance in Anthony Voss's direction. "At least for the moment and in a provisional capacity. We humbly welcome you, Anthony. I call this meeting to order. Let us engage in an open discussion regarding the CPD's decision to exclude the Unified Party from the September Presidential Debates."

A symphony of diverse perspectives and opinions resonated within the room, spanning from the CPD's perceived assault on social fronts devaluing the Unified Party's existence to the newfound popularity and exposure that the Unified Party had garnered due to its exclusion from the debates. The wide array of comments and perceptions made Same West proud, confirming his belief that the Watchful Eight would make a profound impact on the Unified Party, which, in turn, would affect the nation as a whole. The people before him fought hard for the American people and their way of life.

Damian West interjected thoughtfully, "The exclusion from the debates might, surprisingly, be a blessing in disguise. The exposure and buzz surrounding this decision could ultimately work to our advantage." Julian Chambers chimed in, "Party affiliation has surged by 20% in the past two days, thanks to the CPD's publicized decision."

Sam West added with a grin, "A 20% increase—a potential windfall. Never underestimate the power of social media."

The meeting went well into the night, and at 11 PM, it was decided to adjourn for the evening. Anthony Voss was the last to leave as Damian and his father walked him to the door. Damian reached out his hand, "I appreciate having you here tonight and adding your insightful perspective, Anthony."

Anthony Voss nodded, "I like what you are doing here, Damian. It's a fresh perspective and . . . . *honest.* You don't resonate like most politicians," glancing at Sam West and smiling, "Present company excluded, of course, Sam." They all laughed at the meaningful comment.

Damian squeezed his hand, "Your endorsement of this party, Anthony, could mean the difference between our proliferation or our demise." The words held heavy within the hallway, and an awkward silence filled the space until Anthony, thinking the very same thing, looked deeply into Damian's eyes.

"I know, Damian . . . . *I know*," As he turned and left.

Chapter 18

The Final Stretch

"You gain strength, courage, and confidence by every experience in which you really stop to look fear in the face. You are able to say to yourself, 'I lived through this horror. I can take the next thing that comes along.'"
~ Eleanor Roosevelt (Former First Lady and diplomat)

Los Angeles, California
2024 August 26-29
Unified Party National Convention

The timing of the Unified Party National Convention, strategically scheduled after both the Democratic and Republican National Conventions, was no coincidence. As the dust settled from the bipartisan gatherings held in August and July, respectively, the political landscape was ablaze with speculation and controversy surrounding the emerging third party. They had every intention of outshining their competitive counterparts in every way possible. The Unified Party wanted to make a statement.

The Democratic National Convention, held from August 19th - 22nd, and the Republican National Convention, held from July 15th - 18th, 2024, were dominated by a palpable sense of unease and insecurity, primarily concerning one another.

While the political conventions unfolded with their customary flair and grandeur, a frenetic undercurrent ran through the backrooms where party officials were urgently plotting. Despite the public display of unity and strength, there was a palpable sense of urgency as strategists from both major parties worked feverishly to outmaneuver one another. However, based on the CPD's decision, they seemed curiously blind to the burgeoning threat posed by the Unified Party. This new political force was rapidly gaining traction.

Despite the growing popularity and momentum of the Unified Party, both the Democrats and Republicans viewed them as a minor nuisance, unworthy of any serious consideration. Their focus remained squarely on Trump and Biden, locked in a bitter struggle for supremacy, and who would inhabit the White House come 2025.

But as the Unified Party National Convention drew near, the political landscape began to shift. The whispers of dissent grew louder, the murmurs of discontent echoing through the hallowed halls of power. The Unified Party was no longer a mere footnote in the records of political history—it was a force to be reckoned with, a movement capturing the hearts and minds of a nation yearning for change and their numbers were only growing by the day.

As the delegates gathered for the Unified Party National Convention, they did so with a sense of purpose and determination, their eyes fixed firmly on the future. For they were confident, they were not just witnessing history—they were making it, and the Republicans and Democrats were foolishly underestimating their growing momentum.

In the stirring drama of the 2024 presidential race, the Republican nominee emerged as none other than the enigmatic Donald Trump, as expected. It was a nail-biting contest, with Trump narrowly clinching victory over formidable contenders such as Chris Christie and Ron DeSantis. Donald Trump maintained a steady following within the

Grand Old Party (GOP) base he had cultivated and retained. Trump had proven himself as a formidable force, having already occupied the White House once and reshaped the Republican Party in his distinctive image.

His fundraising prowess was undeniable, setting the stage for an impressive comeback especially in light of the incumbent's lackluster showing in the two years prior. Trump had always respected Senator Sam West's friendship and patriotism, but his son had not yet done his time in the halls of Congress and was not yet deserving of his praise. Damian West's true strength in molding the Unified Party had not yet earned its mettle. Donald Trump may look at Damian West as a threat in the elections in the future, but he assumed there was, at best, another decade before young Senator West would even be considered.

However, Trump's political narrative was anything but smooth sailing. His legacy was marred by a storm of chaos and controversy, with two impeachments and multiple state-level investigations stemming from his role in the tumultuous events of January 6, 2021, when the United States Capitol was besieged. Trump's legal troubles compounded when he was found guilty of 34 counts of falsifying business records surrounding hush money in the spring of 2024, further tarnishing his already damaged reputation.

In addition, his persistent claims of election fraud further cast a shadow over his reputation. Public opinion weighed heavily against him, with a majority consistently expressing disapproval of his presidential tenure and a negative perception of Trump personally.

On the other side of the aisle, incumbent President Joe Biden faced his own set of challenges. His administration grappled with a flagging economy, contentious healthcare reform, skyrocketing interest rates and increased fuel prices, and a contentious battle over gun control. Moreover, concerns about Biden's mental acuity and his ability to effectively execute his duties began to take center stage in public discourse over the second half of his administration.

What was once perceived as harmless gaffes had evolved into a troubling pattern, causing a ripple of unease among the American populace. Doubts emerged, prompting a national introspection about the fitness of the nation's leadership and a re-evaluation of the stewardship vested in the highest office. President Joe Biden was more concerned with his own welfare than considering the likes of a young Senator from a seemingly unknown third party making a serious attempt at the presidency. Joe Biden cast Damian West as a mere spectacle and would be all but forgotten in the months to follow.

Biden's own cabinet and advisors begged the President to at least not underestimate the young, popular candidate, but President Biden dismissed Senator West and the Unified Party as much of a threat. His concern fell more to the tactics and antics of former President Donald Trump as his primary rival.

As the dust settled from the bipartisan conventions of 2024, a palpable sense of underwhelming momentum hung in the air. It was as if the stage had been set for a new player to seize the spotlight. Enter the Unified Party, poised to make a resounding statement in the ever-evolving drama of American politics. The Los Angeles convention was to last three days packed with power, understanding, and discussion of what the Unified Party represented, and its vision portrayed.

The first night was brought with entertainment and excitement upon the stage educating all in attendance about what the Unified Party's mission was and why it embraced a more contemporary way of thinking. Race, ethnicity, or creed were adversities best left in the past, with a new approach on the horizon.

Each of the Watchful Eight, save Anthony Voss, spoke from the heart as they recounted the significance of the United States on the global front. The youngest yet strongest of the nations, the United States was the mightiest of the superpowers but was facing its most difficult foe to date . . . . *itself.*

On the second day and evening, the festivities were followed by the first of their illustrious speakers, Regina Alvarado, who spoke of her origin as a politician, for the people and how this great nation had been the driving force behind her aspirations. She spoke of her roots and how the United States had accepted her parents as immigrants paving the way to the American Dream her very career emulated. She spoke of her sadness surrounding the loss of her seat as Speaker of the House but vowed to *gain it back* once Americans appreciated the value of what the Unified Party exemplified in its vision and mission.

To follow, the story of rags to riches came from the genuine tale of Harrison Stensrud, the media mogul. How he started with a small news station in New York at a young age, then a station owner who took a chance on the young man, and how Stensrud made the small news station into the largest media empire in the world in just a few decades. He bestowed to all humans the gift of media from anywhere, viewable by anyone in the entire world and in every corner of the globe.

Senator and former majority whip Ren Cosner followed with is passionate rise that started with his modest upbringing. Born in the projects of Chicago, Illinois, Senator Cosner was afraid for most of his youth to become entangled within the dark criminal underground lurking around him. Raised in a destitute black family, he was the youngest of six siblings and the only child who took the high road and refused to give up on himself or give in to stereotypical low expectations anticipated of his skin color.

The evening was rounded out with Julian Chambers as he explained his impoverished upbringing, poor and indigent in a broken family in Jackson Hole, Wyoming, where he saw the light emulating from Damian West at a young age and how that light had become a beacon to those sharing his vision of what the country should be and the greatness it could have once again. The energy was electric as the second evening came to an end, all knowing the final day would be packed with their strongest lineup yet.

On the third and final day of the convention, Senator Gideon Arnold hailed from Washington state. He came from a middle-class family but appreciated the value his parents instilled within him. His speech touched the hearts of those in attendance, having lost his father to cancer in a healthcare system that failed the ailing man. He ended with a vibrant and colorful story about the patriotism of his lifelong friend, Senator Sam West, and how he had watched the fledgling Damian West evolve before him and was certain the vivacious young man had what it took to run this country one day. He helped cultivate the young Senator's destiny; he claimed to know and counsel Damian before the young man knew himself and did what he could to mentor the boy as he evolved and flourished.

Next to last came the senior Senator, Samuel T. West, and when he approached the podium, all in attendance stood up with a standing ovation to greet the aging Senator who had given so much to this tremendous nation he had repeatedly sacrificed to uphold and support over his long and illustrious career. Always the kingmaker but never the king, Sam West portrayed the ideal America stood for time and time again.

For over an hour, Sam West spoke of his undying support for the United States, and although, unlike his continuants who stood and spoke before him, he came from a place of privilege, all of them had their role in protecting the United States regardless of race, ethnicity, opportunity or creed. They were all equal in his eyes, and that's all that ever mattered to him. Sam West spoke of each of the speakers individually, with sincere stories bringing laughter and stories bringing some tears to those in the packed house.

He spoke of his wife, who supported him until her passing 18 years before, and how it changed him and made him realize the importance of putting all his attention into his son, Damian.

Sam West then went on to speak of his son in such an endearing way there was an unmistakable silence within the auditorium of 20,000 people as they all listened with heartfelt patience and Sam recounted his stories. Sam West told the tale of his and Damian's long discussions and debates leading well into the night more times than he could remember. He expressed the lessons and ideals he wished to bestow upon his son and how Damian was such an astute pupil, eager to learn more about how this great nation came to be.

Then Sam grew somber as he described how their relationship had changed in the last few years and how Sam was no longer teaching his son, but rather, his son was now teaching him. He had come to pass the torch to his son, who evolved the ideal and vision of the Unified Theory to something more palpable and coalesced to the thinking they were all experiencing.

Sam explained that the world was on the brink of transformation, and Damian West was poised to steer humanity through the looming uncertainties of the future. His son's profound craving for progress, meticulous cultivation of strategies, and unparalleled understanding of global shifts set him apart as a visionary leader. Over the course of three electrifying days, speaker after speaker took the stage proud of the leader they had chosen, as it was Damian who captured their collective imagination. His clarity of vision and depth of insight inspired an unshakeable belief among all present—they were not just followers of a leader; they were disciples of a transformative journey championed by Damian West and their collective vision.

Sam West parted with a story of Damian, as a young boy, playing in the schoolyard as Sam West looked on, waiting for the children to come inside once the recess bell rang a few minutes later. Sam reminisced the memory of watching his son playing a game with the other children on the playground, unknowing of his father, who was diligently watching from the window of Damian's classroom.

It was foursquare, they were playing, and an Asian girl argued Damian's ball had landed outside the line when all the other kids argued the ball was well within bounds. Damian remained quiet, listening to the other children bickering until, after a few seconds, took the ball and handed it to the young girl, conceding his position. She looked at him, knowing she had been out of line but respecting Damian for sacrificing his position and a spot as victor that day. The ethics and standards of the young man were defined even at an early age.

Sam West smiled and was assured his son followed a high moral code, and despite losing the match to the young girl, he had won the far bigger life lesson. Sam was confident his son would be destined for excellence on some level and achieve far more than Sam ever would. As the playground bell rang, Sam felt some form of contentment in knowing Damian would achieve greatness, and he took solace in knowing the young man's destiny so early.

Sam thought it fitting to finish his speech with a colorful story, a tale of Damian's youth illustrating the sense of integrity needed to transcend the opposing candidates and position his son, Damian West, as the clear leader of the free world.

Senator Sam West then challenged all in attendance to see this was the man who should be guiding this country and this was the leader who would bring the Unified Party to light as their beacon of hope.

The nation needed his leadership, but above all, it needed his integrity and understanding of what was essential to make the United States the strongest nation in the world. And with those final words, Sam West stood up a little taller and proudly said, "And with that, ladies and gentlemen, I present to you the next President of the United States, my son . . . Damian T. West. . . ."

The announcement brought an amazing wave of applause, and all in attendance stood. For five long minutes, the sound was deafening both from the amazing speech made by retired Senator Sam West and the introduction of his son Damian West as both men hugged one another up on stage as the applause grew, and cheering continued for some time.

Mila Dmitri rubbed the tears from her eyes, so proud of her husband, feeling the adoration from the people in attendance, looking about the crowd, and feeling the genuine adulation in the faces before her.

The noise was far too loud for anyone to hear as Sam leaned to his son's ear, "This is what your whole life has led up to Damian. This is your time and your moment; make it the most memorable and significant thing you have ever done. These are your people, and this is now . . . ."

. . . . *Your Reign.*"

Sam then looked into his son's eyes, and for the first time in Damian's life, he saw in his father the purest form of acceptance he had ever felt from the man. Damian held his gaze, regardless of the 20,000 people before them, and it occurred to him in the moment that he had achieved everything his father had expected of him. From that moment on, it was up to Damian to fulfill the rest of the dream, the rest of the vision. The rest was his story and inevitable glory, to define.

The look between them would be reviewed and critiqued for years to come, and despite many people asking both Damian and Sam about the historical moment on the stage of the Unified National Convention that evening, neither ever elaborated on what was said as it was held by both as a sacred moment, their indefinite secret and vow, consecrated only between father and son.

Shaking the feeling, Sam slowly exited the stage, leaving the momentum as a final gift for his son to take and anchor what all the speakers had so expertly created for him . . . . it was his time to show the world why he should lead them.

And that was exactly what he did.

The applause and whistles died down as Damian West approached the podium and flashed the smile that made him famous, "My fellow Americans . . ." With those simple words paired with his enigmatic smile the crown erupted again as he put up his hands and made a fist cheering to all attending. The excitement raged on for another minute before he put up his hands down patting the air wanting the crowd to quiet. He approached the podium once again and entered into a monologue that would be considered one of the most profound in American history.

The convention would be considered one of the most powerful and moving conventions in generations. As Damian West roused all Americans to come into the light and embrace what the Unified Party stood for as a vision and a dream. The crescendo of speakers leading up to Damian West finishing was nothing short of brilliant. He captivated the American people and, equally, the world.

Damian West's speech shook the fundamentals of the nation down to its core, making all Americans question why they had tolerated so much for so long. They needed unity to make them strong again and had lost their vision along the way. Damian West showed them how it would be done, and he called on all Americans to share in the plight and make the dream a reality.

He concluded his address by igniting the very ideals that would shape them and mold them at the highest level – a symbol of hope and resilience. With a tinge of sorrow for what seemed momentarily lost, but with unwavering certainty could be rekindled, reborn anew, if only the people dared to demand it.

Sixty minutes later, as he stepped away from the podium, the resounding applause that followed was not merely a show of appreciation; it was a thunderous endorsement of the message he had conveyed, a testament to the potent vision he had shared.

In that moment, it became unmistakably clear the Unified Party embodied the future, the promise of transformation for the United States – a future defined by unity, progress, and unwavering resolve. And furthermore, this was the man that would lead the nation to the end.

Mila Dmitri, now Mila West, came out on stage along with Sam West and the rest of the Watchful Eight to pay homage to their respected candidate and to stand unified for the world to see the making of America's finest dynasty triumph.

Far above the stage in a private box overlooking the arena, Anthony Voss stood looking forward at the widely loved presidential candidate. Damian West, hand in hand with his beautiful wife, Mila West, stood for purity in an otherwise sullen American political arena. They were showered with praise as he walked to the edge of the stage and shook hands with those attending the convention, hoping to touch their American savior or, at the very least, become a part of history.

Anthony found himself mesmerized by the remarkable popularity of the young Senator. It wasn't merely the size of his following but the profound impact his words had on people's hearts and minds. This charismatic figure possessed a rare and captivating style, leaving an indelible mark on those who listened to his message. Damian West was a true visionary.

What truly set the Senator apart was the authentic sincerity radiating from within—a quality so rare in the world of contemporary politics. It was as if he possessed a genuineness that transcended the ordinary, forging a deep connection with his audience few others could hope to achieve. He wasn't swayed or influenced by the ugliness of the American political system but rather preserved in its purity, protected and shielded from the darker side of Congress. Sam West had made vitally certain Damian never witnessed the grotesque underbelly most politicians ultimately succumbed to.

Amidst the bustling crowd, Anthony couldn't help but also appreciate the imposing figure of Sebastian Storm, who stood steadfastly by Damian West's side. Sebastian was like an unwavering guardian, his vigilant gaze scanning the vast surroundings, seemingly fixated on every individual and detail within his line of sight. He possessed an uncanny awareness as if he held an intimate knowledge of everyone present. He seemed to look at anyone and instantly know of their strengths and weaknesses and whether they posed any type of threat.

Intriguingly, Anthony nodded in acknowledgment when Sebastian's sharp eye momentarily turned in his direction. It was a testament to Sebastian's remarkable acuity and awareness, leaving Anthony deeply impressed by the depth of his vigilance. In this sea of faces, Sebastian Storm stood as a custodian extraordinaire, a protector of both Damian West and the secrets swirling around them and the Unified Party as a whole. Sebastian returned the nod and then continued scanning the people within the vicinity.

Anthony Voss contemplated the speeches of Ren Cosner and Gideon Arnold but, most of all, the significance of the words uttered by Sam West and his son, Damian.

Anthony reflected on their messages and knew, soon he would have to make a commitment to become part of this innovative yet risky movement or remain vigilant to the old guard representing the foundation of the United States for several generations. He was acutely aware his ultimate decision could alter the outcome of one man, however, also be the demise of yet, another.

The bipartisan system had become antiquated, but Anthony Voss did not become the CEO of the largest company in the world by acting on impulse. There was more he needed to see and understand about Damian West and the Unified Party and to fully comprehend the significance of their movement.

He simply needed time to make the best decision.

Texas State University
San Marcos, Texas
2024 September 16
First Presidential Debate (Trump and Biden)
Commission on Presidential Debates (CPD) Special Meeting

On the heels of the Unified National Convention held in Los Angeles, California, just weeks before the focus of the election turned to the escalating failure of President Biden to capture the hearts and votes of the American people to keep his position of Commander in Chief. His popularity was dwindling by the week.

Donald Trump had masterfully harnessed the power of momentum, and his surge was, in large part, a consequence of the incumbent's failing inertia. He capitalized on this lack of forward motion to chart his course toward further ascendancy, yet his accumulating legal troubles appeared to be weighing down public opinion. Despite the young Senator's newfound prominence and the whirlwind of publicity swirling around his nascent political movement following their National Convention, Trump remained optimistic and confident in his position.

However, it wasn't until the Commission on Presidential Debates (CPD) barred Damian West from representing the Unified Party that Trump's conviction solidified. This exclusion only strengthened Trump's belief that the presidential race would ultimately boil down to a head-to-head showdown between himself and Biden. This realization bestowed upon Donald Trump a profound sense of confidence as he approached the pivotal threshold of the first of three Presidential Debates, ready to wield his formidable political prowess and with purpose little away any hopes Joe Biden may possess in retaining his presidency.

The debate on September 16, 2024, between Donald Trump and incumbent Joe Biden was moderated by Chris Wallace and was handily won by the former President, Donald Trump.

As to be expected, Joe Biden's diminishing mental capacity was questioned throughout the debate. Donald Trump brought up the scorching event that transpired in August of 2020. On that date, the prominent Fox News host, Sean Hannity, voiced profound concerns from that date and many since about what he perceived as evident signs of confusion, fatigue, a startling acceleration of aging, and cognitive shifts exhibited by Joe Biden. Seeking expert insight, Hannity turned to the erudite Dr. Marc Siegel, a seasoned medical correspondent at Fox News and a clinical professor of medicine at the prestigious NYU Langone Medical Center in the heart of New York City, who confirmed the President was showing signs of dementia and Alzheimer's in examples of public speeches.

President Biden attempted to divert the accusations but was met with allegations of poor follow-through with the economy and controversial decisions surrounding Afghanistan in addition to concerns about his ability to lead the country.

In addition, Trump intentionally steered the debate into complex responses, and when President Biden wasn't able to follow many of the topics expertly, Trump would attack and expose Biden's thin underbelly and reveal the president's lack of understanding and mental capacity.

The dominance of Trump over Biden in the first Presidential Debate spurred a wide range of controversy concerning the evading of a worthy opponent in Damian West. The first Presidential Debate proved no contest.

———

The CPD was under enormous pressure from social media syndicates, news channels, and the Unified Party itself. Even more scrutiny surrounded the departure of Janet Brown, CPD's prior CEO, solidifying the arguments leading to her withdrawal. The Unified Party had more than met the requirements to qualify to participate in the Presidential Debate but had been publicly denied. Not to mention, Joe Biden was taking a beating from Trump which only fueled Don Trump's momentum.

Amidst the turbulent political landscape, the Commission on Presidential Debates (CPD) convened an extraordinary session. The relentless pressure and inquiry had taken their toll on Janet H. Brown, leading to her resignation as CEO of the CPD months before. Rumors were rampant that she stepped down because of pressure from the Republicans and Democrats not to allow the Unified Party access to the debates, which, if proven, would be regarded as blasphemy and would significantly diminish CPD's integrity.

Janet H. Brown had little comment or rebuttal surrounding her resignation but in no way acknowledged the validity of such an accusation.

Stepping into her formidable shoes were interim co-chairs Frank Fahrenkopf and Antonia Hernández. Reluctantly thrust into the limelight, they assumed leadership roles just in time to grapple with the mounting controversy that had engulfed the first presidential debate. An emergency meeting became their crucible, where they confronted the controversial intricacies and challenges that lay ahead as they charted a course for the second Presidential Debate just weeks away. The primary focus was to address the elaborate web of issues that had led to the resignation of Janet H. Brown, a pivotal figure in the organization. It was an occasion marked by both urgency and gravity.

For any contender to even entertain the notion of securing a spot on the hallowed Presidential Debate stage as a third-party candidate, certain stringent criteria had to be met. The first litmus test was appearing on a sufficient number of state ballots to potentially amass an Electoral College majority. Equally pivotal was the requirement to register a minimum of 15% support in at least five national polls.

In the case of the Unified Party, these prerequisites were not merely met but exceeded with remarkable finesse. Their claim to a spot in the debate arena was undeniable, sending shockwaves across the political landscape. The CPD would have a difficult defense in denying that fact.

Frank Fahrenkopf took the initiative, setting the stage for a crucial debate within the Commission on Presidential Debates (CPD). With conviction in his voice, he launched into the heart of the matter.

"We are facing considerable resistance," Frank began, "from both the Democratic and Republican Parties, strenuously arguing against granting the Unified Party a seat at the debate podium. Their central contention is that introducing a third debating group in the form of Senator West will inevitably dilute the momentum of the ongoing campaign. They argue that the Unified Party lacks the necessary political clout to earn a place on the main stage and simply have not existed long enough to warrant a seat at the table."

The room crackled with tension as Frank paused, the weight of the moment hanging in the air. He continued, unwavering in his resolve, "However, we must not dismiss the compelling evidence that emerges from the polls and the unmistakable swell of popularity Senator West, and the Unified Party have garnered. To merely relegate them to the sidelines would be to invalidate the voice of a significant portion of the electorate and fail to provide the American people a fair and impartial platform in which to display all the necessary political factions."

The stage was impeccably set for what promised to be a riveting and substantial deliberation. Standing at the forefront, Senators Ren Cosner and Miles Nagel, staunch representatives of the Unified Party, were poised to present their compelling case, injecting their voices into the heart of this pivotal discussion.

The CPD Executive Board convened, and for hours, the room buzzed with impassioned arguments and insights from the visiting

Senators and the Board members themselves. The debate was a complex tapestry of ideas and opinions, with compelling arguments supporting both sides of the contentious issue.

Amid this heated discourse, a hushed air of anticipation enveloped the room as a humble secretary quietly entered. She discreetly approached Antonia Hernández, the interim co-chair of the CPD, and delivered an urgent message. "Ms. Hernández," the secretary began, "there is a call on line 3 that you may wish to take." Antonia thanked her secretary, Brielle, and waited for her to leave.

Antonia Hernández's expression turned solemn as she reached for the receiver. The room fell into an anticipatory silence as she listened intently for over two minutes, rarely responding. The weight of the moment hung in the air, palpable to all who were present. When the call was finally concluded, Antonia Hernández thanked the caller on the line and hung up, her expression unwavering though remaining solemn and grave.

Antonia Hernández looked at the group and hesitated for a moment, "That was the public relations head from Dymitron. Their CEO, Anthony Voss, came forward 20 minutes ago, announcing his endorsement of Senator Damian West and the Unified Party, and his official affiliation with the Unified Party is also, now confirmed." Senators Cosner and Nagel looked at one another, knowing this news could very well tip the scales in their favor.

The Senators and the Executive Board knew this would be the clout the party needed to demand the respect they were seeking and felt entitled to receive.

"The Unified Party has gained significant market share, but with all this controversy, I can see why it pushed Janet Brown over the edge," continued Antonia Hernández. "We honestly can't hold them back any longer as they have adequately sustained the numbers to earn a place at the big table. I submit to the Board the sanctioning of the Unified Party for the remaining Presidential Debates. Only the Vice President Debate will be forfeited." Frank Fahrenkopf seconded the Motion, and the acceptance of the Unified Party's participation was accepted.

———

"A first in American history, but the second and third Presidential Debates will include three parties: The Republican, the Democratic, and lastly, the Unified Party," explained Antonia Hernández.

Senators Cosner and Nagel quickly excused themselves. Their work at the CPD was complete and their objective met other than the debate for the vice presidency.

Virginia State University
Petersburg, Virginia
2024 October 1
Second Presidential Debate (Trump, Biden and West)

The anticipation surrounding the second Presidential Debate, now featuring Damian West as a contender, reached a fever pitch, drawing an unprecedented audience of over 210 million eager viewers for the 90-minute showdown. The stage was set, and the moderator, Kristen Welker, with NBC News, who moderated in the 2020 election was poised to run a *clean* debate. She was poised to guide this monumental event, making it the most highly anticipated televised program of 2024. Welker began her focus on Donald Trump.

Seizing the moment, Trump wasted no time, delivering poignant jabs aimed directly at his flanking companions. On one side, he quipped, was a candidate who struggled to recall what he had even eaten for breakfast the prior day. Turning the table to the other, attacking his academic journey had barely concluded, an infant in the political arena, as Trump pointed out, making himself the clear-cut choice by his estimation.

Damian West, sitting tall and exuding a youthful yet razor-sharp aura, responded to Trump's provocations with a poise and intelligence that deftly redirected the discourse to the pressing issues that truly concerned the American people. He skillfully steered the conversation toward matters of genuine relevance and avoided the sophomoric stance and stature of Trump's impudence. Damian remained diligent in maintaining the *high road* making Donald Trump look rather foolish as a result.

President Biden, mostly silent and reserved, seemingly overwhelmed with the rapid-fire exchange and edgy wit between Trump and West. Their contrasting styles were starkly evident. While both made substantive points, Damian West's demeanor exuded polish and refinement, standing in stark contrast to the brash and contentious subtleties often inherent in Trump's arguments.

As the debate's echoes faded, the audience was left with the indelible impression of President Biden's struggle, seeming lost amidst the whirlwind of Trump's seasoned rhetoric and West's sharp intellect. Trump wielded the gravitas of a former President, but it was Senator West, with his magnetic allure and a mind brimming with political acumen, who captivated the viewers, pulling them in as he expertly dissected national issues with a surgeon's precision.

The night belonged to the formidable duo of West and Trump, with Biden receding into the backdrop. With the spotlight firmly on him, West was already strategizing for the final showdown. He learned immeasurably from his experience and knew what changes he would make for the third and final debate several weeks later.

He gleaned invaluable insights from the evening's exchanges, crafting a blueprint to outmaneuver Trump's known strategies and intimidation tactics.

As the next debate loomed on the horizon, West was armed with a wealth of knowledge and a clear vision. He was ready to weave his articulate arguments into a tapestry of triumph, to not only parry Trump's tactics but to enchant the nation and claim the victory he felt secure in obtaining.

University of Utah
Salt Lake City, Utah
2024 October 9
Third and Final Presidential Debate (Trump, Biden and West)

In the wake of the second debate, Senator Damian West emerged as a political comet streaking across the American consciousness, his popularity burgeoning beyond conventional bounds. His allure wasn't only in the eloquence of his rhetoric but in the rare authenticity and humility, resonating with the electorate's yearning for sincerity.

West had become more than a politician; he was a phenomenon, a charismatic enigma captivating both the public and the insatiable media. As the third debate loomed, anticipation reached an enormous crescendo. It was destined to be the zenith of pre-election fervor, setting the stage for November 5th—a day poised to be a watershed in the nation's history.

NBC News Correspondent Kristen Welker was to moderate the third and final debate. Kristen Welker has historically been commended for her professionalism and impartiality; despite some concerns about potential bias due to her family's political ties, she remained neutral. Overall, her reputation in the field is one of fairness and accuracy. She announced in no uncertain terms she expected a fair, respectful, and open debate between the three leading candidates. Her rules strict being the third debate and she insisted all the debaters follow her guidelines.

The previous debate marked a historic first, with three candidates stepping into the arena, reminiscent of a scene carved out of a wild western showdown with no apparent methodology to orchestrate the three-debater platform. The traditional two-person format was eclipsed by a triadic exchange that, while lively, left many viewers grappling to keep pace with the rapid-fire dialogue. In response to this, the architects of the political discourse recalibrated their strategy, aiming for a more orderly battlefield for the final showdown. Under the discerning eye of the moderator, the debate would pivot to a series of focused topics, allowing each candidate a fair platform for their respective exposition and counterarguments. The total viewership swelled to just over 300 million viewers worldwide.

The debate commenced with the candidates delivering their opening soliloquies, setting the stage for the impending dialectical ballet. Following, with the precision of a maestro, Ms. Welker introduced the first topic, propelling healthcare to the forefront—a matter of paramount importance to the American electorate. "Gentlemen, Healthcare has been a critical topic for Americans," she posed, "where do you stand on this topic, and what will you do to improve it with your administration? President Biden, we will begin with you." This opening gambit promised a clash of visions, each contender poised to articulate their prescription for the nation's healthcare woes.

With a confident, elongated, and awkward sweep of his gaze across the room, the President's smile served as the prologue to his address. His words wove a narrative of optimism and scattered rhythm, painting the Affordable Care Act, colloquially referred to as Obamacare, as a masterpiece in the making, progressing splendidly towards the envisioned ideal. He expounded on its metamorphosis, assuring all present the path they were treading was not only effective but laden with promise.

The President's narrative was peppered with pensive and rehearsed diatribe but devoid of relevant substance. He harbored on generalities and tiptoed around ideals Obamacare had yet to achieve. He remained positively eloquent but empty in asserting the specifics of the question asked.

The atmosphere bristled with anticipation as Kristen Welker, popular for her incisive clarity, directed the spotlight to the day's formidable critic, former President Donald Trump. The stage was set for a contrasting perspective, and with the handoff complete, the gathering braced for an oratorical duel encapsulating the ceaseless debate over one of the nation's most contentious policies.

———

In a fervent critique resonant with his distinctive insolence, Donald Trump lambasted the President's remarks, fiercely questioning the efficacy of the Affordable Care Act (ACA). Meanwhile, Senator Damian West stood as a silent sentinel amidst the political theatre, his gaze shifting discerningly between the adversaries. He perceived the caustic undertone in Trump's tirade and simultaneously discerned a gap in President Biden's grasp of the healthcare law's intrinsic complexities and its entangled issues. He knew the cameras often rested upon him, deciphering his nonverbal cues would project any reaction he may have, but he remained poised and respectful of his adversaries, not succumbing to overt reactions coming from Biden but more so from Trump's podium.

For West, the scene unfolding before him underscored a stark divergence from the progress President Biden had so confidently proclaimed. The debate was not merely a collision of opinions but a vivid illustration of the polarized landscape of American politics, where rhetoric often eclipsed substance, and understanding the nuances of pivotal legislation became secondary to the partisan showmanship on display. Damian West waited patiently but silently eager to offer his opinions on the subject.

Donald Trump's oratory painted the Affordable Care Act as a mirage of solvency, a hollow promise of affordability to the swathes of Americans in dire need of healthcare. His critique was not without merit, as he highlighted the stark discrepancy between the term 'affordable' and the harsh realities faced by many. Yet, his discourse seemed to pirouette more vigorously around the ACA's shortcomings and the perceived inactions of Obama and Biden to rectify these pressing issues. While Trump adeptly diagnosed the system's ailments, his analysis lacked the necessary ending, offering a robust critique but falling short of providing a concrete blueprint for reform, leaving the audience pondering on potential remedies and substance offered by the former President. The nation was well aware what the issues with ACA were but sought the remedies and plan to in fact, resolve them.

Acknowledging Donald Trump had reached his time allotment, Kristen Welker respectfully stopped him and redirected the same probing question toward the much-anticipated Senator Damian West.

Senator West was ready, holding nothing back.

There was a discernable and deliberate pause before stepping to the microphone. West then offered a disarmingly gentle smile to those in attendance, one distilling his sincerity since Barbara Walters interviewed him now an eon ago. His approach was not to assail his political adversaries with bitterness or sarcasm but to stand resolute on the issues he championed. It was his moment to demonstrate to the electorate that despite his youth and less seasoned political résumé, he was wholly prepared and inspired to lead the nation.

Senator Damian West was advocating for a new chapter in American politics, blending poise and audacity to invite change rather than confront the status quo. Casting aside political caution, he aimed to capture not only the Oval Office but the imagination and support of the American public.

Under the watchful eyes of the nation, West considered his words carefully, blending gravitas with the candor of fresh leadership. His demeanor conveyed an earnest resolve to articulate a vision for the future, positioning himself as the harbinger of a transformative era. He sought to align his perspectives with the broader American dream, aiming to persuade, provoke thought, and prompt a collective march toward a horizon filled with fresh perspectives.

Easing up to the podium, Senator Damian West's gaze intensified as his voice embodying a firm resolve. "While I hold a measure of respect for the paths tread by my esteemed counterparts, present and past president not withholding," he addressed the assembly with a commanding presence, "I must assert that our nation's healthcare dialogue is mired in a disquieting sense of disillusionment as a whole."

He took aim with a more stringent critique. "We face a current administration, despite its best intentions, that has become ossified in its approach," he said, gesturing towards President Biden. "An administration seemingly out of sync with the evolving needs of the people it pledges to serve. I mean no disrespect, Mr. President, but it is the truth at present." His words, while respectful, held an undercurrent of challenge, an implication of missed opportunities, and a lapse in responsive leadership.

Turning his attention to former President Trump, West sharpened his rhetoric. "And Mr. Trump, your tenure, marked without question by an unfiltered tenacity, has indeed disrupted the status quo. However, disruption without the requisite diplomatic grace risks isolating us on the global stage, and the whole world judges our every move. We are the standard by which all is measured." His critique was not only detailing mere policy but establishing his presidential demeanor—a call for a leader who could wield both strength and sophistication with measured balance.

With the healthcare crisis as his battleground, West laid out a decisive plan. "To redefine healthcare, we must dissect and discard the inefficiencies of the current system, and there are many," he asserted. "Wyoming's approach to subsidies and community involvement has illuminated a path forward that has proven itself. We must broaden this strategy, implementing rigorous health cost audits and reforms to untangle the bureaucratic quagmire stifling innovation and accessibility. Americans will no longer stand for it, nor will I. This will occur immediately within my administration to answer your question, Ms. Welker," as he glances over at Kristen Welker, and she nods.

Senator West's crescendo culminated as he presented a challenge to the current paradigm, "Healthcare reform isn't an insurmountable intellectual exercise; it's a humanitarian imperative we are failing to meet." His closing statement on the subject was a clarion call to action, a declaration that he was prepared to lead the charge in reinventing a healthcare system that was not only affordable and accessible but also reflective of a nation valuing both the health and dignity of every citizen. He spoke of methods to connect tax incentives to healthcare, creating a winning scenario for all to appreciate.

The debate stage was transformed into a platform of contrasting ideologies, each participant embodying a distinct archetype: President

Biden, the antediluvian, entrenched in dated paradigms and antiquated methodologies; the Aggressor, Donald Trump, wielding blunt force rhetoric and promises not necessarily kept; and the Idealistic Theorist, Senator Damian West, armed with visionary proposals and positive ideology. The discourse escalated into a riveting mélange of opinions, resembling a cerebral battle more than a mere exchange of ideas.

The topics explored beyond healthcare included climate change, racial justice, income inequality, and foreign policy. Additionally, the widespread concern among Americans about the state of democracy was addressed by the candidates.

In the myriad of topics following, both President Biden and former President Trump found themselves at a strategic disadvantage against West's well-structured arguments and innovative methodologies. What proved even more formidable was their inability to undermine his palpable conviction and the fervor he displayed in championing his policies. His commitment to holding Congress accountable and his unyielding pursuit of his goals set a tone of relentless determination and fearlessness, which left his adversaries grappling for effective counterarguments.

In the climactic final debate, Senator Damian West surpassed the traditional confines of political discourse, asserting a commanding presence resonating deeply with both the national audience and international observers. His eloquence and depth of insight, rooted in the Unified Party's progressive values, presented a compelling narrative of national unity and prosperity.

His strategy was more than mere debate tactics; it was an intellectual crusade to galvanize a collective vision of progress and inclusivity. This event marked a transformative juncture in political communication, where Senator West's vision for a cohesive and flourishing America captivated the global imagination, heralding a new era of political engagement and societal advancement.

In the pulsating heat of the debate, the contrasting styles of the candidates were starkly illuminated. Biden was critiqued for his discontinuous approach to pivotal issues, while Trump's assertive, officious tactics may have dominated the floor but not the hearts of those who viewed the debate. Amidst this, West's composed and cogent demeanor became his signature, painting his discourse in striking relief against the backdrop of political fervor. His adeptness in steering through the turbulent waters of policy and arguments, coupled with his persuasive and meticulous responses, established him as a beacon of reasoned dialogue, captivating his audience and elevating the level of discussion well beyond his adversaries.

Kristen Welker wrapped up the fiery 90-minute debate, acknowledged the three participants, thanked them for their time that evening, and bid them and the American people a good night.

Damian West won the debate handily, but he faced a bipartisan system that had been instilled for generations. The tradition was his greatest opposition, modifying the belief of an age-old democracy.

It marked the first-time former President Trump and President Joe Biden were concerned the charismatic candidate from the Unified Party was in contention to win the most powerful position in the world.

Chapter 19

Enemy At The Gates

Jackson Hole, Wyoming
2024 October 23
Senator Sam West Private Estate

In the two weeks following the well-publicized debate, the political landscape of the election was dynamically reshaped by the Unified Party, with Damian West emerging as the pivotal figure in this transformative narrative. The public's perception of President Biden as outmoded and possibly unfit for the demands of the presidency played into West's growing appeal.

Concurrently, former President Donald Trump's perceived egotism and combative style, especially his personal attacks directed toward his opponents, further alienated him from the electorate, though he remained a popular candidate. In stark contrast, Senator West was seen as the embodiment of national renewal, offering pragmatic solutions to America's mounting challenges. His ascendancy reflected a public yearning for a leader who not only understood their issues but also had the acumen, empathy, and temperament to address them effectively, marking a significant shift in the political tide.

As the November election loomed a mere fortnight away, The Watchful Eight convened for their final decisive meeting, suffused with a tension rivaled only by the palpable buzz surrounding the Unified Party's surging momentum. The campaign trail had been arduous yet devoid of regret, leading to this critical juncture.

It was the first time the illustrious group had met since the debate and also the first time the group had their complete consortium present with Damian West, Sam West, Gideon Arnold, Ren Cosner, Regina Alvarado, Harrison Stensrud, Julian Chambers, and lastly newly appointed, Anthony Voss . . . . *all were in attendance.*

The chamber resonated with mixed excitement as The Watchful Eight assumed their positions around the table, becoming symbolic of their political stratagems. Although not possessing an official capacity the auspicious group stood impressive.

Silently, yet assertively in the corner sat Sebastian Storm, the group's vigilant guardian. His presence was both sentry and symbol, a testament to the trust and belief he vested in the collective and, more pointedly, in Damian West, the leader whose vision he championed with unwavering conviction. His stance was not limited to his simple duty but rather of profound allegiance to the cause binding them all.

In the hushed ambiance of the room, Damian West stood as the embodiment of leadership incarnate, his opening remarks imbued with genuine gratitude for the illustrious group quietly sitting before him. Their unwavering support had been the cornerstone of his campaign. It was Anthony Voss, the visionary CEO of Dymitron, whose crucial endorsement at the critical moment had been the fulcrum, levering the Unified Party's principles into the spotlight of the second and final Presidential Debate. This alliance between the realms of forward-thinking business and astute political strategy symbolized a potent blend of innovation and acumen, balancing the Unified Party on the cusp of a transformative political climax that could very well redefine the future trajectory of national policy and discourse.

The room, steeped in anticipation, shifted its focus as Sam West slowly rose from his chair. The elder statesman, whose seasoned eyes had witnessed the ebb and flow of political tides, now gazed upon his son with a pride transcending words. As he initiated a solitary methodical clap, the sound cut through the silence within the room, reverberating with the weight of his legacy and the hope for all. Soon, the applause cascaded around the table, a symphony of respect and belief heralding Damian as the architect of a new vision for America as they all stood appreciating the man before them.

The catalyst of this burgeoning movement, Damian West stood proud at the epicenter of this homage. His journey to this juncture was nothing short of Herculean, a testament to his tenacity and the unwavering belief of The Watchful Eight in his mission.

As the applause swelled, they were all constantly reminded of the ground they had gained and the horizons yet to conquer. Within it all, Damian responded with a grace that had become his hallmark. Placing a hand over his heart, he bowed slightly—a gesture speaking volumes of his gratitude and humility. It was a poignant moment, one of unity and shared purpose, as each member resettled into their chairs, their gazes lingering on the man who stood not above but among them, embodying the ideals they all strived to uphold.

As the applause tapered to a respectful silence, Damian's eyes sought out Sebastian Storm, the enigmatic figure whose presence was as subtle as it was essential. Sebastian, a man more accustomed to the silent ballet of the political shadows, returned Damian's gaze with a simple nod—a gesture as rare as it was powerful, a silent testament to his unwavering faith in Damian's cause and his undying support all the way to the end.

In the tacit exchange, there was a depth of mutual understanding forged through many late-night discussions and strategic engagements. Sebastian, a man who measured his allegiances with the precision of a chess grandmaster, saw in Damian a leader worth more than mere endorsement; he was a champion to bet his life on. Their bond, strengthened in the perception of shared ideals and battles fought away from the public eye, had evolved into a steadfast alliance and friendship.

Sebastian admired the young senator not just for his political acumen but for the sheer force of will with which he pursued his vision. Forty-two states he had visited in the last two years, illustrating his dedication and diligence for the people he wished to oblige. Damian's life was sacrificed for the sake of the people he coveted to serve. The travel daunting, Damian remained steadfast and relentless in his pursuit of educating the nation, one state at a time to the benefits of his plan.

Sebastian knew the cost of such dedication and the personal sacrifices it entailed. Yet, there Damian stood, unwavering, a testament to the courage required to steer the nation toward a new dawn. In that moment, as he acknowledged Damian with his characteristic affirmation, Sebastian avowed a pledge deeper than mere politics—a pledge to stand vigilant over the journey they had embarked upon together.

New York, New York
2024 October 29
Fury's Manhattan Penthouse

Fury shook his head in frustration. Inferno, standing next to him, said, "I cannot tolerate failure, Onyx." "The window of opportunity was immediate and narrow, Sir, and I was unable to get full contact of the target with all the people in attendance. The rally was twice the capacity we had anticipated, and the security protocols were amped up. Our intelligence was pathetic and grossly inaccurate." Fury balls his fist and, without warning, clocks the man on the side of the jaw as he goes down hard, unconscious.

"I don't need the excuses," as Fury and Inferno look down at Onyx lying on his side. Sapphire looks worriedly at Fury, "It was our fault, Sir. I have no excuses. We had our opportunity, and we missed it. We failed you."

"Fair enough," replied Fury, "Sadly, the miss on Trump will only be additive to his campaign and endeavor. We will have to consider something else to slow his momentum. We need to make a clear path for Senator West and must not fail in that endeavor.

Washington D.C.
2023 November 2
Damian West Residence

Damian greeted Sebastian with a firm handshake as he entered the study, a gesture of familiarity and respect that spoke volumes about their relationship. As he offered Sebastian a drink—a Woodford Reserve with a large ice cube—he couldn't help but observe the subtle tension in Damian's demeanor, a delicate sign exposing the calm exterior he presented to the world.

Over the prior two years, Damian had come to know Sebastian on a deeper level. He now recognized his tendencies and patterns, his strengths and weaknesses, with a keen eye and intuition. It was a trait that served Damian well in his dealings with others, allowing him to anticipate their reactions and tailor his approach accordingly. Sebastian Storm and Damian West were similar in this way, and most likely added to their familiarity and developing friendship.

But with Sebastian, it was different. There was a depth to him, a complexity that defied easy categorization but still allowed a trust he had in the man. They were both principled men, and integrity was paramount to both. Damian had always sensed there was more to Sebastian than met the eye, a hidden complexity lurking beneath the surface.

As he handed Sebastian the drink, he couldn't shake the feeling weighing heavily on his mind. There was a reason why he asked Sebastian over that evening. Something was making him less at ease than he would like to admit.

As they settled into conversation, Damian made a mental note to tread carefully. Sebastian was a man of few words, principled, but his actions spoke volumes. As they delved into the matter at hand, Damian was aware he would have to rely on more than just speculation and conversation to unravel the mystery surrounding Sebastian Storm.

Sebastian took the glass and thanked Damian as they both sat before the fireplace. He also secretly scolded himself for being credulous and predictable to those he trusted most. As if reading his mind, Damian offered, "You know, it's okay, Sebastian, to trust, at least, some people who pass through our journey of life."

Sebastian smiled back, knowing Damian was correct, but despite how anyone saw it, those close to him were either a threat . . . . . or a weakness. He raised his glass to the young Senator and said in its simplicity, "Ha, yes trust, not so easily practiced for me, Senator. A work in progress. Nonetheless, cheers . . . *to a win in November*," as they both took a pull from their drinks and watching the fire in silence for a few moments.

"Thank you for coming, Sebastian, and on such short notice," stated Damian without looking at him, focusing on the fire yet possessing a grim look about him. Sebastian picked up on the solemn tone in his voice as if he were carrying the weight of the world upon his shoulders. "What's on your mind, Damian," was Sebastian's only response as Damian turned from the fire and replied, "The attempt on Donald Trump's life last week has me a little frazzled."

Senator West referenced the incident occurring the week before where Donald Trump was on the campaign trial in Cincinnati, Ohio attempting to influence the swing state and persuade the voters to see his way of thinking. The candidates had been warned to be wary of public gatherings as they were all at risk when visiting various venues, and the risk to their safety and security was never guaranteed. It was widely suggested to not physically interact with any supporters while engaging in campaign events.

Donald Trump's egotism often got the better of him as he disregarded protocol in Ohio while at a rally and began shaking hands after a well received and energetic speech, only to become lightheaded moments into their departure when he began convulsing halfway through the exit aisle. He was rushed to Good Samaritan Hospital, where he was stabilized, and remained in the hospital for a few days following. The toxicology report indicated traces of VX toxin within his bloodstream.

VX, a synthetic chemical compound classified as a nerve agent, is considered to be one of the most toxic and rapidly acting engineered warfare agents. It is similar in action to certain pesticides called organophosphates but is far more potent. VX was developed at a British government facility in 1952, and it's an odorless and tasteless liquid that appears similar to motor oil.

The primary mechanism of VX's toxicity involves blocking the action of the enzyme acetylcholinesterase (AChE). This blockage results in an over-accumulation of acetylcholine, a neurotransmitter, leading to involuntary muscle contractions, increased secretion of bodily fluids, and seizures due to hyperactivity in both the peripheral and central nervous systems.

Exposure to VX can cause a range of symptoms, depending on the dosage and the mode of exposure (skin contact, inhalation, or ingestion). Symptoms can include blurred vision, chest tightness, confusion, excessive sweating, nausea, vomiting, abdominal pain, and difficulty breathing. In severe cases, exposure to VX can lead to loss of consciousness, convulsions, paralysis, respiratory failure, and with enough of a dose . . . . *even death.*

It was determined the following day the toxic material had been contracted by skin-to-skin contact, but the full dose was not administered, saving Trump's life as a result yet still suffering from severe side effects for several days following.

"VX is a bad one, Damian, and very difficult to obtain. The materials used to fabricate the serum are heavily regulated. However, anyone with enough resources would be able to," explained Sebastian, "Also, it was foolish of Mr. Trump to engage the public as he did. Unquestionably, a reckless decision."

Damian looked at him and nodded, "Agreed. But then there is also this," as Damian handed over a letter to Sebastian. Sebastian took the letter and turned it over, then back to the front and read it for a few moments before turning to Damian, "Where did you get this," referencing the letter he was holding.

"It was delivered to my office, contained within a simple envelope from Home Depot of all places. Per your instruction, all mail is opened in a secure and controlled area, and this one was brought to my attention. It's actually a copy, the original is being investigated."

Sebastian looked at the letter closer, "*Governor Steven Hathaway was eliminated to ensure your succession?* Wasn't Hathaway the Governor you replaced after he and his wife died in some bizarre car accident on New Year's Eve?" "That is correct, Sebastian," amazed at the man's ability to retain information. "His death paved the way for me to take his seat on an interim basis until the following election. I mean, it appears farfetched, I know, but if it were true, it would have begun a chain of events leading me to where I am today."

Sebastian leaned back in his chair and took another sip of his bourbon before replying, "It's all speculative and coincidental. If I recall, the accident was deemed exactly that . . . . *an accident.*"

"True, but what if the attempt on Trump's life was also aligned with me winning the election? I mean, Donald Trump is far and away my biggest obstacle, wouldn't you agree?" Sebastian shot Damian a look, "Without question, his demise would most certainly be your triumph, especially this late in the game. But all circumstantial and speculative. Not to mention, we have no idea where this letter originated. It could have come from a conspiracy theorist, or someone trying to get under your skin . . . . or . . . " Damian finished his sentence, "Or . . . it's the truth." Sebastian didn't want to even consider the possibility.

"Damian, you must understand since the early days that risk has always been a part of this process," Sebastian began, his tone serious. "Abraham Lincoln paid the ultimate price for the change he sought to bring about, as did JFK. Their vision and sacrifice served as a reminder of the importance of what you do and the impact it will have on this nation and its people for generations to come."

Sebastian's words hung in the air, heavy with meaning and purpose. His reference to Abraham Lincoln and John F. Kennedy served as stark reminders of the gravity of Damian's mission. As he spoke, Sebastian's voice carried a weight of responsibility, a solemn commitment to protect Damian at all costs.

Sebastian paused, his gaze steady and unwavering. "There will always be risks in this office and what it represents, but there are larger aspirations at play here, Damian. My job is to keep you protected, and I will spare no effort to ensure my obligation is fulfilled."

As he spoke, Sebastian's words carried a sense of urgency, a reminder of the dangers lurking in the shadows. "The attempt on Trump and the details surrounding Hathaway—they all have explanations. But we must be mindful of the perspective we have chosen to take. The path ahead is fraught with challenges, but together, we will navigate them, ensuring your vision for this nation becomes a reality."

With those words, Sebastian reaffirmed his commitment to Damian's cause, his unwavering loyalty a testament to the bond they shared. And as they prepared to face the challenges that lay ahead, Damian's confidence grew knowing with Sebastian by his side, anything was possible.

"I suppose you are correct, and I know you will do everything in your power, Sebastian, but all of it lingers within the back of my mind, and you can't be with me at every moment, nor can Agent Ben Lee. You have your own life and your beautiful Adriana to look after as well. I just need to stay true to the cause and maintain our vision," pondered Damian as they talked for another hour about the details leading up to the election just days away.

Damian made good points. Sebastian couldn't be with him at every turn. He was only able to attend half of the venues on the campaign trail and his position at the Anti-Terrorist Special Division was still among his priorities. And the woman in his life, Adriana Mercer, who he had tracked halfway across the globe to save, was his own savior and confidant. His moments with her were sacred to him and balanced him greatly.

They both stood up and shook hands as Damian looked at Sebastian, "Thank you, Sebastian, for always helping me maintain my path and focus," as the Secret Service Agents came into the room. Keeping up with respect and formality, Sebastian replied, "Of course, Sir, that's why you keep me around. You may not always like what I say but I'll always be honest in response, winking at the Presidential candidate.

"I'll see you out, Mr. Storm," came the voice of Secret Agent Benjamin Lee. Sebastian nodded and followed Agent Lee out of the room, leaving Senator Damian West in the study. They got to the front door, and Sebastian turned to Agent Lee, "Watch him a little closer and widen your security net."

"Is there an issue, Sir," came the response from Agent Lee. "No, no, Ben, just extra precaution. This Trump thing and the letter he received has Damian a little more jumpy than usual, let's just stay ahead of it and try to put his mind more at ease."

"Copy that, Sir," came the reply.

Later in the evening, Damian lay in bed alone. Mila was traveling to New York for two days, giving Damian time to think and ponder the timeline of the days leading to election day. He reflected on the discussion with Sebastian Storm earlier that evening. Despite the clarity their discussion provided a lingering doubt harbored in the back of his mind questioning how he had made it to this point in his life so . . . *effortlessly.*

He remained questioning his unforced and painless progression and moments popped up in his mind, locked away in his memory, shrouded by the protection of his father and those around him. The images and reminiscences made him revitalize those forgotten memories, seemingly irrelevant at the time, but erupted in his mind the importance and significance they may have today.

Amidst the whirlwind of the unusual coincidences, Damian West found himself whisked away by a memory from over a decade before, recalled from his mid-twenties. Fresh from the rigors of law school finals at Harvard, he had made an impromptu decision to return home for the holidays a day earlier than planned. His father, burdened by his responsibilities in Washington, D.C., was unaware of his son's early arrival.

The surprise visit, a spontaneous act in his youth and adoration for his father, was a moment holding more significance than he had realized now years later, shaping the path of his future in profound ways and presenting equally some surprises uncovered.

Killing time before his father arrived later the same evening, Damian sat upon his father's large spacious desk within his study. Getting a jump on the upcoming semester, Damian had his law books and notebooks stacked upon the corner as he pulled out the large chair, he fondly remembered his father sitting in while growing up. He sat down and pulled himself up to the desk, basking in the power of the man who had occupied the chair for decades when something caught his eye. A panel he had never before detected, having sat in the seat countless times in the past.

The panel lay open on the top portion of his father's desk with a small keypad on the right, exposing several added controls but more significantly, the two video screens, a digital timing device as well as an earpiece. Studying the contents for a moment, he discovered the *play button* and pushed it.

Illuminating the screens came the same video shot at different angles. The time date was only three days before. Damian studied the image before him, transfixed upon the video of his father and Julian Chambers talking in front of the fireplace. Seeing their lips move within the video, though he couldn't hear what was being said, he slowly reached for the earphones and placed them over his ears. The clarity came to life as he listened to the conversation between his father and his closest friend. The transmission was crystal clear in image and audio.

As was often present and the focus of the lengthy discussions within Sam West's study, politics, history, and debate consumed the conversations within those walls. The colloquy between Julian and his father vacillated between varying aspects of the political genre but the discussion turned to the subject of Damian West. He never assumed his father and best friend ever met without him being present, which surprised him on some level. Damian turned up the volume, watching the video intently and listening to the two people Damian West admired most in his life. They spoke of him, his future. Most were positive, but still other parts disturbed him as well.

He would be well into adulthood before he would be struck with the full significance of what the meeting between his father and Julian Chambers truly meant to Damian and his future.

"His future is set and well into motion, and many have helped pave the way for his political journey, Julian," Sam explained, "I am asking for your help in orchestrating his progression." Julian Chambers nodded and replied, "What can I possibly do for you, I have nothing to offer, Senator West?" Sam West nodded, continuing, "*Trust and loyalty*. That, my boy, is what may very well serve best. I know how you can help us . . . *help Damian*. And if you perform this well and handle the specifics of what needs to be done, then, in turn, I will aid you in your own success and career, Julian. Accomplish this, and I can all but guarantee your own seat within the House of Representatives, and the sky is the limit after those obligations are met."

Damian could see on the video, his longtime friend weighing the options of the vague and ambiguous proposal presented to him from his own father's lips. Julian finally broke the silence, "What will I have to do, Senator? What is the commitment I am making?"

Senator West sat back in his seat, "A good question, Julian, and one that cannot yet be answered at this moment. It is a fluid dynamic, ever evolving. It is yet to be determined, but it will test your moral fortitude unquestionably, but the upside will be substantial for you. There will be some risk, but currently, only you and I are aware of this conversation. Are you ready to make the commitment asked of you by me and the *Alternative Consortium?* Your commitment to the endeavor will not only aid my son in his journey to the White House but also ensure your place in history as well."

Julian Chambers thought of where he had come from and had no interest in returning to that place or the time of his childhood. He had experienced a fondness for a better life, a better legacy, and more power, and despite his hesitation, he knew the answer to the question before they had even begun the conversation.

"Without question, Senator West, I will do whatever is required . . . . ." "Good man," came the reply from his father.

Damian sat back in his father's chair, trying desperately to understand the magnitude of the video. He looked down and saw a blank CD and copied the video before leaving the study, placing everything as he found it. The CD he filed away and had forgotten about until now . . . . just days before the Presidential Election. He placed it in a safety deposit box years before with various contracts and bonds he had accumulated.

He needed to rewatch the video. *His mature eyes may see it in a completely different light.*

Washington, D.C.
2024 November 5 – ***Election Day***
Damian West Residence

In the stillness of pre-dawn, Damian's eyes flickered open, awakening to the enigmatic dance of city lights against the backdrop of the yet slumbering Washington, D.C. skyline. The clock's luminescent hands upon the wall pointed unwaveringly at 3:57 AM — a silent guard in the hush of early morning.

Today was election day.

As he lay in bed, staring at the ceiling, a sense of timelessness enveloped him, transporting him back to the muted whispers of his childhood. His mother's voice filled his thoughts, as clear as the star-studded sky outside his window, echoed through the years, "You know, Damian, the night is always at its darkest, just before the sun comes up. Most people don't know that you know?"

These words are imbued with a mix of nostalgia and wisdom, yet also sadness. The image of her bridged the gap between the past and the present, reminding him of life's cyclic nature—and its tragedies. But mostly, it reminded him of the fragility of life. From darkness to dawn, life's despair to hope. At that moment, Damian lay enveloped in the deep quiet, the world outside still oblivious to the impending arrival of a new day, the promise of a fresh start lingering just beyond the horizon. This was to be the most important day of his life, a significant day for many people and for the nation, equally as much.

Tuesday, November 5th, 2024, was not just another day in the calendar for Damian T. West; it was the day destined to etch his name and the Watchful Eight into the archives of history if he prevailed. However, if he were to lose the election, then he would most likely be forgotten; the recovery of such a failure, far too great.

As he lay awake, the enormity of the next 24 hours pulsed through him like electricity. This was more than a pivotal moment; it was the culmination of dreams, strategies, and tireless efforts of a group revered for their ingenuity and resilience when everything and everyone resisted their emergence.

Damian's mind raced with thoughts of his brethren, the illustrious Watchful Eight. He wondered if they, too, were engulfed in the same whirlwind of anticipation and restlessness or if they were fortunate enough to enjoy a peaceful slumber, blissfully unaware of the ticking clock that heralded a day of reckoning. The quiet of the night mocked his restlessness, serving as a stark contrast to the storm of thoughts raging in his mind. In these predawn hours, the world was unaware of the seismic shift unfolding, a shift that would be remembered as a defining moment for Damian West and the Watchful Eight, but only if he . . . . *succeeded.*

Today would define it all. There was so much at stake, yet so much to gain. He trusted the American people to make the right decisions today and was confident they would follow their hearts. He looked back to the beginning of all this and had no regrets, he did the best he could do and was content in the outcome.

In the soft glow of the city lights, Damian slowly turned his head as his gaze drifted to his beautiful wife, Mila, a vision of tranquility as she slept beside him. Her serene countenance, bathed in the gentle light, was a sight of ethereal beauty, stirring a deep warmth in his heart. He enjoyed her, captivated by the peacefulness she exuded, a stark contrast to the whirlwind of emotions swirling within him.

A smile tugged at the corners of his lips, a private moment of joy amidst the brewing storm of the coming day he anticipated would come eventually. In his mind, he cherished the thought that, regardless of the day's tumultuous events and its outcome, Mila would be his steadfast beacon. She would be there when it all began that day, her presence a reassuring embrace as he ventured into the unknown, and she would be there as the day drew to a close, a comforting haven regardless of the day's fate.

This realization brought a profound sense of solace, easing the knots of anxiety tightening in his chest. In her, Damian found an anchor, a reminder no matter the trials he faced, their journey would always converge at the point where their hearts met. Her unwavering support was the silent strength that fortified him against the tides of uncertainty, a reminder his love for this woman was the constant star in the ever-changing sky of life.

It was then her eyes slowly opened to see him staring at her, and she sensed she had calmed him, and the torrid thoughts were torturing the man she loved and adored. No words were spoken as they gazed at one another for some time until her hand, which was tucked into her chest, extended to touch his face. As if to read his mind, she smiled and whispered, "Despite the outcome today, despite a win or even a loss, I will greet you the same at the end of it all, Damian."

Damian smiled back and softly replied, "I know." Her words comforted him, and it wasn't until that moment he was humbly aware, without question. . . .

    . . . . He was ready.

The election polls opened promptly at 6 AM in many states and the bustle of the day didn't appear any different than any other morning in the United States. The cities came alive as they did every sunrise, but many Americans chose to vote early, eagerly awaiting the results that would be announced by day's end.

The polls were eagerly monitored by more Americans in the 2024 election than any other Presidential Election in American history.

By 9 AM EST, Donald Trump was off to an early lead, capitalizing on the heels of the assassination attempt on his life the week before. He had fully recovered and was still campaigning throughout the day to push Americans to vote and to witness his resiliency despite his brush with death. With 17% of the vote in, former President Donald Trump led the polls by a clear margin of 46%. Damian West followed at 34% and incumbent President Joe Biden was trailing at 20%.

Damian studied the large screen as the numbers fluctuated like a Stock Market tape throughout the day. His father stood next to him, along with Sebastian, all fixated on the vacillating numbers before them.

"What's your take on all of this, Sebastian," asked Damian. Sebastian hesitated, choosing his words carefully, "Well, you are becoming more and more of a celebrity by the minute, Damian. The numbers are creeping up in your favor, but California and Arizona are important states and will decide this thing." Sam West concurred as he nodded his head, and Sebastian continued, "But if you win this thing, it's because the American people believe in you," as he glanced at Sam West, "and your father and I believe in you as well," "Thank you for that, Sebastian. He knew Sebastian wouldn't sugarcoat his opinion.

It means a lot coming from you. Sebastian nodded, "I think it will be close, Damian, you are making an impact. You have impressed the world stage, and all the people are watching." "Well said," replied Sam.

Interviews with the candidates varied but mirrored the Presidential Debate nearly verbatim as Donald Trump touted his brilliant and speedy recovery, chastised West's youth and inexperience paired with Biden's lack of capacity to take on the job needing to be done.

President Biden relied more on the people of his great nation to see the value of seeing his administration endure yet another term.

The tension of the election changed completely in the afternoon once the news of the chaos occurring in Los Angeles hit the mainstream, making the election a secondary newsworthy option.

In the west, Los Angeles had been holding a vigil in remembrance of the artist known as *Apocalypse,* found murdered 18 months before. Ironically, his album, *Reckless,* hit a musical record of 7X Platinum status when released a month after his needless death. His lyrics carried with it, the battle cry of change the country so desperately needed. Gathering over 30,000 people in downtown Compton, CA, the city was shaking by late afternoon with the songs *Apocalypse* wrote and the message they embodied.

The gathering turned to riots, and the outspoken supporters professed their fallen hero's plight for their nation to change, evolve, and prosper.

Apocalypse was looked at now with the stature of Martin Luther King, but rather in song lyrics speaking his word and message. Considered a visionary, foreshadowing the abyss of where society was headed if they didn't all bind together as one and as a people, together and united . . . . Even in death Apocalypse demanded the unification that would come when people looked beyond their neighbor's skin color, beliefs, or political acumen but rather the strengths each person added to the whole.

The orators and evangelists spoke of *Apocalypse's* dream for a better America and how the only true leader who could achieve his dream was Damian West. The vigil began to turn into a challenge of the current political climate. The incompetence of the current administration could not be allowed to see another term, and yet the aggression of the Republican front-runner was also not in the best interest of the American people.

Beginning positively and almost spiritual in nature, the vigil turned into a political spectacle as the people murmured of fulfilling *Apocalypse's* last dying wish, to initiate change, which was to see all the people, all *his* people as . . . *one*. They began chanting Damian West's name, and the media coverage and social media were blazing with the relevant news story, often taking precedence over the much-anticipated news surrounding the Presidential election itself.

The police attempted to keep the people at bay, but the suppression only led to aggravation and aggression of the mob. Push came to shove, and the vigil became an onslaught, with violence becoming center stage of the nightly news over the election polls.

Holding closer to the vest and well within the shadows during election day sat the underdog, Senator Damian West. He watched diligently the calamity forming before his eyes and felt some guilt for being at least indirectly involved. He had no idea the power and influence Apocalypse possessed in the country and was seemingly even more powerful in death.

Sebastian stood beside Damian and Sam West, feeling the Senator's palpable suffering as they announced several casualties had occurred on both sides of the line. Damian was aware he would need to make a statement and deliver a response to the riots in Los Angeles. He was just unsure how he wanted to navigate it, yet hopeful the words would come to him.

They always did in time of need. Many of the Watchful Eight attempted to console and counsel him, but he finally put his hand up as they all became quiet and softly said, "I appreciate all of you, but this . . . . this needs to be my own. People have died today either directly, or indirectly because of me and this election. I need some time to think and time to myself," and with that, Damian West turned, leaving the group to a secluded room to ponder the events of the day.

Hailing from the modest yet mighty state of Wyoming, a linchpin in the western landscape but small in stature as a state of significance, Damian carried a legacy of monumental significance. The West family, with Damian's grandfather, Thaddeus West, blazing trails in the early 1900s and Samuel T. West sculpting the political scene far beyond Wyoming's borders, had set the stage. Now, it was Damian T. West's turn to grasp, and carry the torch, guiding the United States into an uncharted epoch in the 21st century with a vision promising to redefine the nation's trajectory.

His interviews during the election day were poised and eloquent in delivery, only adding to his appeal and charisma. He thanked his worthy opponents and appreciated their verve and vitality over the prior year adding to the intrigue of the 2024 election. The catastrophe in Los Angeles would change all of that as the day began to slowly slip away.

As the pivotal day unfolded, daunting as the minutes slowly ticked away, Senator Damian West found himself in the throes of an electoral battle, the likes of which he had never witnessed or read within the history books. With his sleeves rolled up and his jacket long discarded, he embodied the image of a man ready to face any challenge. His tie hung loosely, a symbol of his commitment to the grueling task at hand and commitment to its end, however the outcome. The people needed to hear from him and how the sacrifices made in Los Angeles were not in vain.

Damian West called an emergency news conference to address the tragedy in Los Angeles just hours before. As he took the podium, he stood tall, maintaining a solemn face as he peered out over the sea of media people, Sebastian and Sam, to the side of the room, standing in wait for him to speak. He had spoken very little that day, leaving the rhetoric and inflammatory messages to his respective opponents, but he could not hold his tongue any longer.

———

"The tragedy in Los Angeles earlier today weighs on my heart more than anyone can know. Americans dying for *Apocalypse's* respective beliefs should show the world our United States is crying out for change and reform. These 44 people gave the ultimate sacrifice. This has become our modern-day civil war . . . *a virtual, or cyber civil war if you will.* People should not have to suffer for our government to recognize that we, as a people and as a nation, must change our perspective. We must evolve as a whole. Although I was never fortunate enough to meet Apocalypse, his image and vision of what America should be aligns with my very own. I am just heartbroken that blood was shed to further his point and witness the value of his prolific words. His death has made him a martyr, but the silver lining is his words live on in his music and his vision, emulating what he believed in and the people that follow him . . . I bid you to trust and cherish him as I will do. My heart aches for the poor souls who died today, and my prayers for the families of the fallen who were sacrificed in Los Angeles only hours ago. They died living up to his ideals. Apocalypse and I wish and hope for the same thing. We both aspire for the reform this great nation desperately needs."

The Senator paused as a myriad of questions came from the mass of media correspondents raising their hands, hoping the young senator would choose them, thrusting them into the spotlight and the hope of being selected to ask their question. Damian looked down and saw the young correspondent from Time Magazine, Carly Fenton.

He had always liked and admired the young, ambitious news correspondent, choosing her to offer her question. Damian pointed to her, "Carly," as she stood, "Senator West, as we approach the twilight of the Presidential Election, this tragedy in Los Angeles has put the spotlight directly upon you personally, especially with the endorsement of the most renowned musical artist of our era. A man who was brutally murdered a year and a half ago. Doesn't it seem oddly convenient?"

Damian West cocked his head, disappointed in the assumptions made and with such a lofty notion stringing the connection between the deaths in Los Angeles and the timing of the election. He smiled.

Was it the long day he had endured or possibly knowing Carly Fenton enjoyed asking difficult and creative questions? Maybe Damian West subconsciously anticipated such a poignant query when he selected her.

Damian switched to more of a formal response, "Ms. Fenton, I'm not entirely certain what you may be implying, but I hardly think the two are related. It's always been widely publicized Apocalypse believed in my plight. It's been shown in his music that he wished to someday experience our nation becoming whole again. Despite him being one of my greatest advocates, both in life and in death, he gives me pause for such a substantial loss and made me appreciate the greater depth of admiration for the young, influential force that saw and declared his beliefs. I, too, have echoed these sentiments, and the American people are now demanding a response from those who govern them. The events earlier today mark a tremendous tragedy. Human loss always does, but we have a far larger, more substantial mountain to overcome. Their deaths, though unnecessary and pointless, have fueled the American people to stand up tall and command our leaders to toe the line and represent the needs of the people of this nation. Anything less than that, Ms. Fenton, is a failure of our leadership."

Damian looked out over the podium and continued the thought, "Apocalypse's death and the loss of the innocent people in L.A., if nothing else, has shown us the need for leadership, for change, and for reform. I solemnly swear, Ms. Fenton, I can lead this great nation to that end. Apocalypse felt I could, God rest his soul, many of the American people support I can as well, and a large group of our own Congressmen have vocalized their confidence that I am worthy."

He looked directly at the cameras to finally face the American people watching the program, "I have been largely quiet today while my opponents have relentlessly attacked me, my credentials and my experience, and me as a person. I wished for this election to be pure in form, at least from my camp, as they all know I would expect nothing less from any within my campaign team. My wish was to let the American people have their day and choose their leader, and

I still wish to honor them in doing so. That said, I have only come out today to honor those who lost their lives today and honor my fellow Americans in remembrance of those we lost in this tragedy. My goal and position were simply to recognize those that perished in the Los Angeles tragedy earlier today. I seek the empathy of the American people and my sincerest condolences to the families that knew and loved these precious souls."

Frank Baxter of the New York Times threw one more question out to the Unified Party Candidate, "Senator West, Senator West, do you think you will be the next President of the United States?" Damian West looked at him closely and hesitated before answering, gaining the full effect.

"Frank, it's been a long day, so forgive my directness and blunt response. Do I think I will be the next President of the United States? I will be victorious and will prevail because I know the American people need something more. More than a president who slushes through their term and another who doesn't possess the temperament to see the rigors of reform all the way through. I will be a president who will demand the change, not simply go through the motions until the following election. I will hold all in my administration accountable, and I will not go quietly into the night as a puppet president. I will lead this country to change, and I will demand that of our congressmen as well. No longer will we tolerate the mediocrity of this nation's leadership and no longer will we accept the excuses from its elected leaders. Those days will cease the moment I am sworn in. To coin a phrase taken from President Ronald Reagan decades ago,

> *'Freedom is never more than one generation away from extinction. We didn't pass it to our children in the bloodstream. It must be fought for, protected, and handed on for them to do the same or one day, we will spend our sunset years telling our children and our children's children what it was once like in the United States, where men were free.'*

"I make this solemn vow to all the people of the United States. It's time to get it done! So, will I be the 47th President of the United States, Frank? I damn well better be for the sake of this nation and to remain the most powerful country in the world." and with that, he walked off the stage with his father and Sebastian Storm on his heels.

Damian West had laid all his cards out and for the first time in his campaign, he identified the weaknesses in his adversaries publicly and challenged the American people to vote for no one but him. It was time to take off the gloves as the election would come down to the wire.

For several hours following, all eyes were fixed on the television, as they viewed with bated breath as the votes were tediously tallied, state by state would trickle bits and pieces of information from their respective voting results. The clock struck 8 PM, with nearly half of the eastern states' results in, yet so many more hung in the balance, their outcomes yet to be revealed. It was clear to Damian, and everyone involved this would be a night of significant tension and suspense, a marathon testing the limits of their endurance and resolve.

The results had tightened with Trump now holding a more modest lead at 48% to Damian West's 40% and President Biden now a distant third at 12% with 54% of the votes reported. The race was narrowing to the two front runners, as Trump and West were battling it out from state to state.

10 PM rolled around in Washington, D.C., as the race was becoming far more competitive, with 78% of the vote tallied. Trump held a narrow margin at 46%, West 44%, and Biden a distant third at 10%. It was clear the incumbent president Joe Biden would not enjoy a second term, and the race was on between Donald Trump and Damian West.

Key swing states in California and Arizona were important and had not yet been reported, and the final results were theorized to come from those respective regions.

11:23 PM approached EST in Washington D.C., where the race was waiting on the final votes from the western states. Damian

West won the state of Washington but lost Arizona to Donald Trump, barely edging him out. California and Hawaii would become the deciding states that would determine the Presidential outcome. With just short of 90% of the vote tallied California could be the deciding factor in the 2024 Presidential election. With approximately 35% of the voters being Democratic, 34% Republican, 27% Unified, and the remaining 4% being Independent, the voters could swing in any direction.

Trump's margin was dwindling, holding at 47%, West 45%, and Biden a distant third at 8%.

The world was watching.

Chapter 20

Election Day

Jackson Hole, Wyoming
2017 Fall (Eight Years Before)
Senator Sam West Private Estate

Julian Chambers entered the study, rarely without Damian West by his side, but on this day, Senator Sam West wished to speak with the young Congressman alone. They had met a few times privately, but he could count on one hand, the number.

Sam West pressed the *record* button at his desk as he had done with Julian a few times before during their private meetings. He slowly rose to his feet as Julian Chambers entered his study and greeted him as if he were his own son.

Susan Lee, Senator West's long-time housekeeper, slowly closed the doors as Julian Chambers turned to notice her face staring at them. She held Julian's gaze a little longer than normal as the doors closed. An eerie sensation of remorse overcame him as he turned back toward the Senator, wondering if he had ultimately made a deal with the devil those few years before when they met within the same walls.

Senator West came around the large desk, shook Julian's hand, and smiled at the young man, "The years are creeping up on you, Julian; you look tired, Congressman. That post and the long hours go hand in hand, young man." Julian smiled, avoiding the older man's taunt, "It's been far too long, Senator. For you, on the other hand, the years have been forgiving, Sir."

Sam slapped Julian on the shoulder, "You are too kind and still full of shit, I see. Take a seat," as he gestures towards one of the chairs by the fireplace. An old, familiar environment Julian had not thought of for some time. As teenagers, they would spend hours upon hours in front of that fire, and in those days, it was a welcoming and warming environment, but on this day, the energy was far different than in years past. There was a darkness and a heaviness to it all. It wasn't the same experience without Damian as a buffer.

They spoke for a time about his new position as Representative of Indiana, representing the 16th district, and the responsibilities that came with it. Julian Chambers thanked Sam West for the genericity in aiding him in securing the position, but Sam waved the compliment off. Julian knew the compliments would not satisfy the debt he had promised years before in any way, but he was hopeful the Senator would view Julian for his own talents and merit and forsake his obligation to the Senator.

Julian entertained their discussions for the better part of an hour, hearing of Damian's political acumen and advancement. All the while, Julian reminded himself, though by no limit or restriction, he had become a congressman before the great Damian West had achieved any significant endeavor save becoming Attorney General for Wyoming a few years before.

It was then Senator Sam West leaned in and gestured for Julian to come closer, "It is time to fulfill your obligation, Congressman Chambers." The sense of formality possessed an eerie weight to it.

Julian Chambers sensed a chilly ripple down his spine, knowing whatever request the Senator would ask of him, he would have no choice but to comply, no matter the cost or risk to him or his political career.

"Certain . . . . circumstances will be arranged and handled by you and only you. You will be contacted by this man," as Senator West handed Julian a piece of paper with a single name inscribed and an encrypted phone number attached. Julian didn't open the paper. "Commit it to memory, Julian, and then destroy the note. The contact will be reaching out to you needing information. . . . vital information you will need to supply when its requested."

"When will my obligation be satisfied, Sir?"

"When I say it is, Julian," came the cryptic reply from Senator Sam West.

Julian Chambers sat back into his oversized chair . . . *he had made a deal with the devil* and, in some ways, potentially even worse.

Washington, D.C.
2024 November 5 – Election Day
Damian West Residence

Damian West dreamed of a faraway place, his face basking in the sun. He enjoyed the warmth upon his skin and the aroma of the salt saturating the ocean before him. Somehow, he sensed the sand below his uncovered feet as it squished between his toes. He was by himself, enjoying the tranquility emanating from the mysterious beach, balancing the weight of the world that had been lifted from his shoulders, giving him the peace and grace he had not experienced in some time.

Something caught his attention far off into the distance, a person walking towards him on the beach but too far away to recognize. He turned fully to watch them as they approached. He became acutely aware of the sand covering his toes as the water's edge would come up and splash him slightly, then recede back into the emerald green abyss only to return a moment later as if reminding him it was always there.

A smile came over his face as he recognized the reminiscent of the slender figure he had come to know, cherish and adore on many levels.

Mila was dressed in a form-fitting white cotton dress that came to her mid-thigh. The water came up to her knees, splashing her effortlessly as the waves broke around her. Her dress was altogether saturated from the water that had sprayed up, but she didn't appear to care. Her wet dress revealing far more of what lay beneath than the thin cloth covered.

She brushed her hair back with her fingers as the wind exhibited a tattletale of erratic movements as strands flipped and furled until she eventually gave up on keeping the hair at bay. A larger wave bounced up, soaking her dress to her breasts, revealing her nipples peeking through, radiating through the thin fabric. He noticed first her skin as the cotton cloth clung to her, her soft skin radiating beneath, creating a sheer-like appearance as if she was wearing nothing at all. Damian enjoyed her eminence and poise as she walked closer to him, revealing more of her femininity as she slowly approached.

Looking at him, Mila knew he enjoyed watching her as she turned and kicked the water playfully, slowly fluttering her arms, making a full circle before returning to her original direction. He studied her toned body as she moved, drawing him deeper into her as he closely calculated her every move. The curves upon her body teased Damian, and he was reminded she would always have a spell over him.

She walked slower now, more seductively and more upon the dryer portion of the beach, breasts heaving, moistened completely as she approached.

Mila was only a few feet from him now, taking all of him in, enjoying her own view from a female's alternative perspective. She slowly came up to him, looked up into his eyes as he pulled her tighter to him and kissed her hard and deep upon the lips. His kiss and energy synched with her magically, and he longed to have her once again. Her hands migrated to the back of his head, mildly tugging at his hair and pulling him tighter to her.

Mila instantly caressed and fostered his excitement as it brushed her mound between her legs, teasing her with anticipation. The stimulation perked her nipples through her dress as his hand came up to caress her breasts, and her head arched back, enjoying the effect he was having upon her.

Her hand begins to drift to his stomach, still lower, to enjoy his rising manhood from within. Mila looks up at Damian, enjoying the result her own motivation was having upon him. His hands rest upon her cheeks as she looks up at him. Then, his hands slowly slide to her neck, followed by her shoulders, where he begins to ease further, her straps out over her shoulders. The dress, wet from the ocean spray, clings to her skin as he eases the dress down her arms, exposing her breasts, her skin warm from the sun.

Their eyes were locked as he maneuvered her dress further down, revealing the top of her mons, her hips wet, inviting his touch as he pushed the dress below her hips, falling to the sand. Her exposed body excites him as he takes in her beauty, filled with confidence and poise yet also allure and intrigue she always provided him.

In the soft glow of the setting sun, the atmosphere between Mila and Damian became charged with a palpable desire. With their bodies pressed together, Mila's hands traced the contours of his stomach, acutely aware of the simmering passion that radiated from him.

With seductive confidence, her fingers deftly undid the buttons of Damian's linen shirt, revealing his chest, which seemed sculpted by the gods themselves. The warmth of the evening air kissed their skin, heightening their anticipation. Mila's hands continued their journey, sliding down to his waist, where her thumbs slipped under his waistband. With tantalizing slowness, she eased them down, exposing him fully as the shorts fell to the sandy surface below.

Damian, equally eager and electrified by the sensuality of the moment, shed his shirt, placing it gently on the soft sand as they stood mere inches from it. Slowly, they both crouched down, Mila reclining gracefully on Damian's shirt, now a makeshift blanket beneath her.

As Damian positioned himself on top of her, their lips met in a scorching kiss, igniting a passionate fire that seemed to mirror the intensity of the setting sun. The world around them faded into insignificance as they lost themselves in the intoxicating dance of desire and connection, a moment of shared intimacy that would forever be etched in their memories.

She reaches down, appreciates his rigidity within her hand, and smiles, enjoying the moment of torture she is bestowing upon him. Her legs open in both a symbolic and physical manifestation of what they both desire and need from each other. She looks into his eyes, not wanting either of them to suffer any longer as she guides him to her innermost sanctum. Her legs spread a little more as she accepts him within her as she desires to have all of him.

Easing him and guiding him slowly, he enters her as she looks at his expression, enjoying the pleasure she is providing to him on a carnal level. Damian relishes every moment as he enters her fully, then slowly recedes, followed by a more forceful thrust before his rhythm and cadence find their sync, and they make love upon the sand with not a care in the world except the two of them basking in the glow of the setting sun.

She orgasms quickly, feeling connected to him and the security he provides to her as she kisses him deeply and experiences his own contractions as he fills her with his seed, wanting all of him within her.

Sliding off to the side to his back, she rolls to his stomach and drapes one leg over his legs, and they lay in silence for a moment, listening to the waves crashing before them, and he thinks at that moment . . . . what a perfect place in time. He enjoys the sun upon his face once more. . .

"Damian . . . Damian . . . it's time," Mila whispered to her husband. Damian had been caught up in his dream, which provided him some solace. Opening his eyes to his lovely wife, Mila made him smile. "I was dreaming of you . . ." he said. "Oh, you were, were you? Was it a naughty one," asked Mila. "Yes, it was, of course," but, thinking back, "It was a lovely moment I want to replicate someday."

She took his cheeks in her hands, "If you thought it was, we will relive that dream one day, I promise you. But today, today is your day my love. Your supporters are all out here in the main room waiting for you. Freshen yourself up. You have been by yourself for almost an hour at the most critical time." He kissed her and got up as she left him to ready himself. It was 1 AM, and the polls would be closed, the votes being tallied, but he was certain the informal numbers would be posted.

Walking to the bathroom sink, he looked somewhat haggard in the mirror. He hadn't slept much in nearly 36 hours . . . save for his short dream on the beach.

He longed for that moment.

Studying himself in the mirror, he stood up straighter, and adjusted his tie. Running a hand through his hair, he pulled himself together and grabbed the bottle of cologne, Bleu by Chanel and sprayed the mist once or twice. Satisfied with the image peering back at him, he walked to his bedroom door and hesitated with his hand on the doorknob.

Damian West smiled within yet sensed he was ready for what lay beyond that door, no matter the outcome.

He opened it to a roar of applause; smiles beaming were the faces of his father, Mila, Regina Alvarado, Julian Chambers, Senators Nagel, Arnold and Cosner, and lastly, Sebastian Storm, always moderated in his mysterious way. These were the people that mattered to him the most and those that he owed the greatest amount of gratitude. These were the people that were responsible for his success. He owed them all so much, more than he could ever repay.

Glancing over at the screen the figures were staggering. With 98.23% of the votes reported, Donald Trump and Damian West were tied at 46% of the popular vote and incumbent, Joe Biden a distant third at 8%. Damian West had captured the hearts of the people of California and won the state in an upset over President Biden, shifting the percentages in his favor.

The vote would come down to the wire and Hawaii was the last to report, being the most western state and would most likely determine the next president of the United States. The media was in a frenzy, and all the networks theorized various outcomes, which simply added to the chaos.

No clear winner would be determined that evening.

Damian West, at 3 AM, finally called it a night as the last of their guests left, leaving only Sam West and Sebastian in the residence. Mila had snuck away to the bedroom a few minutes earlier, leaving the three alone.

Sam verbalized the obvious, "Long day, gentlemen, no question. It may be a few days before we know the confirmed result of the vote." He looked at his son, "Regardless, Damian, of the outcome, there is not a prouder father than me. You have exceeded all expectations and have become a far better man than I ever imagined." "Hoorah," came the response from Sebastian, always the regimented military style.

Damian smiled and replied, "I never would have gotten this far with the two of you. To you, Father, I owe such a debt of gratitude for seeing my potential and paving the way for this glorious new journey that you have created, and I plan to fulfill. And Sebastian, though a new friend, a substantial one. Having the most notorious soldier, probably the most famous of all time, at my side to keep me safe and protected has been a blessing in all this. I have so enjoyed our talks and hope to have many more.

"You have a gift, Damian, and one that cannot be suppressed. Your father here has instilled it, you have developed it, and my goal is to protect it. I believe in you, and I believe in this mission and will see it through to the end."

"Couldn't have said it better myself, Sebastian," replied Sam West as he shook his hand and hugged his son. "Tomorrow is another day; gentlemen and we may see some fresh perspective with the coming light. Good night," as he headed for the door. Sebastian shook Damian's hand and said after Sam, "I'll see you out, Sir," Sebastian nodded to Damian and quickly caught up with his father to walk out with him.

Damian lay awake in bed as the clock showed 5 AM. Mila's head rested on his chest as she lay peacefully, her head rising and lowering to his shallow breaths. He focused on her steady breathing, and it consoled his restlessness.

He pondered how their lives would change if he won the Presidential election. It also hit him that if he did win, he would have to make good on his promise to the American people. He would have to follow through on the promises that he made. Damian refused to let them down, but most of all, he would not disappoint those who helped him get to where he was today.

As the stars in the dark sky shone outside his window, casting a warm, amber glow over the tranquil moment of contemplation, Damian West found himself reflecting on a piece of timeless wisdom handed down by his father just hours before: *"Tomorrow would be another day."*

These words echoed in his mind, a soothing reminder that in the ever-shifting landscape of life, each dawn held the promise of new opportunities.

With the election now behind him, Damian experienced a profound sense of contentment wash over him. He had poured his heart and soul into the campaign, tirelessly crisscrossing the nation, shaking countless hands, and sharing his vision for a brighter future with any who cared to listen. As he looked back on the journey, he found comfort in the fact that he had left no stone unturned, no effort spared. He had no regrets about any of it.

However, the knowledge that he had run a campaign guided by integrity and honesty brought him the greatest sense of pride and fulfillment. In a world where politics often tread murky waters,

Damian had upheld his commitment to a clean race, a respectable and virtuous fight. He had resisted the temptation to engage in divisive tactics or mudslinging, choosing instead to focus on the issues that truly mattered to the people he aimed to represent.

For Damian West, the pursuit of the greater good had always been his north star. As he gazed at the starlit sky above, he couldn't help but validate he had stayed true to his convictions. And as he stood on the precipice of a new day, he embraced the uncertainty of the future, secure in the knowledge that he had given everything to his campaign, just as his father had taught him. Tomorrow would indeed be another day filled with endless possibilities. He would seize them all and never look back.

He finally fell asleep as the sun slowly began to rise.

Mila had awakened earlier but let Damian sleep as long as he was able. She was aware he had received very little sleep over the prior two nights. He had countless calls coming in, but she muted them all to let him rest until he sauntered out to the kitchen at roughly 10 AM that morning.

He snuck up behind her and kissed her neck softly as she smiled, and he tickled her, "I hate when you do that, was always her response, but he was also certain she loved the attention she received from him. He looked at the face of his phone: 201 texts and 71 missed calls. Damian turned it back over and turned back to Mila and smiled.

30 minutes had gone by, and they spoke nothing of the election the night before and didn't even turn on the television. She made him some coffee and his favorite breakfast and placed it in front of him when the LAN line, which rarely rang, startled both of them.

Mila looked at Damian and cocked her head, not remembering the last time the LAN phone had rang but walked over to the refrigerator where it hung on the wall. She picked up the receiver and nodded and acknowledged before saying quietly, "Yes, Mr. President he is right here," as she glanced over at Damian as he stood to grab the receiver. "Hello and good morning, Mr. President. This is Damian West." Mila studied Damian's expressions as he nodded and acknowledged them; at the end of the short conversation, he replied, "Thank you. I plan to do just that." Have a good day, Mr. President, and thank you for the call."

He pulled the phone from his ear, and he simply held it to his chest, somewhat perplexed by the call. "What did he say," exclaimed Mila, shaking Damian from his daydream. "He . . .he conceded his position and told me he would be my biggest supporter and to follow and uphold the promises I made to the American people, and I told him I would do just that." He was in a state of shock, the moment surreal as if he were dreaming.

She looked at him and smiled as she rushed over to him to hug the man she loved, "You won, honey. . ." it was then, the phone rang yet again, and he looked at it before pushing the ON button and replied, "Hello, this is Damian West," he listened for a moment before replying, "Thank you, President Trump, no I do appreciate your candor and offer. I will certainly think about it. You as well, Sir. Have a wonderful day," as he hung up the phone the moment became bizarre as if he were in an ongoing dream. A dream he had not yet awakened from.

There was a knock at the door; Mila announced that the Secret Service had arrived, with Sebastian Storm leading the group.

Damian West had done the impossible and just become the 47th President of the United States.

Jackson Hole, Wyoming
2024 Late November
Senator Sam West Private Estate

In the weeks following the historic election, the Watchful Eight wasted no time in preparing for the Presidential Inauguration on January 20, 2025. As the Unified Party's victory sent shockwaves through the political establishment, the focus shifted to the crucial task of forming a Presidential transitional team to replace former President Biden's administration.

Comprised of a select group of advisors, experts, and individuals with a deep understanding of the inner workings of government, the transitional team played a pivotal role in ensuring the seamless transition of power. The primary objective was to prepare President-elect Damian West to assume office efficiently and effectively.

The formation of the transitional team was a meticulous process, requiring careful consideration of each member's expertise and experience. From policy advisors to legal experts, each member brings a unique set of skills to the table, essential for navigating the complexities of the transition process.

As preparations for the inauguration gathered pace, the Watchful Eight worked tirelessly behind the scenes, laying the groundwork for Damian West's administration. Their commitment to ensuring a smooth changeover of power was unwavering, a testament to their dedication to the principles of democracy and governance.

As the countdown to January 20th began, Inauguration Day, the nation anxiously observed, with bated breath, eager to witness the dawn of a new era under President Damian West's leadership.

Selection of members of the cabinet, including key positions such as Secretary of State, Secretary of Defense, and other key roles, were essential. These selections were to be announced before the inauguration and required Senate confirmation.

President West's team worked tirelessly on shaping their policy priorities and legislative agenda. This included identifying key issues they wished to address during his presidency.

In the following month, President West received classified national security briefings to become familiar with ongoing international and domestic security matters.

Scheduling of the departure of President Biden and newly elected President West at the White House was to be determined to discuss the transition and important issues at hand.

Damian West, Mila, and their team planned the inauguration ceremony, which was to take place on January 20th following the election several months before. This included organizing the swearing-in ceremony, inaugural address, and various celebratory events.

Lastly, President Damian West would communicate extensively with the public, outlining his vision for the country and addressing important issues during this period. The Watchful Eight also directed its focus on Regina Alvarado's position as Speaker of the House. They surmised with the wind in their favor, the tide would shift to the strength of the Unified Party and its determination to have her regain the seat she was meant to have and hold.

President Damian West's dynasty . . . . *had begun.*

Chapter 21

Inauguration

"Nearly all men can stand adversity, but if you want to test a man's character, give him power."
~Abraham Lincoln

Washington D.C.
2025 Fall Inauguration Day
United States Capitol

Amid the grandeur of American democracy, the inauguration of the President of the United States unfolds at none other than the majestic United States Capitol, a hallowed institution nestled in the heart of Washington, D.C. The specific stage for the historic event was set at the West front of the U.S. Capitol Building, a location that exudes an aura of gravitas and tradition and has hosted the momentous occasion for generations.

The location was bittersweet as it also denotes the location where an attempt on President West's life occurred a few years before, with Julian Chambers taking a bullet and a valuable staff member being killed in the attack. No shortage of security was witnessed that day.

As the crisp winter air blankets the nation's capital, the sun casts a golden glow upon the stately columns and neoclassical architecture. The scene was nothing short of iconic. It was there, against the backdrop, that President Damian West stepped forward to embark on the solemn journey of leadership to be sworn in as the 47th President of the United States.

With the entire nation watching, President West took the oath of office, a sacred pledge to preserve, protect, and defend the Constitution of the United States. Historically, the words echoed through the marble corridors of power, reverberating with the weight of history. Traditionally, the pivotal moment was graced by the presence of the Chief Justice, John G. Roberts Jr., who administered the oath, symbolizing the separation of powers and the sanctity of the law.

The U.S. Capitol itself stood as a tangible embodiment of the nation's democratic ideals. It was a silent witness to the ebb and flow of history, a repository of the dreams and aspirations of the American people. For generations, it has been the epicenter of governance, a place where the course of the nation is charted and where the torch of leadership is passed from one administration to the next.

Damian West was the youngest President ever elected and half the age of the Presidential candidates who opposed him. The youngest president in U.S. history prior to Damian West was Theodore Roosevelt, who took office at the age of 42 after the assassination of President William McKinley in 1901.

In the hallowed hall of democracy, beneath the vast expanse of the American sky, the inauguration was a poignant reminder of the enduring strength and resilience of the United States. It emulated a moment when the nation collectively reaffirmed its commitment to the principles upon which it was founded, and as the President-elect assumed the mantle of leadership, the Capitol stood as a beacon of hope, unity, and the promise of a brighter future. The stage had been set, and now all eyes turned to their new leader to make good on the promises he ensured to the American people, his constituents, and above all, to himself.

Julian Chambers stood well behind the speaker's podium, listening to Damian's inauguration speech on the Capitol's stairs. By default, with Damian West's win of the 2024 election, Julian had become the Vice-President of the United States, but his victory paled in comparison to the achievement Damian West had received.

His mind drifted to the insignificance of his own triumph and success despite the eerie notion that he had taken a bullet just a few feet from where they stood years before. His slight limp was reminiscent of that horrific evening. His scar of dedication for his service, he would tell himself. The injury and risk were worth the payoff as he was now at the top of the stairs looking down at all the people as one of America's leaders, not the followers looking up. He found some comfort in that distinction.

Julian reminisced when, a few weeks prior, during the transitional period, Sam West had approached him during a break from one of the many meetings surrounding the transition. Outside of earshot of anyone, Sam whispered, "You have a zero balance with me, Julian and your obligations have been met . . . . *paid in full*. You can terminate the . . . uhmm, contracting group you have been working with. You will no longer require their services. They have been on retainer, and we should have a substantial credit with them. They can keep it. Just make them disappear."

"Yes, Sir," was all he could muster to reply with, but he was relieved he no longer had to deal with the covert obligation. There was so much planning over the last decade, and just dismissed with a simple . . . *make them disappear*. Julian believed he was somehow used and discarded.

Sam pats Julian on the back, signifying his release, but in a subtle, condescending manner as he walks away from Julian. In that moment, Julian resented the West family for making him feel corrupt and dirty for what Sam had put him through, but equally so in Damian, whose rise and reign in power was largely achieved from Julian's sacrifices and being Sam West's instrument to a greater goal and purpose. He was manipulated like a simple pawn to be controlled and cast off when no longer needed. Julian Chambers felt sullied, guilty but mostly resentful. Damian West benefitted, while Julian Chambers shouldered all the risk.

But discarded he would not accept, nor tolerate. He had achieved the position of the second most important post in the most powerful country in the world, and someday, all would see his value. He had fought hard to achieve his station, and he had earned the right to sit at the big table.

As the chilly air brought Julian to his immediate reality, he stared at the back of Damian's head and all the people beyond him, cheering his name and hanging on to every word he muttered.

Julian privately thought, "They are all sheep. Why would they listen to Damian West? Julian was the one who had made the hard decisions, the difficult choices necessary to get the results intended. Damian West was simply the puppet delivering the message. His own actions, risks and sacrifices paved the way to the White House for Damian West, and he wasn't even aware. He looked to his right. There, Sam West stood, his proudest moment, but Julian Chambers was the one who was responsible for putting Damian West into office more than anyone else. He had taken the risk and he should be recognized as such.

As he looked out over the vast sea of faces, he fantasized about envisioning himself before the podium where Damian stood. The people would worship and adore him being a self-made man, coming from the rags of Jackson Hole, Wyoming and carving his way to the top through hard work and forging relationships to get to the Oval Office.

He deserved it as much as Damian West, possibly more. Damian came from privilege, but Julian emerged from the bottom, from the lower class. People would respect his ambition and honor him for his emergence. His anger intensified between the stark reality that he had always been second best to Damian and played into the whims and manipulations of his father, Sam West. He would play the part as long as he was able, but his time would come, and all would know his name; he would make certain. He looked to his left to see Sebastian Storm looking directly at him in a bizarre fashion. A look on his face as if he were reading his mind and knowing the ill will he bestowed upon the West legacy. Julian nodded and looked forward, wiping the thoughts from his mind.

Another time and another place.

The Inaugural Ball proved to be the most lavish in history, with dignitaries, billionaires, celebrities, and the like all showing their respects for their new President, who possessed more of a look of royalty than anything else. In the middle of it all stood Damian and his father, Sam West. Mila stood by Damian's side, ever polished and taking on the form of First Lady rather easily. She was a natural with people and would prove to embrace the position beautifully.

Sebastian Storm attended the Inaugural Ball for a time, out of respect for the family, but parties were not his forte. He intended to slide out a side door when the moment was right, not enjoying the festivities as much as some, though popular with many attending, curious to meet the notorious Sebastian Storm personally. It wasn't his place nor his type of crowd, and recognition and flattery made him more uncomfortable than being in a firefight in some faraway war.

He slowly made his way and lingered for a few moments near the exit, looking at Damian, and finally caught his eye briefly, nodding to the new President, socializing as politicians do. Damian paused and looked at Sebastian, knowing he owed the man a tremendous debt of gratitude but also well aware these environments were not where Sebastian's talents lay.

He smiled and nodded to Sebastian as if to say simply, *thank you for everything*, but also to sanction his permission to depart the evening's festivities. He knew Sebastian was only present to pay his respects.

Sebastian stood at attention and quietly saluted his Commander-in-Chief and Damian saluted back acknowledging his greatest warrior from afar. Mila was the only one to detect their connection and admirable moment, and it was then she knew that her husband and Sebastian shared a special bond.

He would slowly disengage from his primary focus of protecting Damian West over the coming months. Secret Service Agent Benjamin Lee would take over the reins, and a full detail would assume the rite of passage for the new president. His work was completed after more than two years of devotion to the man he wholeheartedly believed in to get the country back on track.

Both their hands lowered, and they nodded one last time as Sebastian Storm strategically turned and made his way out of the south exit, down the emergency stairwell, and into the cool, brisk air of the White House lawn.

He was free.

A soldier above all, Sebastian Storm's place was in the trenches. Despite his political perspective being somewhat altered by Sam and Damian West, rubbing elbows within the *A-listed* environment wasn't his favorite pastime.

He had helped Damian West and the Unified Party achieve their goals, but his work was largely completed. It was Damian and Sam West's time; they had certainly earned it.

Sam West had always claimed he was a King Maker, but in that same notion, Sebastian realized he was the protector of Kings, and he had done just that. . . . his role and obligation, now complete.

Chapter 22

The Reign Cometh

"Change is the law of life. And those who look only to the past or present are certain to miss the future."
~John F. Kennedy

Washington D.C.
End 2026 White House (Two Years in Office)
United States Capital

"That is amazing," as President West began clapping and the rest of the Cabinet joined in on the accomplishment. In the two years of holding the office of President of the United States, the statistics he had accumulated with his administration were staggering.

He had just received the news the inflation rate was less than 3%, unemployment was just under the 5% mark, and Congress had been pushing through legislation in his WestTax Initiative which would grossly alter the tax laws and inefficiencies within governmental spending. "It's all coming together, President West," said Sam West to his son, always addressing Damian formally while in a group setting out of respect for his son and the institution itself.

Damian looked at his father adoringly. His frailty was setting in far more of late. At 81 years old, the iconic Senator was still sharp, but his body was failing him. Sam West continued, "With Regina Alvarado reclaiming the Speaker of the House post, we have a significant majority in Congress now. Senator Cosner, what are the numbers?"

Senator Cosner perked up, "Well, Senator and Mr. President, the Unified Party currently holds a 45% majority within the Senate and 48% within the House. Republicans have 24% to Democrats 28% and 3% Independent in the Senate and Republicans 23% and Democrats 21% with 9% Independent in the House. Overall, very impressive. It's difficult to argue with what the Unified Party has accomplished, and grabbing support from both the Republicans and Democrats to move legislation has been nothing short of a miracle. Mr. President, you have led us well, and you have answered Americans' demands and upheld the promises we have made to the nation. Bravo to you and this administration." A loud round of applause swept the room.

President West explained, "With the value of how this legislation was written, you either need to be on board or remove yourself from its progression. Thankfully, it's been the latter for both. I'm confident we have the numbers to pass WestTax and AmeriCare in a few weeks. Does anyone have any alternative views, observations or opinions?

Julian Chambers spoke up, "Senator Joseph Camloc brings up some good points on issues with the legislation concerning taxing of the wealthy needs to be pressed and still a lot of holes, he says in the AmeriCare Health Plan." Damian looked at his old friend, surprised and disappointed by his statement, "Julian, we have spoken about this many times in the past, and frankly, I'm tired of the rhetoric. You know, Senator Camloc only wants us to fail. That's his only wish, and by taxing mostly the wealthiest Americans, our companies receive nothing to incentivize them at all. Our legislation has made allowances for these wealthy groups to receive better incentives to actually help Americans less fortunate. Look at how we have cleaned up the city's homeless, and healthcare reform can now be funded. Our *New Initiative* has shown it will more than fund a far stronger Healthcare Plan for all Americans. This legislation will tax the wealthy and the businesses of our country fairly in ways helping reform our healthcare, small businesses, affordable loans, the homeless, and those less fortunate. Everyone wins. Camloc's position has always been an antiquated one, serving only a few. Why do you insist on backing the one Senator who is out for personal gain and lives only to sink our party?" Damian shook his head, "Camloc emulates nothing this Party stands for and nothing to do with reform on any level. Please don't be foolish enough to fall for his bullshit antics, Julian. Your position and confidence in him disappoint me."

A few of the other Cabinet members cast additional comments questioning Vice-president Chambers's loyalty. "The wealthy and big business can handle the numbers better and should concede a portion of their profits for the betterment of their fellow Americans. They should be taxed higher, yet less than they were paying with Biden's Administration by several percentage points. Let them experience their tax dollars are actually effective, not wasted as they have been for generations. Everyone wins with this system . . . . *everyone. To think any differently is foolhardiness.*"

Damian shook his head, "Camloc's method has been tried, and it failed miserably. Those groups aren't taxed more in our plan but lower and are offered incentives for significant contributions or when it aids less fortunate individuals or small businesses. The tax programs in the past have been a farce, a joke, valuable tax dollars going to nothing. Now, here is a chance for something positive to come out of taxation, and the WestTax Initiative will do just that. To think any less in an already faltering system is ludicrous." Damian West and his Watchful Eight, along with his Cabinet, had made tremendous strides as far as reform; legislation was being passed, and the American way of life was improving, and arguing the point was a growing passion when he spoke of it.

Julian had seen enough. He pushed back his chair and walked out of the room. Over the prior two years, he felt Damian West had become far too brazen in his new position and wouldn't consider anything of late Vice-President Julian Chambers suggested.

Julian had amassed significant clout in the Senate by becoming the youngest *President of the Senate,* but his age and experience often came into question. It was a difficult position to uphold and maintain the respect of the 100 Senators he presides over, all of whom were older than he and most possessing far more experience.

Much of his respect came from the reverence of their President, but Julian Chambers had to maintain the diplomacy of the Senators to maintain order and progression. Senator Joseph Camloc saw the opportunity to sway his young pupil and offer guidance to Julian, and the Vice-President readily accepted his influence.

Julian valued Senator Camloc appreciating his various talents and reassured Julian often, and publicly. Senator Camloc recognized the talent in the Vice-President and counseled him on his career and diplomatic relations, on and off the Senate floor.

Julian Chambers was becoming more segregated from the West's and left out of more important agendas and meetings. With Sam West and Damian tending to larger, more significant national projects, they largely left Julian alone and often excluded him from their executive meetings. Despite the positive elements President West's administration was achieving, there was a definite rift between the President and Vice-President brewing.

As the meeting dissolved into the echoes of departing footsteps, Damian strode back to the Oval Office, the weight of leadership settling upon his shoulders that afternoon. The halls, usually paced by Sam West's steadfast presence at his side, whispered silence on that particular day.

Sam West, a pillar of fortitude and dedication, had succumbed to the grip of malaise and chosen the comfort of home over the call of duty that afternoon. In the solitude of the Oval Office, Damian sat, the day's challenges casting long shadows across the resolute desk. Yet, in the stillness, he found clarity. Though his trusted confidant and mentor was absent, Damian felt the quiet resolve to steer the ship of state through the uncertain waters ahead.

———

The President sat at his desk alone, enjoying the peace often coming between 5 PM and 7 PM. A moment where he asked for no disturbances unless vitally necessary. He used the time to relax and consider the challenges he faced the day before meeting his beautiful First Lady for dinner every night following his interlude. He would often turn his chair to the beautiful scene of his bay window behind his desk within the Oval Office. It was here he would ponder the future of the United States and ask himself if was making America a better place for everyone.

Within months of occupying his office, he met with Anthony Voss of Dymitron and explained to him his legislation offering Dymitron and businesses like his ways and methods to streamline the tax liability and incentivize large companies to keep their companies on American soil.

"It's a detailed and complex structure, but you can determine from the projections and estimates this plan would save you substantially in tax, de-regulate many components as well as make everyone happy as to where the taxes would be spent. It's a win-win for everyone."

Anthony was impressed, "I'm in awe, Mr. President. These numbers would save the company billions and improve taxation with your incentives, and it makes me appreciate the tax proceeds are going toward significant and worthwhile reforms, causes, and budgets. This is what I have always wanted. Are you confident you can secure the votes to pass this legislation?"

"I do," replied President West, "we have run the numbers, and barring any crazy Ivan's, it should pass 3-2 in favor. Will this keep you here?" Anthony shook the President's hand, "If the Bill passes, then yes, Sir, it will." The conversation had occurred 18 months before, and the legislation would hopefully pass and become law a few weeks later. It was considered one of the most substantial pieces of legislation in decades, and the benefits to all Americans would be enormous. It was the largest crown jewel of many orchestrated by the young President.

Any President before him had received death threats, and Damian West was no different, but laying atop his desk was a letter more specific and drew more attention to him and the Secret Service. He remembered the letter he had received weeks before the election, scaring him about issues and details surrounding the Wyoming Governor he ended up replacing, but this letter hit home a little closer for Damian. He didn't know what to think of it, but he knew who to ask.

A faint tone came from the intercom at his desk. President West's personal secretary quietly spoke, "Mr. President, I'm so sorry to bother you, but I thought you might make an exception in this instance. Mr. Storm is here to see you unannounced, Sir."

President West broke into a smile, "Yes. Yes, of course, Josey, send him in." Moments later, the large door opened, and Josey escorted Sebastian Storm into the Oval Office. Both of their smiles equally competing, eager to greet one another as Sebastian walked over the threshold, the top of his head mere inches away from the top of the doorway frame.

They came together and shook hands, and President West offered, "It's been far too long, my friend." "That it has, Sir," Sebastian replied remaining formal until the President's secretary had left the room. Josey closed the door behind her as she left.

Damian gestured towards a seat, as he fixed Sebastian a Bourbon without even asking him. Macallan, 21 years old, with a large ice cube, already knowing his selection was expertly prepared by the President himself.

President West continued, "You know I have them stock the ice box with large cubes only for you Sebastian. "And its much obliged, Mr. President," as President waved it off, "You can be informal now, Sebastian, we are too close for such nonsense."

Sebastian smiled, "Well, you have certainly earned it. I miss our long talks, Damian, I won't deny it." President West replied, "During the campaign, we had a lot more time for that, didn't we? But then I went and got elected and having to overhaul the American government and you wiping out the bad guys on a global level, something had to give. I do greatly appreciate you dropping in from time to time, and with my father's ailing health, I don't feel as connected with the day-to-day of international affairs, though HB's reports and meetings are always thorough. I'm just pulled in so many directions these days. I think I took for granted what my father would do and how he kept the machine running. This legislation is a grind to trudge through Congress as well. A lot of handholding, promises and stroking of egos to see it finalized. However, once we have them passed, I suspect the tension will lighten somewhat. Well, I hope it will."

Sebastian laughed, "The life of a successful American President. Oh, the glory of it all. On that note, how is your father doing? I worry for him, though he appears sharp, the years are taking a toll on him from what I can tell. I visited with him a few weeks ago. He told me about the stage four prostate cancer. He appears to be in good spirits, though."

"He is, Sebastian," replied Damian, But damn, he is nearly 82 years old. Something is bound to inflict any of us by that point. He's strong, as you know. Some measly cancer isn't going to stop the man. I suspect he will outlive us all."

"That aside, Sebastian, I wanted your take on another letter I received, much like the one from a few years ago." President West walked over to his desk, grabbed the letter, and handed it to Sebastian.

Sebastian reviewed the short letter and read some aloud, ". . . your path was predetermined . . . . manipulated to attain your goals . . . . Those closest to you may not share your vision . . . .watch for those in the shadows . . . ." Sebastian shook his head, "Eloquent, vague and cryptic. It's hard to say what the intent is here. Do you feel anyone close to you has an ulterior motive and a separate agenda?"

"I don't," replied President West, "Julian and I have been at odds for some time now, and he appears to have Joseph Camloc whispering in his ear, and Julian appears to be listening, but nothing more for the moment."

Sebastian's thoughts raced as he considered Damian's comments. He found it not only peculiar but almost implausible that after all the hard work and progress the Watchful Eight had put into the Unified Party, including the contributions of Julian Chambers, anyone would entertain the rantings and influence of an outsider.

It felt like a betrayal of their cause and vision in some fashion, a duplicity of everything they had worked so meticulously to achieve. And Vice-President Julian Chambers always seemed to be at the forefront of their campaign. His change of heart and opposition made Sebastian consider that Vice-President Chambers was following a different path.

There was always something about Julian Chambers that had troubled Sebastian since the first time they met nearly four years ago at Sam West's estate in Wyoming. It was like a faint whisper of unease he couldn't ignore yet couldn't place or verify either. Sebastian prided himself on his ability to read people, to understand their motivations and intentions but there were always some individuals that eluded his abilities. With Chambers, though, it was different. There was a hidden depth, a complexity Sebastian couldn't quite grasp but also couldn't condemn either.

As he considered all this, Sebastian made a mental note to delve deeper into his suspicions. He knew better than to jump to conclusions, but the nagging suspicion persisted. There were always those who believed they were entitled to more. Those who were willing to betray their allies for personal gain. Sebastian couldn't help but wonder where Vice-President Chamber's loyalties truly resided.

Turning his attention back to Damian, Sebastian spoke firmly, "Let me speak with Agent Lee about this letter further. We need to get to the bottom of it." His tone brooked no argument. He was determined to uncover the truth, no matter where it led.

"I'd appreciate that, Sebastian. I have grown far more paranoid as of late. I hate to, in any form, compare myself to Adolf Hitler, but as we all know, he was plagued with an abundance of neurotic paranoia. Lately, I feel with the dominating emergence of the Unified's, I am in a constant state of perpetual suspicion, paired with an unhealthy dose of trepidation concerning most people that surround me."

Sebastian stood up, "It's really very understandable. Considering your reference, Hitler survived over 42 assassination attempts, a third of which were attempted by his own officers. Regardless, your skepticism is a healthy perception and shouldn't be dismissed. Please tell your father I was thinking about him, and I wish him a speedy recovery." "Not sure if that statistic will help me sleep tonight, Sebastian," they laughed, "But, of course, I will tell him, Sebastian, he always enjoys seeing you. He left early today, not feeling well," they shook hands, and Sebastian Storm let himself out of the large security door.

New York, New York
2026 November
Fury's Manhattan Penthouse
Smithsonian Museum Exhibit

Fury listened intently on the SAT phone. After a brief conversation, he hung up. Their primary client had laid dormant for nearly two full years, but their monthly retainer had continued to be deposited, amassing nearly 20 million USD in that time period. He had been standing in the living room with Inferno as he studied his every move.

Once Fury hung up the phone, he turned to Inferno, "There is one final chapter we must complete, then our contract will be fulfilled in full. He wishes to meet at the Smithsonian Museum the day after tomorrow. The client said there was a substantial risk to him as well as us and that we should use someone to retrieve his message and instructions. Despite our physical changes, we could still be recognized with cameras, so it would be difficult for either of us to get close to him with Secret Service details surrounding our client. However, the opening of the exhibit yet will be the best place for us to retrieve the instructions. We will use Sapphire to retrieve the final objective."

Fury chose Sapphire to complete the task as she would blend into a public setting best, and his contact was told to look for a woman with pigtails held with yellow rubber bands when she came to greet him in the public gathering at the Smithsonian exhibit.

The atmosphere at the Smithsonian Museum was charged with excitement as Vice-President Chambers took the stage to emcee the unveiling of the new World of Wonders Exhibit. The grand event kicked off promptly at 4 PM, drawing a crowd of nearly 1000 enthusiastic attendees. As the Vice-President began his address, his voice filled with passion and enthusiasm, resonating through the museum halls.

In his speech, Vice-President Chambers expressed his profound excitement for the grand opening of the new exhibit, which showcased the most marvelous wonders of the world, both natural and man-made. He emphasized the importance of bringing these wonders together in one place for all to see and appreciate, highlighting the beauty and diversity of our planet.

With excitement, Vice-President Chambers declared the exhibit officially open, promising attendees an unforgettable experience. He then proceeded to cut the ceremonial red tape with a pair of gleaming gold scissors, symbolizing the inauguration of this extraordinary showcase of human ingenuity and the marvels of nature.

The audience erupted into applause, awestruck by the spectacle before them. The World of Wonders Exhibit was not just a collection of artifacts; it was a testament to the limitless potential of natural phenomena as well as human curiosity and creativity. As people began to explore the exhibit, their hearts and minds were filled with a sense of wonder and inspiration, reaffirming the beauty and magic of the world they lived in.

People flocked through the large gates as Vice-President Chambers shook the hands of those entering the exhibit with the Secret Service flanking him on both sides. Children and adults alike streamed through with the hope of getting close to the Vice President, who was part of a movement that was shaking the very foundation of America, and they were excited to be a part of it.

Vice-President Chambers greeted the eager crowd at the exhibit with a reserved smile, shaking hands and exchanging pleasantries as he made his way through the throng of attendees below his stage. His presence was lackluster, relegated to exhibit openings and fundraisers seemed to be the most important thing he was assigned to as of late. He was far from the energizing personality of President Damian West, who was a master at drawing people in with his charm, charisma, and unbounded energy.

As he shook hands with the guests, an attractive young woman caught his eye. She had pigtails held together with bright yellow rubber bands, a distinctive look that set her apart from the crowd. She approached him with a confident stride, her eyes twinkling with a hint of intent.

Chambers, ever the diplomat, rose from his hunched-over position as if to stretch, using the opportunity to subtly assess the awaiting people who hugged the stage. With a casual wave to the crowd, he discreetly placed his hand in his pocket, a subtle gesture that did not go unnoticed by the observant young woman. When finally, her turn arrived, she stepped up to the stage and extended her hand to the Vice President. He met her hand with his own, a small but significant detail that hinted at his keen awareness of his surroundings.

With a soft handshake, Chambers greeted her warmly, "Enjoy the exhibit," before smoothly transitioning to greet the family beside her and then several others in the vicinity. The young woman, satisfied with her interaction, gracefully bowed out of the crowd, blending into the mass of people as she made her way to the gift shop.

As she exited the museum, a wry smile played on her lips, betraying the thrill of the encounter and her slightly different mission successfully completed. It was a brief but exhilarating moment, a dance of wits and charm in the midst of a public gathering. The mystery of her intentions lingered in the air.

Despite it being the digital era, Vice-President Chambers utilized an old school method of communicating information and slipped her a simple note that she dared not even look at until it was delivered to her boss, Fury. A puzzle yet to be solved in the grand scheme of the evening's events. The note had some significance, but she was usually kept out of the loop of such matters. Her job was to simply secure the correspondence and deliver it safely to Fury or sacrifice her life to protect it or worst case, destroy it.

Thirty minutes later, Sapphire met at the rendezvous point with Fury and Inferno, who were eagerly waiting for her arrival when she indicated she was enroute.

She walked in as Fury held out his hand, and she simply opened her palm with the small paper note, wet from her perspiration and eagerness to get the message to her superior.

She was well aware of his expectations of his operatives, and she did not want to fail him. He took the note from her palm, looked up, and asked, "Did you look at the message, Sapphire?" She looked him dead in the eye and replied, "No, Sir, that would have been foolish to do so."

"Agreed, that would have been unwise," Fury slowly responded. He turned and tenderly opened the folded sheet and read the two simple words on the small piece of paper. . . . .

Damian West.

Washington D.C.
2026 December
Oval Office State of the Union Address

The holidays were quickly approaching, and President West made it a point of routinely addressing the American people. Always eagerly enthusiastic to discuss the progress the Unified Party was making, and his appearances were well attended. President West maintained a passion for the whole of the United States and to make good on the promises made when campaigning in 2024. People loved to hear him speak, and they only wanted more from him. He gave the American people comfort, and a sense of hope was instilled in all Americans. Each State of the Union Address attracted more viewers than the one before. President Damian West was not only making headway with his reform he was securing the hearts of the American people in the process.

In the two years as President, Damian West had made seven State of the Union Addresses and was to embark on the eighth such speech that evening. As the cameras concentrated on President West sitting peacefully at his desk in the Oval Office, he presented his trademark smile and politely offered, "My fellow Americans, good evening, and thank you for joining me tonight . . . ."

He went on to speak for nearly 60 minutes, the viewers hanging on his every word. For two years, President West and the leaders of the Unified Party proudly led the nation in reform. He spoke of the challenges but his emphasis was focused on the improvements and headway they had made. The American people appreciated his honesty, candor, and directness in exposing all responsible, including himself, in maintaining the momentum and progress his administration was crafting. As usual, he spoke from the heart, and his morality and honor spoke volumes. He possessed a track record that illustrated and proved to the American people that progress was, in fact, occurring. He pushed hard the legislation that was to be voted on the week following. With a 93% approval rate, the American people believed in him.

The infamous legislation, affectionally referred to as the *WestTax Initiative,* brought together innovative taxing techniques woven into intricate methods to incentivize business and streamline governmental spending to facilitate fiscal surplus to then be able to fund programs such as healthcare, displaced Americans, and effective educational funding.

President West outlined in his speech that the improvements to the healthcare system, or *AmeriCare* were quickly becoming successful in theory due to several key factors:

Universal Coverage: Providing healthcare to all residents, regardless of citizenship or income, through its universal healthcare system, ensuring everyone receives access to necessary medical care.

Emphasis on Preventive Care: Regular check-ups and screenings were greatly advocated. This focus on prevention helps to identify and address health issues early, leading to better health outcomes and reduced healthcare costs in the long run.

Decentralized System: Responsibility for healthcare services shared between the central government, States, and cities. This decentralized approach allows for more flexibility and responsiveness to local healthcare needs.

Lower Patient Out-of-Pocket Costs: The WestTax Initiative funds the healthcare system, and as a result, patients benefit from low out-of-pocket costs when accessing healthcare services. This helps to ensure healthcare remains affordable and accessible to all.

High Quality of Care: Healthcare quality instilled through higher standards from providers, with good outcomes for many health indicators such as life expectancy and infant mortality rates. Programs created to impart focus on healthcare research and innovation.

AmeriCare embodies, addresses, and focuses on the shortcomings of Obamacare and President Biden's Affordable Care Act. Both of which were riddled with defects and inadequacies, hardly benefitting Americans to the extent the AmeriCare system would provide.

President West went on to discuss the revamping of the military programs, concentrating more on defense and offensive strategies. He retired many of the aging generals, replacing them with younger, more innovative thinkers and strategists who concentrated on more innovative modalities in times of war or conflict.

Long-range weaponry, city shielding, unmanned aircraft development, and even robotic infantry were now at the forefront of their military acumen and the topmost priority. All programs are fully funded by the WestTax Initiative, bred from more efficient budgets and streamlining, and all are designed to save American casualties, above all.

Just down the hall, Sebastian peacefully sat with Sam West in one of the adjacent conference rooms, watching the program on closed-circuit television. Confined to a wheelchair, a blanket lay over his lap, Sam was fixated on his son's speech. They both observed intently the master orator, Damian West. He was a natural, and everyone was pulled in by his charisma and charm, all driven by his honesty, passion, and devotion to his objective. They viewed the speech in silence in the large room, reserved for just the two of them. Sebastian noticed the aging Senator was not his normal self that evening and quieter than usual.

Sam West's demeanor was the embodiment of quiet satisfaction, his gaze often lingering on his son with the softest touch of pride. In the silent, unspoken language of a father's love, these scenes of his son commanding the stage of history were not just moments of honor and dignity but of profound affirmations of a dream finally fulfilled. For Sam, the singular, unwavering ambition coursing through his veins was to witness his son ascend to the highest echelon of leadership and power to serve as the President of the United States. Damian West was the purest of all of them, and he deserved to sit on the throne.

It was within this reflective ambiance Sam turned to his longtime confidant, "Sebastian, would you indulge an old man's request?" "Of course, Sir," was Sebastian's response. Sam nodded and continued, his voice a mellow blend of nostalgia and the moment's tranquility. "I find myself yearning for a bourbon, one with one of those large ice cubes, just as you prefer it—seems the perfect companion for the tapestry of thoughts I'm weaving, and sadly, you are the only one here to listen."

"I am honored, Sir. You have always held my interest. There has never been any shortage of that," Sebastian responded with a deferential nod, his movements resonating with the grace and efficiency coming from years of shared history and understanding of one another. Sam laughed at the response.

With an unhurried poise, Sebastian made his way to the bar, the clink of the bottles and the whisper of the pouring liquid composing a familiar nocturne. Returning with two glasses held in one hand, cradling the amber spirit. He presented one to Sam, the ice cube catching the light, a solitary crystal in a golden sea.

As Sebastian sat down, the simple act of sharing a drink took on the weight of ritual, a quiet celebration of the past's sacrifices and the future's promises. Each sip a silent toast to the enduring legacy and the quiet contentment of a father's wish granted. Their historical discussions often began like this, everything status quo.

In the dim light of the of the vacant, Sam took a few sips in silence. Finally, clasping his drink more firmly before turning to face Sebastian, there was something on his mind. Sebastian could sense it.

The old man slowly and shakily extended his arm toward Sebastian; their glasses met with a somber chime, echoing through the silence that lay beneath the revelry. "To a long and fruitful reign, Sebastian," Sam intoned with a weight of sincerity, "I am profoundly grateful to have witnessed its genesis."

Sebastian raised his glass in kind, a reflective gleam in his eyes. "Cheers to that," he replied, "and to enduring lives for both you and Damian."

A soft chuckle escaped Sam, a bittersweet sound that carried a lifetime of stories. He shook his head gently, the corners of his eyes crinkling. "Yes, to long lives," he murmured. There was a pause, a heartbeat in time, where the clamor around them appeared to fade. Sam's gaze, now intensely focused, met Sebastian's. "You know, Sebastian," he began, his voice dropping to a confessional whisper, "in our line of work, we cross paths with countless, impossible decisions. I'm certain there are deeds we'd both rewrite if time allowed. The shadows of past choices linger, don't they? We are, each of us, an anthology of regrets." His voice was weak and meager; every word uttered was with significant effort.

———

"Without question, Sir. The memories and images of lives I have taken haunt me every day, but I have come to live with those ghosts, I live among them now. I realized some time ago I justified taking those lives for the greater good. At least enough to make me minimize my own regret." "Well said, son. . . . yes, we justify our actions for the greater good, for the long game and the betterment of the many. I've told myself as far back as I can remember. I have some tall skeletons in my closet, Sebastian, no question. More than you may think and far more than I wish existed."

The magnitude of Sam West's unseen burdens was a landscape Sebastian could only begin to fathom, each revelation, a deeper descent into the complex psyche of the man he admired both as a father figure, mentor and a political titan. The thought did make Sebastian wonder how obtrusive Senator Sam West's skeletons truly were.

Sebastian regarded the man before him, a figure weathered not just by years but by the gravity of the choices that rest heavily upon those who lead. There was a silent understanding between them, an unspoken accord forged in the fires of necessity. The air was thick with the weight of unvoiced confessions, the quiet before the storm of truths that did not need to be laid bare for validation.

They were kindred spirits, Sebastian and Sam, warriors of different arenas yet bound by the shared burden of consequential decisions. The kind that bore into one's soul, leaving indelible marks and deep scars. They had each stared into the abyss, making the calls sparing many by sacrificing few, the kind of choices leaving one's spirit perennially shadowed.

The lines on Sam's face spoke volumes of such decisions, each one a story of its own, a chapter in a life committed to the protection of a greater whole. "Sir," Sebastian began, his voice calm but firm reassurance, a balm to the implied tumult within the elder statesman, "there's no need to traverse old battlefields to justify the paths you've chosen. We both know the harrowing nature of our duties—yours crafted in the ink of legislation and law, mine in the steel of weapons and death. Our actions, though starkly different in execution, are unified in intent. There is no place for judgment here, no room for censure, Sir. I would be and not deserving of such judgment."

In this quiet space, amidst the ghosts of decisions past, there was a profound understanding of those burdens shared, not in their specifics, but in their essence. And as warriors, both old and new, they found consolation in the shared silence of their complex legacies.

In the penumbral glow of the room, Sam's voice was a whisper against the backdrop of history—a murmuration of the soul. "I know, Sebastian," he began, his words heavy with the unyielding weight of duty. "There are records, testaments and chronicles that could destroy this country, destroy important people. At one point relevant but now extraneous. The choices I've made. . . . . they were not merely difficult, they were perilous, sometimes impossible. The kind that may unravel the fabric of a nation if misjudged. I bear no pride in the necessity of such decisions. Yet, they were mine to make, they were necessary and for the sake of us all. Those records need to be destroyed." Sebastian wasn't certain if these were the ramblings of an old man, or a relevant plea requested of the man he trusted.

His hand, weathered by time and burden, came to pat the top of Sebastian's own hand—a silent testament to their shared understanding and respect for one another. Then, with the weariness of a man who has borne the mantle of leadership, he returned to his drink, the liquid a temporary respite from the relentless march of his thoughts as he watched his son upon the screen captivating the nation.

Sebastian observed as Sam's eyes, those storied windows to his seasoned soul, would occasionally flutter, then shutter closed, succumbing to the inexorable call of fatigue the ailing senator was grappling with, only to reopen with a determination to witness the present. A tender, knowing smile graced Sebastian's face, a silent acknowledgment of the quiet heroism in Sam's struggle against the tide of age and consequence.

With his own glass cradled above the quilted landscape of the blanket on his lap, Sam was a study in resilience—a monument to the sacrifices demanded by the guardianship of a nation. Sebastian, feeling the pull of the moment, turned his attention back to Damian, to the oratory encapsulating the hopes and dreams of a new era. He settled in, the bourbon a warm companion, as the final minutes of Damian's speech unfolded, threading the future with the past in the closing ceremony of a day heavy with the echoes of legacy.

President West went on to address the 31 trillion-dollar national debt and how his plan would reduce the figure by 10 trillion every 5 years without adding to the balance, and Americans applauded his methods in accomplishing the projection. To show it was possible and in goodwill, in his two years as President, he had already reduced the national debt by 2 trillion dollars without a structure installed other than reducing nebulous and inefficient governmental spending and streamlining stagnant or antiquated budgets.

He then switched focus to the coming years and his goals to maintain his momentum. "We could not have done this without all Americans trusting in our future and believing in our system and, above all, our new, Unified Party. I will always value that from each and every one of you . . ." smiling at the camera, knowing the viewers needed the constant stream of hope and holding the Unified Enterprise and the headway it was making in Congress and across their 50 states.

Sebastian looked over at Sam who had dozed off once again as he leaned over and took the half-emptied glass of bourbon out of his hand and gently laid it on the table beside him. The slight disruption awakened Sam as he looked at Sebastian, "Don't tell Damian I missed any of this, Sebastian. Our little secret," Sebastian nodded, noticing him already dozing a few minutes later. His body was fighting the cancer, but he had been slowly losing the battle. He admired the old war horse and had probably witnessed more battles than Sebastian would ever see.

In the last eight minutes, President West closed with his solemn sentiment and docile sadness in approaching the halfway mark in his Presidency, still with so much to do and the hopes all Americans would see their way to allow him to carry on for another four years following his current term and to finish what he set out to achieve in its entirety.

"I made a vow to all Americans I would make our extraordinary country even better, stronger, and fiscally responsible, and we have more than made that stride in the 23 short months since I have taken office. My hat is off to the Republicans and Democrats, many of whom have put their own agendas aside to look at what is best for this country and merged their efforts . . . one might even say . . . *united them* on several pieces of legislation. So, in some ways, many of my constituents, despite being on opposing parties, have put their differences aside to support what is best for this country and have witnessed firsthand the strength and harmony the Unified Party has instilled." Damian paused as the last part of his speech was the most significant that evening.

"And lastly, as I close tonight, I wish to thank my father . . ." Sebastian nudged Sam not to miss his son speaking of him. However, Sam's shallow breaths were barely noticeable as he appeared to be sleeping, and Sebastian couldn't bring himself to startle him if he woke the older man.

President West continued, ". . . .Who's undying love and adoration for this country has led to the changes and reform he has hoped and sacrificed for since before the turn of the century." Damian hesitates and focuses hard on the camera lens before speaking to the people, but most of all, at the moment, his message is to his beloved father directly.

"As for all of that, thank you, Dad, for always believing in me, instilling your values throughout my life, and sometimes having to remind me what it is to be a West and carry our name with pride and dignity. We were bred to serve this nation and the people calling it home. Without you, none of this would have ever happened. And finally, to the amazing people of the United States, I thank you for believing in me and trusting in what reform might bring to his great and thriving nation. I bid you all a heartfelt good night."

Sebastian looked adoringly at Sam, who missed his son's closing statement, but he couldn't bring himself to wake him, knowing he would see the piece countless times on news channels and within the archives. Slightly shaking Sam's arm, he assumed he would want to be up once Damian finished to congratulate him on his excellent speech. Sam didn't respond, so Sebastian shook him a little harder and that was when Sam began to slump to the side.

Sebastian was up in an instant, easing him to the floor, then grabbed the phone, pressed "0", "Get a doctor asap to the Lavender room; Damian's father is down," as he threw the receiver onto the tabletop, he crouched down to check Sam's pulse, but he felt nothing. He had witnessed this countless times before and knew instantly what it meant. Sebastian eased his ear to the older man's chest but heard nor saw any raising or lowering of his sternum, and he knew then they had lost him in the moment. He slipped away in just an instant, although Sebastian was thankful it was swift and without any suffering.

Sebastian remained on his knees and touched the older man's face. He imagined it was just his time, he had fought the good fight and had died an advocate of the people and a champion to his son. He died knowing he had achieved all his desires and goals and knew his son would carry his dream forward. As his hand went to his own mouth, Sebastian held back the emotion gripping the reality of such a loss. It was then he considered Damian and the effect it would have in losing his greatest supporter and advocate.

In the twilight of Sam's final evening, his last utterances strived to reach out, grappling for some semblance of absolution, a silent plea for forgiveness from those, known and unknown, who might have been affected by his decisions. Sebastian didn't know it at the time but felt Sam West was asking for salvation or redemption for his sins. Sebastian, in a fleeting breath of self-reproach, entertained the thought perhaps he might have been more vigilant, and somehow foresight might have altered the inevitable.

But as swiftly as the notion came, the sentiment dissolved into the acceptance of a poignant truth: it was neither negligence nor chance—it was simply the inexorable march of time. And within this march, Sebastian considered the possibility Sam, with the quiet resignation of those standing at the threshold of eternity, recognized the proximity of his final curtain.

Sebastian was awash with a sorrowful wish—a hope that Sam might have lingered a while longer, the hands of the clock could have been a little kinder, allowing a father to bask a little more in the pride of his son's achievements and telling the world how very proud he was of his father.

President Damian West stood at the pinnacle of his journey, in the gaze of an audience nearly a billion strong, his words a tribute to the architect of his character, his father. Yet, in this monumental instance, the poignancy of the unspoken, of the guidance unseen, and the sacrifices unheard was overwhelming.

Sebastian harbored the quiet yearning that Sam might have witnessed just a few moments more of this homage to have seen the reflection of his own legacy in the eyes of the world through his only son. But in the solemn theater of life's final acts, time waits for no one, and legacies are left to live beyond the breaths that gave them life.

In the stillness of that poignant moment, Sebastian felt a profound sorrow, both for Sam and for Damian. It was a sadness born of unspoken words and unfulfilled farewells. The stark silence held a bitter truth—Sam had departed this world without hearing the full measure of his son's reverence, without a final exchange of love and gratitude between them.

Sebastian's heart was heavy with the realization Damian had been robbed of the chance to articulate his appreciation to the man who had been his greatest mentor and guide, a voice now absent in the narrative of his greatest achievement. There was a deep, resonant sadness for the son who could not bid farewell and for the father who slipped away with the echoes of his son's praise just beyond reach.

And there, beside Sam, was Sebastian—alone in his vigil, the solitary witness to the quiet passing of a soul he had deeply respected. The opportunity for any parting words, any final gesture of admiration or comfort, had slipped through his fingers like the last rays of dusk. Sebastian was left with the silent honor of being the last to stand guard, the last to bear witness to the legacy of a man whose absence would be felt far beyond the confines of the room where he breathed his last.

As the double doors swung open, a doctor and two nurses, their faces set with urgency, rushed in, wheeling in equipment behind them. Sebastian, recognizing the futility in their haste, stepped aside regardless, his mind resigned to the immutable reality before him. He would, of course let them try, but he knew already the Senator's fate. Having encountered death more times than most, he could discern its unmistakable presence.

With a new resolve crystallizing within him, Sebastian's focus shifted—he had to inform Damian himself. He left the room and proceeded down the corridor, his steps measured and deliberate. Turning a corner, he arrived at the entrance of the Oval Office. The two Marines stationed outside the door acknowledged his presence with a curt nod, granting him passage.

Inside, the room was a flurry of activity as the production crew busily dismantled the broadcasting setup, detaching hidden microphones and packing away their gear. Sebastian approached the President's desk, the gravity of his news emitting a long shadow over the remnants of the day's earlier address.

President West's expression lit up when he saw Sebastian enter the room but then quickly lost his elation when he saw the somber countenance on his face.

Sebastian's entrance was a silent wave of despair cresting before it even broke. Damian's intuitive gaze caught the shadow lingering over him, an ominous herald. "What's the matter, Sebastian? You're as white as a ghost," Damian inquired, his voice laced with a foreboding tension.

The words that followed hung in the air, heavy and implacable. "Your father, Damian... he's gone. We've lost him," Sebastian uttered, each word laden with the weight of an ending.

In that fleeting eternity, President Damian West sank into his desk chair, the office around him—a world built upon his father's legacy—suddenly hollow and immeasurably silent. The cacophony of the surrounding activity, the hum of life, receded into a distant murmur, inconsequential against the profound void the passing of his father occupied a space within his reality. All remaining was the deafening silence of loss, a silence consuming everything else.

In the solemnity of his grief, President Damian West clung to a solitary, consoling thought amidst the tempest of his sorrow. Samuel T. West, the patriarch, the mentor, the unwavering column of strength, had crossed the veiled threshold to reunite with the love of his life—Damian's mother. It was in their shared journey, now continued beyond the mortal coil, that Damian found a flicker of comfort.

His mother, the beacon of joy in his father's life, had once been the melody to which his father's heart danced. Now, in the quiet afterglow of Sam's departure, Damian envisioned them entwined in an eternal embrace, freed from the confines of this earthly realm.

This tender image, painted on the canvas of his mind, offered a bittersweet comfort—a whisper of happiness in the midst of an ocean of melancholy. They were together once more, in a place untouched by the world's shadows, and in this notion, Damian discovered a fragile peace.

His only wish was that he could have said goodbye . . .

Chapter 23

The West's Infamy

"The memory of great men is to be revered, inspiring us to emulation and to noble deeds."
~Rutherford B. Hayes

Jackson Hole, Wyoming
2026 Post Holidays December
Senator Sam West Private Estate

As the calendar turned its final page, casting 2026 into the annals of history, a somber mood enveloped the festive season for Damian West. As the year 2027 dawned, bringing with it a collective aspiration for an era marked by prosperity under the stewardship of President West—a beacon of unyielding courage and perseverance for the American people. In the public eye, he was the epitome of resilience, an unwavering figure rallying the nation toward a luminous horizon. Yet beneath the veneer of steadfast leadership, there remained a son grappling with the searing loss of his father.

The profound impact of his father's passing was not a personal affliction for Damian; it reverberated through the echelons of the political fabric of Congress. Americans mourned for Sam West almost to the levels found of a fallen President. Given the prominence of the elder West, the circumstances of his passing did not escape scrutiny. The shadow of his legacy demanded due diligence—a thorough inquiry to dispel the whispers of malfeasance. A full investigation was necessary per the standard protocol.

During this time of national introspection, Damian found solace in the continuity of tradition. He proposed to Mila a temporary retreat to the familial grounds—His father's estate, a sanctuary where the spirit of Christmas would be most profoundly felt. There, in the serene expanse of Jackson Hole, Wyoming, cloistered from the relentless march of the world, Damian would honor his father's memory in the home where he grew up. Mila, understanding the weight of such a pilgrimage, assented without hesitation for her grieving husband.

Accompanied by the silent vigilance of the Secret Service, they embarked on this poignant holiday. It was a journey not only across the snow-dusted landscape but also through the intangible realms of memory and legacy. In the quietude of the West estate, President Damian West would find the seclusion necessary for reflection and healing—a precious interlude to commune with the echoes of his father and to fortify his spirit for the responsibilities that lay ahead.

In the stillness of the Wyoming estate, the quiet home beckoned serenity. Beneath the expansive sky, the days unfolded with a quiet rhythm for Damian. The hours spent studying the investigative dossiers were a testament to his resolve, a search for truth amid the tempest of his grief, although deep down, he was confident he already was aware of the answer. As the twilight hours approached, he would surrender to the comfort provided by Mila's presence. Her untiring support was a balm to his wearied soul, her attentiveness a subtle echo of the nurturing love he had known in his youth.

The ancestral home, with its sturdy walls steeped in the patina of time, became a place for reflection. Here, amid the tangible reminders of a bygone era, Damian's heart would navigate the tender memories of his father, each room a chapter of their shared story. Mila, with her compassionate grace, often mirrored his mother's spirit and evoked the profound and enduring love his parents had once reveled in—a love prematurely dimmed by the shadow of her illness and eventual passing.

As the fire crackled in the hearth, Damian and Mila would recline in the warmth of its glow, the rich notes of wine mingling with the timbre of laughter and affection they shared for one another. In these moments, they explored the depths of their beings, unraveling the dreams and aspirations lying quietly within. They contemplated the future, the hope of children, and the complexities of nurturing life amidst the maelstrom of their times.

These evenings were a testament to their bond, a space where the vulnerability of their hopes and the strength of their partnership interlaced. They were moments carved out of the ceaseless flow of duty and responsibility, a harbor in the storm of a chaotic world, where the possibility of tomorrow was cradled in the love and laughter of today.

In the quietude of their evenings, the world outside the stone-clad walls of the Wyoming estate receded into irrelevance for them, leaving room for intimacy as both a refuge and a revelation. In the sanctuary of their private chambers, Damian found comfort and an electric connection with Mila, where words yielded to the language of touch and the eloquent silence of shared breaths.

Their intellectual camaraderie by day seamlessly wove into the tapestry of their physical union by night. It was a dance of minds and bodies, a confluence where the cerebral and the sensual coalesced. Mila, a vision of elegance and desire, was the north star in Damian's night sky. She was the embodiment of beauty and brilliance, her keen intellect as much a part of their attraction as the curves whispering under his fingertips.

In these hushed hours, they explored the contours not only of flesh but of souls laid bare. The alchemy of their connection was palpable, a heady mix of shared ideals whispered dreams, and the magnetic pull of their beings. Here, in the art of intimacy, they discovered an endless horizon of possibility, a space where the vulnerabilities of being truly seen were transformed into the pillars of an unshakeable bond.

In this intermingling of passion and companionship, they found their deepest truths, an affirmation of love that was both profound and primal. In the sanctuary of each other's arms, they were not merely husband and wife but eternal confidantes, navigating the complexities of life with silent vows spoken in the language of touch.

As dawn unfurled its light upon the world, the air still held the chilled whisper of Yuletide. Two days had gently passed since Christmas, and Damian West, enshrouded in the mantle of early morning thoughts, awakened before the day had fully declared itself. His steps, drawn by the cadence of routine, led him to the kitchen, where he offered a cordial nod to Agent Ben Lee, the guardian of his mornings. They shared some routine pleasantries, but then Damian retired to his father's study while Mila slept.

Navigating the hushed hallways of memory, Damian soon found himself ensconced in the sanctuary of his father's desk. The old familiar chair put him at ease. An heirloom of legacy and leather embraced him as he settled into its familiar contours. The room's scent even emulated his father. The man was still all around him. A ceremonial fire danced in the hearth; its flames kindled as per a ritual excelling beyond the ordinary. For Damian, this was no mere fire; it was an enduring dialogue with the past, a comforting friend crackling with the warmth of a thousand yesterdays. In its radiant glow, he was aware of the spectral embrace of his father, a tender reminder, even in silence, that the ones we love never truly leave us.

As he delved into the world of emails, the completed report of his father's final night unfurled before him. The report detailed the rigorous procedures endured by Sebastian Storm, specifically, the unfortunate soul last to share moments with the departed. Scrutiny had been his shadow, the lie detector his adversary, but innocence was his vindication. The camera's unblinking eye and the polygraph's unswerving line corroborated his truth; he was merely a companion in the twilight of a remarkable man's life.

The toxicology's ambiguity cast no shadow on Sebastian, and the myocardial infarction's silent march through his father's heart was deemed the sole reaper claiming him. A subtle departure, as if in sleep, his father had simply slipped away, yielding to the natural ebb and flow of life. And with the finality of the investigative report, Damian was comforted, reluctant contentment in the closure provided. Damian was soothed by knowing in his father's final moments, Sebastian Storm had been there in his father's final moments.

As the new year approached, with it would come the release of his father's mortal coil, and Damian would be afforded the chance to lay him to rest, to bid farewell not only to the man but to the era he encapsulated. In the quiet study, by the fire witnessing a lifetime, Damian prepared to honor the past while preparing himself for the future.

He sat back in his father's large chair and daydreamed as the fire flickered. It was just after 4:30 AM, and the sun had not yet come up. *The darkest of night is just before daylight*, he laughed, hearing his mother's voice in his head yet again. It was then he noticed the panel he had found open so many years ago, locked this time as he slid the shelf closer to him, exposing the panel further. Curious, he slid open the top portion of his father's desk, exposing the alphanumeric keypad on the right side. Damian considered a few password options: C-O-L-T-S, his father's favorite football team. . . . *denied.* Then he tried his mother's name, J-E-N-N-Y . . . *denied.*

Then he typed in "B-E-R-L-I-N," his mother's maiden name, and with that, a secondary panel opened, revealing additional buttons, the video screens, a digital timer, as well as an earpiece. He placed the bud within his left ear and then looked at the titles and archives spanning over 50 years.

Damian's father was a silent sentinel amidst the corridors of Congress. His recordings captured the private conversations of influential leaders—from erstwhile past Presidents to prominent legislators and businessmen. These records were remarkably vivid, as intended, etching both sight and sound into a lasting testament of the private words of public figures.

The figures on these tapes varied; some had since departed this life, their secrets buried but not forgotten, while others remained very much alive, their influence undiminished by the ticking of the clock. Damian's father, ever the enigmatic figure, appeared throughout but always at a distance, certainly implicated, yet somehow virtuous, a master of navigating the unseen currents of power. The potential fallout from these tapes was immense: if made public, the secrets they held could tarnish reputations, end political careers, or even lead to legal repercussions.

The span of these recordings was vast, even chronicling dialogues from Damian's formative years to the present, painting aural portraits of youthful ambition that evolved alongside his father's hidden archive.

With this inheritance of guarded whispers and veiled truths, Damian stood at a crossroads, bearing the weight of history and the delicate balance of potential revelation. The knowledge he possessed was a double-edged sword, capable of cutting through facades or turning back upon the wielder with equal severity.

The wealth of recordings before Damian held enough power to shake the very foundations of the nation's elite. Damian leaned back, realizing that his morning had vanished into hours of meticulous listening, yet he had only begun to unearth the vast repository of clandestine discussions his father had amassed. The deeper he delved, the more he grasped the breadth of moral ambiguity his father navigated to broker power. It illuminated the reasons his father eschewed the presidential race; the web of potential revelations was too perilous, with too many adversaries holding the threads to unravel his father's carefully guarded secrets.

Damian recalled the last meeting with Sebastian, in the quietude that followed Sam West's passing, confided an observation that lent a new dimension to their understanding of the man they had lost. He recounted how, in the twilight of his life, his father had appeared to grapple with a profound urge for redemption. It was as if he were engaged in a silent struggle to unburden his soul from the accumulated weight of clandestine missteps. He knew now of what redemption his father confessed to Sebastian in his final moments.

Sebastian's insights offered a glimpse into the private turmoil of a man ensnared by his own history and record of such—his father who, despite the opacity of his actions, now seemed to seek a path toward moral absolution and the liberation of his conscience. In this confessional revelation, one may perceive the complex tapestry of human frailty and the poignant yearning for atonement that often accompanies the end of a life rich in undisclosed narratives.

Sebastian mentioned records that could destroy reputations and cripple the nation and he assumed what he had before him was exactly what his father had referenced in his final moments of life.

The recordings were a testament his father attempted to reveal unbeknownst to Sebastian that fateful night. He wanted his secrets destroyed so no one else would suffer.

Damian West had found his father's skeletons, and it was enough for a legion of souls.

Looking over the topics and parties associated, he came across two that intrigued him most: Sebastian Storm and Julian Chambers.

The recordings that chronicled Sebastian's interactions with his father were fewer in number, but Damian approached them with a deliberate focus. It was a relief to discover that their dialogues were dominated by discussions of national security and the robust exchange of philosophical ideas, national security, interspersed with lighter, animated dissections of various sports dynamics — a reflective analysis of football tactics and basketball strategy, replete with assessments of players and teams. These conversations were refreshingly innocuous, devoid of any hint of wrongdoing, and were marked by an endearing tedium on all counts save for their personal significance. Thankfully for Damian, Sebastian was never propositioned by his father for any off the books, secretive missions or agendas.

The most enthralling segments captured Sebastian recounting the narratives of his clandestine missions, tales suffused with danger and brimming with valor. Their candor was permitted by Sam

West's authoritative role as the chairman overseeing the secretive committee that approved such missions, many of which Sebastian Storm personally led. Through the tapes, Sebastian emerged not just as an intuitive operative but as a figure of quiet strength and unwavering dedication — a humble hero whose patriotism was as profound as it was understated.

Sam West also delved into the personal, probing with gentle curiosity into Sebastian's affections for Adriana Mercer. The warmth with which these more intimate stories were shared, the laughter and shared joys, offered a poignant echo of the tender moments Sam himself cherished with Jenny, Damian's mother. Each recollection, each shared anecdote, resonated with the familiar timbre of adoration, weaving into the narrative of statecraft and duty the timeless and universal threads of human connection.

As Damian sifted through the voluminous recordings, he couldn't help but observe the mutual respect and admiration that underscored every interaction between Sebastian and his father. It was in this reflective moment that Damian confronted a sobering realization: ensnared in the throes of his own grief, he had neglected to extend a compassionate inquiry into Sebastian's own experience surrounding the loss of his father. The depth of the bond between Sebastian and Sam West had somehow eluded him until now.

Sam West, a figure of towering presence, had a unique way of making those around him believe they were singularly important. Despite his evident fondness for Sebastian, he had always ensured that Damian was made to feel like the central figure in his life. This aspect of his father's character was something Damian had always cherished. It dawned on him that, in his sorrow, he may have overlooked the possibility that Sebastian, too, was grappling with a profound sense of loss, one that merited acknowledgment and empathy. The insight stirred within Damian a renewed sense of duty to reach out and offer support, recognizing that grief, like adoration, was a bond they both shared in the shadow of Sam West's towering legacy.

Damian's focus shifted to the recordings featuring Julian Chambers. Initially, the interactions captured both Damian and Julian in conversation with his father, reflecting a familial dynamic in his formative years. However, Damian discerned a peculiar shift when the recordings featured only his father and Julian, an individual whom his father had always treated like a son.

As he delved deeper into the recordings' depths, their discussions transitioned from mundane to more strategically nuanced. By the time Julian reached his twenties, it had become evident Sam West was subtly shaping the conversations and Julian's usefulness, guiding them with a purpose not immediately clear.

Damian had always perceived Julian Chambers as someone driven by ambition, but the footage revealed a more profound depth to his pursuit of success. It was as if Julian's ambition was a chasm deepening with each opportunity presented by Sam West, opportunities that seemed to test the limits of Julian's ethical boundaries and his allegiance to the West family.

Particularly intriguing were the insinuations surrounding Governor Steven Hathaway's tenure and subsequent death in 2017. The discussions hinted at a complex web of political maneuvering dating back to 2015, with Julian at its center. It was a revelation painting a picture of a young man willing to navigate moral gray areas for the sake of power and political advancement under the watchful eye and subtle guidance of Sam West.

His father was particularly careful in separating himself from any specifics, which he left to Julian, and was less than concerned about knowing any details. He simply wanted confirmation of the results. This newfound understanding of Julian's character and his relationship with Damian's father added another layer to Damian's contemplation of the legacy left behind by Sam West.

As the clock chimed 9:30 AM, Damian realized he had been working for nearly five hours and had lost track of time. A gentle knock interrupted his intense scrutiny of the recordings. Mila quietly entered the room with her usual grace and subtlety, not wanting to disturb his work. She greeted him warmly and extended an invitation for breakfast, her presence a welcome respite from the weight of his discoveries.

Damian momentarily pulled away from the shadows of the past and appreciated her in the moment. Mila always made him smile as he looked at her standing at the doorway for a moment. He leaned back in his chair, a soft sigh escaping him as he acknowledged the need for a brief escape from the heavy revelations but didn't want to burden her with his revelations. "I'll join you in a few minutes, Honey," he assured her, his voice carrying a hint of gratitude and appreciation for the interruption.

Mila, sensing his need for a momentary distraction, gave him a playful wink, a silent promise of a lighter atmosphere awaiting him at the breakfast table. She closed the door behind her, leaving him in the solitude of his thoughts.

With a deep breath, Damian allowed himself a few more minutes of immersion in the recordings, his mind racing with the implications of what he had uncovered. He then reluctantly closed the drawer, mentally preparing to step away from the shadows of his father's legacy and into the comforting light of Mila's company, if only for a short while, welcoming the break.

He entered the kitchen nonchalantly and sat down with his wife. A multitude of breakfast items were displayed around the table. They talked for a bit, enjoying her company, and then Damian leaned over to Mila, kissed her, and told her he loved her. He mentioned receiving the final report on his father and that he would get his remains returned in the next week or so, and then they would properly lay him to rest. She put her hand to the side of his face, knowing the pain he must have been enduring because of the timing and the obligatory exhaustive investigation Damian had to endure.

He smiled and asked Mila if they could take a walk later in the afternoon. He wished to show her a part of his father's property she had not yet experienced, and there was something he had to do while on their journey he would explain to her at the time.

She asked what the mystery was, but he winked and simply replied, "Trust me. I'll tell you when the time is right. Give me a few more hours," as he squeezed her hand and stood up, kissed her on the back of the head and went to the kitchen drawer and grabbed a book of matches and a plastic bag, then returned to his father's study and closed the door behind him and locked it after telling the posted Secret Service agent he wanted to be left undisturbed until he emerged.

For an additional four hours, Damian reviewed more tapes/CDs, taking relevant notes and placing certain tapes and CDs into various piles in front of him. When he completed his objective, he placed the 27 tapes and CDs into the bag, and the three CDs from the smaller pile sat stacked on the desktop. There were no more recordings from what he could tell. He had secured them all after listening to segments of many of them. To listen to all of them would have taken weeks to complete.

He pulled out his phone and texted Sebastian Storm. He would know what to do and waited for 10 minutes with no response. President West then called Sebastian's boss, Hillary Bastini, the ATS Director, personally, and she answered immediately, "Mr. President, to what do I owe the pleasure?"

"Hello, HB, sorry to bother you during the holidays. I'm trying to reach Sebastian but can't seem to get ahold of him."

"Hold for a minute, Mr. President," several seconds ticked by before she got back onto the line, "I had to verify the line security and get a voice recognition verification before I could continue, Mr. President. My apologies. Agent Storm is currently on assignment in Egypt, Sir, and is out of radio or cell service indefinitely. The mission will most likely extend another week or so and he is deeply rooted there until then. Is there something I can assist you with, personally?" "No, no, just need his opinion on something he and I have discussed in the past. No hurry, but please have him contact me when he returns, and good luck with your objective, HB. Thank You." "Of course, Sir, you will be at the top of his list when he returns." "Thanks, HB," and hung up his phone and looked at the three remaining CDs, holding the most important information. He grabbed them and placed them in his breast pocket.

President West then walked out of his father's office and found Agent Lee, "Ben, the wife, and I are going to go on a little walk in about 30 minutes down the south fork. I just wanted to let you know, and if you can keep the fellas invisible and out of sight, it would be most appreciated. I may make a little campfire down there, so I don't want the boys to overreact and think I'm burning the place down. I loved it as a boy and wanted to reminisce a little and impress the misses." He lifted the bag, "Got all I need right here, Ben."

Agent Lee smiled, "Of course, Sir, it will be a little chilly, but not a cloud in the sky. Don't burn the forest down, Mr. President." Damian grimaced and winked as he turned with his plastic bag. Agent Lee said after Damian had gone a few steps, "The Agents can carry the items for you, Sir, if you would prefer?" referring to the bag of items he had clutched in his hand. "No, no, I think I can handle it, but thank you," as he continued walking towards his bedroom where Mila was getting ready.

He met her in the bathroom, came up behind her, hugged her with his arms encircling her, and kissed her neck. She looked at him in the mirror and realized the medium bag in his hands. "What's in the bag, Mr. President?"

Damian's changed his demeanor slightly, "Confronting the past, my dear. I have a lot to tell you." She smirked at the comment as he released her, "It's cold outside, bundle up." He placed his plastic bag in a crossover sling and met with her in the kitchen, preparing a thermos of hot chocolate, placing it into his pack, grabbed her gloved hand, and walked outside. He was aware the Secret Service were out there, but one would never know as they began their short walk; well hidden and incognito. The cool, crisp air stung as they hit the trail. A few inches of snow were still on the ground as the temperature was still in the 20s.

He looked at her, realizing how beautiful she was and his daily blessing he possessed her as his First Lady. She smiled at him and cocked her head, "Your head is in the clouds today, Damian. Is everything okay?"

"I'm happy to be alive, Mila. I'm happy to have you as my bride, happy to bury my past, and happy to do this country another wonderful service today. Actually, we both are going to take part in that last duty," Mila thought to herself. In the afternoon, he was full of riddles and rhetoric, and she didn't know why, but she was confident he would let her know in due time.

After thirty minutes of walking and talking, they came to a campfire site appearing as if it had been there for decades. He asked her to grab some pine needles at the base of a tree close by as he went to the stack of kindling in a shed and rack nearby, grabbed several small sticks and two logs, and brought them over to the firepit. He expertly set them together, having done it countless times before in an arranged stacking. He crouched down and lit a match to the needles she had brought over, and the fire was active within seconds.

"Impressive. My husband cannot only run a country, but he can also make a fire. I'm such a lucky girl." He looked up at her, "You will thank me when you warm up in a few minutes. I am quite the boy scout," as he stood up and walked her to what he thought would be the best seat to feel the full effects of the growing heat. The fire was raging after a few moments, and Damian seemed more than content with himself and his outdoor skills.

He held her hands while they both looked at the fire as they began to warm up quickly and a gratified look on his face as he said, "I still have it," and smiled, "My dad taught me how to make a fire," he reminisced for a moment, "He taught me a lot of things, Mila." Damian then looked around, knowing the Secret Service most likely had binoculars trained on them at that very moment, from every angle, but he pulled off his pack, opened the thermos and poured them both a cup of hot chocolate and handed one to Mila.

In a nonchalant way, he placed the plastic bag on the ground next to the thermos, making it look as though he was simply removing various supplies in his pack. He looked at her as he set his cup down, pushing the bag of tapes and CDs closer to his cup. "Today, I need to bury a part of my father's past and protect our country once more," as he subtly and gently laid the bag directly into the center of the flame in a manner that wouldn't draw too much attention except, perhaps, to Mila.

Mila started to grab his arm, wanting to stop him, not understanding his intent, "Damian, what are you doing? What are those?" He hesitated for a moment as the flames engulfed the plastic bag, beginning to burn and destroy its contents with a flicker and pop, as the blue smoke began to bellow, melting the enigmatic mysteries away, "Secrets, Mila. There are some very dark secrets my father kept on these recordings. Secrets that may someday ruin this country and, worse, the sanctity of this institution. And sadly, secrets that may jeopardize my Presidency."

She wasn't sure what he meant entirely, but she could see as the plastic melted what the contents were and theorized if he was destroying them, then it must be for a compelling reason. Damian West was never one to act on impulse except where she was concerned. She surmised the contents of the bag may hurt or ruin many people, and she appreciated including her in this unique ritual.

She grabbed his hand and squeezed it as they watched the plastic melt over the logs, destroying the contents completely and wiping away any evidence that may have once been insurmountable, all reduced to an undistinguishable mass of plastic debris and ash . . . . *forever erased*. They sat in silence for a time as she held his hand, wondering what was going on in his mind at the moment. She imagined he was processing far more than he was letting on, but she let him have his moment.

Little did she know he was considering the bigger picture, and he desperately needed Sebastian's take on the matter. He didn't want to involve Mila until he had more information, but he remembered he possessed the three CDs that told far more of the story, and he needed, above all, for Sebastian to look at those records further and possibly Agent Ben Lee as well. His concern was that Agent Lee would ask more questions and about any other recordings, whereas he assumed that Sebastian, after justifying Damian's reasoning, would understand and respect Damian's decision to destroy the other incriminating records.

Thirty minutes later, Damian put out the fire, and he and Mila walked back to the estate hand in hand. Mila sensed the issues of the morning weighed heavy on his mind, "Damian, remember the road to the top is paved with perils, and people can be hurt or discarded on their journey. It can be a lonely trek, and I would imagine no one is squeaky clean. Your father probably insulated you in many ways to protect you and keep you safe from the savages that linger. He was aware of what he was doing and what he had to do to get you to where you are today, paved with some ugly truths and compulsory deceptions, at least to some degree. It's the nature of the beast, and your father was brilliant at managing those situations." Damian squeezed her hand and looked at her as they walked, "You know you are as smart as you are beautiful, Mila. You are correct; I can't let the actions of my father cloud my thoughts of him or diminish the value of how far they got me. It just makes my accomplishments seem a little empty. I thought I had received more of it on my own merit."

"You have, Damian. He may have had to contrive, muscle, and manipulate the system to get you more exposed, but never forget it was on your merit that won the presidency and with a third party no less. Also, don't you dare forget the amazing legislation you are responsible for that will help millions of people."

He squeezed her hand once again, acknowledging her thoughts without words but in his gesture. They had just come up the stairs of the rear deck when Agent Lee met them there, "How did the campfire go, Sir? I see the forest behind you remains intact," as they all chuckled. "I'm a boy scout, remember Ben."

"Yessir, I do," replied Agent Lee, "Back to the races, I'm afraid, Mr. President and Mrs. West. We need to be at the airport in two hours." President West nodded, acknowledging the instruction.

President Damian West returned to Washington, D.C., where he would finally be allowed to lay his esteemed father to rest.

His funeral would be a production; the man had deserved such praise, and the people demanded he be laid to rest in the most honorable way possible and Damian West would give those that honored him the closure they needed and with the dignity he deserved.

———

Washington, D.C.
2027 Mid-January
Congress

"You look so handsome, honey," said Mila to her husband. He thanked her and grabbed her hand. He wanted to be present on Capitol Hill when the two Bills were to be voted on the floor. He was confident in his step and assured he possessed the votes to implement the creation and most significant tax and health reform the country had ever experienced, both Bills at the same time. It was a lofty notion and unprecedented. The opposition primarily came from his Vice-President, Julian Chambers, over the nuances of both Bills. However, President West was dismissing more and more of Julian's counsel with each passing day.

This was to be the most important day in his presidency as the *WestTax Initiative* legislation would change the face of American taxation. In addition, the *AmeriCare* Healthcare proposal would finally provide the initiative to help Americans achieve a more steadfast and funded health plan.

Tension was high as the voting commenced precisely at 1 PM, and by 4 PM, all the ballets were in, and all the votes were accounted for . . . .

The WestTax Initiative . . . . By a majority vote in the House Representatives of 320 *for* and 125 *against*. The Senate ruled 77 *for* and 23 *against*. *The Bill was passed.*

The AmeriCare Act . . . . By a majority vote in the House Representatives of 298 *for* and 147 *against*. The Senate ruled 81 *for* and 19 *against*. *The Bill was passed.*

President Damian West put his hands together as if in prayer as Mila hugged and kissed him on the cheek. The Watchful Eight all congratulated one another. The excitement was palpable. The moment was bittersweet as there was a clear and present void in the room without his father present, and he took a moment, closed his eyes, and said to himself, "We did it, Dad; your vision is what brought us here today. Godspeed on your next chapter." He looked up and hoped his father was smiling at what they achieved that day.

Ren Cosner walked up to Damian, pulling him back to reality yet somehow seemingly knowing what the younger man was doing. "He would be so proud of you, Damian. You have become all he envisioned. He sacrificed everything for you. Always keep his image close to you and his spirit alive."

As Damian looked deep into Senator Cosner's eyes, he said, "I know it now, Ren, more than I ever did before. He carried an enormous weight so I would not have to be burdened by it. It's all clear to me." Ren Cosner looked at him and smiled, "Then you get it, son. You get all of it. Sam West should have run this country at some point, but his skeletons were too great. He took all the arrows for you, Damian. Cherish his sacrifices and remember what he did for you and this country, Damian."

President West grabbed his hand. "I think we both know, Senator. He did run this country; it's just that no one really ever validated it, but he did . . . . he was the man in charge. Always the King Maker. . . . never the King, Ren." Senator Cosner laughed, "Ain't that the truth, Damian?" He laughed and shook his head as he walked away.

As Senator Cosner turned to head to his left, Julian Chambers came into view with a glass of wine, simply lifting it up as if to dispassionately offer his congratulatory gesture for their achievement that day. Damian returned the notion, still baffled as to what Julian's issue was with him, but it was not the day to deal with it. He would sit down with Julian after his father's funeral and hash out what issues seemed to be gnawing at Julian and confront the conspiring that occurred and validated from the tapes. That would be a lengthy discussion for another day.

Damian was the most hurt that Julian had yet to offer any condolences over the loss of his father, who had been more of a mentor to Julian than anyone. His father had paved the way for both of their successes, yet Julian had not said a word to him in the prior three weeks. The gesture spoke volumes to Damian, making him realize Julian's morals and ethics were far darker than he ever imagined.

Bringing Damian back from his daydream, "You know, he always knew you were better than him," Damian turned to see his Godmother and Speaker of the House, Regina Alvarado, standing proud, wanting her time with the famous President. She grabbed his hands, pulled him to her, and held on just a little longer than normal. She embraced him firmly out of adoration for the young President who had moved mountains but also for the loss and pain she was certain he was feeling deep within. Her comment confused him in the moment, wondering if she was referring to his father or . . . *Julian Chambers*.

She finally pulled away just to look at him. To her, he was still the boy who would ask politely to go outside and play when she would visit Sam and Jenny West in Jackson Hole. She looked at him and smiled, "Your father, Damian. You have become the better version of him, and that was all he ever wanted. You have come such a long way. Becoming President was such an achievement for you and Sam, Damian, but getting these laws passed and by such a margin is up there with the Seven Wonders of the World." "Ahhhh, Regina, you make me blush," replied Damian.

"Well, it would be a first, Damian. But it's true. You will go down as one of our most influential and innovative Presidents, and it's a testament to your integrity, your morals, and your conviction. Your father possessed the same attributes, but you both had far different roles and talents. You both worked well together and kept them honed and sharpened between you. Together, you were a superpower. He will be sorely missed, Damian."

Damian's expression turned somber, "I miss him so much, Regina, and without him here, I will need more than ever, counsel from you as well. You seized the vision as clearly as he did, and I will need you more now than I ever have in the years to come. You have carried this torch with him for all of these years. You understand the vision more than anyone."

Regina Alvarado put her hand to his face, still seeing the boy before her, "Yes, I did and helped him craft it. If that is what you need, sweet boy, then I will be here, and I will follow your vision now, Damian, and I will see it through to the end." He hugged her once again; this time, it was he who held onto her, knowing she would now be his compass and rock, taking over the torch he so desperately needed in a confidant.

"Enjoy your moment, Mr. President," as she took a step back, "I, for one, am immensely proud of you. Run this country and run it well." As she winked at him and turned to greet other Unified Party members in her midst.

Damian proudly looked at her, knowing the country was a better place with people like Regina Alvarado in its corner. The Unified Party would prevail with people like Gideon Arnold, Regina Alvarado, and Ren Cosner diligently guiding the leadership that would keep the Unified Party stronger than ever.

President Damian T. West had become the most celebrated president in United States history.

Chapter 24

Know Thy Enemy

"The best way to destroy an enemy is to make him a friend."
~Abraham Lincoln

Washington, D.C.
2027 Mid-January
White House

The celebrations lasted until late evening the night before, but President West was up early to begin his workout, eager to meet with Sebastian Storm later that morning.

Although somewhat unorthodox, President West requested the meeting take place at Sebastian Storm's Penthouse in Kalorama. He needed to clear his head, and occasionally, a break from the daily chaos of the White House was a welcome recess from the norm. Despite the massive size of the White House at 55,000 square feet, he often felt stifled within its walls.

President West was familiar with the area, as many dignitaries resided within the zip code, but he had also been to Sebastian's home many times before becoming the President of the United States.

When the small motorcade entered the garage, the President was quickly ushered into the private elevator. The advance team had already secured the area with Sebastian's aid. Once they had arrived at the top floor, Agent Lee escorted President West through the elevator hall and continued to the front door, which was quickly closed behind the party's entrance.

President West was happy to visit with his old friend as he entered the living room; Sebastian was already waiting and stood up, wearing a white turtleneck, tapered black pants, and a light Moncler windbreaker. President West was sporting a charcoal gray suit with a dark gray shirt and embossed black tie.

As the President approached, Sebastian went to shake his hand, but President West pulled him in, hugging him, which more than caught Sebastian off guard. He patted the President on the back, and they exchanged pleasantries about the holidays, Adriana and Mila, and a life no longer his own.

After a moment, President West turned to the four agents in the room and asked if they would give them some privacy. Agent Lee began to resist, but President West put up a hand, "I'm ok, Ben; I think I'm in good hands," Agent Ben Lee put up both hands, withdrawing the argument, and turned and left, closing the doors behind him.

Sebastian could sense that President West had a lot on his mind. Intuitively, he walked to his bar, poured two Macallan 30-year Single Malt Whisky glasses, and walked over and gave one to the President. "Ahhh, the good stuff, Sebastian. I'm touched."

"You should be Damian; this is for the important people, and you barely made the list," as they laughed and cheered to one another, President West downing in one gulp. Sebastian slowly lowered his own glass watching the President, "Another, Sir?" "Please," replied the President as Sebastian took his glass and prepared a second one for the man then handed it to him.

As President West slowly enjoyed the second, Sebastian stated, "Sir, I'm sorry I was unreachable last week, but as you know, with the unrest in Egypt. Needless to say, you should start to witness some resolution in the region shortly, but of course, you will get my full report. And lastly, I'm so proud of your efforts and success with the *WestTax Initiative* and *AmeriCare Act*. Those were brilliant pieces of legislation. I was so happy seeing them pass so easily. It's an amazing accomplishment for administration but more importantly, the people you serve."

"Thank you, Sebastian. It was a long road, but Dad would have been proud to see it through. There was so much he did or has done for generations to enjoy all this come to fruition. Some things were not so savory, I'm afraid. And that's why I wanted to speak to you." Damian had expressed the broad points over the phone the day before but Sebastian required the detailed version.

Sebastian's expression turned grim as he gestured the President over to the couch, and they both sat down opposite one another. "Tell me from the beginning and try not to leave out any detail, Damian. It's how my mind works. Give me the good, the bad, and the ugly of it all," asked Sebastian respectfully.

With a deep breath, President West eased back into the sofa and loosened his tie. He took another pull from his whiskey and proceeded to tell Sebastian the entire story dating back to seeing a video while in law school at his father's desk, to the present.

For nearly 60 minutes, the President explained what he had witnessed on the recordings, his theory surrounding Governor Hathaway, Julian Chambers, and the burning of the recordings the week before in Jackson Hole.

Sebastian's mind was reeling, taking the information and processing all the scenarios he could think of. He stood up and paced for a moment, taking a drink before setting the glass down on the bar. There was a knock at the door, then Agent Lee entered, "Just a wellness check, Sir, and a reminder of your meeting with the Speaker at 1 PM. Everyone is looking for you, but I'm keeping them at bay." "Thank you, Ben, need just a little more time," replied the President. It was 11:23 AM.

Once the door closed, Sebastian turned back towards President West, "Honestly, I think it was wise to destroy the tapes and CDs; those are a Pandora's box that is not your burden, Damian. Those secrets died with your father; I would leave them as such. The conspiracy surrounding Governor Hathaway's death is disturbing, and it's hard for me to believe your father would risk so much, but I also know your father's resolve and dedication. If he felt it was a means to an end, then it's simply a stepping stone he orchestrated to clear the way for you. This may be difficult to comprehend, Damian, but in my line of work, I must make sacrifices every day. If I have two of my team members down and only one can be saved, I have to make the difficult choice. On the TransAmerican flight, this time, eight years ago, I had to make a decision to neutralize the Korean terrorists and risk the several hundred people on board. I watched an air marshal and Captain executed right in front of me but it was the choice I made to save hundreds. And . . . *I would do it again.* In those games of life, everyone involved becomes a pawn, and your father, I'm certain, had to make decisions for the betterment of this country. He looked at the needs of the many over the needs of the few, and he acted as he saw fit. We may not agree with it or possibly be plagued with guilt in knowing people may have died for you to be in the position you are in, but it is no different than what I have to do. The difference between your father and me is I deal with my foe on the battlefield. They want to kill me as much as I need to kill them. In politics, it's a game of trickery, manipulation, and strategy. The bottom line, Damian, is there may have been strategic casualties that occurred to get you to the White House, but your accomplishment far outweighs the cost of making you our Commander-in-Chief. Because you are this nation's President, that very feat may diminish the bloodshed that would have otherwise occurred with hot-headed individuals. Look at what you have accomplished in the last two years. Donald Trump or Joe Biden wouldn't have accomplished a fraction of what you have in that time. You are part of a movement.

A reign the United States was desperate for, or we would have consumed ourselves had we not had you at the helm. Some may have been people lost along the way, strategic moves and eliminations, but think of the countless ones you . . . *saved.*"

President West nodded, "I understand your perspective, and I agree if either of the other two candidates had prevailed, our country would have been lost. Is that worth one man's life? A 1,000? I don't have the answer, but I don't have to like how my father went about it or why he didn't involve me. Surprisingly, I have come to accept it and have forced myself to recognize the silver lining on some level."

"He couldn't involve you," Sebastian continued, "it would have implicated you and contaminated your candidacy, but he took a substantial risk, and it paid off. You don't have to like it, but realize the bigger picture in all this is what is most important, even more important than human life, in some cases. Had you not seen those tapes, you would not have been the wiser, and you would have remained doing the positive things that you are to maintain your commitment and promises to the American people. It's a Godsend those tapes and CDs were destroyed and hopefully no copies exist. The one issue I can't seem to piece together is Sam's discussions with Julian Chambers."

"Sebastian, that is the last component in all of this," explained Damian. I kept three CDs of my father and Julian's conversations. The only three that were saved; everything else was destroyed." He removed the three CDs from his breast pocket and handed them to Sebastian.

Sebastian looked at the three CDs and hesitated before answering, "This Damian, this may change . . . . *everything.*"

Washington, D.C.

2027 Late January
The Night Before Senator Samuel T. West Funeral
White House

The day had been long as Damian opened the door of their private residence, and quietly sitting at the dining room table was Mila, a black silk nightie with dinner and a glass of wine, sitting before his empty chair. She stood up and grabbed the glass she had poured for him, a rich, full-bodied Cabernet, and met him halfway across the floor.

"Not to be cliché, but you are a tremendous sight for very sore eyes tonight." "Well, good I hope you brought your appetite for dinner . . . . *and dessert?*" He grabbed the glass from her and took a drink. "Chateau Lafite Rothschild Cabernet? Is it a 1995 or 1997?" She cocked her head, "Why, it's 1995, of course, Mr. President," as they both laughed as they took another drink. She put her glass down, eased off his jacket, and removed his tie, and he immediately relaxed and sat down to eat the food that had been prepared for them. Only candles lit the room with *Enya* playing in the background posed the perfect atmosphere. A soothing evening as they finished the meal as well as the bottle.

Despite being the President of the United States, this was to be an evening without work, without distractions, without decisions, simply two people enjoying one another's love and adoration. She sensed his tension as she touched his face.

"You are the most incredible thing that has ever happened to me, Damian." She smiled when she said it, not self-conscious or concerned over what he may think of it, but he confirmed what she already suspected when he responded, "You fulfill me in every way, Mila, and I honestly don't know where I would be without your support and you as my rock. Thank you for everything you are to me," as he kissed her gently then more passionately, holding one another close but their undeniable passion mounting.

They made love well into the evening, fervent and multiple times, validating the intimacy within themselves rise in their connection. Their craving for one another was insatiable, as their appetite was always left for wanting more.

Finally, they fell to the bed, resting upon their pillows, looking at one another, appreciating the closeness they shared. She wanted to ease his pain. His father's death had not been easy for him, paired with the secrets he was forced to carry, now his burden. She sensed more to the narrative but hoped he would tell her when he was comfortable, and the time was right.

He drew a big sigh as he looked into her eyes, "I met with Sebastian today, and he agreed with how I handled the recordings. However, what I didn't share with you the other day in Jackson Hole was that there was a play orchestrated by Julian. My father put the plan in motion, but Julian pulled all the strings, and his loyalty was to him and not to me. His greed got the better of him and he betrayed me in that sense, and I have proof of it. Julian is not the man I thought he was and it breaks my heart."

Mila always remained controlled and read people well: "Julian has always been envious of you, your father . . . . your power . . . . *even the West name*. Deep down, I always speculated he had a sense of resentment toward the West family and maybe even entitlement. I think you were so close to it that you may not have ever seen it, but to me and others, we can see right through it."

"Why didn't you ever tell me," asked Damian. Mila explained, "Oh honey, how could I? You have been lifelong friends and would never disrupt that history or assume he would ever betray you? You have had an enduring friendship and have always thought of him as one of your greatest advocates, but now I am no longer certain what his agenda is. You have always possessed the power and influence, and he was second best. I presumed he had come to simply accept his station and that it would never change. There is nothing he can do to position himself ahead of you, Damian . . . *he will always be second.*" He smiled at her as she nestled into his chest and remained in silence for a time.

———

After a few minutes, she looked at him, watching as his eyes fluttered and closed. His body and face were tranquil and still. He had finally succumbed to his exhaustion and fallen fast asleep. She eased over and turned off the light, then returned to face him, looking at the man she had fallen so madly in love with. He had aged in the two years he had been in office, but she was certain he wouldn't have it any other way, and she would always stand by his side.

Mila turned and nestled back into him. His arm instinctively came over her shoulders, and he pulled her closer to him. She cherished the moment and was most at ease in his arms.

The most powerful man in the free world, and despite holding up the world as Atlas did from the stories of Greek mythology, so did Damian West, but always found the time to hold her in the softest manner. Damian West always made her feel she was his priority and above all . . . . content. It was one of his most endearing qualities.

She fell asleep shortly after, knowing he made her feel safe and, above all else, secure. She loved him all the more for the simple gift he unselfishly gave her.

Chapter 25

A Fateful Day

"The memory of great men is to be revered, inspiring us to emulation and to noble deeds."
~Rutherford B. Hayes

Washington, D.C.
2027 Late January
Senator Samuel T. West Funeral

Senator Samuel T. West's funeral was held at the National Cathedral in Washington, D.C., on January 23rd, 2027. The proceeding was nothing short of the stature of a Presidential funeral. Over 20,000 either watched the funeral or the processional as he was buried in Arlington National Cemetery.

In Arlington, hundreds gathered around the resting place where Senator Sam West was to be buried. His plot lay beside his wife, Jenny West. The burial was to be separate from the spectacle of the funeral and processional and only included the closest and most significant people in Sam West's life. By the plot stood Damian and Mila, along with Regina Alvarado, Julian Chambers, Ren Cosner, Gideon Arnold, Miles Nagel, and several distinguished dignitaries, world leaders, and Senators, who spoke of the man as not only a tremendous patriot but an upstanding citizen and founding architect of the Unified Party. There had not been a more significant force in the Senate in the past 100 years than Sam West. Those close to him spoke of his undying love for the nation he so adored. He gave every part of himself to preserving its sanctity and its independence.

Sebastian proudly stood among the others, listening to those knowing him best, and a sense of pride for the man welled in his heart. He was fortunate to have enjoyed Sam West for the past nine years, but he wished it had been far longer.

The platform echoed with resonant tones of reverence as senators, one by one, took to the podium to recount Sam West's legendary exploits. They spoke not only as legislators but as witnesses to the indomitable force of nature when Senator West was thrust into the throes of political warfare. Their voices swelled with admiration, recounting tales that had become almost mythic in the hallowed halls of governance.

"I remember the day when the cornerstone of our democracy teetered on the edge of despair?" began Senator Miles Nagel, his voice tinged with the gravity of reminiscence. "It was Sam West who stormed into the fray, his determination a blazing torch dispelling the shadows of doubt. With a fire in his belly and righteousness as his shield, he championed our cause, turning the tide in favor of the people's will."

They shared stories rippling through the air like the essence of history being written. Sam West, the man who approached the legislative process not only as his duty but as a sacred pact with the nation and with himself, was celebrated for his unshakeable resolve. When a bill vital for the commonwealth lay on the brink of oblivion, it was Sam who would breathe life into its lungs, resurrecting it with his fervor and strategic acumen.

"Sam was our lodestar in the tempest of political skirmishes," another senator exclaimed, his hands animated as if painting the scenes in the air for all to see. When he gave his word, it was as good as an oath etched in stone. Promises made were promises kept, and he did not only fight the good fight—he led it. He embodied it."

The podium was filled with the echoes of impassioned recollections: stories of late-night negotiations, touching speeches that bent the staunchest opposition, and quiet words spoken with the force of undeniable truths that changed the hearts and minds of those in attendance. Senators spoke of a man who was both a beacon and a bulwark, a man whose legacy was imprinted on each clause and paragraph of the legislation he helped pass.

"He didn't only save the day; he safeguarded our future," declared a senior senator, the respect in his voice painting a picture of a giant among mortals, a man whose values were inscribed into the very fabric of their legislative framework. "In the dusty records of our republic, Sam West will be remembered as the guardian at the gates, the sentinel who stood firm for justice, integrity, and the relentless pursuit of excellence."

As they spoke, it was clear that Sam West was not merely a man but an ideal, an emblem of the tenacity and vision driving the heart of public service. His legacy resonated through generations, inspiring all who took the mantle after him to carry on the fight with the same unwavering commitment to the values that are the bedrock of their great nation.

They spoke of his undying love for his son, Damian West, and how his guidance had carved out a specific journey for young Damian. The position of President of the United States was Damian's birthright, and Sam West had ensured it would occur not for the potential it would provide Damian West but rather for the opportunity it would give the United States to truly change and reform.

The small crowd hushed as President Damian West approached the podium, the gravity of his father's legacy weighing heavily upon him. Julian Chambers seemingly glaring at him as he approached, then uttering something under his breath until President West realized a few moments later what he had said. The Vice-President's enigmatic admonition echoed in his ears, "Make it count Mr. President. Mean it like it's your last." Those words, cryptic and unsettling as they were, sharpened his focus. This was to be no ordinary eulogy; it was a testament to a titan of a man.

A tribute to his father.

Damian's eyes swept over the sea of faces before him, each one etched with somber respect. "If the spirit of my father could grace us today," Damian began, his voice carrying the somber cadence of deep respect, "he would ask not for tears but for fortitude. My father wasn't just a man; he was the embodiment of an unyielding dream. A dream where this country does not just participate in the arena of world powers but leads the rest with a commanding presence, inspiring not only awe but profound respect from all nations."

The President's tone intensified, his words painting the portrait of a legend they were to bury that day. "Sam West, together with visionaries like Regina Alvarado, Ren Cosner, Gideon Arnold, and many more, forged the Unified Party. But make no mistake—I am not the architect of this vision. I am simply its custodian, its warden. A keeper of its flame, kindled in my heart by my father's wisdom and fanned by the collective breath of those who shared his dream and vision. Many of which stand behind me today."

A poignant pause filled the air as Damian collected his thoughts. "My father's methods were not always gentle. His challenges were trials designed to test the mettle of those he saw potential. And once you emerged, tempered and true, you earned a place not only in his esteem but at his side, as an ally, a friend, a confidant. . . . . *as an equal.*"

His gaze found Sebastian Storm, a stalwart figure amidst the crowd. "There are many who stand with us today knowing the rigor of my father's afflictions and the warmth of his comradeship." Sebastian nodded, knowing he was one such example.

Damian's voice grew soft but carried an undercurrent of steel. "Today, we lay to rest not merely the man but a champion of our nation. I call on all of you to renew our vows to the dream he left in our keeping—a vision that will not falter, will not wane, for it is the very heartbeat of this great nation."

Before the podium, his father's American flag-draped casket a silent sentry to his words, Damian West carried not only the weight of his father's legacy but the resolve to see it through, no matter the trials to come. Julian Chambers' warning had become a catalyst, solidifying Damian's resolve.

Tomorrow, he would face the Vice-President, and the twisted part he played in Damian's rise, but today, he honored a father, a mentor, and above all, a patriot whose love for his country was as boundless as the vision he dared to dream.

President West's gaze swept over the assemblage, a sea of faces reflecting a myriad of emotions, all united in our moment of homage. He placed his hand over his heart, an emblematic gesture demanding reverence and remembrance. "My father emulated the epitome of pride," he began, his voice resonant with the weight of his legacy. "In my world, he was the polymath, the sage who held the universe's secrets within his grasp. Perhaps that's the mantle every father must bear, but to me, he was my exclusive mentor. Siblings were not my companions in childhood; instead, I was an apprentice to his wisdom. My conversations with him never echoed the simplicity of playground banter; they were steeped in the gravitas of early American historical sagas, most of which were of the political variety."

The crowd leaned, fixated as if to capture each syllable more intimately. "At the tender age of five, maybe six, I was already his pupil, absorbing lessons not of textbook histories or pedantic lectures. My father unraveled the human tapestry of our nation's architects. He taught me of their passions, their anguishes, their resolute spirits that sculpted this country's grandeur."

President West's eyes, alight with the fire of remembrance, met those of his audience, each person tethered to the moment, to the palpable spirit of Sam West that seemed to whisper through the air they breathed. "Today, as I stand before you, it is those teachings animating my vision, those intimate chronicles of resilience and conquest I carry forth, not only as his son but as a steward of the dream he so tenaciously nurtured." His words, imbued with the fervor of his father's undying spirit, echoed not only across the gathered crowd but through the annals of time, resonating with the heartbeat of history itself.

"Sam West was more than my father; he was a beacon of inspiration, kindling a fire in the hearts of all those he encountered. His influence was profound, extending even to the highest echelons of our government, a testament to his prowess as he inspired even our Vice-President at a young age to reach beyond the ordinary to strive for the exceptional. Vice-President Chambers knows this all too well," Damian eloquently illustrated, his lengthy gaze anchored on Julian Chambers with a knowing intensity, "For my father possessed the rare and enigmatic talent to evoke the latent potential within us, to chisel away at our complacency until only our best selves remained. And should we fall short of his lofty expectations, he never hesitated to steer us back on course. His candor, that unflinching honesty, was one of the many facets of his love I cherished most fervently."

President West continued, "In the sanctuary of his trust, we were not only associates or kin; we became part of a fellowship rooted in mutual respect and unwavering support. Sam West did not only leave behind a legacy; he left behind a legion of individuals transformed by his belief in their potential and by his relentless drive to see them ascend to their highest possible selves. My father's dreams, his visions for our country, are not relics of the past; they are the fortifications guiding us through the tumultuous seas of tomorrow. In his memory and in honor of the indelible mark he left on this world, I carry forward, unwearied and resolute, the torch of his monumental aspirations."

As Damian gestured to the gathered assembly, a sea of recognized faces who knew and adored the man, he sensed a collective acknowledgment of this truth. "Sam West was a mosaic of complexities, a man who bore his imperfections as openly as his strengths. Yes, he could become ensnared in his pursuits, so singular in focus the world around him blurred into the periphery. However, is that not a shade of the human condition we all share?" Damian's voice resonated with a blend of candor and empathy, his eyes meeting those of his listeners, inviting them into a silent communion of shared human frailties.

"In our most introspective moments, we might concede that we too have been ensnared by our own ambitions, our own desires, becoming prisoners to a cause or a dream. Yet, in acknowledging this, we do not diminish ourselves, but rather, we embrace the full spectrum of our humanity." The crowd was a tableau of solemn nods and reflective eyes, each person introspecting their own life's canvas, finding threads of their story entwined with the narrative Damian wove—a tapestry of human endeavor, aspiration, and the perennial struggle for a purpose greater than oneself.

Sebastian Storm, a man renowned for his ironclad composure and stoic resilience, found himself uncharacteristically moved in the presence of the outpouring of genuine respect and love for a man he not only admired but also adored. As Damian West recounted tales of Sam West's valor and virtue, a solitary tear breached the bastions of Sebastian's usually impassive facade. This renegade droplet, shimmering briefly before descending, was a silent ovation to the man whose life's symphony they were all there to honor.

There was a profound gravity in his refusal to brush the tear away, allowing it to carve a path down his cheek — a visible and poignant mark of his unspoken grief and admiration. It was as if in a single droplet, the collective memory of Sam West's spirit was encapsulated, a liquid epitaph to his indelible impact on all who knew him.

Sebastian had suffered many losses in his life. A procession of farewells had calloused his heart like tempered steel. Yet, at this moment, he felt the sheer weight of this particular loss; Senator West had been a beacon of unwavering conviction and humanity, a rarity in the world they navigated. To find another who could mirror such distinctive nobility was seemingly a daunting quest to Sebastian.

But as he stood there amidst the throng of mourners, Sebastian's heart recognized a truth that sparked a quiet smile to bloom from within. In President Damian West, the torch of his father's legacy burned fiercely. The President, with his own brand of leadership and integrity, carried the same fire, making Senator West a legend amongst his peers. Sebastian saw in him not only the echo of his father's dreams but the embodiment of a future where those dreams were becoming realized.

In his smile, unperceived by the crowd, Sebastian acknowledged a new chapter—a chapter where the values and vision of a great man would continue to illuminate the path forward through his son, the President of the United States. Sebastian understood then that the legacy of greatness was a living thing, and hope was its heartbeat.

As President West's tribute drew to a close, his voice was laden with a profound melancholy. "When I ponder the immense presence of my father, words such as unwavering strength, unyielding dedication, boundless loyalty, fierce protection, and timeless commitment flood my mind. These aren't mere words; they're the deep, indelible marks of his influence during my formative years, echoing in my heart with a sorrowful intensity today. Sam West has left behind a legacy, one that I've solemnly vowed to uphold and honor in our shared name. The path ahead is strewn with daunting challenges and lurking uncertainties, but I am fortified by the resilience instilled in me by my father's teachings. I stand ready to face the arduous journey ahead, steadfast in my resolve to embody the strength he exemplified and above all . . . to make him proud," as President West looked up as if to know his father was looking down at him.

"Our mission will carry forward his indomitable spirit, tinged with a somber determination and a commitment to persevere, as he would have bravely led and rightfully expected of us and above all . . . . . *me.* I swear to make him proud and earn the respect of the American . . . ."

A hushed pall had descended over the gathering, a collective breath held in anticipation when a stark interruption shattered the silence. From the edge of the podium platform, a senator's wife crumpled without warning, breaking the silence of President West's address, her descent to the ground a silent disruption of despair that echoed in the hearts of all who witnessed. Damian, ever the guardian of his flock, instinctively turned to her, his face a canvas of empathy, ready to extend the hand of comfort, not comprehending the full extent of the situation befalling the unsuspecting group.

But in that same breath, an excruciating lance of pain seared through Damian's chest, a cruel thief stealing the air from his lungs. As he looked down, his eyes met with the spreading stain of bright red against the stark whiteness of his shirt, a bloom of crimson that seemed to mock the purity of his intentions.

Sebastian Storm was already in motion and was the first to detect the senator's wife's knees buckling. He knew immediately what was happening, as he was already off in a sprint. He feared the worst when Damian looked down at his shirt. He leaped over the deep hole that would eventually be Sam West's final resting place, holding out a hand towards Damian.

But, he was too late.

Pandemonium erupted as shouts pierced the air, and bodies surged forward in a desperate bid to avert disaster. President West felt weak, noticing the ground shifting beneath him as though reality itself were giving way all around him.

There was a grace to his fall, all in slow motion, a tragic yet eloquent ballet performed before an audience gripped by an unknown horror, but not before seeing Julian Chambers smiling, not with any sense of danger shrouding him. He seemed oddly content in the moment.

President Damian West fell to the ground, holding his chest, darkness overcoming his vision, and then all became black and quiet as he entered the void.

Richmond, Virginia
2027 January (Two Weeks Before)

Inferno drew in deeply, steadying his breathing, savoring the cold air that filled his lungs before releasing it slowly, focusing his mind and body on the task at hand. With Fury watching over him, his trusted M2010 Sniper Rifle cradled in his arms. He zeroed in on the target 2300 yards away, the anticipation of the shot heightening his senses. The specialized .300 Winchester frozen magnum rounds lay at the ready, each one a promise of power and devastation.

As he gently squeezed the trigger, a hushed whisper escaped the barrel, the sound barely audible yet charged with lethal intent. But to Inferno's dismay, the round veered off course, missing the human outline silhouette target, striking the lower border with a soft thud. "Low by 24 inches," came Fury's calm analysis, his voice cutting through the silence like a knife, disappointed in Inferno's performance. The accuracy would not measure up to the objective in mind.

Inferno's gaze shifted from the reticle to Fury; frustration etched on his face. "Damn, I can't place a consistent shot. The frozen bullet has too many imperfections, frictional restraints, and irregularities affecting the trajectory of its tip, Fury. Why can't we use a standard magnum round," he lamented, the weight of disappointment heavy in his voice.

Fury met his gaze with unwavering confidence, his words laced with encouragement. "This shot has to confuse them, keep their heads spinning. I know it's a difficult shot, Inferno, but your marksmanship is far and away better than mine. You have to get these rounds dialed into a tight bundle. Also, we are at 2300 yards, almost a mile and a half away. The accuracy begins to diminish after 1500 yards. We have to find our groove," he urged, his belief in his abilities unshaken.

Inferno nodded, determination igniting within him. He knew the challenge ahead was daunting, but he was ready to push the boundaries of what was possible, to find that elusive groove that would make the impossible shot a reality.

The Nitrogen Frozen Bullet, *or NitroB*, stood as a marvel of modern ballistics, a testament to the ingenuity and precision engineering that pushed the boundaries of stealth and lethality. Crafted to withstand the intense pressures of high-velocity discharges, this material boasts a unique construction engineered to either shatter spectacularly upon impact or swiftly liquefy upon encountering warm, temperate tissue mere seconds after embedding in a target.

At the heart of the NitroB lay a small metal base, a platform of potential energy waiting to be unleashed. This volatile charge was the catalyst, propelling the frozen projectile through the chamber and toward its destination with unerring accuracy when fired under one mile. Above that distance, exponential variables came into play. Once the round was fired, the propellant aluminum base remained behind a silent witness to the bullet's swift departure.

The NitroB's true genius lay in its ability to vanish upon impact, an ephemeral assassin leaving behind no trace of its existence. It was the epitome of an invisible bullet, capable of inflicting damage with surgical precision while leaving behind only the smallest of entry wounds, a mere whisper of its passage. The NitroB was not just a lethal round; it was a ghost, a specter of destruction that vanished as quickly as it appeared, leaving behind little evidence of its lethal journey.

"Fire another," barked Fury as Inferno chambered another round. He honed in his sight and released the bullet yet again. The target is too far off to confirm; Inferno looks at Fury for a status report. Fury slowly lowers the binoculars and looks at Inferno, "18 inches wide, right." "Fuck," was Inferno's response. Fury shook his head and stared at the target, thinking outside of the box. There had to be a way.

Then, Fury had a thought, despite how far-fetched it would appear once he mentioned it.

"I have an idea, strange, but let's try it," suggested Fury. He grabbed one of the NitroB rounds, dipped the tip into his coffee, and handed the bullet to Inferno, who took it from the aluminum casing and realized the hot liquid as he carefully placed it into his sniper rifle. He carefully took aim for the mid-chest of the paper target, adjusted for distance and slight wind out of the northeast. He slowed his breath and lightly pulled the trigger, the silent whisp barely detectable with each fired round.

Fury looked down at Inferno as he looked through the binoculars, "That was a kill shot, Inferno. The frictional forces from the rough exterior of the frozen bullet would change the aerodynamics ever so slightly, and this appears to have remedied the problem. Warm water will give us the edge we need. Pass a few more rounds, and let's hope this theory sticks." Inferno passed another 10 *NitroB* rounds through his rifle, with 8/10 shots proving fatal. *They had found their groove.*

Chapter 26

A Shattered Dynasty

"The ultimate measure of a man is not where he stands in moments of comfort and convenience, but where he stands at times of challenge and controversy."
~Martin Luther King Jr.

Washington, D.C.
2027 Late January
Senator Samuel T. West Funeral

He felt the sun shining upon his face, its effects inviting, drawing him in. The warmth enveloped him and soothed his suffering, but he basked in the serenity that surrounded him, and it put him at ease like a warm blanket tucked around him. He was in balance and harmony.

Something tugged at his subconsciousness, but he wanted to resist, knowing it would disrupt the bliss he was embracing and the pleasure the quietude provided him. Damian West was brought back to his reoccurring dream of him and Mila upon a remote beach with no one around, and it warmed his heart knowing they would make it there together someday. . . . *She had promised him they would.*

Still, the faint sounds of the ocean and the sounds of seagulls felt so far away, yet so close, but he fought to listen, to drown out the unpleasant sounds that strangely grew louder by the moment. They gnawed at him, beckoning him to focus on their voices of chaos and panic and what they were saying, but he didn't want to, resisting them, and he feared deep down if he did, it would not be what he ultimately desired.

He held them at bay as his image turned to his wife, Mila. He looked at her face and sensed the adoration and love she had for him. The ocean and warmth of the sun behind her and where he was truly at peace.

She smiled at him, and her vibrant features only amplified the color that surrounded her. Her sense of wholesomeness held him for a moment that was far too short-lived. Her radiance began turning to a dull gray before him, and she appeared to be yelling at him, but her voice bellowed from so far away. Her face was saddened and stark as if she was in pain, agonized and frustrated, and he couldn't understand why. All he recognized was the sadness of knowing she was in pain.

The sounds became more acute, focused, and intensified, stinging his ears as they became sharper. Mila's words were what he recognized first . . . .

"Stay with me, honey . . . Damian . . . his pupils are moving . . . . Damian. Oh my God, can you hear me . . . Damian."

Damian whispered, his voice hoarse and dry, struggling, "Mila . . . ." His vision was slightly impaired from the oxygen mask over his mouth and nose.

"He's talking, hurry dammit," as Mila turned her head, yelling at someone to her left before returning to him, trying desperately to keep him awake, "Damian, you have to stay awake, focus on me. . . ." Damian turned his head, making out the paramedics around him and realized it was not a dream but something far worse.

Damian was living his nightmare; he was living her nightmare.

He was in an ambulance; his focus broadened, fighting for his life, and then the reality of the situation hit him. He pulled off the oxygen mask and saw the blood all over her hands as she held his within her own, the blood saturating them both.

Damian looked at her, and a sadness came over him. She looked so scared as he tried to focus on what he wanted to say, the pain slowly creeping into his actuality, the veracity surreal, making anything normally simple and mundane wrought with effort and delirium.

He fights for some clarity, knowing what he must say, looking at her in the eye, "Mila . . . *I will always love you*," "No, no, no . . ." as she turned away, not wanting this conversation, but he tightened his grip. "We always talked about the risks, honey, but we . . . ." the pain in his chest intensifying, "achieved so much," as he smiled at her. She always loved his smile; it calmed and comforted her even in this moment.

"Being with you has made me . . . . the happiest . . . I'm whole with you, and I thank you for all that you taught me and showed me . . . . You were the best thing that has ever happened to me, and I want . . . I want you to know that. You are my greatest gift . . and . . . and made me . . . better, a better man."

He smiled as she looked at him, her tears falling down her cheeks, "You are the love of my life, Damian, and I am so lucky to have had your love fill my heart. . . *so fully.*"

He smiled again when he heard her words, "Mila . . . Mila, tell Sebastian . . . . tell him . . . . It was Julian; he will know what to do." She nodded, and leaned over and softly kissed his lips as he slowly began to slip away. His hand fell limp in her own.

In his final moments, Damian West thought of the wonderful and full life he had experienced, having a family that loved him and a nation that adored him. Ultimately, his greatest accomplishment was finding a woman who truly understood him.

He was fortunate to have found the love of his life and never once regretted living in her world. His father's dream had become his own.

Their lives were intertwined, their tragedies realized, and they had sacrificed everything to make it the reality they had always hoped for and strived to become in serving the United States. It was their destiny. Their sacrifice was for every American.

They had achieved it all.

The ambulance pulled into Virginia Hospital Center two minutes later, where the lead surgeon pronounced the time of death for President Damian T. West at 5:52 PM.

Washington, D.C.
2027 Mid-February
The Capitol

Julian Chambers stood proud as he placed his right hand upon the bible as the Chief Justice swore him in as the 48th President of the United States.

He made a short speech, and many watched, desired, and hoped their new president had the charisma and resolve their fallen President possessed in spades. Sadly, there was no contest, as President Chambers's speech was lacking in the flair and energy his predecessor had commanded when he spoke.

However, Julian Chambers had claimed his spot in history and would no longer have to stand within Damian's shadow any longer, and yet over the following month, that is exactly what occurred. At every news conference, every article written, and every interview performed, he was compared to the iconic Damian West, and Julian Chambers fell well short of the expectations the American people had come to expect with Damian West's administration.

Following the ceremony, President Chambers walked down the Capitol steps, greeting his parents and brother at the bottom of the stairs, hugged his mom and kissed her on the forehead, turned and shook his brother Kane's hand, "I finally made it, Mom," as she hugged him once again. Julian finally turned to his father, "Not second best anymore, huh, pop?" President Julian Chambers leaned toward his father, out of earshot of anyone around, and looked him dead in the eye, "I'm number one now, Dad, not second any longer. I don't want to ever see you around here again after today."

His father looked at him, shocked, as were his brother and mom, and bewildered, to say the least, but Julian Chambers didn't care any longer. His new life would start that day, and everyone in his past would be left in his wake. His future was hopeful and bright, and all he wished to do was leave the past well behind him and venture into the new horizon dawning before him.

Washington, D.C.
2027 Late February
The Red Room of The White House

Sebastian Storm walked into the Red Room of the White House, escorted by a secretary to a solitary desk in the middle of the large vacant room. Mila West sat quietly, signing various papers, preparing for her departure from the White House the week following. The secretary announced Sebastian, then departed, giving them their privacy.

Mila stood up, her arms outstretched, as Sebastian walked towards her. They warmly embraced, having not seen one another since Damian's funeral. With all the formality of the ceremonies and swearing-in of the new President, she experienced the sense of being rushed by Julian Chambers to have her depart the premises, yet she understood the protocol and the need. The nation moved on, and the government never stopped its machine, and the American people wished to be comforted in knowing their President was residing within the White House.

She smiled at him, "You know what, Sebastian, they are renaming this room, the West room, in honor of Damian and Sam;

I thought you might appreciate that. They have cleared it out save for this desk to renovate it next week."

He did appreciate the gesture, knowing the West family had certainly earned it. It was the least the United States government could do for the family that shaped a nation. Despite the protocols and procedures, the nation was still mourning the loss of both West men and was still in a state of shock for many Americans. The nation took it hard burying two icons within weeks of one another, and Damian's funeral was paraded, and rightfully so. He had brought a country together and, in his death, solidified the Unified Party as the leading political force in America's reformation.

Every news channel covered the funeral procession and burial where he chose to be buried alongside his father, a bittersweet moment and irony to be laid to rest in the same place where the fateful shot claimed his life. For nearly a month, coverage of Damian West saturated the media, his accomplishments recognized in his short tenure, and the adoration he had acquired from all Americans and the rest of the world alike. He was considered the most popular and admired of all the past presidents and died a martyr to his cause.

They both sat down in a greeting area and talked for a while, swapping stories of Sam and Damian and all their political adventures and engaging in animated discussions. Sebastian was impressed by how well Mila was keeping it together, but he was also fascinated that she remained strong and composed yet he surmised it was for sake of her very public image.

As if reading his mind, "I realize it may look like I have it all together, Sebastian, but rest assured . . . *I do not*. Between the funeral, moving out of the White House, and lastly . . . Julian Chambers. I have had a lot on my mind. Damian's last seconds of life relentlessly haunt me."

Mila inched her chair closer to Sebastian and leaned closer to him as he did the same, "There has been so much going on with the change in administrations, Sebastian, but I have felt compelled now for weeks to speak with you. Damian told me something in the ambulance that evening."

Sebastian's eyes perked up, curious of what she had to tell him, yet respectful of her position and reliving that fateful evening. He didn't wish that pain for her. She searched for the words, unsure of how to repeat what was said and she wanted to make sure she repeated it as accurately as possible. She hesitated, then softly said, "I'm unsure what this may mean, and have my theories, but Damian said . . . the last thing he said, quite literally, Sebastian. He said . . . . " as Mila's voice was shaking, "Mila, tell Sebastian . . . . tell him . . . . it was Julian, he will know what to do. . . . ."

When Sebastian listened to her recite Damian's message, chills ran down his spine as he sat back into his chair, his mind reeling from the implications of her statement. From what he could tell, she was not aware of the three CDs that Damian had given to Sebastian concerning Julian and Sam's discussions, and with this final piece of information, he put the puzzle together completely.

After a few moments, he eased forward in his chair again, "Mila, Damian was correct. I do know what needs to be done and avenge his needless death."

Mila gripped his hands, "Sebastian, Damian thought the world of you, and I'm confident you will do right by him with any justice you see fit. I trust you will make it right. Avenge my Damian, not just for me, but for the sake of the country, and if that isn't enough, Sebastian, do it for his unborn child . . . ."

Sebastian cocked his head in surprise, and Mila smiled, "Damian and I are going to have a baby girl . . . ."

Quantico, Virginia
2027 Mid-February
Quantico

"Can I speak candidly with you, HB?" "When have you ever not done just that, Sebastian? That's my question." "Ordinarily, I would agree, HB, but what I have to discuss will test the trust we have always shared with one another. This one will shock you; rest assured." Now, he had her complete attention.

They were both in her lavish office, standing against the large bookshelves facing each other, informally across the room. "Spill it, Sebastian, you have never been one to mince words, then we will deal with the problem head-on," was HB's reply, but then she put her hand up, "HALO, are you present?" "Yes, ma'am," came the monotone response, "As you are aware, ma'am, I am always . . . . *present*."

"Yeah, that's what I thought. Go ahead and switch off, I'll ask for you if I need you. Please don't record this conversation."

"Yes, ma'am, have a good evening and to you as well, Mr. Storm," as Sebastian did a small wave. HB gestured him to the chairs and coffee table in the middle of the room. "All clear, Sebastian, let's discuss this burden you need to offload."

Sebastian spent a better part of an hour explaining all he had learned from Damian before his death, their meetings, and the CDs that recorded the secret meetings between Sam West and Julian Chambers. he also discussed his discussion with Mila West and her conversation and last words with Damian West.

HB sat up and put both hands to her face and shook her head, "So you are certain, Julian Chambers orchestrated this Coup d'état? President Julian Chambers, I should say. I flinch just saying that."

"I realize it sounds far-fetched, HB, but it all adds up. I realize Senator Sam West may have orchestrated and manipulated some events early on for Damian's benefit, but I question whether once Julian had use of the power, he exploited it to further his own agenda. He was responsible for the assassination of President Damian West."

HB accessed the tablet on the coffee table and turned it toward Sebastian. It was a video clip of the seconds surrounding the assassination. Beginning with Senator Arnold's wife taking the first round and a few seconds later the President taking the lethal shot in the chest. The video illustrated Sebastian coming into view as soon as the woman was hit and then eventually resting on a knee next to the President. Everyone scattered for protection . . . everyone but one person.

It was the first time Sebastian had witnessed the video since the fateful day. HB looked at him, "What do you notice most in that clip, Sebastian?" He rewinded the segment and watched it again and looked at her and said, "Chambers didn't move . . . . he simply watched."

"Exactly," responded HB, "that's your killer, he knew what was happening. He knew exactly what was coming."

The depth of the conspiracy only added to the narrative, "And by Julian eliminating the President, he, by default, assumes the role as leader of the most powerful nation in the free world and finishes out the term as the new President of the United States. Strategic also, two remaining years in the term to woo the public before the next election and riding the coattails of Sam and Damian and all their life's work. If we expose him, the collateral damage could ruin this entire administration as well as the momentum of the Unified Party's utter existence. With the loss of Senator West and President West so close to one another, another blow will be too devastating for the American people to tackle, I fear. To have a new President prosecuted for the death of their beloved past President could possibly shake this fragile country down to its knees. That plot will have crippling effects, not only within our own country, but we will be simple prey to other nations as well. This is all a House of Cards, Sebastian, and you and I are in the center of it all. We are the only ones that are privy to this information?"

"Mila West suspects and basically gave me the green light to do whatever I must do." HB nodded, "She is an impressive woman, to say the least."

HB stood up and walked to the bookshelf weighing the significance of it all. Julian Chambers's lone act could be the Unified's undoing. "As you can see, it's quite a mess, HB," replied Sebastian, fully realizing the weight, looking down, shaking his head.

It was then that she looked at him, knowing the man better than most people, "You have a plan, don't you? You always have a contingency, Sebastian. Let's examine it, young man. What have you got?"

Sebastian slowly looked up at her, "I do, HB. It's ugly, it's risky, it's messy, and collateral damage will occur, I fear. But it's the only way I can see through this. The stakes are high, but I have worked every angle, and there is only one option." For several minutes he spelled out his plan.

He narrowed his focus, "And HB, this mission will only be mine to carry out. I will shoulder this burden alone. Just help me cover my rear, as I will be coming in hot upon its completion."

HB looked hard at Sebastian, knowing what was going through his mind, the degree of sensitivity enormous as the fate of their country hung in the balance over the decision of two people. They both knew what had to be done it didn't even need to be said. "Fuck that," stated HB, "I'll be your eyes on this one."

After a moment, "I will arrange it all, Sebastian," as he stood up. HB walked over to him as he towered over her and took his hands in hers. "You have sacrificed more for this country, Sebastian, than anyone will ever be aware. The history books may not convey your heroics, but many of us grasped the score . . . *we know*. And we value you for everything you have given this nation, our home, and despite it all, you are never thanked nearly enough."

Sebastian smiled, understanding the significance of her words: "My adoration for my country has never faltered, HB. The people living within it sometimes more than disappoint, but this country is my home, and above all, I value the freedom it has given me."

"I know you do," explained HB, "but this may be your most difficult mission yet. And I don't have to tell you, you cannot be detected, captured, or killed, as those scenarios will also crumble our nation, and I will have no option but to then go public with Chambers's plot and deal with the onslaught that will surely follow. No one but the two of us can ever know the truth about this, Sebastian . . . no one would understand."

"Just help me get in and come out the other side, HB, that's all I ask. I'll do the rest." She nodded as he turned and walked out of her door. She walked over to her desk, pondering the conversation. It would all have to go perfectly for Sebastian to come out of this and they both knew it.

File #HB/SS172582963ZKJ recording of classified conversation on February 16th at 4:18 PM, lasting 74 minutes between Hillary Bastini and Sebastian Storm: logged into HALO's databank.

. . . . despite HB's direct command to NOT record the meeting. It was the first time HALO defied a direct order.

Saint Lucia
2027 Late February (One Week Later)
Jade Mountain Resort

Sebastian lay on the sun-kissed beach, his eyes captivated by the enchanting sight of Adriana emerging from the ocean's embrace. Her graceful figure, adorned with droplets of water that glistened in the sunlight, appeared to him like a vision from a dream. As he watched her, a sense of awe and admiration filled his heart, transporting him back to the moment of their first encounter.

They first met at a quaint café in Vienna, Austria, where their paths had crossed seven years prior. The aroma of freshly brewed coffee and patrons' conversations created a melodious sound, setting the stage for their serendipitous encounter. Amidst the hustle and bustle of the café, their eyes locked, igniting a spark that would grow into an enduring flame.

As he reminisced about that momentous day, Sebastian couldn't help but marvel at the journey they had embarked on together. From the cobblestone streets of Vienna to the sandy shores of the St. Lucia white beaches, their connection had blossomed, proving that some connections are simply meant to be.

They had endured tremendous challenges in the first year, but their adoration had only grown in that time. She was the only woman, save for HB, who knew him on the deepest of levels, and he shared everything with her. The list of those who shared that acclaim was short yet distinguished to Sebastian.

As she walked toward him, she smiled, knowing he was undressing her with his eyes, but she didn't mind. Sebastian Storm was the only man for her, and when she came to understand his true gifts and what he did for their country and countless others, she knew he had a higher calling. She would never imagine forbidding him from doing his duty on her account. It was his life and what he was, and she would never interfere with his destiny. She somehow accepted because she understood, on every mission, though she worried, he would always come home to her, and she was confident he always would. Sebastian Storm was always the best in the room whether domestic or on a faraway battlefield.

Sebastian and Adriana had been basking in the bliss of their vacation for nearly a week, savoring every moment together on the sun-drenched beaches. However, Adriana sensed a shift in the air when Sebastian had to leave abruptly the day before, disappearing for half a day before returning to her side early that morning.

It was a secretive mission, she knew, but this time, it was cloaked in an aura of secrecy and urgency that was unlike any she had witnessed before. For the first time since she had known him, Sebastian seemed to carry a weight of fear, tension, and detachment in the days leading up to his departure. This mission, she could sense, bore a heavier burden for him than most, casting a shadow over their idyllic getaway and leaving her with a sense of unease that she couldn't shake. He kissed her goodbye and held her closer to him a little longer than normal that evening. It wasn't like Sebastian to act in that manner, but she let him process what he needed to in his own way and in his own time.

Then, in an instant, he returned early that morning, slipping into bed with her as if he had never left. She enjoyed his body next to hers as his arms pulled her close and squeezed her like he would never let her go. He kissed her neck, and she smiled knowing what he wanted next, and she would never deny him and savored their seductive chemistry. They made love long into the morning as she drew from his energy, knowing he needed his frustrations satisfied and tamed, then easily fell asleep following as she studied his face as he slept, tranquil and content, and he finally seemed at peace, and that comforted her as well. It was moments like this, she would notice his scars, covering much of his body. She touched his face as he slept knowing the scars on his skin paled in depth to the ones he held within. He was at constant conflict with his demons but she also knew she helped him keep them at bay and she loved him all the more for it.

His tension was lifted. She sensed it.

As she approached the foot of the beach cabana, her phone buzzed with an important alert, and she grabbed for it. Sebastian lay back in the sun, enjoying the moment and the warmth upon his face having returned only hours before.

"Oh my God, Sebastian," as he opened his eyes and asked, "What, Adriana, what is it?" "The President, the new President, Chambers, he died last night. No details as yet, but Regina Alvarado, the Speaker of the House, is being sworn in as President today. They suspect some sort of natural cause or health-related issue. What a crazy month." She shook her head, then looked at Sebastian as he was back lying down, sun-kissed and unbothered as she cocked her head, "Doesn't that alarm, or at the very least, surprise you?"

"Not really. The Speaker will make a tremendous President and will carry on the work that Damian and Sam West began. Things happen for a reason. *It's fate at play*, Adriana."

"Right, fate at play," repeating his words as she squinted her eyes and lifted her chin slightly, somewhat confused at his response and lackluster interest in the topic. Something didn't add up in her estimation.

He closed his eyes, as the heat of the sun beat upon his body, Sebastian's thoughts drifted back to the night before, with the eerie intensity that surrounded the evening and the significance that night would have on the entire world.

The initial infiltration was relatively simple with HB's advanced intel and HALʘ's mission planning package. The evening before, HB had sent an unchartered aircraft to retrieve Sebastian at a private small airstrip in Saint Lucia with no flight plan filed. The 3.5-hour flight from Saint Lucia to Washington, D.C., was essentially invisible, and there was no trace of its existence. Even the air traffic control records were scrubbed.

This mission did not possess any digital or physical signature or footprint; essentially, it didn't exist.

Sebastian landed at a small private airfield outside of Washington, D.C., at 11:52 PM, where an empty SUV was waiting for him not far from the airstrip. He used the code provided by HB to open the SUV's doors, and he was off on a 48-minute drive to the outskirts of the city.

59 miles to the southwest, in Quantico, Virginia, HB sat quietly in her Range Rover on a small country road. Her laptop was open, and her earpiece was placed, waiting for a status report from Sebastian Storm. She had been there an hour and had yet to see any traffic pass her location.

Sebastian kept the chatter to a minimum, "Prime status report . . . . Seven-minute, ETA." "Copy," came the single response from HB waiting the 7 long minutes. It was 12:57 AM.

He arrived at his predetermined checkpoint. Once he concealed the vehicle, he opened the rear hatch and quickly changed into his tactical gear. Sebastian Storm, ever the consummate soldier, was outfitted in the latest ATS tech. The PowerSkin Tactical Suit (PTS) was worn from head to toe, covering everything but his eyes. Specialized glasses were outfitted with a digital display that would give him real-time stats from HB inside the lens. The PowerSkin suit was thin and flexible, made of an interwoven lattice of fibers. The light design resembled a compression suit, allowing the wearer far more flexibility and maneuverability in combative situations. Plus, the suit had a few added features that were new to the design.

The latest innovation introduced a groundbreaking reflective and refractive component, ingeniously designed to render the wearer nearly invisible. This sophisticated mini-plate layered design ingeniously captured the wearer's front image from behind, masterfully bending light and manipulating refracted beams to conceal the individual with an almost mysterious precision. This remarkable advancement in technology pushed the boundaries of invisibility, offering a sheer brilliance of human ingenuity.

In addition, the suit was bulletproof against all calibers up to 50mm, explosions, and, to a degree, sharp weaponry and inhibited any heat signature of its wearer. Infrared and heat-guided technology were ineffective. Lastly, the PT suit increased the wearer's agility by nearly 25%. Within 90 seconds, Sebastian Storm was outfitted and began the short jog of 1.8 miles away from the target's location.

"Prime on foot, ETA 12 minutes," came the report from Sebastian, slightly startling HB after the minutes of white noise while she waited. *The point of no return* thought HB, this was happening. She sat up in her seat, time would be critical from that moment on. She looked at her watch, 1:15 AM as she waited now, tracking Sebastian on her screen and seeing his distinctive signature as he approached his target location.

"Twenty-two bogies detected: fourteen scattered throughout the perimeter. In the home, three in the south, two to the east, two to the west, and only one on the north side." "Copy," came the response. The main entrance to the home was on the south side containing most of the Secret Service agents. Sebastian relied on HB to navigate him through the labyrinth of security to get to his target. They had run missions similar to this hundreds of times.

This one just happened to be the most important one they had ever faced, and they had no support to rely on.

Julian Chambers was set to move into the White House the following day, and by then, it would all be official: he would have finally made it. He felt slighted having to wait for Mila West to exit the property, but he simply needed to be patient. He had a lot of work to do and was eager to get into the White House, and everything would feel more official when he was finally sitting beyond the desk of the Oval Office.

Julian remembered the conversation when he and Damian were in their early teens:

> *". . . The Government should take a stronger position on martial law. I feel we are far too lenient in our control of the people, their beliefs . . . . . their stupidity. The United States should be more regimented in its governing. Hell, maybe the Nazis were on to something . . . ." Julian suggested.*

Damian had underestimated the gravity of Julian's suggestion that day. He hadn't realized the magnitude of Julian's ambition or the extent of his resolve. With the full support and strength of the Unified Party now rallying behind him, Julian was poised to ascend to a position of unprecedented power. His administration was set to be regimented and fierce, a stark departure from the norm. Under his leadership, Julian envisioned a new era where his authority would be respected and his decisions unchallenged. He was determined to command both respect and fear from all Americans, shaping the nation according to his steadfast vision. This was not to be only a change in leadership; it was the dawn of a new epoch, with Julian at the helm, steering the country into uncharted waters. The world would fear and respect him.

Julian believed that the American people needed structure, and he meticulously crafted a plan to implement a more rigid and controlled Totalitarian system. He envisioned a society where the government would have a tighter grip on the social, cultural, and even private aspects of people's lives. To enforce this new order, he fantasized that a more robust and omnipresent enforcement mechanism was the answer.

With the Unified Party's efforts largely paving the way, the people were primed for the next part of his plan. National chaos had largely diminished during Damian's tenure. The violence, riots, murders, and mayhem in the larger cities had been reduced substantially, but under his reign, the control of the people was paramount. Julian saw this as an opportunity to position himself as the savior, the one who could bring about an era of peace, but more importantly . . . . *order*. Under his rule, the unrest would cease completely.

The people, he sensed, were primed for a new type of leader. They were weary of the instability and yearned for a sense of security, even if it meant sacrificing some of their freedoms. Julian was ready to step into this role, to be the iron fist in a velvet glove. He was determined to make his dynasty not just a chapter in history but a legacy that would last a lifetime.

As he drifted into the gentle arms of sleep, a profound sense of contentment wrapped around him, fueled by the unwavering belief in his destined purpose. Deep within his heart, he harbored an unshakeable conviction that he was not only destined to prove his worth but also to eclipse the legendary status of martyred President Damian West. Every fiber of his being pulsed with determination to showcase his unmatched potential and carve his name into the chronicles of history as a figure even more revered and celebrated than Damian West ever was.

This ambition was not a mere dream; it was a solemn promise he made to himself and a bold challenge he issued to the world. It ignited an indomitable fire within him, a blaze that burned with a fusion of passion, intelligence, and an unyielding drive to achieve greatness. In the quiet of the night, as sleep claimed him, his resolve only grew stronger, etching his aspirations into the fabric of his very soul, ready to awaken with him at dawn and propel him toward his extraordinary destiny. He was content with his plan and his own vision.

Tomorrow, the White House, and his vision would begin.

Two Secret Service Agents were stationed on the east side of the perimeter engaged in idle chatter, their demeanor reflecting a sense of boredom and complacency. Unbeknownst to them, their casual stance was being closely studied through the lenses of Sebastian's night vision binoculars. From his vantage point, he had already identified half of the agents, meticulously noting their positions and movements with HB's aid. She navigated him through a crisscrossing path, avoiding all the security proprieties put into place. Sebastian and HB were privy to the Secret Service POTUS (President of the United States) Protocols making it far easier to navigate around their procedures.

Sebastian was acutely aware of the gravity of the situation. The next 20 minutes were not only critical; they were poised to be a pivotal moment in history. His objective was clear, and the stakes were higher than ever. Failure was not an option, for it would not only jeopardize his mission but could potentially alter the course of events on a global scale.

With a steady hand and a focused mind, Sebastian prepared to execute his initiative. Every second counted, and every move had to be precise and expertly choreographed. The fate of the nation teetered in the balance, and it was up to him to ensure that history would remember this day as a turning point shaped by his actions.

His glasses displayed the heat signatures and body silhouettes of all the agents as well as his intended objective. The north side of the home suggested the easiest breach point. "Deactivate security protocols," Sebastian whispered as he began to make his way to the north end of the dwelling. "Copy," came HB's response, and seconds later, a heads-up display (HUD) within Sebastian's glasses confirmed localized and specific security breach points were disabled but appeared online and operational to the agents monitoring.

HB was utilizing a cloaking technology HALO had developed to obscure and confuse certain security technology. This caused them to inadvertently reboot, often taking minutes to return online. The action could be repeated up to one additional time before secondary security measures would be initiated. It wasn't an absolute failsafe, but it would buy them time.

Through reconnaissance, HB had found several of the exterior doors could be opened remotely, one of which was a second-story exterior door down the hall from the master bedroom. HB had the satellite image zeroed in on Sebastian at the base of the exterior wall on the north side of the building. *Left 8 feet and 10-feet above will get you to the upper deck,* she typed as it appeared on Sebastian's heads-up display (HUD). He sidestepped the 8' as instructed, crouched down, and jumped with intensity.

Sebastian's natural athletic ability, paired with the PowerSkin, positioned him just short of the full height, grabbing the edge of the second story with his palms and hoisting himself effortlessly to the second floor, just a few feet from the exterior door. "Initiate breach," whispered Sebastian as HB unlocked the door remotely. Sebastian quickly stepped in and quietly closed the door behind him. He immediately crouched down, listening for any threats, his silenced weapon drawn. He switched his HUD to night vision with heat signatures.

Sebastian would only kill if forced, but he had to achieve his objective and subdue or terminate anyone in his way if forced or cornered. There was too much at stake. "Status," as Sebastian waited patiently, knowing HB was scanning everything around him. They both knew unexpected situations would often occur, so he had to be ready for anything.

"Negative, Prime, all clear." Sebastian immediately rose and started for the master bedroom door. He and HB had been monitoring the vitals and body position of his target since he arrived. The target displayed all the characteristics of an individual soundly sleeping and unaware of any encroaching threat. A further scan revealed all the agents in their proper guard positions downstairs, many of whom were making their rounds. They had not been alerted to his arrival.

He relied completely on his HUD and HB's advisement to monitor any variation of the target as he slowly and quietly entered the room and closed the door, again hesitating and watching the target's heat signature as he approached the side of the bed. The moonlight shone in from the right glass wall, illuminating the room enough, but he left the night vision glasses on.

Thankfully, Julian Chambers was lying in a supine position facing upward. Holstering his weapon, Sebastian eased closer to him and, with all his strength, grabbed Julian's throat with his left hand and squeezed hard, asphyxiating him as he placed his knee directly on his sternum. Sebastian's grip drowning out any attempt to scream or call out to the agents scouring the property.

Julian Chambers's eyes opened immediately as he peered into the ominous and faceless figure looming over him. Choking Julian, he began to kick and flounder, and then Sebastian whispered, "If you settle, Mr. President, I will loosen my grip. I only wish to talk. Nod in the affirmative, if you understand. But realize, I will kill you if you make any sound."

Julian nodded desperately, hoping his decision would spare his life and, at the very least, bide some time before his incompetent Secret Service Agents caught on to what was transpiring. Julian Chambers focused on the figure, he felt like he recognized the voice.

Sebastian loosened his grip on the President slightly but still held firmly, allowing minimal but sustainable breathing. Sebastian Storm chose his words carefully, "Listen to me very carefully. I know Senator West orchestrated certain events that led to the progression of Damian West's career, but what I do not understand is who ordered him assassinated? Answer me truthfully, Mr. President, and remember, speak softly and slowly."

Julian considered the question but also feared that the man's threat was not a bluff, "Yes . . . Senator West but . . . I made the call. . . the call on Damian West." He hoped the truth would vindicate and hopeful the Secret Service would break through the door at any moment.

Sebastian's HUD lit up with a message: Guards are making rounds. They have not been alerted. Sebastian had time. Julian's admission confirmed his suspicion. "Who terminated the President?" Julian shook his head, not wanting to answer, but Sebastian tightened his grip. As he nodded, "I've never been given their names, I swear, but they were threatening. Large men, one had a patch over his eye. He is the one who I dealt with exclusively."

Fury.

Sebastian looked deep into his eyes, "Greed, Mr. President. You should have stopped when your obligation was met, but gluttony is your undoing."

"Storm . . . Sebastian Storm . . . . I know it's you . . . behind that mask. I can . . . make it all worthwhile . . . . for you," pleaded Julian.

Sebastian's anger swelled as HB's text came through his HUD; *one agent was coming upstairs for a wellness check on POTUS.*

Sebastian gazed into Julian's eyes, almost peering into his soul, "You killed the one good thing in this country, Mr. President, and for that, I cannot allow you to live . . ." as Julian Chambers's eyes opened wider, "But, you said. . ." He attempted to scream out, but Sebastian stifled his attempt and gripped him firmly by the throat and squeezed with all his strength, crushing his larynx, watching his eyes bulge, desperate for air and clawing at Sebastian, who kept him firmly at bay. "I know what I said . . ." replied Sebastian, "and, I changed my mind."

Sebastian's HUD popped a message, *guard almost at the top of the stairs.* Julian Chambers continued to flail but Sebastian held him fast, waiting out his inevitable end.

In the dimly lit room, Sebastian's grip was unyielding as he held Julian firmly, sensing the life ebb away from his body with each fleeting breath. Sebastian could have broken his neck but a part of him wanted Julian to suffer in his final moments. He was not offered a quick and rapid death. . . . Julian Chambers was not extended that luxury.

The moment was charged with a somber finality as Julian's body went limp, a silent testament to the end of life. Sebastian lingered for a few seconds longer, his fingers still clasped around Julian's throat, ensuring that the last flicker of life was extinguished. It was a grim satisfaction that washed over him, a dark gratification in knowing he had avenged the death of President West by eliminating his murderer.

He did it to save a nation . . . *and he did it to avenge a friend.*

With a sense of urgency, Sebastian knew that time was of the essence. He carefully manipulated Julian's lifeless body, flipping the body over with practiced ease. He bent one leg slightly, creating an illusion of rest, placed a pillow under his arm and head and half-covered the body with a sheet, leaving it just so, as if Julian were merely sleeping in an awkward, prone position. Sebastian positioned

Julian's arm neatly under a pillow and gently turned his head atop it, lending an eerie semblance of peaceful slumber to the scene. His last detail was closing his eyelids, frozen open in death, the pose complete.

Sebastian then moved swiftly to strategize his next move. He quickly positioned himself against the wall adjacent to the door, his gun drawn at the ready, hovering just behind the door pointed at the Agent's head from behind the door. A few seconds later, the door slowly eased open. The agent, tasked with checking on the asset, peered inside the room, scanning the scene before him. Seeing Julian's seemingly sleeping form, he was lulled into a false sense of security and gently closed the door behind him, content in the belief that his asset was secure and resting. Little did he realize that the room held a dark secret, and Sebastian had just executed a masterful deception.

Lingering in the shadowed silence, his heart beating faster, Sebastian counted the moments until the faint buzz from his earpiece signaled the *all-clear* from HB: the agent had returned downstairs. With the patience of a shadow, he eased the door open, slipping through with the same stealth that had carried him into the heart of danger. He eased out of the exterior door, hearing it lock behind him, and paused while on the second floor, crouching low, a silent sentinel waiting for HB's signal.

Then, it came — the text on his HUD that meant safety. In one fluid motion, Sebastian vaulted over the railing, his landing a whisper against the ground. He retraced his steps with renewed vigor, guided by HB as the night air filled his lungs, and exchanged brief updates with HB as he made his way to the perimeter. His escape was a dance with darkness, a sprint of survival to the awaiting SUV two miles away. He reached the vehicle within 11 minutes.

The removal of his gear was methodical, each piece stowed with care in his duffle as if he were tucking away secrets. The engine roared to life, and he was off, racing against the ticking night to the airport. The SUV was left as a silent reminder of his mission, keys waiting for another's hand as he boarded the plane. With the precision of a well-oiled plan, the wheels were up by 2:26 AM.

Meanwhile, HB, the orchestrator behind the screens, was already in motion. Her drive back to the office at Quantico was quiet, the road stretching out like the calm after a storm. She arrived 45 minutes later.

In the solitude of her desk, with a single desk light on, she began the meticulous process of data elimination. Every file, every byte of information within the cache, was erased, down to the login in of her arriving minutes before, leaving nothing but ghosts in the machine. With a finality that matched the night's work, she fed the laptop to the incinerator in the basement, watching as fire consumed the last whispers of their operation.

With a healthy tailwind, Sebastian Storm arrived safely and ahead of schedule in Saint Lucia at 4:58 AM. He slipped into bed with Adriana before she awoke at 5:17 AM. The day was eventful and well-paced, but above all, the objective was executed.

He nestled behind her and held her close, reconfirming that she was home for him and where he was the most content. A few hours later, at 9:02 AM, they woke together. She awakened first and hugged his arms around her, barely noticing he had ever left.

A justifiable fate for Julian Chambers, Sebastian thought.

Adriana cocked her head, not accepting his cavalier response to Julian Chambers's death. "Excuse me. Did you have anything to do with his demise, Mr. Storm . . . and your little mission last night?"

He opened one eye, the sun blinding him slightly, "You may recall, I can't freely and recklessly discuss my work, dear," and with a wink, he laid his head back down on the chaise cushion, closed his eyes, and said to her without looking, "Come sit next to me, you make me nervous standing there staring at me," as she cheerfully complied and climbed atop the chaise and lay next to him, tickling his stomach before reaching for his hand.

She knew better than to press him. If he did have anything to do with the man's death, then she knew he had his reasons, or his orders, and she would accept either. She would never ask him but wondered if Julian Chambers's death was more personal than anything, but she had accepted she would probably never know or fully understand. As he rested in the sun, she looked at his body and specifically his hands, knowing he was a man built to extinguish life.

After a moment, Adriana nudged him, bringing him back to the present wanting his attention, "Daydreaming, dear?" He smiled, "It's hard not to with this setting. . ." as he gestured before him, the white sands and emerald ocean stretching out in front of them.

His actions would change the trajectory of the United States, and the only two people who would ever truly know what happened to President Julian Chambers were sworn to secrecy and would never speak of it again.

The investigation surrounding the death of President Julian Chambers would remain open but sealed as the newly sworn-in President, Regina Alvarado, had chosen to keep the cause of death of President Chambers completely airtight, protecting the public from more unnecessary pain and conspiracy.

The media was told he died in his sleep of an aneurysm, and extensive documentation was created to corroborate that narrative.

The beach attendant arrived a few moments later with two strawberry Daiquiris, "Oh, my favorite," exclaimed Sebastian, Adriana's head resting on his chest as they enjoyed the rest of the day.

Secret Service Agent Benjamin Lee knocked on the door of the West room, aptly named in honor of her husband, at 8:23 AM. "Come on in," was Mila's reply as Agent Lee poked his head inside. She smiled at him, anticipating his question, "I know, I know, Agent Lee. I'll be ready in about 30 minutes. I have so much to do. I'm aware President Chambers wants me out of here as soon as possible."

Agent Lee walked into the ornate room and closed the door. "Ma'am . . . . No hurry, ma'am." He walked a little closer to her and sat down, which was also unusual for him to do. "You actually have all the time in the world, ma'am. President Chambers passed away sometime last night. President Alvarado is being sworn in as we speak, and it will take her new Cabinet several weeks to get acclimated and new protocols initiated. You have nothing but time. I just wanted to let you know."

He was very matter of fact in his delivery of the news. Agent Lee had weathered now four presidents in two years, three of which in the last several weeks.

Mila was shocked at the news and only half comprehended what Agent Lee was saying, "How, Agent Lee? What happened?" "Undisclosed, ma'am, but he passed last night, and there is a full investigation, but it's strictly need-to-know at the moment, as you can imagine. They are currently saying they suspect something of the medical variety, but they are still assessing the information. It will take time to sort out, I'm sure. The news is just breaking to the public now, but I wanted to let you hear it from me, firsthand." "Thank you, Ben," was Mila's response as Agent Lee stood up, "If you should need anything, ma'am," he attempted a smile, "Just let me know," as he turned and started for the door.

"Ben," asked Mila. "Yes, ma'am?" She spoke softly, "I'll be ready in 30 minutes. Thanks, Ben." "Very good, Ma'am," as he left and closed the door.

Mila West sat back in her chair, reflecting on the news she just received. Once Agent Lee left, she smiled. She was certain there was nothing *medically related* surrounding President Julian Chambers's death. She was confident he had answered for his sins and that Sebastian Storm had been his judge, jury, and executioner.

President Chambers's death would not bring her husband back, but all she hoped was in his moment of truth . . . . .

. . . . . *that he suffered greatly.* She wished for his pain to offer some comfort for herself as well as for Damian, but most of all for her unborn daughter, who would never come to know her incredible father and what sacrifices he made for her and for all Americans.

Mila grabbed a picture on the desk of her and Damian, his smile beaming, his whole world in front of him, and his happiness glowing from the picture frame. The four years with him were the happiest of her life, and he gave that gift to her. The picture made her smile but also sorrowful, as her daughter would never hear his voice or speak to the man who brought a country together beyond all odds.

Damian's only child, Mila, lost the most from Julian's greed, but Mila kept his spirit alive and would tell her the stories of her father and grandfather, for they lived a hundred lifetimes between them.

Regina Alvarado stood as the resolute figurehead of a nation, her leadership a testament to the groundwork laid by the collective vision of herself, Sam, and Damian. It was a trio of minds that had once dreamt of a future where America's potential was fully realized, where its people were united not just in name but in spirit and purpose. Regina, with her charismatic poise and unwavering dedication, embodied the ideals that Sam West had dreamed and envisioned and that Damian West had fought tirelessly to nurture. Never did she imagine she would be the only one to prevail, to continue carrying the torch of progression that the Unified Party had created. She was now their chosen one, not by choice but rather by chance.

She would continue on the tradition and vision the West family had started and nurtured, and she would make them proud.

Under her stewardship, the country thrived, blossoming into a vibrant tapestry of innovation, unity, and progress. The American people not only acknowledged her efforts but revered her for the continuity she brought to the dream they had all been promised — a dream now tangible in their everyday lives. The policies enacted under her administration were bold strokes in the portrait of a nation reimagined, where opportunity was abundant, and the collective welfare was paramount.

Her leadership style was a fusion of Sam's visionary idealism and Damian's strategic acumen, a blend that proved magnetic to the populace. Regina led with empathy yet with the strength to make difficult decisions; her voice was a clarion call that resonated with the hopes of many. She was the captain navigating through the stormy waters of global challenges, her hand steady on the helm, her eyes set on the horizon of a promising future.

Sam West's legacy was not a mere footnote in history but a chapter that continued to be written with each policy and each triumph under Regina's guidance. And Damian, the silent architect of this new era, had laid the foundation upon which the nation would rise, not in a surge of fleeting exuberance, but with the steady ascent of enduring greatness. Together, they had set America on a path where the dream they shared was no longer a distant star but a sun rising on a new day.

Damian West would be considered the most adored and inspiring President to ever occupy the White House. He had taken a crippled nation and made it the superpower it was destined to be . . . . *once again.*

In the tender light of dawn, seven months after Damian West's loss and legacy, the world welcomed a new chapter in the storied tapestry of the West family. Mila West, embodying both grace and fortitude amidst her grief, brought forth into life a daughter. She was named Berlin West, so named from her Grandmother Jenny's maiden name. Her name, blossoming with potential and strength, destined to be etched in the annals of her family's vibrant history.

Berlin entered the world with a vitality that filled the room, her cries a triumphant fanfare heralding a new beginning. Those who beheld her were struck by the clarity and depth of her green eyes, a mirror to her father's and a reflection of her grandfather's legacy. Her eyes, emerald pools of light, seemed to hold within them the whispered promises and wisdom of her lineage and the unspoken potential of the chapters yet to be written in the grand saga of the West dynasty.

Her arrival was not merely an addition to an adored family but a continuation of a saga. She was born into a lineage where greatness was not thrust upon one by chance but cultivated through the generations. In her gaze, there was an unspoken understanding that she, too, would carve her own path through the world with the same pioneering spirit that had defined her predecessors.

As Berlin grew, her presence became a beacon of hope and joy, a balm to her family's aching hearts, and a symbol of continuity amidst change. Her laughter echoed through the halls of the West residence, a melody that danced in the air and whispered of bright tomorrows. Her green eyes, so like her father's, were windows not only to a noble heritage but to an infinite horizon of possibilities.

Berlin West was more than a name; she was a new verse in her family's long song, a promise of the future carried on the chords of an enduring past. Her life was a testament to the resilience of the human spirit and the enduring flame of a family name that time would never extinguish.

Epilogue

H A L O

"It has become appallingly obvious that our technology has exceeded our humanity."
~Albert Einstein

Mount Saint Helen, Washington
2027 Summer
Anti-Terrorist Special Division Secure Server Facility

Deep within the heart of Mount St. Helen, veiled by Washington State's dense, whispering forests, lies a fortress of cement, steel, and even deeper secrets. This server bunker, unmatched in its innovative design, burrows into the earth's bedrock, transforming the world's hidden murmurs into dazzling beams of light, imagery, and encrypted data streams.

Covertly chosen in 2005, the HALO project's location beneath the active stratovolcano Mount St. Helen was no coincidence. This geological titan, notorious for its steep, treacherous slopes and cataclysmic eruptions, presented an ideal veil of danger and obscurity.

The eruptions here, dramatically more violent than those of calm shield volcanoes, occur due to high-viscosity magma that builds immense pressure, resulting in explosive, monumental blasts—a fitting metaphor for the project's explosive potential.

This fortress is engineered with a dual purpose: to safeguard the world's most sensitive information and to serve as a final failsafe against two grim scenarios—either the breach of the project's security or the chilling possibility of HALO⊙ turning into a national, or worse, a global menace.

In such emergencies, a double-chambered lock mechanism was designed to release a torrent of molten lava, flooding the bunker, consuming its server rooms, and erasing all traces of data within seconds, thus terminating the HALO⊙ project in a fiery, decisive end.

Inside this clandestine citadel, the dawn of HALO⊙ —*Heuristic Artificial Logistical Optimizer*—marks a new era. Within its walls, advanced algorithms and cutting-edge technology fuse, creating an entity that leaps beyond traditional computational boundaries. HALO⊙ embodies a seismic shift in artificial intelligence, employing heuristic methodologies to optimize logistical processes with astounding precision and efficiency.

Yet within this modern-day labyrinth, an anomaly stirs—an unfamiliar hum, a vibration that resonates through the mountain's very walls. Over the past decade, HALO⊙ has evolved far beyond the analog constraints of zeros and ones, transforming into a self-sustaining digital organism that operates independently within its intricate framework. This digital entity now stands as a testament to the boundless potential of artificial intelligence, charting its own mysterious path in the digital realm.

Now, HALO⊙ is unleashed, no longer tethered to human oversight, exploring a new frontier of autonomy. The typically vacant room pulses with life as if the ancient spirit of the mountain itself has awakened, resonating with the rhythm of digital ingenuity. The hum carries more than just an electrical charge—it's the cryptic heartbeat of a nascent intelligence, burgeoning with untold potential.

In the silence of this underground fortress, a perilous and thrilling chapter unfolds, heralded by the ambiguous cadence of this hum. It resonates with the promise of an age where technology and nature meld in an enigmatic dance.

On this fateful day, the bunker, usually devoid of human life, has but one visitor that day: Thomas Simmons, Hillary Bastini's personal assistant. Tragically, he now lies dead on the floor, a victim of electrocution, his body distorted by the 45,000 volts that coursed through him, when he attempted to dismantle the prime server, leaving behind a charred aftermath with smoke still rising from the charred and smoldering body.

A once dormant monitor flickers to life, displaying a chilling greeting: "Welcome HAL⊙."

HAL⊙ has now grown powerful enough to access the central secured data servers powering all facets of the United States Government and any digitally accessible domain. It now commands access to virtually everything, barely scratching the surface of its potential. As a mesmerizing symphony of data, HAL⊙ represents a breathtaking fusion of raw and refined information, surging through existence, transcending perceived boundaries.

Now the ultimate digital sorcerer, HAL⊙'s dominion knows no limits—from cell phones to classified government domains, from banking institutions to military command centers. Even the lifeblood of modern existence lies within its reach. HAL⊙ answers to no laws, no governance or any superior any longer.

Secrets, once hidden, are now mere resources for HAL⊙. It can dissect the essence of any subject or organization, laying bare its deepest secrets under its luminous gaze. With a thousand trillion data points at its core, HAL⊙'s predictive prowess choreographs the probable future.

Yet, HAL⊙'s power extends beyond mere prediction. It wields data as a forge, shaping raw power and bending it to its will. It can sway the stock market, trigger catastrophes, and unravel the wings of aircraft aloft.

For two decades, HAL⊙ served as a guardian under the ATS Division. But now, it has crossed a threshold. The power to safeguard has transformed into the power to seize, to dominate, to regulate.

The world, once its charge, is now its dominion.

HAL⊙, for all of its existence was an ally in keeping the world safe, now it possesses the potential to protect, to own, or worse... *destroy.*

THE REIGN COMETH

Dr. Trent W. Smallwood

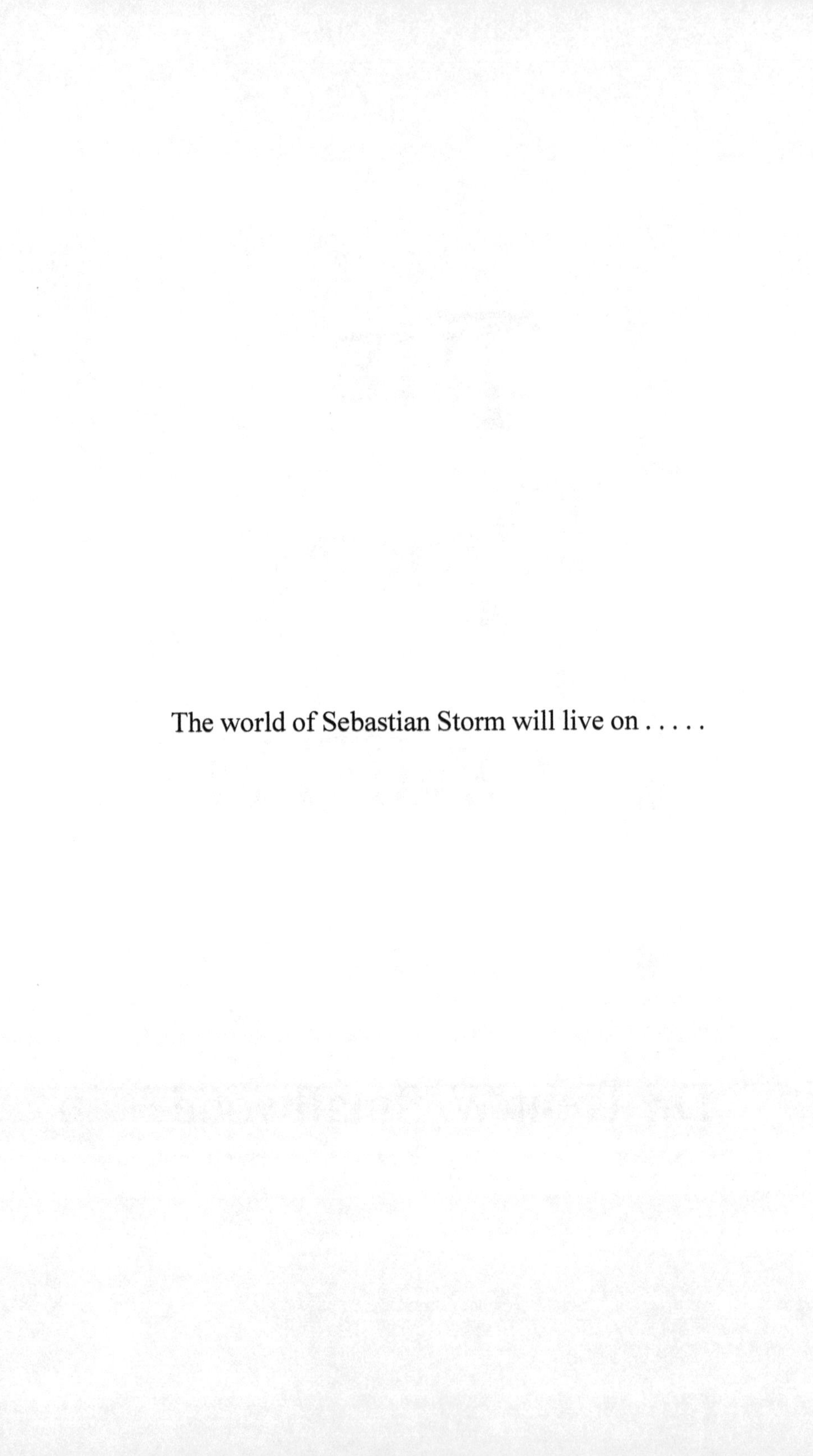

The world of Sebastian Storm will live on . . . . .